ABBY
CITY GIRL IN THE COUNTRY
Erotic Romance

KERRY JAMES

About the Publisher

4Fun Publishing, a member of **BLVNP Incorporated**, 340 S. Lemon #6200, Walnut CA 91789, info@blvnp.com / legal@blvnp.com
NOTE: Due to the highly emotional reaction of some people to works of erotic fiction, any email sent to the above address that contains foul language or religious references is automatically deleted by our anti-spam software and will not be seen. All other communications are welcome.

DISCLAIMER

Abby

City Girl in the Country

Erotic Romance

By: Kerry James

© **Kerry James 2014**
ISBN: 978-1-68030-134-2

PROLOGUE

Last night's winds had finally blown themselves out; all that was left was an occasional gust. The accompanying rain was now little more than moisture dragged from the foliage, yet still with the ability to soak the unwary. The gusts that blew the autumn leaves around like dervishes would suddenly evaporate, leaving the leaves to Last night's wind had finally blown itself out; all that was left was an occasional gust. The accompanying rain was now a little more than moisture dragged from the foliage, yet still with the ability settle in clusters of red and brown, until another gust picked them up to swirl and then settle in another corner; the eddies vanishing as swiftly as they arrived. Thomas Tregonney knew all about these conditions, having seen them for the past twenty-eight years ever since he came here to assume the position of stationmaster. He had seen all the weather that this tiny valley in the south west of England could experience. Hot dry summers, when the rails shimmered like light dancing on water; cold winters when rain and snow would make the long haul up the bank from the junction almost impossible for the tiny locomotives. Almost impossible except that they had made it, the loco drivers had pride in their job, and would employ all the tricks in their repertoire to keep the train moving, but then they, like Thomas, were Great Western Railway men.

He closed the door of the house and locked it; the first time ever in all those years that he had done so. He wore his uniform, not the plain double-breasted jacket and trousers provided by British Railways; until recently they had been hanging in his cupboard where they had always hung; but his first uniform, that of the GREAT WESTERN RAILWAY; he had always thought of his erstwhile employer in capitals giving that company the importance and respect he felt its due; this was the only uniform he would ever wear, scorning any other. The wing collar was threadbare in places and the black tie shone with continual use. He settled the pillbox cap on his head, the red embroidered initials of the GWR entwined over the peak the only colour in the uniform, pulled the front of the frock coat tightly together and strode down the gravel path and up the slope of the platform.

As he walked this short distance it had been his habit to count the wagons in the goods sidings, always a reliable indicator of how well the local economy was performing. For years he could rely on at least a dozen trucks and vans awaiting the pick-up goods train. On market days there would be more and even at this early hour of the morning the cattle pens would be filling with lowing and bleating beasts destined for South Molton. Now they were empty, as were the sidings themselves.

His station was a single platform affair, with waiting room and offices seemingly too large for just that single platform. Even though he realised that he had no need, he still worked in the habit that those years had engendered. The platform was inspected thoroughly for signs of weed growth, or cracked paving slabs, which could trip the unwary passenger. Little point as no passenger would ever wait here again, little point as no train would ever again pull in to discharge travellers or pick up. Little point as there were no more porters who could be detailed to pick the weeds, sweep the paving, or renew the white line painted on the very edge of the platform. Instead there was just Thomas and his lonely station.

It had been this way for two months since the last train had run, British Railways having decided to close the line, an act of vandalism, according to Thomas; preceded by months, when trains would run at times when experience indicated that no trains need run, yet did not run when that same experience indicated that there were passengers in need of trains. Thomas thought that this was a deliberate policy designed to make the case for closure. He had made his protests, bombarding his superiors with complaints; telling them that this was not the way to run a railway; his letters had been acknowledged, but no action was forthcoming. Decisions had been made far away, and the actions of an insignificant stationmaster at an insignificant station in an insignificant valley would have no influence on that decision.

For the last five months after the remaining porter had been transferred elsewhere, Thomas had done what he could to keep the station tidy. He did this despite the fact that in April that year, he was sixty-five and officially retired, although no notice had been issued for him to quit the station house. The waiting rooms had been swept every day, metal and woodwork polished; often with polish and dusters purchased from his own pocket. Even when the track gangs were withdrawn, and the rails became crowned with rust, and the ballast choked with weeds, Thomas still cared, going down on the track running through the station to painstakingly pull every weed that showed its head; determined that HIS station would not show the air of neglect which others might and that it could still fulfill its function if required.

Occasionally, one of the villagers would make the mile and a half walk to share a moment with him, to reminisce on how it used to be; or discuss the weather; and he would from time to time make that same walk in the reverse direction to drink a pint at the Combe Inn and eat a sandwich for lunch. His was a constant dream that one day the bureaucracy would see its errors and the service would be restored. That dream ended when a poster miraculously appeared on the notice board at the front of the station announcing that the track would be lifted in January the next year. In all his years here, no poster was displayed unless Thomas gave his approval, yet all of a sudden, the poster was there. No one had thought to enlighten him, nor consult. They had taken his trains away, now they had taken his station away. Thomas was now superfluous.

Thomas was and remained a diligent railwayman; duty was paramount and took precedence over everything, even his family. He was allowed one day off every week, yet rarely took advantage of it. Trains ran seven days a week and as stationmaster, Thomas would meet every one of them. Many branch lines would not have a Sunday service, nor did this branch, the Combe Lyney branch, until the First World War. The military authorities had insisted on Sunday services, much against the opposition of the Presbyterian Fathers in Paverton, the terminus of the line. Troops under canvas on Exmoor needed to be moved at any time, even Sundays, so the Sunday service was set in place. Those same troops also needed some entertainment when Sunday passes were granted.

The Presbyterians had succeeded in ensuring that the Magistrates allowed no Sunday opening of the local Pubs, so the Tommy's crowded on to the trains bound for Combe Lyney and South Molton, where the Pubs were open. The returning trains were met by the stationmaster at Paverton, an Elder of the Methodist Church, who declined to work on Sunday but nonetheless met the trains and with Bible in hand, harangued the well-lubricated soldiers with promises of Damnation for desecrating the Lord's Day. To men destined for the bloodbath of the trenches in France, his words had little impact; many knew they were heading for Hell in any case. The Sunday trains remained, even after the War had ended. Thomas knew all this because the Railway was a family, and like a family there was always an older aunt or uncle, or in this case a retired railwayman who would visit to sit in the sun on the platform, and could be easily persuaded to relate the tales of yesteryear.

Having walked the length of the platform, Thomas returned to the station buildings, and brought out the broom from the office. Methodically he swept the waiting room, and the office, sweeping outwards towards the covered porch. The waiting room and the office formed two gableswith a porch in between, usually known to the staff as the glasshouse, a glassed area with an open exit to the platform. It was a nuisance and a blessing. A nuisance because at this time of year the leaves would gather in the lee it created; a blessing for in Spring and summer it was ideal for propagating plants which would then go to create the floral platform displays of which he had been rightly proud. All GWR stations were encouraged to garden, and the Company would happily supply seeds and bedding out plants. The GWR also organised competitions for the display, and on one occasion, Combe Lyney had come second in the area competition.

He swept slowly and thoroughly, taking care not to sweep the leaves out on the platform where they would be picked up by the wind and soon find their way back into the porch, but instead gathering up the piles and putting them into a sack. At last with all the leaves gone, he swept the paving in the immediate area of the platform. These old paving slabs many laid in 1874 when the station was built, were pitted and scarred by the thousands of feet that had trod them. Thomas himself had added to this with his heavy boots for this was his beat.

He met every train and it was here outside the entrance to the office that the guards' compartment would stop, the guard and Thomas exchanging greetings as well as small parcels and company paperwork. Thomas would then patrol the platform to where the locomotive was, to glare at the driver even when no infringement of the many rules could be found. As the trains were rarely more than two coaches long, never occupying more than half the length of the platform; that made it a relatively short walk.

He went into the waiting room with a duster, running it carefully over the long bench still showing its coat of grey but worn through to bare wood on the arms and the leading edge of the seat, where so many hands and bottoms had rested. He straightened the few surviving leaflets and timetables, offering services that would never happen and left, locking the door after him. Next was the booking office, and at the rear of that his own tiny office, a desk; bolted to the wall to stop it falling over; with an antique Remington typewriter and an ancient Chubb safe. He knew not what British Railways would do with these, but they were the property of the railway so would be kept secure. Another door was locked, another chapter of his life closed.

As he left the Porch, he noticed that the clouds were building up again in the west, a sure sign that rain would once again be with them. Walking down the slope of the platform, he paused to look both ways, and listened, before crossing the track. It would not occur to him that this was not necessary, as no train would be coming; it was just another habit of his lifetime's service, drummed into him by his first stationmaster at Par, who reinforced the lesson with gory details of the foolish souls who had perished, caught up in the wheels and driving rods of a locomotive. That some of these stories were fanciful never occurred to Thomas, at fourteen he was prepared to believe anything that his elders and betters cared to tell him.

He crossed the track, turned right and made his way towards the goods shed. Here the desolation was greater, the rusty rails, hiding amongst the weed growth seemed intent on tripping him. They had been disconnected from the running line when the signal box was demolished. Soon, along with the running line, they would be lifted by the last ever train; a crane and a number of flatbed wagons would make their way up to Paverton and then descend ripping the rails from the ballast behind it as it came. With that final act, ninety-three years of service to the valley would end. He gave this a little thought as he approached the goods shed. The rails ran up to the great doors, underneath them, and inside giving enough room for two or three wagons to be unloaded. Set into the right hand door was a smaller door, which Thomas had to duck through. Inside the shed the rails were still bright, although splattered with pigeon droppings.

The shed was perfumed with the aroma of the multitude of goods that had passed through its doors; the sweet smell of apples, the must of wheat and barley, the eye-watering sharpness of paraffin and oil, cattle cake, fertiliser, all mixed together into a fragrance of the treasure which lay at the heart of the Great Western. For it was goods traffic; not the passengers; that was the commercial reason for the railway. The goods supplied the dividends the shareholders of the GWR came to expect; year in, year out without fail. Goods did not need fancy and expensive accommodation and carriages. Goods didn't complain about slow trains, nor about being cold and rough handling. Goods created the greatest income for the lowest outlay. British Rail didn't seem to understand this and wanted to abandon truck loads and parcel traffic in favour of train loads, thereby giving the road transporters a free hand with this business. Therefore, it was no surprise to Thomas that when the goods ceased to flow, the passenger income was not sufficient to justify the line.

Thomas climbed up onto the goods deck by way of the small steps set into the end and walked to where he had set an old vegetable box. Picking it up, he shook it and out fell a desiccated carrot, half gnawed by one of the mice which had moved into the shed all those years ago, and which despite the cats that generations of railway men had set to work, thrived on the produce stored almost every night. The mice had fed well, the cats had fed well and grew too full to be bothered chasing the mice, preferring to doze under the sun or sleep in the relative warmth of an open truck and then occasionally inadvertently locked in. How many cats had been shipped off to another part of the country in all those years would never be known, nor would the numbers who would arrive at Combe Lyney in the same way. Traps and cats had never, in all those years, resolved the problem of the mice and pigeons.

Thomas set the box on end, and climbed up; allowing a nod of satisfaction as the rope and noose he had set yesterday was at the right height. He looped the noose around his neck, and with no further thought, rocked his feet on the box until it fell over. He made no sound as the noose tightened around his neck, for that was not his way, no complaint, just acceptance. Not even when the tautening rope dislodged his beloved cap. It fell to the dusty floor, as Thomas Tregonney hung swaying, and with eyes closed waited for death. His duty was done.

CHAPTER ONE

Abby had little difficulty in getting to this point, on the B3227 from Taunton heading towards South Molton, and guessed that somewhere on this road she should see a sign indicating her turn. Yet as she drove further and further into Devon she became uneasy that no such sign had revealed itself. Navigation became more of a problem as she drove deeper into the countryside, signposts, when you could find them; indicated a destination which then received no further mention at all upon succeeding signs. High banks on either side of the road meant that she had little clue as to where she was, the only point of reference was the ribbon of road unwinding ceaselessly and vanishing under the bonnet of her car and the occasional signs for some oddly named village or hamlet. As she passed through villages such as Wiveliscombe and Bampton, she wondered if she had gone wrong, and seeing the sign that said South Molton was just five miles farther on, decided that indeed she had gone wrong. Swearing mildly under her breath, Abby was giving thought to turning round and retracing her path.

Suddenly, she caught that breath; there was the sign. Leaning gently against the high banks that enclosed the road with a vigorous growth of Ivy as camouflage, she would have missed it had she not been driving slowly looking for a place to turn. It was a peculiar sensation, and her heart was beating furiously as she made the turn. A name that had previously existed only in hearsay and on a map was now a fact. Her mother had mentioned the name a few times without thinking, but would not be pressed on its significance. When her mother had died, Abby was nineteen, there was no reference at all to the name in her personal effects, which were few, there was no birth certificate, and the only official document she could find was an out of date passport, giving the birth area as South Molton. Abby's history consisted of just her mother's death certificates, and her own birth certificate. Abby now realised that she could have obtained a copy of her mother's birth certificate, but as is the way of things she had not thought logically at the time. She would repair this oversight as soon as possible. She wondered why her mum had a passport, as she had never travelled abroad.

Combe Linney, as Abby spelt it, was not even marked on her road map, and she had to resort to the Ordinance Survey to discover the location; again there was no place spelt Linney, but there was a Combe Lyney, near South Molton, and she assumed that this had to be the place. Its sum total consisted of two black oblongs, and a round dot with a cross on top, presumably indicating a church. There were no A or B roads that ventured anywhere near the place. If this wasn't the back of beyond, then it was pretty close to it.

The mystery could not be investigated immediately as Abby had after her mother's death, to consider the business of life, a job, somewhere to live. Her mother had left her little, but a stubborn trait that helped Abby survive the numerous jobs she took in the financial and insurance trade; making tea and coffee for surly men and women who viewed her simply as the office gofer.; They would have been surprised if they had known that Abby did not merely put their drinks in front of them, but closely studied what they were doing. They didn't know because Abby was invisible, unimportant, not even missed when she left to go to a better job, using all she had learned to pack her C.V. She was twenty-five when she started in the city as a proprietary equity trader, the years of watching and learning placed her in good stead. She would not say that she was a brilliant trader, there were many more that could turn sixpences into sovereigns at the drop of a hat, but she was intuitive, and with no family to call upon her time, was content to work all hours to achieve her goal. In a business where employers counted the hours almost as important as the success, she was regarded highly.

The commitment to her work had left a gaping hole in the rest of her life, particularly the social side. Starting early, and rarely getting back before nine or ten p.m. left her too exhausted to explore the nightlife that abounded about her. The one indulgence was her flat, a rather luxurious two-bedroom apartment in a block in Kensington; reasoning that with all the hard work and hours she put in, she deserved a base where she could relax comfortably. A fleeting affair with a co-worker that fizzled quickly when his wife became suspicious, was the extent of her forays into anything that could be called a social life; but then the skills that she needed for a social life could not be described as highly developed, lacking the experience that would enable her to discern those who would care for her, from those who would simply use her. Her closest friend was Roz, a glamorous woman who lived in the same flats, who described herself as an escort. Abby could guess what that euphemism concealed, but not being judgmental had never thought less of her for that. Roz had been helpful to Abby, advising her on dress and make-up to fill the void left by Abby's mother; a woman who had little knowledge of these feminine arts herself, but then holding down three cleaning jobs would have given her little time to acquire, or require, these talents. The help of Roz and Abby's cheque book allowed her to assume a confidence she didn't always feel.

She was quite tall for a woman at five-foot-eight, and had inherited a slim figure, which seemed to maintain itself no matter what junk food she consumed during the hectic working day. Light brown hair that she described as mousy, but Roz insisted was dark blonde, cut short for easy maintenance, level brown eyes, and a full mouth that smiled easily. She would never describe herself as beautiful, and most days her looks were secondary to working efficiency, but on the couple of occasions that she had been out with Roz to parties, and under her tutelage had put on the glam; she had been subject to lots of male attention. The problem was her social skills could not stretch to flirting, and with the appropriate responses not given, the man soon lost interest, and she returned to her flat alone, with no prospect of that situation changing. She lived and worked in one of the most vibrant cities, yet stood on the outside, an onlooker, unknowing of the rules that would let her join.

This situation did not bother her too much, although sometimes she looked wistfully at those who seemed to have so much going on in their lives. If she had ever been part of the social whirl, and was then excluded, it might have given her some pain, but what you have never had, you do not miss. Spare time, the little that she had, was spent reading, usually books about the Industrial Revolution, which had become her hobby, and watching the Discovery channel on Sky. Holidays had been a luxury she could do without in her need to pursue a career, consisting usually, as in this case, of a few snatched days, alone and exploring some place that had been significant in the industrial past, the mobile phone ever to hand in case she had to return. It had taken all those years before she finally decided to try and resolve the conundrum. Now she was just a few miles from somewhere that could be very important or of no consequence at all. As she drove, a prick of fear came to her mind. Was she doing the right thing? The old adage was now forefront in her head. Be careful what you wish for, as your wishes may sometimes become true. Was she about to turn over a stone that had something ugly underneath? Hesitancy and fear almost overwhelmed her, and she let fate make her decision. If there was somewhere she could turn round easily, she would do it and forget this obsession. If there was no chance of turning then she would go on.

The road was so narrow that any vehicle coming in the opposite direction would involve one or the other reversing in difficult circumstances for some distance; she hoped it would be the other. It wound its way tortuously between high banks, never letting her have a sight of anything more than fifty yards ahead, until it emerged on an embankment just a few feet above a marshy area. Another of those old road signs declared that the embankment was unsafe for any vehicle over 30 cwt. Abby could just remember from her school days what cwt. meant, one and a half tons! The embankment rose to a bridge spanning a river, dropping back down the other side to a few more yards of embankment; then plunging back into the high banks and starting to climb. Just before her view was cut off, she noticed to the left, a series of brick arches, carrying some other form of transport across the marsh. Beyond the banks was a forest of mixed trees, some deciduous, some conifers of unknown types, she recognised Beech grown so tall that it arched over the road, creating a tunnel of foliage.

The road was obviously used but rarely; with detritus of mud thrown from the corrugated tyres of tractors covering the crown; that rich soil supported a good growth of grass that brushed the underside of her car. Streams seemed to prefer the road to their normal courses as her tyres splashed through water almost every yard of the way. The lane climbed gradually, ascending into a valley she could not see. Then out of the trees a rock built abutment reared at the side of the road, another set back a little could be seen on the other side, no deck connected them, the railway, for she felt sure it would have been a railway, long gone. Possibly, she thought, the reason for the low viaduct she had glimpsed across the marsh. The road continued to climb, but more steeply now climbing out of the forest, although the high banks still hemmed the road. Occasionally, a gateway to a field would afford her views of the stupendous Devon countryside, with irregular small fields lying seemingly at random over hills of varying height as if a patchwork quilt had been thrown carelessly over an unmade bed. To the southwest they stretched away to the foothills of Dartmoor, and to the northeast to Exmoor, only fleetingly glimpsed.

She drove carefully not wishing to rush headlong into any problems the way might present. The lane continued to twist and turn, passing even narrower lanes, which vanished between the hedgerows within the space of a few yards, unmarked on her map, and unsigned by the local council, as if their purpose was a secret, known only to those who had business in these parts. She felt she should have reached somewhere by now, and pondered the comments that had been made to her that West Country miles are longer than miles measured elsewhere in England, possibly she wasn't in England any more. As she drove round yet another tight bend, she caught her breath, for suddenly the vista of the valley opened before her, and equally as suddenly the lane disappeared from in front of her car. She braked urgently. The lane now descended, at an impossible angle, so steeply that Abby felt it would be safer to abseil down. An ancient road sign leaning, drunkenly into the hedgerow, its black and white pole pitted with rust, the sign at its top, surmounted with a once red triangle informed her that the hill was one in four. 'That's never one in four,' she informed the sign, 'that's vertical.' Locking the automatic into low gear, she tentatively started the descent. The whine of the engine rose to a crescendo, dying away as she used the brakes and then rising again as she let the car run against the brake of the engine. At the very least, she thought, anyone approaching the hill from the bottom would hear her, and not attempt the climb until she came past. At last she reached the bottom and broke out of the hedgerows and trees, onto the valley floor. There had been nowhere to turn at all, so fate had decided for her.

The lane followed the valley for some distance, passing a few small Cob cottages, each attended by barns and outhouses. The small, undulating fields upon which cattle grazed, seemingly unfazed by the passing of her car, just merely lifting their heads for a moment to look incuriously, and then returning to their patient cropping of the grass. The banks were not so high now allowing a better view of the surrounding country. The valley was not flat, but undulated smoothly, rising to small coppices, and hillocks that fell gently down to the river which flowed at the valley bottom. The road and the river kept a sort of company, the road having more sense of direction although it still could not be called straight, as it traversed many small hills and side valleys, while the river meandered. Sometimes it was completely out of sight and then abruptly returned those same small hills and side valleys brushing it aside in its journey along the valley bottom.

Another of those old road signs with the red triangle appeared, this time warning her of a junction. Negotiating yet another bend she came upon the junction. No white lines in the road to observe, just another lane of presumably equal importance, or equal unimportance joining. The road seemed to veer to the right so she went that way, at the last minute noticing a faded sign showing left for Combe Lyney, one and a half miles. She couldn't believe it, all that way and only two and a half miles covered! The stories were true; West Country miles were longer than English miles. As she was committed to the right hand road she carried on and immediately drove over a slight hump. On top of the hump set into the road were railway lines, once covered by road stone, but now revealed by the traffic, which over the years had thumped across them wearing away the tar and grit surface. Abby had been very interested in History at school, particularly the Industrial Revolution and the urge to explore such artifacts of the industrial past was never far away. Impulsively she determined to have a look at this one, stopping where the lane seemed a little wider while switching off the engine.

Leaving the car, she took her first breath of the Devon air, her head swirled with its effect and she almost staggered, a glorious rich soup of scents enriched with oxygen assailed her senses and as she breathed deeply filling her lungs with the potent mixture she felt as if she had grown an inch. At first she was astonished by the silence, but as the engine noise which had accompanied her for the last two hundred odd miles faded from her ears, she realised that the silence was punctuated, no accompanied by the gentle rustle of the river and the chatter and flurry of birds. The day was typical of late March. The sun was there but often hidden by the clouds, which hurried over the valley. When they broke for a moment, she could feel the warmth that the sun promised, but too soon the clouds ganged up and became overcast once more. The birds that she heard seemed to time their chatter and flight to coincide with the sun's brief appearances, as if they were unsure whether it was the right time to be nest building. Most confusing for them she thought. Getting out of the car had also brought their bluster to a momentary halt, and as she moved a scatter of small birds burst out of the hedgerow into a brief flight, only to disappear just as suddenly back into the hedge, a few yards farther away.

She walked back to the level crossing. The rails ended abruptly either side of the road; presumably the scrap men didn't want the cost of resurfacing the road to recover just a few pounds of scrap steel. At one side stood a weather-beaten solid post, easily one foot square, the remnants of white paint still clung stubbornly to its side, yet gaping regular holes in the face proclaimed another purpose. Abby reasoned that this must have been the post for the level crossing gate, and searched for its twin on the other side, but that was nowhere to be seen. Where the lines had been though, was easy to spot. No one had bothered to reclaim the land here, unlike the more urban areas, where the price of land made such a task economical. Westwards the line had curved away, following the valley. Eastward the railway bed became much wider, as if there was something more important for the railway to do, and about four hundred yards away were some old buildings.

There was no gate to prevent her so Abby wandered along the way, uneasily at first as if she expected someone to come out and shout at her for trespassing, but more confidently as she made progress and no such challenge came. The way was almost choked with bramble and nettles, and footing was sometimes hard to find. She discovered that the bed was a series of undulations about fifteen inches apart, and wondered why, until she stepped on to an old and crumbling piece of wood, which was where one of the dips should be.

She then realised that the undulations were the result of the old rails and sleepers being lifted from the ballast. The way was becoming more difficult now, and after almost tripping over a loop of wire half buried in the old ballast she decided to retrace her steps. Warm from her walk, she opened her car thankfully and turned on the air-conditioning. Shortly her temperature returned to comfortable, and she drove on, finding a place to turn around and then following the sign for Combe Lyney. The lane was now allowing her a much gentler route, without the sharp bends of earlier, and she could take more notice of her surroundings.

This was lucky, as otherwise she may have missed the overgrown lane leading off to the right, and the small finger sign, which announced STATION. In two minds whether to explore or not, she stopped the car. Again, impulsively she decided to investigate and ventured up the approach. It was only short, and soon she found herself in a small yard. She gazed around. The yard would have once been cobbled, but now all that remained was some evidence of the hard-core, cratered and broken, with weed and brush that sprang through the cracked cobbled top helping to complete the task of reducing the top surface to gravel.

The station stood forlorn in front of her, a single storey building, built with rugged local rock. The building consisted of two gabled ends, joined by a single storey building running between them. The gables contained a single window each, whilst the joining part contained just two windows and two doors. The windows were all barred with planks nailed across. Next to the window in the left-hand gable hung a board with the heading "GREAT WESTERN RAILWAY." Below was a space, which Abby assumed from the tattered remnants of paper pinned to it, would have been for notices. To the left of this gable was a double wicket gate, hanging open, set in a diagonally slatted fence that extended off to the left for ten or so feet before vanishing into overgrown shrubs and bushes. To the right of the station building about one hundred yards away was a house, built in the same style as the station, but two-storied, with a steep roof. Projecting from the roof was a chimney; the bricks laid in a twisted style like legs on an antique table, and topped with tall terracotta chimney pots. Abby was certain that this house would have been for the stationmaster, who obviously lived on the job. Like the station, all the windows were boarded up. Beyond this house the remnants of a gravelled track leading off towards some more buildings about two hundred yards away, these she recognised as those she had seen from the level crossing.

Abby locked her car and walked slowly toward the gate, she looked round cautiously for anyone who would question her presence here, but the place was deserted. Emboldened, she negotiated the hanging gate which half blocked the entrance and walked onto the platform. The platform side of the building was very different. The gables were deeper and the gable ends had shallow bays with three narrow windows. Between the gables there was a large porch. She didn't venture in as the winds, rain and the seasons had combined to fill the place as a natural lee with piles of rotting leaves. There was also the suggestive rank smell of animals. To the right as she stood facing the station building, and beyond the wicket gate was a simple wooden structure more like a large garden shed, but with an awning stretching out over the platform. There was only the one platform, yet there had obviously been two tracks. The track bed was only partially obscured by weed, the ballast she could see clearly stained black with oil, which presumably had prevented the weed invasion. Looking to the east, the line had run through a small cutting, partially choked with vegetation but for a track, beaten out by foot, which wound its way through the brush, and the occasional small tree.

Westward the weed had again taken possession, and all she could see was a crude buffer stop, made from old sleepers set in a sea of brush, gorse, and bramble. She walked the length of the platform, which was quite short, much shorter than those she could remember from the odd times she had travelled by rail. Some of the paving remained, but much was missing. Also missing were the items that old pictures of stations had told her should be here, benches, cast iron lighting standards, enamelled advertising boards and the signs. Returning, she caught sight of one sign, which had survived. It was close by the wicket gate, but seemingly thrown down into the track bed, and broken in two. She could just make out some of the lettering - All Passengers MUST shew - the rest was indecipherable. She pondered the ramifications of the capital letters, and the spelling of 'show'. This was obviously a railway company with a sense of importance.

The day was drawing in now, with the sun no longer able to show from behind the clouds. It was time to find some accommodation. Wistfully leaving the station, she turned right onto the road to Combe Lyney, and drove the mile and a half, West Country miles again, until she found the village. It was a scattered collection of old Devon Cob cottages with some later half- timbered additions. There was also a small estate of the concrete system-built houses so beloved of the councils, placed seemingly without thought just off the road leading to a bridge over the river, and spoiling one of the beauty spots of the area. Abby found the Combe Inn easily just opposite the squat Norman church. Elsewhere this would now be a theme pub, she thought, with a silly name, and mock beams to replace the real beams that were the structural frame of this building. There was a little car parking space, enough for two or three cars in front, but at this hour of the day it was empty, the Inn also seemed deserted.

She walked into what would appear to be the pub's only bar, to find no one, except for a dog, which lay on its side before a slumbering fire. It looked up, thumped its tail once against the flags, and unperturbed carried on dozing. The bar was low-ceiling with beams which were without doubt the real thing, various small chairs, table, and settles were set around, none of which were part of the set and stereotypical pub furniture seen everywhere else. Indeed they, for the most part appeared one-offs in every way, as if they had been bought by succeeding generations, trying to copy the style of the previous, but adding their own unique touches. Around the walls were old photographs, men in uniforms of various kinds, group scenes, cricket teams, football teams, many of which contained the same personnel, and others that had no obvious purpose. The room was divided into two distinct sections by the bar itself. To the left as a patron entered the furniture was plain, without frills. Wooden seating extended along two of the walls, with tables placed about three feet apart standing in front. Upon the third wall hung the inevitable dartboard, with a very washed-out blackboard to one side. The blackboard had seen much use, and was scored and pitted from those darts that had missed their target. No longer completely bBlack, with chalk ingrained into the surface, the scores of the last game to be played overlaid the scores of previous games, which were still visible. Abby wondered how any player could be really sure of where they were in the game. To the right of the bar, the furnishings were much improved, upholstered chairs and stools clustered around polished tables. Abby approached the bar.

"Hello," she called. Allowing a few minutes for whoever was in charge to come to the bar, she called again. "Hello. Is anyone there?" She accompanied her call with a couple of sharp slaps on the counter. There appeared to be a response this time for movement could be heard as if from the depths of the earth. Eventually, through the door at the back of the bar, came a plump woman in her fifties, clothed simply, and wearing a flowered pinny! Abby had not seen one of those for years, except when a nostalgia programme on T.V. showed old adverts from the fifties. The face was unlined and healthy, with a broad smile.

"Hello my dear," the woman said, "how can I help you?" The accent was a slow, easy burr.

Abby returned the smile. "I was wondering if you have some accommodation for a few days? A single if you have one."

The woman's smile grew even broader, if that were possible. "Of course we have, although we don't often get visitors this early. The place may look old but we are up to date. En-suite bathrooms and such like. How long will you be staying?" The mention of en-suite bathrooms cheered Abby considerably; she had had visions of cold night trips to a cheerless communal bathroom.

"Oh, I would think about four or five days."

The woman nodded her head as if in conversation with herself and then upon reaching agreement addressed the visitor. "Right, well I'll put you in the back room, nice view over the valley, and away from the noise here in the front. You'll have to give me a few minutes to get it made up. Breakfast comes with the accommodation, but will you be wanting an evening meal?"

Abby's thoughts had not extended that far, but decided that it might be better to say yes and be sure, rather than trying to find a meal elsewhere, she hadn't seen anywhere for the last few miles that might offer dinner. "Yes please."

Again, the woman nodded her head in her conversation with herself. "Would twenty-five pounds a night be alright?" She asked cautiously.

Abby took her turn to nod. "Yes that would be fine, how much for the evening meal?"

The woman's smile returned. "Oh bless you my dear, that's included." Her smile widened at the look on Abby's face. "I cannot promise you a wide menu at this time of year, but if there's anything you would like in particular, I'm sure we can do something. Now let's get you a cup of tea, and you take a seat. Oh, and I'll get you the book to sign. Sit yourself down, and make yourself comfortable, and if that dog makes a nuisance of himself, just tell him to bugger off." With that she was gone.

Abby wandered through into the lounge, and selected for herself the chair that looked most comfortable. She wondered if she would be expected to eat down here. Normally, she would only feel comfortable eating alone in her room, or going out to some anonymous restaurant, where the prospect of others trying to engage her in conversation would be minimal. That concern she set aside as the warmth of the fire cheered her, the day was now almost gone, with a chill setting in. The dog looked up and deciding that there was no point in making a nuisance of himself, got up, turned around a couple of times and then lay down in exactly the position he had been in before. Presently, the landlady bustled in with a tray of tea.

"Ah, there you are." As if expecting that her guest may have decided to go elsewhere. "That dog isn't making a nuisance of himself?" And without waiting for a reply, shouted at the dog. "Gorn, bugger off." The dog raised himself and with the expression so truly described as hang-dog slunk away, no doubt wondering once again at the peculiarity of Humans. "Now I'm sure I've brought anything, yes milk, sugar, and strainer. You enjoy your tea. Oh and here's the book. Perhaps you could fill in the details, no hurry." She bustled away saying, "I'll get your room ready."

Abby sat and pondered the tea. A strainer! That meant leaf tea. She hadn't used anything but tea bags for years, in fact she never had. Her mother had used leaf tea when Abby was a little girl. Carefully she lifted the lid on the pot, yes, leaf tea. Now should she stir it?

Probably a stir would do no harm. She then poured the tea through the strainer; it was a dark rich brown in colour, adding milk, and half a teaspoon of sugar, she drank. God! It was wonderful. How could it taste so different? It was a completely different drink to the hurried bag in a cup with hot water poured on that she was used to. She would have a second cup, now that was very unusual. Picking up the book, Abby then filled in the normal details.

There had been no entries since October last year, how do they keep going, she asked herself. She was finishing her second cup, when the landlady bustled back into the bar.

"All ready for you. Oh good, you've signed the book." Picking it up, she read Abby's details. "Did you enjoy..." Her voice trailed off as she read Abby's name. "Tregonney, now that's an unusual name. I'm sure someone here has mentioned that name, but I can't recall when, or for why, but that was years ago, I've never heard of anyone else with that name, and you from up Lunnon, that's peculiar, do you have any relations, hereabouts?"

Abby was slightly embarrassed, but agreed with the landlady. "I have never heard of anyone with the name, and there's none in the phone book. I believe my family originally came from around here, and I suppose that's one of the reasons I've come down here."

The landlady had her secret conversation with herself and agreed on a conclusion. "I'll ask Sam when he comes in, he's in his eighties but still knows everything about Combe, every village has got one like Sam, and he'll know if any of your family are still around. Oh I forgot to ask, would you like to eat in your room, or down here?"

It took a great effort for Abby to say in none too firm a voice. "I think I'll eat down here, if that's all right?"

The landlady nodded her head in confirmation. "Now let's get your bag in from your car." She bustled outside with no doubt that Abby would be behind her. Abby got outside to see the landlady staring contemplatively at her car. She looked up as Abby approached and said. "If you don't mind I'll get Jack to put your car round the back. I wouldn't like any damage to happen while you're here."

Abby was taken aback. "Damage? Here?"

The landlady looked at Abby. "This may seem like the peaceful and law-abiding countryside to you, and it is in the main. But we still have some silly devils about," and her head moved jerkily sideways, indicating a direction, which Abby felt may have been in the general direction of the few council houses, but couldn't be sure. She unlocked the car with the remote control, and flipped up the boot. She had but one case, which she pulled out, only to have it taken off her by the landlady.

"I'll carry this for you," she stated firmly, "and if you leave the keys with me, Jack will move your car." Abby would have protested, but too late as the other woman had set off briskly back into the pub. Locking the car, Abby followed. The woman was waiting for her by a door at the back of the lounge. "Do I call you Miss, Mrs., or Ms. Tregonney?" she asked pleasantly.

"Well actually its Miss, but do call me Abby." The smile flashed on the face like a lighthouse beacon.

"Oh that's good; I can't get on with all these fancy terms now. Please call me Mary, and my husband's name is Jack, well it isn't, not really, his actual name is Arnold, which he can't stand, so he tells everyone its Jack. Now you watch these stairs." She changed the conversation without pausing or taking breath. The door opened to reveal a small lobby. To the left was the back wall to the bar. This was home to various charts and a large board with cup hooks running down vertically, all the hooks but one had keys hanging from them. Opposite this panel was the stairs and alongside the stairs a hallway, which Abby presumed would lead through to the kitchen.

Mary lifted a key off the wall and took the stairs "We may have modernised a lot of the facilities, but we cannot change the stairs. Whole place would fall down if we did." Abby could see what she meant; the stairs had undergone a metamorphosis over the years and had been repaired piecemeal. Whilst the general trend was upwards, the risers and steps sloped indifferently to the vertical direction, even at times giving the impression that the climber had stepped downwards instead of upwards. The corridor on the upper floor had obviously suffered the same fate. Abby made forward movements, but the changing angle of the floor sent her bouncing from one wall to the other, much like a pinball machine. Mary managed without problem, the years of practice enabling her to adjust her balance for each variation, walking the corridor much like a sailor negotiating the deck of a ship in heavy seas. The bedroom she showed Abby, was in complete contrast.

"Mind the little step," Mary said as she opened the door. Here the floor was flat, and close carpeted. Abby could walk quite normally. She said as much to Mary. "Well we couldn't have guests crashing around in the middle of the night," Mary replied, "so we had a false floor put in. You've come at the right time when it's relatively peaceful, before we get busy, now you get yourself sorted and have a rest, and we'll see you later."

Abby unpacked her bag, hanging her few clothes in the spacious wardrobe, and setting out the contents of her wash-bag in the bathroom. She examined the controls of the shower, and tried them carefully. A spray of freezing cold water, which after a few moments became boiling hot, rewarded her. Adjusting the temperature control seemed to have little immediate effect, but patience finally presented her with a suitable temperature. Leaving it to run, she went back into the bedroom and undressed. Feeling considerably refreshed from her shower, Abby dressed in slacks and a simple blouse, recognising that the Combe Inn was not a dressy place. She sat for a while and considered the day. Not a bad start, only five minutes in the place and definite confirmation that someone with her family name had lived in the locality, perhaps her mother? Even if that proved to be a red herring, then she had an old railway to explore, so it would not be a completely wasted journey.

At five past seven, she re-entered the bar, and Mary gave her that engaging broad smile. "I've set a place for you close to the fire, would you like a drink first?"

"That would be good; could I have a white wine spritzer please?" Mary nodded her secret agreement to this request simply asking if Abby would like tonic or lemonade as the mixer, and sat Abby down.

"I'll bring it through to you. Now I've got some nice soup, would you like some with a roll?" This was asked in such a way that Abby thought Mary would be seriously dismayed if she refused so agreed to the suggestion. The table had been laid for a gargantuan banquet, judging by the numbers of knives forks, spoons, and utensils waiting her use. As she would normally microwave a supermarket frozen meal, the only utensil that Abby would usually wash was a fork or spoon. The cutlery set out here would last her for days! Abby looked up as a man of medium height approached bearing her glass.

"Hello," he said, "you'll be Abby; I'm Jack, Mary's husband. Nice to have someone staying here this early." He handed Abby the keys to the car, "I've moved your car round to the back, nice cars those BMWs. Mary says your family came from round here." Like his wife Jack seemed to have the facility of talking about two different subjects scarce taking a breath, nor with a change of tone, and all seemingly within the course of one sentence. Abby smiled, it seemed so easy to smile at people in this place.

"Yes, well I believe so, but I don't know much about my family."

A look of consternation passed over Jack's face. "How can that be?" He asked. "Have you not got any?" A question that in the city would be viewed as an invasion, but down here was asked with genuine concern.

"I was an only child, and my mother didn't talk about her family. She died when I was nineteen, so I have no real knowledge of any relatives." At that moment Mary arrived with what seemed like a gallon of soup, and immediately scolded her husband for his impertinence.

"Leave the child be, and let her eat." Placing this huge bowl of soup in front of Abby she ushered her Jack away.

Abby broke a bread roll and spread some butter on it, she popped it into her mouth and picked up the spoon, which was quite heavy, turning it over she could just make out faded Hallmarks, and the name "ELKINGTON," a name she had never heard of, but who obviously made good cutlery. She stopped as the flavour of the bread and butter attacked her taste buds. It was so good, the bread light yet with none of the floury sogginess of the bread she would buy supposedly fresh from the supermarket, the butter with a wonderful creamy taste with just a hint of saltiness. The soup was also superb, yet she could not identify what kind of soup it was. Realising how hungry she was, Abby spooned the soup and ate the rolls with enthusiasm, only stopping when reason told her not to satisfy her appetite, or else she would not be able to eat any of the pie that Mary had promised. Relaxing in her chair, she looked around at the now occupied bar. There was no one on the posh side, but the other side had gained a few customers. They sat and stood in little groups, talking and drinking, with occasional bursts of laughter, their eyes sometimes straying toward her, as a curiosity, and averting sharply if they thought she was looking. Abby smiled inwardly to herself, supposing that yes, a stranger at this time of year would be the subject of questions. Mary came rushing back.

"Oh you haven't finished your soup; I'll come back again shortly." Abby forestalled her.

"No, I have finished, it was very good, but if I had had any more I would not be able to eat another thing."

Mary was nonplussed. "Well most of them round here would be complaining that I hadn't given them enough." .

"What was the soup?" Abby thought to ask. " It was delicious."

"Leek, potato and onion," replied Mary.

"Oh yes, I've seen that in the supermarket, I shall have to get some when next I go." Mary laughed.

"You'll not get that in the supermarket, made right here in my kitchen that was, fresh vegetables this morning."

Abby blushed, frightened that she may have offended Mary. "No, you're probably right, I don't think I shall be able to buy anything as good as that in the supermarket."

Mary smiled contentedly. "I'll be back in a minute with your pie."

The pie was as generous as the soup, golden crust of pastry that melted on the tongue, steak and kidney that dispersed flavours both subtle and rich. Potatoes and vegetables lightly covered with the aromatic gravy that leaked from the pie. Abby had consumed a facsimile of this meal before, which could be classified merely fuel for the body. Those meals could not be compared to this in any way. Mary was again upset that Abby did not eat all that was put in front of her, imagining that the food was not to her liking.

"I can get you something else." Again Abby had to reassure her that such portions were well beyond her capacity. "Well if you're sure then," Mary gave in, "would you like some coffee or tea?" Abby opted for coffee, which she drank slowly, wondering if she would be welcome at the bar. In London she could have gone into a pub and ordered herself a drink. She could have, but rarely did, her lack of social confidence precluding her, but here she felt older attitudes would prevail, and didn't want to make anyone feel uncomfortable, least of all herself. Mary came to the rescue, bustling in to clear the table and leaning down, whispered, "If you would like a drink, Jack won't mind bringing it to you here. It's a lot more comfortable than the bar." The problem was resolved so simply and diplomatically, allowing Abby a choice, but at the same time indicating that her presence in the bar might discomfort the other customers.

Jack brought the whisky and water she had ordered and lingered awhile asking if she had enjoyed her meal. He was as relieved as his wife to learn that Abby had indeed enjoyed the meal, but that the quantities had defeated her. He went on to again ask about her family. Abby was happy to talk, as after all this was partially the reason she had come to the area.

"I was an only child, and as far as I know there are no cousins, aunts, and uncles whatever. Mum was vague about her past, and even after her death I was not able to find much to help. There was no personal correspondence, solicitors' letters or anything like that. I found an old passport, and all that told me was that she was born near South Molton." Jack mused.

"And your name is Tregonney. Was that your Mother's name as well?" Abby nodded her head in confirmation. "Tregonney.... Tregonney, wait a minute." and he disappeared round to the other side of the bar. He was back in a minute dragging an embarrassed man with him. "This is Will." Will nodded his head.

"Evening, Miss," he muttered.

Jack went on. "Will has lived around here for getting on thirty years, if any one knows something it will be him, apart from Sam, Sam Perry, whose been here all his life."

Will perked up because his local knowledge was being sought. "The only one who knows more than Sam is his missus, who knows everything, can't even turn over in bed without 'er knowing."

Jack turned to Will. "This is Miss Tregonney, who thinks her family may have once lived here about." Will didn't need to think long.

"Tregonney, why that could be the Tregonney who was stationmaster, hang on I'll tell you his name. What was it now? Yes," he exclaimed with pride, "it was Thomas, yes that was him Thomas Tregonney, mind you, I didn't know him, I didn't come here until nineteen sixty-eight, but I heard his wife had died, and I believe there was a daughter." He shook his head in puzzlement. "Don't know what happened to her." Will finished his little speech with a broad smile on his face, pleased that he could recall these details so quickly. Abby was elated, her grandfather, it had to be her grandfather, and he had been the stationmaster! No wonder she had felt an affinity for the place. She knew then that she would go back to the station tomorrow, to explore more, and see the place that her grandfather had worked, and possibly where her Mum had spent time as a little girl.

Jack ushered Will away, and returned straight away. "You have just given them all something to talk about. They'll be dredging their memories now. Come tomorrow evening and you could have enough to write a book. Do you think that Thomas Tregonney is related?" Abby nodded.

"Yes it has to be, as Mary said, it's not a common name. He could be my grandfather." She thought for a moment. "Please tell Will thanks for me, and do you think I could buy him a drink? She rummaged in her bag, and came up with a five-pound note, which she proffered to Jack.

"Put your money away, I'll give Will another pint, even though he's had enough already, and charge it to your bill. If they thought you was buying drinks for anyone who could tell you something about your family, they would be making up stories from now until mid-summer."

Abby sat with her thoughts for a while, and drank a little. Eventually she picked up the book she had brought down with her and settled down to read. A quiet but firm 'ahem' startled her and looking up she saw Will peering round from the bar. He lifted a pint glass, and nodded his head in thanks, Abby smiled at him and he withdrew, flustered. The book proved difficult, as she couldn't concentrate, and when she found herself reading the same page for the third time, gave it up. Mary came to join her at her usual bustling pace, and for once sat down.

"It's memory lane round there. Jack's ears are flapping like he'll take off in a minute. Lumme, they say women talk, they've never heard this bunch, mind you a lot of its quite fanciful, but that's country folk for you, a good tale can always be improved with a bit of embroidery. By the way you have been adopted. Jack says you think this Tregonney could be your grandfather. That makes you as good as a local." Abby had to smile; it gave her a good feeling in a way, as she had never really belonged anywhere before. She said as much to Mary.

"Mary, I've been here for what? Six hours. It's silly, I know, but I feel at home already. Probably because for the first time I know where my family came from, I know it was years ago, but I have found out something about me, and who I am."

Mary regarded her guest with affection, and patted her arm. "I reckon you'll find out a lot more before too long." She got up and seeing that Abby's glass was empty asked if she would like another. Deciding that she may not sleep too easily tonight, Abby thought she would have another. Mary brought this for her and also brought a glass of Sherry for herself. "Jack's coping easily tonight; so if you don't mind I'll sit awhile with you." Abby was happy to have her company, and they sat chatting comfortably, Mary in the manner of most women asking innocuous questions that filled in her knowledge of what Abby did for a living--was there a special man in her life, where she lived, and could eventually give a fairly accurate guess as to how well-off she was. She would be shocked later when she realised that she had seriously underestimated that aspect. Mary, being a woman, was now convinced that fate had brought Abby to this valley for a purpose; she was also fairly sure what that purpose was.

Abby for her part was quietly pleased with herself when she eventually retired to bed. Not just because she had found a link to her family; her logical brain told her that it was only a possibility, but her emotions crying out for sustenance would not admit anything but that it was a fact: The other reason for satisfaction was that for the first time she could recall in many years she had spent a whole evening in company, talking easily about everything and anything, and it had been simply done, none of the uncomfortable pauses as she searched for something to say, no asking fatuous questions to maintain a conversation. It all happened so naturally and easily. What was different this time? Why, here, was she relaxed and to an extent outgoing? Whatever the reason it didn't matter, the evening had been enjoyable and Abby retired to bed with a sense of accomplishment.

CHAPTER TWO

Abby slept better than she would have thought with the luxury of an opened window filling the room with the soft country air. She was wakened early, well, early for her, just after six, not by the crow of a cockerel, as she would have imagined but by the insistent blare of sheep. She looked out of the window to the meadows that came close to the wall of the Inn, and then stretched up rising gently at first and then more steeply to a copse on the skyline. The meadow was well populated with sheep, attended by lambs, which would occasionally try to eat the grass. Finding this not to their liking, they would rush back to the ewes and none too gently attack their mothers' udders. Abby was amused by the antics of these lambs that she supposed should be soft and cuddly things, and not demanding little tyrants. "Shouldn't you go 'Baa', not screech like that?" she castigated them.

There was a discreet knock on the door; hurriedly putting on her robe, Abby opened the door. It was Mary, with a tray. "Heard you got up, so I brought you some tea." She slid past Abby and put the tray on the dressing table. Abby was happily surprised.

"I haven't had tea brought to me in the morning for years, thank you."

"Well everybody's got to be spoilt sometime, haven't they?" Mary laughed. "Breakfast will be ready whenever you are. What would you like?"

"Oh, a couple of slices of toast will be fine."

Mary was offended. "Toast? Toast?" She exclaimed with indignation. "You're not going out of here without a proper breakfast inside you. What would people say if they thought I had just given you toast?" The rebuke was delivered with such firmness that Abby had to concede.

"Well perhaps egg and bacon."

Mary was mollified, and left the room muttering to herself. "Toast indeed."

If the tea that she had enjoyed yesterday afternoon was a revelation, the tea she drank that bright morning would have to be heaven. Abby stood at the window, the day was bright with a clear sky, and a light wind ruffled the grass in the meadows and sent the tops of the trees in the copse dipping and swaying. The first cup of tea went down so well she poured another. She had often heard of people saying that their spirits had lifted, and had doubted that such a thing could happen, until now as standing there she knew that her spirits had indeed lifted.

Dressed in a sweatshirt and jeans, she came down to find breakfast laid for her in the lounge. A large glass of orange juice awaited her on the table, from which Abby sipped. Presently, Mary bustled in bearing a platter full of eggs, toast and bacon.

"I've poached the eggs and grilled the bacon, I thought you might prefer it that way." she said with a friendly smile on her face. Abby looked with horror at the mountain of food before her.

"I couldn't possibly eat all this."

Mary interrupted her. "Gorn, you got to eat something, look at you girl, you're almost skin and bone." She stopped abruptly as Abby's eyes filled with tears. "Oh child, I didn't mean to upset you," she said with alarm filling her face.

"No, no, I'm not upset, it's just that those words were almost exactly what Mum used to say." Mary sat down in the chair next to Abby and put her arm around her shoulders.

"I'm sorry, Love, I should have thought. I suppose it is just what my mum would say, and I guess most mums at some time or other. Mind you, my mum wouldn't say it now." She opened her arms wide to demonstrate her ample proportions. The gesture made Abby laugh, pull herself together, and forced the brightness back into her voice.

"Yes, they probably have. I'll do the best I can with the breakfast, but don't be upset if I cannot finish it all." Mary smiled again and nodding her head vigorously in that way of hers, left Abby to eat her meal. She was once more surprised at her hunger, or was it the flavours, which seemed to be so different to those she was used to back in London. It was strange, though, none of these foods was alien to her, she had eaten eggs and bacon before on many occasions, but at no time had they conjured up the tastes she now enjoyed. The flavours complimented each other so well; no wonder people put them together. Yet the supermarket variety lacked the fullness and definition of these, the package may have described the content as fresh, but Abby's knowledge of the market told her that 'Fresh' was anything from twenty-four hours old to four days old. Was this that elusive quality called freshness?

Despite her newly found appetite, she could not finish the meal, and guiltily pushed the plate away. Sipping yet another cup of tea, she reflected that she ought not to go too far from the village today, as she would certainly need to use the loo after all this liquid.

Mary returned empty handed, much to Abby's relief, as she had visions of a plateful of toast appearing. "There, you didn't do too bad." she bantered.

Abby was intrigued. "Does everyone eat as much as that down here?"

"Oh no," laughed Mary, "that was only half a breakfast for most round here."

Abby sat back and stared with astonishment. "You're pulling my leg."

Mary grinned. "Only a little bit." She collected the debris from the table. She was just about to take the plates away, when as an afterthought turned and asked. "Had you any plans for the day?" Abby wondered if Mary was about to suggest anything, but felt that she would rather just wander around rather than have a specific goal in mind, so replied.

"All the driving yesterday has left me quite tired, so I think I shall just walk around getting to know the place." Mary nodded.

"Best thing, if you want anything to eat at lunchtime just pop in, there's always something available."

Abby had been telling the truth when she said she didn't want to drive anywhere, but walking was another matter. Her bag contained the required clothing, something she had learned from other breaks after being caught out in a number of downpours. She had in addition a handy-kit, which contained some basic first-aid items. Therefore equipped with good shoes, light rainwear, warm sweater, and a small rucksack containing, spare socks, some biscuits, a glucose drink, and the handy-kit, she left the Combe Inn, and set off down the lane for the old station. There was hardly any traffic on the lane so she was not required to walk in the gutter, where puddles left from the last rain still waited to soak her shoes.

What little traffic there was consisted of a couple of tractors, the drivers of which raised an arm in greeting upon seeing Abby. She was puzzled when one driver not only raised his arm, but called out. "Mornin', Miss Tregonney." She was certain that she had not seen him in the pub last night, so how did he know her name? It was not a question to concern her for more than a moment, however, as by now warmed by the exercise, she was starting to enjoy the walk. If the one and a half miles had seemed long when she drove this way yesterday afternoon, it was becoming a marathon now. She wondered if she had taken the right road, then told herself that was ridiculous, as there was only one road, she could not remember seeing that tree yesterday, nor that cottage. It was only when she looked back and could not see the cottage that she realised that the bend in the lane, and the hedge hid the cottage from sight when coming from this direction. Thus re-assured, she walked on, and soon was rewarded with the sight of the old sign pointing to the station.

More boldly this time, she approached the old building, after all she now had a personal interest, one might almost say a family interest in the station. Nothing had changed, but everything had changed. The platform still as dilapidated as yesterday, but now touched by a hand she could relate to. Granddad; although it seemed strange to refer thus to a man she had not known; had walked this platform, had touched these few remaining artifacts. Here he had gone about his work. In her mind's eye she could imagine a figure, striding up and down, quietly giving instructions to the porters, (were there porters?), waiting to greet the trains, nodding to the drivers, whilst looking pointedly at his pocket watch, exchanging the time of day with the guards, and importantly giving the right away to start the train on its journey once more. Strangely, although she could see this figure, dressed in a railway uniform, and wearing a cap to denote his authority, she could not see a face.

"What did you look like, granddad?" she mused aloud. "Were you tall, mum was tall for a woman. Were you handsome, and gentle?

Was your hair brown, black, blonde, or grey? Black, I think, because with your name you were probably a West Country man. I expect you had brown eyes, Mum's were brown, and so are mine. Have I got your brown eyes?" She stopped herself then, alarmed by the first watering in her eyes a prelude to genuine tears, as melancholy for a family she had never known swept over her.

Abby recovered her composure after a moment or two dwelling in sadness and deciding not to go down that route again, wandered down past the house at the end of the platform. She stopped and looked again with the sudden realisation that this was in all probability her grandfather's house, this was where her mum had spent her early years and had had grown up. The tears did flow now; this strange place that she had looked at so rationally yesterday, a catalyst for all the emotion that she had denied over the years since her mother died. Suddenly it was there in front of her, the past, not her past, but a past that in a way she owned, that she had never known about. "Damn, damn, damn, why did I come here?" Abby was beginning to think that perhaps this was not such a good idea. Eventually her tears dried, and she used a wipe from her handy-kit to dry the tear salt from her cheek. "Good job I didn't bother with make-up today, otherwise mascara would be all over the place."

This done, she stood for a while, looking at the house. Despite her earlier emoting, she would have liked to get in there, but the boarding firmly nailed into place deterred her, perhaps it was better that she didn't, not from the emotional point of view, but she felt sure that the house was now occupied by other, less wholesome beings, such as rats. Wanting to get away for the moment, her gaze fell upon the old buildings just a hundred yards down the track, and set off quickly to avoid the re-surfacing emotion. She followed the little path, which wound through the masses of gorse and nettles. It became obvious that this path was a remnant of what had once been an access road, periodic clearings showed the road bed, or rather what had been a road bed, but now being swallowed greedily by the weeds. She became aware, as she had yesterday, of the busy and prolific bird population. The flutter and flitter of wings all around, heard, but only occasionally seen, as a bird would dart down, and lift, carrying some wisp of grass or straw. She had heard as well, the rustle from the undergrowth. Sensible enough to realise that whatever creature lay hidden there was probably more afraid of her than she of it. Nonetheless a shiver crept down her spine, she was a city girl after all.

Her trek brought her nearer to the derelict buildings and she could now tell that one would have been a small house, the other, a goods shed. The hand that had designed the station had designed these, using the same rugged stone. The goods shed boasted large doors to which the rails had evidently approached and presumably carried on inside. High windows were set in the wall above head height presumable denying the workforce of any excuse for stopping work. It had a foreboding, almost gloomy look about it which Abby dismissed as purely invention on her part. The path ended here just short of the buildings and opened out into a large gravelled area. Walking to the left, she encountered the undulations where the sleepers had been lifted from the track bed. From this viewpoint she could see quite plainly how the track would have curved into the goods shed, and also that another track would have run alongside. To the right of the shed she noticed a foundation of what would have to have been a small but substantial building. Why leave the others, yet pull down this one, she wondered to herself. She pushed her way through the weeds, and getting closer spotted the large gap in the base of the foundation.

"The signal box!" she exclaimed, "of course, the frame inside must have been worth recovery. Easier to tear the building down to get it out than take it to pieces inside." Pleased with her deduction, she turned her attention to the small house, which was a smaller version of the stationmaster's house, but single storey and not so grand. Situated here she assumed that it would have been provided for the signalman.

"Hello, can I help you?" The voice startled her, and she turned to see the owner of the voice, a man, sitting a chestnut horse, on the other side of the hedge forming the boundary between railway and field. His voice may have carried to her, but there was no way that Abby was going to be able to shout a reply, so she started to wade through the weeds towards the rider.

"Be careful," he called, "there are lots of bits of old iron scattered around."Hhis warning was opportune for at that moment, Abby stepped on a long iron bar, which appeared to be hinged to a plate in the ground. She kept her balance, just, and continued until the gorse formed an impenetrable bar to further progress. She looked up, to find she had narrowed the gap to just ten or so feet.

"I'm just looking around, is that all right?" If she had expected a reply straight away, she was mistaken, for the man was staring at her with astonishment. Abby looked around to see what it was that had so discomfited him, but could see nothing. When she looked back, his face had adopted that bland look, of people who hate to let others see their emotions.

"Perfectly all right," he replied gruffly, "land belongs to no one now, just be careful of adders though, plenty about in that scrub. Good day to you." He lifted his crop in good manners, and urged his horse to walk.

How peculiar, she thought, someone who starts out to be friendly, and then goes all stiff and formal on you. If she had realised the shock in the rider's mind as he rode away, she would have revised her opinion. Abby retraced her steps to the station, with her mind active. On the one hand she was moved with her emotional response to these surroundings, a deeper emotion than she would have thought, being used to calm, clear-headed, analytical, processes of the mind in the midst of the shouting almost chaotic world, which was the trading floor. Yet her logical mind was telling her that she would only understand her grandfather's world if she researched the history of the line, and the society of the time. If there was ever a question in her mind about returning to this place, even with the strange emotions it stirred, then it was now resolved. She stopped in the forecourt and looked back at the station buildings, trying to imagine what it would look like during its working life, immediately she knew where she would start her research. There would have to be a local library, which would also probably possess a photographic archive. "That's tomorrow sorted."

With a goal in mind, Abby's steps which had become listless, regained their spring, and she turned back towards the village. On her walk to the station this morning she had noticed a sign for a public footpath, perhaps a diversion to see where it went would be in order. She found the sign within half a mile, in far better repair than other signs around here, but then a pressure group as well organised as the

Ramblers Association obviously punched well above its weight, and of course the opinion of the actual landowners counted for very little. The sign indicated the footpath leading to "Huish Coppice." Abby turned on to the path, which, ran alongside a small field for a hundred yards or so before turning abruptly left. The turn indicated by a simple wooden sign with a foot seemingly branded into the pointed arm. The path was now gloomy as it was bordered by hedgerow either side. A tractor had used the path at some time carving deep ruts that were filled with dank, slimy water. She had to take extreme care finding the driest footing. Again the path turned, this time to the right, thankfully the tractor had driven straight ahead into a field, and the footing was much more firm, the hedge was to one side only now, and as the path gained height steadily, the hedge got lower, until it had vanished altogether. The path led over a hump in front of her, and upon gaining the crest she was back on the railway!

Abby looked around to orient herself. To the west she could just see the station, and looking east the line curved away to the right eventually leaving her sight in a cutting. Once more she was astonished that the farmers had not reclaimed the old track bed. The boundaries were still clearly marked, sometimes by hedges, sometimes by fencing which appeared to be maintained. Of the track itself nothing remained. Satisfied she knew where she was, Abby set off along the footpath once more. Another sign appeared guiding her steps to the east, this time on a course, which paralleled the railway. As the railway entered the cutting, the footpath climbed, eventually leading away at a tangent, rising steadily. The copse on the hill in front of her was obviously Huish Coppice, and with the rise in elevation she was gaining a clearer view of this part of the valley, and also the village. The copse was apparently the same one that she had seen from the window at the Inn that morning, the railway in its cutting being totally obscured from Combe Lyney, the meadows creating the illusion that nothing intervened between village and hill.

Warm from her climb, Abby paused at the top, and took a glucose drink out of her rucksack. She noticed a stump and Abby gratefully utilised it for a seat. From here the area was spread out in a panoramic view. The station away to the west, the old line curving through the fields and meadows before vanishing below her, and the village, its houses and Church set out like a model in front of her. As she studied it, the shape of its development became clear. The original settlement, she could recognise by the old cob cottages, clustered, haphazardly around the Church. Behind the Church on slightly higher ground a larger house, probably the manor, she thought. And the later stone and then brick built houses, which filled in the gaps. Why the gaps, she asked herself? Then of course were the latest additions, the concrete system built houses, likely put there by the local council. It was probably wrong to call it a village, as there were no more than about forty houses in total, the earliest buildings close to the Church, and the later set further away, part of the community but maintaining a distance. As Abby sat, she was struck by the absence of traffic noise. Traffic noise was part and parcel of the city, even through the small hours of the night, the rumble and growl of cars, buses, and goods vehicles were a constant factor, to which city-dwellers became inured. When walking the lane, which had to be the main thoroughfare, this morning, the only vehicles she encountered were tractors. Even now as she sat the only sounds were those of the wind in the trees behind her, the occasional bleat of cattle, and the muffled grumble of a tractor, working in a field to the right of the village.

It really was most pleasant here. The sun warmed the land, the breeze, and this little enclave where she sat. Ruffling in her rucksack she found the packet of oat biscuits she invariably carried, and munched one contentedly. She had never intended to return to the Inn for lunch, even though she may have given Mary that impression. The truth being that the breakfast she had eaten at Mary's behest would suffice her for the rest of the day, particularly when faced with the prospect of an equally gargantuan evening meal. Far better to just sit, enjoy the view, and breathe the fresh air. A horseman rode along the hedge two fields away, but was too far for her to tell if it was the man she had encountered earlier on, she watched his progress for a while until he rode into another field further away, leaning down from his horse to unlatch a gate, moving his horse through, and then leaning down again to re latch it. Perhaps he never gets off his horse, she thought.

The day had moved on and Abby was amazed to find how time had passed in doing nothing. Rising from the stump, she started to make her way down the path. She had not gone too far before the rider appeared in front of her, it was the same man she had seen before at the station.

He raised his crop to the brim of his cap again, and remarked. "Pleasant day isn't it?" Abby was amused to find his attitude warmer, although it could not have been called unfriendly before.

"It's really nice." she replied, "I've just been sitting up there enjoying the view." He looked up to the copse where she pointed.

"Ah, Huish, yes it's one of the best spots. Often go up there myself, good place to think." He paused, "You wouldn't be the Miss Tregonney, who is staying at Combe Inn?" He asked. Abby stared in surprise.

"Well yes, I am, but how did you know that?"

He grinned. "Small place, Combe, if you haven't been here for at least twenty years, you get watched like a hawk, never know, you could be a spy for the Russians."

Abby repaid his grin. "It seems to me that the Russians had no use for you until you had lived anywhere for at least that length of time."

Now the man laughed aloud. "Oh wonderful, someone with a quick mind, just like your m... eh. Mike." He stumbled over the last word, and his horse seemed to jump a little.

The rider made a great fuss about gentling the horse, and changed the topic quickly. "Must get this one back to her stable, she will be wanting her feed. Perhaps I shall see you around, good day." He lifted his crop in salute once more and urged the horse, quickly moving across the open meadow down towards the crossing. Abby was astounded, again he had turned distant in the space of a second or so, and what was it he was going to say, 'just like your m...' and then 'Mike.' That didn't make sense, as she knew no one of that name, and the rider could not possibly know if she did or didn't anyway. If she was fanciful she could think he was going to say mum, but that wasn't possible either. Abby made her way slowly down the hill, half hoping that she would see the man again, just to tell him that she thought he was ... was what? Well did it matter; anyway he had a nice grin. Then another thought struck her: she had been making conversation! No long pauses as she searched for the right words to say; no embarrassing silences, she had even managed a humorous comment, well the rider had thought so, even if he did ride off almost immediately afterwards.

Mary was waiting for her when she got back to the Inn. "Oh there you are. I wondered if you were going to be back at lunchtime, I got quite concerned when you didn't."

Abby immediately apologised. "I'm sorry, Mary, but I rarely eat anything during the day, and after the breakfast you gave me I wouldn't have been able to eat a thing." Mary handed her the key to her room and in a low voice told her that someone had been inquiring about her. Abby was not too surprised, and ventured a guess that it was a man on a horse.

"Oh you've met him," cried Mary, "that'll be James Comberford, he owns the estate. How did you meet him?" Abby didn't want to go into too much detail, but just said she had seen him out on his horse and passed the time of day. She could tell that Mary was not satisfied with this answer and avoided any further questioning by saying she was quite tired and would go upstairs for a rest. In truth Abby was quite tired, she had walked more today than she had in a long time. The prospect of a cup of tea, and a comfortable chair to sit in had many attractions. Once in her room, she made some tea, and wandered to the window, opening it to look out at Huish Coppice, whilst she drank. It was obvious that Mr. Comberford had made the enquiries, as on their second meeting he knew her name, but why? Small communities were naturally inquisitive about strangers, but there was something about Mr. Comberford's manner that spoke of something more than just innocent curiosity.

The fatigue that Abby had used as an excuse was not so much an excuse as she had thought. Deciding to lie down for a while, Abby had fallen fast asleep, and it was much later when she awoke. Glancing at her travelling clock, she saw it was seven-fifteen. Quickly she rose, amused by the unusual doze, something she never did back home, indeed at this time she was normally to be found still in the dealing room, with the prospect of at least another couple of hours work in front of her. She showered, which re-established her usual vigour, and dressed quickly in slacks and a blouse. A simple gold chain around her neck gave the outfit just a touch of dressiness, and she was ready to go down.

As she walked into the bar, she was astonished at the reception extended to her. She made her way through with greetings ranging from, 'Good evening, Miss Tregonney,' through, ' Miss Tregonney,' to a simple, 'Miss,' all given with a nod of the head, a half smile, or in some cases a suggestion of a finger being raised to where a forelock would be. She returned these regards with smiles and made her way through to the lounge, which was yet again empty, except for the dog lying in the identical position before the fire as yesterday. She took the same chair as last night, as the dog raised its head, and thumped its tail in recognition. Jack was immediately hovering asking if she would like her usual.

Abby laughed happily. "Jack I've been here for just one day and already I seem to have found a new circle of acquaintances, and my drinking habits are noted for posterity, yes please I would love a spritzer." Jack nodded, pleased that he had given her cause to smile. "Be right up," he affirmed and hurried away. Abby was quite amazed with herself. She was actually talking easily to people, without the diffidence she normally felt. Perhaps it was because of these people who treated her with such friendliness. A few minutes later, Mary appeared bringing Abby's drink.

"Hello, Abby, here's your drink; now what would you like to eat tonight? I've got some lamb stew, or if you like a nice trout. Jack took a couple out of the river this morning, that won't take long to grill one. Sorry it's not a posh menu, but..." Abby stopped her.

"Mary I leave it up to you. If it's as good as last night, I know one or two so-called gourmands who would kill to get at your food." The smile of satisfaction on Mary's face was all that was needed.

"Right," said Mary, "My lamb stew is the best you will ever taste, even though I say it myself, you'll see" and she swished off to see to the food.

The lamb stew was the best Abby had ever tasted, the fresh succulent lamb tinged with a herb that she couldn't place, served with dumplings that seemed to have no trace left of the fat in the suet, and slices of crusty bread, which Abby spread thickly with the butter, not presented in little packets, but slabs of the stuff, golden yellow, glistening in a dish. Abby then did something that would be completely infra-dig at any other eatery, she used the last of the bread to wipe round the plate, not wishing to waste a morsel of the stew, so good did it taste. Mary came back just in time to catch her.

"Well, I can see you enjoyed that, would you like some more?"

Abby apologised for wiping round the plate. "But it was so delicious."

Mary beamed, "If you hadn't have done that I would think I was slipping." Abby sat back in the chair, as Mary asked if she would like some pudding. She shook her head. "If I continue to eat like this I shall go home and have to buy another wardrobe."

"Nonsense, girl, you could do with putting a few pounds on; you're like a scrap of nothing. Well if I cannot persuade you to any more, shall I get you a coffee?" Abby felt she could manage that, and Mary collected the dishes and went off to get it. She returned with the coffee, and sat down.

"Sam has come into the bar, let him have his first pint, but would you like to talk to him later?" Abby didn't have to think at all.

"I would like that, but only if it's no trouble, should I come round to the bar?"

Mary shook her head. "No you stay where you are, I'll fetch him when it's right. Jack will put a pint in his hand don't worry about that. Oh and Sam's a good sport, he won't want to know anything you don't want to tell him."

It was about twenty minutes later that Mary brought Sam round. Abby had built a mental picture of this man; based upon the comments that Mary, Jack and Will had made. Sam was nothing like this imagining; being of average height, wiry, and not looking anything like the eighty odd years he was supposed to be. He greeted her politely, and sat down at her invitation. He surprised her by opening the conversation.

"If Mary hadn't told me your name, I would have known who you were anyway, you're very much like Marion Tregonney. And you kept the name as well?" Abby knew that this last comment was a question, posed in the roundabout way that she was becoming used to. She decided not to prevaricate but tell Sam the truth.

"Mum never married." Sam digested this information, with a pull at the beer that Mary had brought. Mary hesitated about leaving, and Abby asked her to sit down, grateful for her company. She was pleased that Sam didn't mention any of the platitudes most people seem driven to offer upon learning that someone was illegitimate, and his next question set her aback.

"I know a fellow shouldn't ask a lady her age, but how old are you, Miss?" Abby was confused, as she seemed to be answering the questions, not Sam, which was the original intention. She answered anyway.

"Thanks for calling me a lady, I'm thirty-four." Sam's eyes steadied on her, and she could see some kind of an understanding and then great sadness creeping into them, and he muttered, almost to himself.

"You poor, poor, frightened girl."

Abby heard him and thought he was talking to her. "I'm sorry; I don't understand why you say that."

Sam apologised, "Forgive me, Miss, I didn't mean you, I was thinking of your mother. She left the village one day without a word to anyone, not even her father, just disappeared and nobody ever heard from her again. No one knew why. Now I know why."

It was Abby's turn to start understanding, and pain started to tighten around her heart. She asked her next question with a suspicion of what the answer was going to be. "When was this?"

Sam looked at her with pain in his eyes. "It would have been the summer of nineteen sixty-five."

Her dire suspicion was confirmed. "And I was born in November." There was a silence, broken only by Mary's gasp as she too realised the consequence. Abby could not stay, upsetting her coffee as she jumped up from the table and rushed to her room, where the tears that had threatened earlier finally flooded from her eyes. She cried not for herself, nor for the grandfather, whom she had never known, her tears were for her mother, who had borne all the sorrow and troubles alone, with no one to confide in, no one to share the burden. Sixteen years old, alone in a city where loneliness afflicts many, but few with a new baby to feed, clothe and protect. She wondered how her mum had managed, and could only half imagine the terrible times that she had suffered.

Mary and Sam sat in silence, until he began to speak, bitterly. "Damn Tregonney! He loved his daughter, she was all he had left in the world, but he was so unbending; so afraid of showing his feelings; never once as far as I know did he ever tell Marion he loved her. No wonder that when she was in trouble, she ran away, rather than tell her father. If only once he could have shown her the slightest emotion, he would probably have kept his daughter, and known this nice lass, his granddaughter." He stopped to think for a moment. "If she couldn't tell him, surely there was one of us she could confide in? We all failed her, just when she needed good friends the most." Mary wanted to ask questions of him, but decided that it would probably be best if she went up to comfort Abby instead.

"Stay here, Sam; I'll see if the girl will be coming down again." Sam nodded.

"If she doesn't I'll be here tomorrow evening, that's if she wants to talk."

Mary left to go upstairs and Sam took his empty glass back to the bar. His bar companions looked worried and one ventured to say, "Miss Tregonney looked upset, Sam, was there bad news?"

Sam just shook his head. "We both discovered something that was upsetting. If the girl wants to tell us about it she will in her own time. If not, no more will be said." The others nodded, this was a small place, here in this valley, curiosity was one thing, prying into someone else's affairs was different, and Sam knew that none of them would mention the subject again, not to Abby, not to Sam himself, and certainly not to any outsider. Sam had no doubt that eventually the circumstances would be known by everyone, but that would only happen with time and with the hurt having been healed.

When Sam got back to the farm that night, he was pleased to see that Mavis, his wife was still up. Without preamble he said. "There's young lady staying at the Combe, name of Tregonney."

Mavis looked up. "Tregonney?"

"Yes."

"That stationmaster was called Tregonney, would she be any relation?"

"You remember his daughter, Marion?"

"Yes." Then her memory cleared. "The one who disappeared!"

"That's her, and this girl is her daughter, she is called Abby."

Mavis thought for a while. "Wasn't Mr. Tregonney's wife called Abigail?" Sam nodded his head. "Well it's nice to know that Marion settled down. Is she there as well?"

"No, Love, you don't understand. She's Marion's daughter, and her name is Tregonney." He waited for a moment then said. "Sadly Marion is dead."

Mavis stopped and stared at Sam with understanding coming to her face. "Ah!"

Sam went on. "Marion didn't marry, and from the dates it is obvious that she was pregnant when she ran away."

Mavis was stunned. "But how could she be, she was only a child."

Sam shrugged his shoulders. "Sixteen, I think."

Mavis sat there with misery shadowing her face. "That poor child. How desperate she must have been, running away from her family and friends. There should have been someone who she could turn to surely?"

Sam had already thought this one through. "Obviously not. I can understand why she couldn't tell her father, I mean you know what Tregonney was like. I don't think I would like to give him bad news. But it hurts and angers me that none of us was close enough to the girl, that there was no one for her to talk to. She must have been so frightened, so desperate. It is painful to think of." He sat silently for a moment. "But who could it have been? That's what I would like to know."

Mavis was thinking furiously. "There's none around here who would do that. That I can say."

"Oh come on, Mavis. Men and boys have been getting girls pregnant for time immemorial."

"Now you don't understand. They could have but they would have done the right thing, not leave her in the lurch. You did!"

Sam looked aghast at Mavis. "What do you mean I did?"

"You thought that Roger was an early birth, Sam Perry. But when you walked me up the aisle I knew I was pregnant. Only a month mind!" Sam looked at his wife incredulously.

"What a time to tell me, after all these years." Mavis smiled in that way that women do when their men show incredible lack of awareness.

"Didn't make a difference to us at the time, we were already engaged and the church planned, so why tell you?"

Sam smiled fondly at his wife, who after all these years could still surprise him. He lapsed into silence for a while, Mavis watched him shrewdly. "What are you thinking, Sam?'

"Oh nothing really."

"Sam Perry! I know you well enough by now, come on, what is it?"

"I was just thinking that our daughter would be about the same age as Abby." Mavis smiled, she knew Sam would have been thinking that. It had surprised them both when Mavis got pregnant again after all those years. Sam was in his fifties and Mavis ten years younger. She thought she had gone through the change. After the initial shock they were happy about it, but three months in to the pregnancy Mavis was rushed to Taunton with abdominal pains. Just a few hours later she miscarried in the hospital. The Doctor told them it would have been a girl. They had already decided on a name for a boy and a girl. The baby would have been Sophie. She and Sam had borne the tragedy together, accepting that that was the way it happens, and stoically reasoning that Nature decided that the child wouldn't have been healthy. She leaned across and put her hand on his arm.

"Well, Abby hasn't got a father, and girls always need a dad, so you had better look after this one."

Sam nodded. "Reckon you are right. But it's not as if she was ours." Mavis had always realised that the loss of the daughter hit Sam far more than her. Funny this thing that men had, they wanted to father sons, but would treasure a daughter far more.

She looked up as Sam brought them back from the past. "Well, Memory Lane is a lovely lane to walk down, so whilst you are strolling, see if you can try and work out who could be the real father of this girl."

Mavis nodded. "Yes I'll give it some thought." Then another thought struck her. "We had some photos! Reg Purvess took them. I wonder if I can find them. Be nice if we can show the girl what her grandfather looked like."

"After all these years?" Sam exclaimed. "You will be lucky."

"I haven't thrown them away, I am sure. I'll find them." She hurried away, leaving Sam with a wry smile. How typical of Mavis, he thought. Eleven at night, and she would now turn the house upside down searching for something that could easily be found in the morning. Also how typically Mavis that she had only now thought fit to tell him that she was pregnant when they married. He supposed he should have known when Roger was born so soon, but assumed that it was an early birth. Other memories now came to him, meeting Abby Tregonney is the catalyst for nostalgia. He could not be sure when he saw Tregonney first. But it seemed as if he had always been there. He didn't realise at that time that Thomas was tutored deeply in the systems of the railway, and it didn't matter what station he was at, the systems and the paper trail was always the same. The same records, bills, chits and ticket procedures. The only thing that changed was the name of the station and the district office. So whenever Thomas had arrived at Combe Lyney, he would have fitted in seamlessly.

Sam then remembered when he first met Thomas. Sam would have been eighteen and started taking the milk down to catch the dairy train. He grinned to himself. He had left with a flea in his ear. Later he had got on easier terms with Thomas. Not friendly terms, Thomas would never go that far, but easier. Sam was at the station quite frequently, either delivering churns for the dairy, collecting empties and sacks of fertiliser, cattle feed, or any of the myriad of supplies that the farm would need that it could not provide for itself. The railway would deliver home, but that was at an added cost, and Sam's father was always careful about added costs.

Back at the Combe Inn, Abby sat in her room, not crying now, the tears just glistening patches on her cheeks. She stared at the window, now just a frame for the darkened skies, and wished that she had never started this search for her family's background. Then the logical side of her mind came into play and she reasoned that her not knowing the truth would hardly undo the desperation and unhappiness of her mother's life. She asked herself, 'Why?' Why couldn't her mother approach her father and tell him the truth, what was so terrible about her plight that she had to run away? Abby knew that if she had gotten herself pregnant, her mother would have been there to help, of course there would be recriminations, but even so Mum would have never turned her away. So what was it about her grandfather that her mother felt unable confide in him? Her search now took a new turn, no longer just about history, and places, but now concerning the mores and emotions attached to her family.

CHAPTER THREE

Abby did not return to the bar that night. She had a fitful sleep, eventually dropping off into an exhausted doze. She was awakened by an urgent knocking on the door just around eight-thirty, Wrapping her robe about her, Abby opened the door, it was Mary, who was very concerned that Abby had not appeared for her breakfast earlier.

"How are you, child? We got worried that you didn't come down for breakfast." Abby smiled listlessly, walked over and switched the kettle on. "Now don't you worry about that, I brought some tea up with me." And Mary stepped back outside the door, and picked up a tray, complete with steaming teapot, toast, butter, and marmalade. Abby slumped into the chair, and Mary bustled around, picking up Abby's clothes which she had discarded haphazardly last night, straightening and folding, all the while taking glances over her shoulder to see how Abby was.

"You don't need to do that, Mary, I'll do it in a minute, I'm not normally as untidy."

Mary stopped and regarded Abby sympathetically. "It's not a problem, Abby, if I had had a shock like that, I don't think I would worry too much about the mundane things in life. Sam was really upset you know; he was quite uncomplimentary about your grandfather. He didn't know why your mum had taken off and now he knows, he's quite bitter." Abby was grateful for a little bit of comfort, and somehow the fact that Sam was disturbed too did help.

Mary poured tea for them both, and took the other chair. "Things were different then," she said, "not many girls could have told their parents that they were pregnant and too many girls in trouble ran away, had abortions from back street butchers and ended up in hospital, or on the mortuary slab. Trouble was that the older generation wouldn't talk about nor accept that sex existed, at least not until you were married, or over thirty. We heard about the swinging sixties, but it didn't happen much outside of London, certainly didn't happen down here. Your mum, God rest her soul, took a very brave course, and if she could see you now would be so proud of you, so proud that she would tell you that all the trouble she had, was worth every moment."

Abby looked over the rim of her cup with gratitude. "Thanks, Mary." She paused, "Have you got any children?"

A shadow of sorrow passed over Mary's face. "No, Jack and I were never lucky that way." Her expression was enough to tell Abby that this was a regret that would not leave Mary, ever. But they were of a generation that did not complain about their situation, didn't demand help from the Health Service to get their perceived 'rights;' they just got on and handled life as it happened. She walked over and put her arm round Mary, and gave her a kiss on the cheek. The great beaming smile that rewarded her was ample proof that the unintended hurt was forgiven and forgotten. "Now Miss Tregonney, what are you going to do today?"

The road to Paverton left the village and crossed the river. It wound its way through the valley in a switch back manner, dipping, swerving but generally on an uphill gradient. The river, road, and from the glimpses of embankment that Abby noticed, the railway, were now being pressed together by the confines of the narrowing sides of the valley. The railway had to take a more meandering course, to maintain the easiest gradient possible, so as she drove Abby would see the remains of the track bed, first on one side, then on the other. Signs of the work that its builders had to do were evident in the bridges and small viaducts, which had carried the railway over farm tracks and streams flowing down from the hills to join the Lyney River.

There was less sign of habitation now, just an occasional solitary cottage set well back from the road, with the faint trace of smoke drifting upwards from the chimney. The river, which had gradually narrowed, could no longer be called anything other than a large stream. As the road twisted, Abby had caught sight, when the trees allowed her, of a large brick viaduct in the distance which spanned the road, stream and valley. Drawing level with the structure it became obvious that this was for the railway; leaping from one side of the valley to the other, as ever keeping the gradients easy. The road too crossed the stream about half a mile further on, a much taller structure than previously. From this bridge, Abby could see back down the valley; a superb view of the ground she had covered since leaving Combe Lyney.

The road now emerged into moorland for five miles before dropping down into the town of Paverton. The contrast between Combe Lyney and Paverton was most marked. Combe Lyney with its white cob cottages, mellow brick, and thatched roofs, a contrast to Paverton's grey, dull, stone built houses, with slate roofs, each looking like a miniature fort, built to withstand the elements. As she neared the town centre, the streets became narrower, with higher curbs, which Abby had to consider when she pulled to the side of the road to allow an oncoming vehicle room to pass. The centre was dominated by what was obviously the market square, the Town Hall on one side could not be mistaken for anything else, and there too was the Police Station, next to the Magistrates Court. Another side of the square was devoted to a Church, its simple design denoting the Methodist adherence of the West Country, and finally a small row of shops to complete the four sides. Abby smiled to herself, the four cornerstones of English life, Bureaucracy, followed by Legal, Spiritual, and Practical, it was amusing to note that the bureaucrats had built for themselves a larger, more ornate edifice than any of the others.

There was no market today so Abby was able to park in the market square itself; even where the inevitable pay and display notice invited her to buy some time. She was astounded by the prices, used as she was to paying London rates of two pounds or more for just half an hour, here the same money would bring her an entitlement for the whole day! Happily, she paid the ransom, and embarked on an exploration. She was looking for a library, and did not need to search too long, as outside the Town Hall a finger post pointed her in the right direction. The library turned out to be part of the Town Hall building, its entrance tucked away round the corner. Inside the atmosphere was of calm sobriety, the reading room to the left of the entrance, but untroubled by customers.

The lending library door was opposite, and the reference library straight on. Abby entered, and was immediately disappointed; the demand for reference reading was obviously small, as were the facilities offered. There was a librarian's desk just to the left of the door, and to the right along the wall was a table, obviously intended for the use of visitors. A young woman sat behind the desk reading an official looking volume, and making notes in a notebook, she looked up from the book with a questioning expression. Abby noted a nametag giving the girls name as Toni and explained. "I'm looking for material on the Lyney valley, with particular reference to the old railway. I would especially like to see any archive photographs you may have."

The young woman's demeanour brightened considerably. "A serious researcher! We don't get many of those; fact is we don't get any. The Tourist Information Office could easily answer most of the enquiries we get. Now let's see what we've got, it won't be much I'm afraid, you'll probably have to go to Taunton for in-depth material." She got up and came round the desk. "I'll show you the shelves and leave you to browse." Abby followed her through the tightly packed bookshelves, and they stopped in the Historical section.

Toni pulled out five books from various parts of the section telling Abby. "You will find that these cover the area generally, some will make reference to the Lyney Valley, but could be quite sketchy, Taunton will have much more detailed histories, but you have to wade through pages of facts and figures to find what you're looking for. I'll leave you to look, and in the meantime I will try and find something about the railway in the industrial section."

She was about to leave when Abby held her back by the arm. "This is very helpful of you, thanks."

Toni gave her a mischievous grin. "It's much more interesting than researching Parliamentary Returns. I needed a rest from all those self-important worthy's." Abby took the volumes that Toni had selected for her to the table and sat down prepared for research. In pursuit of her hobby she had often done this sort of thing and had refined her approach. The contents list were usually just rough guides, the index was the place to start, using a key-word, and then listing the page numbers given for each. No sooner had she sat down and she realised she had not brought a pad and pencil. Toni was equal to the occasion, and re-appeared with another couple of books, a pad and ball point pen.

"Thought you might find these useful." Abby smiled her thanks and started. The first two histories covered too large an area to warrant more than a cursory mention of the valley. The third made no mention at all save a note about the confluence of the Lyney with the River Bray. The fourth had more to say, but this only about the valley as a route used by a column of Parliamentary forces during the Civil War after the attack on Dunster Castle. Another page mentioned the building of the railway by the Bristol and Exeter Railway Company. Here Abby was confused, she had imagined that the line was Great Western, and had been built by that concern. Who or what was the Bristol and Exeter? She made a note on her pad to start looking for references, another key word! The last book gave her the most information, with a description of the valley, with paragraphs about the quarries providing good granite, and another, which yielded Alabaster. It was from this volume that she discovered that the Comberford family had owned nearly all the valley at one time, and that their tenure went back to Elizabethan times. She scribbled furiously, making notes of interest on the pad as well as more key words to continue her research.

She then turned to the last two books that Toni had brought for her. Primarily concerned with the industry of the area, the railway network was written about only as an adjunct to such industry, mainly quarrying, that existed. These two books were very slim indeed. They did however give her another tack to take, as they both mentioned in the bibliography a book about Exmoor Farming. Abby collected her note pad, and picking up the books she called to Toni. "I'll just put these back."

Toni shook her head. "No leave them on the desk here. I have to record visitors and the books they refer to. Did you find anything of interest?" Abby showed the notes she had made, and the list of further research she would make.

"It's a start, but I suspect there's a lot more to do."

Toni examined her lists, and ticked those books she could get. "They'll be here in two days, if you want to come back."

Abby thought about it and replied. "No, thanks all the same." I'm only here for a few days, so I doubt that I shall be able to make much use of them. I'll find them in the British Library."

Toni's eyes widened. "Oh, you are serious in your research then, are you writing a book?"

Abby laughed. "No nothing as serious as that. I suppose I'm looking for my roots, my family lived in the valley a long time ago and I just want to know about the background, and how they lived. I've no other relatives to ask so I'm just casting around for anything that will build up a picture."

Putting the notes away in her handbag, Abby prepared to leave when Toni said. "I'm just going for coffee, would you like to come?"

This took Abby by surprise, but she nodded. "Yes, that would be good."

Toni picked up her bag, and led Abby out of the Library' "There's a nice place just across the road."

Once they were seated with their coffees, which Abby had paid for, Toni leant over the table in a conspiratorial manner. "You know, one of the quickest ways to find information is with a local solicitor. Do you have proof of your identity?' Abby delved into her bag, and brought out a sheaf of papers, amongst which was her birth certificate and her mother's long expired passport. She showed this briefly to Toni, who told her that there were only four long-established solicitors in Paverton.

"Most people at one time or another have need of a solicitor, and they never throw anything away. A pound to a penny, one of them has dealt with your family, and will still have the file, dusty it may be, but it will be there, and as the only surviving family you have every right to anything they have." Abby hadn't thought of this, and doubted that her grandfather would have used a solicitor, but it was worth a try. Changing the topic, she asked Toni what she was studying so intently in the library.

"Some of the local councillors seem to think that the library staff are here purely to do secretarial jobs for them, work incidentally which should go down as election expenses, but of course doesn't. I was looking up references for one of them, which he will use in his canvas leaflet, shouldn't be done really, but as he's my dad, how can I refuse?"

"Well if it's for your father, I would imagine that it all right," suggested Abby.

"Not when I'm doing it in my employer's time, and my employer is the council," replied Toni with a grin.

Refreshed after her coffee, Abby followed the directions that Toni had given her and started looking for solicitors. The name, Tregonney, meant nothing to Bedwas & Jameson nor to Wheatley & Co. the third Solicitor, Mackenzie Davis & Partners could not help either, but suggested she try Chorister Brooks & Son, who had been in practice in the area longer than any others. She found their offices tucked away just off the main road upon which she had arrived in Paverton, coincidentally it was on Station Road. If there were such a thing as an archetypal solicitor's office, then this was it. Heavy oak panelling supported the theme of gravitas and sobriety with which the profession deemed it appropriate to welcome their clients, a highly polished brass bell sat on the desk in the reception room, and a small notice next to it invited her to push the plunger to summon help. Abby did, and shortly a young lady, completely out of place with the surroundings came to see if she could assist.

Abby explained as she had in three other offices. "My name is Tregonney, my family at one time lived in Combe Lyney. To the best of my knowledge I have no other relatives, and I wonder if this practice had at any time any of the family as clients, and if so I would be grateful for any information you can give me." The young lady had to give this some thought, and then said that it would be helpful if an idea of dates could be given.

"I would think prior to nineteen-sixty-five," replied Abby.

The girls face crumpled, obviously she had not even been born then. "I'm sorry but I couldn't help you, being that far back but if you don't mind waiting, I will see if there is someone who can help you." Abby sat down. The wait was likely to be uncomfortable, as the chair was one of those seemingly designed especially for waiting rooms--a high, wooden back, with the seat covered in polished hide as hard as iron. Magazines were available for those interested in Horse and Hound, or House and Garden, but reading really was out of the question as there was only one pitiful bulb to illuminate the room leaving a visitor in perpetual gloom. Abby waited patiently, until she sensed rather than heard someone approaching the door to the offices. A middle-aged man came into the room.

"Miss Tregonney? My name is Brooks, the grandson part of the company name." He extended his hand to Abby who stood and they shook hands. Mr. Brooks was initially inclined to explain that he was sorry but could not help her, having no recollection of the name on their client list, but something about Abby made him re-assess the situation. This was not some poor relative desperately casting around in the hope that a long-lost rich relative had left them a legacy, here was a calm, self-assured woman, who had confidence, and did not seem in need of a bob or two. Used to judging people quickly, he equally quickly made up his mind. "I myself am not aware of anyone of that name as a client, but I have only been with the practice for twenty years. If I could ask you to wait a little longer, I will ask our Mrs. Forbes, who will undoubtedly be of greater assistance. She is out of the office at the moment, but is expected back at any moment, would you mind waiting a little longer?" Abby indicated that she had no objection, and resumed her hard seat. Just as he was leaving, Brooks asked almost as an afterthought. "Oh could we get you a coffee or tea, perhaps?" Abby wondered if refreshment in this place would be dire or plain unpalatable, so declined.

It was about ten minutes later, just as Abby's backside was becoming numb; an elderly woman came in through the street door, and would have swept through without stopping until she saw Abby.

"Is someone attending to you?" she inquired.

"Yes, I have seen Mr. Brooks," Abby replied.

"Oh good," the woman replied in a manner, which suggested that it probably wasn't so good. She then went through the door to the inner office. Two minutes later she was back.

"I'm Mrs. Forbes, I understand you are inquiring about Tregonney." Abby prepared herself to go through the whole story again, but the woman forestalled her. "Mr. Brooks explained the situation, and to tell you the truth I do recall the name, but in what connection I cannot remember. However it would have been Mr. Brooks senior who would have been involved, I'm sure he would remember. Thirty years ago is no problem for him, yesterday, now that's a different matter." Abby smiled digesting this information and asked.

"Perhaps I could make an appointment to see him?"

Mrs. Forbes had a doubtful look on her face. "Well Mr. Brooks senior is retired from the practice, for some years in fact. I don't know if an interview would be possible." She saw the disappointment on Abby's face and relented. "It's most irregular, but I will telephone him now, and see if he could come in, perhaps tomorrow if that would be convenient for you?" Abby agreed, and resumed the hard chair as Mrs. Forbes went off to make the call.

Five minutes went by, and then another five, Abby's backside was now completely without feeling, after a further ten minutes Mrs. Forbes was back.

"I'm sorry to keep you waiting, I had to let the phone ring for quite some time, he never answered a phone in this place, and hasn't got used to the fact that he has to do it himself now. But good news, he seemed quite conversant with the name, and will come in tomorrow to see you, would ten o' clock be convenient?" Abby was pleased that this uncomfortable wait would at least result in some advance.

"Yes, that would be fine." Mrs. Forbes nodded, and then relaxed and smiled.

"It's obviously important to you, I'm sure you will find Mr. Brooks can tell you a lot. In the meantime I have to go down to the cellar, and retrieve the file and other things, although I shall be surprised if it can be found easily after all these years. I shall see you tomorrow then."

Abby left the building with excitement rising. Just two days here and she knew more about her family than in the previous thirty odd years. She returned to her car, but decided to pop back in the library and thank Toni for the good advice. She was just in time as Toni was just about to leave. "It's my half day," she explained, "I get the freedom of Paverton once a week for half a day." the look on her face suggested that the freedom of Paverton was not as endearing as it sounded. They walked out of the library together and Abby told her what had transpired. Toni was really pleased, not just because Abby had got a result, but also because her advice had worked. Their path had taken them back into the market place and Abby stopped by her car. Toni drooled over the car. "Is this yours?" she asked, and when the reply was affirmative, could not contain her envy. "If I worked at that library for the next forty years I could never afford a car like that, not unless I married a rich man, and there are not too many of those around here." Abby felt that her gratitude was possibly not enough, so offered Toni a lift to wherever. "Thanks all the same, but it's only a five-minute walk, tell you what though, if you're coming in tomorrow to see that Solicitor, pop over afterwards and we'll have coffee." Abby smiled and agreed that she would indeed have coffee with Toni tomorrow. Toni gave a little wave and carried on across the square, eventually leaving it down a side road.

On the journey back which she drove quite slowly, Abby ran through in her mind the information she had gathered so far, first her grandfather, how long he had been stationmaster, from what little she knew it was certain that he would not have reached that position at an early age, and most certainly would be promoted to it from another station. Abby had realised long ago that she was illegitimate, so the shock was not that, but of realising how desperate and lonely her mother must have been, and also of knowing that her grandfather had no idea that he was a grandfather. Then there was the strange Mr. Comberford, who she was now certain had known her mother. The more she thought about it, she was convinced that he had been about to say mother. But how could he have known? He had talked to Mary that was clear, so was it impossible that he would work out the relationship? Sam had done that easily. So Mr. Comberford must have known her mother. It was quite simple to put two and two together and get the correct answer. Any other theories and she would be making up conspiracies. Abby is pragmatic, and the shocks that she had received were behind her, she was now determined to discover as much as she could from Sam and make sense of her family, hopefully she could make a start tonight.

CHAPTER FOUR

Sam was cautious at first, as he didn't want to upset the girl anymore than he had already, but with Abby's reassurance that she was fine, he was more at ease. "I had long known that I was illegitimate," she told him. "That doesn't upset me. What did upset me was realising that mum had just walked away from here when she had a family who could have helped her."

Sam nodded. "I was just as upset. Your mum running away was one thing, but realising that she was with child when she did, really angered me. We all knew your mum, and knowing that she couldn't confide in any of us, especially her dad, made me very sad. I just wish that... Oh well it's no good going over that, it won't help at all, too many years have passed." Abby wondered what he was going to say, but didn't press the point knowing that as Mary had said, when they don't want to tell, they won't say anything.

She decided to bring the conversation around to her grandfather. "What was my grandfather like?"

Sam smiled affectionately at her. "To tell the truth girl, I don't really know how to describe him. I won't describe him physically, my missus reckons she has a photo of him somewhere, and she started turning the house upside down at eleven o' clock last night. But don't worry, if it's there, she'll find it. Apart from that I suppose I would say your grandfather acted as though his job was the most important thing in the whole wide world. I never knew him once to appear anywhere without his uniform, and it was always cleaned and pressed like he was going on parade in the army. You knew when he was around, his uniform always carried the faint smell of mothballs."

"Excuse me, Sam, but what are mothballs?"

Sam chuckled. "Mothballs were small pellets which you hung in the wardrobe. Supposedly the aroma, it was camphor, kept the moths away, don't know if it worked too well though, most of our clothes had small holes where the moth had been." He carried on. "His boots, you could see your face in them. He was brought up in the traditions of the Great Western Railway, and although every other railway man was pleased when nationalisation happened, not him. That was the blackest day of his life, and he refused to give up the styles and trappings of the Great Western. To the day he retired, he still wore that funny pillbox cap with the initials on the front, and his frock coat. Everything that British Railways did was wrong, because it was not Great Western, and he told them too, no wonder he never got any further than Combe Lyney. I don't know if he applied for promotion, if he did, well he didn't get anywhere, I don't even know if he was disappointed, if he was he never showed it, not your grandfather, he still did his job every day as if the district manager was watching him constantly, and for him, there was only one way, by the book, perfectly!"

Sam paused to take a long drink from the pint that had appeared as if by magic at his elbow, brought by Jack who nodded to Abby, letting her know that it was paid for. "He wouldn't accept any standard but the best, from himself, and particularly from the porters, strewth; he could, and did, make their lives a misery."

Abby listened intently, building a picture of this martinet, who was now coming to life. "Was he born here, in the village?"

Sam shook his head. "No, he was a Cornishman, don't know exactly whereabouts, but he was certainly Cornish. Tregonney, you know, Cornish name." Abby could have kicked herself, she wasn't thinking straight.

"So when did he come to Combe Lyney?" she asked.

Sam had to think about this. "Before the war it was, now was it before or after the abdication, yes after, I'm sure after, so that would put it about '37 or '38," he thought a little bit more then stated confidently. "Nineteen-thirty-eight. That was it. I was still a lad at the time, he would have been in his late thirties, and even then he acted as if he was late fifties. How he managed to get that lovely girl to marry him I shall never know, she came with him, Stationmasters had to be married, you see. Mind she looked frail even then, not surprised she was taken early."

Abby interrupted. "Taken early, she died?"

Sam looked at her with sympathy. "Yes, girl, she died, pneumonia it was, would have been about nineteen-fifty-eight, she never was very healthy." Here he stopped again and his eyes grew cloudy as he wandered back into a past that was gone forever.

Abby waited patiently, wanting to ask about her mother, but not wishing to disturb his thoughts. Sam roused himself, and as if he had read her thoughts continued. "You'll want to know about your mum. Lively girl, had your granddad's colouring, very little of your grandma in her. Had a lot of spirit, right little tomboy as I recall. After your grandma died, she was left very much to herself, didn't get into trouble though, always interested in what was going on. She came into the milking parlour one afternoon, and insisted on being shown how to milk, got it right too, cow's are very sensitive to who's milking them, and if it's not right will get quite vexatious, and won't milk freely. She would come most afternoons after that and help, then her father found out and put a stop to it."

"Why?" asked Abby.

"Because his daughter was going to be better in life than a farmer's wife," replied Sam, "don't ask me why being able to milk a cow, automatically made her into a farmer's wife, but that was how he thought, he was a bit mazed about it. Same as when the signalman, Purvess his name was, showed her how to pull the levers, and answer the bells. Your grandfather really carpeted him, and no mistake. Funny thing, he could have had him sacked, if the district superintendent had found out about it he would have been, but according to Purvess, it never even went into the weekly report."

Abby digested that, it seemed so out of character with the man that Sam had been describing. "Why would he do that?" she asked.

"Don't know," replied Sam, "some would say, it would have reflected badly upon him, allowing his daughter to run around the station yard, unchecked. But I think the real reason was because he might have felt guilty that he wasn't giving his daughter the attention she should have. Anyway nothing more was ever said about it. He was strange in some ways, your granddad. He seemed determined that your mum should better herself in life, but never did anything about it. Oh, she went to school, I don't know how she did there, must have been alright though, she always had a way with words, but your granddad never seemed to spend time with her. It was the job, porters worked shifts, signalman had plenty of time to relax during the day, stationmaster, well he was on duty from first train in the morning until last train at night, and then he would be in his office, balancing the book, writing letters. I reckon your mum brought herself up." Abby was entranced, this was not only her family Sam was talking about, and he was also talking about a way of life that had vanished. She was hungry for more, but realised that Sam came into the pub for relaxation with his friends, and not to tell her the story of her family. She gave him the opportunity to leave it for a while by excusing herself to go upstairs.

When she came down, Sam was in the bar part of the pub, talking with some of his friends. Abby went straight past, not wishing to take him away but Sam caught her eye and indicated that he would join her in the lounge shortly.

It was little more than two minutes before Sam followed her and sat himself down, prepared to talk as long as Abby wished. He was quite happy talking about those times, the more he spoke the more he remembered. Abby was concerned that she was selfishly monopolising his time, and said as much. "Don't you worry about that girl, the talk in there is all about the weather, the grazing, livestock, and the bloody government. It was the same last night, and it will be the same tomorrow night. I get to sit down and chat with a pretty young lady, and it seems I don't have to buy me own drinks either. If you and Jack are in cahoots you can leave off now. I'm enjoying myself, I don't need free beer to persuade me to something I enjoy."

Abby laughed delightedly, she quite like being called 'girl,' it was a long time since she had thought of herself as that. "Tell me, Sam, you seem to have known my grandfather reasonably well, yet you must have been of quite different ages, how was that?"

Sam took another drink before replying, "Well, I was working for me dad on the family farm, and as I said earlier, the milk run was one of my jobs. Those days you didn't have a tanker come round and collect the milk. You had to get it to the station, for the train. One collection early in the morning, and the other late in the afternoon. I used to take it down in churns, at first in a cart with a horse, and later we got a small Jowett van for the job."

Abby interrupted here. "Jowett, what make was that? I've never heard of them."

Sam chuckled. "I'm not surprised. Made a little utility van, with an air-cooled, horizontally opposed engine, more like a motorcycle engine. Got no power, struggled up hills when empty, put any sort of load in it and you would have to get out and push. They made a car too, called the Javelin, very smart design for the time, looked fast, but it had the same engine, so the looks were all it had. Don't know when they went out of business, must have been the mid-fifties some time."

Sam returned to the milk business. "I had to get to the station twice a day, and got to know your grandfather reasonably well. He was always there, didn't matter what time of day, he was there. I can remember well the first time I went down with the churns, I was well pleased with myself, having unloaded the cart, and got all these churns on the platform, near to the edge, so that the porter wouldn't have far to turn them. Suddenly this voice put the fear of God in me, he didn't shout, but his voice would stop anyone in his or her tracks. 'What do you think you are doing,' he says. I said something about making it easier for the porter, and back he comes, 'I'll decide whether to make life easier for my porters, and as they are lazy excuses for what porters should be I'll make life as hard for them as I wish. Now, while we are about placing churns on the platform, would you pray tell me how my passengers are to get past the obstacle you have erected for them?' My first thought was to say that at half past five in the morning, there was little likelihood of passengers, but I thought better of it, mind you he didn't wait for an answer, and went on to ask. 'Perhaps you would also tell me what is going to happen to your milk, if the train were to be delayed, which it will not be as this is the Great Western Railway, but if it were, your churns will be sitting there in the sun, warming nicely, will they not?' I could see immediately what he was getting at, and started to move them back under the platform awning. The next thing I know he is there beside me, moving churns faster than I have seen, he just pulled the top slightly toward himself, and then rolled them on the bottom rim. In no time at all, seven churns moved into the shade. That's what was sometimes difficult to understand about your grandfather. He would rip you off, and make you feel a complete idiot one minute, and then he was helping you. I never made that mistake again."

Sam drank deeply of his beer. "I reckon I made that trip to the station hundreds, no thousands of times. As I grew older I got to know him better but not well, I don't think any of us got to know him well. In those days everything and everyone who arrived here came by train, and everything that went out went by train, so the station was an important place for all of us, and we all knew Thomas Tregonney, who he was and what he was, and we all had dealings of some kind or another with him, but that was as far as it went. He would come in here for his lunch most days, still dressed up in his frockcoat, and that cap, a bit like a French general's, but could never socialise. The porters could be in the bar, so that stopped him having his snap in there, because he was their boss, and obviously couldn't socialise with them, he probably thought they would take advantage. If the lounge was empty he would come in here and sit down with his drink, but if anyone like old Mr. Comberford was here then he was stuck. He sort of hovered just inside the main door, neither one thing nor the other. It was better for him in the good weather, as then he could take his drink outside and sit on one of the benches."

Abby was fascinated. Sam was talking about a social code that had vanished. She could and did socialise with her subordinates, with no problems at all. It amazed her that her grandfather was bound by a system that put him in a social no-man's land.

"Why couldn't he drink here when Mr. Comberford was in?"

Sam considered her question, wondering how to answer. It was a question like the one about mothballs, it was to do with time, none of his contemporaries would dream of asking such a thing, the answer was part and parcel of their life, you instinctively knew about class. Who was your peer group, who was lower than you in the order, and those you would consider your betters.

"It's difficult to give you a reason," he began, "Mr. Comberford was the landowner around here, and would be the best customer that the railway had. Your grandfather would know that whilst on the surface, Mr. Comberford was happy to do business with him and be civil, although he had little option, as there was no other way of moving goods in and out, he would not be happy about sharing the lounge with someone who he considered to be of the lower classes."

Abby was a little indignant about this, her grandfather, "Lower class!"

Sam sensed her feelings and carried on quickly, trying to explain. "Anyone who didn't own land was of a lower class to Mr. Comberford. All of us who were around then were lower class to Mr. Comberford."

"But surely you weren't," said Abby, "you had a farm?"

Sam shook his head "No, girl, my family were tenants, Mr. Comberford owned our land, and we paid him rent. So my dad drank in there."

This was getting confusing for Abby. "So, he didn't have a problem with the porters?"

"No, but then he wasn't their immediate superior. In fact I'm sure your grandfather could have taken a drink quite easily in there, the porters would have moved away to the other end of the bar, and given him space. They wouldn't have a problem, other than they couldn't moan about their stationmaster. The problem was Thomas Tregonney's. He must have felt that he couldn't associate in any way, because of his position."

Abby was still angry. "Just wait until I see that Mr. Comberford again, I'll tell him what to do with his class."

Mary laughed. "Oh don't go giving Mr. James a hard time. It wasn't him, it was his father." Abby stopped, of course it couldn't have been him, and Sam was talking about a time fifty years ago.

She had realised that Sam once started would have talked on at length, but she felt guilty all the same, so decided that she would leave him to enjoy his drink in peace with his friends. She had surreptitiously looked at her watch and it just past eleven. "Sam, it has been so interesting listening to you, but I am really tired, it must be the air around here, not to mention Mary's wonderful meals. Would you excuse me? I should get to bed now."

Sam looked at his watch, a wonderful pocket watch, the plating highly polished from years of use.

"God bless you Girl, look at the time, I must be away myself or the missus will give me hell. You sleep well, and I'll be happy to see you tomorrow night, that is if I haven't bored you too much."

Abby told him that she would love to talk some more, and on impulse leaned over and kissed his cheek. Sam went a bright scarlet, but the broad smile on his face left her in no doubt that he was delighted. Some of the other patrons, who were leaving noticed, and cheered bawdily.

"Just you wait until I tell your missus, Sam," cried one. "She won't half give you what for." Abby walked back through the bar to a chorus of good nights from those remaining. Happy, she returned their greetings and made her way to her room.

With Abby gone, Mary turned to Sam. "So, when are you going to tell her?" The happy smiling face was gone and the tragedy that Sam had told her about was giving her great trouble.

"I don't know, Mary," replied Sam, "it just don't seem right to just come out with it. I'll find a way."

Mary's expression didn't alter. "You can't leave it forever, she'll have to know, and you'll have to make it soon. I don't want her going back to London with that piece of news awaiting her if she comes back."

Sam nodded his head miserably. "Yes, you're right, Mary, I'll tell her tomorrow

Abby awoke to the sound of rain hammering on the window. Rising, she walked over and looked out on a grey, squally day, of great clouds billowing up the valley from the West, driven by a wind, which bent the trees of Huish Coppice with its force. In many ways Abby was relieved that the weather was bad, otherwise she would be tempted to walk down to the station and immerse herself in its atmosphere, but this time in brighter colour imbued with greater knowledge of her grandfather. But she remembered the Solicitor, she had promised to see him at ten o'clock. Looking at her watch she was relieved to see that it was just past seven, an hour which had rarely featured in her life in London. So it gave her time to conduct a more leisurely introduction to the day than she would normally enjoy.

Mary was bustling around as usual when Abby came down to breakfast and greeted her with that beaming smile. "What would you like for breakfast this morning?" she asked, "and don't tell me just toast."

Abby laughed. "To tell you the truth, Mary, I do feel quite hungry this morning. Could I have some scrambled egg on toast?' Mary seemed quite pleased that at last Abby was going to eat properly, and went off to her kitchen humming. The scrambled egg when it arrived looked like a great yellow mountain, steaming, and running with little rivulets of butter. Alongside were two rashers of Bacon, grilled crisp. Abby would have protested, but the delicious aromas kicked her salivary glands into gear, and she attacked the plate with delight. In short order the two rashers had been consumed and half the mountain, when the full sign went up and Abby pushed the plate away. Thus fortified she could contemplate the day ahead. Wondering what revelations this day would bring, after all, every day so far had brought her nearer to her grandfather, whose existence hitherto was only a biological fact, and also to her mother, who she now realised had once been a young, carefree girl.

The rain was easing when she left the Combe Inn, enough to make driving a little easier, but not enough to avoid her getting soaked running round to the back of the Inn, where the car had been parked. The wipers swished steadily as she drove the road to Paverton, soon clearing the road film from the screen; their steady arc sporadically interrupted as droplets of rain, shaken from the trees by the gusting wind bombed the car, and spattered the windscreen like bullets. Her initial thoughts that the rain was easing were dashed upon reaching the moorland at the top of the valley. Here the elements ruled absolutely, the wind hurling slabs of rain horizontally across the road, whipping the gorse, bracken and occasional beech into a moving undulating mass, more akin to a stormy sea than open country. Even the sheep had sense to take cover, as she had a fleeting glimpse of a small flock huddled into what appeared to be three walls of a ruined cottage. Abby would later find out that this enclosure and others like it were specifically built for this purpose. She was glad to leave the moor behind as she descended into Paverton, for whilst the rain still fell, the wind had been left behind. As she drove towards the square her car splashed through rivers of surface water cascading down the hill like a torrent, she understood now why the gutters were made so deep.

Deciding that leaving the car in the car park and walking would be a little unrealistic; she turned off the square and down Station Road to where Chorister, Brooks and Son were situated. The road was lined with double yellow lines, but today Abby was prepared to pay any fine levied, she didn't want to arrive looking like a drowned rat. She was happy to see that others felt the same way, as cars were parked along the pavement, as if the parking regulations did not exist.

Mrs. Forbes met her in the reception, and hearing Abby's explanation about leaving her car on the yellow lines, assured her she had nothing to worry about. "We don't have a warden here, except in the summer when they come in like a posse, twice a week from South Molton. The police don't bother with parking regulations, unless you're causing an obstruction, so don't worry at all, you are quite safe." Mrs. Forbes seemed have warmed a little from yesterday. "Would you like to come through, Mr. Brooks, senior, is here already, which is a wonder." As she opened the door through to the offices she went on Sotto Voce, "When he was practising he would keep clients waiting an hour, and be surprised when they complained. Not many did though, in those days the Solicitor ranked alongside the clergy and the doctor, as someone who had a greater calling than most mortals." The stern matriarch sounded to Abby as if she regretted the passing of those days. A door was opened and Abby was ushered in to an office, to meet Mr. Brooks senior, who got up out of his chair and extended his hand to shake hers. "This is Miss Tregonney, Mr. Brooks," Mrs. Forbes announced in a loud voice.

"Thank you, Mrs. Forbes, I am sure that Miss Tregonney would like a cup of coffee, I certainly would." Muttering that she would see to it, Mrs. Forbes withdrew. Mr. Brooks was a tall, well-built man with a thick thatch of grey hair and bushy eyebrows to match. Abby would have expected him to be soberly attired as most Solicitors, but presumably having retired Mr. Brooks had forsaken the uniform. Instead a check shirt, no tie, well-worn jacket and flannels with brown shoes were his preferred mode that morning. Abby was a little shocked. Brown shoes! Different modes applied here, nobody would ever wear brown shoes in the city.

When Mrs. Forbes was safely out of earshot, Mr. Brooks grumbled. "She seems to think that because I am old, I must also be deaf. Please, do sit down, Miss Tregonney." Abby sat, and immediately thanked Mr. Brooks for seeing her. "Nonsense, think nothing of it. I have a client file and Instructions, which have not been carried out. Hopefully today, I can finalise the work that I started over thirty years ago." He took a file from a side table and placed it on the desk in front of him. From her position, Abby, who had become accustomed to reading material upside down in the chaotic environment of the trading world, could see clearly the label. THOMAS TREGONNEY. Mr. Brooks looked up and said. "We must observe the formalities first, would you by any chance have your birth certificate with you?" Abby nodded and delved into her bag for the document, attached by a paper clip was her mother's death certificate. She also handed to him the expired passport. Mr. Brooks nodded vigorously. "Excellent, excellent. You don't have your mother's will by any chance?"

Abby shook her head. "Mum didn't make a will, but I do have the probate, not with me but I can send it to you." Mr. Brooks waved his hand in a gesture that suggested that would be acceptable. He opened the file and the first document was a copy of her mother's birth certificate.

He sorted through the papers in the box. "You will appreciate that I have to be certain that you are the immediate family and sole surviving relative of Mr. Tregonney. I knew from Mr. Tregonney that your mother was an only child. Mrs. Forbes accessed the B.M.D. files online, I wish we had been able to do that thirty years ago, progress eh? Anyway her results together with these documents are sufficient proof that you too are an only child, so I can proceed. I must admit that I was curious that your grandfather should bother to make a will. Admirable, though. I wish more people were as conscientious. There was no estate to speak of, merely some personal effects of little value. However, when I heard of the unusual circumstances of his death, his insistence became a little clearer."

Abby interrupted "Unusual circumstances? What do you mean?"

Mr. Brooks looked at her with an anxious and nervous glance. "Well, yes unusual, eh, ahem," he cleared his throat, "you don't know how your grandfather died?"

Abby shook her head. "No, was it an accident or something? I had assumed that it was a natural death."

Mr. Brooks was now even more flustered. "Oh dear, oh dear, ah here's the coffee." A young lady came into the office bearing a tray with two cups of coffee, milk and sugar, also a plate of digestive biscuits. He seemed grateful for the interruption, and having made sure that Abby had the coffee to her liking, attended to his own. Abby, however was impatient to hear to what circumstances Mr. Brooks was referring.

"Mr. Brooks, please tell me, how did my grandfather die?' He regarded her with sympathy.

"My dear, I have spent many years as a Solicitor, and having retired thought that I would never have to perform an unpleasant task like this again. I cannot wrap this up in flowery language. I am sorry to tell you that your grandfather committed suicide."

Abby sat there stunned. She couldn't believe it. After all the stories that she had heard from Sam, she had seen her grandfather as a strong, determined man, not one to let life's troubles get him down, and yet she was now being told that he had taken his own life. She gathered herself. "Thank you for telling me that, Mr. Brooks; it cannot have been pleasant for you. Could you tell me how?"

He regarded her sympathetically. "The coroner brought in of misadventure, but the truth was that your grandfather hanged himself." Abby absorbed this new information without expression. Now her own character came into play, she wouldn't dwell on his death, however horrible, she could allow herself to think about this later, but she wasn't going to break down with grief here in this office. His sympathetic look remained with him, but he had seen the steel come back into her expression and mentally agreed with her that the business before them was more important. "We collected the effects mentioned in the will from the undertaker, and made the usual enquiries for next of kin. No one in the village knew where your mother had gone, nor if she was still alive. We placed advertisements in the local papers, and in The Times, which are the normal organs for tracing relatives, but after twelve months, having no replies to our enquiries, the file was placed in our archive storage. Today there would be little trouble in finding someone, unless they were determined to be lost, everyone is on a computer in some government department or other, but back in sixty-seven there was little chance." He continued. "As there was little or no estate to speak of, we took our fees from the capital that was there. I hope that you will find that procedure acceptable, there is a full accounting of the monies found and those spent in the file. Your grandfather did have a small life insurance, but because he was a suicide they declined to pay out." Abby told him that she was sure that his actions could not be faulted. "Now," he said, "the effects." and he lifted to the desk a box-file. "First there was the will, I will not read it now, and you may peruse it at your convenience. In effect it wills everything to your mother, with the usual paragraph concerning prior demise etc. I am sure that you were the sole beneficiary from your mother's will, so become the same from your grandfather's. I should at some time like to have sight of the probate, if that is possible, just a formality of course." He paused to sip from his coffee. "The effects are documents, a journal, some badges, this watch and these keys. I believe these were gathered by the police at the time." He held up the extra large pocket watch, complete with chain. Although it had lain in this box for so many years, the years before, of constant use had polished it to a shine; only partially diffused where the original plating had been worn away. "The watch may be of some value, I am told they are keenly sought after by collectors of railway memorabilia these days. Particularly when they bear the initials of the railway on the face." He showed Abby the face.

He took the documents and a large quarto-size notebook from the file and laid them on the desk in front of Abby. The watch he placed on top. The last item in the file was a small oblong box, very like a jewel case, which he opened; inside the similarity was continued as it was lined in what appeared to be a green baize cloth. The contents were two small badges, which proclaimed in intertwined initials, G.W.R., and one other; a more modern badge, which had the word "Stationmaster," set in the original British Railways motif. Abby sat there with a stone in her stomach. This was the sum total of her grandfather, all those years of unremitting work, and these few items were his legacy to his daughter.

Mr. Brooks had watched her face carefully. Like his son, he had weighed Abby's motives, and decided that money was not her quest, in fact he would be prepared to bet that this young lady was already very comfortable in that direction. Her search was for some roots, and this exchange was but a small part of that search.

"Would you like me to leave you alone for a while?" he asked kindly.

Abby looked up with a wan smile. "No, that won't be necessary. Is there anything that I have to sign?"

Mr. Brooks pushed a paper towards her. "Just this acknowledgement of receipt of the bequest."

Abby signed the paper where he pointed. "More importantly, is there an account outstanding, I am sure that your searches would have been relatively costly."

Mr. Brooks shook his head. "Please do not worry about that, if there were an outstanding account, it will have been written off quite a few years ago." He knew well that there was a shortfall between the monies recovered and the expenses, but he decided that it might be a sensible thing to have Miss Tregonney leave with a feeling of goodwill. There might be some further service that the practice could perform. He helped Abby collect the various items together, and suggested that she use the box-file, "It will be more convenient to carry that way."

The rain had ceased completely when she left the office, and blue sky was showing between cushions of white cloud scattering across the sky, driven by the same winds from the south west, which earlier had brought the downpour. Abby put the box-file on the back seat of the car, and decided to drive back to the square, where she parked and again bought a ticket, notwithstanding Mrs. Forbes' assurance that there would be no parking warden for some weeks. She then strolled around the corner to the library for the promised coffee with Toni.

Toni was not at her desk when Abby entered the reference library, but the sound of the door closing behind Abby soon brought her out from the racks where she had been. She was delighted to see Abby, "Oh, hi, Abby, how did it go?" The question rekindled Abby's pain, and it obviously showed on her face, as Toni's face immediately fell. "What happened?" she asked, guiding Abby to a chair.

"My grandfather! He committed suicide."

Toni was shocked. "Suicide?" she repeated, "suicide. Oh my God, how awful for you." Haltingly, Abby told her as much as she herself understood, of Thomas Tregonney's life, her mother's running away, and the closing down of the Railway. As she spoke the picture became clearer, and she could start to imagine the complete and utter despair that her grandfather may have suffered. Was this the way it happened, perhaps? Probably only Sam could pour more light on the affair. Her growing understanding, helped her, and she was soon able to mention the coffee that Toni had invited her for.

"You're sure you will be all right?" Toni asked, and with the affirmative nod, brightened. "Oh by the way, I've found something for you," and with a flourish produced from her desk a slim bound volume. Abby looked at the title, 'The Railway to Paverton.' Quickly she flicked through a few pages. It wasn't a weighty tome but her cursory glance convinced her that some of the information she sought would lie within its pages.

Toni had gone to get her coat and when she returned Abby held the little book up. "Where did you get this?

"Oh my Dad had it. I doubt he's ever read it though. It was written years ago by one of the librarians, who was something of an amateur historian. He published a number of books like this on the town, and the area, mostly boring, because he tried to mention all the local worthies, whether they merited a mention or not. Councillors were expected to buy a copy, well they would, because they like to see their names in print. I shouldn't think any of them have been read apart to check that he had spelt their names correctly." Whilst Toni was doing all this talking which revealed a healthy disregard for politicians, she had steered Abby out of the library, and across the road towards the cafe, where they seated themselves comfortably in the window seat.. Abby put the book in her bag, and of course paid for the coffee when it arrived. In response to Toni's question, she relayed the events in the Solicitor's office. Toni seemed a little disappointed, probably expecting a revelation of a bequest of unclaimed wealth. And she was certainly dismayed at the descriptions of the lapel and cap badges and the watch. Abby was amused at her reaction, and teased her by suggesting that the journal might reveal some juicy secrets. They finished their coffee quickly, as Toni had seen the head librarian returning from his break, which was taken at the nearest public house. She would have to get back, but before doing so, extracted a promise from Abby that she would come back and see her again, "When you have written your book."

Abby didn't go back to the Combe Inn immediately. It was just after twelve, and to return would probably mean being dragooned into eating one of Mary's superb, but huge meals. Instead, she drove slowly towards the station. The wind had dropped and the skies cleared, allowing a bright sun to start warming the air. The station dripped water wherever the guttering had broken away, but Abby was pleased that under what was left of the canopy, dry areas existed. She still had in her bag the little book that Stella had given her, and she skip-read various pages. The author had not been too concerned about the places the railway passed through to get to Paverton, and Combe Lyney rated just about one page. No mention of personnel, except of course for the Comberford family. It was understandable that the major landowner in the area would be mentioned. The book seemed to be written as if Paverton was the goal for the railway, until Abby read of the quarries that had existed in the valley. If she had learned anything from her hobby it was that in the early days of railways, passengers were secondary to goods, and she was certain that it was the quarries that attracted the promoters.

The sound of horse's hooves startled her, and looking up she saw James Comberford riding along the track bed from the direction of Huish Coppice. He saw her and urged his horse up onto the rough remains of the platform. Abby thought for a moment he was attempting to intimidate her, but he stopped the horse about six feet away and touched his crop to his cap. "Miss Tregonney."

Equally seriously, Abby replied, "Mr. Comberford." She felt for a moment that she should drop into a curtsey and giggled at the thought. The giggle surprised him and he moved abruptly in the saddle unsettling the horse.

"I usually have to crack a joke before someone laughs at me. If I have amused you, please tell me how, is my habit buttoned up wrongly, of are there bird droppings on the shoulder?" His voice was quite level but a grin played around his mouth.

"I am sorry, I wasn't laughing at you. It was something that Sam said yesterday evening. It would seem that my grandfather couldn't drink in the lounge if your father was there. Not the same class it would appear. When you raised that whip, and said so seriously 'Miss Tregonney' I had this insane idea of dropping into a curtsey. That's what made me giggle."

James appreciated the anachronism and stretched the grin on his face. "I am sure that a curtsey is something not called upon from many ladies these days but I believe you would have carried out the manoeuvre excellently. My father had a number of antiquated ideas, one of the reasons why his circle of friends were mainly boring old f..." Abby knew what he was going to say, so when he stumbled over the word she filled in the gap.

"Farts, was the word you were looking for."

His grin grew even larger. "Yes, that was the word. Incidentally, when I get down to the Inn, I drink in the bar."

Abby responded to his grin, it really was very attractive, and shading her eyes from the sun, looked up at him. "I am glad to hear it."

James sidled his horse nearer to the unkempt hedge that lined the back edge of the platform. "Would you mind if I dismount?" Abby indicated that she wouldn't mind, thinking that some of the antiquated ideas of the father also existed in his son. The good ones, like manners.

James threw his leg over the horse's shoulder, and slipped to the platform, the horse took a step or two nearer to Abby and James gentled. "Come on, don't be a silly old beggar, Cass." The horse quietened, and Abby walked to its head and stroked its muzzle. This gave Abby an opportunity to appraise Mr. Comberford. She reckoned that he was about four inches taller then she with light brown hair cut short in a military style. He was slim and held himself easily. Whilst not handsome, he had regular features which were enlivened by the grin which seemed to play around his mouth almost constantly.

Cass twitched her ears forward, and pushed gently against Abby, inviting further stroking.

"Well you seem to have no trouble with horses, do you ride?" Abby didn't reply immediately, as Cass was thoroughly enjoying having her muzzle stroked, and her ears gently pulled.

"Sorry, no, I cannot say I ride, well sort of; I have ridden once or twice, but there's not much opportunity in London."

James nodded. "Well we will have to see about getting you up on a horse whilst you're here. You will see much more of the valley from horseback, than you will from that car of yours." She thought about that and what he said was true, but she wasn't sure that her riding skills were up to it.

"That's kind of you, Mr. Comberford, but I shall only be here for another couple of days."

"Please call me James, I don't go much for that Mr. Comberford title," Abby smiled.

"And I'm Abby, pleased to meet you, James." She held out her hand and he shook it.

"Abby, presumably named after your grandmother Abigail." She was taken aback that he should know this, when she had only in the last day or so learned her grandmother's name. Realisation came, she was the newcomer, and James was part of the valley.

"It's marvellous that everyone around here knows details about me and my family that I am only just putting together. What else do you know that I don't?"

James smiled then and an impish gleam came into his eyes. "Well, as Bernard in 'Yes Prime Minister' would say, I don't know, Prime Minister, because I don't know what you don't know." Abby had a fleeting acquaintance with the programme and understood the reference.

"Well when I have finished grilling Sam, I will start on you, Ve haf ways of making you talk."

James nodded. "Well you can try, but I'm just a country bumpkin really, so don't expect revelations." Abby thought that country bumpkin was the last label she would apply to James Comberford, his manners and speech indicated a good education.

Abby busied herself with the still nuzzling horse, which at that moment decided that the little patch of green grass was far more inviting.

"So, did you know my grandmother?"

James shook his head. "No, I was very young when she died, I knew of her though, in a small place like this everyone knows everyone, even those who have passed away, are still part of the community as if they had never died."

Abby pushed on. "You did know my mother, then?"

"Marion, yes, I knew her. Bear in mind though, that she was about seven years older than me, and that is a great difference to an eight year old and a fifteen year old. So you couldn't say we were friends, but we said hello, and she did take pity on me when your grandfather chased me off the station. It always seemed so unfair that she could have the run of the place, and I was regularly sent packing." Abby did some quick reckoning in her mind, so he was nine years older than she, he looked younger than forty-three.

"From what I've heard from Sam, mum didn't quite have the run of the place."

James shrugged his shoulders. "Well it seemed like that." Abby decided not to ask if he knew about her grandfather's suicide, she felt it was something best discussed with Sam and Mary, as she was certain that there was something that Sam was hiding from her last night.

She didn't want James to wander off just yet, so she asked him about his family's involvement in the valley. "Your family would appear to have been here for quite a time, you get frequent mentions in this little history."

He leaned over to look. "What one is that, oh yes, my father said it was written more with personal ambition in mind than historical fact. There's a copy somewhere at the house. In answer to your question, yes, we have been around for some time. My great, great, plus a few more greats, grandfather had a small farm, and by dint of a little smuggling, poaching and other nefarious activities, eventually came to own most of the land in the valley. My, we were grand then, but since the turn of the century, what with taxes and all, the family have descended into a sort of gentrified poverty. We maintain the standards of course, by not appearing to work, and living off the rents, and one or two investments. It's a hard life really." Abby caught the sardonic inflexions in his voice, and knew that he was indulging in economies of the truth. She turned and began to walk along the platform, pleased when he gathered the reins and leading the horse fell into step beside her.

"So if it's as hard as all that, why don't you sell?" He looked at her in shock.

"Sell? Never! Look around, look at all this beautiful countryside; can you think of anywhere better to live?" She had to admit that he had a point. She had become more attached to the place with every day that passed. Not because of her own family links, but for the peace, and the feeling of well-being that had cloaked her since her arrival.

"So what do you do all day, except ride around, pop in to the pub at lunchtime, and generally oversee the serfs?" Her bantering tone was unmistakable, and he replied in the same vein.

"Oh well I tumble one of the serving girls in the morning, have a good breakfast, ride out and throw a poor family onto the streets, take a leisurely lunch at the Inn, whilst a groom stands and holds the horse in the pouring rain, get back to the house in time for a rest before dinner, then cards with me cronies, who of course deliberately lose, then bed. Oh yes, it's a hard life." Abby was laughing now.

"If you tumble the serving wenches then there could be a lot more of your family around here than one would think."

James was affronted. "Do you think we don't know what to do? If the silly girl gets herself in a delicate condition, she gets paid off and sent away, come on now, us ruling classes have our standards." He suddenly changed tone. "Except we are not the ruling class, that's if we ever had been." He pointed at the old track bed. "That changed the world forever."

Abby caught his change of mood and a tone that sounded like regret in his voice. "You sound as if you regret the railway coming here."

He shook his head. "No, it wasn't the railway, that did the valley a lot of good, but it started a process of change, which eventually destroyed a way of life, for good or bad. The process went on and ironically destroyed the railway itself. It's still going on, and people are caught up in it like a treadmill, never being able to stand still and take stock, but forever having to push forward, or lose their place. Here thankfully, we are little affected. We can actually enjoy being alive and living in this beautiful valley."

They had reached the old approach now and James admired Abby's car. "Always thought that I would like one of those, too expensive for me, though. I'd have to drive to Paverton to fill it up, cost a gallon of petrol just for that, diesels best round here."

Abby protested. "Isn't diesel fuel more expensive than unleaded petrol."

James nodded and then winked. "Yes, but red diesel bought for a farm tractor carries a lot less tax. Not supposed to do it, but an occasional fill has been known."

Abby was still laughing as she climbed into the car. "You know when you were talking about your great, to the nth power, grandfather. Well he is not the only one who practices nefarious activities; it must run in the family." James grinned wickedly. As she drove out, she suddenly stopped, "If you want to drive this, you're welcome, anytime."

James had mounted Cass. "I'll take you up on that, but you have to ride a horse in return. Oh incidentally, I hope you didn't think I was being rude that first time we met. You know you look very much like Marion, and I was taken aback when I saw you properly, it was as if I had seen a ghost."

Abby shook her head. "I was annoyed at the time, but realised later it must have been a shock for you, so I forgive you." James inclined his head in acknowledgement, lifted his hand in farewell and turned Cass away, as Abby put the car into drive and turned towards the village.

CHAPTER FIVE

Abby had completely forgotten about her mobile phone, and that evening after changing she turned it on, to see if there were any messages, there were a few, but the most important was from her deputy on the team, pleading with her to come back. 'That holding has gone ballistic, and we need you here now.' That resolved her diary for the immediate future. They wouldn't need her back there unless something important and profitable was brewing.

Mary knew that something had happened as soon as Abby came down for her meal. The brief interlude with James Comberford had cheered her up and enabled her to forget the terrible event of how her grandfather had died. This had returned as she changed in her room, and was uppermost on her mind. Abby just toyed with her food and replied absent-mindedly to Mary's questions. When Sam arrived and came to the bar for his drink, Mary just whispered out of the side of her mouth.

"She knows." Sam was troubled. He knew what Mary meant, and he was aware that he ought to have told Abby. What he didn't know was how she knew. Now he had to somehow explain why he hadn't said anything. He lingered at the bar for a while, unwilling to face the girl. Eventually he had to go and see her, as the longer the delay, the greater the guilt. As he walked round into the lounge, Abby looked up, and smiled. The smile gave him hope that this interview would not be as difficult as he feared. Abby asked him to sit, and immediately told him that she had seen her grandfather's solicitor that day. The one question was answered, he hadn't known that Tregonney had a solicitor, how the girl had found out he couldn't fathom, but she was probably quicker mentally than him. "I know how grandfather died, I'm a little hurt that you couldn't tell me yourself, but I can understand. What bothers me is why. Do you know?'

Sam was relieved to be let off so easily, but nonetheless felt he should apologise and explain.

"Yes, I should have told you, and I fully intended to tell you this evening. I'm not very good with bad tidings, but you had a right to know, and I'm sorry that the information had to come from a stranger, it should have been me." He paused. "It was a bad day for all of us. Your grandfather used to come in here a couple of times a week for a drink. When a few days had gone past and he hadn't been seen, Alf Watson, who was the landlord here then, asked Trevor Williams and me to go down and check on him. He wasn't at the station, no reason for him to be there, but you never know, so we walked on down the track to his house. We knocked and called but got no reply. I was going round the back to have a look, see if I could spot anything, and Trevor had wandered off over to the goods shed. Suddenly I heard him calling. He had found your grandfather. He had hung himself from one of the beams. He stayed there and I ran back here."

"Ran?" Abby interrupted.

Sam grinned. "I was a lot younger then. Alf phoned the police and ambulance and that was that. They came and took him away. There was an inquest of course, they returned a verdict of misadventure. I think Mr. Comberford had talked to the coroner, to avoid a suicide verdict. They were going to bury him here but Alf reckoned that he should be buried back in Cornwall, where he was born. The undertakers agreed, but had to charge for the journey, and we all had a whip round for it. Mr. Comberford was very generous. They found out where he was born from the railway. Trevor went down and as he said after, he was the only one there beside the minister. I don't know exactly where it was, somewhere near Par I believe. I suppose I should have asked Trevor, but he died about fifteen years ago, so I reckon he can't tell us now!" All this came out in short stilted sentences, as if Sam was hurrying to explain all the circumstances as quickly as possible.

Abby had listened as Sam stumbled over the events. It had become obvious during the telling, that he, and presumably others in Combe, felt some guilt over the affair, as if they should have recognised the desperation that her grandfather felt, and in some way could have prevented the tragedy. Abby's understanding as Sam had recounted what he knew of her grandfather, and the events that one by one had assaulted him, brought her to the conclusion that he had taken his life because everything that he counted of importance had been taken from him.

She said as much to Sam, who nodded slowly, giving thought to what she had said. "Yes I reckon that just about sums it up. I would imagine that most people round here would have come to that conclusion. I'll tell you now that a lot of us felt ashamed, after all he was one of us, and he'd lived here for nigh on thirty years. We should have been closer to him."

Abby laid her hand on his arm. "I don't think that you or anyone else can be blamed. From what you have said, grandfather's attitude towards others would keep them at arm's length. He doesn't sound like the sort of person who would share his troubles with anyone. My mum was just the same, her running away was proof of that." Sam gave her a quick smile of thanks. Mary, who had strangely enough sat there silently, suggested that they all needed a drink, and without waiting for the reply rushed off to get them. She returned with glasses of whisky, her sovereign remedy for moments of sadness and emotion.

They barely had time to taste their drinks, when cries from the bar caught the attention. Abby heard only one shout clearly, which was 'Come to drag your old man home then, Mavis' followed by good-natured laughter. The commotion continued with a woman's voice reaching higher decibels than any of the others.

Abby heard Sam groan. "That's my missus, can't go anywhere without she's laying into someone for some infringement of the code according to Mavis." Abby expected a virago to come into the lounge, instead appeared a very small elderly neat lady, carrying a very large handbag, her face aglow with self-satisfaction.

"Hello, Mavis," called Mary, "how are you, not upsetting my customers I hope?"

Mavis shook her head. "Upsetting them, no, they enjoys a bit of shouting, that lot." Without pausing for breath she addressed Abby, "Now you must be the young lady who has been bringing my Sam out every evening. If he weren't so old I might have suspected something, but his days of shenanigans are over. How are you? Sam said he knew who you were straight off, and for once he is right, I can see your mother in you well enough. It's really good to see you, can I call you

Abby?" Taken aback by this relentless barrage of words, Abby would realise in time that Mavis always talked like a machine gun.

She stood up saying. "It's nice to meet you Mrs. Perry," extended her hand, which Mavis ignored, moving inside to reach up and plant a kiss on Abby's cheek.

"Now call me Mavis. Sam! You going to sit there all evening and not get me a chair and I'll have a port and lemon." Sam moved a chair, which was only about twelve inches behind Mavis, six inches towards her, and she sank down without really looking to see if there was a chair at all, merely expecting that Sam had made sure there was. Sam made to go for her drink when Mary stopped him.

"I'll go, Sam, I should check that Jack's o.k."

Mavis leaned forward and grasped Abby's hand. "I suspect that Sam has given you the bad news about your grandfather's death by now. But there's no more to come, so take the word of an old lady and don't worry about it, it all happened too many years ago." Abby decided not to explain that she hadn't heard this from Sam, sure that he would tell Mavis later. "I've been rummaging at home and I've found some old photographs, would you like to see them?"

Would Abby like to see them was obviously a rhetorical question, the answer very plain on her face, the eagerness showing. In any case Mavis had every intention of showing the photographs. She delved into the cavernous bag she had brought with her, producing a small package, wrapped around with a rubber band. The band was taken off and the first photograph thrust under Abby's nose. It was plainly years old, dog-eared with crease marks running across. She could recognise the place as the platform at Combe Lyney station, as it had once been. There were two figures in the photo, the first, who dominated the frame was a tall, sparse man, wearing an old-fashioned frock coat, and a small pillbox cap. He had been photographed striding towards the photographer and his body language said he wasn't too pleased to be the photographer's subject, looking as if he had more important business to attend and a photographer was getting in the way. Abby knew that she was looking at her grandfather and the picture swam out of focus as her eyes misted over with tears. An arm came round her shoulders, and she sensed without looking that it was Mary, whilst Mavis took her hand again and patted it gently. Presently she was able to extract her hand in order to search for a tissue. Drying her eyes she thanked them for their kindness, and picking up the photo again examined it closely. It was too old, and the quality too poor to make out much of her grandfather's features, but it was clear enough for her to see the trimmed moustache he wore, and deep hooded eyes. Poignantly she noticed the two small GWR badges, one on each lapel of the coat, now in her possession.

"Do you know when this was taken?" she asked Mavis, who shrugged her shoulders.

"No, I can't even remember how we came to have it, unless Sam knows."

Sam shook his head. "I can't say for certain, but I think it would have been late fifties. Why the photo was taken I can't say, but I seem to recollect that Reg Purvess left it in the bar, that's him on the left; he was the signalman."

Mavis produced the second photo, which was another view taken along the platform. Steam swirled around the front of a small engine standing there with its train. The driver leaned out looking back along the platform. Abby would later understand that it was probably the fireman. Great Western engines were different insomuch that the driver was on the right-hand side, not the left. Her grandfather stood there with his back to the camera, frock-coat and pill-box cap on parade, also looking back down the platform, his left hand extended towards the engineman, not to shake his hand, but imperiously cautioning patience. In the distance toward the back of the train, doors were still open, and porters were loading a crate.

Sam was more informative now. "When trains arrived, your grandfather would be standing just outside the booking office, with his watch in his hand. He never said anything, but if the train was late, the driver knew that it would go into the report, and the look that he got from your grandfather would've ruined anyone's day. He waited until the train stopped, and woe betide the driver again, if he didn't stop it accurately and your grandfather had to walk to the guard's compartment. The guards were really of equal status to a stationmaster, so they would greet each other as Mister Tregonney and Mister Metcalfe, or whoever it was, but Metcalfe was the usual guard on the passenger trains. Then your grandfather would take his walk down the platform, looking in all the compartments so that if a regular and important passenger was travelling, he could salute them and greet them properly. He arrived at the engine just seconds before it was due out, and always, but always would chide them for some misdemeanour, like improper use of the whistle, or black smoke. It didn't matter what, but they would always leave with a flea in their ear."

Abby was astounded. It was the use of the whistle that intrigued her. "And what was improper use of the whistle? The mind boggles with the possibilities."

Sam laughed. "Well you may not believe it, but the G.W.R. had a very strict code about whistling. I cannot tell you all the details, it would take a railway man to do that, but an infringement of the code was considered seriously. I know that before any engine moved the driver had to give one short whistle; I think they called that a crow or a pop, I am not too sure about that." Mavis was impatient to get on, so before Abby had really exhausted the subject of whistles, a third old photograph was placed in front of her. The Inn was the backdrop, its appearance little changed, with three people sitting on the bench in front. Her grandfather was still recognisable despite not wearing his cap and frock coat, but the other two gave Abby's heart a sudden start, a small thin, woman looking incredibly frail and a young girl. She knew without asking that this was her mother and grandmother, she looked at Mavis who nodded her head, a sympathetic expression on her face.

"Yes, Love, that's your mum and grandma." Abby smiled and said no more for a while, just looking at the photo, her eyes brimming with tears. Sam was about to say something, but his wife, given that sixth sense by years of being together, just looked at him before his mouth opened and shook her head. Her expression saying let the girl have a moment. Sam nodded.

Eventually Abby stirred and asked Mavis. "Do you think I could borrow these photographs for a while and have some copies made." She knew a computer specialist who could re-generate the photos.

Mavis waved her hands dismissively. "You don't need to borrow them, they're yours, keep them." Abby smiled her thanks, not being able to say too much at this moment for fear of breaking down with tears. Mary had left a little while ago and now returned with a tray of tea. She believed that either whisky or tea was needed for emotional moments. Her eyes watering, Abby nodded her head vigorously. Tea was exactly right.

With the tea half drunk and her spirits restored, Abby broke the news that she would be returning to London the next day. Mary was disappointed that she would not be staying longer and Mavis added her voice to the entreaties to stay. "I've only just met you and it would be nice to get to know you better."

Abby put their minds at ease "I shall be coming back later in the year," she couldn't resist a little teasing, "but I have to get off some of the weight that Mary's cooking has put on me, and Mavis, I shall want to question Sam a little more, if you don't mind.".

"Mind?" Mavis snorted "I shan't mind, it will get him out from under my feet, and so you will be doing me a favour."

Sam himself seemed quite pleased with the idea. "But I shall be buying my round, do you hear?" Abby picked up her bag, the photographs, and made her goodnights; this time with kisses all round.

Mavis chuckled. "There you go, Sam, young girls kissing you, bet you thought those days were long gone hey?" Sam assumed the shade of red that he had worn last night from the same treatment.

Abby packed most of her clothes that night, except for those she would be travelling in tomorrow. These few days had changed her more than any of the other breaks she had taken. Researching industrial history was dry, and academic, it did not challenge her emotions. Now here was a history in which her family had been involved. The urge to delve further was overpowering, to research in detail the story of this little line and understand her grandfather's part in it. There were other reasons too, because she had learned a lot about her own family, and gained another extended family. In addition, thoughts had started creeping into her mind about her future. The calm and beautiful valley was seductive, and ideas were surfacing of trying to combine a life here with her career in the city, which were very beguiling. She was amazed that in the space of these four days, so much information had been revealed, but these were only cameos, odd scenes which did not and could not present the whole picture, she wanted to know more, it was personal now, not just historical statistics. In London she would find answers in the wealth of the museums and libraries. This would give her the skeleton, putting flesh on the bones could only be done here, and she would be coming back to do just that.

CHAPTER SIX

Coming back to the office on a Wednesday, when her plan had been not to return until Monday, was not too unusual. When things broke it was understood that it didn't matter where you were or what you were doing, you got yourself into the office, it was why the job was so well-paid, and the bonuses were so good. Andy her deputy was right, this was a big one. A holding that she had bought some time ago, a position she had to defend on a number of occasions was starting to boil; already the bank had trebled its original stake. "If I hadn't heard from you I was going to sell," Andy had informed her.

Abby's gut-feeling was to hold on for another twenty-four hours or so. "Even if they drop a point or two, we are still way ahead, but I reckon that they will go a little bit higher." She was right, the following Monday the quoted price showed a further increase. "O.K. sell," she made the decision. The holdings were snapped up in next to no time, she had just made eighty million pounds for her bank, the bonuses on this deal were going to be very good.

As she expected, within a few days, she was asked to drop in to the director's office. Steve was all smiles. "Great coup, always knew you were going to pull it off. There's going to be a very nice share out of the profits, and I'll make sure the board know who masterminded the whole operation." Abby smiled cynically, Steve had been the one who had put her under pressure to pull out of the position. Now of course he would tell the board that the whole thing was done under his direction. This was typical of Steve, smiling Steve, smooth Steve, permatanned Steve, Teflon-coated Steve; who viewed all women in the office as tethered game for his hunt; who had seduced Abby with ease; she, falling for his promises, and naively believing his glib words; that is until she found out that his marriage was not on the point of collapse, and that Steve only perceived their relationship as an excitement, an interlude between the periods of hustle and chaotic office atmosphere.

He went on, "The reason I have asked you in, is to chat about Andy. He's done a good job with you, but I feel he needs some experience elsewhere, so I would like to put him in Futures for a while, possibly send him to New York, get the feel of the place. What do you think?" Abby made the right noises, she knew the decision was already made. Within a year or so Andy would return, but this time as her boss. The glass ceiling had finally arrived, it had always been out there somewhere, but she had never hit it before. Now here it was, her face pressed up to it, looking at the power and prestige at the other side, but never to be able to join that party. Skirts and the city didn't mix. When she left Steve's office, the feelings that Combe Lyney had engendered returned. Only a few months ago she would have fought tooth and nail to defend her position, but now other considerations had entered the equation. Yes, she did have to consider her future. Her job here was probably safe for another year or two, maybe three or four, but she had to acknowledge that one day she would be burn out, the pressures and stress getting to her so that she would miss things, and mess up on deals. Then the call to the director's office, and it would probably be Andy then; would be for her resignation.

That night back at her flat in Knightsbridge, Abby sat and gave the question her undivided attention. Financially she was secure, the profit sharing scheme the bank operated had given her a very nice nest egg, all invested wisely, if safely. She could spread her portfolio a little wider to take in some of the more volatile investments, which with careful management would mean an income at least the equal of her present salary. Her flat, which had taken a huge chunk of capital to buy, would now fetch at least three quarters of a million. She didn't need to work any longer, she worked because it was a challenge, gave her a buzz. What could she do though, if she moved down to Combe Lyney, she couldn't see herself milking cows?

Since she had been home she had not had the time to look through her grandfather's papers. Deciding that the questions she was asking herself did not, at this moment, have an answer; she turned her mind to her inheritance. The will was a fairly standard document; it assumed that her mother would still be alive, although the phrase, which Mr. Brooks had inserted "present whereabouts unknown" indicated his anticipation of the actuality. There was also the usual clause regarding the possible demise of the beneficiary, with the estate devolved to her issue. Was that a hint that her grandfather may have been aware of such a situation occurring? No, it was a pretty standard clause, inserted into most wills. Abby turned to the other papers in the file. The first that she picked up was on old, cheap paper yellowing and musty. The heading was simply GREAT WESTERN RAILWAY, nothing ornate, no coats of arms, dated 13th November 1938. The letter appointed Thomas Tregonney as Stationmaster at Combe Lyney. The letter went on to require him to take up his new post by the 1st December.

Having heard from Sam how important this job was to her grandfather, she was not surprised that he had kept this letter. A pocket-sized card came next, an identification card issued by the railway, the neat, art deco-style GWR logo in a circle on the top left corner. The card authorised the holder to be on the lines and premises of the Great Western Railway Company in the execution of his duty. The name Thomas Tregonney was written in copperplate, with his grade stationmaster, underneath. It was signed, carefully, the signature fully legible, by her grandfather. The card seemed to have no reason, but Abby caught a clue from the printing at the bottom of the page, which required the card to be produced at any time by request, and also that a signature may be required as proof of identity. Perhaps this had something to do with the war?

There were other letters, one dated March 1966, from British Railways, Western Region, addressed "Dear Tregonney," concerning his impending retirement from the commission's service, and advising him the amount of weekly pension he could expect. The other was a printed card, acknowledging his retirement on the 30th April 1966, and thanking him for his fifty-one years of service. The card was pre-printed with just the date and length of service to be filled in by the typist. At least, thought Abby, they addressed him as Mr. Tregonney this time.

She turned to the diary, or rather that which she supposed to be a diary, for it wasn't, at least the sort of diary that Abby would expect. The pages were filled with what she now realised was her grandfather's own writing, the beautiful copperplate letters so carefully formed, that anyone could read without difficulty, and appreciate the time it would take to write in such a way. It could more properly be described as a daily journal, not detailing his life, and that of his family, but the daily minutiae of his work. She read that on the 23rd August 1949, the 6.18 a.m. was three minutes late on arrival, the name of the driver, Albert Perring, recorded for posterity. Also recorded were the number of empty churns to be unloaded, and the number of full ones to be loaded. The passenger figures for each train of the day, often woefully small, and sometimes none at all. Some entries made little or no sense at first glance, until she realised that this tome served as a record of traffic, which could be used as a reference for future requirements, thus the entry regarding the number of cattle trucks for 3rd October 1953, 'three cattle trucks for South Molton Market insufficient, four will be required in future,' there was one entry on 14th May 1949, which defied her deductive process, 'Milk traffic increasing, order four Siphons for both early and late Milk trains,'

Abby realised that to read all of this would give her an insight into the working of the station, and the railway, but no more awareness of her grandfather than she possessed already. The thought suddenly entered her head that perhaps she never would. Remembering Sam's words, 'we all knew Thomas Tregonney, who he was, what he was, we all had conversation of some kind or another with him, but that was as far as it went.' If the only people still alive, and who remembered her grandfather, couldn't throw any more light on him, then did she have any hope at all? Possibly the trick of knowing him was in the railway he served, and his own writing, terse as that may be.

She picked up the little book 'The Railway to Paverton' and started to read. Her first impression of the book was indeed correct. It was quite typical local historian stuff, heavily tinged with sycophantic references to the local powers that were at that time, with their names worked in whenever it was possible. It did give the framework, and explained the position of the Bristol and Exeter Railway, as an independent company, so closely aligned to the Great Western Railway, that its nominal independence was in reality a myth. It shared the great engineer, Isambard Kingdom Brunel, and the reality became official on the 1st January 1876, when the G.W.R. took over the Bristol and Exeter.

The line to Paverton was a branch; in effect a branch off a branch, as the Taunton to Barnstaple line was regarded as just that. It was constructed in 1874, just two years before the G.W.R. took over, and was made to Brunel's broad gauge of seven feet and a quarter inch. Abby had read about this gauge, supposedly the smoothest and fastest, yet doomed from infancy as standard gauge or narrow gauge, as the Great Western derisively referred to it, covered the rest of the country.

Abby was interested to read that the Lyney Valley route was not the initial choice for the railway, but the Comberford family lobbied forcefully for the railway to come up their valley. No doubt, she thought, that if his family were as unscrupulous as James would have her believe, there was a pay-off for them somewhere along the line. There was little further reference to the valley after that, Combe Lyney was mentioned as an intermediate stop, and there was also reference to another stop, known as Lills Platform together with a siding, but no indication of where this was. Abby wondered if this could be the site of the quarries mentioned early on in the tract. The book was mainly concerned from then on with the arrival of the railway in Paverton, and the festivities enjoyed by all and sundry, a six course luncheon for the worthies, an ox-roast for the navvies, beer flowing freely, and a dance for all in the market square that night. This gave the author even more opportunity to mention names. Abby presumed that the names of 1874 would probably be the family names, still important in 1937, when the book was written. The next major step forward was when the line was converted to standard gauge. This was on the 14th of May, 1881, and the work was completed within the day. Abby marvelled at this undertaking, thinking that it wouldn't be done nowadays, the unions, and the jobs worth from the Health & Safety KGB would see to that.

From that day forward the author had trouble filling his pages, as nothing else extraordinary happened at all. It was as if the railway went to sleep. There were details of the services that were offered; from just three trains each way a day in 1874, increasing to the maximum ten trains each way in 1908, but no service on Sunday. The service declined in 1922 to seven trains each way, and that is where it stayed, certainly until 1937, but somehow or other a Sunday service was now in place. Abby realised that the author was writing about passenger services. Goods trains it appeared were not timetabled, although they were regular; at least the morning goods always ran, and the milk trains always ran. Quarry traffic ran 'as required.'

Of course the book did not say anything about the closure. In 1937, such a thing would have been impossible to contemplate. She could imagine the behind the scenes manoeuvring when the Beeching Report (she was sure it was about this time), recommended closure. How the local bus company would assure the Traffic Commissioners that it could provide a service equal to, if not better, than the train. Abby wondered about this, as in the time she had been in the village, she had never even seen a bus. The little book was interesting. It was, she had no doubt, accurate on dates, but short on the detail that Abby wanted. It told her little about what the railway did, and the characters who played their part. Serious research was required.

As she lay in bed that night, Abby's mind returned to the question of her future. She was convinced that now there was no future for her at the bank. She was unconvinced that she wanted a future at the bank. Should she go back to Combe Lyney? Somehow she had felt a belonging in the place, at any rate if not permanent it would be a good place to consider her plans. Her mind decided, wait until the bonuses are paid, and then resign. Mary would allow her accommodation for as long as she wanted, Abby was certain of that, and she could then take stock and come to a decision.

The next few weeks passed in a blur, Abby had little time to give even a minute's thought to her dilemma, with the pressure of work now that Andy had departed for New York. Her workload had increased by having to train the new recruit to the team, and watch constantly to salvage something out of the losses he was about to incur. Eventually at the beginning of July, with the holiday season eroding the activities of all the major exchanges, Abby could once more contemplate some time off and a renewal of her research. Steve had warned her that the bonus would be 'pretty good,' and the arrival of the statement, together with a payment slip confirmed that. A pay cheque not far short of a million pounds was not unusual in the trading fraternity, and amongst people, who were used to dealing in hundreds of millions every day, did not represent the same values as it would to someone who slaved all year for a modest twenty-five-thousand pounds. The tax deductions were frightening, but still left her with a capital sum which invested with the acumen she had shown up to date, would keep her comfortably for some time. The thinking was all done, without a moment's hesitation, she wrote out her resignation and left it on Steve's desk. If he was going to make a fuss she would soon hear about it, in the meantime she had other things to do.

On her way home she stopped off and called at a bookshop in Knightsbridge. Abby was amazed at the number of books published about the G.W.R. References to the Bristol and Exeter were scattered liberally through a number of them, so selecting those in which the index indicated the most mentions she walked to the pay desk with seven publications in her arms.

The young male cashier was momentarily taken aback by this purchase; on a subject that he would classify as solely a male interest; by this lady, and made some small talk. "You seem to have got yourself a lot of reading here." Abby would not normally have made too much conversation in this situation, but reminded herself that Toni had been a good fount of information, decided that discussing the topic may not do any harm.

"Yes, there's a little branch line that I need to research, I'm hoping that these will help." The young man paused, his conversation exhausted, customers did not normally reply quite so readily.

Luckily for him a manager was standing by at the time and was able to pick up. "You could do with talking to Mr. Brasher, he is an absolute mine of information about the Great Western Railway. He's writing the definitive history, it's only taken twenty years so far, but if he does not have the information you want, then no one else will be able to help you."

Abby nodded, wondering what Mr. Brasher would be like. "He does sound like the person who could help me; do you know if it would be possible to speak to him?" She gave her credit card to pay for the purchases as the manager thought for a moment and offered.

"He comes into the store most Mondays, he uses us as a reference library, and we cannot really refuse as he has spent a lot of money here. Tell you what, give me your number, and I'll ask him when he next comes in, and let you know." Abby signed the credit slip for the books, and wrote down her mobile number on a piece of scrap paper, which she passed to him.

"Thank you, I live quite close, so I can get here within ten or so minutes, if that is convenient."

The manager read the number and nodded. "Leave it with me; I'll do what I can."

Abby spent the weekend immersed in the history of the Bristol and Exeter, and then the Great Western Railway. She slouched on her sofa, the books scattered around, opened at pages, which had relevant chapters, so that she could refer back quickly. Coffee cups, some half full of cold liquid, abandoned as her interest quickened, a dirty plate or two, the remains of a snatched meal, straight from the freezer, micro-waved, and hurriedly eaten, but only when the pangs of hunger became so great that she was forced to put down her books. Some of the histories were simply a chronological fact sheet, devoid of human interest, with lists of tonnages carried, and coal burned. Others tabled locomotives built, allocated to various sheds, re-built, serviced, and finally condemned and cut up. Authors of some of the books tried to get into the minds and characters of the men who were the company servants, this she found more interesting. These were men like her grandfather, who took on a job for life, and gave unstinting and poorly rewarded service. They were a breed of men who did not watch the clock for any reason other than to keep the trains running on time. She was gratified to learn that her grandfather was not alone in being something of a solitary person. It would appear that most stationmasters were neither fish nor fowl. Their job set them apart from other railway men, who would have been their natural companions, yet they could never integrate into the society of the town or village they served, partly because they were rarely locally born; unlike the porters and signalman who were; and because they were men who had gained their promotion from the lower orders and after years of diligent labour, had been placed in authority over the men from whose ranks they had risen. The Railway pursued a policy of promotion from within, and it was likely that a stationmaster would be moving on within a few years to another slightly more prestigious post, again a situation that didn't encourage integration. Abby felt slightly better upon reading this, as she had previously thought that this aloof attitude was a personal characteristic of her grandfather.

One constant theme, which ran through these books, was the attitude of superiority that the Great Western exhibited towards other railways, as if the company was in the vanguard of development and service. The attitude was similar to a religion whose High Priest was at Paddington. Paddington seemed always to be referred to in hallowed terms, from whose portals the word was spread like a liturgy throughout the system. This was exemplified by the daily ritual of keeping the company telephone lines clear of traffic and open at ten o' clock each morning when a tone would be broadcast from Paddington to enable all stations to synchronise all watches and clocks.

The company would never buy in a service or product that it could provide or manufacture itself, and even those items that it had to bring in from the outside world, like whisky, were given Great Western labels, and then marketed as superior to all other brands. Even the success of the L.M.S. in later days was claimed to have originated with the G.W.R. as the man responsible, Mr. Stanier, learned his job at Swindon. Abby admired how the company sold itself and its services to the nation, exuding an aura of dignity and stability, yet ever alert to the chance of new and increased business, creating demand with clever advertising, where demand had not previously existed. It had style, but was never so grand that it forgot the grass roots, with as much attention paid to the running of the humble branch passenger train, as to the imperious passage of the famous named expresses. In its dealings with others it impressed with its presentation, the best notepaper, heavily embossed with a grand heading, internally the cheapest paper would do. Prestige and parsimony hand-in-hand.

She was amused at the ceremony which accompanied the departure of all trains, the manner in which the station staff would stand and indicate by the raising of the arm that their section of the platform was clear and safe, how the stationmaster or leading porter would, when all these indications were correct, turn and raise his arm, and blow a whistle to the guard, who self importantly blew his whistle, and raised his green flag for the train to depart. He didn't wave the flag, he displayed it, holding it open so that there could be no misunderstanding. Finally, the driver would give a short whistle, which Abby learned was known as a 'pop' confirming what Sam had said; and no locomotive would ever move without this warning, and then open the regulator starting the train on its journey.

The lore and traditions of the Great Western amused and enthralled her, so much so that she had to remind herself from time to time of the main reason for buying these books, grandfather's branch. She didn't realise it at the time but she now thought of her grandfather in a more possessive way, and the line up the Lyney valley as his branch. It was in this area that Abby was disappointed. The branch from Taunton to Barnstaple attracted a lot of mention, from its inception when it was known as the Devon and Somerset, sponsored by the Bristol and Exeter. Problems beset the enterprise from the start, entailing the interruption of construction work at least once. The line up the Lyney valley received little notice, except for an odd sentence in two of the books, which mentioned the quarries as the reason for its building. Abby was gratified to find that her thoughts on the matter were borne out, Paverton was served as a by-product of the intended quarry business, as it required little extra capital expense to extend the line there. There was no other history mentioned, and Abby could only assume that the branch, which in effect was a branch off a branch, lived and died according to the fortune of the main branch. Disappointing though this was Abby was thoroughly absorbed by the books, as they gave her a tremendous insight into the world that her grandfather knew. The ethic of service that was the Great Western ran through from the lowliest ganger, to the superintendent of the line, and obviously infected her grandfather. If he was made the same as others mentioned in these books, then this service was his dues to the society in which he lived, notwithstanding that same society could treat him with uncaring disdain.

The parallels of their lives was ironic, all the hard work over the years, which counted for naught as expediency took priority. True she was financially secure, which her grandfather could never have been, but she was surplus to requirements, as he had been, she had been treated uncaringly, as he had been and she was without family, as he had been. Tears of self-pity welled in her eyes, as for the second time, she mourned for a family she had never had.

On Sunday, the half expected call from Steve came. "Abby, what is this rubbish you left on my desk. I cannot believe that you did this. Who are you going to? What have they offered you? Come and see me tomorrow, I'm sure we can negotiate a new package for you."

Steve's agitation was obvious in his voice, and it was some time before Abby could reply to the barrage of questions aimed at her. "Steve, I am not, repeat not, going to another bank. I am taking a sabbatical if you like, to assess my life and where I want to go. You know as well as I, that I have no future at the bank, except to do what I am doing now. And that is because I wear a skirt. In twelve months' time, Andy will be back from New York, and will to all intents and purposes be my superior, with a better package, even though he's not half as good at the job as I am. But then he's a bloke, and I'm not. That's the way it works, Steve, and it doesn't matter how much you deny it, I know the writing is on the wall. At this moment I am undecided about taking action against the bank for constructive dismissal. I am sure that there are lawyers out there who would love to take the case; and would love even more the fees they will get out of it." There was a silence at the other end of the phone. Too many of these actions had succeeded, and the banks were very nervous. Abby had spoken without thinking, but her tack was right, and gave her some pleasure, handled carefully, this was a chance to pay Steve back for his treatment of her.

Eventually Steve spoke again carefully, as he was also aware that his treatment of the female staff could be part of any action. "Abby, you know that we appreciate your work immensely, there was no suggestion that you were going to be passed over, we just wanted Andy to gain more experience."

Abby interrupted him. "So why did you not ask me if I would like to go to New York?"

There was another silence, broken by Steve, who changed direction. "Look, Abby, if you are determined to do this, I will accept your resignation, but let's not have any more talk about lawyers and actions. Tell you what, if you would put in writing that you will not be joining a competitor, either now, or in the future, then I am sure that I can talk the directors into a little severance payment for you, how's that sound?"

"Well," she said, drawing it out as if she was making a difficult decision, "I could go along with that, but what sort of extra bonus would we be looking at? Restricting my options for the future is a little unethical to say the least, there would have to be compensation for my agreeing to that."

Steve was happier now, back on ground with which he felt comfortable. "I would think they would be happy with fifty K." Abby laughed aloud. She had to haggle; otherwise Steve would not be able to tell his co-directors how he had whittled down her extortionate demands. But fifty K was ridiculous.

"I bet they would be happy, Steve, you know damn well that a court would take my past earnings into account, which includes this year, and my future potential, and your wish to handcuff me, and other things which I am sure you would not want mentioned in court. An action could cost the bank five to six hundred K. Plus the costs, which would be astronomical. In addition you are asking me to sign a voluntary restriction of trade. This signature has to be worth a lot more than that. I'll tell you what, I'll save you the costs; just pay me the million, and that will be that." For the next three quarters of an hour the negotiations continued, until at last they agreed a figure just over seven hundred thousand.

Having agreed, Abby was content to write the letter he wanted. "Steve, you will get your letter."

He had other ideas. "No, Abby, for this sort of money there will be an exchange of letters; I want you to acknowledge the agreement we have. When I have that I will write confirming our acceptance."

"No, Steve, you put our agreement in writing first, you can make it conditional if you wish, but I want that offer in writing before I sign away my rights."

He grumbled about this, asking if she didn't trust him, but agreed. "Oh, and Abby, I don't think it would be a good idea for you to come into the office again, I wouldn't like others to get to know the details of our agreement." That suited Abby well; the thought of working three months' notice with Steve being snide at every opportunity did not enthrall her one little bit. She put the phone down, and found she was shaking. She hadn't really expected a pay-off, but with the first inkling that one could be available; the hand she played sounded a lot cooler than she felt. Now she had burned her boats. Suddenly she punched the air and yelled 'yippee.'

She spent the rest of the day absorbing the financial pages of the Sunday papers, and collating their information with her own. Working in the city gave access to all kinds of rumours and tips. Acting on those tips could be construed as insider trading, a notoriously difficult charge to prove. Now, however, as she was no longer inside, so to speak, Abby felt quite happy to plan her investments, which took into account some of the information she had gleaned. With something like two million pounds to use, she put together a well-balanced portfolio balancing secure gilts, with long-term growth, and reliable income stocks with some wild card risks. Tomorrow she would see a friend, Peter Adams, a stock broker whom she knew she could trust, who would make all the arrangements for her.

CHAPTER SEVEN

Monday dawned, and it really did feel as if it was the first day of the rest of her life. Peter, who she had known for years, was absolutely dumbstruck when she told him the news. "Abby, what are you going to do?" Like Steve, he was sure she had a deal going somewhere. With her reassurance that nothing like that was in the offing, and that she would be living in Devon for the next few months at the least, he shook his head. "I don't know, what's in Devon?" Like a lot of city people, he could not imagine life anywhere else.

"Peter, have you ever thought about my surname?" She asked. He shrugged his shoulders. "Tregonney is a West Country name, that's where my roots are."

He thought she was mad, but respected her business acumen, particularly when he examined the plan she had put together. "Shrewd," was his comment, "I like this, good returns from day one, and capital builder, any losses will be more than balanced by the growth stocks, but if they come off good profits to be taken. Good Lord! Do you reckon that one?" He pointed out one particular company. Abby just tapped the side of her nose. "Oh I see," a very knowing tone. "In that case, perhaps you wouldn't mind if I made a little investment there too?" Abby smiled.

"Go ahead, if my information is good, and I have no reason to believe otherwise, that could buy you your roller. But Peter, don't go mad; we don't want to attract attention." They agreed on the purchases, which Peter would begin immediately.

Abby went out into a muggy day, very close, with just a hint of rain in the air. Her mobile rang, and she was in two minds whether to answer, until she saw the number displayed on the screen, which was not one she recognised. Pressing the green button she announced herself. It was the bookstore manager, who told her that Mr. Brasher was coming in this afternoon, and would be happy to talk to her. "Great, I'll be there, what time do you think is best?"

The manager laughed. "Well if I were you, I would make it about two o' clock. When Brasher gets going you will have difficulty in stopping him." Abby grinned and said she would make it about two, and rang off. She made for home quickly, reasoning that if this Mr. Brasher was as knowledgeable as she was given to believe, then lots of paper would be needed for note-taking.

It was as an afterthought, that she grabbed the box-file containing her grandfather's papers before leaving the flat, perhaps Mr. Brasher could explain some of the abbreviations and codes used in their writing.

The manager she had met before was just inside the door when Abby arrived. "Miss Tregonney, I will take you down to Mr. Brasher." As they walked he enquired if she had started reading the books she bought.

"I have finished them, well not quite true," Abby explained, "I have read all the references to the line I am interested in. but there does seem to be a paucity of information about it."

The manager nodded, as if he understood. "Well if you could let us have the name of the line, I am sure we could find more references for you. Ah here is Mr. Brasher. Mr. Brasher, this is the young lady I spoke about, Miss Tregonney." Abby could hardly believe her eyes. Mr. Brasher was a tiny, rotund man, sparsely haired, with a small squashed face underneath spectacles that could have doubled as telescope lenses. The most remarkable aspect was his style of dress. Each item, suit, shirt, tie, spoke of quality, yet had evidently been put on with absolutely no thought to colour or co-ordination-- blue suit with a lime green shirt and a tie that boasted various colours of bright hue, none of them blue or lime green. He was obviously a man with no feminine influence in his life.

Abby held out her hand. "Hello Mr .Brasher, my name is Abby Tregonney." Her hand was shaken timidly, and he mumbled something like, 'pleased to meet you.' Abby was taken aback by this somewhat lacklustre greeting, and wondered if the manager had put pressure on him to talk to her. She was later to find out that Mr. Brasher was very unsure in female company. The manager invited them to sit at one of the tables that dotted the store. Once seated, Mr.

Brasher seemed to relax a little and without social preamble, asked how he could help.

Abby had not been sure how much of her family background to tell him, but his initial greeting had convinced her that he would not be interested in this at all. "I have recently taken a holiday in the West Country, a village called Combe Lyney, in the Lyney Valley. There was a railway there and I was interested to learn as much about it as I could. Unfortunately the books that I have been able to get hold of, don't mention it much. I was told that you were something of an expert, and could probably cast more light on the line."

Mr. Brasher brightened considerably. He could discuss this easily without having to make the small talk some women wanted. "The Lyney Valley line, yes, I'm not surprised you haven't been able to find much. Most historians concentrate on the big picture, and small branches such as this are rarely mentioned. That's something that I'm trying to put to rights, I am writing a complete history, you know, and I mean complete. The Lyney Valley line, yes. It should never have been made you know, there really wasn't any point, but that's hindsight of course." He delved into the large shoulder bag that he carried with him, flicking through reams of paper, until he brought out the relevant sheets.

He cleared his throat. "It was supposed to tap the mineral traffic that was thought the moor could produce at that time. Lills quarry produced regular traffic for a while, but after the second war, never more than a couple of trains of half a dozen wagons a week. That was part of the original prospectus; the other part was the iron ore traffic. The man who owned most of Exmoor was granting licences for mining iron ore at the time, what was his name now, I've got it here somewhere, ah yes, Knight. Small pockets of the ore had been mined for years, but not on an industrial scale. There were schemes aplenty, one including the building of a railway to take the ore to Porlock, and then to South Wales, as they did from the Brendon Hills through Watchet. The Bristol and Exeter thought that if they got a railway up to the Moor first, then they could have all the traffic and would route it through Barnstaple. Trouble was that the ground was so faulted, and there was so much water, they never managed to get ore in commercial quantities to the surface anyway. So the line existed on the traffic from Lills quarries, the agricultural traffic, and the passenger traffic that came from Paverton and Combe Lyney."

Abby was amazed, although he had got his notes, Mr. Brasher hardly referred to them at all. He wasn't finished and went on. "Fiscally, it was always on dodgy ground, and returns would never have been able to repay the capital account, but for one thing. The way the land was obtained. Usually land could be bought, sometimes at an inflated price, sometimes using the powers of compulsory purchase that were included in the Acts of Parliament. This line for most of its length was built on land obtained by way-leave, from the Comberford family."

Abby stifled a laugh, that family again, but the term way-leave was unfamiliar to her so she asked the question. "What does that mean?"

Mr. Brasher preened himself; his expert knowledge was again being sought. "A way-leave was basically a lease system. The land was granted to the railway for a fixed number of years at an agreed rent. The way-leave was renewable, but should the land cease to be used for its original purpose, the land reverted to the owner. Similarly if a change of purpose was intended, the way-leave had to be renegotiated. With the Lyney Valley railway, the rent was set very low, far lower than comparable rents elsewhere, although it was not a system used much, if at all, in England. Very popular in Scotland though! Without that rent, which really should be described as a peppercorn, the railway would never have been viable, as it was it was a borderline case for most of its life."

Abby's cynical city mind was working. Without realising she spoke aloud. "The Comberfords were up to something."

Mr. Brasher looked surprised. "You know of the Comberfords then," he asked.

"I have met the present Mr. Comberford."

Mr. Brasher acknowledged this by raising his eyebrows. "You could be right though; part of the deal was the station at Combe Lyney, far larger than really required for the traffic. I would imagine also that free first class travel would also come into the deal, although this may not be written down on the agreement, it was a common request from the landowners. There could in addition be other ways to collect rent, for instance a toll on every wagonload that passed over the line or for every wagonload that originated from the goods yard."

Abby gave a short cynical laugh at that. "That sounds like the Comberfords, an invisible tax on their tenants. They collect the rents, and then collect on the goods the tenants send out. Tell me, would that be possible?"

Mr. Brasher smiled for the first time. "Oh yes. You must remember this was a little branch line. The big railway companies were promoted and run by big businessmen. Their shareholders would be prominent people, and institutions, so it would be very difficult to put anything past them. But small lines like this would be promoted by the local businessmen and local landowners, often holding all the shares between a few men, who got a big railway company involved, to operate their line. Often the tactics and morals of some these local people were, shall we say, less than ethical. Whilst the line was technically independent I am sure that there were some, who, and I am looking for the right word here, creamed, I think is the expression, some off the top." Abby noted his remarks, something to throw, in the most light-hearted way at James Comberford.

Mr. Brasher interrupted her thoughts. "Tell me, Miss Tregonney, of your interest in the line, it is personal, isn't it; or is it coincidence that your name and that of one of the stationmasters at Combe Lyney are the same?"

Abby was taken aback, she did not realise that his research would have been in such depth. She saw no reason not to tell the truth. "My grandfather," she said simply.

"Ah, your grandfather. Do you know much about him?"

She shook her head. "No, I don't, I never knew him. My mother's dead, so the only information I have is from those who had contact with him at Combe Lyney."

Mr. Brasher busied himself in his voluminous bag once more, saying. "Let me see if I have anything on him. You know the trouble with the G.W.R. is not that the facts are not down on paper, they all are. The problem is finding them. This is also the problem with my filing system, I have the information, but sometimes I am damned if I can find it. Today is one of those days. Wait! I have it here." He pulled out a sheet, which he waved triumphantly. "Now let's see. I cannot give you a life history, just the significant dates as they appear in the records, but I will fill in as much as I can with generalisations typical of the time. Thomas Tregonney joined the G.W.R. as a lad porter in 1915 at Par. He would have been doing the most menial of jobs, sweeping, cleaning, and filling the lamps."

"Filling the lamps?" Abby broke in.

Mr. Brasher nodded. "Yes, terrible job that, all the signals had an oil lamp behind them, so they had to be replaced every week, whatever the weather. It usually fell to the most junior of the staff, and with some signals, especially the distant signals, very often a mile or so from the station, you can imagine how unpleasant a job when it was raining or snowing. Climbing the ladders in those conditions was enough to break anyone's will, not to mention a leg. More than one has fallen and been seriously hurt." He paused and then continued. "Your grandfather went to Lostwithiel in 1919, being confirmed as a porter there; and then to Truro in 1927 as leading porter. Truro was a large station and would have many grades of porter, so he would have been issuing tickets at times but mainly supervising the lower grades of porter. He was doing well."

Abby was astounded at this comment. "Doing well? It has taken from 1915 to 1927 to become a senior porter."

Mr. Brasher smiled. "Yes, that was doing well. You must appreciate that the railway service was a job for life, not just a stopping off point in a personal career plan. Many men at that time were out of work, and the railways had more applicants for jobs than positions to fill. So getting a promotion with every move, even a small promotion, was doing well." He referred to his paper once more. "In 1936 he had a trial as a relief stationmaster, spending time at any number of stations covering for illness, or holidays. That was a very difficult job, never being in one place long enough to know the staff, or to discover their little tricks, and trying to pick up on paperwork that the incumbent has let slide. He must have done it well enough though as he was appointed to Combe Lyney in 1938." He looked up at Abby. "Small stations like Combe Lyney, and there were lots of them, were the obvious choices for newly promoted stationmasters. They could be watched from a distance. If they made a mistake then it would not matter too much. If they did well they would soon get the chance at another, but larger, station. If their performance was alright, but hardly inspiring, then they could be left there to serve their time out without holding up others who were destined for better things."

Abby thought about those words, 'left there to serve their time out.' Is that what happened to grandfather, forgotten and neglected? She said as much to Mr. Brasher

"I think that would be putting too harsh an interpretation on the matter," he replied. "The times were unusual. Within a year of his appointment, the country was at war, and although railway men were a reserved occupation, it did not mean that promotion and staff movements were as normal. There would be cuts in the timetable, exceptional trains would be run, normal hours of duty went by the board and men who were in place, and knew how to do their job, were invaluable, left there to get on with it, working very much on their own initiative without constant supervision from the hierarchy. No, your grandfather's contribution would have been important. After the war, it took time to get things back to normal. The railways were in a terrible state, and nationalisation was the preferred option to re-vitalise the system. That of course opened another unusual circumstance, insomuch as under British Railways appointments could be made to anywhere from anywhere in the country. I don't know many men who would voluntarily move from the West Country to the industrial Midlands, or the North, but certainly for men outside, a move to the West Country was very much desired. Applications for appointments in the South and West were always plentiful, not so in other areas. Your grandfather would have applied for more important appointments, of course he would. Probably though they were never for appointments outside the G.W.R. area. He would have been G.W.R. through and through, like a stick of sea-side rock, it would never occur to him to apply elsewhere for a position."

The situation was becoming clearer to Abby. "So his isolation was to an extent of his own doing?" Mr. Brasher shook his head. "Only partly. The war was a turning point in our social history. Your grandfather had grown up and worked in a system where loyalty and application had their own reward. He would have understood and approved a practice that promoted men only after they had demonstrated those qualities, and proven that they were competent in the job. After the war that ethos was turned on its head. There were plenty of jobs available as Britain rebuilt itself. The returning servicemen, young, fit, were found well paying work, very often attaining situations which hitherto would only have been theirs after years of diligent employment. Young men were impatient, they would no longer wait around for dead men's shoes, after all they had risked their lives and won the war for the country, they wanted their reward now. There were lots of other jobs they could go to. Employers found that to keep these men they could no longer follow the old system. The railways were no different. As the fifties moved on, new ideas, new locomotives, diesels and electric were coming in. It required men who were conversant with the new technologies, or who could learn quickly. Men like your grandfather would most likely abhor and obstruct such developments. They had no place in the new railway."

The way that Mr. Brasher had said this gave Abby reason to believe that he didn't altogether approve of the changes that had taken place. "You don't sound as if you liked that new railway."

He shrugged. "Like it or not, it happened. The railway had to become a profitable business, not a public service, although the G.W.R. and perhaps one of the other railways had managed to combine the two. We went from a system where very few villages were more than three miles away from a railway station, to a system that seemed to believe that people only wished to travel between big cities. Given that the cities house fewer than 40% of the population, then the railways are ignoring 60% of their potential customers. And they call that good business!" He shook his head. "You, young lady, will probably label me a Luddite, against progress, and maybe I am, when that progress doesn't actually improve things. I remember what it was like, and do so with fondness, for I was young then, so it is my nostalgia for the days of my youth that is speaking. Allow me that memory. It does appear to me though, that the ethic of service to the community has been lost somewhere along the way." Abby's working life had been imbued with the attitude that profit was all. Banks were not sentimentalist, and cared little for those who suffered in the pursuit of their profits. Yet the little she had learned during her stay at Combe Lyney was starting to make a persuasive argument in her mind that perhaps capital should be more attentive to the effects its decisions have on society at large. She would never be convinced of any argument that capitalism was the wrong system; but she was beginning to think that its policies ought to take into account social deprivation as well. Mr Brasher had started packing his files away, obviously with the intention of leaving. Abby started to thank him for his time, but he waved her thanks away.

"Please, Miss Tregonney, think little of it. I have enjoyed talking; you probably gather that I could bore for Britain on this subject. I would stay longer, but I have an appointment."

Abby had more questions to ask, and with a moment of inspiration, she opened the box file.

"I have one or two items here that were my grandfathers bequest. Perhaps when you have the time you could look through them and explain their significance." She handed the journal to Mr. Brasher; the effect on him was electrifying. He sat down again and with trembling hands leafed through the journal.

"I don't believe it, it's wonderful, a journal. And it appears to be complete. It's amazing. You know they were encouraged to keep these, but few ever did. This is magnificent, look at the writing, beautiful copperplate, and it's all here. Fantastic." He looked at Abby, "You probably don't realise how important this could be, do you?" Abby shook her head, bewildered by his reaction. He explained. "This is a record of the working of Combe Lyney Station, the running of trains, punctuality, the fluctuations of goods traffic, and passenger traffic, the special requirements, and requisitioning of stationery, oil, coal, everything. With this we can piece together the daily working of the branch, and used in conjunction with Bradshaw it will build a complete picture of the line within its environment. May I borrow this? Please let me, it will be invaluable."

Abby was happy to let him have the journal, if he could decipher the codes and oblique references, then he would be doing her a favour. "Of course, I'll let you have a complete list of the code names."

Abby interrupted him. "Just tell me one for the moment, what was a siphon?"

He smiled. "It was a ventilated truck for milk churns."

Abby pushed her luck a little. "I understand that the drivers used two types of whistle, a pop and a crow. I know they used the pop when starting a train, but what was a crow?"

Mr. Brasher nodded. "A crow was a long whistle, at least three seconds. It was used to alert signalmen usually, that they should set the road for a siding, or that a locomotive was coming off-shed. Sometimes if there were more than one siding that could be used, multiple crows would be sounded to indicate which siding the train was to enter. There was a strict code for the number of course; otherwise all sorts of confusion could be had." He smiled as he remembered something. "At Weston Super Mare there were three sidings a train could enter. One was called Rookery siding, and there was a sign up for enginemen before they reached the signal box. 'Three crows for Rookery! They were always amused by that." Abby thanked him for his help.

Mr Brasher had more to say. "If it would be convenient for you I shall be happy to meet you here again next Monday, I'll let you have the journal back, and will probably be able to set out the daily working of the station. It will give you more ideas about your grandfather's daily routine." Abby didn't want to hang around in London for a week, with little to do, and explained that she would be going down to Combe Lyney within the next two days.

Mr. Brasher was unconcerned. "That will be no problem; I will send the journal and my summary to you down there, if you would give me the address. Don't worry; it will be safe with me. I shall keep it very securely, I promise." That settled her mind, she would phone Mary today, and see if she had a room for her.

Mary was delighted to hear from Abby. "Abby, we will be so happy to see you back here, Sam has been most miserable, without you to talk with. Don't worry about anything; your room is ready for you." Abby was surprised and comforted that the news of her impending return could cheer Mary up so much.

"I shall be down tomorrow afternoon."

With that settled, the business of packing now occupied her mind. She had not bothered to take too many clothes when she went down before, as she knew that it would be for a few days only. Now it could be for a few months. She would have to return to London, now and again, but hopefully not often, until she had decided on the future for herself. Abby was thankful that she lived in a flat, she had an efficient security system installed as a consequence of her irregular working hours, so that now all she needed to do was turn off the electricity and water. Her post was delivered to a box downstairs in the lobby, and a note to the caretaker would ensure that it was forwarded. That done, she could set off with an untroubled conscience.

CHAPTER EIGHT

Abby had seen the valley for the first time in late March, when the weather could only suggest a vision of the summer to come, and the foliage was just a clue to the verdant picture of the valley in high summer. Now in early July, those promises were fulfilled. The trees of Huish Coppice swayed gently to a slight warm breeze, and raised and let fall their leaves like petticoats at a dance. The late afternoon sun shone strongly on the meadows and cattle clustered gregariously in the deep shadows under the trees. Sheep lethargically grazed the higher pastures, as if even the ongoing task of eating was too strenuous an exercise in the heat. The air was so still that the droning of a tractor from much higher in the valley carried; heard, but not seen. Everything was as Abby remembered, yet different. She was a visitor no longer, now she felt as if she was coming home. The Combe Inn extended the same welcome, the door open, no one in attendance except the dog, lazing in front of a now unlit fire. Yet again, the dog, raised its head, gave that one thump of its tail, and resumed its leisurely dozing. Abby approached the bar, and called. "Mary."

The response was immediate and Mary bustled in, obviously from the kitchen as she dusted flour from her hands. The welcome was most genuine; no one could fake the wide beam that split Mary's face. Wiping her hands on her apron, she rushed round through the door at the side of the bar, and flung her arms around Abby kissing her cheeks both sides. "Oh Abby, it's so nice to see you again, we have missed you. Jack will be delighted, as will Sam and Mavis and the others, not to mention Mr. James. He has asked if you would be coming back, you know. Now how long will you be staying? Your old room is ready for you, and we are happy to have you here as long as you want." As usual all this came out without Mary pausing for breath, and at the same time nodding her head.

Abby smiled back, as Mary's beam was contagious. "Mary, it's good to see you again, and if it's all right with you I shall be staying for some months."

Mary stopped short. "Some months?" she repeated, "Why, what has happened? Have you lost your job or something?"

Abby hastened to re-assure her. "No, nothing like that, in fact I have resigned, but I'll tell you all about that later. But is it all right to stay for a few months? If it's inconvenient, I could find somewhere in Paverton."

Mary shook her head brusquely. "Of course it's all right, you don't think I would have you going anywhere else, do you?" She sounded offended at the idea. "You stay as long as you want. Now where are your cases, in the car? I'll get Jack to bring them up for you. Let's have a nice cup of tea first, just you sit down, and I'll bring it through." She then called Jack, whose voice carried up from the bowels of the earth.

His footsteps sounding as he climbed up from the cellar. "Abby!" His grin was as infectious as Mary's beaming smile. "It's really good to see you again; I won't shake hands, as I'm all dirty from the cellar."

Mary interrupted him. "Never mind about that now, Jack; fetch Abby's cases from her car; and take them up, will you?"

Jack nodded. "I'll put the car round the back as well, the grockles are about now, and some of them are none too careful about parking. Have you got the keys, Abby, or are they in the car?'

Abby gave him the keys. "The luggage is all in the boot."

He nodded and went off to get her cases. Mary called after him. "Just you wash your hands first, Jack Elvesly." He waved his hand in acknowledgment.

Mary was going off to make the tea, but Abby forestalled her. "Mary, what or who is a grockle."

Mary laughed. "A grockle is a type of visitor. They charge around the country, never getting out of their car except to eat and drink something, or take a few photographs. They think the countryside is very pretty, but reckon that the farmer's new barn or silage tower shouldn't be allowed, as it spoils the view. The smells of the countryside offend them, silage, dung, and the like, and they get really upset if they get mud on their shoes. They don't spend money with us, but seem to think that our toilets are public facilities, then at the end of the day, they go back to the caravan they have hired for the week and eat the food they stocked up with from their local supermarket before they came. That's a grockle." Mary thought a little and continued. "Mind, we don't get too many round here, the roads are not marked except on the most detailed of maps, and we don't have a McDonald's or KFC. But we get enough to do well out of cream teas most afternoons."

Whilst Mary was attending to the tea, Abby wondered if they thought that she was a grockle, but then discounted the thought, after all, Mary was unlikely to have said anything uncomplimentary about grockles if she, Abby, was one herself.

Mary bustled back with the tea tray. "Would you like to sit in here, or outside? The sun will have gone off the front by now, and it will be quite pleasant."

Abby didn't need to think too much. "Outside please, Mary. Air conditioning in the car is very good, but you do get the feeling you are breathing stale air after a while." They sat at the bench table, which was, realised Abby, where the photo of her grandfather, grandmother, and mother had been taken. The bench would probably be a replacement, but the location remained the same.

She said so to Mary. "Yes, Love, it would have been here. Strange isn't it, how life has a habit of going full circle? Such a pity that your granddad never knew about you. Still, these things happen." Without taking breath, Mary launched into another conversation. "Now what's going on in your life?"

Abby took the breath that Mary hadn't. "Well, I resigned my job, for a start. I realised that although I had enjoyed it immensely and it paid well, very well, it wasn't going anywhere. Perhaps it was me, getting to an age when other things could be more important. Perhaps it was coming down here, and discovering the truth about my family. I don't really know. I suppose that I had just become dissatisfied. The catalyst was seeing my deputy being prepared for higher things, and knowing that I had gone as far as I could. So I left. I can manage for a while without worry, and I could not think of a better place to contemplate the future than right here."

Mary nodded. "Yes, there is no better place for you. Now you just relax, Abby, and enjoy your time here, get out now that the weathers fine, and get some colour into your cheeks. We'll put some good food inside you, and before too long you'll feel a different person." Abby groaned inwardly at the thought of the good food that Mary intended she should eat. She would really have to be careful or else her weight would soar.

Jack came out and took a seat beside Mary. "Luggage all sorted, the car is round the back," he grinned at Abby, "really nice to see you again, I expect that Mary will have given you the third degree by now, and she'll tell me what she thinks I should know later. Did you have a good journey down? I would imagine that car goes well and comfortable too. Bit different to my old Land Rover eh?" Abby relaxed; enjoying the tea and the gossip that Mary could now regale her with. Some of the people mentioned were unknown to her, and Mary was careful to explain their links to people that Abby did know. From time to time cars would pass by and a hand would wave indicating a local, others would slow and stare, and then drive on, with Mary and Jack murmuring under their breath, but simultaneously 'grockle.' Abby soon saw for herself the giveaway behaviour and could identify them almost as swiftly as Jack and Mary.

The afternoon slipped away easily in this relaxing way, until Mary stood. "I must get on, what would you like for your dinner this evening, Abby?"

Abby was happy to eat whatever Mary produced, but made the stipulation. "Small portions please, Mary. I cannot manage the amount you used to put on my plate."

Jack grinned. "That's all right then, there'll be more for me."

Mary scolded him. "Just typical of a man, always thinking of his stomach. You'll have what you're given, and be grateful." Mary collected the cups and saucers and piled the tray to take back. "See you about seven, is that O.K.?"

Abby nodded. "Yes, that will be fine. I'll go and unpack."

Abby took a lot longer to unpack and put away her clothes than she had on her previous visit and was thankful for the large amount of hanging space the wardrobe provided. At times she was surprised with some of the things she had brought, which included four quite dressy suits, and blouses, now she wondered why she had bothered with them, they would never be required downstairs, it was not that sort of a place, and she couldn't imagine being asked out to a smart restaurant; or was there such a possibility? Putting these thoughts on one side, she completed the unpacking, with some small ornaments and a photograph of her mother in a little silver frame, together with the photo of her grandfather, grandmother and mother taken outside the Combe Inn. This had been restored by one of the staff at the bank, who had the necessary software on his computer. She was after all going to be here for some months, and may as well make the room a little more homely with these small touches.

One of the first things she had done was open the windows fully, allowing the breeze to blow gently through the room, now she leaned out and drank in the air and the view. If she had previously had any doubts about what she was doing they were now dispelled. The calm of the valley soothed and brought her peace. If in her mind the question why she was here had existed; now it was answered. This is where her family had lived, and however tenuous the connection, it was a root to hold on to, when before she had been rootless. She felt at home here, a feeling she had never really enjoyed before. If she was to embark on a different direction in life, then here was the place to start that journey, because this was the base to which she could always return.

That feeling was reinforced during the evening, as the regulars who had seen her before, made plain their delight at her return. Dressed as she was in denims and a sweatshirt, she no longer felt that she had to stay in the seclusion of the lounge, and after finishing a superb casserole joined the throng in the bar, enjoying and joining their chat and jokes, some of which were at the expense of the grockles, and replying time after time, to the enquiries as to her health and how long she would stay. It was always gratifying when they expressed pleasure at her extended stay. At around nine o' clock, the door opened and over the head of the crowd she noticed Sam entering. If she hadn't seen him she would have been alerted anyway, as a voice called out. "Hey up, Sam. Your lady friend is back, oh hello Mavis, I didn't see you there"

Laughter came from all sides, and Sam's face turned bright red, but it didn't matter, as Mavis using her elbows to good effect; burrowed her way through all the drinkers, and threw her arms around Abby "Love, it's so good to see you back here. Sam's missed you; he's had to put up with the conversation of these turnip heads here. How are you? Let's go and sit down, then we can talk in relative peace." Mavis as ever took charge, and led Abby round to the lounge. Mary joined them very shortly, bringing with her a spritzer for Abby, a port and lemon for Mavis, and her own drink, which looked like a gin and tonic. Once they were all seated comfortably, Abby had to go over the whole thing again. During the explanation, she noticed Mavis looking shrewdly at her, and she stopped almost in mid-sentence. In the silence that ensued, Mavis said, "You must have done all right for yourself, I mean if you can live off your capital for a while."

Abby wasn't surprised. It was obvious that Mavis had a head on her shoulders. Rather than going into the detail, Abby replied casually. "I can manage for a while, but I shall have to find something to do."

Mavis nodded. "Well, there's not much around here, so I suppose you will have to leave us again."

Mary was indignant at the thought. "Oh Mavis, Abby's only just come back, and you're talking about her going away again. Let the love have some peace and quiet for a while." At that point, Sam came to join them, for which Abby was thankful. He had taken the edge off his thirst at the bar and brought a tray with a repeat order for his wife, Mary, and Abby. The smile that Abby gave him brought the blush to his face once again, and he sat down uncertainly, wondering what he had interrupted.

Abby took his hand in hers. "It's so nice to see you again, Sam." He blushed and looked quickly at his wife, who was laughing softly.

"You silly, old beggar," she said, "you never used to blush like that when you took me into that haystack, all those years ago, did you?"

Sam grinned. "If my memory serves me right, it was you that did the leading."

Mavis chuckled unashamedly. "Well if I hadn't, we would never have got together, you being so backward in coming forward, eh?" She leaned forward. "You know, Abby, he must have taken all of six months to pluck up the courage to ask me out, and even then I had to stand there and tell him that if he didn't ask right then, his chance would have gone forever. I wasn't going to wait around." They all joined in the laughter. Any difficulty that Abby may have felt over the questioning of her finances was dissolved, and the conversation moved on light heartedly from there.

Abby was tired after her journey and went to bed shortly after ten o' clock. Just after she had gone, Mary turned on Mavis. "You had no right to talk about how much money she had, just like that, you could see she was embarrassed."

Mavis was unrepentant. "I don't think she was upset, but I'll tell you one thing, Mary, that girl is very well off. If you read the papers, you'll know that what she was doing was very well paid, and did you cotton on, when she said she had a flat in Kensington? Well if I'm to believe what I read, then property like that is worth hundreds of thousands."

Mary was aghast. "How much?"

Mavis repeated. "Hundreds of thousands."

Mary carried her gin and tonic to her lips with a trembling hand. "Good grief, I always felt that she was comfortable, you know, from the little things that she has said, but never that well off."

Mavis smiled with satisfaction. "And you know the nicest thing about her, is that she doesn't flaunt it. I don't want to see her go; she should stay here in this valley; it will do us all good here in Combe to have a proper family up the hill. I know just the right situation for her, and you know what I mean."

Mary looked at her sagely. "You might be running ahead of things there; but yes I think I do know what you mean. Mind he did come in and ask about her, you know, if she was coming back."

Mavis was not aware of this, and her lips pursed as she nodded her head. "That's interesting. Oh well, time will tell, time will tell."

It was just after six o' clock when Abby awoke, an hour which had hitherto been a stranger to her. The light streaming through the thin curtains had brightened the room, which she supposed was the reason for waking at that hour. Pulling back the curtains, she greeted the day. The sun had begun warming the air, which seemed to vibrate softly with the gathering warmth; soon the shadows under the trees would deepen as the full strength of the light became real. In the meadows, the cattle and sheep were busy cropping the lush grass, preparing for the midday sun when it would be too hot even for them. Abby felt herself totally refreshed from the night's sleep and despite the early hour was ready for the day. She put the kettle on to make tea, and cleaned her teeth whilst waiting for it to boil. She stood and drank at the window, something she had done often on her previous visit, as habits go she thought, this was one hard to beat, the pleasure of the tea, and the view she enjoyed lifted her spirits as little else would.

She showered and dressed in jeans and a T-shirt, a pair of comfortable moccasins on her feet, and went downstairs. Mary was surprised to see her so early. "What about you, then," she cried, "bit early for you isn't it?"

"I slept well," Abby laughed, "and when I woke up, it seemed a pity to waste any of the day."

Mary agreed. "Well it's going to be a hot one, if you are out in the middle of the day, wear a hat; you have got one haven't you?" Abby assured Mary that she did indeed have a hat, and also said that she was going for a little walk before breakfast. This reminded Mary that she had to make sure that Abby was well fed, and the consequent negotiation was settled on scrambled egg, two rashers, and just one round of toast. Mary was not at all pleased with the result of this discussion believing that two eggs, three rashers, and two rounds of toast was the very minimum for anyone before venturing out for the day.

Leaving the inn, Abby turned right to stroll down towards the river bridge. To her left she could see the Church. It sat on a higher level to the road and because of this, appeared at first to be quite a large structure. However, as her perspective changed, she could see that it was really a very simple construction, a chapel with grandiose ideas. The nave was not long, and the tower squat, both sitting firmly on their mound, as grey as the rock which was the foundation. Scattered about the churchyard were numerous simple gravestones, some straight like soldiers, others tilting at varying angles. From the road, Abby could not read names, but reckoned that even close up it would be difficult as almost every stone was decorated with the greens and browns of lichen, the haphazard patterns creating a look somewhat similar to the photos of the world taken from a satellite. 'I bet there's a few Comberfords in there.' The thought sprang into her mind unbidden, and she mused upon this almost obsession of hers with the Comberford family. Was it just because of the slighting of her grandfather, or because of their influence and shaping of the valley? It was ridiculous really, they had done nothing more than many others, looking after themselves and their interests. Or was it because she liked James Comberford, and somehow thought she should not. He had that light self-denigrating sense of humour that appealed to Abby, and she had to admit to herself that she wanted to meet him again. Putting these thoughts out of her mind she walked on.

Further down the road, she noticed another lane leading around and up the hill behind the Church. Through the variegated greens of the foliage she caught an occasional glimpse of a much larger house. It had to be at the highest level of building in the village, and without thinking she knew instinctively who owned that house. She decided to ignore this, she wouldn't be seen to be peeking at the place, and determinedly she walked past the lane and continued round a bend towards the river. The road dropped away now, and to her left was the small estate of council houses that could just be seen from the inn. There were only half a dozen of them, and to her eye looked as if the tenants cared for them. The gardens were neat and tidy, and if there was a child's bike lying in the path of a couple what did it matter. That didn't compare at all with the conditions of some around London, whose gardens were to all intents and purposes a car-breakers yard. She wondered at Mary's attitude, and thought it was probably the same attitude that so many people would feel, agreeing that such places had to be built, but not in our village, thank you.

The road went downhill out of the village, and crossed the meadows slightly raised above the level, and then gently rising to the bridge spanning the river. She stopped on the bridge and gave in to the imperative that upon crossing a river bridge that you had to lean over the parapet and gaze into the water. This was not a major river, it appeared to flow and ripple gently over the stones lining its bed, a quiet chuckling was its only comment on life. The water was so clear that Abby could see the weeds clinging to the larger rocks and streaming out with the flow. As her eyes focussed better she realised that these were not all in fact weeds, but fish, dappled fresh water trout, who rather than swim energetically all day, just did enough to stay in one place and let the river bring the food to them. How sensible. From the elevated position of the bridge, she could see both upstream and downstream for some distance. Downstream there was the railway bridge, a girder construction, supported by two stone abutments; both set well back from the river itself. The girders were dappled with rust, 'grandfather would have had something to say about that' her thoughts murmured, and she laughed gently to herself, amazed at how the character of the man was becoming real in her own mind. Upstream the river vanished within a few hundred yards into a small gorge, overhung with trees, but its general course could be discovered by observing those same trees, which had grown stronger and more quickly, thriving on the moisture derived from the river.

Abby turned to stroll back, the thought of some breakfast raising hollow grumbles of hunger in her stomach. The toot of a horn startled her as a Land Rover swept down the road from Paverton, and over the bridge. It passed her, but immediately braked. As she drew level she could see the driver leaning half around in his seat and pushing the slide glass window open.

"Good Morning, Miss Tregonney," said James Comberford, "out and about early, I see." Abby could not but help smile, as his grin was certainly infectious.

"Good morning, James," she replied, consciously using his first name, "yes, I had to get up early, it's all these sheep and cockerels, who have no consideration for us townies, and insist on making a racket as soon as the sun has got over the horizon," she paused, "and you, are you out early, or just returning late from the night's excesses?"

James pulled a face. "Night's excesses? In Paverton?" His tone was incredulous, "No, Abby," following her lead he used her Christian name, "it's what we country folk have to do, so we fit the preconceived ideas of you townies."

Abby laughed. "You mean you got up early just to impress me, I'm flattered, but tell me, you don't seem surprised to see me, how did you know I was here again, I've only been in Combe Lyney for one night?" James did not answer her directly; instead he offered her a lift, which Abby accepted.

Once the Land Rover was underway, which it did with clouds of blue smoke from the exhaust and much missing and catching from under the bonnet, he answered her question. "Well you saw Sam and Mavis last night, their son, Roger, who farms the land now, has a daughter, Elizabeth, who comes up to the house, and mucks out the stables, in exchange for riding whenever she's at home. I saw Liz this morning and she told me that that posh lady was back, so I knew it was you. Simple really. Nothing happens in a small village like this without everyone knowing the next day."

Abby realised that it was as James said, news travelled fast. "I don't know about being called that posh lady, or that you should jump to the conclusion that it had to be me. I'm not posh. I'm the granddaughter of the stationmaster; you can't get much more downmarket than that."

James chuckled. "You drive a BMW; you have some important job in London, and live in Kensington, that's posh to us." They had arrived outside the Combe Inn, and James brought the Land Rover to a shuddering halt.

Abby turned to him. "I might drive a BMW, yes, I had a job in the city, no more, and the flat will be on the market shortly, so I'm going to be losing the posh. Thanks for the lift; this Land Rover's an experience after the BMW, when you drive it, you'll see. Shall I see you around?"

James gave his grin. "Oh yes, you'll see me around, I never go far from Combe Lyney now."

Abby went in to find Mary, and her breakfast, for which she was ready. The grapevine worked even more efficiently here, as Mary appeared almost immediately, and indicated the table laid for Abby. If Abby had known that Mary had noted her manner of arrival and with whom, and that after bringing Abby her breakfast would be on the phone to Mavis, she would have been quietly amused, as it was she gave no further thought other than to eat. One thing she did ponder was the last remark of James'. He had said 'I never go far from Combe Lyney now.' The emphasis she was sure had been on the 'now' as if he had travelled away from the valley, and it had not been a pleasant experience.

It was her intention to drive around and discover the area, but first she would have to get some petrol. Mary was polishing glasses at the bar, eagerly awaiting Abby's departure so that she could phone Mavis. "Mary, I need some petrol for the car. Do I have to go towards South Molton or is there somewhere in Paverton?"

Mary gave this some thought. "I don't really know, I'll ask Jack." she called into the hinterland of the pub, and Jack answered.

He came into the bar and beamed at Abby. Mary explained the need for petrol. "No problem, there's a garage in Paverton, just off to the right of the Market Place. It's closer than South Molton." Abby thanked him and said for both their benefits that she would take a drive, to see the country, and not to expect her back before the evening.

Jack gave her a recommendation. "Go see Porlock, nice little place, and if you drive along the coast you'll get to Minehead, it's full of beer-bellies and tattoos at this time of year, but there's a preserved railway there, you might find that interesting." Abby thought that it would indeed be interesting, anything that would increase her knowledge of how the railways were run fifty years ago, could only be of help in understanding her grandfather.

The road to Paverton she now knew quite well, and finding the garage was easily done. She filled up with unleaded fuel, noting the price per litre. The parking may be cheap around here, but the cost of petrol was way above that which she was used to paying in London. With a full tank she consulted her map and decided to drive over Exmoor towards the Brendon Hills. Rather than using road numbers she listed mentally the names of the towns and villages she would drive through; Exford, Luckwells Bridge, Wheddon Cross, Dunster, and then to Minehead.

The Moor was not as she expected, anticipating the wild, gorse covered, and windswept moors of Northern England. Whilst some parts did indeed resemble those moors, stone and earth embankments enclosed for the most part Exmoor, the fields they created populated with sheep and even cattle. The road that she drove was lined with beech, the trees bent by the prevailing winds. From time to time she would pass old buildings, some derelict, others showing signs of continued habitation. The road itself was well maintained, and wide, not like the lane which ran up to Combe Lyney, and although it avoided the steepest gradients, by threading its way round outcrops and hills, did manifest some quite extensive earthworks, to ease its path. Where the road ran across what she would call true moorland the most stupendous views were obtained, otherwise the beech lining the road restricted her line of sight. Exford came almost as a shock, the road descending steeply into another verdant valley to the bridge over the infant river Exe. A hotel close by the bridge and numerous houses, all in good state, proclaimed this as a much-visited place. The references to Lorna Doone, confirmed the tourist status, although she felt doubtful if the many visitors would be familiar with the book. She laughed to herself, 'shame on you Abby, you haven't even read the book yourself.'

The 'B' road enabled her to drive faster, the road having more gentle curves, although the hills and dips were still quite severe. She was still not able to see much of the Moor though, as the stone and earth banks had become covered with vegetation, hawthorn, gorse, grasses, and of course the inevitable beech. It was only when going downhill on a fairly straight stretch that she was able to see the Moor and its vistas. She came to Luckwell Bridge, diving down one side of a valley, over the bridge itself, and almost immediately ascending. The road curved to the right, and too late to make the turn she noticed a signpost for Dunster. In two minds whether to carry on or turn back, she came to Wheddon Cross, and realised that the turn before was simply an avoiding road for the difficult left turn at the cross roads here. The A396 ran gently through a wooded valley, following the river Avill, which she imagined ran all the way down to Dunster, and then onto the sea. Dunster itself was an experience, the road becoming so narrow through the village; that traffic lights had been installed to regulate the flow of traffic, even so, the lorries and buses coming the other way seemed to have little clearance. When the lights allowed her into the town it was as if a time warp had transported her back to the Middle Ages, cobbled pavements, old houses, and right in the centre a beautiful wool market, all supervised by the lordly castle, sitting high on its mound. She would have slowed down better to appreciate the sights, but for the traffic which had followed her, a large white van breathing heavily down at the back of her car, its body language telling her she was holding it up. She drove on through, resisting the urge to see everything at once, mentally cautioning herself that she would have plenty of time, outside the main tourist season to explore.

The road to Minehead turned left outside the village, and Abby could once again drive a little faster. Not as fast as the white van would like, however. In what seemed like a suicidal move it passed her cutting in abruptly as a car came the other way. The driver of the other car was obviously making pertinent comments on the ancestry of the van driver as he and Abby passed. An island loomed, with the signs showing straight on for the town centre, and one of those brown tourist signs telling her right for the West Somerset Railway, which she presumed would be the preserved railway that Jack had mentioned. She turned right along a relatively new road, passed the inevitable Tesco, and McDonald's, and was brought to a stop by the flashing red lights of a level crossing. A shrill whistle caught her attention, and a steam engine, gleaming in polished green, copper and brass shining drew a train of chocolate and cream coaches across in front of her. She let down her window, and the evocative smell of steam, hot oil, and sulphur wafted into the car. As soon as the barriers lifted, she moved off, and following the signs drove along the front, past Victorian buildings which could have started life as hotels or perhaps family homes but were now converted into shops and arcades, and found the station tucked away on the left, the buffers right up against the pavement. Abby was lucky enough to find a parking space in the small car park adjacent to the station, and wandered onto the platform. The station offices were to her right, a booking hall first, then a shop, then other offices. She walked past them, dodging to the left and the right to avoid the passengers streaming down the platform towards her. There were two lines, one at the platform and the other running parallel, past a building that she would recognise anywhere as a goods shed, it was similar to the one at Combe Lyney, but this one was obviously now being used as an engine shed. At the road end of the second line stood a hulk only just recognisable as an engine, standing on just six wheels. What could they possibly do with that, she wondered; it didn't look as if it would ever again run. In the opposite direction, the second line ran alongside a water tower, a huge tank standing on a slim post. From the base of the tank a jib extended, and offered at its end a large flexible tube, from which dripped water.

The train she had seen crossing the road was now standing at the platform and the engine having left its coaches coasted with soft hissing and pants slowly down the line towards where she stood. It was a medium-sized locomotive, with sloping water tanks on each side. It passed her and stopped with a groan of the brakes, the chimney right up against the buffers. The driver was hanging out the other side to her looking back. Abby followed his line of sight, and heard the clunk as the points changed. A man dressed in blue overalls stood by two levers just at the end of the engine shed, and raised his left arm towards the driver. The whistle sounded, and the engine moved backwards, crossing over to the outside rail, and slowly approached the water tower, there it stopped and one of the crew she presumed would be the fireman climbed on top of the engine tanks, and lifted the fill covers. His mate on the ground grabbed a chain and with it swung the jib until the man on top caught the chain and pulled the jib over the locomotive tanks, now the purpose of the flexible tube (later Abby would learn they called it the bag), was revealed as the fireman dragged it up and dropped it into the engine's water tank. She was amazed at how casually the men clambered over the locomotive, or walked around it at ground level, touching the wheel bosses with the backs of their hands, and even leaning in between the wheels, ministering to some unseen, but nonetheless vital oiling point. All the time this was going on the engine stood there steaming gently, hot water dripping from pipes, hissing softly like a powerful but docile animal, awaiting the attentions of its driver.

Abby watched fascinated, and a sudden thought entered her head. This was a scene that her grandfather would recognise instantly, the timeless rituals and routines of the steam railway. Fifty years ago, no a hundred years ago, it was done in exactly the same way. The overalls would be a little different, the demeanour of the men would be a little different, but the activity would be unchanged. Her attention was more defined now, as if what she was seeing could bring her closer to Thomas Tregonney.

The water pipe was swung away, the fireman closing the water tank cover with a clang, and scrambled down via the steps at the buffer beam. The driver climbed to the footplate, soon to be joined by the fireman, who turned his attention to the firebox, shovelling in eight rounds of coal. Then both men manning either side of the footplate, checked around, and the whistle sounded. A great roar of steam issued from pipes at the front, and the locomotive slowly moved again. Whilst all this had been going on, intending passengers had been walking up the platform towards the coaches, but few seemed in a hurry to take their seats. Many had walked to the head of the train, and Abby realised that they would be waiting for the locomotive to couple on. Regretting that she had left her camera in the car, she debated whether to fetch it, but decided that she may not get back in time, so she too walked hurriedly to the head of the train, just in time to see the locomotive backing down.

The attitudes of the crowd were various, from the dads and older men, who remembered the days of their youth, and looked upon the engine with fondness, and perhaps a little pride that they knew (or imagined that they did), all about steam engines. Mums who knelt down next to their children, exhorting them to look at the puff-puff, the baby name bringing expressions of disgust to the faces of the enthusiasts. The children reacted either in sheer wonder at this snorting machine, or clamped hands over ears, and cried to be taken away. Cries, which fell on the deaf ears of their fathers, who embarrassed, could not, or would not give in to such cowering. The cameras clicked as treasured scenes were committed to Kodak, or Fuji, followed by the darting run of the cameraman to find another angle, much to the annoyance of those who used camcorders, whose footage was despoiled by yet another head popping up in the viewfinder. In the midst of all this, the engine crew went insouciantly about their job, coupling up, bringing the oil lamp from the front, which was now the rear, to the rear which was now the front, and hanging it on its bracket, the fireman once more attending to his fire, then turning a lever under the driver's seat, and leaning over the side looking down, appearing satisfied when another sound, a hum with a slight ringing tone on a higher note, joined all the others.

At last all seemed ready, the intending passengers retreating to claim their seats, and the fireman now concentrating his attention towards the rear of the train. Doors slammed, then opened to receive a late arrival, and slammed again. The platform cleared to leave just two men. The guard who stood about the middle of the train looked both ways, and then turned to the other man, a porter, who stood near the rear of the train, who raised his arm. The guard, looked back to the station entrance and satisfied that there were no more late passengers, turned, raised his green flag and blew his whistle. The fireman called across to his mate, 'right away.' The engine whistle sounded one short 'whoop,' which Abby was delighted to know she could describe authentically as a 'pop,' and with steam boiling out at the front of the engine, it gently eased the train into motion, followed by the sudden and sharply defined blasts from the chimney, as the regulator was opened wider. There had always been a certain ceremony about a departing train, Abby thought, particularly from a terminus, but the spectacle of a modern diesel or electric train departing could not compare in any way to that of a steam train. The steam engine announces itself in a magnificent and spectacular way, demanding that the spectator pay it attention as it went about its work.

Abby watched the train as it drew ever further into the distance, down a long straight track. Even when the coaches could not be seen clearly through the heat haze, and the tracks wavered and danced, there was still a plume of steam and smoke rising into the blue sky to draw the attention. At long last just as she thought she had seen the last of the train, there came faintly to her ears another whistle, a last reminder. She turned to walk down the platform, and for the first time noticed another locomotive, previously hidden by the coaches of the departed train. This was a larger engine, also resplendent in shining green paint, with a copper trim to its chimney, and perched on top of its boiler what looked like an upturned coalscuttle, brass brightly reflecting the sun's rays. This had a tender, with the initials G.W.R. picked out in gold paint. Upon the cab side its number 7820, and curved over the splasher of the middle wheel a name "Dinmore Manor." Whiffs of steam curled away from the chimney, and from a copper pipe under the cab, an occasional drip of hot water. There was no one in attendance on Dinmore Manor, excepting the last of the photographers on the platform, who stood, crouched, scrambled on a few paces then crouched again in their pursuit of the perfect picture. Abby walked on, careful to move behind the photographer, and came to a bench of the type long associated with railway platforms. The weather was so good that she sat, just to enjoy the ambience. Gulls cried overhead, wheeling in the bright blue sky, the sun was warm, in fact could have been too warm, but for the temperature being held in check by the constant light breeze. From the engine shed came the hum of some machinery, Dinmore Manor sizzled quietly, Abby felt really content. She had been sitting there for perhaps fifteen minutes or so, when an older man came down the platform. He was wearing blue overalls and jacket, with an engineman's cap upon his head. Without wishing to stare, Abby could not help but notice that the trouser legs of his overalls were held with bicycle clips.

He walked slowly along and approaching the bench, asked quietly if she would mind his sitting down. Abby smiled and replied. "No, of course not." He thanked her and sat at the other end of the bench. For a while nothing was said, until Abby's thirst for knowledge got the better of her. "Are you connected with the railway?"

He nodded slowly, and indicated Dinmore Manor. "I shall be taking her out with the next train."

She then asked him. "Have you been driving for long?"

He smiled, "Forty years or so."

Abby's next question surprised him, not the usual what is it like to drive, or what is your favourite engine, but, "Is this what it was really like, or is this just make believe for the tourists?" He looked at her, deciding that she wasn't a critic, sneering at them for playing trains, but earnest in her question.

"No, this isn't what it was really like; it can't be, can it? The true picture was not just the railway, but the times as well. Look around; all we have here is a small part, based mainly on the engines that have been saved. The coaches we use are from the sixties, not at all representative of the way people travelled even as late as the forties and the fifties, when the stock used on a local train down here was probably built in the twenties, or even earlier. That building being used as an engine shed, the old part, was the goods shed, and those tracks over there would have been full of trucks, waiting to be unloaded, or ready to go with the next goods. The real engine shed was behind us, where the car park is now, small shed it was, with a turntable and a couple of short roads. If we were to be really accurate, then there would be as many goods trains trundling down this line as passenger. Almost every station had a goods shed, and the pickup goods stopped at every one and shunted trucks in, and out until it had the train made up. A pick up goods train leaving Taunton with thirty trucks could arrive here with thirty trucks, but only about six of them would be part of the original train. There would be what was called express goods, which would come straight through, but express wasn't really the word to describe an unfitted freight that rarely exceeded twenty miles an hour. No, Miss, we can only re-create part of the scene, but even so it is important. We keep alive skills and knowledge, and as well as entertaining people we give them an insight into how the railway operated. It's funny in a way, but there are young people now, whose only experience of travelling by train is on a preserved line like this, behind a steam loco. The car serves them for every other purpose." The man lapsed into silence.

Abby didn't want the opportunity to pass, as here was someone who had worked the railway at the time of her grandfather. "My grandfather worked on the railway, he was a stationmaster, not far from here. I didn't know him, but from what I've gathered he was a difficult person. He spent all his life on the railway, but had nothing at the end."

The man looked at her closely; he could see the sadness in her face. "I know quite a few men who finished like that. When I joined in nineteen fifty-four, I was twenty. I'd done my National Service, and already tried one or two other jobs. I started as a cleaner at Bletchley on the old L.M.S."

Abby interrupted. "I thought that the nationalisation happened in nineteen forty-eight."

He laughed. "It did, but the men still thought of themselves as L.M.S. men, like G.W.R. men, old habits die-hard. I suppose the L.N.E.R. men thought the same. I don't know about the Southern though. The Southern was always different." Abby was inclined to ask why, but instead filed that away as a question to ask Mr. Brasher at some time. The man continued. "It was at a time when lots of men were leaving, retirement for the older ones, and well the younger ones didn't like the hours and dirty conditions, so I progressed through to firing and driving quite quickly. It was strange though, I was working alongside men who had spent forty years getting to the top link, and suddenly I was there in next to no time. I don't suppose they liked it too much. The older men had worked for all that time, and were now coming up to retirement on a pension that would hardly keep body and soul together. They had gone through the war, experienced all the problems after, cheered when the railways were nationalised, expecting that it would all change. It didn't though, the owners might be different, but it was still the same bosses, and the conditions didn't change either."

Abby didn't quite know if he was trying to show his sympathy for her grandfather, but his words did help a little, knowing that many other men were in the same boat. "So you come down here to drive steam locomotives in your spare time?"

He shook his head. "No, Miss, I took early retirement, same as lots of other men, my wife originally came from this area, so we moved down here. I drive because I always enjoyed driving steam, and as I'm local, it's easy for them to call me in when the volunteers can't make it." He stood, collected his bag, and told her he would have to take over Dinmore Manor now, "but if you're here again, say hello, it's been nice talking to you." He gave her a cheery wave and moved to the edge of the platform. After looking carefully in both directions he dropped down to the track and crossed the lines to the engine. Abby pondered his comments, yet again she was aware of the separateness, she could think of no other word that seemed to be part and parcel of railwaymen. There were other things to puzzle, like "unfitted freight," and "top link." She had felt too daunted to ask. Perhaps Mr. Brasher would have an explanation for her.

Abby's logic told her she should leave now, but the emotions stirred by these sights wanted to stay, and stay she did, wondering what would happen next. Whatever was to happen next migrated to the back of her mind, as the calm of the place permeated her thoughts. She sat back and just enjoyed the quiet that had descended over the station with the departure of the train. That was odd she thought, all that activity and suddenly it all stopped, only the seagulls wheeling overhead brought movement and sound, the harsh cries 'aark, aark' assaulting the ear. After a while even that grating sound was lost as her consciousness no longer heard it. "Dinmore Manor" sat quietly a curl of steam coming from the top of the boiler, and occasional spurts of hot water from a pipe under the cab. She imagined she could actually hear it simmering, a gently comforting sound. Sitting there, warmed by the sun and soothed by the gently voice of the engine, she closed her eyes. She awoke with a start, wondering for how long she had dozed off, and also what had awakened her.

That question was answered fairly swiftly; as it was the whistle of an engine that had startled her awake. The beep, beep of the warning at the level crossing as the barriers came down was a response to the whistle, and with the gates safely in place the engine opened up to draw the train over the level crossing and into the station. The signalman came out of his box to receive the token, and the train gently coasted along the platform. The locomotive was the twin of "Dinmore Manor," but named "Odney Manor." The train halted, and crowds of travellers alighted from the coaches. Mums, dads, kids, grandmas, grandpas, and dogs, milled about, and sorted themselves before making their way back down the platform to the exit. A scene not too far removed from that which must have existed years before, when the railway was the prime mover, and Summer Saturdays meant family holidays. The children would be excited, wanting to get their first glimpse of the sea. Dad would be harassed, ensuring that all their luggage, (except that which was sent in advance), was gathered together. Mum was trying to cope with the children, possibly wiping their faces with a damp flannel, to remove the dirt and grit collected by the journey, a consequence of heads which would insist that the only way to travel was at an open window, despite dire warnings of retribution from their parents. Grandmas eased aching limbs, and tried to straighten flowery, Polyester dresses creased from the extended journey, as ever, the train was much delayed. Grandpas would show much technical interest in the locomotive, seemingly apart from the turmoil on the platform behind them. All these things were so similar to the scene today, with the exception of the luggage, as now the travellers were simply on a joy ride, and the train wasn't late, well not too late.

Whilst all this was happening, "Dinmore Manor" had moved, up and was in the process of backing down to attach itself to the set of coaches, which were now refilling themselves with new passengers. The guard strolled up towards Dinmore, resplendent in peaked cap, and uniform, the cap and uniform liberally trimmed with gold braid in every possible location, the ensemble completed with a Rose for a buttonhole. He spoke briefly to the driver, before retracing his steps back down the platform. Abby would learn that it was incumbent upon the guard to inform the driver of the number of coaches, and also if any request stops had to be made. Doors were now slamming, as porters patrolled ensuring that all those who wished to travel were safely in their seats. The guard now stood by his compartment, awaiting the all clear from the porter at the back of the train, who was busy ushering the final passengers into the last coach, advising them to walk through the train to find seats. The ceremony moved towards its close, with the guard's whistle and green flag, the response from the driver with a short whistle, and the great clouds of steam boiling from the locomotive, creating a mist through which it pulled the train to start its journey. Abby was moved by this spectacle, a timeless event that drew her inevitably back, and closer, to her grandfather, whom she could see in her mind's eye as part of this, not just a figure from the past, who happened to be related to her, had granddad seen this scene, and been part of it? Yes, of course, many times, and had his senses been moved by the ritual, the sounds, and the smells? She felt somehow that that was so; his allegiance to his job, and the company that employed him could only have been part of the tie that bound him to the railway. He would have been active in all this, a figure of authority to whom all other railway employees would defer, imperiously directing passengers into compartments, porters to carrying suitcases and parcels, and with frequent and obvious references to his watch would remind everyone that there was a timetable to be kept here. Abby smiled to herself as she pictured the scene.

With the departure of the train, the station lapsed into that torpor again. The platform deserted apart from her and a couple of photographers who were packing their equipment. Odney Manor had come to a stand by the water tower, although there seemed to be no moves to fill its tank. Of the crew no signs were to be seen. Abby sat for a while longer, telling herself that she should move on. She looked at her watch, and was horrified to see that it was quarter past three, what had happened to the time? As if the realisation of the time had reminded her stomach, it suddenly groaned and announced its empty condition. This was silly, she had rarely eaten at lunchtime, and never before had hunger pangs disturbed her, so why now? Ignoring her stomach's immediate demands she determined to wait and do justice to the meal that Mary would certainly place in front of her later this evening.

Back in her car, Abby consulted the map. As she had overstayed at the West Somerset Railway, it would now be difficult to spend any reasonable time at Porlock. She decided that she would make her way back to Combe Lyney, but taking a more leisurely route. The map indicated that the A39 and then the A396 would take her towards Taunton, but she could turn off either between Washford and Williton, or later before Bishops Lydeard and cross the Brendon Hills and find her way towards Wheddon Cross. In the event she followed the A396 up the valley towards Bishops Lydeard, delighting in the names of the villages signposted off the road, Bicknoller, Stogumber, and Crowcombe, which she discovered was separated from its railway station by at the least two and a half miles. She recalled something that Mr. Brasher had said, that the G.W.R. was not too concerned that its stations should actually be in the town or village it purported to serve, it was uneconomic to divert the railway from its best line. Besides the best customers to use the railway would be the gentry, who would have horse and carriage to bring them to the station. The lower classes could walk. The journey was pleasant relaxed motoring, the roads not at all suitable for fast driving which suited Abby, the tailback caused by a tractor not causing her any inconvenience, unlike the driver of a Blue Saloon, who demonstrated his impatience with constant lunges to the off-side, not achieving anything as oncoming traffic continually frustrated any passing manoeuvre. Abby was pleased to see the signpost for the B3224, which was where she intended to turn, convinced that the saloon driver would shortly make an impossible overtaking move with possible disastrous consequences.

The B3224 took her towards Wheddon Cross, and judging from the road signs for Crowcombe, and then Stogumber, on an almost parallel course to the road she had just used. She smiled wryly to herself, so much for her map reading! This road climbed steadily into the Brendon Hills, passing cottages that were now far removed from the prosaic and utility purposes for which they were built. Never had Thatch looked so pristine, nor did Cob walls gleam so bright, indications that the current owners had cash to invest in their upkeep, capital gained from commerce that was unlikely to be agricultural. Beyond Elworthy the road gained the crest of the hills, and ran relatively straight and level for some miles, she was tempted often by signs indicating roads to Bampton and Dulverton, and the curiously named Wimbleball Lake but ignored them, reasoning that there was plenty of time to explore in the weeks to come. It was therefore with some surprise that Abby arrived back in Combe Lyney earlier than she would have thought. Therefore instead of going to the inn, drove instead to the old station. It wasn't strange that this place attracted her so much. She felt a warmth and comfort here, where her family had lived and worked. Wandering along the platform, she tried to marry the images she had seen at Minehead, with the scene of desolation evinced here. Try as she might, she could not conjure up the rails of shining steel, the trucks standing motionless awaiting their next load, or the picture of the platform itself, never crowded as Minehead was, but with at least a few intending passengers. She sighed with the frustration. This jigsaw had all the pieces except the most important, and it would be with a good imagination alone that she would see it complete. It was with a slight despondency that she returned to her car and drove the mile and a half to the inn.

Abby was astounded with the activity that surrounded the inn. Cars were parked; filling the meagre parking places at the front, and the road either side was similarly filled. She turned into the drive leading to the back of the inn, but was unable to follow it all the way, as the gate was closed. Leaving her car nosed to the gate she went around the back to find a flustered and slightly perspiring Mary, laden with a tray full of cups, saucers, tea-pot, milk, scones, a pot of thick clotted cream, and another of strawberry jam. The yard was dotted with trestle tables, each under a sun umbrella with lounging customers chatting or attending seriously to the cream tea placed before them.

Mary smiled grimly at Abby, and whispered. "Cream Teas for Grockles."

Abby almost laughed, but restrained herself sufficiently to ask, for Mary was obviously under pressure. "Can I help?"

Mary shook her head. "Almost all done now, but it's been pandemonium all afternoon. Go sit yourself down and I'll get you some tea shortly." Abby did as Mary bid, but feeling a little guilty, until she saw Jack emerge from the back of the pub, followed by a young girl in her teens, both similarly laden with trays as Mary had been. Seeing that Mary had help made her feel a little better. The young girl was faster than Jack at unloading the trays, and came straight over to Abby.

She smiled. "Hello, can I get you anything?"

Abby shook her head. "No thanks, Mary is going to get me some tea."

The girl regarded Abby, and suddenly said. "You're Miss Tregonney, aren't you? I'm Liz."

Abby was caught for a while trying to remember if she should know whom Liz was. Suddenly she remembered. "Oh yes, you help out in the stables for James Comberford. How are you?" She offered her hand and Liz shook it.

Then in that easy manner which most of the people in the valley seemed to have she sat down, and asked. "Are you going to come here to live?"

The question caught Abby unawares, not because she hadn't thought about it, as this was something that had floated around her mind, but because of the directness of the approach. "I haven't really thought about it that much, it's a lovely place, and somehow I feel that I'm at home here. Having said that I have still got to earn a living, and I don't know if there's much I can do around here."

Liz looked at her with astonishment. "Oh! I thought you were quite well off." The girl's simple honesty caught Abby for a second time, and the thought of the gossip that must have been bruited about, tickled her.

She broke out laughing. Liz sat there wondering what she had said that was funny, until Abby explained. "I'm not laughing at you; it tickled me to think what the gossip must have been."

Liz's face cleared. "It would be nice if you came to live here, there's not many young people like us around. Mr. James would be happy; I think he quite likes you."

Liz was going to go on, but an interruption came from Jack, who leaned over Liz's shoulder and said. "Lizzy, it would be a great help if you served customers, instead of sitting down gossiping with them."

Unabashed, Liz got to her feet. "O.K., Uncle Jack, just going." As she walked away she turned back to Abby. "I'll get you your tea." Putting the emphasis on the 'I'll' as if to make the point, that others who had promised had failed to deliver.

Abby smiled up at Jack. "I'm sorry, it was my fault, and I shouldn't have kept her."

He grinned. "No, it wasn't your fault. Lizzy will take any opportunity to stop work and chat. She just can't help herself. If you want to publicize anything, tell Lizzy, you can be sure that within twenty-four hours, half the county will know."

CHAPTER NINE

Abby spent the next few days exploring the surrounding country. She found Porlock, Lynmouth and Lynton taking the cliff railway from the one to the other. Another day and Barnstaple, Torrington and South Molton were on her visiting list.

She parked her car, and on foot explored all these places, thus discovering a most delicious cream tea in Dulverton, which she enjoyed guiltily, first because it was a temptation she couldn't resist, and second because she knew that Mary would be hurt to think that she could eat a cream tea anywhere else but at the Combe Inn. The contrast in the landscape was remarkable.

In the north in the hinterland of Lynton and Porlock, the moor met the sea with tall cliffs, broken only by the river valleys at places like Lynmouth and Porlock.

Away from the coast the moor folded itself, with a succession of interleaved, steep sided valleys. To the south of the moor, the hills became softer and rolled away gently towards the Exe valley, Cullompton and Exeter.

The weather stayed fine for her, and she adapted by wearing her shorts and just a T-shirt. Mary's advice about the sun was sensible, and Abby had dug out an old brimmed hat, which shaded her face, something for which she was grateful, when she realised, standing in the shower, how her arms and legs had tanned, the contrast to the white of her body being quite startling.

Every day was a voyage of discovery, as the area revealed its secrets to her, and as a consequence of the day, every night was spent in deep sleep, awakening early refreshed and in eager anticipation of the new day ahead.

It was a surprise therefore on the morning she came down to breakfast, and saw the thick, brown envelope on the table addressed to her. Opening the package, she found her grandfather's journal, a thick sheaf of papers, and a covering letter from Mr. Brasher.

Dear Miss Tregonney,

First, I must thank you for allowing me to read your grandfather's journal. The G.W.R. encouraged its servants to keep this kind of personal record but unfortunately few were so meticulous, as to actually write it up every day.

This record has really been most enlightening for me, and I have taken the liberty of photocopying the whole. I hope that you will not mind. Of course it goes without saying that when my book is published, a credit will be made for the invaluable information obtained from this record.

The accompanying notes I have made to give you some idea of the life and working arrangements of a stationmaster, such as your grandfather; under the auspices of the G.W.R. and later, B.R., although there was very little change at first. Much of the information was already to hand, but I have been able to update my knowledge with the benefit of the journal. I hope that this will give you some insight into the circumstances of your grandfather's working life.

In addition I have reviewed my own notes of the history of the line, with the benefit of the Journal, and enclose an up-dated copy of the same.

Please do not hesitate to get in touch, at any time, should you have any queries, or seek further information.

The letter was signed simply 'Brasher' The letter and the manner in which it was signed was so typical of him, Abby thought, a somewhat unworldly, English gentleman, who would treat anyone with courtesy and kindness, regardless of their station in life, who no doubt would be Church of England, even though his appearances there would be limited to those few important occasions of life, and whose love and zeal for the past greatness of one particular aspect of his country, marked him as an eccentric.

Abby was now in a quandary. She dearly wished to read this treatise, yet the day had already been earmarked for a trip on the preserved railway. In the end the decision was made by the climate. The fine weather continued and it would be a good day to be out and about, whereas reading the notes could wait for an evening or the time when the weather broke, as it most certainly would. She consulted Mary on this, who agreed that this fine spell would come to an end shortly.

"We'll have some rain soon, that's certain, but only a couple of days, then it'll start getting warm again." Her mind also came up with another reason, it would probably be better to read Mr. Brasher's words after she had investigated the preserved railway in greater depth, as she would then be able to visualise more clearly those aspects to which he was referring. It is amazing how the mind can find logical reasons for one's preferred action. Abby finished her breakfast, surprised that she actually cleared the plate, 'my appetite is improving,' she thought, and then examined the waist of her slacks, no; they didn't appear to be tighter, so she could not be putting on any weight. She had told Mary where she was going, something that Mary somehow had insisted upon, 'you never know,' had been Mary's reason, and made her way around to where her car was parked.

As she drove out, she noticed James's Land Rover, pulling in to the front of the inn. She stopped. James waved and jumped out quickly to come over to her. "Good Morning, Abby, are you off somewhere interesting for the day?"

She squinted up at him, through the strong morning sun. "Hello, James, yes, I am going off to play with some trains."

The well remembered grin came to his face. "You're not going to drive one I imagine."

Abby laughed. "Hardly, just spending a lazy day riding and getting atmosphere." She paused, "Was there something in particular you wanted?"

He hesitated and then said. "Well I was going to ask if you would like to come up to the house sometime, and meet Jason."

Abby was nonplussed. "Meet Jason, who is he?"

The grin on James' face got wider. "He's not quite a 'He' nor a 'She'," James was enigmatic, "Jason is the horse you are going to ride."

Abby was immediately on her guard. "Me, ride? Oh no, whatever gave you the idea that I would be riding a horse. I may have ridden on a few occasions, but that was on very docile creatures, in the park, no obstacles, and no galloping. I am certainly not going to ride a horse around here."

James then played a dirty trick. "Oh that's a shame. I thought we might follow your grandfather's railway up and down the valley, and it's really the only way that you could see it properly."

Abby was hooked. "You swine," this was said with a smile. "Well I don't know, it sounds like a good idea, but how big is Jason?"

"Not too big, only about sixteen hands and I know he would behave himself with you."

Abby picked up on the words behave himself with you. "What do you mean? Behave himself with me; doesn't he behave himself with others?"

James hummed and aahed. "Well you see he's a Gelding, but he doesn't seem to realise that he's got bits missing. He sees men as a threat to his territory, but he's fine with ladies. Just come up and meet him, you'll see." Abby thought about it.

"Alright, but if he's not very controllable, then forget it."

James brightened. "How about this evening, I'll come down and pick you up, say about seven thirty, is that O.K.?"

Abby nodded. "Yes, that will be fine, now can I go and play with the trains?" Those words were said with a smile on her face, so James would not be upset, his grin returned.

"Yeah, go on, Casey Jones."

Abby filled up with unleaded petrol in Paverton; at the garage she had cause to visit a number of times in the last few days. Her BMW was perhaps her only real unnecessary luxury. In London it was used little if at all, here she had enjoyed driving roads that were not clogged with traffic, the car showing her much of its potential for easy, comfortable motoring. The downside was the amounts of fuel that she had used; it was not exactly frugal with petrol. The pump attendant, a functionary rarely seen in London, had been slow to react to her presence when she had first visited, now came quickly to fill her car, allowing her the service that went with being a good customer.

"Good morning, Miss Tregonney; shall I fill it up?" He had, she thought, obviously remembered her name from the credit card vouchers, she was unaware that Jack Elvesly had mentioned to him that Abby's family was local; it put her into a different category of customer, although it made no difference to the price per litre.

The Moor had put on a different coat after the last few days of warm, dry weather. The longer grasses had become a silvery brown that shimmered like water as they bent and swayed with the wind, which the sheep nosed aside as they searched for the new short tender blades underneath. The gorse and heather had become a uniform dull lifeless green, giving the Moor a mottled look like army camouflage. The road was now well known to Abby, and she drove confidently, but not quickly, enjoying the bright sunlight from the comfort of her air-conditioned car. It seemed to her that now that her journeys took less time, maybe the famous West Country miles were not so long as rumour would have it. It was therefore with surprise that she came to Minehead a good fifteen minutes before her estimate, leaving her with time to wander as she waited for the first departure at ten fifteen. It was a little unreal. Rarely had she travelled by train, she did not count the tube as a train, and this trip would be a significant experience. The experience would be more intriguing as the method of operating was one, which had been abandoned more than forty years ago.

She walked to the head of the waiting train. "Dinmore Manor" was the locomotive, but she was a little disappointed that her friend of the other day was not on the footplate. Finding a seat was no problem, as there was little custom for this service.   It was not surprising therefore that promptly at ten-fifteen the train pulled out.

Later, she would review this day with mixed emotions. Abby had somehow been expecting her grandfather's world to come alive, to see a steam railway run as it had been in his time. But as her friend of the other day had pointed out, it wasn't, nor could it be. Setting her disappointment aside for the moment, Abby had enjoyed her day. The admittedly slow but comfortable journey had lulled her, and beguiled. There was a quality of theatre about the line. The rhythmic clatter of wheels over rail-joints, something that seemed not to exist with modern railways, was an overriding theme, interrupted by the differing acts which were the various stations along the way, each with a character of its own, the slumbering of Dunster and Washford, the quaint charm of Stogumber, surely a name that could only originate in the West Country, to the bustle of Williton, where trains crossed, and

Bishops Lydeard where the engine was uncoupled to run around before making the return journey. Looking back, Abby would realise that whilst none of them could substitute for Combe Lyney, yet each had some aspect that could be Combe Lyney. It had been a long day as Abby had not simply come back on the first train, but had taken time to explore, mainly at Bishops Lydeard, and at Williton. She had heard that a restoration of a large engine was in progress at Williton, and had hoped to be able to see this. Unfortunately, visitors were not allowed in the shed. All was not lost, however, as one of the porters, (could she really call these volunteers, porters?) had told her to come in September, at the gala weekend. "Shed will be open then, Miss." She would be back in September. One thing that she did see, and which gave her quite a shock, was the museum at Bishops Lydeard. Without being told, she knew that it had once been a goods shed, as it closely resembled that which still stood at Combe Lyney. Confirmation came from a book she discovered in the shop at Bishops Lydeard, which concerned the stations and buildings on the railway. The Bristol and Exeter Railway had built the goods shed! Once more that name appeared, a ghost from the past. Now she thought, I can read Mr. Brasher's story, hoping that he will explain this complicated relationship between the Devon and Somerset Railway, the Bristol and Exeter Railway, and the Great Western Railway.

Abby upset Mary, by declaring that she was not very hungry, and would like a light meal that evening. To assuage Mary's dismay, Abby explained that the day had been very hot, and that had affected her appetite. Mary's idea of something light was two grilled trout, together with a salad, which would have kept a whole warren of rabbits busy. Abby knew better than to complain, and daunting though the plate was, made the best of the meal she could. Mary returned at regular intervals to spur Abby on to greater effort, at the same time making small talk about the day, and how had Abby enjoyed herself. At last Abby put down her knife and fork, and admitted that she could not eat any more. The look of disappointment on Mary's face was only removed when Abby innocently remarked that James was calling for her at about seven-thirty. "He is going to introduce me to this horse of his, Jason, which somehow or other he thinks I am going to ride."

Mary's face assumed a bland look of disinterest. "Oh, you're going riding are you, that'll be nice."

Abby hastened to squash that idea. "No, I am not going to ride, James seems to think that it is the best way to see the valley, but I have serious doubts." Mary was busy tucking away this nugget; there would be lots to discuss with Mavis tonight.

"Well actually, I think he's right, you can't see much of the valley from the road, and you couldn't get into too much trouble if James was with you. Anyway, if Lizzy can ride that Jason, I am sure that you will be able to."

James was late, arriving at ten to eight, apologising profusely. It didn't worry Abby as she was starting to adopt the country habit of loose time. An appointment at seven thirty actually meant any time between seven fifteen and seven forty five, so ten to eight was only five minutes late, which really was of little consequence. She was also quite amused at James' embarrassment, she had considered, or rather he had given the impression, that he was one of those men who was always in command of a situation. To see him now so flustered was an eye-opener. Abby found this quite endearing. The lapse did not last long, as he eyed her dress. "How do you suppose you are going to get up onto a horse wearing that?" he asked.

Abby bridled, and replied a little icily. "I thought I was just going to meet the horse, I had no intention of riding it." James caught the tone in her voice and easily soothed the exchange.

"Well you would certainly do a good job of charming Jason, as you would charm anyone, dressed like that. But just in case we can persuade you to mount, would you mind putting on something a little more suitable?"

Abby relented. "As you ask so nicely, I will, but I am giving no guarantees about anything else. Give me five minutes." She raced up to her room, to re-appear in a little more than the five minutes dressed in a sweat-shirt, chinos and boots. "Will this do, sir." Her tone sounded submissive, but her stance belied the tone in her voice.

James grinned. "That is better, if I had to give you a boost into the saddle, I wouldn't have known exactly where I would have been able to put my hand before." The grin did it again and Abby couldn't keep up her disgruntled attitude.

The smile came to her face, as she appreciated the somewhat ludicrous situation. "Come on then, let's go and meet this horse."

They climbed in to James' old Land Rover, which coughed and spluttered before catching and running relatively smoothly. James backed and filled and turned on the road, before accelerating away past the Church. He turned up the lane, which climbed in a series of gentle bends, and then sharp left into a gravelled drive. A forlorn name board hung at an angle beside the drive, "Lyney House," no grand name to celebrate the Comberfords, she thought. Rhododendrons, hawthorn, laurel and beech hung heavily either side of the drive, battling for light and space within which to grow. James did not slow down and the Land Rover bounced from pothole to pothole, lurching sideways into the bends with the shrubs scraping along the sides, as it passed. The drive turned left quite abruptly, and the house came into view. The twists and turns of the drive had disorientated her but soon she understood that they had circumnavigated the churchyard, and were now at the back of the Church. As she had expected this was the house she had seen from the road, that morning after her return to Combe Lyney. It did not add up to the sort of place that romantic novelists might have described. In essence it was an Edwardian country house, built in the grey, rustic dressed, granite of the area with cornice stones of a slightly lighter colour. There were two frontages in effect, one set slightly further forward that the other. Large sash windows to ground floor and first floor rooms alleviated the dull grey stone. One of the downstairs windows was a shallow angled bay. The roof was slate, with gables breaking up the outline. The gables did not reach to the full height of the main roof. The main door was approached by way of a simple glass porch in a corner formed where the one frontage extended forward. To the right clustered various outbuildings, which Abby presumed would be the stables, and garages. A full-grown beech shaded the left of the house, with one branch growing perilously close to the slate roof. From a distance the look was very Horse and Hound magazine, closer inspection revealed pointing that had fallen away, peeling paint, and a sash window slightly crooked in its frame, which Abby doubted would ever be opened for fear of it falling apart.

James swung the Land Rover around in a great circle, thumping over the ever-present potholes.

"Do you always greet your guests with this obstacle course?" she shouted to James over the roaring of the engine.

He glanced over at her whilst steering with one hand, the other waved expansively at the surroundings. "This is smooth compared to some of the roads round here." He was forced to grab the steering wheel with both hands as a particularly deep pothole whipped the front wheels in a novel direction, straight at a hawthorn. Persuading the vehicle to resume its intended direction, he pulled up with gravel spraying at the front porch. Turning off the engine he looked at her. "Welcome to Looney House.

Abby wondered if she had misheard him. "Don't you mean Lyney House?"

He grinned mischievously. "I know what I mean." He jumped out leaving the door open, and strode round to her side. Abby had started to open the door, but realising his motives, allowed him to extend the courtesy. As she got out he murmured. "Mother will be watching and she is very hot on manners." Abby was taken aback, at no time had he mentioned a mother, nor had anyone else. It was stupid of course; to take for granted that his mother would not be around, and why was she worrying about a mother, anyway. She had no designs on him did she?

James was obviously not intending to introduce her, as he led the way to the right, and the stables, where awaited this horse she was supposed to ride. They walked into the cobbled yard and Abby was happy to see Lizzy, who was sweeping up muck with a huge broom, and then shovelling the pile she created into a bucket.

She straightened up and greeted Abby with a smile. "Hi, Abby, I'll go and get Jason out." She then disappeared into a box, re-appearing in no time leading the horse. Jason seemed to be a little reluctant, and Lizzy explained. "I've given him an hour or so of schooling, but it would probably be a good idea to give him some more. Here, hold his head, and I'll get the saddle and tack." With that the halter rope was in Abby's hand, and Lizzy had gone. Jason stood quietly for a while examining Abby, and then decided that as she was new, he could throw his weight around a little. He began to pull away, and toss his head.

At that moment James behind her said quietly. "Hold the halter firmly, and talk to him."

Abby thought great, what do you say to a horse, but nonetheless she pulled the halter firmly down, and said calmly. "Just because you're big, does not mean you can boss me around, now stop clowning and stand still." She went on in the same tone, meaningless words, and Jason quieted. His big brown eyes still watched her warily, and his great nostrils opened wide to take in her scent. Maybe the signals he was getting did the trick, but more likely it was the return of Lizzy with his saddle and tack. With the skill developed through long experience she had Jason in his bridle, and the saddle on his back in next to no time, moving under the horse with little fear to tighten the girth. James had vanished but returned shortly leading Cassie, the mare. Now that Jason was saddled up, James and Lizzy looked expectantly at Abby, who looked at Jason, who turned his head to look back at her. She didn't know how she would get on to this huge beast, on the few occasions she had ridden before, there had always been a mounting block.

Lizzy seemed to realise the problem and came round beside her. "Bend your left leg and I'll give you a boost into the saddle." Abby did as she was instructed and was amazed as Lizzy literally propelled her off the ground, it was more by luck than judgement that her right leg went over the saddle and she found herself sitting like a sack of potatoes in the saddle. Lizzy adjusted the stirrups and fitted Abby's boots into them, at the same time whispering to her. "Keep your heels down." The reins lay slack on Jason's neck in front of her and she picked them up. The horse started forward immediately as if she had given him the signal to walk on.

James had mounted Cass and riding alongside, leant over and pulled Jason up from the bridle. "I thought you said you had ridden before?" he accused her.

"I have, but only a few times, and on horses that were very gentle, well behaved, and knew exactly what to do even when the riders didn't."

James gave that grin. "Oh well, you just sit on top of Jason, and we'll walk around a bit until you get the hang of it." Without waiting for a reply he urged Cass on and Jason walked on too.

Abby did not find the walk too difficult, as they followed James out of the yard and onto the gravel in front of the house, the horses hooves made a shushing sound as they walked around in a large circle. This allowed James time to see how Abby coped. Lizzy had come out as well, and walked close by Jason, giving Abby instructions, getting her used to bringing Jason to a halt, making him move on again, and turning him left and right. James watched closely, and satisfied that she knew enough not to fall off, he suggested that they move on and up the hill behind the house.

Abby agreed. "But only as long as this horse doesn't have to go any faster than this."

James smiled and replied. "No, not really, but perhaps we might get into a canter." The grin erupted on his face again.

Before Abby could reply, Lizzy came running out and alongside Jason proffering a riding hat to Abby. "Put this on," she called. Abby accepted the hat leaning precariously down to grab it, and put it on with one hand. Jason had ignored the commotion and walked placidly on, following Cass who was now walking down the drive towards the gate.

They turned left at the gate and followed the lane upwards. It was another of those lanes that obviously did not carry a tremendous amount of traffic. The surface was rough and pitted, with a central core of muck supporting a healthy growth of grasses. The unkempt hedgerows crowded in leaving just enough room for the two horses and riders to pass between them. Abby had somehow coaxed Jason alongside of James, although she was not too sure that she was in control, it may have been Jason's instinctive need to lead, and not follow. The horse seemed determined to walk under branches, which would have brushed Abby from his back, if she had not ducked, and no amount of pulling on the reins would make him alter his course. James watched this unequal struggle for a while, all the time the irrepressible grin hovering close to his mouth.

Eventually he leaned towards Abby and told her. "Jason is a bit thick, give him a nudge with your left boot to turn him right and vice versa and pull the reins over sharply. He's cross-trained." Abby was grateful for the information, but her efforts remained ineffectual. James again leaned across.

"Give him a good boot next time, don't just tickle him, make him know that you're the boss." The advice seemed to work, with the next branch looming closer, Abby gave Jason a hefty kick with her left heel, and the horse obediently moved over.

They climbed for some time and Abby was surprised when James told her it was nearly a mile and a half. The height of the hedges diminished, and eventually Abby was able to see more of the country. She had to admit that you certainly could see more from the back of a horse; but she wasn't going to let on to James, just yet. They approached a gate, and she decided to exert her authority over Jason a little more, guiding him towards the gate, and gently but firmly pulling the reins to bring him to a stop. Here was a vantage point that allowed her to see far more of the valley. To her left through trees she could see the roof of Lyney House, beyond those the Church steeple, and to the right of that the village, the thatch and slate roofs, showing as glimpses between the trees, which seemed to predominate from this angle. They were high enough here for her to make out clearly the line of the railway, and she could follow it easily as it curved sinuously through the valley, crossing the river, towards the old station. From there on it could be traced by the cuttings and embankments, still clearly evident after all these years, yet not intruding on the hillocks and woodland that marked the lower valley. James had turned Cassie round and rode back down to stand alongside her.

Abby continued her observation for a while, and then without turning to James said, "It's rather pretty, isn't it?"

He didn't say anything for a while. Then clarifying his thoughts, "When you see something every day, you can sometimes lose sight of its value. Then it takes someone else to point out the obvious. Yes it is pretty. It's taken a few hundred years to make it that way, and it wasn't really planned, but that's how it ended up."

Abby turned in the saddle. "You know you are a little bit of a philosopher in a way."

He looked startled. "What makes you say that?"

"Well, what you said just now, and before when I was down the first time, we were at the old station when you said something about the railway changing all your lives."

James looked perplexed. "I can't really remember, was I maudlin at the time?"

Abby laughed. "No you weren't, but you had dropped the superficial flippancy you practise." She could feel James getting uncomfortable, so changed topic slightly. "It must be wonderful to own all of this."

The horses, sensing that they might stand here for a while had now stretched their necks down and cropped the lush green grass that grew at the side of the gate. James looked at her. "Own!" He queried "I own it in the pattern of inheritance, as my father did, and grandfather. But it's not mine to sell, it has to be passed on to the next generation. And if that wasn't enough reason, how could I sell the lives of all these people, who have worked their land for years, good times and bad, now mostly bad. They own the land more than I do, as it is their sweat that has made it productive. No, if I cannot sell this land then I don't really own it, I'm just borrowing it for a while." He stopped, seemingly embarrassed at this rather long speech. Abby regarded him thoughtfully. She had made the mistake before of presuming to understand him, and as before he had brought her up short, having to rethink her opinion of him.

James pulled Cassie up, and Jason assuming that something was about to happen raised his head also. "I think we should head back now, Lizzy will be waiting to settle these two in their stalls, and if we are late, she won't have much drinking time left." He pulled on Cassie's bit, and turned her head. Abby did likewise, but felt that Jason obliged her, rather than actually following her command of the reins. They made their way slowly down the lane. "How do you feel on Jason?" he asked.

"I shall probably be very sore in the morning, but he is as you said, accommodating to my inexperience."

James laughed. "If you speak to Lizzy she will let you have some ointment to relieve the soreness. Now I should tell you everyone will know you have used it as it smells to high heaven, but it is effective."

Abby smiled ruefully. "I think I should rather take the hot bath routine in that case, people here seem interested enough in my movements, without my broadcasting the situation."

He looked across at her with that grin again. "You don't need to worry about that, Lizzy knows, and she is the local propaganda service. Tomorrow everybody will know."

Lizzy was polishing tack when they rode into the yard, and promptly took charge of the horses, looping Cassie's reins through a bracket while she unsaddled Jason, and led him off to his stall.

As she passed Abby she whispered. "If you are sore at all, I have a good liniment." Abby declined politely, smiling to herself as she took note of James's warning. He had disappeared, but returned as Abby left the yard.

"It would be polite of me to introduce you to my mother. But she has a bit of a headache and has gone to her room. She sends her apologies, and would you like to come up one afternoon and take tea?"

Abby was grateful for the headache, she didn't feel like being introduced to the Comberford matriarch, wearing Chinos and a sweatshirt. "I quite understand, tell her I would love to come to tea one afternoon." Abby felt a little unreal. She had known that James' mother was alive, but somehow in her conversations with him felt that she didn't affect his life at all, her intuition told her that the headache was merely an excuse, in order that their meeting should be more formal. The other thing that disturbed her was the assumption that this meeting was quite important.

They hopped into the Land Rover and James drove them back to the Combe Inn, exhibiting his usual lively style of driving. As he hadn't asked Abby if she would like to freshen up before leaving the house, Abby excused herself immediately to go to her room. She had though asked him if he would like a drink, and James went to the bar to wait for her. Abby decided to change out of her chinos into something a little more suitable for a drink, at the same time wondering, if this could be construed as a "date," she hadn't had one of those in a long time. She had now become used to using the door to the bar, rather than the door to the lounge. Any feelings of discomfort by being in the bar had long vanished. By the time she came down,

James was involved in a lively conversation with the other customers, including Sam. She assumed it was something to do with farming judging by the odd terms that flew out of the group, and decided that no, this was not a date, she stayed at the end of the bar ready to order a drink realising that she would probably see little of James for the rest of the evening.

Mary gathered her up on a progress through the bar, and sat Abby down at the table she always seemed to use. "Now my dear, would you like one of your spritzers?"

Abby was about to say yes and changed her mind. "No thanks, Mary. I think I'll have a vodka and tonic tonight."

Mary raised her eyebrows. " Was it that bad riding Jason?"

Abby laughed. "No, he was very good. At times I wondered who was in charge, but he didn't give me any problems."

Now it was Mary's turn to laugh. "I know, Lizzy popped her head through the door while you were upstairs, and in about two minutes told everybody what was what. I'm glad you didn't take up her offer of the liniment though, It would take days for that smell to wear off, and you would have to wash everything it came into contact with."

The mention of washing clothes sparked a thought for Abby. "You have just reminded me, is there a laundry or launderette in Paverton so I can get some washing done? I shall need to get some done soon."

Mary shook her head. "No, no my dear, you just leave things out that you want washing and I'll take care of them. I'll put a basket in your room."

"Mary, I can't have you washing for me as well, you do enough round here."

Mary's smile had vanished. "I have a load to do anyway, and the little you put out will not add to the work at all, besides I can't have you going up to Paverton to do your wash, what will people think of me, Mavis wouldn't be very happy with me for certain. No you put things out like I said, and don't worry, they'll all be done properly. Now I'll get you your gin, no vodka and tonic." There was no arguing with her.

Abby sat nursing her drink listening to the voices coming from the bar, the decibels raised and lowered, as the discussion went on, with periods of calm, as the loudest voices presumably took a drink. She was therefore surprised when James appeared and sat down on the stool facing her.

"I'm sorry I left you alone, most ungallant as my mother would say, but farmers are the same the world over, they always have something to talk about. Can I get you another drink?"

Abby declined indicating that she still had plenty in her glass. "I really should get you a drink, after your kindness in allowing me to ride Jason."

James' infectious grin came and Abby knew he would say something flippant. "Oh, I think in that case you should buy Jason a drink for his allowing you to ride him." Abby's laugh was heard the other side, where Mavis had arrived only moments ago, and seeing Abby and James together had opted to join Sam and Mary at the bar. Mavis and Mary exchanged looks, with a slight nod of heads.

Sam caught the unspoken exchange and groaned. "God what are you women up to now; can't you leave well alone?"

Mary laughed, but Mavis with her more fiery character bristled. "Just leaving the two young people to get to know each other, and besides it would be good for James to get married, after all he's been through he deserves a sensible wife. That girl in there would be just perfect for him."

Sam knew his wife well, and unlike most was not afraid to bite back on occasions. "I don't suppose the fact that Abby is probably well off has got anything to do with it now, would it?" There was nothing that Mavis could say to that; her transparent motive would give Sam an inward chuckle for many months to come, it was not often that he was able to leave her lost for words.

Mary charged into Abby's room the next morning without waiting for the reply to her hefty knock at the door. "We are going to have a good thunderstorm today, if I'm any judge. Be right though, clear the air and the weather will be much more pleasant after. Got you some tea." She placed the cup on the bedside table. "Now, where's the washing you want done, good day to get it sorted, as there'll be a good drying breeze after the storm." Abby had already packed a bag with her dirty things, ready to take them to Paverton, or wherever the laundry was. Mary seemed to home in on these without being told, and picked up the bag. "Now don't you worry, Love; these will be done with care. I'll sort out the things which need hand-washing." Mary bustled around picking up one or two other things, which she judged would need washing. Then she looked at Abby, "Usual breakfast?" She asked raising her eyebrows with the question. Abby just nodded, lifting herself up in the bed.

"Thank you, Mary... for the tea, and everything else." Mary went slightly red with embarrassment, but flashed her beaming smile and rushed out.

Abby lay back for a while to relax, sipping the hot tea, and enjoying the warmth of her bed whilst listening to the rain now pattering against the windowpane. Her memories of her mother had dimmed over the years, but Mary's caring, motherly attitude, brought back feelings that had long been forgotten. Perhaps it was the sense of loss that they both felt, Abby for her long dead mother, and Mary for the child she had never borne. It was a kind of symbiosis; they each gave the other something they missed. It was strange that here she should feel so welcomed. Perhaps it was the ghost of granddad, and the guilt that the villagers felt over his isolation, although from all accounts; that was self-imposed; and then his death. Perhaps it was guilt for her mother, running away because there was no one she could talk to.

These people had welcomed her as no one else had done, and indicated that she was one of their own. Abby had come here to make life decisions. Was one of those decisions being made for her? Should she stay here? Staying at the Combe Inn on a permanent basis was not an option, but possibly somewhere in the village? If she did stay, what could she do to earn a living? She knew that her investments would keep her for the rest of her life quite comfortably, that was not a problem, but doing something was. She had grown up accepting that hard work was an imperative, her position today was a result of hard work, and accepting rebuffs and insults from the city, which did not approve of females. Her determination had got her through. It was, she thought uncharacteristic that she had accepted this final proof of the glass ceiling, but there again, perhaps there comes a limit to the number of times one can rap on the window without answer, and the deal she got added a very nice sum to her capital wealth. But was it strictly necessary to be in the city to work? Being online with a good computer could offer her opportunities. These thoughts she put to the back of her mind, another day would be sufficient, for today would be a good day to read Mr. Brusher's writings; there was a comfortable chair in the room, and she knew that Mary would provide her with constant hot drinks.

An hour later, with one of Mary's breakfasts sitting well inside her, she sat down to read.

CHAPTER TEN
Thomas Tregonney

At first the valley was all black, a black so still and thick it had substance. The sky was not black however, as countless stars and the Milky Way splashed a kaleidoscope of silver across the wide expanse. Gradually from the east though, the sky lightened, transforming the black to indigo, the panoply of silver gradually faded and then vanished when the indigo metamorphosed into purple and then to blue. The hills evolved from dark indistinct masses, to a grey green as the aura of the rising sun in the east chased the night away; the dark shadows shortening and fading in the increasing light; revealing detail hitherto shrouded in darkness, the buildings, the long platform, goods shed and signal box. Tendrils of mist crept silently through the cuttings, and up to the platform transforming it into an island lapped by a grey misty sea. In the fields dark shadows resolved themselves into cattle and sheep, blinking in the increasing brightness. The warming light dissolved the mist and the tracks gained definition, turning from gunmetal grey to silver, flashing darts of white light as the sun's rays caught them.

Down the track, a late fox paused whilst crossing the line, his brush held horizontally behind him, a front leg lifted, as he listened and scanned carefully in each direction; senses alert to any danger. Satisfied, he continued his journey, now loping alongside the track; using the last remnants of mist as cover, towards an earth somewhere in the tall stand of trees that men knew as Huish Coppice. From the chimney atop the signal box, a thin wisp of grey smoke rose, as the signalman coaxed the embers of the previous day, returning the stove to life. The air was still, and all was quiet, until the Blackbird, sitting high in the tree that gave him a view of all his ground, gave voice to the new dawn. This was a signal and like one piece of an orchestra at a time the other birds became vocal too, building to a crescendo then fading as the daily toil commenced once more. Away over the hills, a Buzzard began his day of lazy circling, wings spread to catch thermals or the lightest breeze, incessantly searching the fields below for the unwary small rodent.

Thomas Tregonney closed the door quietly, so as not to wake the girl. He stood in the porch of the station house for a few moments, breathing deeply and filling his lungs with the clean crisp air. After a lifetime of early starts, he had come to enjoy this time at the beginning of a day, when it was calm and peaceful. The railway was a twenty-four hour activity, and although a branch like this would not run all night, its business started long before the first train was due; and didn't end until long after the last train had gone.

zHe glanced down at his boots to check the polishing, they gleamed, no sergeant-major could have found fault there. His wing collar was pristine too, although it was held together more by starch than fabric now. Next he tugged the frock coat down at the back, to clear the crease that inevitably formed just below the collar, and then pulled the two halves together at the front. They still met as they had done when he first put the coat on, but they had never been buttoned up, it caused a bagging and creasing that he would not countenance. The pillbox cap suffered from the constant soaking and drying that was a natural consequence of his job. It had not shrunk, he took care to stretch it after any soaking, but the red initials of the GWR surrounded by a wreath of gold above the peak had become faded, and worn. Abigail, his wife, had been good with a needle; all girls then learned to sew; and she had made a satisfying repair of the embroidery, but his thick fingers had never been nimble enough to make any kind of a job of it, consequently the lettering that was supposed to read GWR now pronounced an approximation of those initials, and the unknowing would read them as CWE. Despite all this it was clean, and the black visor reflected the morning light, just as it done that year he had came here and proudly worn it for the first time.

In his office at the station hung a new cap, the British Railways cap, flat-topped, and with a badge proclaiming "Stationmaster," over the visor. Thomas had no use for it. He had not worn it at all from the day it had been issued to him in nineteen-forty-eight. He didn't need a label telling passengers who he was; the style of pillbox cap issued by the Great Western Railway, the wing collar and frock coat, all worn with dignity; identified him immediately.

Now, even junior staff, were issued with the standard cap, not that they bothered to wear them. There was no distinction attached to his position any more. Perhaps if Abigail had lived she would have taught Marion, their daughter, still asleep in bed, to sew. Marion was quick, and he felt sure that she would have been able to restore the badge to its proper splendour. But what was the point now, the line was run down, already rumours of closures were circulating elsewhere. He didn't know what future this branch would have, or how much longer he would have to wear the cap.

Be that as it may, there would be no slackening of the standards at Combe Lyney. Straightening himself up, he started up the gravel path that led to the platform, the chips crunching noisily under his boots. Opposite to his right on the other side of the tracks a thin wisp of smoke rose from the chimney of the signal box. Reg Purvess, the signalman leaned out of the open window to call, 'Good morning, stationmaster.' Thomas acknowledged the greeting with a jerky arm, somewhere between a wave and a salute. Purvess would already have brewed a pot of tea, the first of many, which, no doubt, would be shared by the footplate men and the visiting ganger, who would make a contribution of an occasional rabbit, mushrooms or wild onions, gleaned from the embankments and fields that bounded his length. The enginemen would also enjoy the fruits of this gleaning, and if from time to time coal would accidentally drop off the engine, strangely close to the ganger's cottage; well it was all part of the country railway's unofficial custom. The quality of the tea would be thick and strong, as the pot was constantly replenished a teaspoon of leaves and fresh water bulking the remains of the last brew. Then of course the pot was never thoroughly washed, the dark liquid that issued was obviously to their taste.

Purvess would now be busy, polishing and cleaning as if the district superintendent was to make a visit today. The superintendent would not be coming. Reg knew that as well as Thomas, because this backwater was of so little importance now that inspection visits were a thing of the past. Nonetheless Purvess kept the box spotless. The levers and brass instruments shone, the thin linoleum would be mopped every day, and a duster was always ready to hand as no lever would ever be pulled without that scrap of cloth between hand and metal. Thomas was just as particular at the station. It was an ethic ingrained from his induction, the proper way, the Great Western way. Thomas thought that Reg, although only in his late twenties, was a competent man in the box, even though he joined the railway after the demise of the GWR, but his father had been a GWR man and Reg had obviously inherited the ethic from him. True he had a tendency to cut corners but Thomas was always alert to this possibility, and insisted on proper procedure at all times. The railway, especially the G.W.R., had been patriarchal and encouraged sons to follow fathers into service, giving them precedence over other applicants for work. It was one of the ways that railwaymen would fit easily into their jobs, knowing the pattern of shifts and also gave rise to the ability of railway workers to recall anecdotes from the past.

Thomas had little authority over Purvess, although theoretically he had jurisdiction over everything and everybody within the station limits; but practically he had no sanction to apply, as the signalman could not be replaced at the drop of a hat. He would like to have done so at the time he found Marion working the box whilst Reg attended to his allotment, a patch of ground on the line-side close to the box. There was no real danger as Reg could hear the bells, and there wasn't much traffic on the line these days. Nonetheless, Marion was an unauthorised person, and she was only fourteen years old! He would have liked to take Purvess out of the box and suspend him. The problem would have been that the only person who appeared to be able to work the box in Purvess' place was a fourteen-year-old girl! His anger hadn't lasted long; in fact it had been tempered by the pride he felt in his daughter that she could master the procedures in the first place. Not that he told her so. He felt that his praise, could have given the impression that he condoned this behaviour.

Thomas continued his short walk to the centre of his kingdom, the station, counting the trucks and goods vans in the siding as he did. There was the usual assortment awaiting the 'goods' for returning empty. Very little goods traffic originated from Combe Lyney now. As ever, he mentally noted anything that would need attention, stopping to examine discrepancies that required closer inspection such as an intruding weed, or a sign that needing paint. He brought from his pocket a little notebook into which he scribbled a brief note. These notes would be transcribed into his journal on arrival at his office. Later these tasks would be given to the lad porter, Bob Fairworthy, who was thus denied any chance of joining Purvess in the signal box, for a mug of that indescribable tea, at least until his jobs had been completed to Thomas' satisfaction. The leading porter, Alfred Anson, would arrive with the first train down from South Molton where he lived. This would be an empty stock working, designed to form the first train in the up direction from Paverton.

Over the years, valley people had become aware of this working and would frequently make use of it, with the help of an obliging crew. This placed Thomas in a quandary; he would like to have charged the fare for their journey, but his returns would have brought the situation to the attention of the district office, who would have censured the crews involved, as theoretically the passengers would not be covered by insurance. Thomas had little choice but to let it go. There were compensations, however, as from time to time, a freshly plucked and drawn chicken, vegetables with aromatic soil still clinging to them or the first pick of new fruit, would appear on the doorstep of his house. The locals did not believe in something for nothing. There had been a time when Anson would have been expected to be at the station well before the first train, using any means of transport to make the journey, walking the four miles if that's what it took. Now the dispensation had to be made, otherwise there would be no leading porter. So the empty stock working would pause just long enough for Anson to jump out of the guards compartment, together with any other informal passengers, who Thomas would pretend not to see. Therefore, he timed his arrival at the station just after the empty stock train had gone through.

The leading porter would collect tickets, ensure that important notices were displayed, and would also double as the goods clerk. There were not that many trains plying the branch these days, but Thomas had no intention of allowing his porters an easy time during the hours between those trains. Not that Thomas himself was allowed any relaxation; as hard as he drove his porter, he drove himself harder.

The station was a much grander affair than most would think necessary for this small village on a small branch line. The Comberford family were major shareholders in the line when it was built, and as such could insist on a suitable monument to their participation. That the line had never made a profit under any of its owners was immaterial. The Bristol and Exeter had insisted upon a full staff, as did the Great Western Railway. Nowadays British Railways, with its cumbersome bureaucracy, were probably unaware that they were maintaining a station far too large for the traffic it created, nor that they were paying wages to two porters, when one would have been taxed to find a full day's work. Into the breach stepped Thomas Tregonney, who found work to ensure that neither porter was ever idle.

Thomas walked up the platform ramp. Already the station was the scene of activity. From a small van, milk churns were being unloaded to a trolley, which would then be wheeled through and placed on the platform, close to where the ventilated trucks, known to the G.W.R. as siphons would stop. From five-forty-five until six-thirty, half a dozen farmers would arrive in a variety of vans, wagons towed by tractors, or even horse drawn, to offload their milk. The first up train always conveyed two or three of these siphons, taking milk from Paverton, Lills Platform, and Combe Lyney, down to South Molton, where they would be shunted and coupled to a larger train bound for Torrington and the Creamery. Anson was stacking parcels on another trolley. Later there would be a goods train, but small parcel traffic would go with the first passenger in a parcels van, or the guard's compartment. Thomas stopped to check the labels, he could remember well the days when there would have been a special parcels train, the days when everything into the valley and everything out of the valley was conveyed by rail. The days when there would have been at least half a dozen siphons to pick up milk churns, which would stand four to five deep, covering one hundred feet of platform. Then the cattle dock would be full on market days, the air pungent with droppings, and the ear challenged with the lowing of the cows. Now, increasingly the milk went by road, as did those cattle, which were still sent to market. The little used cattle dock now sprouted lush grass, growing exuberantly from the rich nutrients left by the cattle.

He was glad to see that Fairworthy had helped with the churns; left to themselves, the farmers would leave them all over the place. Fairworthy, under Thomas's tutelage, had made sure they were placed neatly, so that loading them would take as little time as possible, the timetable was God; and everything that could be done, would be done, to keep the trains on time. No one would point the finger at Combe Lyney as the cause of late running. When the station was first built there had been no Canopy extending out over the platform, but the G.W.R. had built an extra structure sometime in the early thirties, presumably to give shade for the increasing numbers of churns. The churns no longer blocked the access to the station building. Fairworthy would then go on to sweeping out the porch. This was sometimes unofficially referred to as the Greenhouse, a feature, which for some reason was particular to stations in this area. It occupied the space between the two gables, which on the platform side were deeper than the approach side. There was some weather protection from a half glazed partition, but with no door to cover the access opening this was of dubious efficiency. With wind in any quarter except from the northwest, dust would blow in, entailing the sweeping, which was the first job of the morning for the lad porter. Inside and to the right was the ticket office; whilst to the left was the waiting room. Thomas nodded to Fairworthy as he walked past, his intention as every morning to walk the length of the platform, again noting anything that needed attention. He was pleased that this morning there appeared to be nothing untoward. This being the case, his mind worked on the tasks that might be imposed. The platform edging could of course be re-whitened; the flowerbeds could also be in need of attention. 'Good,' he thought, that would keep Fairworthy busy for most of his shift.

The stationmasters' office was at the back of the booking office, and shared with Anson when he was issuing tickets. He removed his coat, as he entered dressing it on a hanger that then went on the back of the door. He kept his cap on. He opened the safe, an antique Chubb affair with a large key. A child could probably have cracked the safe; but the paltry sums kept within would hardly tempt any but the most desperate. Taking the ledger and cash-box, he sat down to enter into the ledger the previous day's takings. Every ticket supplied to them as their stock was registered at the district office. As Anson issued the tickets, each had to be accounted for together with the requisite fares. Thomas had to balance these transactions and return each day the account sheet; and the cash, which went in a leather pouch; marked clearly "Combe Lyney" with the guard of the first up train. With no till, just a cash drawer, and the uncertain mathematics that Anson exhibited, often there was a discrepancy. Thomas had learned over the years to hold onto the surpluses, to offset the inevitable losses. Even so on occasions, he had to put his hand in his own pocket to make up a balance. Now he worked quickly. The first service would be due in twenty minutes and it was a matter of pride to Thomas that he had never missed getting the pouch onto the train on time. He scanned down the ledger, holding his pen just above the paper, and mentally adding the column, pounds, shillings and pence all at the same time. Satisfied that for once the value of tickets issued equalled the cash received, he wrote out the dockets, and put them together with the cash in the pouch, clipping it shut. It locked automatically.

A distant whistle told him that the train would be arriving soon. Automatically, he checked his pocket watch. He lifted his coat off the hook and taking a brush from the desk drawer, energetically brushed the coat down. Satisfied that it was clear of lint, he put it on. With the pouch firmly clasped in hand he left the office, through the ticket office, and strode out onto the platform. Glancing down the line he ascertained that the home signal was off, the board lowered to forty-five degrees from the horizontal; the so-called lower quadrant signalling in the Great Western manner; and paced slowly two or three steps in either direction, the pouch clasped in front in both hands. A commotion at the end of the platform drew his attention. Arthur Gill, a local dairy farmer had just arrived with six churns. Calling for Anson and Fairworthy, he told them to help get the churns into place, and approaching Gill he chided him. "Mr. Gill, now you know what time the train arrives, the same time it has arrived for the last twelve years, and you know that this being the Great Western Railway the train will arrive on time. So, why do you always turn up at the last minute; giving us inconvenience and possibly disrupting the timetable?" Arthur Gill just smiled weakly, an apologetic smile at having inconvenienced not just the Great Western Railway, but more importantly Thomas Tregonney. Quickly the churns were wheeled into place just as the train, hauled by the G.W.R.'s maid of all work, coasted into the station.

This was a six-wheeled locomotive with water tanks seemingly slung on either side of the boiler like panniers. Indeed these engines had always been referred to as pannier tanks. This particular locomotive had recently been shopped for a heavy overhaul. Thomas viewed with distaste the new livery. It had emerged from Swindon painted in British Railways unlined black with the crouching Lion and wheel emblem on the side. Behind the loco were the two siphons, placed there so that they could easily be detached at the junction; and then two compartment coaches. The coaches were trundled up and down this line, eking out their last days in passenger service. Once when they had been new, they would have worked out from under the soaring bays of Brunel's High Church in Paddington, rubbing shoulders with the elite coaching stock forming the great expresses; 'The Cornish Riviera,' 'The Red Dragon,' and 'The Cheltenham Flyer;' expresses hauled by the elegant racehorses of the silver road, the kings, and castles. Later they would have gone to the second division, cross-country services, and now they were here. The Great Western Railway never threw anything away, refurbishing and repairing locomotives and stock to get the maximum value for their investment. From his waistcoat pocket, Thomas pulled his large pocket watch and checked the time.

The line since Lills Platform had been on a downgrade. The pannier tank, therefore, had little work to do, and just as the loco arrived; the safety valve blew off with a great gust of steam. The fireman quickly turned the injector on, to cool the boiler, but knew that the stationmaster would have words to say on the subject. The train stopped, so that the guard's compartment was precisely where Thomas was standing.

"Good morning, Mr. Metcalfe." Thomas stepped forward proffering the pouch.

"Good morning, Mr. Tregonney." The Guard took the pouch and with Thomas observing placed it into the locked box through a non-returnable flap. At South Molton, the box containing the pouches from Paverton, Lills Platform and Combe Lyney would be transferred to another train, which would take the Exe Valley route to Exeter, where it would go to the district office for checking. Anson was making quick work of loading the parcels into the luggage compartment and would shortly join Fairworthy in loading the last of the churns into the ventilated wagons.

Thomas approached the engine. "Look busy, here he comes," muttered the driver out of the side of his mouth to his fireman. The man was busily checking water levels when Thomas looked into the cab.

"Fireman," he barked, "you know well enough that safety valves should not blow off whilst in the station. Please ensure that there is no repetition. Driver, you were one minute down. Why?"

"Two minutes late off Paverton, Mr. Tregonney, don't know why, just didn't get the board." With this excuse the driver checkmated the stationmaster. Thomas couldn't berate him as he had done well to get a minute back. The driver knew, as did Thomas, that there was no point in checking. Thomas could only do that through his colleague at Paverton, who would not want to waste time answering questions on such a trivial matter, just to please a martinet like Thomas, who at one time or another had upset just about everyone on this line. Anyway, the signalman would probably cite operational reasons for not pulling off the starter, such as a sticking point. Thomas gave him a dark look, knowing that to investigate with his colleagues at Paverton would be a waste of effort.

He looked up the track toward the signal that stood at the end of the platform. "You will observe that our starter is now off; I trust you will make a smart get away when your guard gives you the flag." He turned on his heel and marched away towards the guard's compartment once more. The churns were now finished loading and Fairworthy was closing the van doors. Thomas checked that the drop bolt was securely in place, and approached Guard Metcalfe, who was standing at his door awaiting Tregonney's confirmation that everything, and everybody was aboard. He looked at his watch again, checking the time. "Right away, Mr. Metcalfe," called Thomas.

"Thank you Mr. Tregonney." Metcalfe gave a short blast on his whistle to attract the driver's attention, and raised his green flag. He didn't just wave it, he held the shaft in one hand, and the other hand stretched out the flag by the corner, so the driver would be in no doubt that he had been given the green. A short "pop" on the whistle and the train moved off.

Thomas checked his watch again. He called to his porters. "Smart work, away on time from one minute down."

Alfred grinned at Bob, as the stationmaster went back into his office, "Always economical with praise is our Mr. Tregonney."

Bob shrugged his shoulders. "It's that bloke Gill, he's always late, if he would for once get his milk here on time we could have got the train away early."

Alfred regarded his young companion with a withering look. "So we get the train away early, what will happen? Nothing. What praise will we get? None. Because it's early the train will be held at the junction and all we will have to show for it is sweat and blisters. No point in working your socks off, it makes no difference."

He walked away towards the ticket office. There was little chance of passengers this early, and those that would appear would have weekly seasons anyway. He would check though, and if it was all quiet he would make his way ostentatiously to the goods shed; giving the impression that he had work there, and then when Thomas was no longer on the platform he could slip away for a mug of tea with Reg in the signal box. No such opportunity for Bob Fairworthy though, for Thomas emerged from his office once more, carrying in his hand the little slip of paper that Bob knew would be his tasks for the shift.

"Ah, Fairworthy, have you changed the lamps yet?"

"Just going to do that, Mr. Tregonney."

"Good. Now when you have done that, please check all the fire buckets, the gentleman's facilities will need to be mopped out, and then the flowerbeds will require tidying. I noticed one or two weeds coming through the platform slabs at the north end, please attend to those as well."

"Very good, Mr. Tregonney."

The lad porter set off to the lamp poom built in to the front of the station building, another peculiarity of this station. Usually at most stations, a separate corrugated iron hut was used for this purpose, a precaution against fire. Today was Thursday, the day for replacing the oil lamps that illuminated the red and green spectacles on the signal arms. The oil lamps would burn for eight days. Unlocking the door, he collected two replacement lamps, trimmed and filled, one for the up home signal and one for the up distant, and began the long trek to the signal. This was situated in the cutting by Huish Coppice, and was three quarters of a mile from the station. Today would be a good day for this job, a pleasant walk in the warm sunshine, even a chance, once out of sight to lie back beside the track and have a cigarette. In winter, he hated it, with rain sleeting in on the Southwesterly winds, he would arrived at the distant with his back soaked through, climbing the steel ladder to the lamp would be treacherous, and then on the way back his front would be soaked in its turn. The wet weather gear supplied by the railway was efficient except in high winds, when it tended to act either as a sail, speeding progress outward, and impeding progress inward; or as a parachute, at all times trying to fly above his head; either way the soaking was inevitable. The down distant was even worse, the signal standard being on a slight embankment, where the wind and rain ruled without mercy. In those conditions, climbing the ladder to pull the old lamp off and replace it was extremely dangerous, he thanked his lucky stars that it only had to be done once a week.

Thomas worked quietly at his desk; a relic from the thirties, scarred, damaged and repaired on more than one occasion, it was now secured by an angle iron to the wall, as the joints were so sprung that nothing else would save it from wobbling. He was reading the latest promotional literature special rates, and changes in timetabling. He would select those items, which would be of benefit to the potential customers in this area, and later today would write to the largest outlining the offers, and enclosing a handbill with the details. He could never decide which would be better; to write longhand, or to use the ancient Remington typewriter that had been issued to the station in nineteen-forty-nine. The problem with the typewriter was that the punctuation, needed a double shift; the first shift was for capitals, and the second for punctuation; and he was constantly forgetting to do this. His typed letters therefore tended to take twenty minutes to half an hour for a simple two paragraphs, and would contain many erasures or overtyping and as he would normally send out twenty such letters, he found himself working well into the evening to complete this work. He could as a matter of course write in copperplate, but this could take almost as long. The sorting proved to be far longer than he originally thought, as two of the special rates would at first glance appear to be the same, as he puzzled over this his hand instinctively went to his waistcoat and pulled out his watch; he was no longer amazed that this now unconscious action happened when there was four or five minutes to the arrival of the next train.

The service that had triggered this was the first down passenger due at eight fourteen. He put on his coat and walked out onto the platform. This was the train, which would take most of the village children to school in Paverton, his daughter included. The children waited quietly, knowing that the stationmaster's displeasure would be incurred by any larking around. Thomas nodded to Marion, pleased to see that she was well turned out as usual, her school uniform neatly pressed and clean. It was a source of pride to him that she would get herself up in the mornings, breakfast, wash up, and dress, in plenty of time to catch this train. His personal sense of duty and integrity applauded his daughter for these similar attributes. Yet apart from that nod, he would not acknowledge her in any way. He was the stationmaster and he was on duty.

The engine could be heard now, working hard on the almost continual climb from the junction close to South Molton. When it approached the down distant, the driver blew the whistle, and moments later the train appeared. It came over the level crossing and as it approached the signal box, came almost to a complete stand, the fireman leaned down and handed a ticket to Reg, who had come out of his box to collect it. The regulator was opened again briefly, and then closed, the driver allowing the train to coast into the station. The engine was one of the little tank engines so often used for lightly loaded passenger trains, with four coupled wheels and two trailing wheels. Almost everything about the engine was on the diminutive scale, with the exception of the vast polished dome on top of the boiler, which seemed completely out of proportion to the rest of the locomotive. The coaches were the two, which had formed the last up train. As ever with a train, even though they travelled twice a day, there was a sense of repressed excitement amongst the children as the train drew to a halt, and there was some jockeying for position in order that they could share a compartment with their best friend; or that some other child could be excluded from their select group.

Thomas' stern gaze would put a stop to the more physical of this selection process.

The train stopped predictably with the guards compartment just where Thomas was standing. The guard / stationmaster acknowledgment intoned just as before, except that this time the guard was the other regular on the line, George Bird. Combe Lyney's stationmaster was not one for idle chat, which was strange in a way, as that position was a solitary occupation, and other railwaymen, were probably the only people that they would come into contact with on a regular basis. Bird knew of some stationmasters who relished a chat, and would return to a topic that interested them with the regularity of the timetable, picking up two minutes conversation with a guard every time that train returned to his station, as if the last words said on the subject were only a minute ago, instead of an hour or so. Thomas supervised the embarking of the children, walking slowly down the platform ensuring that all the doors were closed. As he walked he peered into each compartment, and acknowledged regular travellers with a nod, or in the case of first class, touched his cap. He wasn't much called upon to do that these days. Anson was standing at the picket gate, having examined or collected tickets of those passengers who alighted.

As he passed, the stationmaster enquired, "All correct?"

To which Anson replied, "All correct, Stationmaster." Thinking to himself, "How can it be any other way with only three passengers to deal with?"

Thomas arrived at the engine, just as the down starter signal dropped. The train could not depart yet as the driver was not in possession of the token, which Reg would be bringing now. The fireman was leaning out, watching the activity on the platform. Thomas called across to the driver. "Driver, it isn't required in the rule book that you sound your whistle at the distant, or have the whistle codes changed in the last twenty-four hours?"

The driver had been ready for this. "I thought I saw an animal on the line, Mr. Tregonney, but I was mistaken."

Thomas nodded, this was in the rule book. "Very well, Driver, but you should be careful, or our signalman would believe that you wanted to come inside." This was the railwaymen's colloquial for leaving the main line to enter a siding or loop. The fireman, trying hard to keep the grin off his face applied himself studiously to the rear of the train, where Reg Purvess was just walking up the platform with the token for the next section; he handed this to the driver who checked that he had the right token.

The guard had just placed his whistle between his lips; and with his pocket watch in hand, he waited until the minute hand reached twenty minutes past. Thomas had his watch in hand as well, also checking the time; he raised his arm to indicate that the time was right. The guard blew his whistle, and the green flag was shown. The driver tugged the whistle chain just once, and immediately opened the regulator, being on the far side of the cab, his comment to his mate, "And that's in the rule book as well." It did not reach Thomas's ear.

Whilst the train had been in the station, there had been considerable bustle, the idle chatter of the children, the opening and slamming of doors, the hiss of steam from the engine combined with the crackle of water dropping on to the hot surfaces. Yet the moment the train departed there was silence, except for the sounds of the engine away in the distance, working hard on the bank towards Lills Platform. This was the extraordinary characteristic of branch line stations. Five minutes of hectic activity and then an hour or more of tranquillity. The platform was deserted as the staff went about the jobs that passengers rarely saw. Thomas to his never-ending paperwork, Alfred Anson checking in the tickets he had collected, and Reg Purvess wandering back down the track to close the level crossing gates, and then returning to his isolated signal box. A viewer from the distance would see a deserted station, with apparently nothing happening, giving rise to the impression that railwaymen lead an idyllic life. Only was there an occasional movement as one or the other of the staff would make a brief appearance walking out of one door, only to enter another.

In the office, Thomas pecked carefully and laboriously at his ancient typewriter, grinding out the letters to his potential customers.

His hand went instinctively to his pocket and consulted his watch; he called out to Anson. "Anson, goods due in forty-five minutes, is everything checked in and loaded?"

Anson had been sitting quietly, enjoying a few moments of calm. "Yes, Stationmaster, I am just going now over to make sure nothing else has arrived."

Thomas did not look up from his typing. "Do that if you please?" Framed as a question, this was more an imperative. Alfred knew this and reluctantly left the ticket office.

And so the watcher from the distance would have seen Anson leave the building, stroll down the platform, descend the ramp, and cross the line on his way to the goods shed. He passed Bob Fairworthy, who was just returning from the down distant having completed the task of replacing the oil lamps.

"If you get the chance, come over and help," he shouted, "I've got one large crate to load." Bob raised his hand in acknowledgement and continued on his way, stopping at the lamp room where he stored the exhausted lamps. Within the next couple of hours, he would trim the wicks and re-fill the lamps so that working spares were always available. He walked up onto the platform wondering whether to just go over to the goods shed, or tell the stationmaster first.

He opted for the safer of the options and went in to the office. "I have completed the lamps, Mr. Tregonney, the leading porter has requested help with a large crate, shall I go now, or is there anything else you wish me to do?"

Thomas looked up wearily from his typing. "Go help load the crate, you should know well enough now that that is the priority."

"Yes, Stationmaster," replied the porter, and backed out quickly, before Thomas could add any more sarcasm to his reply. Typical, he thought. If he hadn't said anything he would be in trouble for not letting the stationmaster know where he was. You got it in the neck for doing something and also for not doing it.

In the signal box, Reg Purvess had re-filled the kettle and put it on the stove in anticipation of the arrival of the goods. His timing was right for at that moment the bell gave one ring, Reg immediately pushed the plunger once to signify that he was alert. The bell then rang three times followed by a pause, then four times with another pause, then once, signifying that the goods wished to enter the section. Reg set the signals and points, and sent back the same bells he had received. The moment the passenger had cleared the section he had set the block instrument to show 'line clear.' A few minutes later he got the bell code for "train entering section." He acknowledged this and set the block instrument to "train on line." The line was divided into sections known as 'blocks,' and the signalling system ensured that only one train could be in any block at a time. Having done this he ambled down to the level crossing to open the gates. In many places these gates would be interlocked with the signals, so the signal could not be cleared unless the gates were open for the train. Due to the amount of traffic this had never been thought necessary at Combe Lyney, and more than once a signalman who had forgot, watched horrified as an engine smashed through the gates. The crossing gave access to the goods yard and the dirt lane that led to the old mill, and so little traffic used it these days that it would have been easier to leave the gates shut, only opening them when a wagon required access to the yard. That would probably have happened were it not for Thomas Tregonney, who of course insisted on everything by the book; therefore Reg had to make this walk many times each day.

The goods ran as it had for years on the same timing, irrespective of the fact that there was little work for it these days. Where once it would be a dozen vans and half a dozen wagons, all to be shunted and reformed, a process taking up to an hour or so; now there would be three or maybe four vans and two open wagons, and the shunting could be accomplished in twenty minutes. The demand had changed but the timetable hadn't; and the goods would have to wait for the up passenger from Paverton. The crew were quite happy as this gave them an hours' break to drink Reg's tea and gossip in the box. In the goods shed, Alfred and Bob had manhandled the heavy crate into one of the two vans standing on the goods road. Bob, with regret now had to return to the station to carry on with Thomas' job list. Anson made the final check that all the crates, and boxes had been written in the rate book, that the vans had the destination labels clipped into the carriers, one for Exeter, and one for Taunton, and settled down to wait for the goods.

Thomas bestirred himself, glancing once more at his watch. Whilst the goods train would not be dignified at every station with the attendance of a stationmaster, he felt it incumbent upon himself to oversee the proceedings from a distance. Therefore he was standing on the platform when the goods arrived and made its way slowly into the goods loop, again hauled by the six-coupled pannier tank. It stopped to the accompaniment of the clanging buffers, as the un-braked wagons closed up to the wagon in front. Reg set the points for the head-shunt, a short length of track on which the guards van could be shunted to clear the vans and trucks that would be detached here, and the little round ground signal turned to clear, the guard, it was Mr. Metcalfe again, waved his green flag from his van, and slowly, groaning, the train set back, until the guards van was placed well into the head-shunt. Anson had wandered down and ducked under the couplings to release the guards van from the train, which was then allowed to pull forward leaving the van in the head shunt. Anson and Metcalfe then discussed the wagons to be dropped off, the wagons to be picked up, and with the contribution of the driver who had now joined them, how and in what order it would be done. With so few wagons nowadays it was relatively simple. Twenty years ago, the train was so long that many of the wagons had to be shunted on to the running line to give them the space to carry out the shunting, very often delaying the up passenger, which had to be held at the distant. Forty years ago they would have had a shire horse to pull individual vans into place, reducing some of the many engine movements.

The shunt took place, again with the characteristic clanging of the buffers, and the groans of bearings in which the grease lubrication had gone solid. From the vantage point of the platform Thomas watched carefully, anxious to notice the shunting practice that would save time, but was deemed unsafe according to the regulations. Those involved in the operation were well aware of this scrutiny and took care not to give reason for censure, not that they would have, as Metcalfe said. "With so few wagons there really is no need to cut corners." Reg Purvess was little involved, as once the train had entered the goods loop, it was effectively 'out of section,' and moving trucks over the various points was effected with ground-based levers. Nonetheless having closed the level crossing gates he leaned out of the window in his box, and watched the process with interest, he was after all, a railwayman, and would no doubt tell Anson and Metcalfe where they had gone wrong, once they had their hands around the mugs of tea he would provide.

Thomas returned to his typing, he would have almost a full hour at this task before the next up passenger. Yet again that curious peace returned to the station. Thomas was working in his office. Anson, Metcalfe and the crew of the engine were drinking tea in the box with Purvess. The engine stood quietly simmering at the head of the now reformed train; occasionally attended by the fireman to keep the boiler quiet. The only person that could be seen working was young Bob Fairworthy, who had mopped out the gentlemen's facilities, and was now lethargically, weeding the flowerbeds along the platform. Most railwaymen were quite keen gardeners, either by inclination, or necessity. The Great Western had encouraged this by allowing line side plots to be cultivated for vegetables; very welcome to a family economy used to living on a low wage; and making seeds available for station gardens and hanging baskets. Bob had not joined, or so he thought; to become a gardener and had incurred the displeasure of the stationmaster more than once by 'weeding' plants that did not require weeding. He was learning, though, and was starting to show some enthusiasm for the job.

In the box, the signalman, driver, fireman and the guard, supped noisily at their mugs of tea.

The fireman, who was only in his twenties, took it upon himself to remark on Tregonney's habit of watching the shunting movements. "It's almost as if he doesn't trust anyone else to do the job right," he complained.

Metcalfe laughed. "Our Thomas is quite able to pull a few stunts himself." He commented, only carrying on when Reg asked him to explain the comment. "I remember one I was told about, it was during the war. The Yanks were up on the Moor for exercises, and as they couldn't go anywhere without all the comforts of home, the number of trains that went up to Paverton was considerable. Well on this one day, the Yank movements officer down at Molton assembled quite a long train of wagons, and despite the fact that the stationmaster told him that it wouldn't fit into the loops, sent it off. They had put a large Prairie on from Taunton, so the crew didn't know, and the pilot had only been up the line twice before, so although he had signed for the route he didn't know what length of siding we had here.

"Hang on," interrupted the fireman, "the regulations wouldn't allow that."

"No," replied Metcalfe, "but this was wartime and a lot of things like this happened."

The driver nodded. "Yes I heard tales of crews having to drive on to all sorts of unlikely places, remember when that hall ended up somewhere near Sheffield, it was over-gauge for the line, and took quite a few platform edging stones off, the crew were so far away from home they thought they would be interned for the duration."

Metcalfe grinned, he knew the story well. He continued. "There was no trouble until they got here, when it had to go in the loop. It was of course too long. They stood there for some time with the crew, the guard, and the signalman all scratching their heads. Then they heard the whistle of the up passenger at Lills platform, and the panic really set in.

That's when Thomas Tregonney came onto the scene. "Split the train," he says, "get as many wagons as you can into the good shed road, and then get the rest into the loop." Well they did that, but it soon became obvious that there were still too many wagons; the last wagon was still fouling the turnout. "Right," says Thomas "we'll get them right up into the down head shunt." Now that would have been o.k. but the loco couldn't get behind the wagon, because they were still fouling the point, and of course it couldn't haul them into the head shunt as it would trap itself. Thomas beckons the driver to come with him into the shed, where he points to a great coil of Manila rope. "Do you reckon that that would take the strain?"

The driver looked at the rope and then at Thomas. "You're not thinking what I think you're thinking?"

"Well you tell me another way of clearing the line," says Thomas.

The driver thinks about it and says. "Mr Tregonney, I'll do it, but get everybody well away, because if that rope parts it will kill anyone nearby." So that's what they do, attach the rope to the wagons, and the back of the loco, and the driver takes it slowly up the main line, until the rope's taut, then gradually the wagons move up the goods loop into the head shunt, where because they had no braking on, they demolish the stop block, and the lead wagon drops two wheels off before they stop. That clears the line, except for the loco, which had no place to go, so they attach it to the front of the up passenger when it arrives and send it back to Molton, double headed. Then it came all the way back light engine! By this time Thomas had managed to get a shire horse from one of the local farms, and they moved sufficient of the wagons for the loco to assemble the train again, except for the wagon that had dropped off. That stayed there for days until they could get the breakdown crew up."

They all laughed at this story, and Reg Purvess ventured the opinion that it was all make-believe.

"No," says Metcalfe. "I know it happened because the driver was my dad. There is one other thing though. The wagon was full of supplies for the Yanks, which included a couple of cases of whisky. Needless to say they weren't in the wagon when it eventually got to Paverton. Their laughter was heard all over the station site, and Bob cursed his luck that he could not be with them.

Metcalfe was not done yet. "If there was something that Thomas loved; apart from the Great Western; it was cricket. He turned out for the local team from time to time. He was quite handy as a slow bowler, off-breaks, leg-breaks, the googly, he could do them all, as well as a rather tasty faster ball, which got him quite a few LBW's. Problem was that Thomas could never stay for the whole match. He had to get back here for the seven fifteen."

Reg interrupted. "He didn't have to; it was Sunday, his day off."

Metcalfe grinned. "Yes but you know Thomas, he didn't like to leave it for anyone else to do. Probably thought the leading porter would derail the train or something. So it was important that Combe Lyney won the toss and elected to field first, and then at least they would get the benefit of Thomas's bowling, before he had to leave. Of course he was never available for away matches." He took a sip of his tea. "I was told about another dodge that Thomas got up to. They were playing Bishops Nympton, and there had been a stoppage for rain, so the whole match which was a bit of a needle match was late. Well the Bishops Nympton team would always catch the eight thirty-five, but the way this match was going it probably wouldn't end until about eight ten, and it was going to be nip and tuck for them to get to the station in time. The train was in on time and the driver was very surprised that when he stops, Thomas goes down in the six foot and starts to examine the outside cylinder very closely. So the driver gets down as well and wants to know what Thomas is doing. Thomas explains the situation and the driver goes along with it, as Thomas said he would cover the report. Thomas gets back on the platform and tells the few passengers that there was a slight problem with the engine, says to those who ask that it could be gland-packing. Wouldn't you know it but the problem disappears the moment the Bishops Nympton team run onto the platform. I heard later that he wrote in the late report that there was a suspected leak from the cylinder, so the driver could not get into trouble."

The fireman laughed and said. "Go on tell me the driver was your dad again." Metcalfe nodded.

"Yes, it was. Thomas would not have dared pulled that stunt unless it was someone he knew."

The sun was well up now, and heat was building. Bob had undone his waistcoat, and rolled up his shirtsleeves, as he bent to his task. Although he was some distance away from the signal box, it was so quiet that he heard the 'ting' of the bell. Knowing that this would herald the arrival of the up passenger, he straightened, and leaving the bucket he used for the weeds, started back down the platform, dressed as he was.

His fates were never so kindly, that he was unnoticed by Thomas, who appeared on the platform just as Bob walked past the porch. "You will not be greeting the service dressed like that, I trust?" Thomas growled.

Bob held up his hands, which were dirtied with soil. "I was going to wash before I buttoned my waistcoat, Mr. Tregonney." Thomas could not argue with the sense of this and merely grunted,

"Carry on." He of course was wearing his cap and frock coat, despite the heat. Bob walked on, a smirk on his face and the unspoken comment, 'gotcha,' in his head. Any victory, no matter how small, was sweet.

The bell had also stirred others back to life. Reg was pulling signal levers, the engine crew rejoined their locomotive and Metcalfe his van. Anson appeared on the platform and took his place by the wicket gate to collect tickets. The ceremony had started again. The train arrived, and left, leaving a handful of passengers trickling out through the gate, some to a waiting car, most to walk the mile and a half to Combe Lyney.

Thomas did not wonder why the station was so far from the village it served, this was often the case with country railways, laid down at a time when two or three mile walks did not deter folk. The better classes would have carriages to bring them to the station, so they would not have complained. Now attitudes were different, people would not use a mode of transport that was not convenient for them, and increasingly bought their own transport.

With the departure of the passenger train, the goods could resume its slow journey to Paverton. Reg set the points, and with much groaning and clanking the train cleared the station and commenced the uphill struggle towards Lills Platform. It was at this time of the day that Thomas would make his way over to the signal box. Part of his responsibility was to sign the train register, a record that Reg was required to keep, listing all train movements and their times, in and through the section. It had once been the time to await the "signal," a tone broadcast from Paddington over the company's private telephone lines that enabled all stations to synchronise their clocks. This was the end of the first part of Reg's shift and he would 'switch out' the box. He worked what was known as a split shift-- coming on early, working late when there were more trains; with a break in the middle of the day, when there were less train movements. Switching out created one long section from the junction with the barnstaple line to Paverton, controlled by the boxes at those two points. Thomas climbed the stairs to the box and knocked on the door. The door carried a sign marking it 'Private' and even Thomas would observe the courtesy of knocking.

Reg was speaking on the telephone, the railway's private line, which connected the signal boxes. He was confirming to the boxes at either end of the branch that he had switched out, although they would already know this from the bell codes and the line indicators.

He waved Thomas in. "Good morning, Stationmaster, there is tea left in the pot, would you like a cup?" Thomas accepted, not just because he had to remain on good terms with the signalman; but also because they lived close, in railway houses, and his widowed mother would shop for Thomas when she went to Paverton. Reg's father had been on the railway, and had been killed by a shunting accident at South Molton.

Sipping his tea, which was stewed to an extent that not even the sterilised milk could disguise, Thomas tried to make small talk, not a skill with which he was at ease. "It's a warm day today," he was standing there in his cap and coat, with perspiration trickling over his forehead.

Reg smiled. "That it is, Mr. Tregonney," thinking to himself, why didn't Tregonney take off that stupid coat. "Saw Marion going off to school this morning, you will be proud of her, the way she has adapted." This was a reference to the death of Abigail, Thomas' wife, and Marion's mother just three years ago. Thomas was cautious; he was unsure of the signalman's attitude towards Marion. Particularly after the incident when Marion had operated the box, she must have spent quite some time here to learn the skills. Reg was in his late twenties and was going out with a girl from Combe Lyney; surely he would have no interest in Marion? Reg didn't have any interest in Marion, apart from the fact that he felt sorry for her, especially as Thomas was always too dedicated to his job to have much time for her.

"Yes, she is a good girl."

Anxious to change the subject, Thomas moved on to ground upon which he felt safe. "Not too much on the goods today."

Reg agreed. "And it's getting less all the time."

Thomas nodded. "Time was when we would have need of every inch of the track out there, just to clear the line for the passenger, and then to add to the problems, there would be the quarry trains. I don't know what we will do when it starts picking up again, I shall have to see if district will put in some improvements." He finished his tea. "You will be going off now, let me sign the register." Thomas did that, but not before scrutinising the page to make sure that everything was in order.

"Thank you for the tea, Reg, I shall see you later." He left the cabin, and Reg rinsed his cup out with hot water, and hung it on a hook to drain. Funny old Bugger, he thought, aloof and throwing his weight around one minute, and then quite reasonable the next. Then he laughed to himself, if he thinks that things will get better, he's kidding himself. The whole system is falling apart; soon there will nothing left. Reg was realistic, he had been looking at other jobs, and felt that he could in all probability get another box. It would mean moving, he had talked with his girlfriend, Gladys, and she had agreed that if that happened they would marry and she would move with him. He checked around the box, closed the damper on the stove, and left himself, locking the door on the way out.

CHAPTER ELEVEN

Reading Mr. Brasher's summary had helped Abby understand her grandfather's work but also had raised many other questions. Not so much as about his life and work, she realised that was something she could never fully appreciate, but more about the line itself. She wanted to put substance to the places about which she had read. It occurred to her that James' suggestion that riding along the old track-bed would provide a much better viewpoint to appreciate the valley and the line in that context. She determined to ask him at the earliest opportunity. In addition she would like to know what happened to the other people mentioned, Reg Purvess, Alfred Anson, and Bob Fairworthy. Perhaps she could ask Sam again, although she felt he would probably be heartily sick of her questions by now.

That evening, Sam and Mavis didn't come into the Combe Inn, Mary explained that they had gone to Molton to visit Mavis' sister, who was not that well. James did, however, and although he made a show of talking to everybody, he gradually made his way along the bar to Abby, who forsaked the Lounge and occupied a corner and was talking to Jack and Mary, whenever he was not pulling pints, and she was not darting off here and there. When James arrived at Abby's side, Jack and Mary both found work to do at the other end of the bar. Well in truth, Mary found work for them both, almost dragging Jack away; she was beside herself with glee, it was rare that James came in two nights running, and the thought of phoning Mavis to report this added to her delight. Of course she wouldn't just come out with it, this was gossip to be savoured, and teased out of her, all the while frustrating Mavis who as ever would want to come straight to the point. Eventually, Mary's curiosity got the better of her, and taking advantage of the fact that James' glass was in need of re-filling, she moved down to where they were talking.

She was disappointed in that the conversation revolved around little more than the rain that had deluged the valley that day. Mary reached over and indicated James' mug.

"Yes please, Mary, would you like another drink?" he enquired of Abby.

"Thanks, can I have a vodka and tonic?"

"And a vodka and tonic for Abby," he repeated the order to Mary, who, in order that she could overhear as much of their conversation without appearing rude, pulled James' pint, and poured Abby's vodka as slowly as she could, and was delighted to hear, when Abby asked if she could take up James' offer of riding along the track bed. "Of course," he replied, "although I did wonder if riding Jason for the first time, might not have put you off." He grinned.

Abby had felt some muscle strain from the saddle, but she was damned if she would admit it to James. "Not at all, I quite enjoyed the experience, and I think that you were right when you said, riding the old line will be much more informative than driving, or even walking." Abby deliberately deferred to his superior knowledge, something that she had rarely done with any man before, but an innate feminine instinct told her that this was the right thing to do. James nodded, pleased that his advice had been accepted. Mary was aware of what Abby had done, and inwardly congratulated her.

James of course did not realise that the flattery had been a little false and accepted the comment as a true admission of his good judgement. "Well, when would you like to do it, I'm afraid that tomorrow is out, I have to go to Taunton, but Friday would be fine, if that suits you?" Friday would suit Abby well, it would give her an extra twenty-four hours to recover from the slight saddle soreness that yesterday's outing had left her with.

Mary had been listening and felt that she could offer something. "As you will probably be out for most of the day, would you like me to put up some sandwiches and a flask?"

Abby looked at James for guidance. "Will we be out that long?"

He thought they would. "There's no point in hurrying, and there is a lot to see, so I think yes, we will be out for most of the day."

Abby turned to Mary. "That would be very kind of you, Mary. Are you sure it's no bother?" Mary was aghast at the suggestion that a few sandwiches and a flask of tea would be a bother, although her mind was already working on a suitable menu. Bother? This was grist to her mill.

Later in her room, Abby thought that perhaps she should write to Mr. Brasher, thanking him for the information he had sent. She had brought her laptop computer with her and normally would have emailed, but she doubted that Mr. Brasher had even heard of the Internet, much less have an e-mail address. Heaving a sigh, she drew out the few sheets of writing paper she possessed and began to write. She chuckled gently to herself; this place really had got to her, now she was communicating just as her grandfather had done way back in the forties and fifties.

Abby drove into Paverton the next day to post the letter, and also to drop in on Toni. Timing her visit right, she was just in time to catch Toni on her way for morning coffee. Toni was delighted and grabbing Abby's arm, hurried her across the road to the café. "Now bring me up to date, have you learned anything new?" Abby once more had to go through the story of her resignation, leaving out details of the financial nature of her severance, and telling Toni all about Mr. Brasher's story, including the background of the valley railway. Toni laughed upon hearing the accurate history. "So much for the librarian's history," she commented. "And how are you getting on with James Comberford?"

The question came out of the blue and took Abby by surprise. "How do you mean, getting on with James?"

Toni's eyes twinkled. "Well you did say before that you had talked to him once or twice, and word has reached what passes for society in these parts that James has become friendly with someone new to the area, and you referred to him simply as James, which would indicate a little more than a passing acquaintance."

Abby's face blushed a bit, and she smiled, "I suppose that we have struck up a friendship."

Toni laughed triumphantly. "I knew it. And of course you have put one or two noses out of joint. But are you sure it is just a friendship?"

"Don't read anything into that," replied Abby shaking her head. "Although I am going to be around for a month or two, I shall have to earn a living, and that is something I can't do in Combe

Lyney; so eventually I shall be leaving. There's no future for me here" she paused and feminine curiosity overcame her, "Anyway whose noses have I put out of joint?"

"There are some who had hopes in that direction," Toni said mysteriously.

"Not you surely, Toni?"

"Oh good God no, I want to get out of this place, not get myself mired in and we know that James will never leave here now." Again. The emphasis on the "now." Abby was determined to get to the bottom of this.

"That's the second time I have heard that said. Is there a story there?"

Toni looked at her in surprise. "Well you know he was in the army, don't you?"

"No, I didn't."

"Yes, he was in the Parachute Regiment. Went through the Falklands War and got himself decorated. He came back and resigned his commission. From what I can gather, he doesn't like travelling further than Taunton now. I don't know what happened to him out there but something obviously did."

Without thought Abby muttered, "Oh poor James." Toni kept her thoughts to herself upon hearing the comment. Whatever Abby said, her feelings were perhaps a little more than just friendship.

Abby drove back to Combe Lyney knowing that she had not told the truth. She did not need to earn a living, she needed to earn a life. Combe Lyney was seducing her. The location, the people, and more than those; as if they weren't enough, her roots were beguiling her to stay. She discounted James as a reason. He was charming, amusing, and good company but Abby had managed to get through without a man as part of her life. She had some occasional adventures, which were mildly diverting, but they had never been more than that, perhaps because she had never committed totally in her mind to the relationships. Consequently her life had been one of hard work, coupled with a detached observation. She was part of life, but never affected by it. Here for the first time that attitude was changing. She was conceiving a love for the valley and the people who lived here. They accepted her and involved her in their community without asking for favours or help. Without thinking she drove straight through the village and along to the old station. Unconsciously, she had become used to this place as somewhere she could think, perhaps hoping that her grandfather's ghost would still be around to help her deliberations.

Abby would have been amused to realise that others had noticed this behaviour and approved. Mavis and Mary had discussed this, after Sam had reported her frequent visits to the site.

"The girl needs somewhere to think," said Mavis, "and where better than the place her mother grew up. Leave her be, is what I say, and let her make her decisions in peace." This was, of course, ironic coming from Mavis who was determined that Abby should assume a place in the village that she, Mavis, had elected for her, a situation that at this moment had never entered Abby's head.

Mary without guile had pointed out to Mavis, "Yes, that's alright, as long as she makes her mind up the way you think it ought to be." Mavis nodded, unaffected by the sarcasm.

The station exerted its usual calming influence over Abby. She wandered the platform allowing the tranquility of the place to wash over her. The very peace that she sought here, ostensibly to help her deliberations, was subtly influencing those deliberations. The ambience of the place was diluting any sense of freewill that she erroneously believed was hers. Although Abby didn't realise or recognise the fact, Combe Lyney station was not the right environment for the decisions she was tussling with; so that when she left to return to the Inn, Abby still believed that she had a choice, unaware that the insidious atmosphere had worked on her emotions. Only later would she realise that. Collecting Mr. Brasher's papers from her room, she made her way outside to sit at one of the tables and continue reading.

Mary appeared after some twenty minutes with a tray of tea. "I've got some nice scones and cream if you would like," she offered.

Abby laughed delightedly. "If I eat as much as you seem to want me to eat, that poor horse will not be able to carry me tomorrow."

Mary laughed too. "Don't you believe it, girl. Look at you, there's hardly anything of you." She went on, "If I was your mother…" There she stopped abruptly, realising that this was an area that could upset Abby.

Abby understood immediately and put Mary at ease, "If you were my mother you would be telling me that I don't eat enough to keep body and soul together and that you hadn't slaved all day to put good food on the table, and have me turn my nose up at it." Her voice changed, "I miss Mum, but the hurt has gone, and it's nice to have someone like you, who worries about me in the same way that she would have." Mary's eyes nearly filled with tears at the compliment.

She turned away, saying. "I'll get another cup, I could do with a cup of tea myself."

When she returned she had her emotions under control. Abby took charge and poured tea for them both and then asked the question that had been lurking around her mind for some time now.

"Mary, I have known for years that I was illegitimate and have never concerned myself about it. But coming here and learning so much about my family prompts a question that I never thought I would ask. Do you know, or do you think Mavis and Sam would know, who my father was?" Mary was silent for a moment. She, Sam and Mavis had more than once talked about the possibility of Abby asking this question and Mavis had elected herself spokeswoman if Abby were to ask.

For Mary, the answer was easy. "I can't help you, Love, you know that Jack and I only took over the pub fifteen years ago. You had best talk to Mavis." Abby nodded her head. Mary went on. "It was thirty-five years ago, if nobody at the time knew that your Mum was pregnant, why would they have reason to suspect there was a man involved?"

Abby nodded again. "I think you are trying to prepare me for disappointment."

Mary shook her head sadly, "Sometimes finding out the truth could be the disappointment."

Abby looked up sharply at her. "Do you know, Mary? That is very profound. But nonetheless I shall have to ask Mavis at the first opportunity." She went on, "When I was young I imagined all sorts of reasons why I didn't have a dad, I invented stories for myself about him, that he was for instance an explorer, lost in some unfathomable jungle or working secretly for the security of the nation. I didn't feel deprived, just a little different. As I grew up, I realised that not having a father was one of those things, that never having, I didn't miss. It wasn't important and I haven't thought about it for years until coming down here and discovering that I did have a family, that mum had had a mother and father. Whilst you know that biologically that must be, its only when you put a face to a vague concept that it becomes real. If mum ran away because she was pregnant, then it follows that my father must have been from this area."

Mary shook her head. "No, Love, in those days, the West Country was one of the main holiday regions in the country, plenty of tourists, far more than now, coming here from all over the country." Abby sat quietly absorbing the truth of Mary's argument.

But not wishing to let the conversation get too depressing her innate sense of fun re-emerged. "You mean I could be the result of a holiday fumble?" Mary was shocked, until she noted the grin on Abby's face. Relieved that Abby could still find humour she relaxed.

Abby then changed the subject. "Now, what are you putting in the packed lunch tomorrow? Jam sandwiches and a bottle of water would do me." The laughter was back in her voice.

Mary laughed too. "No, nothing like that, I thought a few dry biscuits, and possible a bit of hard cheese. That will do fine as long as you cut the furry bits off." The gloom had lifted as suddenly as it dropped before. With their mood restored to its normal good-humoured balance, the conversation moved on until Mary, having finished her tea, decided that the kitchen required her attention once more. Abby resumed her reading.

That evening brought a message from James, who had popped in on his return from Taunton. He would pick her up at eight o' clock the following morning. The message also contained the injunction 'wear comfortable.' Abby's enquiries of Mary brought a blush to both their faces.

"You will spend a long day in the saddle; don't wear anything too tight around the hips and bottom," was Mary's interpretation of the instruction. Abby's giggle said it all, realising that James was trying, in the most genteel way, to spare her embarrassment later. Mary also added some advice of her own. "Don't drink too much this evening or tomorrow morning; you can't duck behind a hedge as James can." Abby's shoulders shook with suppressed laughter, there was definitely humour in this surreal situation. This, she thought, was definitely a date with a difference. Then the thought struck her, was this a date? The few dates that she had were often never repeated, or ended up with pressure for Abby to be more 'friendly' than she wished to. She doubted that this would be the case tomorrow. Her musing was interrupted by the arrival of Sam, who insisted that he was going to buy Abby a drink for a change. Abby asked for a vodka and tonic, reckoning that a short drink would comply with Mary's advice.

Sam knew about Abby's ride tomorrow with James and invited her to call in at the farm, which wasn't far off the track. "Mavis will want to kill the fatted calf and lay on a full spread for you, so I won't tell her you may be coming by. That way I shall be the only one to suffer afterwards, for not letting her know that you may call. I'll leave it up to you." Abby thanked him and asked how they would find the farm. Sam laughed. "Oh Mr. James knows the way, don't worry." She realised that of course James would know and felt quite stupid for a moment.

They chatted for a while, until Sam suddenly said, "I almost forgot. I think I may have found out where Reg Purvess is living. I believe that he's in Cullompton." Abby heard this information with mixed feelings, one of which was trepidation. She was aware from the conversations she had with Sam and Mavis that Reg and her mother were what could be called friends; and to Abby he could be a suspect for paternity. Sam noticed the expression on her face and forewarned by Mary who had telephoned Mavis that afternoon, could read Abby's thoughts. He leaned over and whispered in her ear, "I know what you are thinking, the answer's definitely no. That is of course if you haven't dyed your hair." Confused, Abby looked at him. He smiled. "Reg was a real carrot top, and nine times out of ten, children will inherit that colour. Are you red underneath that blonde hair of yours?"

She relaxed. "Sam, can you read me that well?"

He shook his head. "No, Love, but we knew that it was only a matter of time before you would start wondering. Mavis has racked her brains and can't think of anyone who was close enough to your Mum. But I'll tell you one thing, it wasn't a casual affair; your Mum wasn't like that. Whoever he was, he meant something to her." Abby was grateful for the kind words and impulsively kissed Sam on the cheek. Sam of course turned the bright red that was his usual reaction to gestures of affection.

Mary chuckled delightedly as she walked back down the bar, wiping her hands on a towel. "Sam, you will just have to get used to being a sex object."

Abby's mind churned the somewhat peculiarity of Reg's hair. "Isn't it unusual for a man from this area to have red hair?" she asked Sam.

He shook his head. "There were quite a few Scots shepherds who came down here in the middle eighteen hundreds when they were establishing large scale sheep farming on the Moor. It wasn't too successful. Some went back, some stayed, intermarried, and made new lives for themselves. You'll come across a few Scottish names and colouring from time to time."

Abby excused herself about half past nine. An early night would be useful if the following day was to be quite long and she wanted to review some of Mr. Brasher's' notes. His history was far more complete than the little book that Toni had given her and Abby wanted it fresh in her mind for the expedition tomorrow.

CHAPTER TWELVE

James arrived at twenty to eight the next morning, riding Cassie with Jason on a leading rein. As Abby was still eating breakfast, Mary asked James if he would like some breakfast as well. He eagerly accepted, walked the horses to the back of the pub, and looped the reins around the back of one of the bench's. He joined Abby at her table, immediately pinching a piece of buttered toast.

"Don't you eat breakfast?" she inquired.

James nodded, with his mouth full, he eventually managed to say, "Yes, but that was some time ago."

Abby looked at him in amazement. "Some time ago? What time do you get up for God's sake?"

"Usually half past five, things to do, you know?"

Abby shook her head. "And there I was, thinking that you just laze the day away." At that moment, Mary arrived with a plate full of crisp Bacon rashers, fried eggs and tomatoes.

"Good grief, that was quick, Mary," James exclaimed.

"Well I was doing this for Jack when you arrived. It seemed easier to let you have this and I'll do some more for him."

James looked a little sheepish, "Will you tell Jack that I appreciate his sacrifice?"

"I wouldn't worry," said Mary, "he doesn't know you've got his breakfast. I'll cook some more for him in a moment."

She left them to their meal, only to re-appear with the flat packages and flask that contained the packed lunch. "Will these fit in the saddle bags?" she inquired of James. His mouth, being full again, he nodded. Abby was amazed with the speed with which James tucked away his breakfast. Food has never been of primary importance in her life, at least until she came to Combe Lyney, but even here, with the delicious meals that Mary brought to the table, she had taken care to ration her intake, ever mindful of her figure. James however seemed to have no such inhibitions, yet showed no signs of over-indulgence physically. He must, she thought, be one of those lucky people who never put on weight.

James drained the last of a mug of tea, and turning to Abby with a smile on his face, enquired, "Ready?"

Cassie and Jason were standing with their heads together as Abby and James came out. James fitted the packed lunches into a saddle bag on Cassie, who turned her head to see what was being done and then placed the two flasks into the saddle bag on Jason, who side-stepped skittishly as if to avoid this indignity. Abby had brought a small bag with her, containing those essentials that no woman would be without. James looped a leather strap through the handle and secured it behind Abby's saddle, he gave her the hard riding hat that thoughtfully he had brought with him.

"Right, come on then, I'll help you up, bend your leg, or if you wish step up onto the bench." Abby approached Jason cautiously and opted to climb on the seat of the bench. James stood the other side of Jason to stop him moving away and Abby threw her leg over the saddle and mounted with little difficulty. Taking the reins up, she remembered that Jason needed a good hand and pulled him up firmly when he started to walk. James had mounted Cassie in the meantime, and turning his head looked to Abby, who similarly goaded Jason into walking. James lead the way not out onto the road, but to a five-bar gate situated in the rear fence of the yard, leaning down he unlatched it, gesturing to Abby to go through, he followed, allowing the gate to swing to behind Cassie, and re-latched the gate.

"I thought it would be easier this way, rather than going down the road."

Abby looked about curiously, "Won't the farmer mind?"

James shook his head. "No, I don't mind," he grinned at her, "don't forget, as you pointed out the other day, I own all of this land."

She grinned back. "How silly of me, Droit de Seignure and all that."

He laughed. "That's right, so do you feel safe being out with me today?"

"Of course," she replied, "besides I have got Jason to protect me. You did say he sees men as a threat."

James nodded ruefully. "Yes he does, oh well I had better behave myself today." Funny thing, thought Abby, she could never visualise James not behaving himself.

She surveyed the landscape wondering where they were going. "O.K., where are you taking me?"

He pointed towards the corner of the meadow, "We'll get onto the track bed there, just beyond the cutting, I thought we would go up the valley first, you get some really good views of the line from up there."

"Is that near to Lills Platform?" she asked.

He looked across at her. "Good Lord, how did you know that?" Abby explained that Mr. Brasher had sent her all these notes and that it was a name mentioned quite frequently. They had arrived at the corner that James had indicated, and passed through the gate, and up onto the track. Turning to the left, they walked the horses easily along the track bed, which at this point was starting to rise on an embankment.

Abby could see the girders of the railway bridge ahead. "Are we going to cross by the bridge?" she asked.

"No, I don't think it would be safe enough for the horses, you can walk across on foot, but there are one or two gaps that you have to look out for. We'll ford the river there, it's only about eighteen inches deep."

As they approached the bridge, James led them off the track and down the embankment at a slight angle. The dressed rock abutments loomed up on the right, as they descended the bank of the river, both Cassie and Jason stepping into the water without hesitation. The horses splashed through the river, which in summer drought was not flowing particularly quickly, both horses stretching their necks down to snatch mouthfuls of water. They would have stopped if allowed but James urged Cassie onwards and Jason followed. They ascended the embankment once more and regained the track, walking on. Abby could see the definite rise as the track aimed itself across the meadows towards the valley side, where the climb became more pronounced and she wandered at the effort the old steam locomotives would have made to ascend this incline. The pathway had been narrow for a while and James had to lead the way but it widened once they were off the embankment, and he dropped back to ride alongside. The track hugged the valley side, and as they climbed the views became ever more striking.

He pointed to a cluster of farm buildings, "That's Gallow farm."

Abby followed his pointing finger. "Should I know about that?" she asked.

He looked puzzled for a while and then understanding came to him. "Sam and Mavis' farm," he explained.

"Oh, you know that Sam has asked us to call in, don't you?"

He pulled a face. "I know." He said with a long-suffering air. Seeing his expression Abby hastened to say.

"We don't have to, I don't think Sam would mind."

"You're right." James agreed with her. "Sam wouldn't mind, but Mavis would. I'm prepared to bet that she's got binoculars on us at this very moment, and when we come back this way, if we were to go straight past, I would never hear the end of it, so we will go and call." They rode on in silence for a while, as the track rose ever higher up the valley wall, and the trees closed in on both sides. They had on a couple of occasions come down off the embankment to cross the road, the decking having been lifted off the bridges. Intermittently there would be a break in the foliage and Abby caught breathtaking views of the valley below. The scenery reminded her a little of the journey on the West Somerset Railway, where the railway turned away from the coast and climbed into the valley. It was in this section that the locomotive was working at its hardest. Abby remembered the sounds and in her mind they were replayed, but relocating them to this climb through the Lyney Valley. Here, as there, glimpses of the valley below were enjoyed but briefly through gaps in the trees, or where one tree in particular had grown tall, inhibiting growth underneath. James looked back to her and tilted an imaginary coffee cup in front of his lips.

"Coffee?" he called.

Abby nodded, "Wonderful idea."

They stopped, and dismounted at one of the breaks and took the time to enjoy the panorama. Away down to the left she could see the roofs and the Church of Combe Lyney, set out like a model village.

Below the riverine bush indicated where the river flowed and to the right she could make out the arches of the viaduct, still some distance away. She looked at her watch and was astonished to see it was half past ten; they had been riding for two hours.

"How far have we come?" she turned to James as he poured coffee from one of the flasks.

"About six miles." He handed her a cup, which she took gratefully.

"I can't believe it, it doesn't feel as if we've done any distance at all."

He grinned. "I would think that about three o' clock this afternoon, you will certainly feel that we have done some distance."

Abby smiled back at him. "Well, Mr. Comberford, if I do, you certainly will not know about it. Besides, I am enjoying myself too much to worry about that now." They enjoyed the coffee in a companionable silence, Abby standing where she could take in the vista, James sitting on the bole of a tree, watching the horses. Cassie and Jason, their reins looped casually over a convenient branch, stood quietly occasionally snuffling about cropping the rich grass which grew hereabouts.

Finishing her coffee, Abby turned to James. "Shall we go on?" He nodded, and taking her cup, stowed it with his in the saddlebag.

Abby walked over to stand by Jason. "You will have to give me a leg up this time," she remarked.

"A pleasure ma'am," he smiled, "mind you, if you stay any longer eating Mary's food, it may not be."

Abby laughed. "You mean that if I put on any weight you won't want to know me, or are you asking me to leave?" He just shook his head, grasped Abby's bent leg, and boosted her into the saddle. God, she thought, I'm flirting, and then a second later, and he is too.

James having settled in his saddle waved his hand airily towards the track. "Lead on." Whether under guidance from Abby or not, Jason did lead on. The track was more overgrown here, so again that had to ride in single file. The steady ascent continued, but gradually they came out of the tree line and into an area half way between forest and moor. Here the grades lessened, as they neared the top of the climb. Once again they were able to ride side by side.

"Is this still Comberford land?" Abby asked of James.

"Yes, it is," he replied, "we will get to the quarry soon. Just after that the line crosses the valley by the viaduct. That marks the end of the estate."

"How far to the quarry?"

He thought for a moment. "About two miles and another half mile beyond that to the viaduct."

"And how far down from Combe Lyney does the estate extend?"

There was a grin on his face now as he answered, "It extends down as far as the forest, that's on Crown land, about six miles." Abby did some quick calculations in her mind. The valley was some two miles wide at its widest but narrowed considerably towards the top, so allowing for that the estate was some fifteen square miles. She was busily working that into acres, when James said,

"Eleven thousand four hundred acres; give or take an acre or two. About thirty-five percent is in pasture, the rest is moor and forest."

She looked across to see him laughing. "You rotter, does everybody know what I'm thinking before I say anything."

He stopped laughing, but soon the irrepressible grin took command of his face. "Just because us lives in the sticks, doesn't mean us is thick," he used a grotesque version of the supposed country dialect.

Abby joined in the laughter, but got her own back. "You do that accent awfully well," she replied, using Sloan speak, "did you have to go to school especially to learn it, or does it come naturally?"

James' shout of laughter echoed across the valley and startled Jason into skittering sideways. James edged Cassie over and grabbed the rein to settle Jason. Abby was a little unsettled, but as soon as Jason resumed his gentle walk, she regained her composure. "I don't think I shall try to be humorous for a while, it doesn't seem to be good for my seat."

James was contrite. "Sorry about that, I had quite forgotten that Jason could be a little twitchy at times." The incident had put a slight dent in the good humour that they had shared, but it was soon forgotten.

James then changed the conversation completely. "The other day, you mentioned that you had resigned your job and that you would be selling your flat; there's nothing wrong I hope?"

Abby considered for a while and then replied. "No, not really. I suppose I had gone as far as I could in the job, the city and women have a peculiar relationship, you are welcome as long as you understand your place. I could have gone on, fighting the system, and when I think about it, if I hadn't come down here, I probably would have done just that. But this place changed me and I decided to take some time out, and re-assess my values and ambitions."

James nodded. "Yes, this place does have that effect." He paused in thought. "I didn't think the glass ceiling existed anymore."

Abby smiled ruefully. "Don't you believe it? It's still there, not officially of course, not P.C. You can fight it, or as I decided, get out. But not without winning a little victory first." James was astute enough to realise that a little victory would be financial compensation, but manners dictated that one didn't ask about that, even if he had wanted to.

"So what are you looking to do?" He asked.

Abby looked at him. "At this moment I am not thinking about that. Right now, this is the most important thing in my life, finding out as much as I can about me, about my family, and my roots. I know it sounds crazy, but I need to find my place, and a kind of peace." James said nothing, knowing all too well the emotions that were running within Abby, hadn't he suffered the same way?

They rode on in silence for a while. As they rounded a gentle curve, Abby could see the formation suddenly become double width, right where this started, and almost completely covered in bramble was a buffer stop, constructed of bent rails. "What is this place?" she asked James.

"This is Lills Quarry siding, the actual quarry is over there." He pointed off to the right, "It's not too far."

"So this, presumably, is Lills Platform."

"Well sort of, there is a platform about four hundred yards further on. That is Lills Platform." Abby's urgency communicated itself to Jason, who quickened his pace a little. Within a few minutes, Abby could see the remains of the platform. Built almost entirely of sleepers, set on a brick base, it had lasted well, probably because the sleepers were soaked in creosote, or some other preservative. She walked Jason alongside the platform and whilst some of the sleepers were starting to crumble, she could see that most were still strong.

"Amazing, isn't it?" She remarked to James, "Over thirty years since the last train and it still stands."

"Well they built well in those days. I think this is an excellent place to stop and discover what Mary has put in those packed lunches. I don't think we will be disturbed by a train and I'm quite hungry."

He had manoeuvred Cassie alongside the platform as well swung his leg over the pommel and alighted onto the platform. Abby did likewise, finding it much easier with the platform at the height it was. James produced a long rope from his saddle and haltered the horses, giving them sufficient rope to wander a little. They then turned their attention to the lunch. Mary had indeed gone to town. Crusty bread rolls, filled with fresh salad, hard-boiled eggs, tomatoes, pate, fruit, the contents went on and on.

"James, I am never going to get even half way through this. You did say you were hungry, didn't you?"

James surveyed the spread. "Yes I am hungry, but judging from the amount here, I reckon that Mary thought she had to feed the horses as well. We'll never eat all of this, but what are we going to do with it all. You can't take it back or Mary will be really upset."

"What do you mean, when I take it back? You are surely not going to chicken out on that."

"Yes, I was. I don't think that she would be too hard on you. I, however, would definitely get the wrong end of her tongue."

"Get started, Mr. Wimp, we'll work out what to do with the leftovers, when you're stuffed to the gills." They sat on the platform with their legs dangling over the side, the repast spread out between them. They started on the pate and salad rolls.

Abby picked up the flasks. "There's coffee left in this, and I presume that the other is tea, what would you prefer?" Instead of answering, James jumped down off the platform and walked over to Cassie.

He rummaged in the saddlebag and turned around with a big grin on his face. "I wondered if you might like to indulge in something a little more refined." He held up a bottle of white wine and two glasses. "The bottle was very cold this morning and has warmed a little, but I think it still drinkable, what do you say?"

"I think it is absolutely perfect, Butler! Pour me some wine." The wine was very drinkable, and still chilled despite the increasing heat of the day, a fact demonstrated by the horses, which extended on their long halter and had moved to some shade.

"How did you manage to keep the wine so chilled?" asked Abby.

"Well I have a small cool bag, which had been in the fridge overnight, together with the bottle, and it has worked quite well. After all we can't be drinking warm wine now, can we?" The last part of his sentence had been spoken with the accent of a Pukka Sahib.

Abby giggled, "Are you always as well-organised as this?"

"I'm afraid not." James shook his head guiltily. "This was my mother's idea. She was always the organising one in the family. My father let her make all arrangements for whatever. He was good at running the estate and quite astute. The fact that the estate is still extant is testimony to that. But in everything else, he was hopeless. She even had to put out his clothes for him; otherwise he would have left the house in the morning dressed like a scarecrow."

"He sounds like Mr. Brasher."

"Who's Mr. Brasher? Oh yes, your railway man. What was he like?" Abby could remember him quite well. The way he dressed, Mr. Brasher would not meld into the background.

"He was a lovely little man, when you got to know him. Everything he wore was top quality, but completely uncoordinated. He has a lifelong ambition to write the complete history of the Great Western Railway, and nothing else matters. I would imagine he has some private income; otherwise I wouldn't imagine that he could devote the time to the project that he does. It was amazing though, we started talking about this line, and within minutes he had all the details to hand. Your family got mentioned a bit, as having been instrumental in building the line, together with speculation that all was not quite as above board as it should be."

James burst into laughter. "Oh wonderful, the evil Comberfords of Lyney, what were the old devils up to?" "

"It's only speculation, but free travel, and possibly a hidden levy on all goods coming in and going out was part of the trade-off."

James still had the grin on his face, obviously not upset by the possible slander of his family name.

"It would have been my great, great, great grandfather, although I may have missed out or added a great or two. That must have been where my father got his acumen from." He paused, "pity it hasn't been passed on to the present generation." He looked at Abby. "So what else did you learn about the line?"

Abby thought for a moment. "Well this quarry was one of the main reasons for building it."

James looked astonished. "The quarry?"

"Yes, also he said that there was talk about large deposits of iron ore on Exmoor and that the Bristol and Exeter Railway wanted to get a line here first, to get the most traffic; but in the event the ore was too difficult to extract, something about faulting, and wet conditions. So although there was traffic from the quarry, it was mostly rock for building. The other traffic was agricultural from the valley."

James mused for a moment, and then laughed, a little cynically. "If there was a kickback for my ancestor, he must have been very disappointed when the ore traffic didn't materialise."

Abby was suddenly struck by a truth. "Of course, it would have been the iron ore that provided the largesse and there I was thinking that he was out to rob his tenants."

James looked hurt. "Oh Abby, how could you think that any Comberford could have been so low as to do something like that." The expression on his face belied the words.

Abby regarded him thoughtfully. "You know the acumen has passed on, you immediately saw the true reason for the toll, shall we call it. I didn't, and after the work I have been doing, I should have seen it straight away."

"Thank you, lovely lady, I do try to hide my light under the bushel, but sometimes the rays escape." Abby warmed a little to be called "lovely lady."

She hid her pleasure by scolding him. "Yes you do, you show the world a flippant and cynical face, but underneath you are quite sensitive." She stopped. To go any further would invite a conversation she wasn't ready for. James, to his credit, also realised that this wasn't the time or the place.

They finished as much of the lunch as possible, but were dismayed by the amount left.

Abby picked up a couple of apples. "Can I feed these to Jason and Cassie?"

"Yes, of course, slice them in two first, and then be prepared for their demands for more." Abby did that and the horses accepted the tidbit eagerly. As she walked back to the platform, Jason followed her, nudging her in the back.

James smirked. "See, give them a little, and they want more." He had been packing what remained of the food, and stowed the packs back in the saddlebags, taking care that everything they had brought with them, they would take away.

"Can we look at the quarry?" Abby asked.

"Look as much as you want," James waved his arm around in a half circle.

"Where?"

"There," he indicated again the area he had pointed to. Abby looked more closely and realised that what she had taken for a natural bowl in the hillside, was in fact an area where the hill had been blasted away. Expecting to see raw rock, the area was now covered in vegetation and small trees. As her sight adjusted, the straight lines of the foliage became obvious, following as they did the strata left by the quarrymen. She looked at James with a sheepish grin on her face. He had that insufferable smirk of having been proved right.

His sense of justice asserted itself almost immediately. "I can't blame you for not seeing it, even though you were sitting right in the entrance, it's amazing how quickly the shrub and growth take possession." She accepted his attempt at conciliation.

"Is it possible to get in there, or is it dangerous?"

"No, it's O.K. You will probably find that someone has been in recently."

"Is it still being used?"

"Well, not officially, there's no blasting anymore, but the locals will scavenge for small rock and the like, there's plenty of that around. Come on, we'll leave the horses here, and go and take a look." He shaped to take her hand, but then thought better of it and led the way through the small stand of trees that fringed the floor of the quarry. "Careful!" he pointed down at the footing. The reason was a length of rail, embedded in the residue created by pulverised rock and water that had set like concrete.

Once through the trees, the remains of the quarry was even more obvious, with the rusted remains, of what could have been a crushing plant, standing gaunt and skeletal amidst piles of partially crushed rock.

"So who or what was Lill? That this placed should be named after."

"Well I don't know who the original Lill was, or where he came from. I expect he had a licence for the quarry, bought at great expense no doubt, from one of my forbears, but I wouldn't have thought that it brought him riches."

"Why do you think that?"

"If the family had made a lot then one of his descendants would not now be driving a taxi in Paverton."

"Oh, probably the expense of quarrying the rock was too high, or perhaps the toll that the Comberfords charged excluded profit for the unfortunate Mr. Lill." James gave a theatrical gesture of resignation.

"There you go again, is there any ills in the world that you cannot lay at the door of my family?"

Abby laughed. "No, in fact my city background applauds them for their profit motive."

James' expression was again theatrical, exhibiting great surprise and cried loudly, "At last, recognition for the Comberfords."

Abby giggled. "Don't let it go to your head, James. I am sure I shall be able to find some criticism to balance the equation."

James was rueful. "Well at least there was some little thing that you could give us credit for." Their walk had brought them to the middle of the flat floor of the quarry; here, Abby could see the remains of the terracing left by the rock-cutters as they brought the hillside down. There was a scattering of rock lying around, hewn from the hill, half prepared for further treatment, but left unfinished when the closure brought to a halt all activity.

There were signs of later work, which Abby remarked upon.

"Yes," explained, James. "From time to time some of the locals will get up here and collect rock to repair dry-stone walls and buildings."

"You don't mind?"

"Not at all, don't forget, that as the landowner, they are actually improving my property." He then looked at her, with a challenging expression and said, "Make something out of that, if you can."

"Oh James, don't take it to heart if I have a little dig at your family from time to time. There is nothing malicious intended; in fact it is probably a little jealousy on my part. At least you have a family that you can trace back for generations. I have a history only as far as my grandfather." He was immediately apologetic, without thinking he stepped towards her and took her hands in his.

"Abby, I'm sorry, I didn't mean to snap."

Abby shook her head. "You didn't snap, James. I should apologise to you, it was all light-hearted banter, and then I went and turned into something else." James had kept hold of her hands and Abby made no attempt to withdraw. He's going to kiss me, she thought. A thought quickly dashed as James, realising the intimate situation, let go her hands, his face becoming slightly red, and suggested that they ought to return to the horses. Abby nodded her agreement, and turned to go, hiding her face from him, as a little glow suffused her cheeks.

They found the horses a little restless, seemingly eager to continue the ride. Abby led Jason over to the platform and used that to mount.

"Are we going back now?" she called to James who had taken the time to ensure that first Jason's and then Cassie's girths were still tight.

"No, we'll go a little further, up to the viaduct." Jason had already decided that it was time to walk on, and started before Abby was completely ready. She pulled sharply on the rein.

"Hey, I'll tell you when to go." She used a firmer voice than ever before and Jason stopped and switched his ears back.

James began to laugh softly. "I'm glad you're getting him sorted. Now give him a good dig in the ribs." Abby did so, and Jason walked on again, his ears still switched back, as if awaiting another command. Leaning forward, Abby rubbed Jason's ears. Talking softly, she told him that they would get on much better if he would follow her instructions. James listened with a grin on his face.

It wasn't very far to the viaduct, the track gradually turned though almost ninety degrees to the left, and suddenly it was there. The valley was much narrower at this point and the viaduct had been built to take the railway across to find easier gradients on the other side. The track was blocked. Heavy timbers fixed firmly to the rock portals, prohibiting their access. Although someone had broken down part of the timbering and a narrow track wound its way across, indicating that some foolhardy souls had used it recently. James stopped and waited for Abby to stop alongside him.

"Is it safe?" she asked.

"Yes. You could walk across with care, but I wouldn't take a horse over."

"Why's that?"

"Well the structure is quite safe but the deck has quite a few pits, I wouldn't want a horse to put a leg in one of those, probably break it. If you want we could walk out a little way, give you a tremendous view of the valley."

"If you think it's safe. That would be great."

Without thinking about it, Abby lifted her leg over the saddle and slipped to the ground. She led Jason a few steps and looped his reins around a post, which stood conveniently from the side of the track. She looked again at the post and realised that it was an old rail. She remembered what Mr. Brasher had said about the G.W.R., that it threw nothing away but recycled it, she had seen that at Lills platform with old sleepers becoming a platform deck, and now here, an old rail used for some other purpose, probably as a fencing post. James used a similar post for Cassie's reins and waited for Abby to join him. Just as she was doing so, she remembered her camera, which was in the bag of essentials. She ran back, pulled it out of the bag and joined James with a cheeky grin on her face.

"Ready, Sir."

"Now be very careful," he said as he climbed over the blocking timbers, "the footing can be a little loose." Abby followed him over the timber and they set out on the little track that previous walkers had made. There was weed and thistle covering most of the track bed and as they slowly made their way out, Abby noticed the pits, some of which seemed to be very deep.

"How have they come about?" she asked.

"I think it's where the waterproof layer has broken up, and the rain gradually washes the infill out of the piers."

"James, is this safe?" a little alarm creeping into her voice.

"Oh it's safe enough, if you stay on the path."

His words failed to reassure her but the view of the valley, which opened up as they moved further out overcame her fears. As they approached the middle, she forgot her fear completely, and opening her camera looked for somewhere to take some photographs. The view was such that she was spoiled for choice, so settled for firing off a series of shots; the quiet beep as the camera became ready to take another picture accompanied her adjustment of stance as she panned slowly from one side of the valley to the other. She turned and looked up the valley, although the view was not quite as spectacular, she took another series of photos in the same manner. She finished by taking one of James, who had moved to one side and was gazing reflectively down the valley.

He didn't realise that she had taken this shot, until he turned and caught her with the camera pointing at him. "Why spoil a perfectly good set with my picture?" he asked.

"Oh so I can show all my friends back in London the Lord of the Manor." He grinned.

"You mean the Lord of the Muck Heap."

"Oh no, in fact there's some of my girl friends who might think he's rather handsome; but those would be the ones without much taste, of course."

"Of course," his grin grew wider, "and you would have to tell them how distasteful it was for you, having to slum it down here."

"Absolutely, so distasteful, that I'm thinking of buying somewhere to live down here."

The words were out of her mouth before she could stop them. Suddenly what had hitherto been just a thought bouncing around her head, became more of a reality. It astonished her and James was astonished also. He recovered quickly.

"Well, in that case, you had better remember who owns the land around here and how iniquitous and tricky the Comberfords are in their dealings."

"James, you wouldn't take advantage of a poor innocent girl, would you?"

"Of course, as you know, I do that every morning, before going and throwing a few peasants out of their homes."

"In that case, I'll just have to be very careful."

They had started walking back. Abby looked around. "The wind has died." There had been a persistent warm breeze all morning.

James shook his head. "No, it's the parapet."

She looked at him. "The parapet?"

"Yes, it diverts the wind upwards and anything on top here is in the lee, you'll see, when we get back you will feel the wind again." His words were true, the moment they stepped out from the protection of the viaduct, Abby could feel the breeze again.

"How remarkable."

"They knew a thing or two, those Victorians."

The first part of the ride back down the valley was passed in silence. Abby wondering why she had blurted out the possible intention to live in the valley. James giving consideration to how he would react if that actually happened. This was not an emotional decision, but a practical one. It had always been his family's policy to keep the land intact. Apart from the railway, this had been achieved. If Abby were to decide on residency, he felt that she would not want to be a lessor. There were some cottages available, but to rent; and much as he liked her, he would be unable to sell her any of the property. He would like Abby to be around, but refusal to sell might drive her away. Neither was a course he wanted to happen. The horses were allowed to set their own pace and ambled quite contentedly onwards. When the track was wide enough, they walked side by side, with their heads nodding together in their gregarious nature, their riders deep in thought.

They were well on their way down when Abby saw a furtive movement in the trees off to the left.

"James, there's someone there."

"Where?"

"On the left, behind the tree." As she spoke, the figure emerged from hiding. She felt James relax.

The figure stood and waited for them to draw abreast.

James spoke first, "Hello, Woody, how are you today?" Abby tried not to look astonished as she took in the man. He could have been any age from mid-fifties to late nineties, dressed in a multitude of what appeared to be cast-off clothing, none of it clean. He was unshaven with a ragged beard that looked as if it had been hacked off with shears. The voice, when it came, belied the appearance; his speech being perfectly regulated with an accent that was only acquired at the very best public schools.

"Good day to you, Mr. Comberford," he nodded in Abby's direction, "Miss." He returned his gaze to James. "Thank you for your enquiry, I am well. An excellent day for a ride."

James introduced Abby. "This is Miss Tregonney, Abby this is Woody."

"I'm pleased to make your acquaintance, Miss Tregonney, would you be related to the Mr. Tregonney, who was the stationmaster?

"I'm pleased to meet you, Woody, and yes, he was my grandfather."

"A gentleman, Miss, he was a gentleman." Abby smiled with pleasure. Woody then addressed James.

"Mr. Comberford, I have been asked for more hurdles, would it be permissible to take the wood from the Lydcott stand?"

"Yes that would be fine," replied James, "would you like to look at Huish as well. I believe that could do with some thinning."

"I'll do that with pleasure. Good day to you, Mr. Comberford, Miss Tregonney. Do enjoy the rest of your ride." Seemingly without disturbing a single branch, the man vanished into the trees.

Abby searched the foliage for some trace of his passage and astonishingly could find nothing to mark the man's path.

As they nudged the horses to walk on she turned to James, "Who was that?"

"That's Woody."

"Yes, you introduced me, but what is he? Who is he?"

James smiled. "No one really knows. He's been around for something like forty years, but it could be more, as people in the valley rarely see him. He could have been there sixty or more years for all we know. We call him Woody, because he lives in the woods, and acts as a sort of unpaid forester. He has no history, well none that anyone has been able to discover."

"He lives in the woods?" Abby was incredulous.

"Yes. There's an old forester's cottage, it's a ruin really, but he's made a home of sorts in it."

"But his voice, it's perfect, now you don't get that kind of voice skulking around in the woods."

"Oh Woody's educated all right, quotations from Shakespeare, Chaucer, Milton and Plato, he's got more literature in his head than most of us have in our houses."

"So why is he here?"

"As I said, no one knows, I would imagine though that he's running away from something, or rather given the years he's been here ran, might be the correct word. He's got so used to the land around here that he can turn up most unexpectedly at times, and as you just saw, demonstrated his movements that are very difficult to detect."

"I don't suppose you charge him rent for the cottage?" Abby asked with cynicism.

James laughed at the sally. "No, as I said it was a ruin. He works for it though, servicing the woodland, and making wattles. My father once offered to pay him for the work, but Woody refused. He didn't want to become a statistic, presumably because he could then be traced. Anyway, he has little use for money. Woody wanted to lose himself, and stay lost. In that he has succeeded, to this day now, one knows who he is, or where he came from."

"This place never ceases to amaze me. Oh and what is a hurdle? I don't suspect it has anything to do with racing?"

He grinned. "When we get down to Sam's place, I'll show you a hurdle or wattle as it's sometimes called." The mention of Sam's place also brought him a solution to the problem of the excess food. "I know what to do with the leftover food."

"Oh yes, are we going to stop and eat another lunch perhaps?"

"No nothing as difficult as that; when we stop at Sam and Mavis', you will have to occupy Mavis for a while, and I will get Sam to help me feed it to his pigs, we did eat all the ham rolls didn't we? It seems a shame about all that good food, but it is better than the look on Mary's face when we bring half of it back, and of course we will eventually eat the food."

The casual reference to the pig's fate reminded Abby how pragmatic country people were about animals. "How do you know that I shall be able to keep Mavis occupied?"

"There's no problem there. I shall announce that I need to talk to Roger about the Lower Penny Acre, and Mavis will promptly march you inside for a debrief."

"I would ask two questions. One, what or who is Lower Penny Acre; and two, what is a debrief?"

"The answer to your first question is a pasture down by the river," James answered. "Two, a debriefing, a question-and-answer session on what has happened today; Mavis asking the questions and you, doing the answering."

"Are your movements of so much interest?"

"Oh yes, to Mavis they are very much of interest." He had a big smile on his face.

Abby had become used to the friendly curiosity of people living in the valley and gradually as the import of his words reached her, she too began to smile.

"Should I embellish the story a little? Descriptions of passionate scenes in the quarry or merely a little innocent hand-holding?"

"I don't somehow think that Mavis would believe anything like that, but a little innocent hand-holding would go down well."

"Damn and I always wanted to be a femme fatale."

"Oh I'm quite sure you could be that."

"Thank you, kind Sir, I'm sure you meant that as a compliment."

He grinned. "Perhaps I did."

James and Abby left the track some way before the river crossing and struck out through the fields, which took them to Gallow Farm. Abby was surprised that there was no reception until they had walked the horses into the yard. Roger was the first to appear, and upon seeing them, shouted in the direction of a small cottage, standing a few yards away from the farmhouse.

"Mum! Dad! Mr. James and Miss Tregonney are here." He walked over and held Jason's reins while Abby dismounted. Abby realised that she had met Roger before, one evening at the Combe Inn, without knowing that he was Sam's son.

"Hello, Roger, sorry to drop in on you unannounced."

"Unannounced?" His voice was incredulous. "Mum saw you going up the track earlier today, and has been on tenterhooks ever since, wondering if you would come by, needless to say all the best China has been got out, and washed, just in case. Dad has been going around like someone with a secret all day, as if he knew you were likely to call in."

Roger was not allowed to say anymore as Mavis came rushing out, wiping her hands on a pinafore, which she was trying to take off at the same time. "Abby, Mr. James, it's so nice you could drop by, come in, don't stand there, you will have some tea won't you?"

"Hello, Mavis, yes I would love a cup of tea." James winked at Abby behind Mavis' back. "Mavis, I would like to have a chat with Roger about Lower Penny, may I join you in a minute?"

"Business, business, it's all you men ever think about." She looked at James accusingly, "I hope you haven't been boring this young lady with talk of farming and cattle all day?"

"Would I dare?"

"Humph, I wouldn't put it past you. Now come along, Abby, and I'll put the kettle on." Abby looked at James who was grinning, and shrugged her shoulders, then followed Mavis who had set off at a determined pace for the cottage.

Abby caught her up, "Don't you live in the Farmhouse?"

"No, Love, when Sam handed the farm over to Roger, we moved into the cottage. It's much more comfortable than that draughty place, and big enough for the two of us. The farmhouse is a family home, Roger and Val can get on with their lives without Sam and me cluttering the place up."

They entered the cottage through the back door, straight into a well-kept and modern kitchen. Wooden fitted units lined two of the walls with a worktop running almost the whole length. Set into the worktop against the window wall was a double sink and drainer. A large scrubbed-top table dominated the centre of the room.

"Now I'm sure you will want to wash your hands, there's a bathroom just through there, to the right." Abby smiled, she would indeed like to 'wash her hands,' even following Mary's advice about drinking, had not prevented a certain discomfort on the ride down the valley. Mavis, like all women, would be aware of the priorities.

Refreshed, she joined Mavis in the kitchen, where the kettle was just coming to the boil. Her hostess was busy setting out cups, saucers, milk-jug, sugar bowl, and various plates all of it lavishly decorated with Acanthus scrolls and leaves, picked out in a dark blue. "Would you like to sit in here, or shall we go through to the sitting room?"

Abby eyed the ladder-back chairs, which were set round the table, each seat was covered with a cushion tied on with strings at the back corners, after the hard saddle, they looked very comfortable. "In here would be fine."

Mavis smiled. "Oh good, I'm much happier sitting at the table, sit yourself down, don't wait on ceremony." Abby sat. "Now," said Mavis, "how has your day been?"

Abby smiled inwardly. "I have really enjoyed myself. The valley is beautiful. James was right, the best way to see it is on horseback. Mary packed us a superb picnic and James even brought a bottle of wine, which was lovely. He's been the perfect gentleman all day."

"Oh," said Mavis in a slightly disappointed tone.

"We walked into the old quarry and he had to hold my hand when the ground was difficult."

"Oh," said Mavis in a much warmer tone.

"He took me out on the viaduct."

"He did what?" asked Mavis in a voice that threatened retribution.

"He took great care of me all the while and I got some great photos."

"He's no business taking you out there, that thing is dangerous, anything could have happened."

"Please, Mavis, don't go shouting at him, he's looked after me and I have enjoyed his company."

Mavis's face cleared. "Well I suppose no harm's done, and if you enjoyed yourself, that's all that matters."

Abby felt a little guilty, as she had been teasing Mavis in the most gentle way, but Mavis appeared not to recognise the tease. She poured, asking Abby how she took her tea, and after pouring one for herself, poured one other, with just a splash of milk, and one spoon of sugar.

"Whose tea is that?" asked Abby.

"That's for Mr. James."

"You know how he likes his tea then?"

Mavis nodded. "Yes, I've made many a cup of tea for him, especially a few years ago, when he came back. He would come up here, and he and Sam would talk for hours."

"You said when he came back, would that be after he left the army?"

"Yes, Love, you know about that then."

"Only that he's been in the army and went to the Falklands. I understand he got some decoration."

Mavis said nothing for a while, as if making up her mind whether to say anything or not. Eventually she seemed to decide. "Well it should come from James himself, but as he is reluctant to talk about it, I'll tell you what little I know. He joined the army in the late nineteen seventies. He got into the Parachute Regiment and they were sent to the Falklands as part of the Task Force. James was at Goose Green, have you heard about that?"

"Only a little. Wasn't a colonel or somebody killed there?"

"Yes, they called him Colonel H. James was there. I don't know what happened but James got some medal, I'm not really sure which one though. As soon as they got back, he resigned his commission and came home to Lyney. He was in a bad way, that's when he would come up here and talk with Sam. I think that James felt guilty about surviving, when so many good men died. It's taken him a good few years to get over it."

"Well I'm glad he survived." For the second time in a day, Abby spoke without thinking, but as so often when that happens, the mind's truth is contained within the words. Mavis kept the look of pleasure from her face, and busied herself with topping up the teapot with hot water. Her pleasure did not come from congratulating herself; indeed, she would have difficulty in expressing her thoughts. Perhaps it was because it was ingrained in her country way of life, the continuity of life. Men did still go away to war, and did get hurt in more ways than just physical injuries. The majority would come home, and home could almost complete the healing process. A good woman by his side, who would care for, and nurture him, was the only thing that would finish the job. James had a few girlfriends, daughters of locals, but none had been more than passing acquaintances. James had shown none of them the interest that Abby created, and certainly none had the privilege of riding out with him for a day. Perhaps this was the woman who could complete the process for James.

Abby wanted to know a lot more, but it was obvious that Mavis either would not, or, could not tell her. Nonetheless it proved to her that an assessment she had made much earlier about James was true; there was a lot more to him than the flippant, glib-face he showed the world.

The subject of these meanderings walked into the kitchen at that moment, with Sam close behind. Mavis looked up, and said wearily to Sam, "I suppose you will want a cup as well?"

"That would be nice, dear." James winked at Abby, as an indication that the manoeuvre was successful. Mavis caught the wink, but believed that it was a sign of their growing closeness. She indicated the cup that she had poured earlier for James.

"Your tea is there but it's likely lukewarm by now, I can make you another cup if you like."

James shook his head. "It's wet and warm, Mavis, and that's all I need."

Sam sat next to Abby, and said, "I understand you have met Woody." Mavis was a little put out, as Abby hadn't mentioned this to her.

"Yes we did, James told me a little about him, a strange character."

"Oh aye," replied Sam, "I have never known anyone manage to keep their life story as secret as he has, and there's some around here who are better than the Gestapo at winkling out people's secrets." Abby could not help but giggle, as she was well aware to whom Sam was referring, James had a broad smile on his face, and Mavis looked at Sam as if she couldn't for the life of her recall anyone who would fit his description. Sam then said to her. "You want to know what a hurdle is?"

"Yes, I do. Woody mentioned them and James acted as if it was some dark secret."

James was affronted. "Hey, hold on, I said I would show you one when we got here."

Abby stuck her tongue out at him. "Whatever, he wasn't prepared to tell me what it is, will you?"

Sam laughed. "If you've finished your tea, you come with me, and I'll show you a hurdle wattle."

Abby finished her tea, and with Sam, she left the cottage. He led the way across to the barn. In the corner there was a stack of what appeared at first glance to be small five-bar gates. Sam pointed to them. "There you go," he said, "they are hurdles." Abby looked closely and decided that they couldn't be five-bar gates, as the end and centre posts were too long, reaching down below the bottom rail by some eighteen inches to a point. The wood of which they were made hadn't been planed, just stripped of its bark.

"What are they used for?"

"When you want to make a temporary fold for the sheep, you can just stick it in the ground to make an enclosure. They're light, easy to carry and fix. The sheep could knock them down as easy as anything, but they're too stupid to understand that."

"And Woody makes these?"

"Yes, it's an old country craft when you thin out the woodland, keep the long straight stems, let them dry out, and use them for a hurdle. Years ago they would use the stems when they was green to make a wattle that was used in building."

"Of course, wattle and daub!"

"You've got it, it was slightly different as it wasn't jointed, but woven, it all depends on the thickness of the wood you've got, but it's still a hurdle-wattle."

James came up to them as they were leaving the barn. "Now you know what a hurdle is. It's easy when you see one, but hard to explain."

"Yes O.K., James, I forgive you."

James looked at his watch. "I don't think we are going to cover the rest of the track today. Shall we just ride down as far as the station? We can do the rest another day." Mavis had reminded him that it probably wasn't the wisest thing for Abby to ride too much as she hadn't ridden that much before. James hadn't really given that a thought, as he was enjoying the day so much. Mavis was encouraged by the look on his face when he realised his unthinking behaviour. Abby was relieved at this suggestion, she knew that she would suffer for this day, but to her, it was worth it.

"That's a good idea, shall we go now?" James nodded and went off to get the horses. Roger had watered them and they had been resting in a stall.

Mavis came out to see them off and Abby wished her goodbye with a kiss on the cheek, Sam waited also, not wanting to miss out, his face bright red with embarrassment, but not wishing to forgo the pleasure of a kiss from Abby.

CHAPTER THIRTEEN

Once back on the track, they retraced their steps of the morning, fording the river once more, and then followed the embankment over the river meadows with the tall mound of Huish Coppice looming ever closer. The cutting between Huish and the village was in shadow at this time of day, the nettle growth much more dense. Abby was surprised when she spotted a tall post, a rusted iron ladder still connected at the top, standing at an angle by the side of the formation. Combe Lyney up distant. Suddenly the purpose of the day came back to her. She was back in her grandfather's territory. Within a few hundred yards the station came into view, they were out of the cutting now, riding along a small embankment, past the spot where she had crossed the line that first time going up to Huish Coppice, and then riding into the station itself.

James had not said too much during this short ride, now he rested his arms on the pommel and looked around. "I have seen this place hundreds of times and still for the life of me, cannot understand why British Railways, or Rail Track, whatever they are called now, has not done something with this site. You would have thought they would have sold it to someone, or even offered it to my father."

A sudden memory came into Abby's mind, what was it that Mr. Brasher had said about the way the land was obtained? A way-leave, and if the land ceased to be used for the purpose of the railway, it would revert to the original owner. "I believe British Railways couldn't sell it, because they didn't own it," she offered.

"Pardon?"

"They didn't own it."

"Then who does own the land?"

"You do." There was a silence.

"I do?" James asked with surprise.

"Yes."

"How do you work that out?"

"Well it was something that Mr. Brasher said, about the land being made available to the railway in what is called a way-leave. In essence, it is a leasing system that is self-renewing unless the railway ceases to use the land, in which case it reverts back to the original owner, and that happens to be you."

"How sure of this are you?"

"Well, Mr. Brasher seems to have done his research very thoroughly, and had looked up all the relevant Acts of Parliament, so I don't think he would be wrong on this. You will probably have to consult your solicitor to have the land register checked, but as no one else has laid claim in the meantime, I can't see a problem with it."

James surveyed his restored land with a jaundiced eye. "Much as I am happy to have the situation resolved, if it is as you say; I can't say that it will mean that much to me. The tenants don't want it, except as a convenient track between fields, so it won't bring me any extra income. Then of course, the revenue will view it as an asset, and will attempt to tax it as such."

It had been a day for Abby to speak without thinking, and she continued in that vein. "You could sell it to me. Well at least this little bit here about the station." Her brain then caught up with her mouth. "No, you won't want to sell, will you, it's land, you will never sell the land."

James was grateful to Abby for seeing the difficulty and letting him off the hook. "Why would you want this?"

Abby had spoken with a gut feeling, an emotional reaction, and she thought for a while before replying, clarifying her thoughts as she did. "I said that I might like to settle in Combe Lyney and I have loved this place; felt an emotional attachment to it ever since I first came here. It just seems right. This was where my grandfather lived, and died; it's where Mum was brought up and I feel somehow that by coming home, granddad's spirit will find some peace, and be happy." She stopped; embarrassed by her words, fearful that James would mock. He didn't.

"That makes sense to me. The valley gives me that feeling, being here, and maintaining the system that my ancestors started. Yes I can understand why you would want to live here." He paused. "I'm glad you understand that I cannot sell the land; that is if it's mine to sell. However, I would be prepared to lease it to you on a very long term, if that will make you happy. Having said that, I should warn you that the place is falling down, and will take a load of capital to set it right."

Abby nodded, now the business brain was working. "What sort of term would we be looking at, and what would the rent be?"

James gave a short dry laugh. "I don't think that sitting here on horseback is the right time or place to discuss such business. We should sit down somewhere quiet and talk about it over a drink. Shall we say tomorrow evening at the Combe Inn? Then we've both had a chance to think about it, and what conditions we are prepared to accept."

"And this is the man who said he hadn't inherited his father's acumen," Abby taunted him gently with his own words. "But will the Inn be quiet enough?"

"Oh yes, if we sit down in the lounge with our heads close together, Mary would crucify anyone who dared to interrupt us. Mavis, of course, would prefer hanging, drawing and quartering."

"So you have noticed that as well."

The grin returned to James' face. "Don't be upset, it's just that they believe it's not right for anyone to be single, and happy."

They turned the horses, homewards, riding back down the formation until the public footpath that crossed the track for Huish Coppice. Here, James turned them off the formation and they took to the fields, riding through a herd of cattle, some of which looked incuriously at them before moving slowly out of their way. James unlatched the gate of the field, and they moved through into a meadow, bright with rippling field grasses, adorned with shades of purple, yellow, red and white. Many hued butterflies fluttered busily over the kaleidoscope of colour.

"What kind of field is this?" Abby asked James.

"A meadow," he replied. "It hasn't been grazed this year but it has been dunged. Next year the cattle will love all this."

"What are all these flowers?"

"The purple is knapweed, the red is betony; I think the yellow is hay-rattle, and all the white is saxifrage, and actually they are weeds or meadow grasses."

"What funny names, and you know them all, I'm impressed. I've never seen a meadow like this before."

James thought before answering Abby's observation. "Modern farming is all about artificial fertilisers and pesticides. Spray the field with those, and within a year or two, all of these meadow grasses will be gone."

"So why haven't you done that?"

"Economics. The market today is so competitive and is only viable if you produce in bulk, to sell at the lowest unit price. The West Country farmer cannot create huge fields that are worked with the minimum labour. Here in this valley, we have even less chance of creating viable units. So there is little point in adding to your costs, when the unit price the market is paying is often below your production cost anyway. We still use the old ways of fertilising."

"The old ways?"

"Yes, the old ways, dung my dear, dung. It's cheap and plentiful."

"If the market price is below your production costs, are you making losses?"

"No, most of the tenants break even, or make a small profit, but that is by only producing in quantities that they know can be sold locally. Economies of scale work both ways."

"That's not very business-like."

James made a face. "Do you really want to end a great day discussing profit and loss?"

Abby shook her head. "No, you're right, it's not the time to talk business, besides I am finished with all of that for the moment. What else can we talk about?"

"Well, I was going to ask you if you would like to come to the Hunt Ball later this year?"

Abby was dumbstruck. "The Hunt Ball, I didn't know you were a huntsman."

James could detect a slight distaste in her voice. "I'm not. But I allow them to hunt on my land, so they send me an invitation. The farmers support the hunt though, and if you have any reservations about that, talk to Sam, or some of the other tenants, see what they have to say." James' tone was a little testy, as if here was a townie adopting a high moral position about something of which she had little knowledge.

Abby heard the unspoken message and backed off quickly. She remonstrated with herself for allowing her distaste of hunting to show. James hadn't said as much, but his tone of voice had hinted, that judging people before knowing all the facts was a recipe for ill-will. She was discovering that life in the country was lived very differently to life in the cities and that attitudes shaped by the paved streets, and high-rise buildings had to be adjusted accordingly. She changed tack quickly.

"What sort of event is this? Is it very dressy?"

"You could say that," replied James. "White tie and tails, pink for the members of the hunt and every lady trying to outshine the rest." Abby was thinking. She would have to get a dress for the occasion, in her thoughts the word "dress" was written in capitals and illuminated. She would have to enlist Toni's help to find the right shop.

"Who will be there?"

"The Lord Lieutenant, some right honourables, and a knight or two."

"Oh so this is society."

"Definitely, well society as it is down here. God knows why they ask me. So will you come?"

"James, I accept your invitation with pleasure."

They had arrived back at the Inn. James dismounted and held the horses while Abby slid down, something she did with a little groan.

James looked concerned. "A few aches?" he asked.

"None that a hot bath will not cure," she replied, "James it has been tremendous, I have thoroughly enjoyed the day, thank you."

"I have enjoyed it too, and don't forget we still have the rest of the track to cover." He had a mischievous grin on his face. "Perhaps when you are ready to get in the saddle again..." He left the rest of the question in the air.

"I'll let you know, it won't be too long, rest assured of that." Abby smiled.

Mary came out of the Inn at her usual pace. "Hello, you two, back earlier than I thought. Did you enjoy yourselves? Mavis called and told me you had dropped in for tea. Are you going to have a cup before you leave?" This, directed exclusively at James, who was emptying the saddlebags of the lunch packs. Mary was watching hawk-eyed and seems satisfied that everything had been consumed.

"No. Thanks all the same, Mary, I shall take these two back to their stables. Liz will be up there by now, wanting to curry them and feed them. Perhaps I shall see you later?" he said to Abby.

"Yes, possibly, but I shall be standing at the bar tonight." They laughed together, as he remounted Cassie, and taking Jason's rein rode out of the yard.

Mary turned to Abby. "Will you want a cup of tea?" she asked.

"Yes please, Mary, a good strong one, and then if I may, is there a bath I can use." There was a shower but no bath in Abby's room.

"Of course, you can use mine, and I'll get you some radox salts as well. Sit down and I'll get you the tea. May as well have it out here, the weather has been so good today."

Abby composed herself for the inevitable barrage of questions. She was resigned to the fact that Mavis and Mary were intent on pushing James and her together, and found amusement in the situation. Not that Abby was averse to James' company, it was very pleasant; but Abby had suspicions that James, like her, would act contrary if too much pressure was brought to bear. Perhaps a word with Sam would help, before the interference created an atmosphere.

Mary returned with a tray of tea, typically she had added some scones, jam and cream.

Abby went on the attack. "Mary, after all the food you gave us in the packed lunch, how could you possibly expect me to eat anything else."

Mary just smiled. "Well you may have felt like something, so I brought it just in case."

The tea was poured and Mary sat expectantly, waiting for Abby to begin. Abby kept Mary waiting. Taking time to sip her tea and savour the sensation of sitting still for a while. She could see the frustration on Mary's face, so she eventually began to talk about the day, describing everything that she had seen, everything that they had done in minute detail. This was not what Mary wanted to hear, and had to be satisfied when Abby told her about walking in the quarry, and James taking her hand. That it was to help Abby over a rough part, would not count later in Mary's recollection.

The longer she sat, the more her aching thighs demanded attention. She reminded Mary of the offer of a hot bath, and soon she was relaxing in the warm scented waters. With time to indulge, she took her mind back over the day. It seemed that with everything she learned, the more questions there were to be answered. One question had been answered, that of where she should live, and that answer had come without thought or discussion. The idea of re-opening the station house as a home; had come on the spur of the moment, yet the prospect filled her with pleasurable anticipation. It was no silly flight of fancy to believe that there was a strong emotional bond directing her plans; she didn't need to ask if her mother or grandfather would approve, if there were an afterlife, she was sure that they were watching and urging this course of action.

Her mind turned as mind's do with no logical link, to the information that life in the valley may seem idyllic, but not profitable. She was well aware that farming in the U.K. was problematical, but this had always been a detached fact, viewed from a distance in the metropolitan manner. Now it was in her face. These people had welcomed her, and made her a friend. Their hurt was becoming her hurt; although she did not for a moment believe that there was anything she could do, except perhaps understand. She would ask Sam smiling at the thought. It was fate that always had her turn to Sam for knowledge, the man who had known her grandfather, who was becoming a surrogate for the man she had never known. It was interesting that it was to Sam that James had turned, when he needed a voice of comfort.

Then there was James, oh dear, she was starting to look forward to seeing him, enjoying his company; never feeling uncomfortable, even in those periods of silence that would always occur when two people spent some time together. She didn't have the need to fill the void with inconsequential chatter, and neither did

James. That was something she liked about him. His flippant and self-deprecating manner didn't annoy her, and she was quite prepared to banter in the same way; but because he never took it to excess, the human, caring side of him was revealed, never far from the surface. None of her few friendships had inspired any feeling of happiness in anticipation of meeting again. Was this the beginning of something more? The cooling water brought her mind's monologue to an end. She returned to her room to find that Mary had anticipated her sudden wish with another pot of tea, freshly brewed on the side table, steam rising gently from the spout. She drank a cup, standing at the window, before letting the fatigue of the day lead her to the bed.

Abby did indeed spend most of that evening in the bar, standing, and endured with good humour the gentle comments regarding her presumed saddle soreness. In an easy way she was discovering, without realising it, the social skills she lacked. If she had examined the question logically, she would have realised that, these people who would be described as simple by urbanites, had much to teach in this area. They didn't form cliques that excluded others, but moved easily from one to another, joining in topics of conversation, and adding humour or pertinent comment effortlessly. She noted James' arrival, and how he would stop and exchange greetings and some comment with almost everyone in the bar, as he made his way towards her, the journey taking some ten minutes or so, to cover just ten yards. Abby had asked Jack to set up a drink for James, so it appeared on the counter as if by magic. He picked up the glass and took a large sip.

"That's good. Good evening, Abby, I won't enquire after your disposition, I gather that plenty of comments have been made already."

"You could say that, but I had a long soak in a hot bath, and that seems to have worked wonders."

He grinned. "Well let me know when you want to finish the exploration."

"Give me a couple of days, and I'll be raring to go."

"Look," he said quietly, "about the Hunt Ball, I may have bounced that upon you, and you may want to re-consider. If you do, I can understand, you may not be comfortable with a load of people with whose leisure pursuits you do not agree." Abby shook her head.

"I do want to go, that is if you still want to take me."

"Of course I do."

"Then I will be delighted to go. But can I ask you a question?"

"Yes."

"Why don't you hunt?"

"It just doesn't appeal to me."

"Is that all?" Abby was getting to know James, and realised that his answer was a palliative, designed to prevent controversy.

He looked a little uncomfortable. "I can agree with the necessity of the hunt, I just don't want to join in. I've seen enough blood to satisfy me."

You're talking about the Falklands."

"Oh you know about that, I suppose I can thank Mavis for that. Yes, that has a lot to do with it."

Abby nodded. "I cannot understand what it was like, but I can appreciate the sentiment; and I'll reserve judgement on hunting until I have spoken with Sam."

She was pleased that he felt he could trust her sufficiently to be honest about his feelings. "Now about the station, what sort of a deal are you going to offer?"

James looked aghast. "Abby, Abby, slow down. This is the country; everything takes time here. We don't go rushing into things. Besides I haven't even thought about it." The truth was that he had, and was very keen to have Abby here in the valley. His first thought to offer the property at a rent she could not refuse, he had rejected; knowing that her business background would not allow her to agree the first offer, and in addition, he didn't want her to see how keen he was that she should stay. Abby was disappointed but concealed her chagrin behind a smile.

"O.K. we'll talk about that later." Mary who had been eavesdropping whenever her duties behind the bar would allow, had only caught snippets of the chat, but had heard enough to put two and two together and make five. She was elated, as she was certain that

James had invited Abby to the Hunt Ball, but she didn't understand the reference to the station. Not that it mattered; this was something she would have to share with Mavis immediately.

Choosing a quiet moment, she left Jack to cope and hurried upstairs to their private quarters. It seemed an age before Mavis answered the phone, and when she did, Mary blurted out her news without the normal preamble that they would have shared. Mavis, like Mary, was thrilled by the news of the Hunt Ball, and again like Mary, could not decipher the reference to the station.

"Perhaps James is trying to buy it back from whoever owns it now," Mary ventured. Mavis thought about this.

"That could be a possibility, but for what reason? The land has been unused since they closed the railway, and it's not as if James can rent it to anyone. Why should he spend money on buying it if he has no purpose for it?"

"Well perhaps he has heard something that we don't know about. I mean could the council be planning to build a new road?"

"I shouldn't think so. After all there's little enough traffic on the road through the village anyway, so why build a new one?" The discussion went on for some time but no conclusion was reached. Mary came down to the bar to find that Abby had gone to her room, and that James was now making his way out, stopping to talk with various groups, in the same way that he had made his entrance. The mystery would remain unsolved for the moment.

Abby broke the news that James had invited her to the Hunt Ball to Toni the next morning. This prompted an early coffee break in order that this could be discussed in greater detail. "My, you are honoured, James doesn't normally attend. In fact I don't think he has ever attended." Abby was equally delighted to hear that Toni would be there.

"My father would not miss it for the world," Toni told Abby. "It's golden opportunity to rub shoulders with all the great and the good, and network outrageously." Abby had got the impression that Toni was never too impressed by her father's motives.

"Oh good, at least there will be one friendly face there."

"So you don't count James as a friendly face?"

"Of course, but you know what I mean, a friendly face besides James." Abby moved on to the most pressing business.

"I am going to need something to wear, could you recommend a good shop?"

"Not around here, you will have to go to Taunton, or Exeter for something good. It does depend on what you want to spend."

"Well I suppose if I saw something I really liked, up to seven or eight hundred."

Toni sat there with her mouth open. "How much?"

"Don't you think that will be enough?"

"More than enough, but if you are thinking of spending that sort of money, you may even have to go to Bristol."

Abby thought about it. "Look, I could do with your help. Is there any chance you could come with me?"

"That's no problem. One advantage of having a councillor for a father, is that I can get time off for civic duties, and this will count as a civic duty."

"What? Helping me buy a dress?"

"Yes, as I am accompanying dad to the ball as his escort, my going to buy a dress for the occasion will count as civic duty. He doesn't have to know that the dress is not for me, any way, I might even buy one, but not for that sort of money."

"Well if you think it's all right. When do you think we can go?"

"The best day would be a Monday; the shops are never as busy; so we will have plenty of time. I think we should go to Taunton first, then Exeter; and if we have no joy at either of those, then we will have to go to Bristol. But we won't be able to get there the same day." Abby hesitated before saying that Monday week would be best, she would have opted for this Monday, but there was a possibility that she and James would be riding again, and that was not to be missed. With this decided, they parted, exchanging telephone numbers as they did, Toni to return to work, and Abby to return to Combe Lyney.

The atmosphere at the Combe Inn that evening was of quiet curiosity, as James came in, and instead of making his usual chatty progress through the bar, joined Abby in the lounge immediately. Sam was a little put out, as he was enjoying his chats with Abby, but Mary made it plain that he should not interfere; even though she had no idea why they had closeted themselves so quickly. For whatever reason, she would encourage their closeness, knowing that Mavis would back her to the hilt.

James started the negotiation. "Have you thought seriously about this? I wouldn't want to hold you to something said on the spur of the moment."

"Yes I have, and the more I think about it the more I like the idea. But have you checked that you do actually own the land?"

"I phoned my family solicitor early today, he seems to think that what you say is correct, he even phoned back later to say that his records would appear to confirm the way-leave, at the same time apologising profusely for not having brought this to my notice before. He will need to check with the Land Registry, and that will take some time, but it would all seem to be above-board. So what do you think you will do with the property?"

"I'm not sure yet, except that I want to convert the house to live in. I am toying with the idea of restoring the station to how it would have looked when my grandfather was working there, but that's just a whim at the moment."

"O.K. First, I am sorry that I can't sell, but I know you do understand. So what I was thinking was a lease for ninety-nine years, at a ground rent of two hundred and ninety pounds per acre. We can do a survey and decide later how many acres you want. For the station building, I would be looking at a fully repairing lease for nineteen hundred per annum. I would also write into the contract a clause to the effect that should I, or my successors, ever decide to sell the land, you would have a first refusal to the property. Now you will have to realise that there is a tremendous amount of work and expense that will be required, and in view of that I have tried to keep the rents down to a minimum."

Abby looked pensive, trying to keep the look of delight off her face. Compared with the prices she was used to; and she knew it was an unfair comparison; this was a steal. She knew however that she would have to negotiate, or James would think it too easy.

"I would imagine that the price per acre you quote is for agricultural land," she reckoned that he would have simply looked at the rents he was charging to his other tenants. "As you yourself said the other day, the land is useless, except as an unofficial right of way for the farmers, correct? So it is not agricultural land."

James was astonished; this was not the discussion he had anticipated. "Well no, but the rent is below that which would be usual for agricultural land anyway."

Abby let that go for the moment. She had always found it a useful tactic to change the point of attack rather than looking for a compromise immediately. "You ask for nineteen hundred for the building. Is that just the station building, or would it be all the buildings on the site?"

"Just the station building."

"And the platform?"

"Obviously the platform."

"I should want to take the other buildings, certainly the station house, and possibly the goods shed and the other house, would you be prepared to look at a package deal?"

"The station house possibly. But there could be a little bit of a problem. Since this new situation has arisen, it occurred to me that I may have a use for the goods shed, so I wouldn't want to commit on that now. The small house is in a very poor condition, I don't think you could do anything with it except knock it down."

Abby had to admire this tactic, by giving the goods shed a possible use, he had diverted her from asking for special terms on what in essence was an unwanted building.

"What about water and drainage?"

"There should be a well for water, and I suspect that there is a septic tank for waste. You don't need to pay for water, but there is a sewerage charge for emptying the tank."

"Right, I will pay you the nineteen hundred, but I would like you to include the station house as well." James set to thinking about this. Abby continued, "Go on, James," she urged him. "After all, you will not get any rent off the place otherwise. And the house is essentially part of the station." James was going to deal anyway, but put on an air of sufferance.

"O.K., Abby, you have a deal."

"Would you be prepared to waive the buildings' rent until such time as the building was fit for occupation?" Now James had to think.

"I could go along with that."

"What do I do about power?"

"I am sure that SWEB will be happy to connect you, the power lines run along the road anyway."

"The ground rent, James, it is a little higher than I would have thought, particularly as the land is in effect useless, what do you say to two hundred and twenty pounds per acre? Don't forget I shall be improving your property."

James groaned. "I'll settle on two hundred and fifty, and buy you a drink to seal the deal." He shook his head sorrowfully, "Where did you learn to negotiate?"

"It came with my territory, James. Now mine is a vodka and tonic, do we shake hands as well?"

She offered her hand.

James took it and shook, but he had a grin on his face, that Abby knew spelt trouble.

"That grin tells me I've missed something. Come on, out with it, where's the catch."

"You will need change of use permission from the Council, they don't negotiate."

Abby suddenly realised that she should have included that as part of James' responsibility. His smile broadened. "You will meet some of the local councillors at the ball, so if you charm the right people, I am sure that it won't be any problem."

"Oh I see; do I have to grease a few palms as well?"

"No, nothing as serious as that, just a smile in the right direction, a little flattery, and you'll be home and dry."

"I'll do my best, now where is that drink you promised me?"

James left for the bar and Abby, looking over her shoulder, saw Sam looking curiously in her direction, she beckoned him over. "I was going to come and see you earlier, but Mary reckoned that you should be left alone. If Mary and my missus are up to something, I shall get rather upset."

"No, Sam, James and I had some business to discuss, and it looks as if you are not going to get rid of me that easily, I am going to take the old station and house, and convert it to live in." The effect on Sam was tremendous, his face lit up, and the biggest smile split his face in two.

"By golly, Girl, that's the best news I have had in years, I'm so happy. Let me buy you a drink to celebrate, oh just wait until Mavis hears." James returned with the drinks. Sam took one look at the drinks and said, "That's no way to celebrate news like this, Jack's got some nice champagne, that's what we need." He was off, leaving Abby and James looking at their suddenly redundant drinks. Moments later, the voices at the bar rose to a crescendo as Sam obviously had imparted this news. Mary came rushing over with tears just starting in her eyes. She flung her arms around Abby, and burbled words, which appeared to convey her happiness.

Then standing back, she accused Abby of not being content with staying at the Inn. "Mary, I have been very happy here; and I will stay for quite some time, if you'll have me, as it will take a long time to get the station fit for occupation."

Mary was somewhat mollified. "Of course we will have you, there's no question of that."

Sam had caught Abby saying that it would take some time to get the station ready. "You are right about that, the first thing will be to open it up, and get Harry Webster to put his terriers in."

Abby looked confused. "What would that do?" .

"Terriers will clear out any vermin in next to no time," James answered.

"Vermin? You mean rats!"

"Not necessarily, but it's best to be sure."

This information gave Abby a little fright, and her expression gave her fears away. Sam leaned over and told her not to worry. "Rats come with humans, they live off our waste, be it food or anything else. I would imagine that in London, there are more rats than you will ever find in the country, and I don't think that the old station has any at all, as nobody has lived there for years. Harry will be grateful though, for the chance to give his dogs some exercise." James felt that he had to put a stop to the euphoria and planning, which might be a little premature.

He coughed and cleared his throat. "Let's not get too carried away, as Abby is aware that all this does depend on the Land Registry recognising that I own the property." Mary's mind went back to the conversation she had overheard, and all the pieces fell into place.

She was not going to let a little thing like the Land Registry get in the way of her perception of the future. Therefore, ignoring James' warning, she went full steam ahead. "I can't imagine how you will turn that place into a home, but rest assured that Mavis and I will help. We can make it all comfy and pretty for you." Sam's eyes rose skywards in their sockets, and he looked at Abby with an expression of 'told you so.'

Those who had been in the Combe Inn that evening took the news home with them, passed on to spouses and families, the gossip travelled along telephone wires, and by word of mouth, so that within twenty-four hours almost everyone in the valley was in the possession of the facts. This was not earth-shattering news, indeed some in the valley had never seen Abby, but knew of her, and in an area where little occurred to disturb the even tenor of life, any event like this would give rise to intense conjecture, with embroidery and trimmings to suit whoever was discussing the subject at the time. It would make no difference to their lives; but it was something new, and would in the course of the next few days be dissected thoroughly, and examined from every angle for implications that could affect them. Mary and Mavis together assumed an air that bespoke prior knowledge, as if they personally were the movers and shakers that had brought this about. Sam chuckled inwardly to himself at seeing them fluffing their feathers. Mavis had swept into the Inn the following evening to question Abby closely about her plans, and involved herself automatically in the execution. Abby realised that without help, she would have difficulty in fulfilling this project, and pragmatically allowed Mavis and Mary to contribute; yet at the same time was aware that without careful handling, the scheme would be taken away from her completely. She was grateful that shortly after she was able to get Sam to herself.

"Well, Girl, you have certainly put the fox amongst the chickens, haven't you?"

Abby shook her head. "I'm amazed at how people here attach so much importance to it."

"No, it's not that. It's something happening, something different. This little valley of ours is peaceful, sometimes a bit boring, as nothing ever happens. Each day goes by the same as yesterday, and tomorrow will be the same as today. The only things that change are the seasons, and our work patterns with them. We don't have traffic accidents, bank hold-ups, burglaries; these things happen elsewhere. So when something like this comes along, the whole valley is livened."

"Well they shouldn't get too excited about it, it depends on James getting confirmation that he owns the land."

"That's one thing I don't understand. How can that be?"

"Well, it is all to do with how the land was made available to the Railway. It would appear that the Mr. Comberford of the time, didn't sell the land, merely leased it. So when they closed the railway, the land came back to the Comberfords. I suppose the original papers were lost over the years, so James didn't know about this."

"Well I don't care how this has come about, if it keeps you here in the valley. I, for one, shall be pleased." Abby blushed, not quite as deep a colour as Sam would, but a blush nonetheless.

"That's nice of you to say, Sam, but I don't know what I am going to do for work. I can live easily enough, but I have to do something or I'll go mad."

Sam heard the words 'I can live easily enough,' but refrained from comment. He decided also, that he wouldn't say anything to Mavis; she had enough to fuel her speculation, without him adding a log to the fire.

"Sam, I upset James a little when we talked about hunting. He said talk to you about it."

"What do you want to know?"

"Well everyone that I know back in London believes that it is harsh and cruel, and without thinking about it too much, I probably held the same opinion."

"There's nothing I can say that will help you. People have these opinions, and no matter what evidence they have to the contrary, cannot change them. There are no rights or wrongs to the situation; but there are practical reasons, which like it or not have to be thought about."

"Such as?"

"Protecting our livelihood."

"But surely a fox cannot endanger your livelihood?"

"It's such a small thing, isn't it? It's got a cute little face, and eyes that seem to twinkle, and it reminds everyone of that nice little dog they have at home, so cuddly, and obedient. Well, a fox is not a dog, and you cannot train it, because it's a wild animal, and if you tried to cuddle it; you would probably be bitten. Anti-tetanus jabs, not to mention a possibility of rabies, would be the next thing on your agenda then. That cute little thing will go into a chicken run at night and kill ten or twenty birds."

Abby interrupted Sam, "Why does it do that?"

"The chicken has a very basic nervous system. You can break its neck and even though dead, it will run away. The fox may think it hasn't killed the bird, so goes on to kill another, then another. It will only take one though. You may think that at the price of a chicken in your supermarket, that it isn't a great loss. Bear in mind though that that fox will do the same every night, and at the end of the week, a farmer could have lost fifty or sixty birds. That is about seventy pounds to him. If you were to lose seventy pounds every week, wouldn't you want to do something about it? If we could keep the hens in batteries it would solve the problem, but the government tells us that is cruel so it exposes the hens to an even greater cruelty, the fox. There's another thing, aA fox will chase sheep. A pregnant ewe, if she's chased, will sometimes abort, now that's fine for the fox, he's got a nice warm meal, which has cost the farmer something like ten pounds. Not a lot of money you might say, but a big sum to a bloke who works something like twelve hours a day, seven days a week, to get an income of eight thousand pounds a year. You are the one that knows about business here. Tell me, if you had a department that was making losses year on year, if you could do something that would turn it around, wouldn't you do it?"

"Well, yes, of course."

"If that process involved making people redundant; you would do that?"

"It's happening all the time."

"So it's all right to cast a man on the scrap heap, possibly never to work again, in the interests of making profits. But it's not all right for a farmer to try and keep his livelihood intact by culling an animal that could ruin him?"

"I don't think your comparison is completely fair but I'll let that go. What I would ask is, is it necessary to kill them in such a horrible way?"

Sam thought the comparison was fair, but wasn't going to challenge Abby. He addressed the topic of how the fox died. "Let me ask you a question in return. Do you like rats?"

Abby shuddered. "No, of course not."

"Well in that city of yours, there are more rats than ever we have in the country. So rats are your vermin. How do they go about getting rid of them?"

"They put poison down."

"Exactly, they put poison down. It's warfarin, which thins their blood to such an extent that they bleed to death. The rat dies in agony, a really horrible death, taking hours, and sometimes days; not to mention the cat or dog that might have picked up the bait inadvertently. But that's one of those things, isn't it? Because you don't want the rat living cheek by jowl with you, and it's dirty, it carries disease. So if something else suffers to rid you of the rat, tough. But the rat is only doing the job that nature intended it to do. You can put poison down in the city, because it will not affect other wildlife. We can't do that here. There's livestock, birds, other mammals, squirrels, rabbits, hares all of which could pick up the bait and suffer. You would be really upset if Mr. Brock the badger died, curled up in agony, for picking up a bait set for a fox."

Abby had to agree with that. "Couldn't you shoot them?" she asked.

"It would take a good shot to kill a fox running at close to thirty miles an hour, and the fox would know you were coming before you had got within half a mile of it, so he's not going to hang around.

You couldn't do it with a shotgun. You could use scatter, but you still have to get very close to it. A rifle would be better but we have to make a very good case to the magistrates for a rifle licence. The other problem would be that the fox would have to be sporting enough to come out in daylight, but they're sneaky, they're mainly nocturnal. Shooting at night with a shotgun or a rifle, heaven knows what would be hit. No, Abby, the only way to control the fox is with the weapon that nature gave us for the purpose, the dog. And the only way to control a pack of dogs is on horseback, because no man can run fast enough to keep up with a running fox, or a running dog. When the dogs catch the fox they behave with the instincts that nature gave them."

Abby nodded. Everything that Sam had said was logical. "It makes more sense when you explain it like that. But I still feel sorry for the fox with the way that the dogs tear them apart."

"I wish I could tell you that they die cleanly, they don't, but they do die quickly. There's one more thing, the hunt manages a kill about once in every two outings, and the fox that they kill is usually old or lame. That is the fox, which raids the chickens most often. A young fit fox will find plenty to eat without coming that close to man. Beside all this, tell me how many foxes do you see on the side of the road, killed by a car?"

"Quite a few."

"They don't all die quickly. And there are more foxes killed on the road, than by the hunt. But they don't ban cars, do they?"

"If this is all as necessary as you say, why is it that people want to stop the hunting?"

"Some hold a genuine belief that hunting is cruel, that I can respect, but others? I don't really know for sure, I can guess, but that is all it would be, a guess."

"Yes, well what's your guess?"

"Evening old scores, punishing people for their political beliefs, but cloaking it under the guise of humanity."

Abby was surprised at that statement. Sam had always seemed so evenly balanced. "Oh Sam that's a bit far-fetched isn't it?"

"Is it? When you have a government-based on a movement, which is essentially urban; that doesn't understand the rural way of life; then the country dweller is always the last in the pecking order. But they don't usually enforce legislation to the detriment of the countryside. The countryside is in essence conservative, and is seen as such by parties that pretend to represent the so-called working classes. If you can find any of those that is, who works as hard as a farmer and for the wage he gets. The problem is that they don't understand the difference between conservative with a small 'c' and a large 'C.' This government however seems to be positively discriminating against the countryside. Allowing four hundred odd professional politicians from the cities, who have never done a proper job in their life and are totally ignorant about life in the country, apart from something seen through a car or train window; to control our lives is unfair. They enact laws and regulations in the name of animal rights, but care little if as a result we are unable to compete with foreign producers who are untroubled by that legislation. They then walk away shrugging their shoulders as if we are to blame for the problems they dump on us. They talk about helping the farmer, but tie up the help in so much red tape that it is impossible for anyone bar a civil servant to understand let alone claim."

Sam's face had grown red, not with the embarrassment he usually felt, but with anger. Abby felt guilty, for bringing the subject up in the first place; but pleased that she was starting to understand these good people.

CHAPTER FOURTEEN

The next day dawned with high cloud, through which the sun would break frequently. It was warm, and Mary considered that it would stay this way all day. Abby had considered going over to the West Somerset Railway again, but Sam's words last night had given her a lot to think about; and after breakfast, her footsteps, as if with a mind of their own, took her to the station. The peace and solace that she would normally find here escaped her today. Perhaps she was wrong to think that she could put down roots in this place, she was growing fond of these people, but had managed to upset both James and Sam, two men who had shown her a different side of the male of the species. Sam, who she had started to view as a surrogate father; and James, who treated her with respect and genuine friendship, without the predatory approach that she had become used to, and for whom her feelings were starting to extend a little past simple friendship. Was the diversity of urban and rural attitudes too much for her to surmount? She sat on what was left of the coping to the platform, and contemplated the situation miserably. How long she sat there she didn't know, until her misery was disturbed by the sound of horse's hooves.

She knew who this would be before she looked up to see James sitting upon Cassie regarding her solemnly. "We don't appear to be in our usual good humour this morning. Is this because we are contemplating the horrendous task of restoring these buildings?"

"No, James, in fact I may not attempt that at all."

"Oh, has anything happened?"

"I don't know. I don't know if I will fit in here. Did I upset you when I questioned your support of hunting?"

"No. Why do you ask?"

"Well I might have upset Sam. I spoke to him last night, as you suggested, and he seemed to get angry."

"If I know, Sam, he wouldn't be upset with you. You asked. I think what Sam gets upset about is those who don't ask, but just condemn from a position of ignorance."

"Are you sure about that?"

"Yes, but if you need to be re-assured, why don't we go and ask Sam?"

"Could I? The only trouble is that I would have to walk back to the Inn to get my car."

"No trouble, I am sure that Cassie wouldn't mind taking us both to the Inn. That is if you don't mind riding pillion behind me." Abby looked concerned about the prospect.

"Would that be alright?"

James didn't reply, he nudged Cassie over to where Abby sat on the platform. "Just put your leg over her rump behind me, and put your arms around my waist, you will be fine." Abby did as she was told, and once settled; James got Cassie walking at a gentle pace along the track. For the first hundred yards or so, Abby was a little worried, but as she got used to the walk, relaxed, and suddenly found the proximity to James rather comforting, so much so that the usual humour that she enjoyed in James' company was restored. "If Mavis could see us now, she would be elated."

James shoulders quivered as he chuckled. "She may not see us, but she will know all about it soon. Mary will see us and that's just as good as putting it out on the B.B.C. news." Their arrival back at the Combe Inn was too soon for Abby, Cassie's rump was not the most comfortable seat in the world, but hugging James had more than compensated for the discomfort. Great credit had to be given to Mary, when she came out and noticed them, not a muscle moved to display her feelings, and she took it in her stride when James asked if she would mind Cassie being tethered for a while.

"No problem at all, you will be going off somewhere then?" she asked incuriously, which was not how she felt.

Abby explained that they were going to see Sam. "I don't know about James, but I would love a cup of coffee before we go." Mary's face split into her beaming smile, which it did whenever she was asked to provide food or drink for Abby.

"Of course, Love, would you like a cup, Mr. James?" James nodded his agreement, and made sure that Cassie was fine.

He tethered her so that she had a little slack to get to the longer, lush grass that grew by the fence. Abby watched as he did so. When he was sure that Cassie was ok he came to join Abby. "As that rattletrap of yours isn't here, you have no choice but to go in my car." Abby told James as they sat down at one of the benches. She noted the glimmer of laughter in his eyes and prepared herself.

"Well you know I profoundly disagree with these luxuries of life, and it goes against all my principles, however as you say there is no choice. I have one request to make though."

"Yes," Abby said resignedly.

"Can I drive, please, pretty please, can I drive?"

Abby was laughing now, her misery of earlier completely forgotten. "Yes of course, but remember one thing, you bend it, you mend it." Mary was pleased. She had heard some of the exchange from where she was making coffee in her kitchen. Instinctively she had known that Abby was miserable this morning, but could not fathom the reason. Hearing her laugh was enough to convince her that whatever the problem, it was resolved. It also cemented her view that James was good for Abby, and that the reverse was also true.

James turned out to be a good driver, treating Abby's BMW with consideration, unlike his treatment of his Land Rover. Abby had bought the car when it was twelve months old, choosing an automatic as better suited to London motoring, with the 2.5 litre engine. She had never sat in the passenger seat before. This was a new experience for her, which she found she quite liked. Their arrival at Gallow Farm went unnoticed, which meant as James remarked that Mavis was not around. They toured the various barns and out-houses searching for either Roger or Sam, and found Sam in a stall, tending to a solitary cow. He greeted them cheerfully.

"Morning, James, morning, Abby, how are you today?" He then astonished Abby by apologising for his anger last night. "Hope I didn't upset you, but I sometimes get infuriated, when I talk about this government."

James nodded sagely. "I know how you feel, Sam. Some of the things they get up to are just plain daft. But what's happening here?" He asked indicating the cow.

"I'm just keeping Jess apart from the herd for a while; she seems to have a bit of fever."

"Nothing that needs reporting?' asked James with a serious expression.

"No, nothing serious, I expect she's ate something, given her a tender belly, but I'm just being careful for the moment, I'll have to milk her though, otherwise she will be in pain." With that he grabbed a plastic bucket, and a little stool, and squatted down by the cow's withers.

"You give names to all your cows?" Abby asked in astonishment.

"Well, they don't mind what you call them, but anything is better than their registration number." He indicated the yellow ticket attached to the cow's ear. "It's the tone of your voice that they recognise."

Abby watched fascinated as first he washed off the cows' udders, and then used a cream rubbed all over the teats, anointing his hands as well, then with the bucket held between his knees, he began to milk, squeezing gently at the teats to send jets of milk into the bucket. Suddenly, she thought of her mum, who had, according to Sam, mastered this technique, until Thomas Tregonney had forbad her. If her mum could do this, why couldn't she? So, in a tremulous voice asked, "Sam, would you show me how to milk?" He looked up at her with a mixed expression on his face, thinking for a while, possibly of the day so long ago that he had taught Marion to milk.

"Let me make her more comfortable." He said. "With this amount of milk in her udders she will be feeling a little sore." He continued to milk until the ringing sound as the milk hit the bucket had softened, the milk now filling half of the bucket.

"O.K., Abby, take some of that cream, and get your fingers lubricated." Abby did as she was told, finding that James was looking at her with that famous grin on his face.

"What's the grin for?" she asked.

"Well if I seem to recall all the stories about milkmaids, they all seemed to be a little on the buxom side. You will have to eat a lot more of Mary's food, before you qualify."

Sam's voice came, muffled as his head was still buried down by Jess's withers. "I reckon you have been reading fiction, not all milkmaids were built that way. Look at Mavis, she was a stick way back, and she's still a stick now. Right, Abby, have you got your hands well covered?" Abby held up her hands to show. "Right." Sam got up from his stool, and held out his hand, with the fingers pointing down. "Now squeeze my fingers in a downward pull." Abby did as he asked the cream making her fingers slip downwards. "A little firmer." She increased the pressure. "That will do fine, now that's the motion you want to use, letting your fingers slip down her teats, expressing the milk. You reckon that you could do that?" Abby agreed that she could do that. "Now get down as you saw me, and try and hold the bucket between your knees. This proved more difficult as the bucket was now quite heavy, but eventually she mastered the technique. The smell of the cow was warm and creamy tinged with manure, not at all unpleasant and not as she had imagined. "Take two teats, and just do what you did with my fingers. Alternating between your hands." Abby grasped the teats, and suddenly milk shot out of the one, missing the bucket completely, splashing instead over her shoes. The cow looked round, aware that different hands were now milking her.

Abby soon found the rhythm, and her aim. "Well! Look at that, James, I'm milking a cow."

"Conversion from city slicker to country bumpkin, in one easy lesson," James replied cheekily.

"Change to the other two teats," Sam suggested. "Do that about every half-dozen pulls." Abby worked on, becoming warm in the process, it was harder work than she had thought, and the heat emanating from the cow, added perspiration to her brow. Abby thought that her efforts were slackening the streams of milk becoming thinner and less powerful. Sam knelt down by her side.

"I think you can stop now, she's pretty well milked out." Abby stretched back with relief, as Sam took the bucket from her.

She stood up and grinned at James. "Well did you think I could do that?"

"I had no doubts at all. But do bear in mind that years ago before machine milking, you would have a herd of fifty to sixty to do, and twice a day at that."

That stunned Abby into silence, as she multiplied the effort she had put in by fifty. "Surely one woman wouldn't have to do all that?"

Sam answered her query. "No, Abby he's just pulling your leg. At milking time, everybody would be in the parlour, and not every cow was as productive as Jess here, some you could milk out in two minutes." He wiped his hands on a clean cloth and then offered it to Abby, "Do you fancy a cup of tea?" Abby was pleased to accept, mainly because she could make use of the bathroom in the cottage, she was amazed that milking a cow could bring on so much perspiration. On the way to the cottage, Sam stopped at the pigs' pen and poured a little of the milk into each of the food bins.

"Why did you do that?" asked Abby incredulously.

"Oh a couple of reasons. First, if there is anything wrong with Jess, it would be foolish to sell on the milk until we know what it is, and..."

"Second," added James, "the creamery will only accept machine milk. They don't think it's hygienic otherwise."

Abby was stunned. "But that's stupid."

"Yes it is, isn't it?" replied Sam.

As they sat drinking tea, Sam turned to Abby, "Not that it isn't nice to see you, but I am sure that you had another reason apart from milking a cow, for coming up here today."

"Well we have sort of covered that. I was going to apologise for upsetting you last night."

Sam shook his head. "No, Girl, I wasn't upset with you, in fact I was pleased that you were making the effort to find out, rather than just assuming. You go on asking questions, if I get in lather, it's not you that does it, it's those silly idiots in Whitehall."

Abby was relieved that the situation had been cleared up. "Now I'm going to put you on the spot, Sam. Did I do as well as Mum?"

Sam beamed at her, "Well if I recall right, your mum spilt more milk the first time than she got in the bucket, so I suppose the answers yes. But Marion came down quite a lot, and got on well, until your grandfather put a stop to it. But if we were still hand-milking today, I would call on you for help, that's for sure." James, of course, could not let this go without a sally.

"You see, come down here with all your airs and graces, and we'll soon have dirt under your fingernails." James had that characteristic look on his face of teasing humour, and Abby could not let that go without returning the serve.

"I thought we had had this conversation before, then you called me a posh lady, and as I said at the time, I'm the granddaughter of the station master; there is no reason for airs and graces." James laughed as he went off to use the bathroom and Abby took the chance to ask Sam what kind of dancing there would be at the ball.

"Oh all kinds, Abby. Mostly proper dancing, but I do believe that there is one of those guys who use a record player, for the young ones to dance to, but that's only for a short while. Why do you ask?"

"Well if what you mean by proper dancing is ballroom dancing, then I can't!" Sam was stunned.

"You can't dance. Surely you could waltz?"

Abby shook her head, "No."

Sam thought for a bit. "What about if you come up here for a couple or three evenings, and Mavis and me, we'll teach you to dance? Mavis was very light on her feet when she was young, she'll get you twirling in no time."

"Oh Sam, that would be great, but not a word to James, please."

"Don't you worry, no one will say a word."

Sam noted when they left, that Abby got into the passenger seat without hesitation. 'The girl's made her mind up,' he thought to himself, 'she probably doesn't know herself, but her emotions do.' Loathe as he was to keep secrets from Mavis, he wouldn't share this with her, 'if I know Mavis, she'll make a song and dance out of it, and probably embarrass all and sundry. Good-hearted but that woman just don't know when to stop.'

James drove back to the Combe Inn just as carefully as before. This amused Abby, "Not driving at our usual frenetic pace, I notice?"

He grinned. "Well you did say that if I bent it, I would have to mend it. The local dealer's price would be well beyond my pocket and I am sure you wouldn't want the usual repair practiced in these parts, a hammer and the welding torch."

"It's a good job that I am fully insured then."

Abby thought for a moment. "When are we going to finish the ride along the track? I'm impatient to see the rest."

"You feel up to it then?"

"Yes."

"O.K., whenever you like."

"Tomorrow? No, not tomorrow, I'm going shopping. The day after, is that alright with you?"

"No problem, Tuesday it is. May I ask, what is your shopping trip supposed to accomplish?"

"Well I shall be buying one or two girly things, but you won't want to know about them. However, the main purpose is to buy a dress for this ball. You didn't suppose that I would be turning up in any old thing, now did you?" James went quiet for a moment.

"I must confess that I didn't really give it thought. So where are you going? Can I offer any assistance?" Abby laughed.

"I can just see you hanging around while I try on dresses. No thanks, James; I am going with Toni, from the Library." James looked bemused for a while then his face cleared.

"Oh Antonia, the daughter of Councillor Wates."

"I assume that it is one and the same, I only know her as Toni. I believe we are going to Taunton first, and if that's not successful, then Exeter."

"Well have a good day, here we are." James turned into the Combe Innwhere Cassie had become the centre of attention of one or two patrons.

Their arrival, with James driving Abby's car, received no comment. He declined Mary's offer of further refreshment and got up into the saddle.

"See you, Tuesday," he called to Abby, and wheeled Cassie away, heading off towards the Church, and Lyney House.

Abby's nose detected the wonderful aroma of cooking, which reminded her that she didn't eat a great deal at breakfast and was hungry. "That smells delicious, Mary, what are you making?"

"That, Abby, is a rib of beef, which I shall be serving with yorkshire pudding, roast taties, and all the veggies. Then there's apple pie and custard to follow, do you want some?"

"Definitely, have I got time to wash my hands first?"

"No problem, I shall have it on the table in about ten minutes."

Abby had grown used to the food here; in her opinion of superior quality and taste to any she had before. This meal, however, spoiled her for anything that would come after. Sitting at her table, feeling completely spoilt and full, she could only reply to Mary's enquiry with one word, 'superb.' Mary's face beamed with satisfaction. Although there were others in the lounge, enjoying equally the repast, it was only Abby's opinion that mattered to Mary, a mark of how she, Mavis and Sam had 'adopted' Abby as their special person. She was concerned though, when Abby declared that there was no way she would be able to eat anything else that day. From the first day that Abby had arrived at the Inn, Mary had felt it incumbent on her to round Abby out, considering that it was unhealthy to be so slim. Abby for her part had battled hard to resist the blandishments to eat more, despite the wonderful meals that Mary would put in front of her, so far she had won the skirmish.

It was almost without thought that Abby got in her car and drove once more to the station. It seemed strange that just a few hours ago, she was here, possibly seeing it for that last time, and now once again contemplating the future in this place. The serenity that seemed to envelope her in this place was stronger than ever now, and she could almost imagine her grandfather's presence. Would he recognise her? Yes she thought, he probably would, after all Sam knew who she was immediately, why not her own grandfather? What would she say to him? 'Hello granddad, I'm your granddaughter, Abby.' How could she explain to him, all that had happened, and how she came to be here? Then a thought came to comfort her, if his spirit still existed, then he was already aware of everything, she had no need to say anything. He would know.

There had been a warm summer breeze teasing her whilst she had been standing on the platform; it flirted about, blowing first from one direction and then another. Abby had taken little notice of it until something brought it to her attention. Maybe it was her imagination, but she was sure that it carried a subtle scent of camphor, bringing to mind the words of Sam, 'you always knew when Thomas Tregonney was around, by the smell of mothballs.' She took a deep breath. Yes it was there, camphor. The feeling was exhilarating, a feeling of being wrapped in a warm towel and cuddled, with the warmth and peace of a family to share. Granddad knew. He was there. Impulsively and with a happy smile on her face but tears in her eyes she called out. "Granddad, I'm home."

CHAPTER FIFTEEN

The next evening, Abby drove to Gallow Farm for her dancing lesson. Sam and Mavis had prepared for this by shifting the furniture in their lounge back against the walls to leave enough space to dance. Sam had opened up what he was proud to call the radiogram, a huge piece of furniture, with large speakers either end and in the middle under an opening lid there was a record turntable. Abby found this fascinating as the spindle in the centre was at least four inches tall, with the top inch kinked to one side. Sam explained that it was possible to load the top part with up to ten records, which the machine would automatically drop into place to play, once the preceding record had finished. Mavis produced with triumph a load of twelve inch records, saying to Abby, "I knew we still had these, and look, none of them have been broken." Abby examined one of the records, surprised at how heavy it was, until she realised that it was made from a hard substance like a brittle plastic. The label in the centre showed not the HMV logo with which she was familiar, but the name spelt in full, running in a half circle over the top with below a picture of a little black and white dog listening at the trumpet of an antique phonograph. The credit on the label was for Victor Sylvester and his orchestra.

Mavis, all businesslike, announced that they would start the tuition with the Waltz. "It's the easiest to do and you really only have to remember the three steps." She then proceeded to coach Abby through the steps, watched by Sam, who then interrupted the proceedings.

"Wouldn't it be better if I took Abby through the steps, then she can see how they fit in with her partners?"

"What's the point of her dancing with a partner?" Mavis immediately bit back. "When she doesn't know the basic steps? I'll show her those and then when Abby understands them, you can dance with her to show how it all goes together."

Abby got the hang of the Waltz quite quickly, and was soon moving around the floor with Sam, who held her at a respectable distance so that she could look down and see how their steps interacted. Then Mavis put on one of the records and the strains of violin, piano, and saxophone filled the room. The most notable feature of the music was the strong beat, which made the music so easy to follow in time.

"Victor Sylvester was renowned for this," explained Mavis as Abby and Sam danced. "He was a champion ballroom dancer himself, so he knew how important it was to keep to a strict tempo." Again Sam took Abby through her paces, with Abby managing the steps with little trouble. It seemed quite easy, as Sam seemed to indicate what they were doing with subtle pressures, either with his hand holding hers, or with an inclination of the body. The proof of this was when he took her through a turn, which she followed as if she had prior knowledge of the steps.

"How did we do that?" she exclaimed. "You didn't teach me those steps."

Mavis laughed. "It's easy. Sam was, no is, a very good dancer. And a good male lead can get you doing all sorts of steps as if it was natural. Now do you think you could do that again?" They went through those steps a dozen times, yet Abby somehow stumbled over them every time.

Sam said to her, "Abby you are trying to think what steps are coming next. Don't! Your feet know the steps, just listen to the music and follow my lead. The steps will come automatically." This worked and Abby again floated around the room in Sam's arms. Later, Abby sat and watched Sam and Mavis dance and marvelled how they seemed to accomplish quite intricate steps together moving as one.

She said as much to Mavis who explained, "Don't worry about those steps. On a crowded floor you will not get the chance to dance those and if you try, will annoy everyone else, because they cannot do them. Just get the basics and you will do fine."

They sat down for a cup of tea and Mavis asked if Abby had got a dress for the ball. Abby described it to her and Mavis suggested that she bring it down next time. "I would love to see it." The look on Sam's face suggested that he too would love to see it. The next suggestion was that perhaps Abby would like to come down to Gallow Farm and dress, and have James pick her up here.

Abby gave that some thought and shook her head. "Thanks for the offer, but I would have to bring everything, my make-up and all the other bits and pieces down here and would be sure to forget something. So if you don't mind, I will dress at the Inn. But could you come up there? I could probably do with some morale boosting before I go." Mavis smiled, happy that she was being involved.

"Yes, Love, of course we will."

Abby was waiting the next morning, sitting on one of the benches at the back of the Inn, when James arrived, leading Jason on the rein. Jason immediately moved to Abby and nuzzled her, then stood quietly, waiting for her to mount. The riding hat was looped over the pommel on the saddle. "I see Jason has fallen under your spell as well," remarked James as he dismounted Cassie and helped Abby mount. Mary hovered with the picnic lunch she had prepared for them; a smaller lunch, totally inadequate in Mary's view, but she acceded due to Abby's urging that too large a lunch would prevent her, Abby, from enjoying the evening meal. James comment was not lost upon Mary, who tucked this morsel away in her memory for future examination.

"Now you two have a good day, and James, don't ride too far."

"Mary, I shall look after Abby as if she were the Queen of Sheba," James replied with the grin just flickering around his mouth, as if he was undecided to be flippant of serious.

With the lunch packed in the saddle-bags, Mary waved them goodbye as they left through the gate and out into the field, heading towards the old station once again. Abby quickly found her seat, and settled comfortably in the saddle. Looking across at James she asked, "So who else has fallen under my spell?"

"Just about everyone in Combe Lyney." James avoided the trap adroitly. "Sam and Mavis especially. Why? Were you thinking of anyone in particular?"

"No. I just wondered."

James grinned. "Talking of spells, I think that you may have fallen under a spell as well."

"Perhaps you would like to explain that?"

"Combe Lyney. I think you might have fallen under the spell of Combe Lyney."

Abby thought about that for a while and they rode in a companionable silence. "Yes. You are right. This place does get to you; I could easily spend the rest of my life here, if only I could find something to do."

"There's so much you could do," replied James. "There's milking cows for a start." The laughter in his voice alerted Abby to the fact that his flippancy was back, preventing the conversation from getting into too serious an area. Abby laughed with him.

"Oh I couldn't do that, grandfather would have a fit, or at the very least spin in his grave."

They were riding along the old railway track now and the old station came into view. This prompted James, "I have some news for you. My solicitor has had a reply from the Land Registry and it is confirmed that I do own this land."

"That was quick."

"Yes, Cobbold usually take an age to do anything, but I think he was so embarrassed that he hadn't spotted the way-leave clause, he felt that he had to move quickly to get back into my good books. So there we have it. This place is now yours as soon as you sign the lease." They had stopped alongside the platform.

Abby looked around and smiled. "James, you couldn't know how pleased I am. I feel at last as if I am connected to something."

"Oh I think I can understand."

Abby came back quite sharply. "No, James, you can't. You have always been here, where your family has lived for generations. You have always been part of this place, and it has been part of you. I have never had that feeling. When mum was alive we rented small flats, constantly moving in order to get a lower rent. Mum was the only family I had, and because she wouldn't talk about it, I had no history. Now I have discovered a history and I am going to own a part of it. You could never understand how good a feeling that is." James, taken aback by Abby's vehemence, said nothing. Abby feeling guilty because she had reacted so strongly was also quiet.

After a while James broke the silence. "I am sorry, Abby. You are right, I did not understand what you were saying." He leaned over and put his hand over hers as she held the reins. "Forgive me."

Abby smiled, turned her hand over and clasped his. "I am sorry too, I overreacted." He squeezed her hand and relinquished the hold.

They had started moving again, drawing level with site of the signal box, and shortly after crossed the lane at the level crossing. Abby had assumed that this lane had only ever led to the goods yard, but from the different perspective of Jason's back could see that another lane had once branched off, heading in the general direction of the river. She pointed this out to James asking where it went.

"That's Mill Lane. Well it was, once, it was never anything more than a track, and I doubt that anyone has been down there for years."

"Mill Lane? So presumably there would have been a mill at the end of it?"

"Yes, a water mill. Nothing left, except a few crumbling walls. The pond and the mill race are still there, but the wheel's long gone. The leat has been filled in."

"So what would they have milled?"

"It would have been for local grains and such. Lasted until the early nineteen twenties, I believe, when it was abandoned.

"I thought that the Valley had only ever supported livestock."

"Livestock has always been the main farming practice, but until the turn of the century, there was always a good percentage of land given over to cereals. That was another thing your granddad's railway changed."

"How so?"

"Well, they would grow wheat for bread, barley for brewing, oats for livestock feed, but all intended for purely local consumption. When the railways came, it was possible to get all these commodities at a cheaper price, because they were grown on a larger scale elsewhere. It was a gradual erosion, but eventually there was no point in cereals here, so the land was switched to pastoral farming and the mill just became redundant."

They were now riding on a low embankment, which James pointed out kept the railway above the level of flooding. "All these meadows will flood from time to time, that's why the cottages were built up there. He pointed to the right, where Abby could see the isolated cottages, built on the side of the valley, not on the valley floor. The track curved gently, avoiding the small hills that encroached, only occasionally had there been cuttings where going around the small hill would have entailed bridging the river.

"So how long has your family lived here?" she asked. "Forget the boysown story of smuggling and nefarious practices. Give me the truth."

James laughed. "Well the truth is not easy. But I believe that there have been Comberfords in this valley from the thirteenth century."

"How long?" Abby was amazed.

"Seven hundred years, give or take. The trouble is that the Church burnt out sometime in the seventeenth century, and they held the only records of Hatch, Match, and Despatch."

"So how can you reckon that your family goes back to the thirteenth century?"

"Tithe records, now held at the County Museum in Taunton. They only tell you who owed tithes on which bit of land, but the Comberfords do show in those records. The name has changed slightly, but it is pretty certain to be us lot."

"What was the name then?" Abby enquired.

"It was spelt differently from time to time, but essentially it was C O M B Y R F O R D E. You know how a person's name would be a corruption of their work skill, or place they lived. I suspect that the name came from some serf, who was a Wool Comber, and lived by a ford. Probably the ford which was close to where the river bridge is now."

Abby thought James was elaborating on a slim fact. "Go on, this sounds like an extreme fantasy."

"Abby, me, fantasise?" He laughed. "No, it's mainly conjecture, based upon some little supporting evidence."

"O.K., I accept the origin of the name, I believe that happened a lot. But, James how does a serf, as you described him, become lord of all these acres?"

"In a close community as this would have been then, it was quite possible that everyone was related in some way to everyone else, so when you have something like the plague come along and kill off close to a half of the population, you suddenly find a new class of landowners, men who had inherited all those small strips of land given to their various relatives as reward for their services to the Lord of the Manor. If they added all those small strips to their own, they could build up a reasonable holding. It didn't happen all at once of course, it would take years, but when the Black Death, after its first onslaught in thirteen forty-eight, would ravage the country for the next fifty years, it was inevitable, that if one branch of the family could survive, they would come out richer than they ever thought possible." He paused for a moment, then went on. "There was something else, some families would be completely wiped out; the plague halved the population in this country between thirteen forty-eight and fourteen hundred; so the holdings of those who died should have reverted to the lord, but if there was no lord around, others could annex the holdings, and yet again increase their wealth."

Abby listened in delight. She had become used to and enjoyed the stories that Sam, Mary and others would relate and now James was regaling her.

"James you are either a born story-teller, or this is the truth. I cannot believe the plague could kill that many people. Now come on, own up, this is all a story, isn't it?"

"Abby, I cannot claim that this is the truth, all I know is that people with this name, or something close to this name, became increasingly responsible for tithes in the late thirteenth and through the fourteenth centuries. As for the plague, yes it did kill all those people, it is well documented. In fact some villages were wiped off the map completely as no one survived there."

"This is fantastic, so where does all the smuggling and nefarious practices come in?"

"That would have come a little later. If you can imagine this guy, now calling himself a freeman, who had all this land, but none of it contiguous. He would have set about persuading his neighbours that the sensible thing to do was to have one large plot of land, rather than a number of separated plots, so how about doing a deal? If they were happy to do so, that was fine. If they weren't, then possibly other means of persuasion could be employed. If our guy had money obtained from activities that were not too legal, like poaching that would help, he could make them an offer they couldn't refuse, so to speak. There would also be land, that wasn't being used. Start farming it, and eventually the law of Adverse Possession would come into effect."

"Adverse Possession?"

"Squatters' rights."

"But surely the Lord of the Manor would have something to say about that."

They clattered over a bridge crossing a minor stream. The horses seem to like the sound of their hooves on the boards and nodded their heads vigorously. James waited until they were back on the embankment.

"Yes, but bear in mind that the Black Death would have been visited upon them just as surely as it had upon the peasants. Their lands could now be held possibly by some distant relative who lived a hundred or more miles away. Back then a hundred miles was probably a two or three-day journey. This relative would probably not even be aware that this distant cousin had died, and that he had inherited the holding. Another fact that comes into the equation is that the lord, if he had survived would not now have hundreds of serfs bound to give him service. They were dead. To maintain his land he was now in a position of having to purchase labour. They tried unsuccessfully to regulate wages but those lords who survived were desperate and would offer higher wages to tempt serfs away. Under the feudal system a serf or villeyn could not leave his village without the permission of his lord. But now they didn't care, all a serf had to do was change his name, and no one was any the wiser. So with all this going on, a shortage of labour, which was becoming expensive anyway, land which was remote from the lords' main location could be forgotten as unviable. The feudal system was dead, and the law of supply and demand started to rule." He grinned. "It was the birth of capitalism."

Abby felt that this story, although somewhat fanciful, could have a germ of truth. She challenged James, "You speak as if you know that these things happened, or is this the conjecture you spoke about?"

"No, History was one of my subjects at 'A' level. I was toying with the idea of reading History at University. But if you want to know more about the period, check it out on the Internet, there's hundreds of references to it."

For a while, Abby had taken little notice of the land they were riding through, their conversation had been fascinating and she was once more reminded of how much she missed her own past. James could, albeit with a little stretch of the imagination, tie himself to a history of some six hundred years. Whilst she, had only recently discovered a family, and a history of little more than sixty years.

The horses plodded contentedly onwards, nodding their heads in that manner that suggested a conversation; with James and now Abby sitting easily in the saddles. The old track bed had meandered lazily between river and the valley sides, enlivened occasionally by a farm crossing, or a small bridge crossing a stream hurrying to join the main river. The land was quite open, just small copses of trees dotted haphazardly on hillocks, or along the course of the small streams. Cattle and sheep grazed and browsed, unfazed by their passage, only the odd individual raising a head to watch them pass. Looking to the right, she could see a road, ascending steeply out of the valley, and realised that this was the road she had taken when she first arrived here. Looking back to that day she felt a sense of wonder that so much could have happened to her, just by a whim to seek a place that her mother had mentioned.

They rode on in companionable silence for a while. James broke the silence when he asked,"So what started you in the city, which I must say is very impressive to many people around here?"

Abby thought for a while before answering. "It was an accident more than design. I started working in an insurance broker's office, and went on from there."

"Come on, Abby, there's got to be more than that."

"Well yes there was. They did very little for their commission, advising customers on the best place to get insurance, the best place always being the company which offered the greatest commission to the broker. I moved into financial services, only to find the same thing. The best investment would always be the one which offered the adviser the best commission, whether it was right for the customer or not. It didn't take much of a brain to work out how it was done, so when I was offered the chance of becoming an adviser, I jumped at it. At that time you didn't need any qualifications. Working with money all day tends to make you a little blasé about it, and the challenge was not how much money you were dealing with, but how much you could make it do. Sometime later, I heard of a chance to work for one of the Merchant Banks, not dealing of course, that came later, but doing administration for the dealers. If you just regard the job as placing papers in the right order, and in the right place, then you will do it for ever. I read the paperwork to try and understand what was happening. I spent time at the online computer as well, watching the movements. Everything else was luck. The director came into the office one day and caught me working at some figures. I had in my imagination taken up an offer a few days before, and made a good profit on my supposed investment. He asked me what I was doing and I explained. He said to keep making the supposed investments, but to keep a full record. He would check them from time to time, and obviously thought I was doing alright. A few months later he told me that I was to start dealing."

James gave a disbelieving laugh. "Huh! Abby, you make it sound so easy. I don't believe that it could be as simple as that."

"Well I suppose it wasn't that simple. I would usually be in the office from about seven in the morning until ten at night, but that was so that I could do all my paperwork, and then have time to work on my imaginary investments."

"Fifteen-hour days!" James was shocked. "When did you have a life? "

"I didn't. I worked Monday to Friday, and then Saturday and sometimes Sunday as well."

"How long did this go on for?"

"Ten years or so."

James shook his head in dismay. "Well it sounds to me as if you have worked enough for a lifetime however you look at it. So now you have the time to start living life. God knows its precious enough."

James' last comment sounded too heartfelt to be just another of his casual lines. Abby realised that there was a memory of the Falklands there, and wanted to ask, but stopped herself, knowing that James wouldn't talk about it. She was grateful that he hadn't asked, even in a roundabout way of her supposed high rewards from the bank. It was ironic, that their friendship was getting closer, but there were still things that neither of them wished to talk about. She once again took notice of where they were riding. Turning in the saddle she could look back and see the valley. The trees patched dark greens and coppers against the lighter green of the pastures. The valley sides rose slowly in another shade of green up to the perfect cerulean blue of the sky. She had heard someone once talk about a big sky; they were talking about the Kansas prairies. This could never be described as a big sky, just a small strip of blue framed by the heights above the valley, but nonetheless the picture was perfect. The various shades of green complimenting the blue of the sky.

With that idyllic picture in mind, she turned to James, "It must have been good, growing up here in the valley."

He thought for a while. "I can't say that I felt that. This was all I knew, so a feeling like good didn't come into it. There was a certain freedom, particularly after my riding reached the standard that father considered safe. Then I was allowed out on my own. I couldn't really come to harm, not with the tenants all keeping an eye out for me. As a kid you accept things as they are, never worrying about why your life was as it was. It was only when I went away to school, that I realised how lucky I had been."

"You went away to school?"

"Not at first," he shook his head. "I went to the school in Paverton until I was eight, then I went to boarding school."

"How did you get to Paverton?"

"On the train. With all the other kids, and that included your mum."

Abby was stunned for a moment; she had never considered something so mundane as her mum going to school. It was obvious to her now, that there wasn't a school in the village.

"That must have been exciting." James smiled as he remembered those days.

"The lads would get up to all kinds of mischief, not at the station of course, your grandfather would not allow any larking about, but on the train, yes. There was many a boy pushed onto the luggage rack, and left there when the train reached Paverton."

"Did that happen to you?"

"Yes." He replied with a grin. "When I was small, but later nothing, probably because they realised who my father was, and imagined that some dire retribution would result from bullying me. It wouldn't have though. Dad seemed to take the view that this was part of the character forming that all boys had to experience." Abby laughed delightedly. James decided that he rather liked to hear Abby laugh, and broadened his smile. The laughing lady delved further.

"Then you went away to boarding school?"

"Yes. That was when I started to realise how good life had been here, and decided that I would always want to live here."

"But you did go away."

Abby almost without thinking had asked the question from which she had earlier shied away.

"Yes I did. Not mind you because I wanted to, it had to do with the gentlemen of Argentina, thinking to grab hold of something that didn't belong to them. Once I got back, I knew that my earlier decision was the right one." James had skied over the topic without delving into the detail. Abby was disappointed. Not just because she was curious, but also she wanted to try and understand something of that which James' had experienced. She made up her mind to try another tack later on.

The character of the valley was changing. The pasture land was diminishing and trees were taking over.

"Are we leaving the farm land behind?" she asked.

"Yes," replied James. "From here on it is pretty well all forestry."

"Yours I presume?" James laughed, hearing the touch of friendly sarcasm in her voice.

"Well some of it anyway. A huge chunk of the forest is Crown Estate."

"How did that come about?"

"More history I'm afraid." James grinned. "Well we're back to the aftermath of the plagues of the Middle Ages. The lords held their lands by gift of the monarch. Kings are different, they could give something away and then take it back if it pleased them, well they could, in those days. If the lord to whom it was entrusted was no longer around, then the king could take it back, or give it to someone else. Often it would become part of monastery lands, and after Henry the Eighth, it again became Crown property. With all these transfers back and forth, and no one really knowing where the boundaries were, odd little bits slipped through the net, so the Yeomen who had grabbed one of those little bits, got to keep them."

"Like the Combyrfordes?" Abby chuckled.

"Like the Combyrfordes." He agreed.

"It would appear that I am not the only one who simplifies these things." Abby remarked lightly.

James looked hurt. "Abby, I am talking about something that happened six hundred years ago. Any way it actually wasn't that simple. Getting the land was one thing, keeping it was an entirely different kettle of fish. In the times of the Tudors, the Stuarts, and then the Commonwealth, it paid to keep your head down."

Abby was intrigued. "For why?"

"Well it was all about religion," James explained. "First you could be in trouble for being a Catholic, twenty years later you could be in trouble for not being Catholic. Twenty years again, and it didn't matter if you were Catholic, but best not to advertise the fact, else you could be suspected of treasonable activity. Later you could be in trouble for being a Royalist, who were suspected of being Catholic and then later still for being a Parliamentarian and Presbyterian. Then it got really silly, you had to be the right kind of Presbyterian else you were in trouble. Other landowners in the area lost everything by becoming too prominent. If you get yourself noticed then you come under pressure to discuss your opinions. Tell everybody what you believe in, and it could and did rebound on you depending on the powers of the day. Through all this the Comberfords seem to have remained unnoticed, managing to keep their little plot of England. There are some advantages to being in the back of beyond. But for something like two hundred years holding the wrong beliefs or thoughts could lose you everything, including your life." Abby was digesting all this history. It had an immediacy that her interest in industrial history had never possessed, it was being related by someone whose family had been touched and shaped by history.

Abby's earlier comment about the changing face of the valley had prompted James to think of lunching before they entered the woodland proper.

"Shall we stop for some lunch? It may be a bit early but I was thinking that we can enjoy the sun here, whereas if we go on, it would be quite gloomy."

"Suits me, where do you think?" James considered and pointed.

"See where there is an accommodation crossing just ahead, there." Abby could see what had been a crossing, by the gates, but had not heard the term 'accommodation crossing' before. She surmised that it was exactly what the words meant, a crossing made to accommodate the farmer who worked land either side of the railway. They arrived at the crossing, which offered a pleasant grassy bank for them. James opened the gate and walked both Jason and Cassie into the field. He looped the stirrups up and left them to graze. He returned with the goodies from the saddle-bags and a blanket which had been strapped to the saddle. Abby noted the cool-bag, which she presumed would contain a bottle of wine.

"Don't you think you should have asked the farmer, before you let them loose?"

"Not a problem. Abe Stone rents this land, and he doesn't have enough livestock now to graze it. I am concerned that one quarter day he will tell me he doesn't want it anymore, and I don't think anyone else will want it, so I shall be down three acres. I hesitate to remind you that I actually own the land anyway. But if I do that you will no doubt find cause to make some comment about landlords and serfs." Abby giggled, as she probably would have made such a comment. Instead she asked a question although she was well aware of the answer, "Quarter day?"

"The day that rent get paid, once a quarter."

They busied themselves getting the blanket down and opening the various parcels of food that Mary had provided. Eventually they found themselves comfortable positions, and James raised his glass of wine to her, and then to his lips. "What could be better," he asked, "a lovely day, good food and wine, peace and quiet, and a pretty girl to share with?" Abby blushed a little, his compliments were more frequent now, and secretly she enjoyed them, even when they were disguised by his banter.

"Well I suppose I should feel safe, after all you are an officer and a gentleman."

"Don't assume too much, I am also the squire around here, and you know what they say about squires." He mimed twisting an imaginary moustache. Abby smiled, and turned to view their surroundings and reflect. She could honestly admit to herself that she had never felt more relaxed in her whole life. Yet again she confirmed to herself the sense in her decision to make a new life here in this valley. The problem of an occupation was ever present, but not a priority. From the corners of her eyes, she took a surreptitious glance at James, who was applying himself wholeheartedly to the food. Her relaxed state had a great deal to do with him. He was good company, solicitous of her well-being and amusing. She wondered if he wanted to take their friendship to another level? Possibly, she thought, but knew that he would never make the first move. Whilst his demeanour was that of a confident man of the world, she sensed a shyness within him that would preclude his making an advance that could be rejected.

James interrupted her thoughts. "Have you thought much about what you will do at the station?" His question brought her quickly out of her reverie.

"I have thought about it a little. My mind is toying with the idea of restoring it to how it looked when granddad first came here."

"Whew! That could be a tall order." He went on. "You know that it is listed don't you. So you cannot change the character of the building anyway."

"Yes, I know. I suppose that restoring it to its original condition would be acceptable?" James didn't have to think about that.

"That would be O.K., but you will have to be careful how you do it, I'll get Cobbold to look into it. But whatever way you look at it, I imagine it will be costly." Abby nodded her head.

"I thought it would, but it's worth it. It's about connecting with my past, or rather my family's past. I would like to see the station as granddad saw it. Oh I know I can't do everything. I can't put the rails back, but the house, the station, the platform, possibly those I can restore."

James mused for a moment. "I may be able to help, I am sure that there are some photographs of the station somewhere at home. I'll have a look."

"That would be really helpful. I was thinking of asking Mr. Brasher to advise me. Perhaps he would even come down. What he doesn't know about the Great Western is not worth knowing anyway."

"You're really serious about this, aren't you?"

"Yes. When can I take over?"

"If it was anyone else I would say let's get the legalities out of the way, but that's no worry, we have agreed so as far as I am concerned you can start any time you like."

"You'll trust me then?"

"Of course."

"Great, I'll write to Mr. Brasher immediately."

"Why don't you phone him?"

"Mr. Brasher isn't the sort of man who telephones people. He prefers to write, and I am sure that he will look upon my request more kindly, if I write to him."

"I think I like the sound of Mr. Brasher," James murmured.

Abby looked across at him. "Yes, I think you would. You too are a little bit of a throwback. No! Not a throwback, a man out of his time."

James was shocked. "How do you make that out?"

"Well it is just your attitude to life. You love it here in the valley, where modern life doesn't intrude too much, in fact from some of the things you have said I get the feeling that you hate where life is going, and would like it to stand still for a while."

"Is that a bad thing?"

"Once I would have said yes, but now I think I am catching the virus. I look forward to living life at this pace."

"See I told you, posh lady to country bumpkin in one easy lesson."

Abby laughed. "Well thinking about the station I think it is going to take quite a lot of money to enjoy this life. Posh lady needs that sort of money to become country bumpkin."

James grinned. "So it takes a boatload of cash to turn from posh lady to rustic, now normally it's the other way round."

Abby felt that she could ask the question that had been in her mind for quite a while. "On that score, what turned an officer and a gentleman into the wicked squire?" The grin faded from James' face.

CHAPTER SIXTEEN

Abby wondered if she had overstepped the bounds, until James suddenly began to speak.

"In many ways I was only playing at being an officer, I viewed it as part of my training really to become landlord here. Oh it was fun and I enjoyed it, that is until the Falklands happened. You know it is rather exciting to enjoy that sort of life, believing that you will never have to put into practice the skills you are being taught. Many officers can go through their entire army career and never hear a shot fired in anger. I thought that would be my situation. Seven years in the army, and then back here." He shook his head, "Unfortunately it didn't work out that way. I hadn't had the time to enjoy the captains pips on my shoulder before I was off to the Falklands. It was cold, wet and thoroughly uncomfortable, and if that wasn't enough the Argies were firing at us!" He was quiet for a while, and then said softly, "I killed a man you know."

Abby not understanding just commented, "I would have thought that was part of war."

James shook his head. "It is, unfortunately, but usually you are detached from the deed. You send a bullet on its way and that does the killing. No, I actually killed a man, only he wasn't a man, he was a boy, and I did it with my own hands. I stuck a bayonet in his stomach, and watched him die. I had his blood all over my hands. He was only young, couldn't have been more than eighteen! What in hell was he doing there? He shouldn't have been there." James stopped suddenly, his face a picture of misery.

Abby leaned across and took his hand, suddenly understanding the misery and horror. James carried on as if he was speaking to himself, "It was when we moved in on Goose Green, we had to be as quiet as possible as we got into position; a shot would have told the garrison that we were there. My company was creeping through this outcrop, rock, scrub and bush, when suddenly he was there, I just reacted. Afterwards I wondered if he was trying to surrender. Sometimes when I look back, I am sure he was trying to surrender. Then at other times that he wasn't... I just don't know. My company sergeant had put his hand over the boy's mouth to stop him from crying out, stomach wounds are very painful. I could see the agony on his face and tears running down from his eyes. He just looked up at me and you could see the question, 'Why? Why me?' When the boy died, my sergeant just said to me 'you or him, Boss,' and carried on." James' voice faded away and he just sat there, clinging to Abby's hand.

Abby heard herself say without thought, "Well I for one, am glad it wasn't you."

If James had heard he didn't react, they both remained still, waiting for the misery to pass. Eventually, James stirred his voice now a little less strained. "I talked a lot with Sam when I got back. He had served as a sniper during the Second World War; sometimes, the army does manage to get the right peg in the right hole. He helped a lot, but as he said he had never killed close up, all he ever saw was a uniform, no details of a face, so it was impersonal." He moved and lessened his grip on Abby's hand, but kept the contact. "Thanks for the comfort. I haven't gone through that for quite some time."

"I'm sorry, I shouldn't have asked about it."

James shook his head. "You are a friend, you should know." He paused, "Sam is the only one who knew about this, and now you. It's not something I would like to be common knowledge."

Abby understood what he was saying. "It stays with me, you know that. Why was Sam the right peg in the right hole?"

"Countryman. He had used a shotgun from an early age, knew how to move about the land without drawing attention to himself, and how to lay up in a thicket for hours if need be without moving. All essential to be a good sniper." Abby nodded, it was simple really, but not the sort of thing that most people would think about.

The sun was now getting quite warm, and their position so comfortable that Abby lay back enjoying the peace and quiet. After a while she realised that it wasn't so quiet, used as she was to the city life where noise is a constant background; she expected the country to be quiet, now she knew that it wasn't. She could hear the crunch as Cassie and Jason cropped the grass, the faint buzz of insects flying around; the flutter of birds grown bold, anticipating that there could be crumbs for them, and faintly on the breeze the ripple of the river. She lay contentedly, only occasionally sitting up to sip at her wine which although now warm tasted delicious anyway. James had moved away a little and was methodically packing away the remains of the picnic.

She watched through half-closed eyes for a while and was prompted to comment, "You are very tidy you know, was that the army training?"

James looked up,. "Yes and no. It's also the Country Code. All this paper and waxed cartons have no place in the country. Cows would eat it, because it smells good, but it wouldn't do them any good. Remember Sam's cow Jesse?" Abby nodded. "The most likely cause of her discomfort would have been something like this, left innocently by some visitor, but causing trouble all the same." He picked up the bottle of wine and held it up squinting through the glass.

"There's some wine left, shall we finish it?"

"Good idea," Abby said with a grin. She held out her glass. "You know it was interesting listening to you talking about your family history. I was fascinated by how they kept out of the limelight and prospered. But how do you know they kept a low profile?"

"It is as much a question of what isn't there, rather than what is there. The local histories of the time mention quite a few names, who aren't around now. But don't mention the Comberfords, who are. So I make the assumption that it was this keeping their light under a bushel attitude that ensured survival." Abby nodded.

"You still do that, don't you?"

He looked curiously at her. Abby went on to explain. "Well in all this time you have never mentioned any strong political adherences, nor any religious ones. Have you never been interested?"

"There is a very simple answer to that. No! No political views except that they are all a little dodgy. And as for religion, I was not brought up as anything, so I have no views on that score. Perhaps my family became non-religious as a way of surviving, go with the flow, say the words, but you don't have to mean them. That sort of thing. The West Country was once very Catholic, but that was at the time of the Tudors and Stuarts. For the last two hundred years or so, it has been Wesleyan in the main. But if you talk to a few round here, you will find that they tend to be Anglican mixed with Wesleyan, but not so much you would notice." The conversation faded away and Abby relaxed.

She may have dozed a while, for it seemed only a moment before she realised that James had packed everything away. Cassie and Jason were standing at the field gate following his movements as if they sensed that the journey was soon to begin once more. Abby didn't move, quite content with the warmth, and the rest she was enjoying until James asked.

"Are you going to lie there all day?"

Abby stuck her tongue out at him. "You were the one who recommended that I should take things a little easier, so don't get stroppy if I follow your advice." Without looking, she knew that smile was on his face.

"I see, gone native, have you?" Abby roused herself and stood up. Grasses had stuck to her back, and she vigorously brushed them off.

"Mary would be ecstatic if she saw these," she bantered. "She'll put two and two together and make at least six."

James restored to his normal humour, grinned delightedly. "Yep, and the phone line to Mavis would be red hot."

Abby laughed. "Is the country always like this, I mean gossip?"

"Of course. Everyone is an object of interest, it's not malicious, but there has to be something more than crops and weather to talk about, so you coming here has been a welcome break from the normal gossip. You would be surprised at the fanciful stories circulating about you."

"Me!"

"Yes, you are new, and a bit of a mystery, so in consequence you will get talked about. As I said, nothing malicious."

Abby thought that over. She found a certain humour in the situation. "How nice to be thought of as a mystery woman." Abby grinned. "And what are they saying about you and me?"

"Oh not much. Just that you had come down here to get away from an unhappy relationship, or that you are writing a novel, or that you are trying to buy the estate."

"Mary and Mavis don't subscribe to those ideas," Abby said dryly. James agreed with her.

"Ah well, Mary and Mavis have their own gossip, which they do not share with anyone else." Whilst this banter was going on, James had released the horses from the field.

Jason immediately broke away and walked over to Abby, snuffling at her pockets. James called across. "He wants his treat, here!" He searched in the saddle bag and found an apple, with his pocket knife he sliced it in two, and gave both halves to Abby. Jason greedily nudged Abby's hand, and she fed him his treat. James had done the same for Cassie, so with both the horses happy, they mounted, and resumed the journey.

The way now entered the woodland, the track bed curving left and then right but always on a constant downgrade. With the trees in full leaf, the area was gloomy, with only splashes of dappled sun creating islands of brilliance. Apart from bird calls and the rustle of the breeze in the foliage, it was quiet. Even the river could not be heard.

"Are we still on your land?"

"Yes, for a while. We shall leave it in about a mile."

"About a mile?"

"Yes. The boundary isn't marked, but I shall know when we are on the Crown property." Abby was used to a system where everyone knew to the inch where their property began and ended.

"Why isn't the boundary marked?"

"Little point as this is not land that can be rented. Too wet for anything but woodland. We will fell trees from time to time, which gives the new growth room to grow, but apart from timber, that is it."

"It's very gloomy here." Abby observed. James nodded.

"It is now. When the railway was running it was much more open. The engines would have worked hard coming up this bit, so sparks would often set little fires in the undergrowth. Too wet for them ever to become big blazes, but it did clear the ground either side of the track."

Another reminder for Abby of how it was when her grandfather was alive. Yet one more piece in the Jigsaw. She came back to the subject of boundaries.

"If you don't mark the boundary, and don't have fences, anyone can walk on to your property at any time, can't they?"

"Yes they can. There is nothing here for them to steal, and they can do little harm. Country people have little objection to people wandering over their land, so long as they observe the Country Code. Don't light fires, don't do damage, and take your rubbish home with you."

"That's a very generous attitude."

"I mentioned once that although legally this is my land, I am really a curator keeping it safe for everyone. It's a lovely country here, it would be churlish to deny entry to anyone who wanted to enjoy this beauty." Abby looked across at James to see if he had that little grin on his face, and was surprised to see that he was being totally serious.

She lightened the mood. "So the wicked squire does have a social conscience." She knew that James would be grinning now, and waited for the retort. It wasn't a long wait.

"Social conscience is merely a nice way of avoiding the truth that I cannot afford to fence the whole thing in." The laughter in James' voice told her that he was once again hiding his true values behind humour.

Abby had taken little note of their whereabouts for some time and was now surprised to see that the track bed was rising on an embankment. Upon closer examination she realised that the track was level and it was the land either side that was dropping away. The curve of the track straightened and in the distance she saw the brick parapet of what appeared to be another viaduct. She remarked on this to James who confirmed that they were to cross the river. "The river is now in quite a deep valley, and the track crosses here and then leaves the valley."

"The railway didn't follow the river all the way?"

"No," James went on to explain. "Do you remember when you first drove up the valley?"

"Yes."

"You may have noticed that the road followed a side valley, and then you crossed over and came down a steep hill into the Lyney Valley proper."

"I certainly remember that hill. What was it? One in four or something."

"Yes it is. That hill was always a problem, especially in winter. Well the railway and the road used the side valley, I assume it was because the Lyney Valley from this point on was Crown Estate, they weren't allowed to build there, Also from the railway's point of view the gradients involved would be too steep."

"So this is where we leave your land?" She asked.

"Just a bit further on," replied James, pointing towards the viaduct.

The track crossed the river by a single arch viaduct, but not so high as the viaduct they had seen on their previous ride. Shortly after that they entered a gloomy cutting, the steep rock sides towering over them, scattered with bush and small trees that had managed to gain a footing in the cracks and crevices. The track here was narrowed by the slippage from the sides, so Abby was forced to ride behind James. The cutting ran for some one hundred and fifty yards, and they emerged into relative daylight, Abby following James as he guided Cassie off the track and descended the embankment. Suddenly, there in front of them was a lane, which Abby quickly recognised as the lane she had driven with caution that first day, the bridge abutments that had drawn her attention then standing to her right. She found it difficult to recall the excitement and doubts she had then, if she had known that it was taking her to a new life would she have gone on, or turned and driven away? Whatever she felt then, now she walked Jason confidently across the lane and following James, up the trail to regain the track bed. She belonged here now, no longer an outsider looking in.

The track was again wide enough for them to ride side by side, and she dug her heels into Jason's flank to urge him on. The horse needed little urging and they were again riding abreast. The land had become a little more open the tree line having receded to allow small fields with a few grazing cattle, the fields bounded by those familiar stone walls covered in ivy and grasses. "So where did the estate end?" Abby enquired.

"Back there when we rode through the cutting."

"This isn't Crown Estate then?"

"No," James shook his head. "It belongs to Richard Welling, Sir Richard Welling. You will meet him at the ball."

"He doesn't mind you riding on his land then?"

James turned to her, smiling, "No, he doesn't mind. This area is difficult for access bounded by the two rivers, the Lyney and the Bray, coupled with the limits on that bridge. It isn't really big enough to make a decent farm, but too big for a small-holder. The ground gets very wet in winter, so you have to take the livestock off. He has tried to sell it to me on one or two occasions, but I am not interested at the price he wants. Even then the same problems apply for anyone who would be interested in renting. I could make it more attractive if I cleared this track bed back to the viaduct, giving it better access, but then it would only be of interest to my existing tenants, and the closest is Abe Stone, and he, I think, is looking to have less land rather than more. You couldn't put dairy cattle on it either." Abby was confused by that statement.

"Why not?"

"Milking. Twice a day you have to milk them, and that means machine milking or you cannot sell the milk. The nearest parlour is five miles away, so your herd would be walking twenty miles a day, wouldn't do them any good, and would affect the yield badly as well." Abby was even more confused now.

"But there were some cattle back there."

"Bullocks." He was grinning widely. "Can't get milk from a bullock."

"It gets very complicated doesn't it?" Abby laughed with him.

"Yes it does. It would appear so simple, here's a field, good grazing, put cows on it, money for old rope. Then the problems come, and suddenly it's not so easy. Something those blokes in Westminster don't think about."

Abby was quiet for a while digesting the import of this. She like most people had thought that farmers led an easy life. It would appear that every day she was learning something new. Her opinions were changing dramatically.

"You said something about the bridge and the limits on it. What bridge would that be?"

"We'll see it in a minute," James told her. "You will have driven over it when you came up the lane, we will take a break there and I will explain." As if on cue, the gradient levelled and a final wide curve brought them to a long, low viaduct. Abby stared in confusion for a while until she suddenly realised that this was the bridge she had seen from the road on her first visit, and looking to her left she saw the embankment and road bridge. Intuitively she knew that this was the bridge that James a spoken of.

"That's the bridge you meant, isn't it?" James had stopped Cassie and was dismounting. He nodded.

"Yes." He tethered Cassie and walked a few paces onto the railway bridge, looking carefully for signs of unsafe footing. Finding none he returned.

"Shall we have some coffee?" He enquired whilst holding Jason's rein so that Abby could dismount. He tethered Jason, and brought the flask and cups from the saddlebags.

"The viaduct seems safe enough for us, but I wouldn't like to let the horses on it. If we walk out you will be able to see better."

They sat on the flat top of the parapet with coffee. Abby looked down at the river, it hardly seemed the same river as that which flowed through the valley, the valley river was bright and urgent, it chuckled as it flowed. Here it was brown, slow and lethargic, meandering between banks of weed.

"So what is the problem with the bridge?" she asked.

"Did you notice when you drove over, the weight limit?" Abby mused for a moment and then it came to her.

"Yes, it said thirty hundred weight."

"Exactly! One and a half tons. Only the smallest of vans could go over that bridge. Any decent size lorry will be seven tons and a bus will be three tons without passengers. So access to the valley can only be from Paverton."

"I thought the sign was just a remnant they had forgotten to remove."

"No that is the weight limit, and has been for the last ninety years," James went on. "When your granddad's railway was running it didn't matter, all goods and passengers went by rail. When they closed the railway it was on the understanding that the bridge would be upgraded to take heavier vehicles. That never happened. My father often tried to get the council to fulfill their promise, he didn't get anywhere as the answer was that it would happen when they could allow for it in the budget. It would appear that many other projects had priority. The bus company said it would provide a service, but that had to come via Paverton. For anyone in the village wanting to get to South Molton, that would mean a round trip of some forty miles, to get to a place that was only seven miles from where they started. Understandably, the locals went out and bought cars, the bus service ran empty for much of the time, so eventually the buses stopped. To be fair to the council, it wasn't just the bridge. That whole lane would have needed to be widened and re-graded. You know how steep those hills are. What I could never understand is why; when the railway was lifted, they never took over the track, and used that to build a new road."

"Perhaps the owner wouldn't sell," Abby remarked.

Abby made the comment lightly, with no accusation. James laughed. "If they had investigated, they would have found out about the way-leave and my father would probably have sold the land without a qualm. But the council didn't look into it, I assume because they really had no intention of doing the work anyway, whatever the circumstances. So it left us like this, partially cut off from the hectic pace of modern society, and the throwback, as you describe it, in me is quite happy with that."

"Why would your father have sold?" Abby was confused. "You have impressed on me the importance of not selling the land."

"If the council had wanted to buy there would have been little choice. You would negotiate for the best price possible, without making the authority go for a compulsory purchase order. In any case dad thought it beneficial for the valley to have the road, so I am sure he would not have put obstacles in the way." Abby now had a smile on her face as she said, "The munificent Comberfords eh?" she teased James. "That's something different."

James followed the tone immediately, "Wonderful, at last you are starting to see us in a better light."

Whilst they had been talking, only two cars had used the road bridge. The driver of one had raised his hand in acknowledgement indicating a local. The other car had driven slowly with heads inside turning this way and that, taking in every sight possible in the time it took to cross the bridge. Abby muttered,"Grockles," which brought gusts of laughter from James.

"Now I know you have gone native. Where did you learn that word?"

"Mary and Jack. They said it was a local word used to describe visitors." James nodded.

"Well sort of, it is used to describe those visitors who are most ignorant and rude. Not for the usual traveller who respects our environment."

Abby felt chastised, "I shall be careful in the future."

They sat in silence for a while, Abby enjoying the peace, the warmth of the sun and a seat which was not moving beneath her. James, sipping his coffee. She watched the river again and wondered why the flow was sullen.

"James, why is the river so different here? Further up it flows quite quickly, but here it's very sluggish." James had been packing away the flask and coffee mugs, obviously in anticipation of starting their return ride. He walked over and looked at the river.

"I suspect it would have something to do with the geology. I believe there is a ridge of impervious granite down there," he pointed away from the valley, "and it has created this area of bog. The river couldn't cut through the ridge so it spreads out and finds many channels to run through. I think the railway bridge was built on the granite, but the road bridge had to have that embankment built, probably why they never improved it, they would have had to put pilings down to get a firm foundation." Abby looked up at James.

"Is there nothing you don't know about this valley?" she asked with a smile.

James grinned and shrugged his shoulders. "It's a legacy of the generations that the family have lived here, and of a little boy who was always asking questions, much to the annoyance of his long-suffering mother and father." His face bore that habitual grin,a grin that could be warming, welcoming and sometimes exasperating. "Do you know that some were rude enough to call me that damn know-it-all?"

Abby had to smile. Not that he qualified as a know-it-all but at the picture conjured in her head. "I'm picturing you as a little boy, in short trousers, dirty knees and torn sweater." James laughed and shook his head.

"Never short trousers, jeans from the very earliest days. Too many brambles and nettles around to wear short trousers. But the torn sweater, yes. I have to admit that." He collected the cups and walked over to Cassie and packed them.

"Are we off then?" Abby asked and James nodded.

"I think we should, bit of a haul back, but we can stop on the way if you want." He brought Jason over and Abby used the parapet of the bridge to mount Jason, who suitably refreshed by the stop was eager to be off.

It is always this way, thought Abby as they rode back. The journey to a place was always more exciting than the return. Yes, she enjoyed riding along with James, and Jason had now learnt to obey her instructions; or perhaps it was that she had learnt how to give them; yet there was a sense of sadness that she was approaching the end of a really good day.

As she rode behind James where the track narrowed, she noticed that he was riding with his shoulders slumped a little, did he feel this sense of sadness as well? The gloom of the wooded area did not help either, the sun was now coming more from the west casting more of the valley into shade. Abby felt happier when they emerged from the woods and the sunlight once again fell upon them. Although there was quite a way to ride yet she didn't want the day to end there, so riding up alongside James she told him how much she had enjoyed the day. "Would you join me for dinner this evening?"

James looked up sharply, "Dinner?"

"Yes, I am sure that Mary would give us a good meal."

James didn't think at all. "I would love that, thank you, but why?"

"You have been so helpful, allowing me to ride Jason, and showing me this lovely valley, which I admit could not be seen better than in the saddle, so it's a little thank you."

"You have no need to thank me," James replied. "It has been an absolute pleasure, and as I haven't ridden this way for some time, the ride was made all the more pleasant for the company."

"Good, I shall tell Mary, I am sure she will do us something a little special." James had that quivering smile about his mouth again.

"I have no doubt of that, she will probably be distraught that she doesn't have any oysters to give us." Abby giggled at that remark, the first time that James had made any kind of a suggestive quip with her. James continued, "Are we going to be formal?"

"Of course not," replied Abby knowing full well that she would put on a dress this evening, and use the lessons she had from Roz, and take more care with her makeup than usual.

"As we are issuing invitations, my mother wondered if you would like to come up to the house one afternoon for tea. Any day this week would suit her, if you are not too busy."

Abby had to give this some thought, not that she wanted to refuse, but about the significance of this meeting. Deciding that there was no real significance, she answered, "I would like that. Would Wednesday suit?"

James nodded. "I am sure it will. I'll let you know this evening if that is ok."

"Will you be there, James?"

"Some of the time, I am sure. I may have to go out though, but I won't let you suffer completely alone."

"You make it sound like a bit of a trial." James laughed.

"No not really. Mother is quite easy to get on with, when she is here. She just makes life uncomfortable for me for the first few days when she arrives. She will be all sweetness and light for you." Abby was thinking to herself that she should have to make another effort for this appointment, when James said, "You don't need to go to any trouble. Mother will probably be in Jodhpurs."

"Oh, does she ride?"

"Yes, Jason is her horse really. When she's here, Jason gets a lot of exercise; else he would be eating his head off all the time." Abby had heard from James before that his mother did not seem to spend all her days in the valley and wondered why?

Emboldened by their frankness earlier she ventured to ask. "Does your mother spend much time away?"

James smiled before answering "When the flat racing season is with us, she's in Berkshire; when it's National Hunt rules, she's everywhere else, as long as there is society to be part of, that's where she is. She has never been happy in the valley you see," James said that as if he couldn't understand why anyone could not be happy with the valley. He went on. "That suits me well. I am left to get on with my life as I see fit. Apart from her spies, of course."

"And what pray," Abby giggled, "have they told your mother about you neglecting your duties to entertain this newcomer to the valley?"

"I would imagine that mother has been briefed thoroughly. I know not what she is thinking, but I can imagine as I would think you can as well."

Abby's face lit up, "Along the same lines as Mavis and Mary perhaps?"

"Got it in one," James nodded vigorously. Abby mentally slapped herself. She was flirting again. Annoyed in one respect but pleased that it seemed to come so easily. Perhaps it was James and the ease with which they could talk and yet not talk together. Neither feeling the need to fill the gaps with inane chatter. She was comfortable with him, never feeling threatened by crude and loaded comments.

They were arriving back at the station. Abby was surprised to see Sam and another man on the platform. She had seen this other man in the Combe Inn and talked with him, yet for the life of her could not remember his name. She was saved when James muttered.

"I wonder what Sam and Harry are doing here?" That was enough of a reminder for her, the name now jumped from her memory. Harry Webster, the man with the terriers.

They rode up, Sam and Harry turned to await their arrival. Abby was the first to speak, "Hello, Sam; hello, Harry, it's a lovely day," she guided Jason towards the platform, and Sam came forward to help her dismount. Abby gave him a kiss on the cheek which brought on Sam's blush as ever. Harry's greeting was more reserved, lifting his cap slightly and murmuring, "Mr. James, Miss Abby."

Sam immediately told Abby why they were here. "Harry and me were wondering how we were going to open up this place for his dogs to check it out. That's if you don't mind of course."

"Oh no, I don't mind at all, in fact I would be pleased."

"Don't want to break a window, or force the door, but I cannot see another way at the moment." Abby could see the problem and was giving some thought as to what she would prefer when a moment of clarity came to her. "Wait a minute, I think I may have keys for the doors."

James turned to her with amazement, "How could you have the keys?"

"I saw granddad's solicitor. There were some personal items and a set of keys. It never occurred to me until this moment that they could be the keys to the station and the house."

"Do you have them at the inn?" Harry asked.

"Yes."

"Well, if Sam and I can borrow them we will try tomorrow, if that's alright with you? I'll bring my tools along just in case they don't fit and we have to force the doors."

"I hope they are the ones," Abby seemed eager. "Can I come along and watch?"

Sam nodded vigorously, "Of course, Abby it's your property after all."

"What time do you think you will be here? Not too early I hope."

Sam laughed. "I would have thought about mid-morning, it will take Harry an hour or so to catch his terriers first."

Harry pretended to bristle a little. "Not likely, Sam, if my dogs get the idea that there is some fun for them here, they will be here before any of us."

Abby laughed, as she remounted Jason, with Sam moving to help her. James had sidled Cassie alongside of Jason to make sure he didn't move away, something that Sam noted silently to himself. They rode off with Abby waving goodbye. Sam smiled and waved back, his inward thoughts adding a lot of warmth to his smile.

Harry watched them ride away, lifted his cap and scratched his head. "I am not really a judge of these things, but it appears to me, Sam, that Mr. James and that young lady are getting rather close."

Sam slowly nodded his head. "Could be you are right, Harry, could be. But don't let on your suspicions to anyone else. You know what my Mavis is like. Give her a sniff of romance and she will have the vicar booked and everything before you can turn round."

Harry was well aware of Mavis's weakness for matchmaking. "Heart of gold, your Mavis. Always remember how kind she was when I needed help. But she's the same as all women. Likes a romance, particularly if it ends with a Church wedding. And our Church has not seen one of those for quite some time. Reckon it'll go that far?"

Sam ruminated, his head nodding slightly, "I would say a fair chance that Mr. James has never treated any girl the way he treats Miss Abby. Perhaps this is the one."

"Well that would be good." Harry slapped Sam on his back. "Just imagine, you could be asked to give the bride away, eh Sam?"

"Rubbish," Sam was scornful. "I am sure Abby has plenty of friends she could ask."

Harry was grinning and shook his head. "Now come on, Sam. It was you told me that the girl has no living relatives. I've noticed she turns to you a lot, so it's a pound to a penny that she will ask you. Of course it will have to be the full rig, you know the tail coat and all. I mean Mr. James will be in full dress uniform, won't he? So you will need the top hat." His smile grew broader as he teased Sam. "Got to do these things properly."

Sam's face was quite red again. "Now don't you start, Harry Webster. You and my Mavis are very much alike, neither of you know when to stop do you?"

The couple in question rode quietly for a while. Until Abby turned to James. "James, why is it that Harry will always call me 'Miss Abby?' He did so then and also when I have seen him in the Combe Inn."

James thought a little. He knew why, but searched for the right way of telling Abby the reason. "It's something to do with the way Harry sees his place in society. Because he places you as one of my peer group, he sees you in my company, so he has to show respect. He always calls me 'Mr. James' so he has to call you 'Miss Abby.'" Abby shook her head.

"But that's not right, I am no better than them, besides, Sam calls me Abby. It's back to the same situation with your father and granddad."

"Yes, but it's a little different with Sam. He is the oldest man in the valley, and you show him respect as that. In addition, you have become close to him, treating him as a father figure, so that makes it O.K. for Sam to call you Abby. But Harry could not, for all the tea in China, be so familiar. I know it isn't how things happen in the modern world, with everyone calling everyone else by their given name, no matter how fleeting the acquaintance. But here, older and different values apply." Abby had a mischievous smile on her face as she replied, "Oh we are back to the throwback mode are we? So why don't they call you squire? You are the squire, aren't you?"

James grinned. "Squire is a title you have to earn, it doesn't just come with the land and the big house. It is a very old style, a bit too old even for me, it never seemed right. One or two did call me that, but I quickly put them straight. To be honest, I agree with you. I am no better than them. They work the land, I am just a sort of parasite even though I own the land. I would be happy if they just called me James, but they didn't think it right."

He then changed the topic. "Anyway, clever girl. How come you manage to find your grandfather's solicitor, I wouldn't have thought for a moment that he would have one."

"I have to confess it wasn't my idea," Abby replied a little shamefaced. "Toni at the Library in Paverton suggested, I asked around. I struck lucky."

"So was there a huge legacy?" he asked with his normal grin.

Abby laughed. "If you can call a couple of keys, a watch and a journal, which Mr. Brasher went ecstatic about, a legacy, well then yes. The personal items were nice to have though."

"It brought you closer to your granddad." Abby nodded and went silent for a while. James did not attempt to fill the void, but concentrated on taking the horses through the gate into the meadow.

They arrived back at the inn. The cream teas were not so busy this afternoon, and apart from one or two curious looks as they came through the gate, and hitched Cassie and Jason to the fence, little was said as they sat down. Mary immediately appeared and beamed her smile as Abby asked if they could have some tea.

"Did you enjoy your ride?" she asked hoping for some tidbits with which she could regale Mavis. Abby's next request gave her all she needed.

"James is going to join me for dinner tonight. Mary, I don't want you to go to any trouble, whatever is going will be good. Is that all right?" Mary's mind was racing, outwardly she kept her calm. She replied casually, "No trouble at all, as long as I put out enough food to feed three, Mr. James will be quite content."

James could not let this slur pass, "Mary, are you saying I eat a lot?"

"No, Mr James. It's just that you seem to believe that a plate should never be sent back with anything on it but the pattern."

"It is simply good manners, Mary, good manners. If someone goes to the trouble of cooking this good food, I should not disrespect their labour by leaving food on the plate."

Mary made no reply to that except, 'Humph.' Leaving no doubts about her opinion. "I'll get you some tea."

Abby was absolutely certain that there would also be scones, jam and cream. She would eat none of it, but knew that James would fall upon the scones with delight.

She sat back to enjoy the late afternoon sun, grateful for a solid seat. James had gone to the horses and was emptying the saddle bags of their lunch. Jason and Cassie were in luck as there were two apples left, which they scrunched with obvious enjoyment. He put the packages on the table and whispered to Abby, "Nothing left but the wrappings. That will please Mary," Abby giggled.

If it pleased Mary, she said nothing, as she placed a tray on their table. As Abby expected, the tray held far more than the tea, for which Abby was gasping. She busied herself pouring tea for them both, remembering that James took one sugar, something that Mary noted; whilst James set about the scones and cream.

Mary watched with a smile on her face for a while and then said, "I shall have to be getting on now, oh by the way, I shall be doing Somerset Pork tonight, but looking at Mr. James and those scones vanishing, I don't suppose he will want much anyway." James had his mouth full at that time, and was unable to reply. He just looked at Mary with a hurt expression on his face.

CHAPTER SEVENTEEN

When Abby returned to her room, the first thing she did was to go through the wardrobe, looking for a suitable dress for tonight. Nothing too formal, this wasn't a Cocktail Bar, but nothing too casual. As she was doing this Mary knocked and came in when Abby called.

"I wondered if you would like to have a bath."

Abby jumped at the chance. "Oh yes, Mary, that would be lovely. What do you think of this?" Abby held up a frock. It was a dark blue, with a little white collar.

Mary looked unimpressed. "A little too business-like, don't you think?" Abby had to agree. Mary moved to the wardrobe and looked through with Abby. She pointed.

"Now that would look nice." Abby pulled the frock out, a Polka Dot button-through in lemon with white spots, a square top and thin straps over the shoulder. Abby held it against herself and looked in the mirror. Mary went on. "The lemon will show off your tanned shoulders." Abby looked more closely, indeed she had tanned quite well, she looked round at Mary and nodded her head.

"Yes, I think you are right."

***

James arrived, wearing immaculately pressed Chinos, pale blue shirt with the collar unbuttoned, and a Linen jacket, which he immediately discarded. He regarded Abby with a jaundiced eye.

"I didn't think we were going to be formal?" The grin forecast one of his sardonic comments. "If this is casual do you put a Tiara on for just a slightly more important occasion?" He went on, "But I have to say that you look lovely."

Abby smiled with pleasure at the compliment. "Thank you kind sir, do I curtsy now?" James grinned. Then Abby went on the attack. "You don't appear to be too casual yourself."

James shrugged his shoulders and held his hands up before replying. "Well let's say I had a sneaky suspicion that you were going to be a little elastic in your idea of casual, so in honour of the occasion I even shaved again." This was said with a smile on his face, and Abby could do little except smile in return, but she did put her hand up to his cheek to check for the closeness of the shave. Was this what they meant about being hoist with your own petard? She sat down whilst James went to get their drinks. Of course James could not go to the bar without some banter from the early evening drinkers, many just in from the days labour, and still in their working clothes. Before he returned Mary had appeared at Abby's side asking if they would like the food served now. Abby thought about it and decided against.

"Could you leave it for a while, Mary? James is getting us some drinks and it would be nice to sit quietly and enjoy those for a while." Mary was only too pleased to do this. As far as she was concerned the more time that Abby and James spent together the better.

***

The food had come up to Mary's normal standard, superb, and James despite demolishing the pile of scones earlier managed to clear a large plate of Somerset Pork with a host of vegetables. They were sitting with coffee and chatting over the events of the day when their quiet chat was disturbed by an increase in noise from the bar. James had his back to the bar and turned round to see what had caused this. Abby looked up, and was curious to see a man staring at her. His face had a look of total surprise, almost of shock. He was medium height, pale-faced with a fringe of ruddy hair surrounding an otherwise completely bald head. James suddenly thought he recognised the man.

"Good Lord, its Reg, isn't it? Reg, is that you?" The man stared at James for some time, and then with recognition clearing his face greeted James.

"Well Mr. James, it took me a bit to place you, last time I saw you was just before they closed the box, late sixty-five that was. You were nobbut a lad then." He approached their table, although speaking to James; his eyes never left Abby's face. James could understand his astonishment, and made an introduction.

"Abby, this is Reg Purvess. Reg, this is Abby Tregonney." This had a surprising effect, as Reg slumped into a chair open-mouthed in shock and then felt in his pocket producing a handkerchief, and proceeded to wipe his eyes. Abby put her hand on his arm, and said gently.

"I am Marion's daughter."

Reg made no reply for a moment, but eventually looked up, his eyes red-rimmed. "I don't understand, I can see the likeness, is Marion here? I can't believe it, I mean how did... No what I mean is." Reg stumbled over words, the tumult in his brain making his thoughts a complete nonsense.

James got up. His innate courtesy told him to leave a man alone when he was emotional.

"I'll get you a drink, Reg, Bitter is it?" Reg nodded, and James walked away. Reg suddenly turned round and called after him.

"Thank you Mr. James." Abby waited until Reg pulled himself together and smiled at him.

"It's good to meet you, Mr. Purvess. I have heard a lot about you. You taught Mum to work the signals, didn't you?" Reg nodded.

"Yes, she was quick, got to know the bells in next to no time. Please Miss, where is your mum? I would love to see her again."

Abby could see no way in which she could let him down lightly. "I am sorry, Mr. Purvess. Mum is dead; she died about sixteen years ago." Sorrow is something that everyone expresses from time to time. For some it is genuine, for others something that is expected of them but not touching their emotions. Abby saw immediately that Reg's sorrow was genuine. The handkerchief was produced again, and no one could fake the grief that Reg was suffering. James arrived with the drinks. He also brought with him a lady who was introduced to Abby as Gladys, Reg's wife. He had briefed her when getting the drinks and she put her arm round her husband's shoulder.

She looked at Abby and gave a wan smile. "He liked your mum, and has worried for years about what happened to her, this is a bit of a shaker for him." Abby nodded, and when Reg had again gathered himself, she asked him if he was alright. Reg nodded.

Rather than having Reg ask question after question Abby felt she should explain. "When Mum left here, she was expecting me. We lived in London, but she never talked about when and where she had grown up. Only once or twice did she mention Combe Lyney. I was working when she died and it didn't really cross my mind to try and find this place until earlier this year. I came down here not knowing whether I had any family here or anything. With Sam's help I have been able to discover a lot, who my grandfather was, and how my mum grew up." Reg listened with rapt attention.

"But you are still Tregonney?"

"Yes mum never married." Reg absorbed this with a disturbed look on his face.

"Do you know who your father was?"

"I have no idea. I have talked with Sam and Mavis, and they have no idea either. I had a silly thought that you may know, but now I don't think you do."

"No I don't." This was said with some anger, "but if I did I would have done for him after letting Marion down like that." Abby smiled at Reg.

"That's good of you to say, but really it is all academic now. I have known all these years that I was illegitimate; not having a father has never been a problem. Mum was all the parent I needed." Reg nodded.

"Yes Marion would have been, always thorough, must have got that from her Dad."

It was at that point that Sam, who had only just arrived at the Combe Inn, came in all flustered.

"Reg, you're here! I am sorry but I got held up." He addressed Abby. "Sorry Love, I meant to meet Reg before and explain everything to him."

Reg stood up and shook Sam's hand. "It's good to see you Sam, after all these years. You don't look a day over sixty, but I know you must be at least one hundred." He smiled, as did Sam.

"Well show some respect for your elders, Lad. I'll have a pint whilst you're at the bar." He leaned down to give Abby a kiss on the cheek, and turned to Gladys.

"Well, Gladys Carter as was, how are you? Sorry day for us when you went off with this fellow. The prettiest girl in the village, gone just like that." He clicked his fingers. Gladys stood up and gave Sam a hug."

"It's good to see you again Mr. Perry. How is Roger these days? Are you working him just as hard as you used to?"

Sam shrugged his shoulders. "I have handed the farm over to him now, so he pushes himself rather than me pushing him. You know he married Valerie Williams, don't you?"

"No, I didn't, but I am not surprised. She always had her eye on Roger, none of us others could get a look in." Reg came back with drinks at that moment.

"Hey, hey, what's this? What's this about you and Roger?" He was smiling.

"That's just the point." Gladys laughed as she explained. "Roger was spoken for long before even knew it, Valerie wasn't going to let any other girl get anywhere near him." Abby was fascinated; this was the gossip of a time when her mother was around. Mum would have probably known all these people and about their attachments and intrigues.

Sam having seated himself nudged Reg.

"You are going to have to talk to Abby, about her grandfather. The girl is very keen to know all about him." Abby nodded with her eyes gleaming.

"Would you mind Mr. Purvess?"

"Not at all, but there is one condition though." Abby asked the condition. "That you stop calling me Mr. Purvess. It's Reg ok?"

Abby turned to James. "See! It doesn't have to be Mr. Mrs. or Miss always." James just waved his hand in resignation. Abby addressed Reg. "And I am Abby. Reg, what can you tell me about my grandfather? Sam has told me so much, but even he says he didn't know him well."

Reg thought for a while. "Well I should start by saying that he was a railwayman through and through; thorough, diligent and always ready to give someone a helping hand. Mind you, because of his manner some people didn't think it was help, more like criticism. He certainly helped me a lot."

Abby looked at Sam. "That doesn't sound like the man you described?"

Sam shook his head. "I said that I didn't know your granddad that well. I would only see him for about ten minutes, twice a day."

"Don't get it wrong Miss Abby." Reg interrupted. "Thomas was like that. All stiff and formal. He was economic with words, I think the expression is, and unless you got to know him well, he came across as brusque. He wasn't really; he just didn't know how else it could be done. When he joined the GWR, it was run very much like the Army. Everyone was addressed by their surname if they were junior to you in rank; Mister if they were colleagues and Sir if they were senior. Passengers were always Sir or Madam, even the young ones. Orders were given, and obedience was expected, the discipline was very strict, you obeyed. If not there were plenty of men who wanted your job. If you were admonished by your superior, you stood and took it, and then said 'Thank you Sir'. No arguing with them either. That was how Thomas learned, and it was a lesson for his lifetime." He took a sip of his drink. "But he was a good man. He would never let anyone down, and he stood up for those who needed help."

Abby was warmed by this description of her granddad; it would appear that he had virtues hidden until now. "Please go on."

Reg nodded. "One of the reasons that I liked him, was because of the help he gave me and my family. My dad was on the railway, and he was killed in an accident at South Molton. If you were related to an employee of the GWR, you got preference over others who didn't have a family connection. But BR didn't bother with that, and when I applied for a job, they were going to offer me a position in Lancashire. Thomas had known my father and wrote a letter that changed their minds, and instead they offered me work in this Division. I first worked in a box as a Booking Boy, learning the ropes, but mainly recording all the trains, and the passing times. Later I did the signals course, and Thomas asked for me to come to Combe Lyney, knowing that the man there was about to retire. As the cottage went with the job, that was important. Me, and my mum were living in rented rooms in Dulverton. So I got the job, and Mum had a proper home to live in. That was your grandfather for you. He never said anything to anyone about it, and never reminded us of his help."

Abby was so happy to hear this, it showed a human side to her granddad that hadn't been discovered before. "I know you were a good friend of mum. How did that happen?"

Reg thought for a second or two. "Well it was after the death of your grandma. Marion was left very much to her own devices. Your granddad would leave the house at five thirty every morning, and wouldn't be back before about nine in the evening. Your mum would do all the cleaning and washing at the weekends, but during the school holidays even that couldn't fill all her time, so she was hanging about doing nothing with no-one to talk to. To tell the truth I was angry with your granddad, because he was so involved with his job that he took for granted that Marion would do all his washing for him, and cook a meal for him, but she was only ten years old! A child! It wasn't right. He was only a hundred yards away, but he could have been in China for all the contact he had with her."

After all these years his anger was still obvious. "One day I asked Marion into the box, gave her a cuppa, and we talked whilst I was working the levers. After some time she started to write up the register for me. Well to cut a long story short she learnt everything about working the box, and even got the knack of pulling off the up Home."

Abby couldn't let this go without asking. "Why was that so difficult?"

"That was the furthest movable signal." Reg told her. "The distant signals were fixed you see. But the up Home was away at the other end of the platform, so you had the weight of the board, plus all the cable run to move. Not easy for a grown man, but Marion would pull it slightly to take off the catch, brace her foot on the frame, get all her weight behind the lever and suddenly surprise it, and off it came. It always made me laugh to see it; there was this little slip of a girl, heaving away at this lever which was almost as tall as she was. Of course her father caught her at it one day, I was surprised that he didn't cotton on earlier. He signed the register every day and didn't even recognise his own daughter's handwriting. Anyway he put a stop to it, well so he thought, but your mum would still come, but knew how to make herself scarce when it looked as if he would visit the box. Thomas even helped with that. His habit was to call at the box before my half-shift finished and sign the register. Of course with your granddad it was as regular as clockwork, always ten o' clock on the dot. The railway worked with a timetable and so did Thomas. Everyone knew it, so he never caught her again." Abby had learnt from Mr. Brasher's notes what a half-shift was, and about the stationmaster signing the Train Register. But she also knew that an unauthorised person in the Signal box was a serious offence.

She asked Reg why he allowed it.

"As I said I took pity on her, yes it wasn't right for her to be in the box, but on a branch like this rules became a little elastic. The only one in authority was your granddad, and if he didn't know, then there was nothing to worry about. Apart from that Marion was a lively girl with a great sense of humour, don't know where she got it from as Thomas certainly had none at all, well none that he showed. The drivers and guards liked her too, and I know for a fact that she had frequent footplate rides down to the Junction and back. She came back with coal dust all over her face and a great big smile lighting up her dirty face. She would drop off when the engine stopped to give up the token, your granddad couldn't see because she was on the blindside as he looked from the platform. She hid behind the Box until the train was in the station, and then dashed across to the house and washed her face, coming out as demure as anything with a face that looked like butter wouldn't melt." Reg laughed heartily at the memory. Abby giggled delightedly as well. She could remember her mother's sense of humour, and her capacity for hard work, obviously learned when she accepted the domestic chores for her father.

James had sat there listening, and nodding his head from time to time. Reg's comments awakening memories. He leaned towards Abby.

"Do you remember me telling you that Marion had the run of the place? Well there you have the proof."

Abby smiled. "I suppose you are trying to tell me that I have to believe everything you say?"

James grinned. "Well almost everything."

Sam had watched this little exchange with a warm feeling, the growing closeness between Abby and James delighted him, but he kept his feelings to himself. This was not a mad passion that would extinguish as quickly as it flared, here were two people who were coming to understand each other, to like each other, and would probably be most surprised when they found that friendship had become Love.

Reg seemed as if he wanted to say something, but stopped. Abby looked at him with a question on her face. He looked at James with a slightly humorous expression and decided to say what he had started. "I was going to say that for all his strict rules, Thomas was not above accepting some bounty from time to time."

Abby was puzzled. "Bounty?"

"Yes. The ganger was very good at providing rabbits, pheasants, a trout now and again, and mushrooms. We all had a share, including Thomas, although he didn't know where they came from. They were just left on his doorstep."

James knew where they came from. "Poaching!" He declared. "Poaching on my land."

Reg grinned. "Well the ganger always said that they were taken from railway land."

James was smiling now. "How do you think a trout could be taken from railway land?" He asked. "Unless the fish managed to jump out of the river onto a bridge."

Reg shrugged his shoulders. "We didn't think to ask." He grinned back at James who acted outraged, but couldn't keep up the pretence, and returned the grin.

"Mushrooms," James commented. "I can understand. Rabbits did have their burrows in the embankments. pheasants now, he would have to be lucky to catch them on railway land."

"Well, Mr. James you know how stupid pheasants are. I am told he would put down some bread crumbs and seeds, then sit there quietly until the silly pheasant came along to eat them. Quick whack on the head and the pheasant's in the bag, or so I understand."

James laughed. Then went on to say. "Well it's a good job then that the railway isn't there now; otherwise I would know where to look if I were losing pheasants on a regular basis."

There was one question that bothered Abby.

"Surely the ganger wouldn't take a fishing rod with him?" Sam, James and Reg smiled in unison.

Sam answered her. "No he would tickle them."

Abby looked long at Sam, trying to decide whether he was kidding her or not. "Tickle them?" Sam nodded. Abby looked confused so he went on to explain.

"There are parts of the river where the trout will sort of hover, in eddies and suchlike. If you are very slow and gentle, you can get your hand into the water and underneath them, and then gently stroke their bellies. It seems to hypnotise the trout. Once you have lulled them you can quickly scoop them out and onto the bank. There you have it. trout for dinner." Abby looked from one to the other and saw that none were smiling, just nodding.

She appealed to Gladys. "Are they having me on?"

Gladys shook her head. "No, Abby. It's quite well known how to do it, especially amongst those who want to take the fish without the owner's permission."

James cleared his throat. "And that was without my father's permission. He took a dim view of poaching, always complaining that the Courts didn't treat the case severely enough. But then he couldn't understand why deportation for life was not still an available sentence."

The smiles were interrupted by Sam. "You do your father an injustice, Mr. James. When the old gamekeeper retired, he never bothered to appoint another. Woody lived by poaching all the time, your father knew this, but never tried to put a stop to it."

"Yes." He agreed. "But he considered that Woody paid for the game in other ways."

Sam had to agree with that, and then changed the topic and addressed Abby. "Have you got those keys, Abby?"

Abby nodded. "Yes they are in my room. I'll go and fetch them."

James got to his feet as Abby left. "I'll get another round in."

Sam turned to Reg. "Abby reckons she has the keys to the station and the house. We are going to open them up tomorrow. Want to come along?"

There was no doubt in Reg's mind. "Yes, of course, but why?"

"Abby is going to live there."

James had returned with a tray of drinks, and on hearing Sam, added. "She wants to restore the station as it was when her granddad first came to Combe Lyney."

Reg was dumbstruck, and then a happy expression suffused his face. "That will be good. A Tregonney back at the station. Wherever he is, Thomas will finally have a smile on his face. Mind though, he wouldn't let anyone else see it." Abby returned and handed the two keys to Sam. Reg leaned across.

"Let me have a look." Sam showed him the keys. "Yes I would say those are the keys, I saw them often enough, Thomas always had them on a little chain loop attached to his belt." He addressed Abby. "Sam says you are going to live in the old house and restore the station. Your granddad would be very happy about that. Did you buy the land from Railtrack?" Abby shook her head, but James answered.

"No. The land always belonged to the estate, but no-one knew it. It was Abby who discovered that, so we have done a deal." Reg didn't enquire into the details, but went on to say.

"If there is anything you need to know, I hope you will ask me."

"That's very kind of you, Reg. I suspect I will need a lot of help as there doesn't seem to be many photographs of the station to work with. I have the ones that you took, but they don't show the station as it was in nineteen thirty-eight."

Reg laughed. "Oh it didn't change much at all. I have some more at home, which I took from the box. I'll sort them out, and let you have them."

Abby's smile said it all. "Have you any more with my granddad in them?"

"I think I have. He hated having his photo taken. When things were running down, we used to get enthusiasts coming around to take photos. Thomas would chase them off. Of course there were some official photos taken, Thomas couldn't do anything about that, so they should be in the archives somewhere, but I don't know where that could be."

James looked at Abby. "From what you have said about him, I reckon that your Mr. Brasher will know where they are, and how to get hold of them."

Abby agreed. "Yes I suspect he will."

Reg surprised Abby then. "Will you want any Permanent Way?"

"Permanent Way?"

"Yes. I know some of the old gangers, all retired now of course, but I was told about some rails that had been lifted, but never sold for scrap. Could be possible to get some. You will have to pay for them, but I could find out." Abby was delighted, the smile on her face saying it all. With rails the station would really be as her granddad knew it.

"That would be wonderful, could you, Reg? I would be ever so grateful."

"It shouldn't be a problem, I will ask next time I see the guys. They would probably be happy to come and lay them for you, give them something to do. Mind I doubt they will be able to do it the old way. They will need a small crane or a JCB now."

"The old way." Abby queried. "What was the old way?"

Reg laughed. "Sweat, muscle, and aching backs. They would place the sleepers, then fix the chairs, the sleepers were pre-drilled at the permanent way depot; and finally they would put the rails into the chairs and hammer in the keys. All by hand. Two men to lift a Sleeper and at least ten men to lift a rail." Abby was amazed; she had thought they would have some kind of mechanical assistance.

"Ten men to lift a rail?"

"Yes, at least ten. They had these grips, like huge pliers, that they would fix over the rail head, lift the rail together on the count, and heave it into position."

Abby was now worried. "No! I would love some rails, but I can't have these old men doing that, what if one were to hurt himself."

"Don't you worry about that, Abby. If they say they can do it, they will do it. Lessons and habits learned from a lifetime are not forgotten. I haven't worked a mechanical box for years, it was all buttons and small levers when I retired, but put me back in a box and I reckon it would take about twenty minutes to get all the old skills back. They will be the same but as I said they will need something to lift and carry the rails, don't think there will enough of them to do that now." Abby still had reservations but decided that she would wait and see what Reg could discover.

The evening was drawing to a close now, and Abby couldn't wait until the morrow. Reg and Gladys were staying at the Inn, so the party broke up. Sam waited for his customary kiss on the cheek, which resulted in his usual broad smile and blush. Reg promised to be there at the station, but Gladys had decided that she would go to see her family.

"I will see you again, won't I?" entreated Abby, receiving assurances from Gladys that indeed she would.

Abby arrived at the station just after ten o' clock to find Sam, Harry and Reg there already. A few minutes later James rode up on Cassie. He greeted them and asked Harry. "Where are the dogs, Harry?"

"They are in the van. Thought it best to get the place opened first, else they would be difficult to control. They're excited enough as it is."

"Good idea." said James. "Well shall we give it a try?"

Sam gave the keys to Reg asking. "Which one is which?"

Reg gave them a cursory look. "That one is for the station," pointing to the slightly larger key, "and that one is for the house." Reg handed the keys to Harry, who was carrying a work bag. He put it down and produced a can of oil. He dripped some on the keys, and approached the station door.

He turned and looked at Reg. "Which door does it fit?"

Reg shook his head. "Doesn't matter, the key fits both locks." Harry gave a grunt which could have signified approval of that system, and proceeded to give both locks two or three squirts of oil.

"Let those soak for a bit, and we will try them. I will go and give the house lock a squirt as well, will help to ease it." He went off leaving the keys with Sam.

Reg held his hand out for them. "If I remember rightly, this door always gave a bit of trouble," pointing to the booking office door. "Thomas had a knack, let's see if it still works." He inserted the key and tried to move it, meeting some resistance at first, but gradually working the key round through ninety degrees. He then pulled the door towards him and twisted the key sharply. At first it didn't move, so he tugged on the door again when suddenly the key turned through to a complete three hundred and sixty degrees. He then relocked the door and went through the action again and again. With each attempt the key turned more easily as the oil worked its way into the tumblers, but the door needed to be pulled tightly outwards each time.

James was concerned. "If that needs to be done each time, it could be difficult for Abby. You might want to think about changing the locks."

Abby shook her head. "No I shall get the knack." She was determined that she would change as little as possible.

Harry now returned being dragged along by two very excited terriers. Obviously eager to be at whatever adventure awaited them. Abby laughed delightedly as they yipped and growled deep in their throats, the fur on their backs raised and their bodies quivering with excitement. Harry approached the door, trying with difficulty to restrain the dogs.

"The doors unlocked." Sam told him.

Harry was surprised. "Well that must have went easy then."

"Reg sorted it. He says there was a knack."

Harry snorted. "Damn railwayman. Always tells everyone there is a knack." He grinned at Reg, who grinned back. Harry asked Sam if he could open the door whilst he prepared to let the dogs loose. The handle turned and the door had to be pushed firmly against the wishes of the hinges which after close on thirty years of inactivity didn't want to yield. Reg lent his weight to Sam, and the door creaked open. Immediately Harry let the dogs free and with barks and growls they leapt through the opening. The barking withered away gradually and Harry looked at Sam shaking his head.

"Nothing in there."

Sam nodded. "I didn't think there would be." He agreed. "Not after all this time, that's if there had ever been any." James watched this exchange with interest. He bent down to where Harry had left his bag of tools.

"Harry, can I use this claw hammer, I can make a start on getting the boarding off the windows."

"Yes please, Mr. James. We may be able to see what we are doing inside then."

Abby was impatient to go inside, but Sam cautioned her to wait until the windows were unveiled.

"If my memory serves me correct, it was always quite gloomy in there, best wait until the light is better." Harry had gathered his now unhappy Terriers, and turned his attention to the other door. Reg explained that this was the waiting room. This time the key turned easily, and again the dogs leapt into the room with excited barks, but they had the same disappointing result. James, helped by Sam had now removed most of the boarding at the windows. Abby cautiously moved to examine the booking office. Reg entered first and beckoned Abby in. They kicked up years of dust from the floorboards which hung around like a mist twelve inches above the floor. The room was totally empty, bare walls once painted cream and brown, now streaked with dirt, There were a couple of what could have been Lamp-holders on the wall, but no sign of any pipe work. The back wall as they entered had a small glass window, with an opening, an inverted 'U', cut into it at the base where a small counter was fixed to the wall. To the left of that an open door invited further exploration.

Reg was just as inquisitive as Abby. "Thirty years." He lapsed into silence. "Thirty years. I can't believe it." He suddenly realised that he should be explaining things to Abby. "That was your granddads office, also the ticket office. I don't know why the door is open, Thomas would never have left it like that. Regulations demanded that it was closed at all times. I suppose that the BR gang left it that way when they cleared the place. Do you want to go in?" This was a largely superfluous question as Abby was already heading towards the office. After all the excitement of coming here to open the station, she was now completely silent as she absorbed the atmosphere, a strange melancholy descended on her, as she touched the walls and the doors that her granddad would have touched every day, where he had been so much at home, in his element. The room was so gloomy and ordinary. She entered granddads office. All that remained was an ancient desk, sagging at one side and held against the wall by an angled iron. There was a counter fixed to the wall where the ticket window was. The counter had an indent where the issuing porter would stand. Reg's voice came to her through her sadness.

"There was an Edmundson machine just to the right of the ticket window, you put the ticket in the slot and it automatically dated the ticket. Your grandfather worked at the desk. He had a very old typewriter. It took him hours to type letters. There was always new promotional rates being introduced, and he had to write to anyone who could possibly be interested to inform them. It was ridiculous really. Those customers that did use the railway had no other choice, and there was no point in writing to the others because they had long ago made other arrangements. Your granddad never gave up though, he would be here until nine or ten in the evening still typing. Marion would even bring his evening meal in. When it got dark he would light the Kerosene Lamp, not that it helped much. They never gave much of a light."

Abby was close to tears. She thought she had shed them all, but the picture being painted, of this lonely old man, sitting here late into the evening, typing letters that would probably be consigned to the rubbish the moment they were received, tore at her heart. She turned to Reg. "Why? Why did he do all this when he knew it was a waste of time?"

All Reg could say in answer was. "That was his job. It was part and parcel of his employment, and he would carry it out no matter how long it took, no matter that it wouldn't do any good. His pride would not let him do any less, he saw it as his duty." The explanation mollified Abby to an extent. She could remember herself in the early days in the City, working away for hours at her supposed investments, so perhaps this gene of integrity had been bequeathed to her.

They walked out and looked in the waiting room. Again, the same bare floor with cream and brown walls. To the back of the room was another, smaller room, with a dingy cubicle leading off. Reg explained that this was the ladies waiting room and toilet. Abby was uncertain that she would have liked to use that under any circumstances. The only item of furniture was the long seat, originally painted grey, but now dappled with worn away paint and dirt. Abby asked Reg why this seat would have been left when all the other furniture had gone.

"I suspect that the size of this would have put the men from BR off. The rumour was that it came in pieces and was assembled in the room. I can't see how they would get it through the door otherwise." James joined them to say that he was going down to get the boards off the house windows.

"Sam and Harry are down there trying to unlock the door, but it is giving them a lot more trouble than these two."

Reg grinned. "I had better come down and give it the magic touch then." James went off and Abby and Reg followed at a more leisurely pace chatting generally about how the station was worked. Reg was impressed with Abby's knowledge. "Have you been talking to someone?"

Abby looked pleased with herself. "I met this lovely old gentleman called Mr. Brasher, who is writing a history of the Great Western Railway. I asked him about this line, and he recited all the details off by heart. He even had granddads name down as one of the stationmasters. He said about the lamps, and how granddad would have started by filling, trimming and replacing the lamps. He said that was a job for the latest recruit. Called him a Lad-Porter." Reg was astounded.

"That's right, they did. Well I never, and he's got all this stuff for a book?"

"Yes. But I don't know if it's ever going to be published. He has been working on it for twenty-five years, and still says there is a lot to do." They were interrupted by a shout from James.

CHAPTER EIGHTEEN

"Abby! Come and look at this." James shouted. They hastened to see the cause of James' excitement, similarly Sam and Harry who were still trying to unlock the door, came round to the front of the house where James was looking in the window he had just cleared. They all joined him and he said. "Look inside." Abby did so, and through the dirt on the glass could just see into the room. As her eyes adjusted to the gloom she saw what had excited James. Furniture! Table, chairs, an old fashioned dresser, with what appeared to be crockery still displayed on the dresser. She looked at James with surprise written all over her face. The others crowded around to look.

"Good Lord!"

"Strewth!"

"Bloody Hell!" This last from Reg, who immediately apologised to Abby.

She smiled. "Don't worry, Reg. I have heard much worse in the Dealing Room, and have used much the same myself at times. But I won't say what language I used as I don't want to have Sam believe that I am not quite a Lady."

Sam laughed. "Abby I am sure that anything you said would not be as bad as Roger and me when we can't get the tractor started. Come on let's get that door unlocked." He hurried off, closely followed by Harry.

The door to the house was at the side, a cantilever porch roof protecting it from direct rain. Harry was wrestling furiously with the lock, which had turned a little but then stuck solid. His struggles were accompanied by a surprising amount of swearing which amused Abby enormously. Suddenly the lock gave up and the key turned. Harry regarded his efforts morosely with the comment.

"Well I have either done it, or broken the lock." He straightened his back and went off to get the dogs which had been tied to some fence work.

Sam looked at Abby. "Do you want to open the door?"

"May I?" Abby's curiosity was evident.

"Bless you Girl; it's your house now. Seems right to me that a Tregonney should open it again." Abby took hold of the door knob and turned it. Surprisingly it went quite easily at first, but then the door stuck, she pushed it again with Sam lending his weight, and slowly the door creaked open. Harry was there with the Terriers, and called. "Stand back." Abby moved to the side and the dogs passed them with the same excitement they had shown before. Their search took longer this time, but the result was almost similar to the station, the excited yelps gradually died away, as the unhappy dogs found no sport until suddenly the yelps and growls built back to a crescendo. Then one dog came trotting out, proudly carrying his kill. A very dirty duster! Harry took the duster off the dog saying "Silly bugger!" and looked at Abby. "Nothing in there. By rights you should be first in, but I'll go in if you want, Miss Abby, just to be certain."

Abby shook her head. "Thank you Harry, but I will do it." Harry nodded and looked at Sam, who also nodded. Abby entered her family home.

***

James had managed to get the boards off all the downstairs windows, so there was adequate light for Abby to see. She entered a large room, dominated by the simple table which stood square in the middle of the floor, its sturdy legs planted seemingly unmoved by time. Ladder-back chairs of the same unfussy design were arranged, two to one side, one to the other, and one at one end. To the left of the door stood a dresser, the top reaching up close to the ceiling with three shelves running the full width. Underneath the counter, were two wide drawers with simple cupped handles, and beneath them two cupboards, one of which was slightly opened. To the right of the door against a window sat a large, shallow Butler sink with a single tap standing tall over it. To the left of the sink there was a grooved wooden draining board, now cracked and warped. Over the draining board screwed to the wall were a row of hooks, one holding a cracked mug.

As Abby turned anti clockwise she saw a blackened, dusty range, and then a door leading presumably to the stairs and the back room. The opposite wall to the main door was empty except for a large, round, wooden cased clock, the hands frozen at four thirty-five. Everything was covered in a fine white dust, even the great clusters of cobwebs which festooned everywhere. Abby stood there with astonishment. The dresser did indeed have a few pieces of crockery. Sam, Harry, and Reg had now crowded into the room, followed shortly at a run by James who, having taken down the boards from the downstairs windows had wanted to be the first after Abby to enter.

Abby turned to them indicating the furniture. "How?" She said no more as the question was obvious. Sam shook his head. She looked at Reg with the question still on her face. He shrugged his shoulders. James had been pondering this question from the time he had unveiled the window. He cleared his throat, and they all looked at him expectantly.

"I could be very wrong." He said hesitantly. "But I would say the house wasn't cleared for a number of reasons, but all connected." Abby waited for him to go on. "It may have been that the crew that cleared the station were told that this was now private property, they wouldn't have a key for it."

Reg interrupted. "They had a key to the station."

James nodded. "Yes it stands to reason that they would have a duplicate for the station, but this house was the stationmaster's residence. Even if they had a key, they couldn't clear it because the contents were his not BR property. They simply boarded the windows and left it. Someone in BR obviously knew that with the closure of the line, the land and buildings became the property of the estate. They could come and take away the items that belonged to the railway, but they couldn't touch this stuff, nor do any damage, which was probably why they left the seat in the waiting room." He thought speculatively about this. "If BR's legal people knew about the Way-leave, it would have been nice of them to inform my father. But then they could have done just that, but knowing dad he could have just as easily lost the letter, or never bothered to read it." Harry to whom all this was academic and not of interest offered to look at the rest of the house.

"Upstairs will be dark." James suggested, "I will need ladders to get the boards off those windows."

Harry thought for a moment. "I will take the dogs back to the van. I am sure I have a torch somewhere. I'll get it."

Abby walked gingerly over to the partially opened interior door, trying not to disturb too much dust and ducking as cobwebs dangled low. She pulled the door completely open to reveal a small lobby. To the right the stairs ascended into complete darkness, opposite there was a smaller room which she entered. This was empty apart from a large Captains chair and a single Iron bed frame. She walked towards the chair with little puffs of white dust rising from her shoes, and touched it gently. She could see her granddad sitting here, but no other sign of a family having lived in the room. Reg had followed her in. She turned to him.

"Just this?" She asked plaintively.

Reg nodded glumly. "After Marion left, and there was no sign of her coming back, Thomas cleared upstairs, and moved in here. It was warmer, because the range backed on to that wall." Abby understood. Emotions chased around her head. It seemed that every time she got closer to her granddad, another poignant situation reared to bring a lump in her throat. She suddenly felt that she wanted to get out, and walked quickly back into the front room and out the door. Sam and James had been chatting and looked up in alarm as she left. James went after her and Reg who had followed made to go as well. Sam put a hand on his arm to stop him.

"Let Mr. James go."

Reg looked at him and realisation suddenly came to him. "Ah!"

Sam nodded. "Yes. I think she will want Mr. James there rather than any of us."

Once she had got out into the yard, Abby stopped. James caught up with her and put his arms around her feeling her trembling. He held her in a comforting embrace rather than a passionate hold. Abby accepted the comfort of his arms without thought. After a moment she began to speak.

"I get annoyed with myself, that these things affect me so much. After all I knew what had happened, yet these little reminders get to me. I saw a few sticks of furniture. Was that all that my granddad had to show for his life? He had worked so hard, yet in the end he had so little." James didn't reply he just held her, knowing that she needed to talk, just as he had done once. "I don't regret coming here. It is just that knowing the history was purely academic. But going in there and touching his stuff made all these pictures in my mind come to life. I was touching furniture that granddad had felt every day and sat in. I felt his loneliness and despair, and I wanted to weep for him." She stopped, keeping the tears away from her eyes, just accepting the sympathy that James' arms offered.

He let her regain her composure, understanding the struggle she had with her emotions, then he spoke softly. "All history is a bit like that, Abby. And family histories especially. If you delve you will always find sadness, tragedy, good times and bad. The important thing to remember though is that somehow the circle balances itself, turns, and for all the unhappiness and bad times, there is good fortune and happiness to compensate. You are the living example of that. You are living a life that your granddad could never have dreamed of, nor even your mum. If they were looking down now from wherever people go, they would have the biggest smiles on their faces, to see you, and your success, and it would give them so much pleasure to know that you are coming home. He and your mum would tell you that everything they suffered was worthwhile to make you the person you are today. They wouldn't change anything." As his words and the truth they contained filtered through to Abby's mind, her sadness gradually melted away to be replaced by the pleasant sensation of his holding her. She began to enjoy James arms for more than just the comfort he offered. Resisting the impulse to burrow even deeper, she looked up and smiled at him.

"Thank you." Abby was very conscious of James' arms around her, which was comforting, but for her also a little more. Wanting to take the warmth out of the situation she mimicked the local accent. "Oh Squire, what would the others say, to see you holding me like this."

"Not much really." James laughed. "After all they all know what Squires are like." He released her with Abby detecting reluctance, and stepped back.

Harry was approaching. "Ah here comes Harry with a torch." There was a forced normality in his voice. Harry did indeed have a torch, so large that it had a handle, and the biggest lens she had ever seen.

"That torch looks as if it would shine for miles." she commented.

Harry laughed. "Very useful at night when you are looking for an animal that may have caught itself in a ditch." he replied. He went straight into the house, calling Sam.

James looked at Abby. "Are you ready to go back in?" he enquired.

Abby nodded. "Yes, I think I have got over the girly stuff."

As she turned to go James said softly. "Not girly stuff, compassion."

Harry was standing in the small lobby at the foot of the stairs. "I'll go up, if you don't mind, Miss Abby. I had a good look at the roof yesterday, and it seems to be intact, but you never know. Pigeons could have got in, in which case there could be some dead ones up there." Abby told him to go ahead, and switching on the torch he made his way carefully up the stairs. From below Abby could hear his boots scuffing the floorboards above her head, and then clumping over the back room. His voice when it came was muffled. "It's all alright up here, come up. I'll shine the torch on the stairs so you can see.' Moments later the stairs lit up. Abby looked up and was blinded by the beam. Harry moved the torch away from her eyes and Abby started to climb. Harry had cleared the cobwebs on his way, although some still brushed her face and hair. Behind her she could hear James following. The stairs finished on a small landing with just two open doors. Harry had backed into the front room as she got to the top and now shone the torch on the ceiling. Such was its power the room was completely visible, and completely empty. Two windows on the front wall and a small fireplace were the only features of an otherwise completely featureless room. Harry gave her a moment to take it all in, then said to her.

"Shall we see the back room, Miss?" Abby nodded, aware that James was watching her carefully, just in case her emotions broke down again. She smiled at him to let him know she was alright. Harry kept the torch pointing at the ceiling. Although very dirty, the ceiling had been painted white, and that was sufficient to reflect the light back down on the whole room. The back room was exactly the same as the front. Perhaps a little smaller, and reversed, But another totally featureless room, apart from the two windows and a hatch in the ceiling. Presumably the loft opening.

Her thoughts were disturbed by Harry's voice. "It may be sensible to go down now. The battery is quite old, and I wouldn't want the torch to fail, whilst you're up here."

Abby looked at him. "Yes of course, thank you, Harry." With

James leading, and Harry following her they descended and came back into the main room where Sam and Reg looked up expectantly.

"Well, Abby, how do you like your new home?" Enquired Sam.

Abby looked around. "It's going to take a lot of cleaning and decorating. I am amazed at all this white dust. Where has that come from?"

Sam grinned. "It's Lime wash, Abby. Good thing too." They were walking outside. Abby had to ask the reason for that last remark."The place was built with Lime mortar, plaster, and the walls and ceiling washed with it." Sam informed her. "That's why it's dry inside." He could see the question of Abby's face before he went on. "Lime soaks up moisture. From the atmosphere and the stone used to build. The Lime plaster inside would absorb any moisture in the air, and it would go through the Lime mortar, and be dried by the wind."

Abby was giving this thought when another struck her. "There's no bathroom!" Her companions laughed.

"No, Abby." Reg explained. "Your granddad would have used a big tin bath, once a week, even if it was freezing outside."

"Yes but what about….." Her voice trailed off, not knowing quite how to talk about calls of nature in this all-male company. Sam came to her rescue, and just pointed her to a wooden lean-to at the back of the house.

"Oh!" She exclaimed.

James had of course been grinning at his exchange. "I told you it would take a lot of money, Abby." He went on. "You will have to convert one of the upstairs rooms into a bathroom, and plumb the place too."

"Plumb the place?"

"Yes. There is no running water. There will be a Well somewhere hereabouts, though." Reg could help there.

"It's down there." He pointed to a low rock-built enclosure, half hidden by weeds on the side away from the station. He continued. "The Lad Porter would have the job of pumping up the water to a tank, which stood next to the well. It supplied just the tap in the kitchen, the station, and my house too. Tanks gone now, but I suspect the Well is ok. It is good water. Mind you, in hot weather the water was always warm when it came out of the tap."

Abby's practical mind was working now. She turned to Sam. "Is there a good local Builder I could use?"

He didn't have to think about the question, answering immediately. "Yes Love. Bloke called George Walker. He's in Paverton, but does most of the work in this area. Good craftsman. He would be useful at the station as well. He does a lot of work with the listed buildings around here."

James agreed. "Yes, he's the man you want. Would you like me to give him a ring, and get him down here to take a look?"

Abby looked pleased. "Yes please, James. I am going to need someone, and if he's your recommendation, then it had better be him." she looked at her watch. It was half past one.

"Oh God! If I am seeing your mother this afternoon, I shall have to get washed and changed. James, you will be there won't you?"

James laughed. "Yes, Abby I will be there a bit later, don't worry though. She's not an Ogre."

Abby smiled sheepishly. Then turned to the others. "I am sorry to rush away like this, please forgive me, and thank you for all the help you have given me today." Sam smiled.

"Go on Girl, don't worry about us. I'll lock up and let you have the keys tonight." Abby smiled and gave him his ritual kiss on the cheek, and was gone.

***

Harry was regarding the ground around the house. It was covered by gorse and windblown self-seeded weeds. "Would be a help if we cleared all this, before George gets started, and that could do with a gate on it." He pointed to the gap where the gravel path started from the station.

Sam nodded and turned to James. "Whole area could do with fencing anyway; do you know how much land is going with the house and station?"

"Not yet Sam." James replied. " Got to get the surveyors down to measure up. Abby's having the house, the station with its track bed and the drive."

Sam shook his head. "Oh come on Mr. James, best thing is to get some fencing up, at least around the house and then calculate the area.

We could do that."

James thought about it. "Yes Sam. Let's do that. It doesn't make that much difference for a yard or two. Do you reckon we should get some gravel down as well? I don't think that Abby will want too much lawn and Flower beds."

Sam looked to Harry. "What do you think, Harry. I have got some post and rail not doing anything. Do you think we could do it ourselves?"

Harry grinned in reply. "Course we could, I have got some post and rail as well. We can get some gravel from Lills, if that's ok with you Mr. James? Sam, it would be a change to see you working again."

"I was going to buy you a pint tonight, but after that comment you can buy your own." Sam had a smile on his face, not seriously offended. Indeed he looked forward to doing this work. It pleased him to be able to do this for Abby.

Reg was now anxious to get away. "Got to pick up Gladys and get home. I'll see one of those gangers tonight, and I'll give you a call tomorrow if the rails are available." He took a look at the house. "It will be good to see the place lived in again. I had many happy years here, and it feels right to have a Tregonney back here. She's a nice lady."

"Yes she is." James agreed.

CHAPTER NINETEEN

The front door to Lyney House was open when Abby got there. She had driven up preferring not to arrive hot and clammy from the walk up the hill. "Hello!" She called stepping forward just across the threshold. She was uncertain whether to proceed further. A door twenty feet away directly in line with the front door opened and a tall, slim, grey-haired lady, dressed in jodhpurs and blouse smiled at her.

"Hello, Abby. Do come through, I have just put the kettle on."

Abby advanced down the hall. "Good afternoon, Mrs. Comberford." For Abby was sure it was indeed Mrs. Comberford.

"Please call me Gwen. Come on in, I thought we could have tea on the patio at the back." The door led through into a large Breakfast room, with a French window which opened onto a paved area outside. Gwen extended her hand, and they shook hands. "It's so nice to meet you at last. I have heard a lot about you, but not from my son, I have to say. He seems most reticent on the subject."

Abby smiled. James had mentioned his mother's spies, and Gwen's comment seemed to bear out the efficiency of her network. "It's good to meet you. Can I do anything to help?"

"That's kind of you. Would you take that tray outside? There is a table and chairs. The table is a bit wobbly, but it should serve. I'll just make the tea and join you."

The table was indeed a bit wobbly, and Abby noticed that a folded piece of cardboard had been used to balance the leg. She adjusted the card and achieved a kind of stability.

Gwen appeared with the tea, and noticed that the table was more stable. "Oh well done. Everything around here either wobbles or is falling down. I have told James on many occasions to pull the whole place down, and build a small modern house. He won't of course. He doesn't seem to like modern things that much." Abby giggled. Gwen looked at her sharply. "You seem to have come to that conclusion too."

"Yes, I called him a throwback the other day. He actually agreed with me."

"Well wonder of wonders. He argues with me whatever I say. You must have the magic touch." Abby thought this last comment may have been said in a rather delving manner.

Gwen switched topics. "I was so sorry to hear that your mother was dead. You know that no-one here knew what had happened to her. CC made a lot of enquiries, but to no avail, she had vanished completely."

"CC?" Abby queried.

Gwen laughed. "Sorry, that was how I called Charles, James' father. CC, Charles Comberford."

"Well it was generous of him to make the enquiries."

"It was this damn valley. CC adopted a very patriarchal interest in everyone. It was his duty in a way, although he had a high opinion of your grandfather. He would have tried for his sake."

"I didn't think my granddad was that friendly to anyone?"

"Oh no. It wouldn't have been friendship. Charles admired your grandfather because of his sense of duty and his integrity. That was very important to Charles." She poured the tea, adding just a little milk to Abby's with half a spoon of sugar. Abby was dumbstruck! How did Mrs. Comberford know how she liked her tea?

"I understand that you don't spend too much time here?" Gwen shook her head.

"No, I have to confess, that unlike CC and James, I am not absorbed by the valley. I prefer to live in Berkshire. I have a lifelong friend there. She is widowed as well, so it suits us both. I only come back here to get some of the fat off Jason, and chivvy James, as he no doubt has told you."

"Yes, he did mention something like that."

"I would imagine that his comments were a little more barbed than just mentioned."

"Yes, perhaps a bit." Abby smiled.

Gwen took up the topic of Jason again. "But from what I hear, I shall not have to be exercising Jason as much in future?"

Abby blushed slightly. "Well I wouldn't say that. Gentle walking was all I managed with him, and I don't suppose that I shall be riding him again."

Gwen looked at her pensively. "Well if you are going to be a resident here, you may as well ride Jason whenever you wish. It will be doing me a favour." Abby picked up on Gwen's inflexion. There was an emphasis on the "here", almost as if Gwen meant Lyney House rather than the valley as a whole. Gwen tilted her head to the side and went on, pointedly asking Abby. "Another one becoming absorbed with the valley?"

"I wouldn't say absorbed."

"What would you say?"

Abby felt that she had to make some kind of explanation. "Mum grew up in the valley, and even though I was born in London and grew up there, I never felt that I was a Londoner. I lived and worked there, but that was all. I came here to see if there was a possibility that I had family I didn't know about, and found an intriguing story. I also found somewhere my family had been part of, in a very small way. Having no tie to anywhere else, this is the best I have got."

Abby had not explained herself well, and knew it, but found it difficult to put into words. Funnily it didn't seem a problem with James; he seemed to know instinctively what she meant.

Gwen gave her a smile. "So the valley will have one more resident. What will you do though? You are obviously an intelligent girl; I doubt that you will find anything as exciting as the life you have led, here?"

"I don't know at the moment. I think I will have more than enough to do with restoring the station and house. After that, I shall have to give it some thought."

"But you don't really have to work. Do you?" Gwen asked. Abby was not taken aback by this direct question. She was well aware that the valley was alive with gossip, and that Mrs. Comberford's spies would have passed this on.

"I cannot do nothing." She replied hoping that this would neither confirm or deny Gwen's question. The evasion only served to firm up Gwen's suspicions. If Abby had to find a job, there would be no reason to prevaricate. Abby continued "The only thing I do well is use the Banks money, and make them even richer than they were. I doubt that I can do that here."

"You may be surprised. When you go to the Ball, you should be prepared for some loaded questions." Abby had long ceased to be taken aback that everyone seemed to be aware of her movements, so Gwen's reference to the Hunt Ball was not worth comment.

"Oh and why would that be?"

"There will be some moneyed people there. Your position in the City is of interest, although no-one is actually sure of what you were doing, except that whatever it was you did it very well. You will find the need to fend off some indirect, even some direct questions. There are some who will always seek free advice, if they think you can give such advice.

Abby laughed at this. "Well, I don't think I will be able to help then. Moving millions of the Bank's money is a long way from advising on investments in the UK. I had to use a Stockbroker to make my own investments, and they are nothing like the sums I worked with."

Interesting, thought Gwen. More reason to believe that Abby, financially, was very comfortable.

"Did you find the job interesting?"

Abby gave that some thought. She had never considered this before. "I suppose I did. Yes! It was a challenge. At least it was when I started, but looking back on how easily I gave it up, makes me wonder if I had not outstayed my time. I know there are those who would say I should have stayed and fought, tried to break the Glass ceiling. But another challenge beckoned."

Gwen smiled now. "Restoring the station and house?" That was what she said, but her thoughts turned to the possibility that James was the real challenge. She did not find this upsetting. Gwen felt none of the emotions that mother's were supposed to have about girls setting their sights on her son. In fact emotion played very little part in her life. She had married Charles Comberford because their families had all agreed that it was a good thing. She had never felt passion for Charles, just fondness, and having given Charles the son he needed, had absented herself from the valley as much as decorum would allow. To her mind it was immaterial if Abby and James should fall in love. Love didn't pay bills. It appeared to her that Abby did have the funds to pay bills, if they liked each other, so much the better. However there was something playing on her mind that would make all this speculation pointless. She got up. "I'll go and make some more tea, James will probably be here soon, and will want a cup."

"Can I help you?"

"No, but thank you for asking. Have a little wander round the garden. It's quite pleasant. Not as pristine as when we had a gardener, but James does a reasonable job keeping it tidy." Abby said she would.

As she strolled down the slight hill past beds of Roses set against huge Rhododendron bushes she realised that Gwen had learnt a lot about her, whilst giving away little about herself. She didn't converse so much as interrogate subtly. She laughed to herself. It didn't matter; it was just a little more to add to the gossip. She was disquieted a little as her hostess seemed to be examining her face very closely; Abby wondered if she had smudged her lipstick or something. Gwen on the other hand was quietly pleased. She had tried for years to get James to come with her to Berkshire, where he could have been introduced to girls who knew what their duty would be, and would comply without complaint. All in vain. Suddenly the valley had produced the right girl without any apparent effort on her part. There were one or two problems. To the first she would have to give much thought, the other was more simple although still a little vexing. Gwen was certain that Abby would not accept a marriage in the same way that girls of Gwen's circle would. She felt certain that Abby and James would want to be in Love. Why? She asked herself. Wasn't it enough that they were well suited? Why did they have to bring love into the equation? Whatever, none of it mattered until the first problem had been resolved, and that meant delving into the past. How tiresome!

She busied herself, filling a kettle and placing it on top of the Aga to boil. She was alerted to James' arrival by the racing diesel and crunch of the gravel as he brought the Land Rover to a stop in his usual manner. He came into the kitchen and briefly pecked her cheek. "Hello Mother, just making tea? Good! I need a cup."

"Good afternoon, Dear. Has it been a good day? I am well, just in case you felt the need to ask. Our guest is walking in the garden."

"Oh good. Has it been your usual interrogation? Or are you going soft these days? No thumb-screws and burning matches eh?" He had a smile on his face so Gwen did not take offence, in fact this was a very natural way for them to converse, and hiding the mutual love and affection they had for each other.

"I have been very kind to Abby, as she will no doubt tell you. She's very nice. Polite and good company, unlike some I could name."

James groaned. He knew that the comment was barbed and aimed at him. He picked up the tray, and carried it out through the Breakfast room to the table. Gwen followed with the Tea. "Go and find Abby. Tell her the tea is ready, I'll get some cake for us." James did has he was bid, finding Abby sitting on a bench.

She looked up and smiled at him. "I understand that you are the gardener these days."

"Well I try. I keep the grass cut and occasionally prune the roses. But everything grows so quickly down here that it is a bit like the Forth Bridge. Finish the job and you have to start all over again." He looked around him and sighed. "I can see jobs here for me that I thought I had completed only last week. Never mind, tea is served Madam." His perpetual grin was there on his face.

"Thank you James, will you escort me back to the Patio?" Abby replied in the same mode.

Gwen was cutting the cake. "Would you like some cake, Abby? I know that James will."

"Just a small slice please, Gwen." She took a bite. "This is lovely. Did you make it yourself?"

James laughed and Gwen looked discomforted even a little bit offended. "No. I do not cook. To tell the truth, James made it!"

Abby was astonished, turning to James she asked. "You made it James? Is this another one of the talents you picked up from the Army?"

He shook his head. "No, I have to cater for myself a lot of the time, and got fed up with the usual Steak and Chips type of cooking, so I experimented a bit, picked up some ideas and tips from Mary and just progressed."

Abby was impressed. "Well done you. I am sure I wouldn't know how to even start cooking a simple meal, much less bake a cake. All I ever do is Microwave a packet of something."

Gwen was cheered to hear this. In her opinion cooking was no occupation for a Lady; they should have cooks to do that. "I keep telling James that he should employ a cook cum housekeeper, and a gardener, but he takes little notice of me."

James turned to his mother. "And I have to keep reminding you that there isn't the money for such luxuries." This was not said with rancour, only a resignation that comes from having the same discussion many times. Abby could see the affection between mother and son, but sympathised with James as it was evident that Gwen found it difficult to come to grips with present day realities.

Abby left about half an hour later, James saw her to the door. "I hope mother was not too much of a strain for you."

Abby shook her head. "No I enjoyed talking with her."

"Good." James seemed relieved. "Shall I see you this evening at the Inn?"

"I shall be there. But first I have to negotiate with Mary about the size of the meal she will want to give me."

She drove off with her thoughts tumbling around in her head. She liked Gwen, she had a feisty character that Abby applauded, but also had many ideas that to Abby were well out of date. She also felt that it hadn't been a conversation so much as an interview. For what position she could only guess, but whatever the situation, Abby was feeling that she hadn't really passed muster. If Abby had realised the turmoil in Gwen's mind she would have slightly different thoughts.

Gwen sat musing on the meeting. She had liked Abby instinctively. She had many times tried to persuade James to come to Berkshire with her. The plan was for him to meet suitable girls who would make an ideal wife and partner. James to her fury had rejected all her blandishments, and to his mother's despair had remained a bachelor with no sign of that ever changing. Now out of thin air a girl had come who was absolutely right for James, and to put the cream on the cake was seemingly wealthy as well. What more could a mother ask for? Gwen should have been ecstatic, but she wasn't. There was a horrible thought insidiously creeping into her mind. A thought that couldn't be brought out into the open, although the circumstance could arise that meant it had to be. It would destroy her hopes, James' hopes, and crush Abby.

Abby had slipped down to Gallow Farm quite frequently, and was now reasonably proficient in the basics of the waltz, quickstep, and the foxtrot, although she remained concerned of her ability. Mavis recognised her fears and put her mind at rest. "There will be so many couples on the floor that you will be shuffling rather than dancing. I doubt that they will play too many foxtrots, or if they do people will not do it properly, but dance a slow quickstep." Abby thought that a shame, as the foxtrot seemed to her a particularly graceful dance.

She was cheered by Sam telling her that she would not make a fool of herself. "You can do those steps better than most people will, so don't worry, and you have a good sense of time, that for most people is the hardest part of the foxtrot." She had enjoyed her lessons and had asked Mavis if it would alright for her to continue coming after the Ball, to learn more. Mavis was delighted, and Sam was looking very pleased as well.

Immediately he started making plans to further her skills. "We will start adding more steps to the basics, which makes the dance much more interesting." To demonstrate he had taken Mavis in his arms and danced the foxtrot in a way that got them around the floor without ever having to do the same steps twice. They glided and turned as one, elegantly and smoothly. Abby was enthralled, and longed to be able to dance like that herself.

Now the Ball was but three days away, and Mavis had vanished while Sam was taking Abby round the room in a quickstep. She reappeared with a large cardboard box. "Abby, I know you have your dress and shoes all sorted, but have you thought about a coat? It may be a little chilly that evening, especially in the early hours, when you leave." Abby hadn't given that any thought at all, she shook her head. Mavis looked relieved. "Well if you are not offended, I would like you to look at this Cape." She opened the box and produced from the layers of tissue paper inside a black velvet hooded Cape. "My mother bought this for me years ago, and it has been stored properly. I checked it the other day, and aired it thoroughly. No Moth or creasing at all. Would you like to use it?" Abby's face was all the answer she needed. Smiling with satisfaction Mavis draped the Cape over Abby's shoulders settling the large hood carefully down her back. It was lined with a dark blue silk, and once she had settled the Cape, Abby twirled delightedly. She was slightly taller than Mavis so the bottom hem came just above her ankles, but as this was where her dress would fall, it was perfect. As Mavis said it had been aired thoroughly, with just a pleasant fragrance of Lavender lingering.

"Damn, girl." Remarked Sam. "You look just as attractive in that as Mavis did."

"Oh Sam!" Mavis's voice had a bite to it.

"Well almost as attractive." Sam qualified his words to sooth Mavis's ruffled feelings. Abby took the sting out of the atmosphere.

"It's beautiful, Mavis. Oh but I couldn't borrow this. I would be frightened if I spoilt it."

"Abby. If you don't use it, it will go back into storage, and probably never be used again. So you take it. It will give me and Sam a lot of pleasure to see you in it."

Abby kissed them both. "I will be very happy, so thank you both very much, for this and all your help in teaching me to dance."

Later, when Sam had gone to the Combe Inn, Abby sat down with Mavis for a while and Mavis made some tea. Abby explained that she was having her hair done in Paverton earlier on the Saturday of the Ball, and would be back at the Inn about three o' clock. Mavis said she would be there shortly after, and would help if there was anything Abby needed.

"Just moral support, Mavis. I shall be a bag of nerves, I know."

"Nonsense Abby. You will be fine."

"Don't you believe it. I have never been to any function like this before."

Mavis was shocked. "You're not serious?"

"Yes I am. All I know is business meetings, and seminars. Standing around sipping sherries and talking money. I mean how do I address a Lord Lieutenant?"

Mavis had to give that some thought, and then said. "Well I am sure I don't know. If I were you I should just follow James' lead. He will know, that's for certain." This thought gave Abby some confidence.

"I am looking forward to seeing James in Evening Dress though." Mavis shook her head.

"Oh no. I suspect that James will be in his Dress Uniform."

Abby was surprised. "But I thought he had left the Army?"

"He did, but he was a Captain, and even though he resigned his commission, he is still on reserve, and entitled to wear uniform. He does so on Remembrance Day, medals and sword as well."

Abby giggled. "I trust he won't have his sword with him on Saturday. He would have trouble trying to dance."

Mavis smiled at the thought as well. "Have you finished your tea? Good. Give me a lift back with you, would you? I want to have a little chat with Mary." The box was placed on the back seat, and Mavis got in beside Abby. She looked around. "This is a lovely car."

Abby agreed. "Yes. One of my little indulgences, we will use it Saturday evening. James is going to pick it up, and give it a good clean. After all we don't want to turn up at Coolton Grange in a dirty car."

Mavis agreed with that. "Oh yes. They will all be there trying to outdo their friends and acquaintances. There will be quite a few Rolls-Royces' and Bentleys, some of them even owned by the people who turn up in them."

Abby laughed. "Mavis, that's a bit cynical."

Mavis smiled as well. "Perhaps. Let us just say that some of the people going only come down here for weekends and holidays, and for events like the Hunt Ball. I don't have any time for them. Not like Mr. James, who lives here, and tries to make things work. And that isn't easy for him either."

Abby was intrigued. "Why is that?"

"Oh I shouldn't say really, but I know of one or two occasions when Mr. James has forgiven Tenants their rent when they couldn't, or wouldn't pay. Them as does it forgets, that money is what Mr. James has to live on, and a quarter or two's rent is a big drop in his income. Not right if you ask me." This was another side of James of which Abby had not been aware. She had an idea of the acreage of the estate, and knew approximately how much per acre it could command in rent. She also knew that not all of the acreage was let, much had no agricultural use, but her business brain told her that James' income from the estate was relatively modest. Unless he had some very good investments, his circumstances were not going to be comfortable. The exchange he had with his mother bore that out. Mavis had gone on. "He's a good landlord, Mr. James. Years ago we would call him Squire. It was used with respect; and has to be earned you don't buy the title with the land: Sam and I, and others, think of him as the Squire. I know he doesn't like that term, but that's how we think of him.

They arrived at the Combe Inn, and Abby drove straight round the back. Mavis carried the box, and Abby opened the door for her. She looked round quickly to see if James was there. Pleased that he wasn't, Mavis brought the box through and Mary opened the door so they could go straight upstairs.

"Mary. " Mavis began almost as soon as she was in the door. "I shall need to get this hung up somewhere so that it doesn't crease. It won't do it any harm to get a bit more airing either. Can you suggest somewhere?"

Mary didn't have to think. "Put it in my wardrobe. It's deeper than the one in Abby's room, and it's got plenty of room."

With the Cape carefully hung, they came back down to the Bar. Sam had already bought a round of drinks. The usual Port and Lemon for Mavis and guessing a Vodka and Tonic for Abby. James still had not made an appearance, and Mary thought that strange, as he had got into the habit of popping in every evening lately. Mavis and she had agreed, happily, that Abby was probably the reason for this. Eventually he did arrive, making his way through the bar, stopping for a chat with every group until he joined Abby. A pint appeared and he gratefully took a sip before addressing Abby. "I managed to speak to George Walker, and he said he could get down here on Friday to have a preliminary look at what needs doing."

"That's quick."

"Well I did say that this was probably a job for which he would be paid promptly. Cheered him up no end."

Mary laughed. "He was in here once having a good moan. Told me that he had done some work for someone in the area, and it took him eight months to get his money!"

Abby thought that was terrible. "In the City all accounts have to be settled on Pay Day at the end of the month. Everybody pays all that they owe, so the money goes around. Everybody gets what they are due, so they can pay what they have spoken for."

James had only a vague idea of what she was talking about, but agreed that it was a good system. "In case anybody is wondering, it wasn't me, obviously. You have seen the state of my house. I can't afford George's prices anyway." As usual his mouth showed his habitual grin

Abby was worried. "I really can't tell this man how much needs to be done, until I know what the place looked like. I have written to Mr. Brasher, but as yet have no reply."

James told her not to worry. "I think that George will understand that. He will be looking at basic work that needs to be done. As the station is a listed building, he will talk with the Heritage Officer from the Council, and the English Heritage people who will let him have all the do's and do not's. They are quite strict by the way. I assume that as they listed the building they will have details, possibly photos to use as a guide."

"What about the house?" Abby asked.

James could not give advice for the house. "I don't know if that is listed or not. I would imagine it is. I think the general rule is that as long as it is restored outside, you can within reason modernise it inside, plumbing and central heating etc. George will know more than anyone, as he seems to do quite a lot of work on historic buildings." Abby was content with that, although worried about how long she would need to be down at the station. James like most men had little idea of the preparations a woman needed for such an important event.

***

Mavis and Mary had listened to this conversation with interest. They had already discussed what sort of curtains and colour schemes they thought the house should have. It didn't seem to occur to them that Abby may have her own ideas. They moved away to discuss these issues leaving James and Abby alone apart from Sam, who despite his wife's signals stayed where he was. James was saying that the clock would have to come down and be restored.

"They are quite valuable you know, so it should be taken out before George starts work. The house would not be that secure once they start work, and an item like that could walk quite easily. There's a specialist in Paverton. Best to take it to him for cleaning. He'll keep it secure until you're ready to move in." Sam then told Abby that he and Harry would be putting up a gate, clearing all the weeds away, and putting gravel down. Abby was surprised and grateful.

"Sam that's really good of you. You must let me pay you though."

Sam shook his head. "No Love, wouldn't hear of it. The post and rail is sitting there doing nothing, and the gravel we will get from the old quarry. There's plenty of it there. I am sure Mr. James won't mind us taking a trailer load or two." James shook his head. "Anyway the work will get me away from my Missus for a while. I love her to bits, but she can get a bit much when I am there all day and every day. Be good to be doing something."

Abby was quite astounded at the help people would offer, with no expectation of recompense. In the city no-one did anything for anyone without a gratuity being anticipated in one way or another. Sam explained. "This is a small community, if something needs doing, everyone will pitch in and help get it done. After all most here will have been friends for years, or even related. So it's natural to help. What does it take? A day's labour, or a few materials, that's very little. But it brings people together, and at some time, the favour will be returned."

James agreed, nodding his head vigorously. "That is one of the things that has bound me to this valley. Call it patriarchal or whatever, I couldn't walk away from the spirit that exists here. My father knew that. He could have sold. He had offers I know. This community looks after each other. That appeals to me."

Abby lightly slapped his arm. "James, you are getting all emotional. That isn't you at all, now stop it."

Suitable penitent, James grinned. "Ok, drama over for this evening." Mavis and Mary had rejoined them and watched this exchange with pleasure, for this was how a couple who were growing attached to each would behave. Sam noted as well, and hoped that his wife would not make too much of it. He was grateful when Mavis made no comment.

Abby then changed the subject. "I shall be back here on Saturday about three o' clock. When will you pick up the car?"

James looked aghast. "I had forgotten that! I won't be back from Taunton until about six. I will not have time to clean it."

Abby's disappointment showed on her face. "Oh well I shall have to see if I can get it cleaned by the garage in Paverton."

Mary had been listening. "No, Abby. Hang on a moment." She went over to where Jack was serving and had word in his ear. He nodded and came back with her, wiping his hands on a tea-towel. Mary was smiling. "Jack will clean the car."

Abby was grateful. "Are you sure Jack? I don't want to be a bother."

He shook his head. "No trouble at all."

Abby smiled and decided the least she could do, would be to buy drinks for them all, she dug in her purse and took out some money. "Thanks Jack. Let me buy my round, and you and Mary have one as well, please?" Another problem resolved.

After the drinks were served, Abby turned to James. "So Mr. Comberford. What time are you picking me up on Saturday evening?

"Probably about nine."

"Probably?" Enquired Abby with a flinty tone, "I have a lot to do, so I need it to be a little more accurate than 'probably'."

Mary was nodding her head. "Mr. James!" She said in astonishment.

"Right, I understand. Well I shall pick you up at precisely nine o' clock. That will be P.M. Or if you prefer the army way twenty one hundred hours." He added with a little grin. "Will that be alright?"

Abby nodded. "That will be fine, James, and I shall, fashionably, be a little late of course, but you won't mind at all, will you?"

"I shall hide my impatience admirably. Mother will approve of your being fashionably late. It's exactly what she would do." Abby had no doubt of that. She felt sure that Gwen Comberford, even if she were ready, would have delayed her entrance for at least ten minutes.

***

When she went to bed that evening, Abby was unable to sleep for quite a while. Her mind was turning over the comments Sam had made about helping one's neighbours, and she aware of how much help she had received, and also how much was about to be offered. She so much wanted to start giving in return, but could not think of how this could be done. Her last thought calmed her mind. The future would bring the opportunity.

CHAPTER 20

The next day dawned cloudy but dry. Now that George Walker was coming on Friday, her plans for that day, which was to lay out her ensemble for the Ball, were brought forward to today. She mentioned this to Mary at breakfast, after scolding her for trying to slip another rasher of bacon, and a slightly higher mound of scrambled egg on her plate. Mary took the scolding in her stride, and even if she had been upset was immediately mollified when Abby asked her help. "I want to lay out the dress and everything else I shall be wearing. Is there somewhere I could do that where it won't be disturbed?"

Mary thought for little more than a moment. "Yes. I'll open one of the other guest rooms for you. I haven't got any bookings so it won't be a problem." She didn't mention that if she had some last minute guests, that room would not be given to anyone. This was far more important.

The day passed swiftly, and Abby was amazed how much she had to do, and seemingly how little time she had in which to do it. The dress, shoes, gloves and cape, were laid out on the bed with layers of tissue paper to keep the dust off. Abby had made a choice from what little Jewellery she had. She looked at a single strand of Pearls, with matching earrings. Mary was willing her to choose those and Abby did. Mary approved, saying that it was simple, but very elegant. Noting at the same time that they had not been cheap, the box they came in had the name of a very well-known jeweller on the inside. It was late afternoon before Abby had a chance to relax, and sitting in her room had caught up on a little more reading of Mr. Brasher's papers together with the inevitable cup of tea.

James had told her that George Walker would be at the station about ten o' clock, and Abby was impressed that he arrived very promptly. He examined carefully both the station and the house.

"I can see straight away that these slabs will need re-laying." indicating the platform paving. "Some will need to be replaced, as they are cracked too much. I will have to talk to a quarry to get the right ones, else they will look out of place, and the Heritage people will not allow it. The station generally is in good condition, just needs some pointing and painting. The Barge boards will need to be replaced. I will have to get details of how they actually looked to make exact copies." Abby asked him if he could put in Electric light and power. He looked a bit dubious. "I shall have to see what the Heritage people say. It's possible as the supply cables run alongside the lane, but they may say no, to that. I can put it in the house, that's not listed, and as I understand you intend to live there, you will need it." He never seemed to stay in the one place, always strolling around the building and stopping suddenly to examine some stonework or structure. He would make notes in his little book making a little humming sound and then move on. Abby had to run a little to keep up with him.

Eventually he ended up back at on the platform. "Can we get inside?" Abby had the key, and tried the lock. The oiling that Harry had given it had worked and copying the knack that Reg had demonstrated she was pleased to open the doors with little trouble. George went inside, again stopping and starting, making his notes and humming to himself. Eventually he looked up and spoke to Abby. "They built well in those days. Everything over-engineered of course, but it has lasted over a hundred years, and will probably last another hundred." He consulted his notes. "Strip and replace the plaster as it is coming away, and repaint. That old desk has the worm. Best to get it out and burn it before it gets in the floorboards. Doubt that there is any rot at all, Lime plaster takes care of that."

"Do you have to replace the plaster?"

"Best. Some of it is coming off already, I can patch, but it's better to get it all off, then we can see the condition of the walls as well. They should be alright, but it would be sensible to make sure. I shall have to replace with Lime-plaster, so when it's painted you will not know any difference." Abby in her brief scrutiny had not seen the damage, but accepted his opinion.

"I don't want to burn the desk. That was my grandfather's desk."

He looked at her with curiosity. "Your grandfather worked here?"

"Yes he was the stationmaster."

He thought for a moment or two. "Right! Well in that case I'll get it collected, and take it to Archie Breed. He can treat the worm, and from what I have seen will be able to restore the desk to as good as new. He's a good craftsman. Cost you a bit though." Abby did not need to think. As far as she was concerned the price would be worth it.

George explained that he was looking at the basics, but he couldn't give her a price until the Heritage Officer had inspected and gave him a list of requirements. "That will be a long list I have no doubt. When I have their report I will be in touch with you to discuss it. Of one thing I can assure you though, it is going to cost you a bit. They will insist that I use materials that are sympathetic to the original."

Abby nodded. "I was prepared for that." She was to find with time that the expression 'cost you a bit' was frequently on George's lips. Abby locked the doors of the station and they walked over to the house. Mr. Walker detoured to his van, and then rejoined Abby with a pair of step ladders over his shoulder.

Abby was happy to see that Sam had arrived. George greeted him immediately. "Hello Sam, long time since I have seen you. Are you well?"

"George, good to see you again. Still bodging jobs are we?"

George grinned. "Only for those as is not quick on paying me."

"Well make sure you do a good job for this young Lady here. Else you will have the whole valley after your blood."

"Don't worry. I'll make sure she's happy with the work." Abby was surprised to see that the upstairs windows had now been cleared of the boarding; she pointed this out to Sam who shook his head.

"Not me, Abby, I suspect that Mr. James did it." Abby unlocked the door to the house. George walked in to start his inspection.

He came out again very quickly. "Miss Tregonney, you had better get that clock somewhere safe as quickly as possible."

Abby was confused. "James said something about that. Why is it valuable?"

"Yes.' Replied George, "From a quick look I would say it is over one hundred years old. Clocks like that sell for over a thousand pounds. Anyone looking in could see it, and it is a bit too tempting."

Abby nodded. The value meant little to her, but it was her family's clock, and that gave it a different meaning. "Could you take it down for me? I'll keep it in my room until I can get it to be cleaned." George nodded and went back to make his survey. Abby stayed outside in the air, watching Sam pace the ground around the house.

The initial impulse to restore the station and the house had been just that, an impulse. But the more she thought about it the stronger her resolve became and she was now making plans in her mind about the funding. She was under no illusions; the commitment would be major, or as George Walker would say cost her a bit. Her thoughts became clear and firm. She would return to London within the next two weeks and pack the remaining personal items in the flat, and put it on the Market. When she bought it she had also purchased an extension of the lease to ninety-nine years. With this cushion the flat would be worth a lot more than if she had remained with the original lease of fifty-six years. The Capital she would release from that should be more than adequate for the work she was putting in hand here. There was no longer any regret about leaving the life she had known for this new one. Her only concern was to find something to do.

Sam returned to her to say that he felt sure that between them, Harry and he had sufficient post and rail to fence off the property. He went on. "Oh and I found the Septic tank around the back"

Abby remembered James saying something about that, or was it Reg? "A Septic tank? I thought that there was drainage."

Sam shook his head. "No Love. Not many here have drainage. About a hundred years ago everything went into the River. The water authority stopped that before the War. Now we have Septic tanks. Get them emptied about every six months." He had a smile on his face as he said. "Abby you will really be back to a rustic way of life here. Water from a well, and a Septic tank."

Abby laughed ruefully. "It will take some getting used to all these privations after the City. I don't even know where the nearest Tube station is."

Sam chuckled. "Well as long as you keep the smile on your face, that's all that matters. Honestly you won't know any different after about ten years. Oh and by the way. What's a Tube?" He laughed and Abby laughed with him.

George rejoined them. "What's so funny?"

"I was telling Abby about the delights of a Septic tank."

George nodded. "Only time you are reminded of it is when you have it emptied. If you have any sense then you go away for half a day."

The little book was produced and George went through his notes, humming as he did so. "Right. No real problems. All the wood is sound, and the fabric is in good condition, perhaps some pointing here and there. There is a Slate Damp-proof course. Unusual in houses of this age, but it was built by the railway, and they built well. Power can be installed, Central Heating if you want it. Use small bore, hardly see the pipes, most will be under the floor anyway. Bathroom, again no problem, I would suggest the back room upstairs, then the large soil pipe will be at the back, goes straight out to the septic. I would suggest that we strip the walls and ceilings, and put dry-liner up. You won't get all that white dust then, also make it easier to run the power and light cable behind. You will have to have a gas tank put somewhere. Has to be away from the house, but also convenient for the tanker to re-fill. The range now... "He thought for a moment. "I would suggest we take out. They were not very efficient, and it was only used for cooking and immediate heat. We could replace it with a gas-fired Aga if you like?"

Abby was doubtful, she had noticed how long they took to boil a kettle. "To be honest I am not much of a cook, so I doubt that I will make use of it. But the range is part of the house and I would not like to see it go."

Sam decided that he ought to inject some realism. "Abby! You will have to decide if you want a Museum or a home. You can't have both. The range would be of little use to you, and you would spend hours cleaning it so George may as well get rid of it. Put an Aga in if you want, or a modern cooker." Abby was a little shocked. Sam had never spoken to her like that before, if she discounted their conversation on hunting.

But his words struck home, she didn't want to live in a Museum. She made up her mind. "You're right. Get rid of the range."

George made a note. Then went on. "I went up in the loft, that's sound. We could put a header tank up there with an electric pump feed from the Well. I'll get the water people in and check the quality of the water. Just a precaution though, Water round here has always been good, it's all this Sandstone, naturally filters the muck out. That's about it, Miss Tregonney, Take me a couple of days and I can let you have a quotation. It's is going to cost you a bit, though." Abby gave this some thought.

"Yes, I like your suggestions, and will go along with all of them."

She stopped as Sam coughed, and looked at him. "Abby, the front door faces North East. We can get a keen cold wind, down here. If I may I would suggest that you have a more substantial porch put on there."

George looked at the door, giving his humming sound which Abby now realised was his thinking process. "I think Sam's right. We could box the porch in and put a second door on, that would sort that out."

Abby was also thinking. "How about putting a Victorian style Conservatory on that side? Could you do that Mr. Walker?"

Sam nodded fiercely. "That would look very good, I must say."

George considered the idea. "The building isn't listed, but we may have to apply for planning permission, depends how big you want it."

"I would think all along that side, perhaps take it round the corner and along the front as well."

"If you do that you will certainly require planning permission. They will be happy though that you don't want to put a modern style up, but we will have to draw the plans up and submit them. Leave it with me. I'll get my draughtsman to come down and we will put some ideas together. You're stopping at the Inn I understand? When I have got some drawings for the Conservatory I'll give you a ring, and we can discuss it." Abby said that would be fine. "If you wait a moment I will get the clock down for you." Abby looked at the house trying to visualise the conservatory on the side. Now that she had stepped back, she thought that taking the conservatory round the front may be going too far. George re-appeared with the clock, which tinkled as he moved. He gave it to Sam, and went back for his step-ladder. Abby re-locked the door. Sam said that he would follow Abby to the Inn and carry the clock in for her.

"Is it heavy, Sam?"

"No, but it is very dusty, you don't want to get this white dust all over you now." Abby thanked him. The kindnesses never seemed to stop.

Back at the Inn, Sam posed Abby a question. They were sitting on one of the benches at the back of the Inn. "I want you to think very carefully, Abby. Do you think you will feel comfortable living down there?" Abby didn't understand the meaning of his question and answered the question she thought he had asked.

"Oh yes, Sam. Once I have got all my bits around me I shall be fine. I know I got a bit emotional when we first opened the house, but I am over that now, that won't bother me again."

Sam smiled and told her he wasn't asking that. "What I am saying is how will you feel when you have moved in? You have lived all your life in the City. Now it's a long time since I have been there, but what I remember most is the feeling of being crowded all the time, by so many people, also the fact that even at night in the hotel it was never quiet, with traffic noise all the time. You have grown up with that, to you that is normal. Now down in your little house, when you go to bed you will be very alone. No other person within a mile of you, no street lights, no noise of traffic either. Look out of your window and all you will see is blackness. After a while you will start hearing strange noises. There will be badgers snuffling around, Dog Foxes barking, and the first time you hear a Vixen screech you will think someone is being murdered. You will have Deer around; you will hear the clack of their horns. All these noises will be a bit unnerving. Grow up with it and it means little, but coming as you do from the City it will be very strange. That is what I am worried about." Abby's enthusiasm was pegged back a bit as his words sunk in. She hadn't considered that aspect. Living at the Inn was only a half-way house. There was laughter, voices and music playing until late in the evening. She often lay awake listening until sleep overtook her. Yes on those occasions when she had woken in the early hours it was black outside her window, it could become oppressive if you let it.

Sam's words started to worry her. "I hadn't thought about it like that. Are you saying that perhaps I shouldn't go to live down there?"

"No Love, not at all. Of course you should go and live there, it's your family home. But what I will say to you is don't think for one moment that once you are there, you have to stay. You will find the winter worst, give some thought to coming back here for two or three months. Or if you would like, Mavis and I would be happy to have you stay with us. But please don't suffer in silence, believing that we would think any the less of you if you couldn't cope with the loneliness." He stopped for a moment, thinking. "There is an upside to it though. The first Owl you see flying low over the fields at Dusk or early morning will thrill you. He flies about three to four feet off the ground, looking for small rodents. They can't see him until it's too late, but he can hear them. Old Barny will perch on a gate post, he's not frightened of you unless you get too close, and when you see his head turn right round to look backwards at you, you will want to laugh, it's so comical"

"Old Barny?"

"Yes, the Barn owl. You will see the Little Owl as well; he's quite small and likes a higher perch, so is a bit more difficult to spot. Mr. James, I am sure, has already pointed out the buzzards, and if you are very lucky you may see a Red Kite, they are mostly over Dartmoor, but some are on Exmoor as well. There are so many more that you will see. Look at the hedges and you will see Dunnocks, Robins, Linnets, Finches of all sorts, and Corn Buntings. You may like to get a book about the Birds so you can identify them. They are quite fascinating."

"Sam, I have heard about all of these except a Dunnock. What is that?"

"It's a hedgerow bird, some call it the hedge sparrow, but it isn't really a sparrow."

Abby liked to hear about the animals and birds, and thought that she would enjoy learning more. She had found her family roots, and a circle of friends she didn't feel she deserved. A new life was beckoning with many new interests, but she felt it wrong that all this could come easily without some recompense. Her determination to put something back into this valley was increased.

"Thank you, Sam. What would I do without you and Mavis to help me?" Sam blushed.

"Well you could buy me a drink for a start." Abby's laugh was all the thanks that Sam needed.

CHAPTER 21

The Saturday slipped by so quickly that Abby was convinced that she would not be fashionably late, but seriously late when James arrived to collect her. She needn't have worried with Mavis and Mary who scurried around like devils to make sure that their protégé was ready. Thus it was that at ten to nine, Mary slipped downstairs and invited Sam to come up and see. He entered the room, looked at Abby and was immediately speechless. Mavis came to him and put her arm around him.

"Our girl is lovely, isn't she Sam?"

Sam had a lump in his throat and could only nod his head, eventually finding his voice. "Yes, she is. Abby you look wonderful." He croaked. The girl in question stood there with a happy smile on her face. The hairdresser had cut and highlighted her hair so that it was now more blonde with brown. Abby had used all the tricks that Roz had taught her, much to the amazement of Mavis and Mary, who had never realised that make-up, could do so much. Her dress of Celadon Green Brocade Silk draped her slim figure to perfection, the bodice was fitted snugly, with broad straps around the tops of her arms leaving her shoulders bare, the skirt flared gently from the waist and the drapes swung elegantly with her movement. The shoes just peeped from under the hem, and Abby's pearls and earrings had just the right touch of simplicity and elegance.

"Will I do, Sam?" She asked.

He couldn't do but smile. "Do girl? You'll make them all stop in their tracks. Yes, you'll do. Mr. James will be proud to have you on his arm. Oh by the way he arrived just as I came up here."

Mary checked her watch. "He's eager! Sam would you go down and ask him to wait in the Lounge, we'll hang on here for another five minutes." Sam gave a half smile, knowing exactly what these women were up to. He paused on his way down the stairs to wipe an eye which had suddenly become misty. His thoughts were of the daughter that never was. She would have looked as beautiful as Abby, going off to her first Ball, and he would feel the same emotions for her, pride and trepidation for his girl going out for the first time to sail on the troubled sea of life.

Abby slipped into bed at quarter to six that Sunday morning, her mind alive with so many pictures of the Ball that she was certain that sleep wouldn't come for quite a while. James had been wearing a trench coat when she went down, and it was only after they arrived and his coat and her cape had been taken that she saw his uniform properly. Dark blue Trousers, very tight, with a red stripe down the outside, a brilliantly red Jacket, shaped over his hips, Maroon shawl collar, black waistcoat, and a blindingly white shirt with a black bow tie. There were Pips on the Epaulettes, and the winged dagger emblem on both lapels. Also on the left lapel were two miniature medals. It was exciting and so glamorous to be escorted by James in his uniform, but she was more excited by James comment on seeing her in her dress. He said nothing at first, just looked with growing wonderment, until at last he was able to speak.

"Abby, you are beautiful!" She smiled with the pleasure of the compliment and a little more colour crept into her cheeks. He held his arm out and her heart quickened as she linked her hand through, and James, filled with pride escorted her into the Ball. They walked through a large conservatory full of colourful foliage and then outside down some steps towards a marquee. James mentioned that the marquee had been erected over the tennis court. Inside the marquee was a kaleidoscope of colours. Not just the dresses of the ladies, the pink tail coats worn by the male members of the hunt added to the spectrum..

So much happened that evening. She danced with James a number of times, so pleased that her lessons had not let her down, and with others who seemed to seek her out. She met so many people whose names she would never remember. Some were merely going through motions, others though seemed genuinely pleased to meet her, particularly Sir Richard Wellings and his wife, Maggie. Both were happy to see her and insisted that they were just Richard and Maggie.

"Sir Richard and Lady Margaret are such a mouthful."

He, she remembered for his obvious respect and friendship for James. It was he who explained the two medals that James wore. "The red ribbon with the blue edges is the Distinguished Service Order, and the other with the little bit of green in the ribbon is the South Atlantic Medal. You get some fuddy-duddies complaining that officially the order should only be awarded to Majors and above. Stuff and nonsense if you ask me. Doesn't matter what rank you are, courage is courage." Abby knowing little about these formalities was inclined to agree.

She was dancing with James who moved almost as well as Sam. During the dance she had to ask James how he managed to get the very tight trousers on, he had laughed. "They have loosened up a little now, but the first time I had to get two of my brother officers to hold the waist whilst I jumped up and down getting them further up my legs with each jump. Oh, and incidentally, they are not trousers, they are known as overalls."

"Overalls!" Abby was incredulous.

Toni had introduced her to her Father, the self-important Councillor Wates. He had held her perhaps a little too tightly as they danced, but had let her know that whatever she planned for the station and house would be alright with the planning committee. She met a Lord something or other who suggested that he would appreciate a chat with her at another time. Abby inwardly smiled at that, being reminded of what Gwen had said about free advice. She also found that you addressed a Lord Lieutenant as simply Lord Lieutenant! Later in the evening, or perhaps early in the morning would be more accurate, they served Breakfast! She was sitting nibbling some toast whilst James was tucking in to Bacon and Eggs. She was joined by Sir Richard, who having relaxed a little and accepting Abby as 'right', referred to some of the other guests as 'Parvenu's'.

She asked him why. "Got plenty of money, but the only investment they make in the country is the house they buy from some poor chap who has to sell to pay Inheritance tax. Got to be polite of course, but I cannot really abide them. Got far more time for chaps like James. Tries to make the land work, gets little thanks and little income from it either." That remark would be bookmarked for later examination. Her mind dwelt on so many things that had piqued her. The music, real music provided by a small ensemble of Piano, Violin, Saxophone, Trumpet and a Drummer who kept the time well, even if his efforts did sometimes drown out the melody the others were playing. When they took a break, a Disc Jockey took over to play a good selection of modern hits, although the music that went down best was the classics from the sixties, to which almost everybody danced. The colours of the dresses, some gaudy, others restrained, inexpensive and elegant side by side. Ladies who worked, and ladies who lunched; partnered by gentlemen who could probably be categorised the same way, some who enjoyed the evening, and others who looked and sounded just bored. Dragged there by a wife who was determined to have a moment in the limelight no doubt?

They had arrived back at the Inn at five o' clock. James drove straight round to the back. Abby implored James to take the car home with him, but he declined. "Walking will help me clear my head." He looked at Abby and thanked her for her company, but seemed unsure of how to take his leave.

Abby helped him. "You can kiss me you know, James." He smiled and leaned towards her. Putting his arms around her he brought her forward until their lips touched. The kiss was soft and gentle, not possessive but one with emotion hovering on the brink. She opened her mouth slightly to see if he would respond. He did, his tongue just lightly touching her lips, and flirting with her tongue. That pleased her, as he took only as much as she was offering, but the indication was that at some time there would be passion there.

He drew back, and Abby kissed his cheek. "Thank you for a wonderful evening, James. It was lovely to be escorted by an Officer in all his finery. I felt quite like a Princess."

He smiled warmly. "You were my Princess and I was enchanted tonight. Now your Frog will leave and let you get some sleep." It was the kiss that Abby would remember and treasure above all the other memories. She knew that it had meant something in their relationship, moving it on from friendship to another level. She lay in bed and hugged it to herself like a favourite Teddy Bear as she fell asleep.

Mary, like any mother would do had slept lightly, her subconscious alive to any sound that could mean Abby returning. It was thus that she heard the car, and crept to the window that allowed her to see out the back of the Inn. The kiss was therefore not as private as Abby thought it would be. She had a warm sense of satisfaction as she got back into bed. Jack rolled over in his sleep, murmuring. "What was that?"

"Abby's back."

"Oh good." He fell back into his deep slumber. Mary would not sleep eager to share this development with Mavis. She thought about getting up to see if Abby needed anything, but resisted even though her curiosity was on an all-time high. She would let her sleep.

Abby did sleep and woke up about noon. She felt a slight headache, although she had drunk very little last night, and a little deflated. Putting this down to the odd hours of the last day, she got up to make herself a cup of tea. Her temperament returned to normality as she remembered the kiss, a secret smile and a slight blush creeping over her face.

The weather was changing now, as autumn announced its intention of barging in on the summer. Clouds gathered high and full in the west, and the temperature had dropped. Abby looking out of the window on some early mornings saw the valley clothed in a soft gossamer mist, with Huish rising out of the white embrace like an island in the warm ocean of the Pacific. Today though the mist had cleared well before Abby got up. She washed and dressed, putting on comfortable clothes, and went downstairs. She enjoyed the greetings that she received from the few regulars who frequented the bar; answering their hopes that she had enjoyed the evening with assurances and smiles. Upon seeing her Mary announced her intention of preparing a breakfast, only to be forestalled by Abby's resolute "No thank you Mary. All I want is toast and coffee please." Mary was prepared to put up an argument, but Abby was adamant. "Just toast and coffee, and I promise I will eat a good meal tonight. Ok?" The toast and coffee did not take very long, and Mary sat with Abby whilst she ate. With some difficulty she restrained herself, and when Abby had finished some toast, and was sipping coffee, she was rewarded as Abby regaled the events of the last evening. Mary laughed as Abby did when talking of the antics that some had got up to, and was serious when she told her of what Sir Richard had said. Abby did not mention the end of the evening and what had transpired at the back of the Inn, nor had Mary expected her to.

This had already been discussed with Mavis, who announced her intention of coming to the Inn this evening. "Just to hear how Abby got on last night."

"Well don't you go asking the girl any awkward questions. And don't mention what I have just told you, else she will think I was spying on her."

Abby returned to her room, having decided to refresh her knowledge with some of Mr. Brusher's notes. As she relaxed more pictures of the Ball came unbidden to her mind. It was strange that she couldn't review the evening as a whole, yet her memory picked out little Vignettes. She had been introduced to a young woman called Amanda, who said 'how do you do?' in quite a cool manner. She didn't chat with Abby for long seeming anxious to be somewhere else. All Abby could remember of their conversation was a comment Amanda made about James suddenly deciding to come to the Ball. "He has never bothered before. Perhaps you know why he is here this year?" The woman looked at Abby with almost a glare as if daring her to answer. Abby made some non-committal remark, and Amanda ignored her, going on to say. "He was once thought of as a good catch, but he's so anti-social that anyone who married him would be imprisoned in that valley of his. He's penniless anyway." She then left Abby, calling to someone on the other side of the room. Abby had been tempted to say, 'but I'm not.' But resisted. Now on reflection Abby remembered Toni's saying something about noses out of joint, perhaps this was one of those noses. She was intrigued by the fact that people seemed to assume that she and James were a couple. Why? Surely they would not imagine that James had invited her for any other reason than as a friend? It was just as well that they didn't see the end to the evening, or they would be confirmed in their suspicion. Abby smiled to herself and then settled down to read.

Abby was aware that her feelings for James had gone further than just viewing him as a friend. Their parting last night was evidence of that. It was not the kiss that two friends would exchange; rather it was the tentative kiss that would prove if they could be close physically. Abby now knew that she would like that intimacy, and was sure that James would as well. For the moment she would be content. There was too much happening for her to complicate matters with emotions. If it was to happen it would.

Her thoughts turned to the business of having to go back to London and clear her flat, prior to putting it on the market. She reckoned that it would take at least two or three days. There were not too many personal items to bring away, after her bleak girlhood there were no family treasures to keep, all she had was the bits and pieces she had bought herself, and they were few in number anyway. Did she feel sad about selling up? She mulled that over and decided no. In many ways it was not a life she had lived there, it was merely an existence, there were no memories to treasure, no magical moments in her life that she would leave behind, and no friends she would miss except Roz, who came and went from her life with no pattern. Yes, she thought. A couple of days would do it. Another thought came to her, possibly James would come up to London and help? Perhaps spending time together away from the valley would help resolve how their relationship would develop. A mischievous smile came to her face. Going away with James would really set some tongues clacking.

CHAPTER 22

Abby was having breakfast on the Monday morning when the phone rang. Mary answered it, and had a brief conversation with the caller, before coming into the Lounge. "Abby, it's for you." She immediately thought it would be George Walker, and was surprised at how quick he had been, when Mary said. "It's Sir Richard Wellings." Abby's surprise showed by her raised eyebrows.

The phone was on the Bar, so Abby walked round. "Hello Sir Richard, how are you?"

"Now Abby, I thought we had covered that bit. It's Richard. I'm well thanks. Have you caught up on your sleep yet?"

"Yes thanks I have. It's good to hear from you, Richard. A surprise as well."

"Well I don't call everybody after the Ball. But I thought I would ring and ask if you enjoyed yourself."

"I did, thank you, very much. Something very new for me I have to say, but very enjoyable."

"It didn't seem as if you were not used to such functions. You fitted in as if you were born to it. Maggie reckons you were the star."

"Thanks for saying that Richard, but to tell the truth I was a bundle of nerves."

"Now, Abby I don't believe that." He laughed. "I rang because Maggie and I were thinking to ask you and James over for some lunch one day. What do you say?"

Abby thought for a moment. "That's very kind of you. I shall speak to James when I see him; I am going to London for a few days shortly. May I call you when I get back?"

"Of course you may. You're not going back to move money around again for that Bank, I hope."

"No, no. I am going to clear my flat and put it on the market."

"Oh? And where is your flat? If you don't mind me asking." Abby explained where the flat was.

Richard listened carefully. Then asked about the accommodation. "It's a two bedroom, serviced flat. Private underground parking with twenty-four hour porter."

"Abby, can I get back to you possible later today or tomorrow. I know someone who is looking for a flat in Kensington. If I were to put him in touch with you, you could save a little on Estate Agents fees. Would you mind?"

"No, not at all."

"And Abby. He is just an acquaintance, not a friend. So don't think I am asking for a special deal. Find out the market price, and that's what you ask of him." Abby agreed with him, although when it came to money she had learned her lessons in the City, and knew the value of every last penny. It hadn't entered her head to offer this man a special price. "I'll get back to you as soon as I have spoken to him. Goodbye, Abby."

"Goodbye, Richard, and thanks."

Abby wanted to ask James about coming to London, but didn't want to do it here in the Inn. She decided to go down to the station for a while. She felt there was a good chance that James would suddenly appear. She was right. He did. He rode up on Cassie about half an hour after she got there.

"Good morning Abby. How are you today?"

"Morning James. I'm well thanks. How are you? Thrown any peasants out today?" The laughter was in her face. He grinned.

"No, I must be getting soft in my old age."

"You didn't look old on Saturday night, gallivanting around the floor." He smiled, and dismounted. Cass followed him as he walked towards her. Abby held her face up, and was delighted when he kissed her. Cass put a stop to that by nudging Abby with her nose demanding a fuss.

"I can do that here," James remarked, "that is if Cass will let me, but if I tried at the Inn, the bush telegraph would be fizzing."

Abby laughed. "Yes I know. I don't think it would be a good idea. I am glad to see you. Richard phoned this morning, and asked if you and I would like to go over for lunch one day. I said I would ask you, and get back to him."

"Sounds good to me, unless he is going to try and sell me that useless piece of land again. Yes, let's go. When do you think?"

"Ah, well there is something else I want to ask. It's a bit of a favour really. I have decided to go to London for a day or so. Basically to pack up the flat, and put it on the market."

"Burning your boats are you?"

Abby nodded. "Yes I suppose you could say that, although the decision was made a while ago. The thing is that I would like some company, otherwise I may get maudlin. It's a big favour I know, but would you come with me?"

Abby was pleased to see that James did not have to think about his answer. "Of course I will come with you." He replied immediately. "When are you thinking of going?"

Abby's thinking had not extended to deciding a day. She thought quickly. "Let's say Thursday, come back Friday. No! The traffic on the motorway will be murder Friday afternoon. What about we go down on Sunday, and come back on Tuesday. That will give me plenty of time."

"Good idea, I'll book myself a Hotel."

"Don't be silly James. There are two bedrooms in the flat. You don't have to worry about my reputation you know."

"I do though. If Mary or anyone round here thought I was staying with you at the flat, they would welcome you back as if you had been on Honeymoon. It will be better if I book a hotel." If Abby felt a little disappointed she didn't show it. She hadn't issued an invitation for them to sleep together, merely creating an opportunity to do so if the situation felt right. She was pleased that James though had the consideration to believe that her reputation was important.

She turned the conversation back to Richard Welling's invitation. "We'll ring Richard later that week. It will be nice to see the Grange in daylight."

"It's quite a place." James told her. "The gardens are very good. They should be. He has two full-time gardeners, and Maggie to get them looking so well."

"Oh, does Maggie garden?"

"No, but she makes sure the gardeners do."

Abby smiled. "Do you think he has a reason for inviting us?"

James shrugged his shoulders. "I wouldn't think so, apart from getting to know you. Very difficult at the Ball, as the Host he is pulled this way and that, trying to keep everything going well. No. I would imagine that it is just getting to know the new resident of the valley."

Abby examined that in her mind, perhaps James was right, it was just simple courtesy that gave the reason. "How's your mother?"

James cheered. "Gone again. Back to Berkshire. At least I shall have some peace now."

"Oh poor James. Does she make your life a misery? She's very fond of you, you know. She's just worried about you."

"Yes, well if that's the case she can stop worrying. I am alright." Abby felt that Gwen would not believe James was alright until he had married. She wondered if James thought of her as a possible candidate, if he did, how would she react? At this moment the answer would be probably negative. Abby wanted to have a meaningful occupation. Something that would sustain her over and above being a wife. James had a meaning to his life here; Abby could not endure just being a consort to his vocation. A reality crept into her mind. James would never ask her to marry him. His pride would not let him, for the thought that she may believe he asked only to marry her money. If there was any asking to be done, Abby felt that she would have to do that or create the conditions for him to do so. She laughed inwardly as she realised that she was the one who was pushing their relationship forward. James must think of her as a brazen hussy, although he didn't seem to mind at all when she invited him to kiss her.

This musing was interrupted as James was asking a question. "Sorry, I was miles away. What did you ask?"

He grinned. "You are going native so fast! I asked if you had thought any more about what you will do with it when the station is done." Abby hadn't thought beyond getting the place restored.

"No. Apart from seeing it as granddad saw it."

"You mean you are doing it as a tribute to him." Abby was astounded. James had just put into words the idea that had never properly formed all this time. She turned to him.

"That's it. That is what I have been doing all this time, but didn't really know it. A tribute to Thomas Tregonney. How clever of you." Impulsively she took hold of his shoulders and kissed him. "Thank you, James." He smiled casually.

"Well if I get a kiss every time I come up with a good idea, then I shall have to think of many." He quipped, and then carried on with his question. "But what will you do with it when it is restored. It will look just as it did, but you will not want to stand here all day and just look at it, will you?"

Abby shook her head, and wandered down the platform a little. Turning around she said. "I suppose in my mind getting it done was all the challenge I needed. I haven't thought beyond that."

He moved to her side and put his arm around her waist. "Well is it going to be a museum? Or just a complete old station, with no rails, no trains, in the middle of nowhere. Do you see what I am getting at?" Abby did see what he was saying, and for the moment had no answer. She stayed where she was, enjoying James' arm round her waist. She thought furiously. He was right, it should have a purpose. But what purpose?

"You must think me stupid, James. I really haven't gone further than thinking about getting it restored. Do you have a suggestion?"

James did. "Well how about turning it into a kind of educational site? You know with old pictures up, and notices printed which explain what the stationmaster and the porters had to do. How the milk was handled, who brought it, and where it went. What goods were handled, what came into the valley, and what went out of it." James' words were starting to excite Abby.

That was the answer. It would have a purpose, and she was sure that her granddad would approve. She turned to him smiling. "James you have the perfect solution. I love the idea. I think that granddad would be really pleased that if the station could not do what it was designed to do, teaching people about his job would be the very next best thing." She hesitated for a moment as a wicked smile came to her face. "I suppose you think that has earned you another kiss?" James too smiled the wicked smile.

"For that idea, something more would be appropriate."

Abby viewed him archly from beneath her eyebrows. "Down Boy. It was good, but not that good." They smiled at each other, a smile that said they understood that this was flirting with a little bit of danger thrown in to add spice. James was happy that Abby approved of the idea. Although he hadn't talked to Sam, his concerns coincided. He thought it would not be good for Abby to be living here, alone, in what would have been a testimonial to the past. Giving the station a purpose would give her a purpose as well.

He had other worries as well. By coincidence his worries had already been aired by Sam. He had lived in the valley for all his life, and apart from the few years spent in the Army, the valley was all he knew. Abby had only known the valley in summer. James knew that the autumn and winter months presented a very different face. Snow was rare, but wind and rain wasn't. The soggy, cold months of December, January and February, would depress even those who had spent their lives here. How Abby would react James could not guess, but he was sure she would be very miserable if she lived here, all alone through those months. He would not say anything that might deter her; he wanted her here in Combe Lyney; but he knew that he would have to ensure that she was not left alone. This was a duty to which he looked forward with pleasant anticipation.

He broached a subject that could create some problems. "If you do this, it would be good to bring the goods shed into the equation. You know by now that goods were far more important to the railway than passengers."

Abby did know, and perhaps subconsciously she had avoided thoughts of going into the building. She prevaricated. "I thought you had found a use for the goods shed?" She asked lightly.

James had forgotten that, and was stumped a little. He then grinned like a little boy, and had to confess his sin. "Yes." He said slowly. "I did say that, didn't I?" Abby nodded with a smile on her face.

"Well Mr. Comberford. Have I caught you out?"

James nodded. "Ok, Abby. I hold my hands up. It was a bit of a negotiation tactic. Perhaps though it is best that we include it in the agreement. Let's say an unofficial part, best sealed with a handshake, eh?" Abby's eyes twinkled.

"There is a better way." She lifted her head and offered her lips. James was perfectly happy to do business this way. He took her in his arms and the deal was sealed in a way that both of them enjoyed. He held her in his arms after the kiss and looked at her.

"Where are we going, Abby?"

She shook her head. "I don't know, James. But shall we just keep going down the road, and see where it leads?"

He smiled. "That suits me. Let's not read the signposts, until we get to journeys end. Mind you, all these kisses are very enjoyable."

Abby turned away with a smile on her face, keeping his hand in hers, to look in the direction of the goods shed. "I know that I shall have to go in there soon. But I am afraid."

"Well I'll go with you if you want."

"I hoped you would, James, but would you be upset if I asked Sam to come as well. I know that if I get emotional, I would want you to be with me. But Sam was the one who found granddad, and..." Her voice trailed off as she couldn't find the words to explain her feelings. James knew instinctively what she was trying to say.

"I am not upset. I was half expecting you to say that. Sam is the link." Abby nodded, that was absolutely right.

She looked up at him. "Why is it that you always seem to know what I am trying to say?"

"That's because I'm a clever clogs." With those few words James lightened the conversation, bringing a smile back to Abby's face.

She appreciated the change in tone. "Ok, Mr. Clever Clogs. How are we going to get away from here next Sunday without the whole valley putting two and two together and making five?"

"By the whole valley I presume you mean Mary and Mavis. Well it's quite simple really, just tell them the truth. If you were to try subterfuge they would see through it in no time, and then put their own interpretation on it."

It was indeed as simple as that. Mary had overheard Abby tell Sir Richard that she would be going to London, so when Abby told Mavis and Sam that evening she was not surprised. Mavis speculated that it would be a lot of work for Abby, in just two days. "Yes, I know it will, so I have asked James if he would give me a hand. It's just the personal stuff I shall keep. I'll get one of those house clearance people to take the furniture away." She addressed Mavis in a conspiratorial way. "James is booking himself a room at a hotel." Abby had put emphasis in the 'himself'. "Do you think he would be offended if I offered to pay for that? After all he is coming to help me."

Mavis' pleasure at being involved was immediate. She gave the question some thought. "Well, I don't think he would be too offended, he won't accept of course. What do you think, Mary?"

"He will be offended. You know Mr. James, proud, to say the least. The idea of Abby paying for his accommodation, no, he wouldn't like that at all."

Sam had followed this with some amusement. He suspected that Abby had raised this as a way of diverting the two ladies away from their suspicions. He decided to play the game for Abby.

"Well you could take him out for a good meal." Mavis and Mary both agreed with enthusiasm.

Mary adding the comment. "You know how James likes his food." Abby smiled, the crisis was over.

"Will you be bringing much back with you?" Mary asked.

Abby thought about it. "I would imagine that the car will be pretty full, but it is just clothes and a few ornaments. Nothing else."

Mavis being practical asked. "Do you have enough cases then; you don't want to be putting stuff into black bags."

"I think so. I have a couple of large cases, and some smaller ones. They should do."

"Well just in case you need them, I will look out some old cases we have got. If you think you need them, come by anytime and pick them up.

Abby had thought she had got over her announcement quite well. Truth or not it satisfied neither Mary nor Mavis, and much to Sam's disquiet after Abby had gone to bed, their conversation was full of the possible consequences. Not that they were outraged, far from it, this to them was further proof that the two young people were getting close. Mavis had not told Sam about Mary's reporting the scene after the Ball. So it was a surprise to him when Mavis mentioned it. It wasn't wholly a surprise to Sam. He had seen the burgeoning relationship in the small gestures that James and Abby used when they opened the station and house. To him is seemed reasonable to accept that they would get to this point. He hadn't shared his thoughts with his wife, not wanting to add more fuel to the fire she was building. He felt that things were going along naturally without interference. He had to say something when Mavis said to Mary. "I wonder if Abby is taking that Birth control pill. Probably not, good thing too."

Mary was with her on that. "Oh yes. If Abby were to get pregnant, James would not hesitate to marry her."

That was it for Sam. "Now listen you two. James and Abby are getting on well enough. They don't need you talking about it like it was in one of those Sunday papers. In fact, if it got to their ears the way you are going on, I would not be surprised if Abby gave up all her plans and left Combe Lyney for good, rather than be the subject of all your gossip. Now put a stop to it the pair of you." Only rarely did Sam talk to his wife like this, but when he did she listened, not without a rumble of self-righteousness, but she listened and understood when she had overstepped the line. This was one of those occasions. Mary had never heard him like this, and it frightened her. She was treading a fine line between friendship and commercial common sense. If her customers thought she was an out of control gossip, they would not be so pleased to patronise the Combe Inn. She exchanged glances with Mavis and could see that Mavis for all her fiery nature was taking notice.

The autumn ate insidiously into the last flirt of summer. With the days getting shorter Abby felt she had little time to get all the things done she was planning. George Walker had phoned and asked if he could meet to discuss the work she wanted done, they arranged to meet at the Combe Inn. She phoned Michael the porter at her block of flats and told him she would be there on Sunday, and then Sir Richard phoned her to tell her that his acquaintance was very interested in the Flat. Abby had gone on the internet and now had a figure in mind. She told Richard what she was looking for.

"I shall put it on the market for seven hundred and fifty thousand, Richard. I bought an extension on the lease, so there is ninety-four years on it, the price reflects that, but it is still favourable for the area, and I will not move on that."

"I don't think that would be any problem." He replied. "From what I gather Bernard needs to move quite quickly. When are you going to be there?"

"I am going down Sunday, and will be returning here on Tuesday."

"Damn. He's will be in Tokyo then, won't be back until the following Friday."

"There isn't a problem. If he identifies himself to Michael, the porter, he will show him around."

"Are you sure?"

"Yes, that will be fine. Give me the name." Richard did that, spelling out the surname as it seemed to have East European origins.

"That's good. I'll leave all the details with Michael, and if your friend wants the place he can put his solicitors in touch with mine."

"Don't worry, Abby. I will tell him. I said before he was only an acquaintance, not a friend, so I am not going to ask for a favour on his behalf. He's well-heeled anyway, been based in Paris, but has to move to London, so will want to complete quickly. When are we going to see you and James?"

"I'll give you a call when I get back next week, if that's ok?"

"I look forward to it. Enjoy your time in London."

Abby then turned her attention to the station and house, she mentioned George Walker's visit to James, who said that as the Landowner he would like to be there. "If you don't mind, of course."

"Don't be so silly, James. Of course I don't mind. As you say, you are the Landlord and have a right to know what is being done with the property."

George had worked out his sums and quoted a figure which left James gasping. Abby didn't turn a hair, merely asking if that was an estimate or a quote. "Oh, an estimate." replied George quickly. "Based upon my inspection. I have spoken to the Heritage Officer, and she will come down with a list of requirements. It would appear though that within reason there will be no problems. Your intentions for the station have pleased English Heritage. They seem to have passed this on the nod, makes me think that someone has put the word in." He gave Abby and then James an enquiring look. Neither of them thought it politic to mention Abby's conversation with Councillor Wates. Getting no explanation he carried on. "I will need to find some details, though. How the Barge Boards were decorated and such. You mentioned someone who you thought could provide some evidence of that."

Abby nodded. "Yes, my contact, Mr. Brasher should be able to furnish all that. I do have some photos taken in the fifties, though I don't know if they will show enough detail for you."

"Anything will be helpful. But the final figure will depend on how much I have to employ specialist craftsman. They don't come cheap you know."

Abby had already made her mind up. "Your estimate is a good guide, but I wouldn't want a variation above say five percent without discussion. Is that acceptable to you?" George nodded. He had already built in an overrun, so five percent gave him plenty of latitude. Abby then made him very happy.

"Would you like stage payments?"

George was very agreeable to that. "That would be good. I'll get a programme of work out for you, and we can discuss the percentages for the various stages."

"Will you get started as soon as possible?"

"I can get men in the house within a couple of weeks. I shall see the Heritage lady next week, wouldn't want to start anything at the station until I have seen her. When we know what we are facing then I can plan accordingly."

James had something to say. "I would imagine that the work will take a month or two?"

George looked uneasily at James, hoping he wasn't going to ask for the work to be done in a hurry.

"Sorry, but I doubt that we will be able to make the house habitable for at least three months. To put a water tank in the loft I shall have to take some of the roof away. We won't be able to get it through the loft access, you see, even though they are plastic these days. Wouldn't want to do that with bad weather. Then there's all the plumbing and electrical work, can't leave that to the jobbing lads. I suspect it will be well into next year before I am finished. You do want it done properly, don't you?"

Abby quickly agreed. "Yes I do, I shall just have to impose upon Mary for a little more time." James was pleased with the answer. It meant that Abby would not be moving in until the better weather next year.

George pulled out some drawings. "These are for the Victorian style conservatory. As you see my man has done two. One showing how it would look with just the side covered and the other taking the conservatory round the front." Abby looked at them keenly. She didn't take long in making the decision; she had half convinced herself already that taking the conservatory round the front was too much.

The drawings settled her mind. "Just the side, Mr. Walker."

He agreed. "Yes doing too much can often spoil the whole thing." He rolled the drawings up."

Abby had been impressed with the drawings, as they had been water-coloured, and gave an impression of garden as well. "Do you think

I could have a copy of that, it's really good?" With good humour George gave her the drawing.

"That's only an impression, you know. Won't look exactly like that when it's done."

"I know, but it will be nice to have it, just to remind me of how it may look eventually."

Abby was getting worried, that she hadn't heard from Mr. Brasher, She had written to him some three weeks ago. Her worries were resolved the next day when she came down to breakfast; the letter was sitting on the table awaiting her. Eagerly she opened it.

Dear Miss Tregonney,

Please accept my apologies for not replying to you sooner, I have been to York for some days pursuing my researches.

I am most interested in your plans to restore Combe Lyney station to the condition it was in during the Great Western period. Your request for information and research was most warmly received, and I have started to gather such detail as I can. I believe that I will be able to obtain some official photographs commissioned by the GWR in the nineteen thirties. If this is possible I shall be happy to make copies available to you for the local Heritage Officer, who no doubt will have to be involved.

As this is a project so dear to my heart, I would be happy to come down to Combe Lyney. Any advice, little as it may be, I shall be delighted to share with you and your builder.

I shall write again, once the relevant information is to hand. I assume that accommodation could be found for me at the Combe Inn.

Thank you once again for inviting me to be part of this work.

Yours sincerely,
Brasher

Everything she was planning seemed to be falling into place. She had no doubt that Mr. Brasher would be able to obtain the photographs, and his knowledge would be invaluable to them with information about the working practices, so that James' idea of the station becoming a heritage classroom could happen. She thought that Mr. Brasher would embrace the idea enthusiastically. Now she had to think of what she would do with all the stuff she would bring back from her flat. Her room here would certainly not accommodate anything more than some of the clothes she would have.

She asked Mary when she came to take her plate away. "Have you had enough, Abby?"

"Mary, you always ask, and I will forever give you the same answer, plenty. May I ask a favour though?"

"Of course.'

"The station house is not going to be ready for me, probably until early next year. Will it be alright to stay here until then?" Mary tutted and threw her head up to suggest that such a question was a waste of time asking.

"Oh Love, of course you can. You didn't need to ask. There's a room here whenever you need, and for as long as you need." Abby smiled her thanks, and then went on.

"I shall bring a lot of stuff back from London with me, is there anywhere I can store it until the house is ready?"

"We'll put it in the room where your dress is." Abby's Ball gown had vanished from her room the day after the Ball. She had a moment's panic, until Mary told her she had hung it back in the closet where it had been before.

"Won't you need the room?"

"No Love. We don't get many visitors this time of year, there are three other rooms, which will do for any that do come, and over the winter we don't get any. So your stuff will not be in the way."

"I shall pay you the going rate for the room then."

Mary looked horrified. "You will not." This was said so firmly that Abby knew that argument would be fruitless.

Mary cleared the plates, just leaving the pot of tea. "It will be nice to have you here over Christmas. We only open from twelve to two, and then Jack and I sit down to a Capon with all the trimmings. Mr. James will come if his mother is away. It's a really nice day. You'll enjoy it. In the evening we go down to Sam and Mavis, they have a bit of a party."

Abby thought she would enjoy the day. She had never really celebrated Christmas after her Mum had died. Christmas Day for her had been a rather lonely event, eating a packaged festive meal; toasting herself with a half-bottle of wine, and getting bored in front of the television; but mainly anticipating getting back to work the day after Boxing Day. She had one question though. "Capon? Not Turkey."

"Goodness no. Of course traditionally it should be Goose, and there's many round here that will have Goose. But Jack can't abide the fat, and I am not much of one for Turkey, too dry for me, so a nice Capon fits the bill. Not too dry, and a really good flavour."

"I don't think I have ever had Capon."

"It's just a cock bird that's been neutered. Makes it put on weight. You'll find it very tasty."

"Mary, if you're cooking it I know I shall."

Mary left with the plates, saying, "I must get on." She wore the wide smile that she usually had when Abby praised her cooking.

CHAPTER 23

Abby and James left at nine-thirty that Sunday morning, Abby without thinking getting into the passenger seat so that James could drive. He took the road through Paverton and across the moor to Wheddon Cross and then down to Bishops Lydeard and Taunton.

Abby was puzzled. "Why did you come this way?"

"There is a lot less traffic on this road. It's a bit longer, but easier so it takes about the same time as going down the valley." Once on the motorway James put his foot down. The car cruised effortlessly and he shocked himself when looking down he realised that they were doing ninety-five miles an hour. He relaxed his foot and slowed the car down to just less than eighty miles an hour.

"It's a good thing I don't have one of these," he remarked, "I could lose my licence in no time." Abby laughed. She was very happy, the idea of having James' company for two days appealed tremendously, and she was very content just sitting there comfortably enjoying the journey. Apart from the road works at Bristol they made good time even allowing for a stop for coffee at Leigh Delamere services.

***

As they approached London, Abby asked James if he wanted directions. "I should be alright." He answered. "Should I make for Kensington High Street?"

"Yes. I am not too far from the station." Abby directed him from the station and then to the underground car park of her block of flats. She gave James the key-card that raised the barrier to the car park. Abby let them in to the entrance hall with her key and they were greeted by the porter, Michael, who had seen them drive into the garage on closed circuit television. "Miss Tregonney, how nice to see you again, have you returned to us now?"

"Yes, but only for a couple of days, Michael. I am putting the flat on the market, and moving down to Devon permanently."

"I shall be sorry to see you go, Miss Tregonney." He looked at James.

"Good afternoon Sir."

Abby hurried to make the introduction. "Oh Michael, this is James Comberford, a good friend. He has come up to help me pack my things."

"It is good to make your acquaintance, Sir." Michael didn't extend his hand as most men would do; rather he stood there at a sort of attention.

James summed him up in no time. "Good afternoon, Michael, not on parade now though." He grinned as Michael relaxed his face.

"Is it so obvious, Sir?"

"Only to someone who has also been in. Sergeant, or was it Sergeant Major?"

"Sarn Major, Sir. The Royal Green Jackets. I suppose it was standing to attention gave it away."

"No Sarn Major. It's the boots." He looked down. "Never forget that lesson do you?" Michael laughed, and kept the smile on his face as he looked down at James' footwear and said without rancour.

"I would put your Batman on a charge, Sir." Instinctively recognising officer material. James hugely enjoyed the joke. "If I may ask, Sir, what Regiment?"

"Two Para."

"Indeed Sir." this seemed to Abby to be said with respect. "I have an oppo who was in that lot.

Name of Diggins, he made Sergeant."

"Not Spade?"

"That's what they call him behind his back. Yes Sir. Then you would be Captain Comberford?"

"Yes."

"In that case Sir, I am very pleased to meet you."

"All in the past Michael, all in the past."

"Yes Sir."

***

Abby had stood there dumbfounded as this male bonding process had gone along. In just a few moments, Michael had found out details it had taken Abby months to discover. Then she realised that the common bond of service would bridge any awkward gaps. She also noticed that Michael didn't need to ask James about his service in the Falklands, he knew, and was gently told not to mention it by James' words, 'all in the past.' She smiled inwardly as she felt a little jealousy creep into her mind. Perhaps she would try to seduce James whilst they were here.

She opened the door and let James into the flat saying. "It didn't take you long to sum up Michael. I have lived here for ten years and all I knew was that he had been in the army. Nothing else though."

"The army does things to a man, obvious to someone who can recognise the signs."

"Yes but you guessed his rank."

"That was easy. Once a man has made Sergeant, he changes and it stays with him. The way he addressed you and stood, that never goes away."

They walked into the flat, and James looked around with interest and a growing unease. There was no sign of the flat ever being a home, no touches that showed the place had been loved. A few ornaments and couple of pictures on the walls. A large couch, a club chair and a television completed the furnishings of the lounge. A few utensils in the kitchen. No evidence that Abby had ever tried to make this anything but a temporary refuge. The sadness he felt for her at that moment strengthened his feelings. He could not allow her to live like this once she got back to Combe Lyney, Abby needed a home, a proper home, and Combe Lyney would provide that.

Returning to Combe Lyney, the boot full of cases, and the back-seat piled with black bags and various hold-alls, Abby was very happy, not just that she and James had got closer over the last two days, but because she had now surrendered her previous life to history. She hadn't instructed an estate agent as yet. Michael was aware of the possible interest by Richard's acquaintance, and would allow him to view the flat when he called. She had left her mobile number and the number of the Combe Inn so that contact could be made. Tomorrow she would call the solicitors, Chorister Brooks and ask them to handle the sale for her. She looked over at James, driving. Their time together had been good, working together to clear the flat and eating together at a couple of the good restaurants that were close by. One was an Italian restaurant, and Abby had worn a dress that showed quite a lot of cleavage which James had found quite delightful. The waiters seemed to think that this was a romantic assignation and like all Italians to whom 'amore' was everything reacted by ensuring the candle on the table was always well placed to cast light on her eyes and a discreet shadow emphasising the cleft between her breasts, making unnecessary visits to top up their wines, and even singing Italian love songs whilst they served them. Abby and James had laughed together and been serious together and silent at times. It seemed not to matter that there were these pauses in the conversation, she enjoying the atmosphere and James enjoying looking at Abby. He had not objected too much when she was determined to pick up the bill for the meals, but had been adamant when she suggested she should pay for his hotel, saying vehemently "no way." Refusing even to discuss the matter. In her mind it was fate that it should be James taking her away from the old life and driving to a new.

Their arrival back at the Inn went mostly unnoticed. Mary appeared with a bland face to enquire if they had a good journey, and helped bringing in the cases and bags. She opened the room that she had set aside for the storage. "Just put them all in here, and sort them out later." Abby was half expecting a cross-examination, and was a little disappointed when none came, but realised that this probably would happen when James had gone home. This he did after the inevitable cup of tea, leaving Abby to face the interview. He winked as he left and Abby smiled giving him a kiss on the cheek saying.

"Thank you, James for helping, and everything." She knew she was teasing Mary. The lady in question was eager to prise out of Abby all the details, but bearing in mind Sam's anger at her and Mavis, decided to leave things for a while. Part of her mind recognised that things were going the right way anyway, so she could be patient. Abby for her part was surprised that there was no inquisition, unknowing that this was something else for which she could thank Sam.

If Abby thought that everything was moving along well, she was in for a surprise, although the problem came from an area she least expected. Another letter from Mr. Brasher confirming that he had obtained photographs of the station taken in nineteen thirty, and some architectural details which may not be evident from the station as it was today. He said he intended to travel down later that month, and asked if accommodation would be available for three days starting the twenty third. This was no problem. She had another meeting with George Walker at the station and the Heritage Officer came this time. This officer, introduced as Ms Eaton appeared at first to be rather out of her depth and was quite abrupt, but when Abby told her of the material that Mr. Brasher would be bringing she softened. Afterwards Abby got the idea that her abrupt manner was concealing the fact that she had not been able to turn up any photos or details from the council records. George told Abby that he would be sending in a crew the following Monday to start stripping out the house. "I'll take all the old furniture out, what do you want to do with it?" Abby had already thought about this.

"The table, chairs, dresser, I shall keep, oh and the big chair in the back room."

George nodded his head. "Ok. I'll get them all checked for worm, and have them cleaned up. Shall I take the range out?"

"Yes please, I'll let you know what I want to replace it with in a few days. What about the sink?"

"That is past its best, Miss Tregonney. I can get a new one, they are still made, and fit it into a work-top along that wall, with drawers and cupboards underneath if you wish."

"That will be fine."

"I will be down here quite often to check on my men, so as it goes along we can discuss the other bits and pieces." Everything was falling into place.

The bombshell exploded at Lyney House. Gwen Comberford returned to confront James. He was surprised to see her back so soon and also surprised that her manner was not as warm as usual. His mother tackled him as he was about to go out. "James, I understand that you have been to London with Miss Tregonney." James was immediately on his guard, when Abby was referred to as Miss Tregonney.

"Yes. She wanted to clear out her flat, and I went with her to help with the heavy items."

"Did you sleep with her, James?" The question, coming from his mother, was like a slap in the face. He would not deny to himself that he had been tempted to try, especially after that Italian meal, but his upbringing had forbad his making any move. Barely concealing the anger that was slowly boiling up he replied coldly.

"I do not propose to answer that question. You have no right to ask it. Indeed how dare you ask it."

"James, you must tell me. Did you sleep with her?" Gwen was also getting angry, not with James, but with the idea that she had to ask.

James got up and walked to the door, but then turned, his face white with anger. "Mother, you brought me up to be a gentleman, you taught me right from wrong, in addition my Army training taught me a lot about how a gentleman behaves, if you like the Officers code. If there is one thing that I learned from you and the Army is that a lady is deserving of respect, and that gossip about this aspect of her life is totally wrong. Abby is no different and on this subject I will not speak. Ever." He opened the door and left. Gwen called him.

He would have ignored her but a tone in her voice spoke of distress. He came back. "James, you are right, and I am pleased that you feel this way, but I would not ask the question without a very good reason. Please tell me."

"No."

"No, you didn't sleep with her?"

"No, I won't tell you. You say you have a very good reason for asking. Well I cannot conceive of any reason that would allow me to answer. But I will listen to your reason." Gwen had thought about this a lot, and the small seed of doubt had grown into a mountain, but she could not tell James the reason, as she felt she would be guilty of a kind of betrayal.

"I can't tell you the reason."

"Well then, that ends the matter."

"You must have slept with her, if you hadn't you would tell me straight away."

"Mother, I will not answer your question one way or the other, because you have absolutely no right to ask it in the first place. You say you have a compelling reason to ask, but will not tell me what that reason is. I will not have the reputation of a very nice woman besmirched. You know well how the gossip around here can get out of hand." Gwen knew her son, with him in this mood, and getting pompous she would not get an answer by wheedling.

She had to give in. It was more important than her guilt. "If I give you the reason, will you tell me the truth?"

"I doubt it." Gwen was beaten, now she had to get to James in a roundabout way. "You don't know who Abby's father was, neither do I. but perhaps you ought to give some consideration to the possibility that it could be your father. Abby could well be your sister." James was stunned. He felt total shock, his mind blank. He couldn't stay and with an angry mist clouding his eyes rushed out into the garden to think. Gwen didn't have her answer but thought she could read into his reaction an acknowledgement. She sat and waited, as miserable as her son would be at this moment.

Fifteen minute later James returned. He had been pacing up and down in the garden, trying to keep his temper in check and turning this possibility over in his mind. "I refuse to accept this; you are labelling my father an adulterer."

Gwen shook her head sadly. "I am labelling my husband an adulterer; that should hurt me more than it will hurt you?" Her voice and face betrayed naked misery.

"What makes you think this?" His voice broke, choked with his emotion.

Gwen smiled sadly. "It was my fault. I left your father alone too much. He was a healthy man, there was enough evidence to suggest he had affairs, but I chose to turn a blind eye. We lived our lives in an expedient way, allowing each other a certain freedom. You knew your father, most of the time he was a bit of a bore but he could be most charming when he wanted something. There being no other apparent candidates for Abby's father, you have to consider there is a chance, an outside chance I agree, that it could be Charles. If he set his sights on Marion, then she would have been hardly able to say no." James shook his head. His eyes were being opened. Most children recognise their parents as being fallible in a gradual process, starting after the child comes to adulthood and culminating when the parent is elderly. It doesn't engender disappointment, more likely greater love. Charles Comberford had died just after James had entered the Army; his faults therefore were buried with him.

James was being forced to acknowledge the truth. That and revelations about his parent's marriage. "No Mother, I cannot believe this. I knew Marion as well, I don't think that she and my father ever exchanged more than two words together, and from what I remember, she wouldn't have been browbeaten."

"Darling, I understand how you feel about Abby." Gwen tried to placate her son. "Your reaction was enough to tell me that. If you really like her we shall have to make sure that she isn't your sister, we should try to get some DNA evidence. Perhaps you could get some of her hair. I believe that would be sufficient for a test." James could see the sense of that, but getting a sample from Abby without her knowledge would be wrong.

"You want me to go sneaking around to get a strand of her hair? I will not do that. I shall have to explain everything to Abby; she has as much right to know as we do. I am certain she will agree. It's this way or nothing."

Gwen had no option but to agree. "Very well. Perhaps you are right. Would you talk to her about it, perhaps ask her to come up here, I don't think it's the kind of thing you would want to talk about in the Combe Inn." He nodded agreement. "James, please answer my question. I don't want to spend the next few weeks worrying about that." James looked at his mother.

"Mother I will not answer. If." He said putting a lot of emphasis on the 'if', "we did, and it was incestuous, then talking about it won't make it undone. If we didn't then it doesn't matter." Gwen shook her head wearily. Part of her applauded James for his integrity, after all she wouldn't admit to any of her adventures, and she brought him up so he was only acting in the way she had taught him; the other part cursed him for being the stubborn fool.

James needed to find Abby as soon as possible. He dreaded telling her of the possibility that they were brother and sister, yet this couldn't be delayed. He had left his mother, with anger, hating her for the presumption she had made. He jumped in the Land Rover and drove viciously out of the grounds. He didn't stop at the junction, simply wrenching the steering wheel to go right, the tyres squealing, heading towards the station. The blaring horn brought him back to his senses. He waved to the driver of the small van he had nearly run off the road, to acknowledge his mistake, and drove on a little more slowly. The near accident cleared his mind. His mother was right; she had no other option but to mention it. Abby was not at the station, he got straight back in the Land Rover and drove back the way he had come to see if she was at the

Combe Inn. Her car wasn't there either. He went in and spoke to Jack.

"Yes, Mr. James, she went out about an hour ago. I think she went to Gallow Farm." James thanked him and gave some thought about what to do. He sat on a bench at the back of the Inn for about half an hour, Mary brought him some coffee, and he was rewarded when Abby's car turned into the drive. She flashed a smile when she saw him, and came over to join him at the table. She poured some more coffee from the pot.

"There isn't another cup, so you won't mind me sharing yours will you?" He had to grin at her cheek, and then the reason for his coming here took the grin from his face. Noticing the swift change of mood, Abby asked. "Is there something wrong?" He nodded with gloom written all over his face. "Tell me."

He found it difficult to know how to start. He had thought not to discuss this with Abby here, at the Inn. Now he wanted to unburden himself as quickly as possible. "Well a situation, no something has come up and I don't really know how to tell you."

"You're married."

He gave a hollow laugh. "No, no, nothing like that. That would be simple. Abby it's difficult so I will just say it. You could be my sister."

Her face went dead. "What?" she eventually managed.

"There is a chance that our fathers could be one and the same."

Abby looked at him, looked away, and then turned back quickly. "This is a joke, right?"

"No, no joke."

She then astounded him. She giggled. Then giggled some more when she saw the expression on his face. She leaned close and whispered. "Then it's a good job, that my amateurish attempts to seduce you didn't work."

The load lifted immediately from his shoulders. "You don't know how many cold showers I had to take when I got back to the hotel."

She laughed with him. "Well then you shouldn't have resisted." She smiled at him fondly. "I know neither the time nor the place." The giggle came again and she whispered. "But you know. Incest has a deliciously immoral ring to it."

"You're laughing at me."

"No James, just trying to see the funny side of it, or I could rant and rave if you wish, but that will not do any good. This is unusual by any stretch of the imagination, I can't get my head round it, tell me. If I were, how would you feel about having a sister?"

"If you are my sister, it will take some getting used to, but I suppose I could come to terms with it after a while. So long as you don't try to boss me about. But I would much prefer to have a lover."

Abby was pleased to hear that that he too recognised their relationship was going that way. "So would I, James. So would I." She finished the coffee in the pot. "This is cold. I'll ask Mary for some more." Mary as usual had anticipated her, and in two minutes Abby was back with another pot of coffee and another cup and saucer. Abby ignored the second cup. "I much prefer sharing yours. Anyway, how did this come up and what do we do?" James explained his conversation with his Mother, leaving out her wish to be told if Abby and he had slept together.

"She suggested that we have a DNA test done."

"That seems a sensible idea. What will we do? Get a doctor in to take swabs?"

He was surprised. "You seem to know something about it?"

"A little bit. One of the girls in the office had a baby, no father in sight, and she accused one of the dealers of getting her drunk and having his way with her. The suggested father and the baby had a DNA test. That was how they did it."

"Was he?"

"No. She was trying it on I think, to get money. Although I would imagine that at some time they had been together. He was known for playing, and she was rumoured to be very 'friendly' with men."

James grinned at the euphemism then wondered how much money would have bought satisfaction. "If we got our doctor to come to the house, would you let him take a sample?"

"Of course. Better to know one way or the other."

"Ok, I'll do that. I'll let you know when he's coming." They sat for a while drinking coffee, the cup being used alternately between them.

Abby's mischievous mood returned. "You know of course that Mary is convinced that we were in bed together for most of the time."

James grinned. "Well we had better put her right."

Abby shook her head. "No, I told you when we were riding that I would like to be thought of as a Femme Fatale, let her think that. Besides I would not want her to believe that my technique was so bad that I couldn't lure you into bed." James smile told her she wasn't out of order talking about this.

"I did say something about cold showers. I know you think that I was inhibited about that. It has been so long since I was in a situation like that, I misread your signals. I thought I would be out of order making a move. I shan't do that again."

"Well to be honest I don't know if I was sending the signals, because I don't have that much experience, but obviously if I decide that I do want you to seduce me, I shall have to make the message very plain."

"You talk as if there is not a little problem to be sorted out."

"To be honest, I don't think there is. I don't feel like your sister, if I was I am sure that there would be some feeling that told me."

"You mean a kind of instinct."

"Yes, exactly. Do you have any feeling like that?"

James looked doubtful. "Actually no. I would have thought, as you do, that there would be some primeval feeling that would warn us we were going against nature. I certainly didn't get that. In fact the very opposite. I don't feel like your brother at all."

"So James, no kissing until we know."

The expression on his face was desolate. Abby had sympathy for him, yet at the same time was happy that not being able to kiss her could depress him. "Think of it as a kind of Ramadan or Lent."

He nodded gloomily. Then brightened. "When it's done, and if it is as we feel, shall we go away for a weekend?"

Abby smiled wickedly. "A dirty weekend?" He grinned.

"I would like it to be so."

"Mr. Comberford, you certainly know how to turn a girl's head. And just in case I will make my requirements plain, I want one room, one double bed, and you and me together in that bed! Preferably without clothes. Now is that understood?" He didn't grin this time, just a very warm smile.

"The message is clear and understood. I am already looking forward to it." Abby leaned across the table and looked down.

"Well, so you are!" Their laughter echoed across the garden and in to the Pub.

If Abby had taken the time for introspection, she would have been amazed at the change these few months had wrought. In her office she had been a Leader, taking command and decisive. In all other respects she was a Follower, allowing others to take control and guide her, not always with her best interests at heart. Anyone who had known her in London would be stunned at the assertive and bold Abby now revealed. Indeed Abby herself was surprised, not knowing what possessed her to behave like this. The other change was her ability to flirt. It may have always been there, was it an instinct that most women possessed? Or was it James who was the catalyst. Whatever the reason, it mattered little; she was quite enjoying being a tease. She was pleased that Gwen Comberford, who after all would know her son better than anyone else, deemed this important enough for action to be taken, sensing in her son feelings for Abby, that made this necessary.

Mary had not heard any of their conversation. She had hovered in her kitchen which gave her a view of the garden, even opening the windows in case she could hear. But Abby and James had their heads so close together, and talked so quietly that all her efforts were in vain. She decided direct action was needed, so boldly marched out to see if they wanted Lunch. James declined as he wanted to get back to the house.

Abby accepted. "Just a little Salad, please Mary, and do you think I could have it out here?"

"Of course Love, best make the most of the weather. It will change soon." She went back to her kitchen, all she would be able to tell Mavis is that they had sat with their heads together for some time, and although James seemed serious at first they were soon laughing together. She felt aggrieved. It was almost as if they were trying to keep something secret!

Abby finished the coffee. It was funny she thought, something which could have put an end to the relationship, had the effect of clarifying the situation. She now knew that James felt something for her, his demeanour had proved that. And the episode had spurred him to propose taking things to the next level. She had little doubt that the test would prove that they were not brother and sister. But a seed had been sown. She would not feel confident until the test was done.

Mary saw Abby walk off after lunch, heading inevitably towards the station. Despite the laughter Abby and James had shared, Mary sensed that there was something that concerned Abby. She wished that she could share the problem. Mary had put Abby in the place that her own child would have occupied in her life. If Abby was hurting, then Mary hurt as well. If she looked at the situation realistically she knew that the so-called plots that she and Mavis had nurtured had been pie in the sky. As Sam had pointed out, the two young people had come together naturally without any assistance from Mavis or Mary. Yet Mary felt a responsibility towards Abby, and wanted to fight her battles, whoever the enemy.

CHAPTER 24

Abby had gone to the station to think and was surprised to find Sam and Harry who had cleared off all the scrub and weeds around the house, and also erected many of the posts. Sam greeted her heartily. "Hello Abby, how are you today?"

"I'm fine thanks, Sam. I didn't think you would be down here so quickly."

"Yes, we thought it best to get the ground cleared before George comes in. He will only dump everything all over, and we would have to wait until goodness knows when to get the scrub scraped off."

Harry lifted his Cap. "Afternoon Miss Abby."

"Hello Harry, you don't waste any time do you?"

"Well I know us country folk are supposed to be slow, But them as says it aren't here when we are getting on with the job."

"So I see."

"We wanted to get the ground cleared off, and a load of gravel down. Be easier to tidy up once the builders have gone." He turned to Sam. "Sam, I am going up to Lills and get a load of gravel now, be about three parts of an hour. Ok?"

"Yes fine, Harry. See you in a bit." With Harry gone, Sam looked at Abby and asked.

"Do you want to be alone for a while?" He could feel that there was something on her mind.

Abby gave that a momentary thought and decided to divulge her problem. After all Sam was the one that James had turned to when in despair. "Sam, do you think that James' father could also be my father?"

Sam was immediately furious that anyone could make such a suggestion. "Who has told you that? The idea is nonsense."

"The idea came from Mrs. Comberford."

"Oh, I see." He thought for a bit. "Well it was known that Mr. Comberford liked the ladies. But I would say that there is no possibility that he was your father. As far as I know he never went down to the station. Any dealings that your grandfather had with him, he went to Lyney House. I doubt that Mr. Comberford ever saw Marion above once or twice in her life. No, Love. Put that idea out of your head."

Abby pondered for a while. "Then why would she say such a thing? Do you think she is trying to put a wedge between James and me?"

"No Girl." Sam shook his head vigorously. "She may honestly believe there is such a possibility. I say she's wrong. Mr. Comberford was stuffy, and a bit of a bore, but he was a gentleman and very conscious of his position. If he played around he did it elsewhere, rather than give people here a chance to gossip about him. And there would have been gossip. Mark my words. My Mavis would have heard, and she couldn't have kept her mouth shut." He stopped and gave the idea a little more consideration. A seed of an idea came to him brightening his countenance. "If you ask me, I reckon that Mrs. Comberford may be playing a game. Yes, I suppose you could say she had grounds for suspicion, but as she was never here that much after Mr. James was born she wouldn't really know how things were. Now give some thought to her trying to stir Mr. James up. She may well think that you are the perfect match for him. So she gives him a bit of a kick. To make him do something about it. You know, threaten to take a child's toy away and the child will want it all the more." He nodded his head sagely. "Yes I reckon that is it. Mr. James is one of the best, but he sometimes is guilty of letting things slide along, and not doing what needs to be done."

Abby thought about that. "Well if she thinks I'm the perfect match for James that makes me feel better. And if there is the slightest suspicion, it is best sorted. We are going to have a DNA test to prove it or not. I don't think it is true, and neither does James." She smiled mischievously and asked. "Sam do you think I am right for James?"

He shook his head with a big smile on his face. He answered her with another question. "Do you?"

Abby hesitated before answering and then with a blush suffusing her face softly admitted.

"Yes. I think I have fallen in love with him."

Sam was filled with pleasure at those words. "I have known Mr. James all his life. He has never treated any girl the way he treats you. I noticed the other day when you ran out of the house. It was James who chased after you, and it was James you wanted at that time. He cares for you, Abby, he probably loves you but may not know it yet, but I have no doubt. If you want him, you will have to push him though." Abby was well aware of that. Sam went on. "You are right for each other. I have thought that for some time."

"I am pushing Sam. I got him to ask me away for a weekend when all this is settled. It's a naughty weekend. Aren't you ashamed of me?"

"No Girl, not at all." Sam laughed heartily. "What better way to celebrate eh?" He winked at her, and then a serious look came to his face. "Abby I wish I could tell you who your father was, I can't. But I am sure I can say who he wasn't. And Mr. Comberford was not. Have your test; I have no doubts of the outcome. You and Mr. James are not related... Yet." Abby touched his arm and smiled her appreciation of his support.

They walked towards the house, and Abby raised the issue of the Goods shed. "I don't want to go in there, but I shall have to anyway. Can I ask another favour of you? When I do go in, will you be with me? James has said he will come, but I would like you to be there as well. It would be a sort of hand-holding thing.'

"Of course, Abby. Just let me know when." He wondered if the rope was still hanging from the beam, and whether he ought to get in there beforehand and make sure it was taken down. He would talk to Harry about that. The sound of a diesel engine disturbed them, as Harry arrived back, a big trailer full of small broken rock and gravel, behind his JCB Tractor the scoop raised high. Sam and Harry were immediately immersed in discussion about where and how they should spread the load. Abby did not want to be in their way, and asked if they would mind if she left.

"No Love, not at all. Harry and I will have this chat about spreading the gravel, and as usual Harry will do it his way."

"And Sam will just get in my way, the way he's always done." replied Harry with a grin, "but don't you worry Miss Abby, it will be sorted properly." Abby laughed and took her leave. She understood that Sam and Harry had known each other for years, and that this ribbing each other was just a way of enjoying each other's company. It brought into focus her lack of good friendship, the sort that stays the course over years. This was another reason to stay here, she had made friends, and she knew that these friendships would keep.

Rather than returning by the road, she walked down the track, deciding to use the Public Footpath coming down from Huish to get back to the Lane. It gave her a chance to think about what had happened, and how she would react if the test proved that she was James sister. She had read stories in the papers about siblings, re-united after being split as baby's, having an unnatural attraction to each other. She wondered if that was happening to her and James. She shook her head. She had to believe that her instinct would have warned her, and Sam's undoubted stance that they were not brother and sister.

It was two days later that James phoned her on her mobile to say that the Doctor would be at Lyney House the next day at eleven. Abby promised to be there, half hoping that Gwen Comberford would have left again. That was not to be as it was Gwen who let her in. James was not in evidence.

"Hello Abby, Thanks for coming up like this."

"It's not a problem, Gwen. I would like to know who my father was. If this will narrow down the search I am quite happy." They walked through to the breakfast room.

"I would offer you a cup of tea, but I don't know if that is allowed before taking this swab."

Abby was pleased to see that Gwen was a little unsure of herself, compared with before when she visited, Gwen had been so collected and in control.

"I think not, but afterwards a cup of coffee would go down very well."

Gwen smiled possibly in relief for Abby accepting the situation so calmly. "It must have been a bit of a shock to you, this business, I mean. It didn't occur to me until I realised how close you and James had become.'

"Yes, it was a bit of a blow. But having thought about it, I have to say that I don't believe it to be true. I don't think James believes it either."

"I just don't know." Gwen looked guilty. "I feel terrible, but I had to raise the matter. You see I left CC alone too much, because I didn't like living down here. What he got up to in my absence I don't know, and didn't want to know. You saying you didn't know who your father was, started me thinking, who it could be. Then, and it was a horrible thought, it came into my mind that it could have been CC. I honestly can't say that he is your father, but as long as there is a possibility…" Her voice trailed off.

Abby nodded and finished what Gwen had been saying. "We have to make sure."

Gwen nodded. "For what it's worth, I honestly hope that you and James are not brother and sister. The anger that James showed me when I suggested it, well I had never seen him as angry before. He's very fond of you, Abby."

"I am very fond of him."

Gwen looked up and Abby could see she was happy about the situation. "Well let's keep our fingers crossed. I think I would be very content to have you as a Daughter in Law."

"Hang on; it hasn't got as far as that."

Gwen smiled. "Oh I think it will. I hope it will, and then I can leave this bloody place for good." Abby could not say anything, knowing that her thoughts had extended that far. Gwen went on. "And if it does, you will have to do the asking. I'm afraid my son is a little backward in coming forward at times. Ah, here's James." The growl of the Land Rover, and the grit scattering over the drive told her that her son had indeed arrived.

***

James strode into the room, throwing a fleece jacket on to a chair. "Hasn't he arrived yet? Hello Abby." Whether from devilment or not, Abby could not say, but she raised her face to him for a kiss. James did not hesitate, and put his lips to her cheek.

Gwen did not turn a hair. "I am sure you could do better than that, James." She said drily.

"Oh yes he does." Abby replied for him. "But we thought it would be better to show some restraint until the tests have been done."

Gwen smiled and whispered to Abby. "I am not your enemy, Abby. But I liked the riposte. Any other girl would have been squashed by that." Abby blushed a little, the comment wasn't really called for. In Gwen's mind though it was proof, however much Abby may deny it, that she was seeing James as 'Her Man' and would jump in to defend him. Gwen approved of that.

***

The Doctor was not there that long. The swabs were taken easily and deposited in two sample tubes, properly labelled for despatch to the Pathology Lab. Doctor Graham assured them he would get the tests done as soon as possible, but even though this was a Private Consultation it would take some time. "There are not many Labs I would trust to do this work, so I reckon it will be four or five weeks before I get the results." He had asked Abby for the name and address of her Doctor.

Having only the Doctor she had seen very occasionally in London, he suggested she came in to the Surgery. "I'll get you registered with my Practice. The records will come down eventually, but they usually take an age so in the meantime I will give you a check up." He gave her a card. "If you would phone to make an appointment."

Gwen had made coffee, while James and Abby saw the Doctor. James couldn't stay, so Abby joined Gwen in the Breakfast Room. Abby had to ask Gwen something. "Gwen, if it was proven that your husband was my father, how would you feel about that."

Gwen stirred her coffee slowly as she considered. "I suppose I ought to feel some antagonism towards you, but I don't think I would. It was all so long ago, and I feel somehow to blame for leaving CC alone so much. If I had been here and did my wifely duty, it wouldn't have happened." She thought some more, Abby staying silent. "Actually I think I might be happy about it, I always wanted a daughter, and suddenly I would have one ready- made, without all the morning sickness and dirty nappies to cope with. Bearing in mind that I do actually like you, Abby, I think I would be very happy with the situation. And who knows if not daughter, hopefully a friend, or even a daughter in law."

Abby had to smile at that. "I said before, you may be rushing ahead a little.'

"No, I think I covered all eventualities. Whatever happens, please don't be a stranger. That's all I'm saying."

"That I won't be. You make very good coffee."

They both smiled at that, and Gwen offered another cup saying. "As you like it so much."

Abby, who for a while had wondered if Gwen was trying to prise James and her apart, was relieved. Sam had said as much and she had not quite believed him, now perhaps she should believe him when he said that Gwen may be trying to stir up James. She had said in no uncertain terms that she thought Abby was right for James. Now all she needed to know was if James thought that as well. In the meantime there was the problem of her paternity. The waiting was going to be the worst part, not knowing was the hardest Millstone.

***

The arrival of Mr. Brasher caused quite a stir. She had written to him advising taking the road through Wheddon Cross and Paverton, something for which she was profoundly grateful when she saw his car. A Rolls Royce! It was not a complete surprise, knowing that whilst he was unworldly, he nonetheless insisted on the best quality even if his colour co-ordination was abysmal; so his choice of car could more or less be predicted. What was incongruous was his small figure getting out of a car so large, and it was large! He would never have got that up the lane. Later she would find out it was a Silver Wraith made in nineteen fifty four, with a body by Mulliners. Mary had immediately said the car should be parked down the back, and Mr. Brasher, without a care, had handed the keys to Jack, who was petrified.

"I can't put that through that narrow gateway, what if I scrape it? It will cost a fortune to repair. No, someone else will have to do it." Mary pointed out reasonably that there was no one else. "Mary, you will have to help. Watch me in."

"I can't do that. I have to go and settle Mr. Brasher in. I am sure he will be wanting some tea. Get on with it Jack." Jack walked around the car assessing the width and length. With those measurements in mind he walked to the gate and eyed it, then looked back at the car. It probably would go through he thought but not without help. The problem was resolved as Harry Webster came past on his tractor.

He stopped immediately, and came over to admire the Rolls. "Good Lord! A Silver Wraith. Mulliner body if I'm not mistaken."

Jack looked astonished. "Harry! You take one look and you know all about it, how come?"

"Always been interested in these, Jack, well, all Rolls and Bentley's really, always wanted to own one. Fat chance on a farmer's income, but I can dream can't I?" He shook his head. "This is a beauty, I mean look at it. Got style, and it's immaculate. Lovely!"

"Well if you know so much about them, you can put it down the back, come on, I'll see you in." Harry was ecstatic. "Never thought I would get to drive one of these. Hang on, I'll take me boots off, don't want to get mud all over." He then regarded his overalls. "Don't suppose you have something I could sit on, my overalls aren't that clean." Jack went off to fetch some towels from the Bar.

Abby was sitting in the Lounge with Mr. Brasher, who seemed much more at ease than when she met him before. He took a sip of the tea, nodded in appreciation, and looked around. "I didn't get to see this place last time I was here."

Abby almost choked on her tea. "You were here before?"

"Yes. It was in nineteen sixty six. About three months before the line closed. There were a lot of closures about that time, and I made it my purpose to travel all of them before they were gone forever. Not the whole country, you understand, just the Great Western lines. I was on the train of course, so I didn't have an opportunity to stop and look around." He picked up his voluminous bag, which Abby remembered from the bookshop. This time he had no trouble in finding what he sought.

"I have been able to get these few photos. Most are original GWR publicity shots, taken in nineteen thirty four. That was the last time the station underwent any major alterations. And I do have a few taken in nineteen fifty two. Those were unofficial photos, taken by an enthusiast." He cleared some space on the table and laid them down. "These are the official ones. As you can see the photography was first class, and shows the detail very well. Unfortunately from your point of view they wouldn't allow any of the staff to be present on the platform at the time, but as your grandfather didn't take up his appointment until nineteen thirty eight, it makes little difference."

Abby studied the prints carefully. "These are very good, I imagine that Ms. Eaton..."

"Excuse me. Miss Tregonney." Mr. Brasher interrupted. "Who is Ms. Eaton?"

"The Heritage Officer."

"Ah!"

"These should satisfy her completely. I believe she hasn't been able to find any such evidence as this. It's a pity they are black and white, though. We can't tell what the colours were like."

Mr. Brasher gave a small smile. "Oh that's a little enough problem. The GWR used standard colours throughout the system. I have plenty of evidence of how the buildings were painted, I can even put you in touch with manufacturers who still have the actual colour recipe."

"Mr. Brasher, you are a marvel."

"No Miss Tregonney, it was the Great Western which was the marvel." He sorted out the photos taken in the fifties. "As I said these were unofficial. But as you can see there was little change. Now, Miss Tregonney, do you think that could be your grandfather there?" He pointed to a figure standing just outside the buildings.

Abby nodded. Even with her eyes misty she could recognise him immediately. It was the uniform and Cap that gave it away. "Yes, Mr. Brasher. That's him."

"I am so pleased. Would you like these improved? I can get better copies you know."

"That's very kind of you. I would like that."

"Leave it with me, I'll send them on to you as soon as possible. I have to say though Miss Tregonney, that he does look a little fearsome, if you don't mind me saying so. I notice that he is wearing the old style uniform of the Great Western, not the British Railways one."

Abby smiled. "I understand he was not exactly pleased with photographers coming around. As for his uniform, I am told that he disapproved of nationalisation, and refused to wear anything but the Great Western one."

Mr. Brasher thought about that and with a small smile nodded his head. "I think I rather like your grandfather Miss Tregonney, he sounds like a man I could have warmed to."

"Mr. Brasher, please call me Abby."

"I would be pleased to. I usually answer to just Brasher. I don't think you would be comfortable using my given name, in fact it hasn't been used for over thirty years."

"I'm sorry but I could not call you anything but Mr. Brasher. It would not seem respectful." God she thought, I have gone all Combe Lyney. He did not say anything to this except smile.

Abby was saved any further embarrassment by the approach of Jack, who held out the keys to the car. "It's safely round the back, Mr. Brasher, and I have taken your case up to the room. Lovely car though. You must feel good driving that."

"I drive very little. It's totally impractical for London."

"Harry said it was the Mulliner body."

"Yes it is. He must know his cars then. They had to make me a special seat and pedals position." He indicated his lack of height. "Otherwise I could not see over the steering wheel." Jack nodded, Harry had said something to that effect.

"Can I get you something to drink?"

"No thank you, not at the moment. I am enjoying the tea very much, though. I have not had tea like this for years." Jack said he would see them later. Mr. Brasher turned to Abby.

"You seem to know a little more about your grandfather?"

"I have been talking to a couple of people who actually knew him. Sam Perry, who has farmed here for years, and Reg Purvess who was the signalman in the late fifties and early sixties." Mr. Brasher pursed his lips in thought.

"Do you think I could talk to them as well. I would be very interested in their reminiscences, particularly Mr. Purvess."

"That's no problem. Sam comes in here most evenings, and I am fairly certain that Reg will come over if we ask."

"Excellent! Now if you will excuse me, I shall go and unpack. Do you know what room I have been given?"

"One moment I will check." Abby went to look at the wall chart, and saw that Mary had written Mr. Brasher's name next to room three. The key was on the hook, so she brought it back.

"Here you are. Room three. Is there anything I can carry for you?"

"Thank you, Abby. I can manage. Shall I see you later?"

"Yes, I shall be here. Will you join me for dinner? About seven thirty."

"I will be delighted. I shall see you then."

***

Abby had worried that Mr. Brasher might find the facilities of the Combe Inn a little primitive for his taste. There was no need, as at dinner he complimented Mary on the room and the comfort of the bed.

"After that drive I felt in need of a little nap. I was lucky to wake when I did, else I should have been late for the meal." Later after dining he was effusive on the quality and flavour of the beef.

"It reminds me greatly of the fare that I remember from my childhood." When Mary had left them with a proud beam on her face, he said to Abby. "That was truly delicious. Do you know where Mrs. Elvesly gets the beef."

"Everything is obtained locally. I am certain that the beef came from a farm within a mile or so."

"Interesting." He went quiet with his thoughts for a moment. "I hope the next meal is as good as that."

"I can assure you it will be." Abby affirmed. "I have had to be very strict with myself since I have been here. Everything is so different from London and the Supermarket stuff I lived on."

"Well if you enjoy flavours like that every day, I can understand your desire to come and live here." Mary brought coffee for them and asked Mr. Brasher if she could get him a Brandy or something.

"I am not a drinker, but I believe that a Brandy would be perfect to go with a perfect meal." Mary smiled and looked at Abby with her eyebrows raised.

"Could I have a Vodka and Tonic please, Mary?"

Behind the bar, Jack was having a panic when his wife informed him that a Brandy was required.
"I can't give him that stuff we usually serve. Hang on, I have a bottle of Armagnac down in the Cellar. Hold the fort here and I'll go and fetch it.' After five minutes he returned with a very dusty bottle, which he rubbed over with a cloth, opened and poured a measure into the Balloon glass that Mary had washed and polished. She took their drinks to the table, where Mr. Brasher was regaling Abby with stories of the railway. Abby looked up and asked Mary if she would let Sam know when he came in that they would be delighted to have him join them. Mary nodded.

Mr. Brasher returned to his theme. "I am very interested in your plans for the station, not just because you will restore part of the Great Western Railway, but also for the idea of it having an educational function. I am all in favour of teaching new generations what the old railway was all about. However I assume that you realise this will be a serious investment."

Abby was already getting used to the costs involved. "Yes. I understand that."

He cleared his throat. "Well, Abby. I don't want to embarrass you, but I would be pleased to help, not just with information and historical facts, but financially as well." He stopped. Far from embarrassing Abby, he had done just that to himself. He twirled his Brandy, swishing the dark amber liquid around the Balloon. "I apologise. That was impertinent."

Abby shook her head. "No Mr. Brasher. Please don't apologise. I recognise that this is something very important to you, otherwise you would not have come down here in the first place. But I do realise the costs involved, and I am prepared to meet them."

"You are very generous to an old eccentric, Abby. But I would like to contribute, if I may. You see I have no family, so the Great Western has been my passion. I have made a Will making bequests to various organisations that foster the legacy of the Railway, so what you intend to do is very close to that ideal."

Abby knew she would refuse the offer, but how to do that without offending him. "Perhaps I can explain myself, Mr. Brasher. This was my grandfather's station. He was here for twenty-eight years. And having everything taken away from him, his wife who died, his daughter who went away, and finally the railway which was his life, he hung himself in the goods shed. James Comberford put it well when he said that I was doing this as a Tribute to my grandfather. I want to dedicate the restored station to him and the life that he led. I do thank you for your generous offer but I feel that I, his granddaughter, have to bear the burden." Mr. Brasher listened carefully, and recognised the anguish that was driving Abby. He understood that taking on the responsibility was a part of that Tribute.

"Very well, Abby. I do understand. I didn't know your grandfather had died that way. You have my deepest sympathy." He paused. "If you will not let me contribute financially, then you must understand that any other help I can give will be given without stint. I will be gratified if all the research that I have done can be of more assistance than just being published as a book. May I give some advice though? The Heritage people do have grants at their disposal for such schemes as this. They will be happy if you do not take advantage of them. I would beg you to get everything you can. Let us say it is one way in which today's Society can salute the service your grandfather gave to yesterday's Society."

That appealed to Abby, and she smiled at the pleasant idea of getting something back for granddad. "I didn't realise that, Mr. Brasher. I will do that. I shall talk to Ms. Eaton about it."

Later when Sam had come in and been introduced to Mr. Brasher, Abby left the two men to chat, and joined James who was hovering at the bar, unsure if he would be intruding. Mary was quick to notice that they did not have the usual air of togetherness, and started to worry. She remembered the day they sat and chatted in the garden, and although they had laughed a lot, she instinctively knew that there was something keeping them apart. Now their attitude and body-language gave her more cause for concern. A phone call to Mavis was now an important matter, and as quickly as possible. She made the mistake of mentioning this to Sam when he left. His response was forceful, and designed to keep them away from the truth.

"Mary, you and Mavis have been scheming and gossiping for a long time, and don't think for one moment it has gone unnoticed. From little things that have been said I think that Abby is getting uncomfortable with it. So stop it now! I shall tell Mavis the same when I get home. Leave them alone." As he left the Combe Inn Sam was feeling a little pleased with himself. Knowing Mary, she would not want to upset Abby, so hopefully her prying would stop. He had also enjoyed chatting with Mr. Brasher, who had let slip his Christian name of Wilberforce. Although their backgrounds were so different, they had the memories of growing up in the thirties to share, and a wistful appreciation of times past. Brasher had questioned him closely about farming in the valley which surprised Sam. He had however answered the questions frankly. The facts seemed to give Brasher some food for thought.

CHAPTER 25

Abby drove Mr. Brasher down to the station the next day, leaving him to wander around at his own pace. It was some time before he returned to her with a smile on his face. "I always get emotional when I see a place such as this. It looks so forlorn and neglected now, its purpose forgotten. But it was once an essential part of an economy that boosted this Country's wealth and social standards to be the envy of the World. Knowing that it will be restored is a source of great happiness for me." Abby agreed with him, but her emotion stemmed from a different source.

"For me it is all about my family. Even though they are all dead, I come here and connect with them. My emotion is finding a family when I grew up not having any."

Mr. Brasher was understanding of her emotions. "I had a family, but rarely saw them. My father was a Diplomat, the scion of an old family, always away somewhere in the Empire. My mother consigned me to a Nanny from an early age, then to Boarding school, then to Cambridge. I think that in all those early years I never saw my mother for more than ten minutes at a time some half a dozen times a year. I doubt that she saw my father much more than that. I saw even less of him than her. They were both killed in a bombing raid in nineteen forty-one. Ironic really, after being apart for most of their lives, they were together when the bomb fell." These few words convinced Abby of her suspicion that Mr. Brasher came from a privileged background. However it would seem that all that privilege had given him less affection than she. No wonder he had become an eccentric, without warmth in his life, just a fascination for this railway.

***

The arrival of George Walker in his van spared them further embarrassment. Abby introduced them. Immediately after the introductions George cast about with a worried look. "Is she not here yet? Typical of her, I have never known her to be on time anywhere." His complaining was cut short as Ms. Eaton drove into the yard the very next minute. Mr. Brasher reverted to his previous uncomfortable mode, and produced the photographs, which Ms. Eaton and the builder examined carefully. She seemed to be relieved as they showed so much detail, and declared that as far as she was concerned this was the specification she wanted. George was a little more diffident. The photos showed Barge boards on the gables carved in a very ornate fretted style. These were no longer present, obviously as some time being replaced by plain boarding.

"I can't do that without proper drawings." He declared. Mr. Brasher rummaged in his bag and produced diagrams that showed them exactly. George examined them, nodding his head and humming all the while.

"Yes, I know a Carpenter who can do that." He said finally. Abby opened the doors to the booking office and waiting room. Pleased that she had mastered the knack that Reg had demonstrated. Ms. Eaton looked around fussily, and made various demands of George Walker. He told her that he had already made an inspection and let her know that he would be removing the plaster, but would re-plaster with Lime.

She then demanded that the place was re-painted with colours as they saw.

Mr. Brasher who had also come in coughed. They looked at him. "I don't believe these are the original colours. It had been changed at some time."

George looked exasperated and a little testily asked Mr. Brasher. "You seem to be well-informed. Can you tell me what colours they used?' Mr. Brasher again delved into his bag.

"All woodwork was painted Brown and the walls a dull cream.' He was flicking through papers as he spoke, then lifted two up, looked briefly at them and pulled them out completely. "Here is an official colour photo showing the scheme, and here," he sounded triumphant, "is the names of paint manufacturers who have the original recipes for the colours." George fell upon these with delight.

"Well that will save us a lot of time." Ms. Eaton was even happier. All her problems were resolved it would seem without her having to do the research herself. She was prepared to leave it all in other's hands. However Abby did not want her to get away so easily. Reminding herself of what Mr. Brasher had said last night. She took Ms. Eaton out onto the platform and asked about Grants towards the cost of restoration.

Ms. Eaton's face blanched. She hadn't expected this. "Well I would have to look into this. It's not as if it was a Public Building is it?"

"I was not aware that it had to be. The station is a listed building and isn't being restored as a home. The intention is to create an area, where people can see how the station worked, what the station master and porters were expected to do, and how the station was a part of the local economy. We are going to place old photos and explanatory notices, so that people can come here and understand."

"Oh I see. An educational site. Best thing you can do is let me have a full costing when Mr. Walker can work it all out. Then we can have a meeting with the Museum and Heritage committee, and the Education Department. They will be interested too. Have you thought about putting in an application to the Heritage Fund of the National Lottery?"

Abby hadn't even thought about that, but wasn't about to let Ms. Eaton of the hook. "Yes. One will be made, when I get the quotation. But as you well know they seem to like wasting that money on all sorts of politically motivated schemes." Ms. Eaton agreed with that. Wishing that more of that money came to local schemes like this, which in turn would not dent her Authority's budget so badly.

"When you have the final costing. Let me know, and I will be happy to help with the application. They do like bureaucratic jargon you know." They agreed that that was the best way to proceed. Ms. Eaton gave Abby her card. "That's a direct line to my desk. Call me anytime."

Mr. Brasher and George Walker had been engrossed in discussion. And George was now satisfied that he could do as complete a restoration as any he had done. Abby re-joined them, and with confidence that there would be grants available, asked George if he would consider the Goods Shed as well for the work.

"I will, but cannot look at it now. I am expected at another job. Can I come down later this week and have a look?" Abby agreed. He went on to re-assure her about the station. "When I am finished it will look exactly like those photos." He declared. Mr. Brasher was happy that it would be. First Ms. Eaton departed, and then George left. Mr. Brasher was still happy to walk around the site. Abby stood there looking at the Goods Shed. She would ask James and Sam, if they would help her over her nerves tomorrow.

She was startled when Mr. Brasher suddenly spoke behind her. "That was where your grandfather met his end?" Abby just nodded. "It is brave of you to consider that. I think some would have just wanted it knocked down."

"I am going to go in there tomorrow. I shall ask Mr. Perry and James Comberford to go with me though."

He nodded his head. "I understand. Obviously I would like to see inside myself, but I shall wait for another day."

"Oh no, Mr. Brasher. Please come. After I have got over the first bit, I would be very keen to have you tell me all about it."

"Very well, Abby. But I shall make myself scarce for a while. If you could let me have the key to the station I would very much like to immerse myself in the atmosphere a little more." She was pleased that he understood the emotion.

Abby brought the topic round to Mr. Brasher's long conversation with Sam. "You seemed to get on well with Mr. Perry last night."

"Yes I did. It shouldn't be surprising, although we are from different backgrounds, we are of the same generation, and had much in common to reminisce about. I gather that he has taken you under his wing, so to speak?"

Abby smiled. "Yes. Sam has been good to me. I quite look upon him as a surrogate grandfather."

"I believe he looks upon you as a surrogate granddaughter. It would give me pleasure if you were to view me as a sort of great-uncle."

"Why! Mr. Brasher, I would happy to do that." He smiled something that didn't seem a normal expression for him. Abby locked the doors and they walked towards the car.

"May I bring up something else, Abby?" She looked at him.

"I was very impressed with the quality and flavour of the beef last night. I spoke to Sam about it, but thought I would ask you before proceeding, in case it embarrassed you."

"I don't understand."

"I have not for years tasted beef like that. My Club, where I dine most days, gets the best available, but cannot compare at all. Would you see me as presumptuous if I asked to buy some and take it back for the Chef to try as well?"

Abby could empathise with his comments about the food. "I have been similarly impressed, and no. I don't think it presumptuous. I am sure that Mary would be happy to provide you with a joint or two. I would suggest that the Lamb and Pork here is in the same league." Abby laughed inwardly, she was starting to reflect his style of language.

He shook his head. "Perhaps a joint or two would be sufficient to start, but later I would suggest a good size cut would be appropriate, a whole lamb and a side of pork if that would be possible. I am on the catering committee at the Club. I have no doubt they will consider the meat to be as good as I think. They may well ask if regular supplies could be obtained. I think they will be happy to pay a premium for meats such as that."

Abby's brain was working overtime. She had considered the food at the Inn to be very good, but her thoughts had gone no further than that. Now as if by chance there could be an opportunity. If Mr. Brasher's Club were to want regular supplies, who else in a selective market could be approached? A niche market for the finest meat would bring in a valued extra income for the farmers of the valley. This she had to discuss with Sam and James.

"I am not too sure of the supply position. I shall have to talk to people about this. But I am sure that something could be done, if only on a restricted basis."

"I understand. Perhaps we could discuss this further. If my committee are as pleased as I have been, I shall get in touch with you."

***

That afternoon Mr. Brasher opted to go to a preserved railway known as the South Devon Railway. Abby questioned him about this and decided that it would be well worth a visit at some time, as from his description it reflected more closely the sort of railway that had existed here in the valley. She wanted to talk to James about the opportunity that Mr. Brasher's comments had suggested. She telephoned Lyney House and having no answer decided that he was probably out and about on Cassie. An impish smile crept over her face, as she thought that if she were to drive down to the station again, he would probably turn up. She was right. It was soon after she got there that she saw him riding along the track from the direction of Huish Coppice. His smile told her how glad he was to see her. Having dismounted he came close, but made no further move to greet her. Abby was not going to allow this. She moved up and raised her face to meet his lips.

"I thought we were not going to do this."

"I don't care." She replied. "Now kiss me properly." After a few minutes when neither of them could speak as their mouths were otherwise pleasantly engaged. James stepped back.

"Whew! You meant that."

Abby had a very happy smile on her face. "We are a very close brother and sister." this was said with laughter in her voice. "I did want to see you, so I thought that if I came here alone, you may well have turned up."

"I see. Am I that predictable then?"

"Oh no. Well only when I want you to be. I just think about you and you get a message."

"You witch." He grinned as he said this.

Abby had a secret smile. "Am I?" He nodded. "How nice. I never thought I could be a witch."

"Yes. A witch and a hussy. You deserve a good spanking."

"Ooh! That might be nice. I may let you do that, one day." They both laughed at the thought.

"Now why did you send me the message?" He enquired.

Abby explained what Mr. Brasher had said about the beef. "He thought that if his committee agreed they would want regular supplies. Could that be done?" James didn't have to think long. "Most of the regular slaughter is taken up by butchers in the area, but I would think that they could increase production. But you had best talk to Roger, Harry, Nat, and Abe about it. They really are the ones who would be involved."

"Would they want to talk about it?"

"They would, but it is going to be difficult for you. Farmers are stubborn, independent blokes. You are a relative newcomer to the valley. Roger and Harry would be alright. But I think that Nat and Abe may not want to listen."

"Nat and Abe?" Abby queried.

"Nathaniel Gaunton and Abe Stone."

"Well you could talk with them, couldn't you?"

He shook his head. "No. I am the landlord. They would view it as interference from the Squire. They have to be persuaded. Your best bet would be to talk to Sam first of all, then try and get Roger and Harry on your side. If they then chat to the others, it will not look so much as if you are interfering."

Abby could see the sense of his thought. "I was going to talk to Sam anyway. If he doesn't come in tonight, I will drive down to Gallow Farm and see him."

"I wouldn't wait until tonight. Go down and see him now, he'll be around the farm somewhere." She agreed.

"I'll go down now."

"Right, I'll ride that way as well. I won't get involved, but if I can add anything I will be there."

***

Abby found Sam without difficulty. He took her into the cottage, where Mavis, ever pleased to see Abby made tea. Sam nodded his head wisely as Abby explained.

"I wondered why he questioned me so much about the farming here. Now it all falls into place."

"What do you think, Sam? I spoke to James and he said he would not get involved."

"Well we would be fools if we didn't explore any avenue that could give us a better income." He drank some tea before continuing.

"Let me get Roger in, see what he thinks." He went off to find his son. Mavis had listened carefully to what Abby had to say.

"Men! Always have to have a conference. It sounds like a great chance to me. But they will have to talk about it, look at it every way, and take so long that it will be months before they do anything." She was dying to ask Abby how she and James were getting along, but mindful of the talk that Sam had with her, she held her tongue. Sam had said nothing about the chat that he and Abby had. Preferring to let her think, like Mary, that any gossip now was likely to upset Abby.

Roger took little convincing. Even so he looked to his father for his agreement. "I like the idea, Abby. What should we do next?"

Abby waved her hands defensively. "Oh no. It's nothing to do with me. Mr. Brasher spoke to me about it and I am merely passing the message on."

Roger didn't agree. "You have to get involved, Abby. I like the idea, and I am happy to talk to the others. But we are all independent businesses. That's no good for your Mr. Brasher. He needs one point of contact. You are the obvious person."

Abby shook her head again. "But I know nothing about selling beef, and I would imagine that lamb, pork and poultry would also come into it. I don't know what prices should be charged, how the stuff is shipped, whether we have to go through a wholesaler, what certificates are needed, nothing."

"That's no problem, we sell direct to butchers in the area, so there is little difference to selling to what to all intents and purposes is a catering establishment. The slaughter house in Paverton is registered, so all carcasses are certificated. Prices? Well I don't know what they are paying in London, but I am willing to bet that it is more than we get around here. I reckon that Farmers Weekly will be a good guide though."

Abby wondered if she should protest again, then thought that she would make a concession. "Well I am not saying I will do it, but I will have a look to see if I can access the information, and think about it. But I am new here. It doesn't seem right that I should interfere." Out of the corner of her eye, Abby saw Sam smile. He was a wily old fox, and saw that Abby was making them come to her, rather than being seen as a newcomer trying to organise everyone. Roger promised to talk to the other farmers as soon as possible. Abby asked him if he thought that Mr. Brasher could have a joint or two to take with him.

"Of course; I'll get a couple of Top and Hips down from the Cold Room in Paverton." He turned to Mavis.

"I'll have a quick cup of coffee, Mum, then I shall have to be off." Abby took her leave, giving Mavis a kiss on her cheek, and walked outside to see James just arriving.

Sam, who walked out with Abby to see her off, greeted James. "Hello again, Mr. James. If you came for the conference, you're too late. It's all settled. But Roger is trying to persuade Abby to be our contact with Mr. Brasher. She's reluctant, so you will have to convince her."

James dismounted and murmured to Sam. "Sam, if you continue to talk with your tongue in your cheek, you are going to bite it off!"

Sam grinned. "Abby played a blinder." He turned to Abby. "But you are going to have to keep it up. Nathaniel and Abe will be the difficult ones."

James agreed with Sam's assessment. "We will have to be careful with them. Try and make it look as if it's their idea. Are you leaving now, Abby?"

"Yes. But before I go, can I ask you both something? Is there any chance that you could be with me tomorrow? I have decided to open the Goods Shed, and I would appreciate you both being there." For neither one was there a conflict. Nothing would have kept either away.

Abby drove down to the station with Mr. Brasher, arriving just a few moments after Sam. Abby had already given Mr. Brasher the keys to the station, and after greeting Sam in his normal courteous manner, he went off to browse around the platform and station building wallowing in nostalgia. Sam's first words to Abby confirmed that Harry Webster was all for the idea of selling to Mr. Brasher's Club.

"He reckons we can get a much better price per carcass. Roger has gone to see Abe, and Harry is going to put the idea to Nathaniel. It seems to me that we are going to need your business brain before too long."

Abby demurred. "I don't know Sam. My business brain as you put it was trained in a very different business than farming."

"Don't underestimate yourself, Abby. Commerce is commerce, whatever the product may be. Roger and Harry will talk the others round, and we will need someone slightly detached from us to handle the organisation, else there will be arguments galore."

They were diverted by the arrival of James in his battered old Land Rover. "Morning." He smiled, and without thinking gave Abby a kiss. Sam had the biggest smile on his face, so pleased that they felt they had no reason to hide their feelings from him. It didn't concern him at all that their parentage was in question. As far as he was concerned there was no possibility that they were brother and sister. "I have brought some tools. I noticed that the door had been boarded up."

"Well I am glad the Army taught you to think ahead, Mr. James." Sam wanted to keep this a light as possible for Abby's sake.

"Yes, but it didn't teach me to keep my boots polished. Did it Abby?' This was lost on Sam, until Abby explained about the porter at her flat, and his comment to James. Sam understood the joke, and immediately compared his boots with those of James.

"Well it would appear that I didn't learn that lesson either, but then it was sixty years ago, so I claim old age as an excuse."

They strolled casually over towards the shed, passing the station house on the way. Sam and Harry had fenced off a large area, installed a five bar gate, and gravelled the enclosed area.

Abby was impressed. "That looks good Sam, thank you very much."

Sam nodded. "Does look a bit better. We cleared away right up to the Well, and where the Septic tank was, so George will have no trouble getting to them." Harry and he had quite enjoyed doing this work as a change from their normal occupation, easily finding loads of gravel at the Quarry. Sam was pleased despite the growing feeling in his mind that Abby would never actually live there.

As they approached the goods shed, James had moved ahead, and used a big claw hammer to ease the wooden battens away from the small door. Sam was standing next to Abby watching this, and could feel her tremble. As the last batten came off, he suggested to James that he, Sam, should get in first, and whispered to him. "Look to Abby." James looked across, and could see the concern on Abby's face. He went to her and put his arm around her shoulder as Sam pushed the door inwards. She looked up at him and, moved a little closer. Sam entered. He was mainly concerned that the rope that Thomas had used, had been removed, he seemed to remember that it had, but wanted to make sure. It had gone. Either rotted away or been taken down by the Police. He emerged. "Phew! It pongs a bit in there. Dead Pigeons all over the place. Come in, Abby, if you think you can stand the smell." Abby hung back a bit, and James removed his arm around her shoulders and took her hand instead.

"I'll be with you, don't worry." Reluctantly she moved towards the small door, as Sam smiled at her and vanished into the interior once again. As they ducked to go through, James caught a whiff of the interior, and quickly dragged a handkerchief from his pocket.

"Here, hold this to your nose. The smell is disgusting." Abby gladly accepted the handkerchief, and ducked through the door.

Whatever emotions she was expecting, vanished with the smell that assaulted her nostrils, even through the handkerchief. Sam was leading the way, kicking the carcasses of dead pigeons away making a path. The live pigeons up in the rafters looked down and ruffled and flapped wings at the intrusion, their soft cries echoing thought the large shed. The rails were still in place, mortared into the concrete floor. Light filtered weakly through the high windows, dirty with droppings and dust. Yet there was enough to see at the far end, a railway van, waiting at the platform to be loaded or unloaded. Abby could not believe that after all these years it would still be there. She looked to James in bewilderment, but he seemed just as surprised.

Sam was also regarding the van. "Well I don't know at all. It was here before." He carefully skirted around that time as it was when Thomas's body was discovered. "But I would have thought they would have taken it away when they cleared everything else." He approached the Van, the side doors were open, and quickly turned to Abby.

"Don't get too close. It has been used by feral Cats, and a couple of them have died in there." Abby summoned her courage.

"Sam. Where did you find granddad?"

He looked at her not really wanting to add to her emotions, but realised that it was pointless not to answer. He pointed to a rafter. "He was there."

Abby nodded and moved to where Sam had indicated. It was an eerie, uncomfortable feeling as she stood for a moment on the spot where her grandfather had last stood on this earth. She looked up. The only sign was a small piece of rope wrapped around the rafter. She was still holding James' hand, and she felt his grip tighten slightly, reminding her she was not alone, she returned the pressure and looked up to him with a wan smile on her face.

"I'm Ok, James, really." He nodded.

A cough from the door got their attention and broke the moment. "Is it alright if I come in?"

Abby was happy to break the emotion. "Of course Mr. Brasher, do." If he was affected by the smell he didn't show it, his eyes lit up as he too saw the Van.

"Good Lord! A ten ton Box-Van." He followed the cleared path and joined them.

"What do you think it is doing here?" Asked Abby.

"Oh they left dozens of these all over the place. It was a case of the left hand not knowing what the right hand was doing. In the hurry to lift the rails they marooned lots of trucks and other rolling stock in places like this. If BR ever discovered the loss, it would still cost too much to get it taken away by road, so they just wrote them off." Abby stood with James, taking comfort in his closeness. Sam had wandered off and was now looking at the large doors. After a while he leaned his weight on the one leaf, and it moved a few inches.

They heard his shout of surprise. "Damn me, they were never

locked!" Abby and James hurried over to join him, and with James adding extra weight, they managed to push the door open sufficiently to reveal a gap that a person could walk through. "It's still stuck a bit, but with a bit of releasing oil on the runners I reckon that Harry and me will be able to get these open all the way. We can get rid of all these dead birds, and disinfect thoroughly. Got to be careful with pigeons, they carry a bug that will lay you low."

Abby disagreed. "No Sam. I'll get some specialist cleaners in."

Sam laughed. "What do you think farmers are, if not Jack of all Trades? If you have spent your life cleaning out cow sheds, and barns, you have all the stuff you need for this little job. Don't you worry, Abby. We can manage this."

James was nodding in agreement. "Sam's right, Abby. He and Harry have all the right equipment and disinfectants. I'll come down and lend a hand."

Mr. Brasher had joined them now. "I would like to come back when it has been done, if that's alright with you, Abby? I would like to explore further, but I am afraid the smell in here is making me feel sick."

Abby, concerned, took him through the gap that Sam and James had opened saying "I could do with some fresh air myself."

After taking a few moments to fill his lungs with air, Mr. Brasher turned to Abby. "I shall write to you, giving you all the details of how the good sheds operated. I wouldn't say it was complicated, but to an outsider it could be confusing at first sight."

One thing was bothering Abby. "What will we do with that van?"

Mr. Brasher didn't have to think about that at all. "Keep it. A little bit of carpentry, and a coat of paint, and I would think it would be ideal as an exhibit in your plans for the station. I can let you have photos of how they were lettered. Do remember that it was goods that were the most important factor in building the railway in the first place. Educating visitors in that aspect is vital."

"Won't BR want it back?"

"Bless you no. They don't use trucks like that now, in fact if you want any more the only source could be preserved railways. Many were bought for pennies, but the enthusiasts cannot afford to restore them. So they are still there, sitting on a siding and rotting."

"Do you think any would consider selling to me?"

"I am sorry to say, Abby, but I doubt it. For them it is a question of 'one day' they will be able to do the work. That day may eventually come, but I suspect in many cases there will be little left to preserve."

Sam and James had tried to close the door, but it adamantly refused to move. Rather than spring the bolts holding the roller track they left it. "Won't matter too much, Sam, at least it will let some air in." James remarked.

Sam nodded an agreement. "I'll be down here as soon as I can. Harry will like the challenge of the doors anyway. If we can get up to the rafters and clear all the nests, it may discourage the birds." They followed Abby and Mr. Brasher over to the station forecourt. Mr. Brasher seemed to have a lot on his mind, and turning to Sam asked if he would allow him some conversation tonight at the Combe Inn.

"No problem. I shall be in about nine o' clock."

Abby tackled Mr. Brasher that evening. She had noticed that he seemed concerned about something.

"Am I taking on too much?" She asked.

"Oh, no, Abby. If I seem distracted it's my concern. To be honest

I have been having serious thoughts about my book."

"In what way?"

"Well, I have been writing for quite some time, taking great care to get all my facts right, trying not to omit the smallest detail. Yet I have just been reminded that I have forgotten to include the most important part. It makes nonsense of all I have been trying to do."

"I don't understand, Mr. Brasher. You seem to have everything at your fingertips, and if not there, in your files. I cannot think of anything you have missed." He had a wan smile on his face as he turned to her and said.

"I have missed out the people, Abby. The people. The railway was run by people to serve people. Just chatting with Sam and you talking about your grandfather, it came to me that this little branch, so insignificant to bureaucracy, was anything but insignificant to these farmers. It would not be too farfetched to say that the railway timetable was their timetable as well, and the services the railway offered influenced what they produced. I have to write a whole new chapter now to cover this topic, possibly using Combe Lyney as an example. Indeed I now realise that it is so important that I may re-write my foreword, to explain this."

"But Mr. Brasher, surely you have done that. You were able to get out the details of my grandfather so easily."

"No, no, Abby. That was just the pure facts. Just a few words with Sam, and talking to you, and your grandfather became a real person, not an item on the service record. I have to get closer, and tell about these people as they were, human."

"Well in that case you really must talk to Reg Purvess."

"Now he was the Signalman, wasn't he?"

"Yes, and he knew my grandfather quite well."

"In that case it is doubly important that I come down here again."

CHAPTER 26

When Sam came in that evening, Abby left him and Mr. Brasher to talk, and moved to a position by the bar, which by now the regulars were coming to know as her place. She had not been there long when a tall lugubrious man who she had seen before but apart from nodding had no conversation, approached her.

He didn't seem too pleased with her. "Miss Tregonney, I will thank you not to get involved in business which is nothing to do with you. You come down here, fresh from your City and think you can tell us how to do things. You know nothing about farming, so please keep your nose out of our affairs. That is all I have to say. Goodnight to you." Abby was so taken aback that she didn't know what to say.

Fortunately Jack had overheard the diatribe. "Nat! If you leave now you will never be welcome in this place again. I would like you to apologise to Abby." His raised voice stopped every conversation in the Bar, and brought Sam to see what was going on.

Nathaniel Gaunton, for that was who he was, furiously pointed a quivering finger at Abby. "That young lady is trying to tell me how I should run my farm. I won't have it. I have got on well enough all these years without a slip of a girl; who knows nothing about farming; offering me advice I don't need."

Sam was not going to stand there and allow Abby to be shouted at. "Nat! Don't you dare point your finger like that, it is insolent. Abby is not telling you how to run your farm. She merely passed on a request from the gentleman who I was talking to just now, about possible supplies, on a regular basis, of produce. That was all she did. She has no wish to get involved any more than that. Now if you don't feel the need to have a new customer you are obviously doing better than you let on. You were always one to have a short temper and jumping to the wrong conclusion. Now calm down, and let us have a talk about this." He led Nathaniel away.

Abby had still not said anything, still shocked at the outburst. Well aware that she may have been thought of as interfering, she had not thought that it could lead to this. Jack put a drink in front of her.

"Here, Abby. Drink this; it will calm your nerves." He then turned to prevent Mary, who had heard the ruckus from her kitchen, going round to give Nat a piece of her tongue. "Leave it Mary. Sam's dealing with it."

Mary was fuming. "I'll give that Nat what for. He is not coming in here and speaking to Abby like that." Jack calmed her down.

"It's all right, Love. Sam is talking to Nat, and I am sure in a moment Nat will be apologising to Abby."

As Abby calmed she realised that Mr. Brasher was left alone, and probably wondering what all the fuss was about. She took her drink and went into the Lounge to sit with him. She explained that there had been a misunderstanding.

"I did not hear it all, Abby, but I did hear Sam say that it was about farm produce. I hope it wasn't anything to do with my request."

"No. Mr. Brasher. It was more to do with the way I went about it. That man thought I was interfering."

"If my enquiry is causing any unpleasantness, then I shall withdraw. I don't want to be the source of discord between you and your new neighbours."

"No, Mr. Brasher, you are not at fault. As I said it is a misunderstanding, and Mr. Perry is sorting it out now. Anyway, Mary has told me that there is a large joint sitting in her Cold Room at the moment. She said it was a top and hip, whatever that is. It will be packed with ice for when you go."

He brightened. "Well at least I shall enjoy some more of this superb meat at my Club. There are one or two members upon whom it will be wasted of course, but that cannot be helped. Can you tell me, who do I have to reimburse?" Abby wondered herself about this, but concluded that the items would appear on his Bill."I would imagine that it will be included on your account from the Inn." He nodded.

"That will be fine. If this is acceptable to my Club, to whom should we address further orders?"

"May I get in touch with you about that? That is where the little misunderstanding lay. There are four major producers in the valley. They need to sort out their own system of co-operation. Farmers it would appear are very independent, and resentful of what they consider outside interference." He gently shook his head in understanding.

"I think I know what you mean. Sam appeared to be very much in favour though." All this time, Abby had been keeping an eye on Sam and Nathaniel, heads close in earnest discussion by the door. She was pleased that eventually Nathaniel seemed to nod his head, and a more benign expression came to his demeanour. They came over to where Abby sat with Mr. Brasher.

"Excuse me Mr. Brasher, but could Nat have a word with Abby."

Abby got up and went to the other side of the room with Nathaniel. He coughed a little and looked embarrassed. "Miss Tregonney, would you please forgive me for my outburst. Sam has explained everything to me, and I realise that I jumped to the wrong conclusion. Unfortunately, as Sam pointed out, it is one of my failings. Please do accept my apology."

Abby was happy to do this. "Mr. Gaunton. Please do not worry about it. I do realise that as a newcomer I should not interfere, and truly that was not my intention. Would you in turn forgive me if it appeared that way?" The smile came to Nat's face.

"Miss Tregonney, there is nothing to forgive you for. May I buy you a drink?" Abby ignoring the fact that she already had a drink on the table, accepted, and they walked to the bar together, where Mary awaited them with a face that could blister paint. She appeared somewhat mollified when Nathaniel asked Abby what drink she would like, and Abby happily asked for a Vodka and Tonic. Mary's temper eased as they chatted without rancour.

However Jack murmuring in her ear. "See, Sam sorted it out." Did not please her, and she snapped at him.

"We're running out of glasses, get some in." Jack grinned, and went off to collect some empties.

**

It is a curious aspect of Life that those who originally may be thought of as your enemy, turn into the strongest supporter. Thus it was with Nathaniel Gaunton, who became a spirited advocate for Abby. Urging the others, not that they needed urging, to enlist Abby's help in encouraging this new customer. Abby spent quite some time accessing the internet learning as much as she could about fatstock and prices. She was aware that this could come to nothing, but reasoned that if it succeeded, she should be prepared. It came as a relief to her when the weather which had been consistently squally, relented and produced one of those fine autumn days of Sun, light breeze, and comparative warmth. She walked down to the station, filling her lungs with clean fresh air, and enjoying stretching her legs. If she had expected an oasis of tranquillity, as she come to expect, she was surprised. Outside the goods shed a bonfire was billowing grey smoke towards the sky. Whilst in front of her house a lorry and a van had been parked. Men were loading her grandfather's furniture into the van. The first thought was alarm, until she noticed the Logo on the side of the van proclaiming it to belong to George Walker. The man himself was there supervising the work.

He greeted Abby cheerfully. "Managed to get the last job completed a little earlier, so I thought you wouldn't mind if we started."

"No, not at all. What will you do with the furniture?"

"I shall take it to Archie Breed, my furniture man. He will check it thoroughly and repair if needed."

"It won't come back looking brand new, will it?"

"No, Miss Tregonney. Archie's good, but I doubt that even he could perform that miracle. It will be cleaned and polished, but it will still look as if it has seen years of service." A shout from one of his men, called him away.

Abby walked over to the goods shed, where the great doors had been slid open and was confronted by an apparition, dressed neck to toe in protective clothing, and whose face was covered by a mask. Heavy black gloves completed the outfit. The apparition waved its arms, and lifted the face-mask. It was Harry.

"Don't come any closer Miss Abby; we are using chemicals in there." Abby stopped where she was, and Harry joined her.

He seemed to be quite happy."Got those doors open." He told her gleefully. "Both ends."

"Both ends?"

"Yes, there are identical doors the other end of the shed." Abby digested that information; no doubt Mr. Brasher would cover that in his notes. Harry was continuing.

"We have cleared the carcasses, and they are being burned. If they were diseased, wouldn't want to just bury 'em. Sam is spraying the place to kill anything that may be left. We'll leave the doors open for a couple of days, so that the chemical airs out."

"What about the live pigeons?" Abby was worried that they had been killed.

"No problem. They all took to their wings, when we started. I have been up and cleared the nests. They were the first things on the bonfire. The birds won't be back for some time. They will come back eventually, they always do. A couple of good cats will keep them under control if you think they are becoming a nuisance."

"How long have you been here?" Abby asked in astonishment."To do so much work?"

"Started yesterday. We will have it finished today. Oh and by the way, we found out why that Van was left here. Seems to have a seized axle. But I reckon I can sort that. Just need to work out a way that I can get my tractor in to lift it." Abby laughed.

"Is there nothing you cannot do?' Harry grinned back at her.

"Spend a lifetime in farming and you get to know how to fix most things without getting specialist help in. Besides it's a challenge and I like that." Another figure, similarly clothed to Harry emerged from the shed. He came over to them, lifting his mask as he came.

"Thought you had gone off for a cuppa." Sam grinned to Harry. "Hello, Abby. See! Things are happening."

"So I notice. Well you are not the only ones who have been doing things. I have managed to get a lot of information about fatstock prices. It would help if I can sit down and chat about it some time."

Harry looked at Sam and nodded his head.

Sam being elected spokesman turned to Abby. "Well we have been chatting about this, and Nat came up with a good idea."

"Yes?"

"Yes, he reckons we should form a Farmer's Co-operative. We will all be partners, and then share equally in the income. But." He paused. "Nat wants you involved Abby, to run it."

Abby shook her head."Oh No, Sam. It's really nothing to do with me, I am an outsider. I haven't been here long enough to understand fully. Yes I can do the research, but I don't know enough to run something like that."

"That's just the point, Miss Abby." Harry added his voice to the discussion. "You are a newcomer. You aren't part of the intrigues and petty disputes. If we tried to run it ourselves, there would be arguments and nothing would ever happen. You do it, and we will all behave ourselves. You are an independent unbiased manager. Besides we need your knowledge of business." Sam was nodding all the while Harry was speaking.

"That's what we all think, Abby. It's up to you. If you don't want to do it, well..." He didn't finish. The obvious thought that it wouldn't happen in that case being left unsaid.

"I am going to have to think about this. I won't say No, neither am I saying yes. Let me mull on this for a day or two." A further thought struck her. "If I say I will do it, I will take advice about how to do it. But in the end it is my decision, no arguments."

"That's why we want you to do it, Miss Abby." Said Harry. "Just so there won't be any arguments."

Sam announced that he was going to continue spraying. "Abby, best you don't stay around here. The fumes can be most unpleasant."

Harry agreed. "Yes, and I am going to put some more carcasses on the fire."

Abby laughed. "Don't beat about the bush; just tell me to go away."

So much for a quiet contemplative morning she thought as she walked back to the village, but at the same time she was pleased. Here was the opportunity to do something, to help, to put her skills to work for the community. She had always known that without something to do, she would not be totally happy here. Without much effort on her part it seemed that her days would now be usefully employed.

The scream of the racing diesel behind her as she approached the village could only mean one thing, James!

She laughed as he braked hard to a stop, and looked out of his window at her. "James that poor

Land-Rover must look forward to the scrap heap as a well earned rest."

"Nah. Built for this type of treatment. Coffee?"

"Good idea. Shall I see you in the Inn?"

"Yes, Ok. Or would you like to come up to the house?" Abby nodded smiling. She ran round to the passenger door.

"I hope you haven't had anything disgusting on this seat."

"Abby I am a Gentleman Farmer." James was affronted. "We don't use our cars for carrying mucky stuff!" Abby hopped up and James let in the clutch. At the house, they made their way through to the Breakfast room, and James put the kettle on.

"Sorry." He apologised. "It is only instant coffee here."

"I grew up on the stuff, so it suits me fine." Said a voice immediately behind him. He turned, and found that Abby was standing close.

"A cuddle and a kiss, please James."

"I was thinking the same thing." They were!

Whilst they waited for the kettle to boil, Abby told James about her conversation with Sam and Harry that morning. He didn't seem surprised. "I suppose you knew all about this?" She accused him.

He grinned. "Well not all about it, but I knew something was in the wind. I saw Nat yesterday, and he mentioned a little." He made the coffee, and they sat down at the table.

"So what should I do?" Abby asked.

"Why ask me?" James shrugged his shoulders. "I should think that you have made up your mind already."

"Well perhaps I have, but I would like to know if you think it is a good idea?"

"Yes."

"Is that all?"

"Yes."

"Oh you are not being any help at all this morning." Abby complained.

"That is unfair." He complained. "You ask me if I think it a good idea and I said yes. What else do I say?"

"Well you could have offered advice on setting it up, and how it should be run."

"But you didn't ask that question."

"Oh being literal this morning as well as monosyllabic."

He got up, and walked to her side, took her face between his hands and kissed her. Her happy smile showed that she wasn't upset.

"Am I forgiven?"

"You keep kissing me like that, and you are forgiven for the next half-dozen times you annoy me."

"Sisters are not supposed to enjoy kisses from brothers as much."

"I have made my mind up. You are not my brother."

"I believe that to be true, but until we have it writing…" His voice faded.

"I know, I know. But it is very frustrating. How long will they take, I am getting fed up with the wait, I want to seduce and be seduced."

"Let's change the subject. Talking about it will not make it happen faster." Abby knew he was right.

"Now about your Farmers Co-operative." James started.

"Ok, what about it?" Abby took a sip of coffee and listened.

"Increasing production should not be difficult. They have the land for pasture, and if they want more, I am quite happy to let more land. You will need to think about Cold storage though. The Abattoir in Paverton will probably have enough room, but they will charge for the space. You will need to get an idea of what demand you will have, how often, and rent space accordingly. You will need to look at refrigerated transport. Again the Abattoir can do this, but a trip to London will be costly. Especially if it only a carcass or two." He paused. "Shall I go on?"

"There's more?"

"Oh yes."

"I need to write this down; do you have a Pen and Paper?" He nodded and got up to rummage through a drawer. He handed her a pad. He didn't notice that there was a letter stuck to the pad, which came away when Abby took the pad from him. She couldn't help but see the heading. It was a Share Certificate. Without a word she handed it back to him. For the next hour, James talked and Abby made notes. At the end there was a mountain of research to do.

"There's a lot of phoning to be done here. My mobile will be red-hot."

"That will cost you a fortune. Come up here and use my phone." James suggested. "The lead will run into here, and you can at least sit down in peace and quiet and concentrate. And more importantly, I can come and bother you frequently." Abby's face showed that she quite liked that idea.

"I will pay you for the calls, James." He shook his head.

"Don't worry about it. If all this happens, I shall be better off as I shall rent more land."

Abby was thinking. She didn't want to delve into his business, but at the same time he was being very helpful to her so perhaps she could be helpful to him. "James. I know it was an accident, but I did see that Share Certificate. Tell me to shut up if you wish." She waited.

He simply said. "Go on."

"Those shares are as safe as houses. But they are also very dull. The dividends have never been exactly great. In fact you could do better putting your money in a Building Society. Could I say something else? Again tell me to shut up. I feel I am being intrusive here." He smiled at her.

"No you are not, Abby. It was an accident, but if you can steer me in the right direction I would be grateful. The investments, such as they are, were all made by my father. I have never changed anything, as I know little about the Stock Market."

"Well I am not an expert.

"Oh yes." He scoffed. "You worked in the City, made loads of money for your Bank, and say you're not an expert. Come on; at the very least you know a hell of a lot more about it than I do." Abby smiled at him. Sometimes he appeared so naïve.

"What I did in the City was far away from Stocks. I bought things, commodities, on the informed suspicion that their value would double or treble in the space of a few weeks or months. Stocks and shares are more about balancing a portfolio to give you income and capital growth. However I did hear things and I may be able to suggest a place for your funds which will give you a better income." He digested what she had said.

"Ok let's have it then."

"Not so fast. Not before I have checked one or two things. Then I'll get back with some Companies that are worth going for."

"If you will, perhaps you could look at the others?"

"Are you sure you don't mind James. It is better to look at the thing as a whole, rather than isolated investments."

He nodded. "I'll go find them. They are in my desk drawer in the Estate Office."

"Shall I boil the kettle again?"

"Yes please. I could do with another coffee."

Abby went through to the kitchen and filled the kettle. She lifted the pad on the Aga and placed the kettle. As she waited her mind wandered. Doing this simple job now, but could she see herself as Mistress here? Her imagination took off, discussing with Cook the menus for the week; there would have to be a cook, Abby's culinary skills would never be up to it. Ordering provisions and other requirements but what else? Abby didn't know. She couldn't see herself sitting down to tea in the afternoon with 'The Ladies', nor could she see herself indulging in charitable works. She would be a working wife, which was why this Farmers Co-operative scheme was so important to her, unless there were children? She was certain that James would want children. She was in no doubt that she could give him a child, her monthly visitor was evidence of that. Would a child curtail her lifestyle? Would she be a good mother? James would be an excellent father; she had no qualms on that score. Perhaps the love she would have for any child she and James had created would overcome any deficiencies she may have as a mother. She would certainly not go away to leave her child in the care of others. She brought herself back to the present with a start, and a smile on her face. However she looked at the future it looked good to her. If the results of the tests showed negative that is.

The future father of her children came back with a small file of documents. "Sorry it took so long. I had to move a pile of stuff to find them." Abby smiled, she was becoming used to the idea that office work was not something that his father had attended to, and James seemed to be cut from the same cloth.

"That's ok, the kettle has almost boiled. I am not used to these Aga's but they do seem slow. George Walker suggested that I have an Aga put in the house. But judging by this experience I don't think I shall. Far too slow for me."

James had that familiar grin. "You will have to get used to the idea, Abby. Everything takes its time here in the country."

"Well this is one thing I have no intention of getting used to." Abby retorted. "When I want coffee, I want it now! Not next week. Now let's have a look at these Shares." James gave Abby the file, and attended to the coffee. Abby turned to a new page on the writing pad, and sat down to examine the investments. She started to write the details down. For half an hour there was silence as she wrote and thought, raised her eyebrows and shook her head as she understood some of the Shares. At last she sat back and took a drink of coffee, and looked at James.

"Well?" He asked.

She shook her head. "Not well." She answered him. "There's stuff here that is so ancient, I cannot be sure they are still quoted. However off the top of my head I would say you are missing out, by about ten grand a year."

"How much?"

"Well give or take a bit. It will depend on how much risk you are prepared to accept. With some risk I think you could better yourself more than that, but if you wanted security, a little less. I shall have to get the latest offer prices for these, to be honest I doubt that they will be exciting. But I will see what can be done."

James thought a little. "Anything you can do, I will be grateful."

"Wait until I get some figures, then see if you want to do anything." He nodded. Abby went on. "Do you have a Broker?"

"Dad had one, but that was years ago. I suspect that he has either retired or died."

"If you have no objections I shall get in touch with Peter Adams who does my broking. I shall explain what you want and he can make some suggestions. His advice is sound and worth following."

"I place myself in your hands, Abby."

A wicked smile came to Abby's face. "Not yet you haven't, James. But when you do, I can assure you it will be a lot more exciting than Share Certificates."

His smile was broad as he said. "Don't do that to me, Abby. I feel another cold shower coming on. We don't have permission to misbehave yet."

He got up and held out his hand. With a question on her face Abby stood and grasped his hand. "Come with me."

"Where are we going?"

"You'll see." He led her out into the Hallway and out the front door, then round to the stables. Cassie and Jason were in their boxes, inquisitive heads straining out of the half-doors, Jason whickered when he saw Abby. James led her on to the other buildings, and opened a door at the back of the stable yard.

"This is the Estate office." He announced. The place was to say the least a jumble. Wooden filing cabinets lined one wall, and a roll-top desk filled another. Cardboard boxes were strewn everywhere, piled on top of each other at crazy angles. Abby viewed the scene.

"I don't think you use this much nowadays, do you?"

"No hardly at all. I was thinking that if you get this Farmers Cooperative off the ground you will need an office." He stopped and waved his hand around grandly to indicate an office. "There is a telephone somewhere. What do you think?"

Abby viewed the place with a somewhat jaundiced eye. "Well it's not the sort of office that I am used to, but I suppose that I shall have to have somewhere."

"I shall clear it out completely. There's nothing here that has any relevance these days. The filing cabinets are there if you want them, all I shall need is one drawer for my estate records."

"Could I get another telephone line put in?"

"I would think so, but why?"

"Well I imagine that the line is your private line, so I wouldn't want you to pay for my calls. Also I would want a Broadband Internet connection, and usually they have to put a new line in for that."

James understood. "Well you can do whatever you want." He said grandly.

"Wait a minute, James. If I use this as my office, won't the members of the Co-operative wonder if you are getting involved a little more than you should?"

He shook his head. "I don't think they would worry about that. Particularly if I am not charging rent for the office. I didn't want to be seen getting involved in the idea of the Co-operative. But now it is going to happen, they will see me going along with their idea." He emphasised the word 'their' Abby chuckled.

"You should have been a politician, James."

"No way." He shuddered. "I could never hold my head up again, being labelled as a liar and a cheat."

"James! At the very least you should charge the co-operative some rent for the office." He shook his head vigorously.

"No. Let's just say it my little contribution to the project. You should know my feelings by now, Abby. I am not here to make a pile of money. My job here is to try and keep this thing going, for my family's sake and for the sake of my tenants. I wouldn't like to be thought of as the guy who made money out of them at every opportunity."

They left the office, with James locking the door. Jason saw them and whickered once more. Abby walked over to him and the horse nodded his head and nosed Abby as she got close. Abby turned to James.

"It would be nice to go for a ride again."

"We shall, but we'll have to pick a good day. How about if the weather looks good for a day, I could phone you. Do you think you could drop everything and get out to ride?"

"No problem. I shall look forward to that." She turned to the horse and stroked his muzzle.

"Don't worry Jason; we'll go out before too long." Suddenly she turned to James. "Richard! I promised to phone him."

James acted immediately. "Come on we will do it now." They rushed back to the Breakfast room, and in next to no time James had Richard on the phone.

"Hello James is Abby with you by any chance. I left a message for her at the Inn.'

"Yes Richard, she's here. I'll put her on." He put his hand over the mouthpiece and said that Richard was trying to contact her as it happened. Abby took the phone.

"Good Morning Richard. How are you?"

"I am fine thank you. I have some good news for you. Bernard has phoned. He likes the Flat and will pay your price." Abby looked at James with a big smile on her face.

"That is good news."

"He wants to do this quickly; can I give him the name of your Solicitor?"

"Yes, it is Chorister Brooks, I know they are in Paverton, but I am not sure of the actual address."

"Don't worry, I know them well. You can leave it to the Legal boys. It will all be done quickly. If Eddie Brooks drags his heels, let me know, I'll put a fizzer under him. Now when are you and James coming over for Lunch?"

Abby looked at James. "When are we going for Lunch?"

"When's convenient for Maggie?" Abby heard muffled sounds and then Maggie's voice somewhere in the background, replying to James's question.

"Maggie heard that and Maggie says anytime."

"Maggie says anytime."

James thought. "Thursday?" Abby passed the day on to Richard.

"That's perfect. Come about twelve, we'll have a drink first."

After she put the phone down, Abby then started to think about what she would wear. James laughed at her worrying.

"Don't worry about that, they will be very casual."

"Are you sure?

"Yes. Maggie will be in Jeans and sweater. I would bet on that. You don't have to dress up."

CHAPTER 27

The next day James phoned early. "The weather looks good for today, so how about taking the horses out for a little canter today?"

"A ride yes." replied Abby, "but canter no. It would be good to be out for a while and I have got nothing on today," she heard James laugh and forestalled his comment, "James behave! I am sure you were just about to make a comment about Lady Godiva."

"I wasn't actually, but now you mention it..."

Abby stopped any further comment."Enough! It will be great to ride, where shall we go?"

"I thought we could go up the valley on the northern side, that way we will get the Sun in the morning, and come back down the old track, when the Sun is in the South West. What do you think?"

"Sounds good to me, I'll go and get some warm clothes on. Oh and I'll ask Mary if she can put together a packed lunch. Shall I come up to Lyney House?"

"Yes, that would be best. I'll go and get the horses saddled ready, what do you think, about an hour?"

"Good thinking, I wouldn't want to put Mary under pressure."

***

Mary had no trouble about producing her usual picnic lunch for four or five people. Abby had to remind her that if she were to eat her fair share, then she would not require much in the way of an evening meal. Mary demurred.

"It's a nice day, but with a little chill in the air, you will be quite hungry later. Now there's soup in this flask, and coffee in the red one. I have put cold beef with mustard in the rolls, and there's a couple of Pork Pies as well, I didn't think you would be wanting any salad today."

The nerves that Abby experienced the first time she rode Jason were long gone. With less fear and greater confidence Abby could enjoy the ride and the scenery and James' company without reservation. They had taken the road that led up the hill behind Lyney House, and approximately a mile and a half mile turned off onto a bridle path that followed the contours of the valley. At first they rode through a wooded area, with very little view to be seen, but gradually the trees thinned and the watery Sun found a way through the foliage. There was little warmth in the light, and Abby was relieved that she had put on warmer clothing, even so James had insisted she wore one of his Fleece jackets, apologising that it was not too clean. Abby had no problems with that, she believed she could smell him on the jacket and that pleased her. James explained that this Bridle path was originally the drover's road, by which cattle were herded to Paverton.

"Why didn't they use the road?"

"This was before the bridges were built, so there were two or three fords on the lower track, they became impassable when the river was running high, and so this was the way they used. It did go back all the way to South Molton as well."

"All the way from Paverton to South Molton?"

"Yes, but higher up the valley the road now uses this route. You know where the road crosses the river higher up?"

"Yes."

"That is where the road was laid over the old Drovers path. In the other direction you can follow the path as far as the River Bray, but beyond that it has disappeared." Abby nodded. It no longer amazed her how the old and the new became synonymous here.

"Do we see the old railway from this side?"

"Yes we will. In fact we can ride along the track bed for about two miles, instead of the Bridle path."

"I would like that." James now had the little smile on his face.

"Of course two hundred years ago the smugglers would use this path.

"Smugglers!" Abby thought James was making it up. "But we are miles from the Sea."

"We are, but smuggling was no good unless you could get the contraband to the buyers. It also made sense to get the stuff away from the coastal areas, where the Revenue men would be most active. There would have been lots of places where the contraband could be hidden. I believe that one of my forebear's, William Comberford may have known more about the business than he ought to."

"Ah, why am I not surprised that the Comberford's would be involved somewhere." James looked over to her with the grin on his face.

"Now don't be too quick to condemn, remember he may be one of your forebear's as well." Abby had to laugh; he had caught her neatly in a trap.

"I thought that Smugglers landed on the South Coast. Being nearer to France."

"They did in the main, but with the profit to be made, particularly on stuff like Brandy and Silk, it was worth the haul round Lands End. The smugglers would not do that journey themselves, but would meet the ships out in the channel and transfer the load."

"Risky, I would have thought."

"Yes, but they couldn't be seen out there in the channel and it lessened the risk as they could bring their contraband in to small coves; of which there were many; where the bigger ships could not go. The Revenue men could not stake out every cove and the smugglers had good intelligence from the locals as to where the Revenue men were. The smugglers were locals, the Revenue men weren't. All they were doing is what you did in the City. Take a risk to make lots of money." Abby smiled broadly.

"Yes, but what I was doing was legal."

James shrugged his shoulders. "It's a funny thing when you think about it, we change our laws over a period of time, and many things that were illegal three or four hundred years ago, are acceptable and legal now. The smugglers were free enterprise blokes; they bought wines and spirits in France and sold them over here. Now they would just take a white Van over and back on the Tunnel train. Same enterprise, different transport."

"Just a little problem of the duty to be paid?"

"How many people go on package holidays and come back with stuff in excess of the allowance yet don't declare it, cigarettes, perfume or booze. Same crime, except two hundred years ago you could be hanged for it. Now it's just confiscation and a fine." Abby ran that through her mind, he was right of course, although she would not tell him so. She had done just that, walked through the Green Channel with an excess of Perfume in her bags. She giggled. James looked to see what had amused her. She explained.

"I've done that, came back with more Perfume than I should. I felt that everybody's eyes were on me, and was so relieved when I got out the other side without being challenged. If I am a product of the Comberford genes, then who was it?" Her memory came up with the name. "William Comberford would call me a chip off the old block." He smiled at her.

"No Abby not a chip off our block, of that I am certain, but Thomas Tregonney would be mortified that one of his family had committed a sin."

"I had forgotten about him. Yes, I really would be in his bad books."

To Abby it seemed that they had now reached high ground, yet the path did not appear to climb. She looked over to the left and could see the valley floor, a collage of varying shades, green fields, and woodland some green, some turning a brilliant rust, grey rock outcrops, and the copper of the Beeches. Interspersed were occasional cottages, some still in the white Cob, and others built in the grey stone of the local granite. Abby pointed them out to James.

"Are those built on your land? "

"Yes." He sounded gloomy. "They are on estate land and I get ground rent on them. But they are residential not agricultural. My father had to sell the properties as he needed capital. I will never be able to get them back."

**

The road from Combe Lyney to Paverton showed quite clearly from time to time, but of the old railway track there was very little evidence. It was remarkable that the railway could sit so well in the environment, yet the road, even a very minor one, slashed a scar across the landscape. The track took them through a small side valley, they splashed through a little rivulet that zigzagged down, hurrying and then pausing in little pools before tumbling down again on its way to join with the Lyney. The path kept to the contour and eventually they rounded the spur that brought them back into the valley proper. Ahead of them lay the Viaduct, the first time she could see evidence of the railway. It was still some distance away and James chose this moment to ask if she wanted a coffee break. Abby nodded enthusiastically. They stopped where there was a good view over the valley. Below a tractor was towing a trailer spreading dung over pasture. James watched intently for a while.

"Geoff won't graze that next year. But the year after that it will be excellent for his cattle."

"Geoff?"

"Yes, sorry, you haven't met him yet. Geoff Corliss, that's White Rock farm. He has more sheep than cattle, and has rights of grazing on the Moor. His Lamb is superb. Very distinctive flavour."

"In what way?"

"His sheep graze on the moor for much of the year. Sheep don't eat Heather as such, but because they browse so close, they will eat young Heather shoots by accident. Just flavours the Lamb slightly." Abby remembered the lamb stew Mary had served, and wondered what the subtle flavour she detected could be. Now she knew.

"I have had some. I had some of Mary's lamb stew. That was the flavour!" After all this time the mystery was solved. "Does he know about the co-operative?"

"Yes, Roger talked to him, and he is quite interested. I suspect he will be asking to discuss this with you very soon."

"How many more will there be?"

"That's it really. There's Fred Bayley, but he is just a smallholder, only five acres. He keeps a few dairy cows, small herd of sheep, a number of pigs and some Goats. Very good vegetable garden though. He doesn't sell any of his stock commercially. Slaughters just enough for his own needs."

Abby was astonished. "How does he survive then?"

James tapped the side of his nose. "Churns his own Butter, makes Cheese with the milk and goats milk, clotted cream. Sausages, Hams. Not certificated, tells the Health and Safety busybodies it's all for his own consumption. But he will sell to those who are in the know as his produce is absolutely out of this world. Pays me the rent in cash. Quite useful really."

"You are making my stomach rumble; I shall have to try some sometime."

"You have."

"What?"

"You have tasted it. You have had Sausage at the Inn, butter and cheese. Mary is one of those who are in the know. Now you are as well." Abby smiled to herself. This place was sucking her in, and making her an accomplice to their irregular dealings.

"So the cash he pays you isn't declared I take it." James shook his head.

"Oh yes it is. The Inland Revenue keep a close eye on me. But I take it out as income, save bothering the Bank."

"Why do they keep a close eye on you? Have you tried to evade tax at any time?"

"No, not me. But father did. Don't know the exact details but they hit him with a huge sum. Went back seven years. That's when he sold those properties; even then he had to borrow against the estate. The mortgage was still outstanding when he died." Abby went quiet. She was certain that no-one else knew of this, and to think that James was prepared to share this with her, gave her a very warm feeling.

"Is it sorted?"

James gave her a smile. "Yes it was sorted a couple of years ago." He was slightly embarrassed, and hoped that Abby didn't think that he had told her hoping to elicit a loan. Abby was equally embarrassed. If there was still monies outstanding would she have offered a loan? She may have done, she couldn't be certain. If she had would he have accepted, probably not, his pride would not allow it, and he would have, in all likelihood, been very angry. Good job the situation hadn't arisen. They finished their coffee in silence, standing apart as if their thoughts had driven a wedge between them. Abby moved closer and snuggled to his side; his arm went round her and held her close. Then he murmured softly.

"I think that sister or no, I am getting to a situation where I will want to make love with you, Abby even if I go to Prison for it."

Abby turned her face towards him wearing the loveliest smile James had ever seen her wear. She reached up and kissed him. "Thank you, James. That is the most wonderful compliment I have ever received.

The path now was quite open and to Abby's eyes level. James looked over to her. "How about a Trot for a while."

"No I don't think so, James. I don't believe my riding skill is up to that." James reasoned with her.

"Abby, as you intend to stay here, it would make sense to improve, then you can ride as often as you wish. Come on," he cajoled, "just a little, say about a hundred yards."

Abby was fearful, but didn't want to show that fear in front of James. "Oh, alright, but just for that hundred yards. What do I do?"

"Well you have to transfer your weight onto your legs, and as Jason trots you will find the way to rise and fall, without slamming back into the saddle. Lean forward, get most of your weight in the stirrups and let your knees grip the side of the saddle." Abby did that. The strain on her legs muscles caused them to quiver.

"This is difficult."

"It will get easier when Jason trots, believe me."

"How do I get him to trot then?"

"Just rap him smartly with the reins and click your tongue a couple of times so he can hear." Abby did that and Jason immediately quickened his pace. The strain on her legs was strong, but she soon found that the rise and fall motion helped a lot. James was beside her, riding easily, but watching her closely to make sure she was safe.

"That's good, you've got it." The horses trotted on and Abby was sure they had gone much further than the one hundred yards that James had suggested. She looked at him in alarm, and he immediately told her to pull back on the reins with both hands. She did so and Jason dropped back to a walk.

"Phew! I don't know if I would want to ride like that for any distance."

James was grinning again. "You did well for a beginner. When you get your leg muscles used to it, you will find it quite comfortable. Then when you get to Canter and Gallop, it is exhilarating." Abby shook her head.

"No James. I shall content myself with walking Jason. That's quite enough for me." Her leg muscles were shaking with the effort, but gradually calming now. "Your mother rides Jason a lot when she is down, doesn't she?"

"Yes, she is absolutely mad. Takes the horse up to the moor and gallops him furiously. I am certain that she will break her neck one day.

Jason arrives back sweating like anything, and Lizzie has to wipe him down and walk him around for some time to calm him." He broke off to point out to Abby the Viaduct which was almost abreast of where they were.

"We can get on the old track soon." He explained.

That was sooner than Abby expected. The Bridle path turned casually to the right, and Abby saw the crossing just fifty yards away. It was obvious from the stout timber posts that were still in situ that the railway had treated this almost as importantly as the crossing at the station. The gates were long gone, but other artefacts reminded the observant of the use that had been made of the crossing. A hard rubble packed with soil and weed was all that remained of the ballast, yet Abby could define where everything had been. The track bed was obvious, unlike the track bed further down the valley, here little use had been made of the way, all it required would be ballast and rails and trains could run once more.

James pointed out the way to the right. "If we go down that way it isn't far to the viaduct."

Abby agreed. "Let's do it." They turned the horses heads and rode side by side. Abby commented on why the track was still evident after all these years. "I mean the track down by Combe Lyney is still there, and has become a agricultural way, but here it is as if nothing has happened in forty years."

"No point. The road and railway ran almost parallel to Paverton, and there is no farm hereabouts that could find a use for the track. The Forestry Commission use it from time to time, but that's it."

Abby thought about that.. "So this track can be used all the way to Paverton?"

"Almost. The station site at Paverton has been cleared, and is now used as a light Industrial site, but you could ride pretty well all the way if you wished." He saw the eagerness in Abby's face. "We will do that, but it would be better to wait until next Spring, the winds across the moor can be pretty fierce."

The track, due to its purpose curved gently through a turn of some ninety degrees, and brought them to the threshold of the viaduct. Abby looked across to where they had stopped on the first ride. It seemed so long ago now. James halted them and Abby dismounted. They were in a small cutting from where the track seemed to launch itself onto the viaduct. This was in the Sun, yet excluded the light breeze that had brought a little chill to the air.

"As good a place as any to take lunch." James suggested. Abby agreed. She looked around for anyplace that it would be more comfortable to sit, There appeared not to be anywhere that offered a seat, so with resignation she prepared to sit on the ground.

"Wait a moment, Abby." cried James, and he delved into his saddle bag producing a groundsheet. This he laid in a place where they could see all the valley, but remained out of the breeze. Abby sorted through the lunch that Mary had prepared.

"That's soup, beef rolls, and there are some Pork Pies."

James ears pricked up at that. "Let me see. Ah yes." He handed them back to Abby with a smile. "Fred Bayley's Pork Pies, well Arabella's to be precise, you'll like these." They ate with an appetite sharpened by the ride and the air, and Abby did like the Pork Pie.

"This is delicious. There's some flavour there I can't place though."

"Thyme and Apple." James informed her. "Bella insists that the secret of using flavouring is that no-one should be able to tell exactly what herb or Fruit has been used. It just adds to the taste experience. Her words, not mine." He was laughing now. "I am unable in my own puny culinary efforts to be as subtle as she is."

"But you keep trying."

"Yes. I keep trying."

Abby was sipping coffee as James walked out onto the Viaduct. Watching him she saw a contented, happy expression come over his countenance. She walked out to join him, taking a coffee for him as well. He didn't say anything as she joined him, took the coffee but continued to look over the valley. She stood in silence looking at him, looking at his valley. She would have said that it was a look of love; she understood that men don't admit to expressions like love. Instead she "You are really happy here."

He nodded. "Yes. Knowledge of other places had convinced me. This is the only place I want to be."

"Well I suppose compared with the Falklands that is understandable."

"No I don't compare with the Falklands. I compare with other places in Britain. I went to Birmingham University for interview. That was when I was going to do a History degree. I looked out of a window whilst waiting and all I could see was rows and rows of houses, and factories. The only green was around the University itself. I thought of spending three years there and that was a dismal prospect. That didn't make my mind up though. The Lecturer who would take the classes was a long-haired hippy. He didn't want to know about my academic record, but mocked me as I had turned up in a suit and wearing a tie, he was wearing grubby Corduroys and a baggy Sweater. I believe he made his decision based upon political beliefs, he was definitely left wing, and I suppose he had me down as a Fascist, reckoning that I came from the privileged classes. Huh! Look at me. Privileged class? I knew I wasn't going to get on there, and to be honest I am glad. I was in no doubt that he would present a perverted view of history. History should be about facts, and shouldn't be taught with a political slant, which tends to slide over facts which don't fit the teacher's bias. It is the student who should be allowed to make up their own mind on the facts presented."

"So you didn't go to University?"

"Yes I got in at Leicester, but within a few months I applied to the Army for a short service commission. The army sent me to all sorts of places, Germany, Belize and of course the Falklands. After that I decided that the only place that had meaning to me was here. The rest as they say is History." They walked back to where the horses were tethered.

James was looking at the sky. "We shall have to be on our way back, I think." He pointed to the sky over the lower valley. "There are some rather dark clouds coming in from the West. I doubt we will have time to get across and ride down the track from Lills. I'm sorry." Abby shook her head.

"No problem, as long as you don't expect to ride at the trot on the way back."

James looked at her with a mischievous smile. "Well if the rain breaks, it may have to be at the canter."

CHAPTER 28

Abby had got used to the easy pace of life in the valley. It came as a surprise therefore when she realised that now there were very few days when there wasn't something or other demanding her attention. She went to Paverton to see the Solicitor, instructing him to handle the sale of the flat, and leaving with him the deeds. Visits were needed down to the house, as George Walker got on with the work, and phoned often to ask some question of her. She finally got to see the goods shed, when Harry and Sam deemed it safe. She went in with Sam, no longer needing James as the emotions of what had happened there no longer assailed her. The stench of all those rotting birds had indeed gone, and she was able to see the place properly. The windows had been washed down and both sets of doors were open so that daylight had once more come to the interior. Harry had manoeuvred his tractor in, and had lifted the Box Van on one side, freeing the wheel.

"Is that safe, Harry?" She asked.

"Well I expect the Health and Safety Inspector would have a fit, but I am quite confident. Anyway I am not going under the van. I don't reckon that the wheel is seized, there just doesn't seem to be any grease in the bearing." He was straining at the nuts holding the axle box cover. "If I can get this greased up well, then it should move. Probably need a bit of persuading, but we are used to that."

"Typical Harry." Sam laughed. "If it's meant to open then Harry will open it whatever. If it's meant to close then he will close it. I remember him opening a window once. He did open it eventually, took the whole damn frame with it as well, he'd forgotten he had nailed it shut years before, because of the draughts."

Harry looked up ruefully. "Trust you to remember that."

Abby was smiling. It was always a happy experience being with these two. "Why do you think there were two sets of doors?"

Sam had already thought about that. "If I remember rightly when they had finished with one van, they would just push it through, rather than having to pull it out and then push in the next one to be unloaded. The rails rejoined with the siding loop the other side. What do you think, Harry?' Harry stood and stretched his back.

"I think you're right there, Sam. Reg Purvess will know. Better ask him when he's next here."

"He phoned the other day." The mention of the name had triggered Sam's memory. "He said he would be over soon. I told him that Mr. Brasher would really like to chat with him. I am to call him next time he comes down." He stopped for a moment then turned to Abby. "Meant to tell you earlier. He's sorry it took so long but he can't get any rails for you. They had all gone. But his mate the ganger says you can have as many old sleepers as you like. He thought it would make it look a little bit like a railway anyway. You will need to pay for transport though, but the gangers are quite happy to come over and put them down. What do you think?"

"I'm delighted with anything they can do. You are right; it would make it look more like a railway. Do I have to organise the transport?"

"No, Reg will do that. Knows a guy who will do it on a Sunday for cash." he winked.

"I see, cash no invoice, no Income tax, no V.A.T." She sang a few bars of the introduction music from a popular comedy show. Sam grinned.

"Good voice you've got there. We'll have to get you into the Church Choir."

"I didn't know there was a Church Choir."

"There isn't, that's why you would have a good voice for it."

Abby got the joke. She smiled broadly. "Are you saying that I cannot sing?"

Harry's muffled voice came from the depths of the Van. "Sam's singing stops the cows giving milk. Compared to him, Abby, you are Lesley Garrett. Gotcha!" His cry signalled that he had got the bolts free on the Axle Box.

He withdrew the bolts and with a sharp tap the cover fell to the ground. "Just as I thought. No grease left at all. Sam! Could you hand me that grease gun. I'll give the bearing some directly, and then fill it up when I have cleaned the nipples." Abby was about to leave when a thought came to her.

"Sam, will you be in the Combe tonight?"

"Yes I shall pop in, anything in particular?"

"I will need to know a lot more about rearing beef cattle; do you think you could give me a quick run-down?" Sam looked at Harry who nodded.

"We'll both be there, and then you can get a much better picture of how it happens." Abby smiled her thanks and happily left them to their labours.

***

Over at her house there was great activity. All the windows were open, and clouds of white dust billowed out. Men wearing protective clothing and masks were barrowing loads of the white plaster out of the door and carefully emptying it into large Polythene bags. Abby decided not to approach as she felt sure that she would be a hindrance. Remembering also that Harry and Sam had warned her away when they had been similarly attired. No doubt the work was a little hazardous. They seemed to be working very hard, and she did not understand why George had told her that the house would not be ready for her occupation until the New Year. However she was comfortable at the Inn, and could wait.

It was to the Inn she now returned. With so many strangers around she couldn't enjoy the peace the station had given her. In any case she needed to decide on a wardrobe for tomorrow, the Lunch with Richard and Maggie. Notwithstanding James' comment about being casual, she was not going to let herself into the trap of dressing down too much. She considered it disrespectful to arrive looking as if you hadn't taken care of your appearance. Mary automatically assumed that Abby had to be fed when she arrived, and it took quite a lot of persuading before she would agree that no food was required. She rumbled off complaining that the girl would starve to death soon. Abby went to her room with a smile on her face to decide on an outfit.

James came in that evening, and without thinking kissed Abby on the cheek. Mary could not hide her expression of delight for a split second, and then her face returned to normal. Abby acted as if this was nothing out of the ordinary, but was secretly pleased. If anyone else in the Bar noticed no comment was made. What Abby didn't know was that the news would be disseminated throughout the Valley, and would give rise to the same talk that had followed the intrigues of Valerie, Roger, Reg and Gladys all those years ago. Time may move on, the names would be different, but the gossip was still the same. Later Abby settled down with Harry and Sam for her lesson in animal rearing.

"We rear our beef cattle in what is known as suckler herds." Sam started. "Abe Stone has a good breeding herd. Got a very good South Devon Bull. The cow suckles her calf until it is about nine months old and weaned. After that it is known as a yearling. We buy yearlings from Abe, and fatten them. The herds are out to grass for most of the year, and only come in when the ground is too wet for them."

"So they are eating grass all the time?"

"Yes." Said Harry. "But we have to supplement, with Oats and Cattle-cake, you will see the troughs in the fields. If we bring them in we feed silage." Abby was taking this in.

"James told me that years ago the farms would grow oats and barley, but not now. Where do you get those from?" Sam came up with the answer this time.

"There's a merchant down South Molton where we buy the cereals. He has supplies that are chemical fertiliser free. Same for cattle-cake. Contains the nutrients without introducing artificial substances."

"So at what stage do you send the beef to slaughter?"

"Usually about two years."

"So you buy all your yearlings for fattening from Abe Stone?" Sam shook his head.

"Buy most, but have to put our own cows in calf; otherwise they will stop producing milk." Abby understood that answer, it was obvious.

"So you have your own Bull's?"

"No. We use artificial insemination."

"Why do that? Surely you could use Mr. Stones Bull."

Harry was really pleased that Abby was asking these questions. It showed she was considering this co-operative seriously. "Well," he explained, "it depends on what you are wanting. If you want beef cattle Abe's bull will give you good offspring South Devon's have a good reputation for beef. If however you are looking for dairy cattle, then you have to have the right pedigree of bull. Use A.I. and you have a wide choice of semen to use. Usually Jersey or Friesian." Abby was finding all this of great interest, but it was not as simple as it seemed.

"But surely you cannot guarantee the sex of the calf?"

"No we can't. Any bulls born will be castrated after they have been weaned for beef production, we call those Bullocks others call them Steers. Some breeds do not make good beef, so the castrated calves of those will go to slaughter at twelve months. We call those baby beef."

"Therefore you have both beef and dairy cattle on your farms?"

"Yes," said Sam, "That way you are getting a regular income from the milk and the bonus when you slaughter."

"Are you organic?"

Sam looked at Harry, who shrugged his shoulders. "I suppose so; we rotate the animals on the fields, so they don't get worms or other parasites. The only fertiliser we use is natural. The supplements are natural as well, so I reckon, yes, we are organic."

Abby was happy for the moment and insisted on buying the next round. "Be prepared though," she said, "I shall be back to ask some more."

Sam was easy with that. "No problem, Abby. You remember what I once said to you, you keep asking questions, it's those who assume without asking that gets me angry."

Abby had assumed that they would use her car to go to Coolton Grange, and it would appear that James believed the same. He suggested that he arrived at the Inn about eleven-thirty. Abby agreed happily. That would give her plenty of time to get ready. James may have thought that she didn't have to dress up, but even for a girl to look casual, it still took a lot of time and thought to achieve the effect.

When they had driven to Coolton Grange before, for the Ball, Abby had not taken too much notice of the way they went. At the time she was too nervous to be able to take in the directions for the journey.

There were no nerves today, and she sat and committed the journey to memory, certain that one day she may have to make the drive on her own. The road to Paverton she was familiar with, but just after leaving the valley, James took a left turn. She had noticed the turn before, but it had no significance then. They followed the lane for three miles across moorland, and then took another left, which descended into another, but broader valley. The drive up to Coolton Grange she remembered as being quite long. They drove over a cattle grid which rumbled and vibrated the car, the track crossed pasture before wending its way through Rhododendrons and another cattle grid to the sweep before the house. Maggie was waiting at the door, and greeted Abby with a smile and a kiss on the cheek. It wasn't a showy air-kiss, but one of good friendship.

"It's so nice to see you again, Abby. Come inside. I saw you turn into the drive. Richard is opening some wine. Hello James! Turning up in style these days I see." James grinned. Abby awaited the humorous response.

"Well I like to drive a Lady in comfort, particularly when it is the Lady who provides the transport, and the style."

It had been, Abby had to admit, a very pleasant day. Maggie was not in Jeans and Sweater, as James had promised, but had dressed similarly to Abby, in slacks and a blouse. A cool Chardonnay before and during an excellent meal of salmon served with a large salad set Abby's appetite at the replete mark. She wondered how she would be able to persuade Mary later on that she would not want a meal that evening. James and Richard wandered off discussing farming problems, and Maggie took Abby in hand, leading her through to the conservatory, to sit and drink coffee.

"You are doing everyone a lot of good around here." She said without preamble.

"Me? What do you mean?" Abby was astonished.

"You are putting a bit of excitement back into their lives." Maggie was smiling.

"I don't know how you reach that conclusion."

"You are giving them a new topic to talk about. That's excitement around here. Makes a change from the normal conversation."

Abby shrugged her shoulders. "What is there to talk about? All I am doing is having the station restored, and making the house liveable."

'Well that is just it. Restoring that old station, means that lots of them are dredging their memories, dragging up anecdotes from the past. You will find that as the work goes on, there will be quite a few visitors who will tell your builder what he has done right, but more likely, what he has done wrong. And then, of course, there is you and James."

Abby smiled inwardly. Maggie it would seem had got around to the topic that she had really wanted to cover. "What about James and me?"

"Oh, come on Abby. It's plain to see that James is very taken with you. Else he wouldn't have brought you to the Ball. Now that is important. Not just to his tenants, but also to others. I must say that it surprised one or two people, not always happily either. Within five minutes of your coming into the Ballroom, most of the ladies had priced your dress to the nearest fifty pounds, and then turned the same colour as your Gown, only with envy. That upset some, as they knew they couldn't compete. Others were upset because you were with James." Abby grinned.

"Yes, I met one who didn't seem happy to see me there with James."

Maggie smiled in agreement. "I think I know who you are talking about." She looked at Abby. "You weren't upset though?'

"No. If you are tough enough to put up with all the barbed comments you get from a male dominated City. That was a mere trifle compared."

"Richard thought you fitted in very well." Maggie told her. "He likes James a lot, you know."

"I gathered that. He was very attentive, making sure that I was looked after."

"Of course he did. He likes you as well. We both do. He was saying later that you two could make the perfect couple."

Abby laughed delightedly. "Not you as well?"

"How do you mean? Not us as well."

"There is so much match-making going on at Combe Lyney that anything that James and I do together would appear to be headline news." Maggie had a broad smile on her face.

"Well that's the country for you. Do you mind?"

Abby shook her head. "No, not really. In fact it is amusing. Anyway…" Abby stopped.

Maggie's head came up in unspoken query. "Anyway what?"

"There may be some grounds for the assumptions." She didn't clarify anymore, but raised her cup to her lips with a secretive smile on her face.

"Abby! Don't stop there. What has happened? Tell me more." Abby took a deep breath. She felt that Maggie would be a good friend. Someone in whom she could confide. She decided to do that as she didn't have anyone else to talk to.

"I am very taken, as you put it, with James. We have got close, but there is a problem." Maggie was immediately concerned.

"Whatever you say stays here, you know that, Abby."

That convinced Abby. "As you may know, I do not know who my father was. No one who knew my mother can offer any ideas. But Gwen Comberford has suggested that my father could possibly be Charles Comberford."

Maggie sat there stunned for a moment. "Complete and utter nonsense." She said vehemently. "Absolute rubbish." She looked around, and changing the tone of her voice said.

"Let's get our coats and take a walk in the garden."

James had promised Abby that the gardens were worth seeing, and even at this late time of the year they were magnificent. With their coats to keep out the chill, Maggie and Abby wandered easily along paths cloaked with shrubs and trees. Coolton faced down the valley, so from the house you had an uphill view over the garden. Abby thought that Lyney House with the gardens looking down into the valley could present a vista superior to this should they ever have a caring hand to tend them. They strolled silently for a while with Maggie pointing out interesting specimens from time to time. Eventually she asked. "On what basis does Gwen make that assumption?"

Abby thought for a moment. "She realised that with her absences from the valley, James' father had opportunity to stray. She just wondered if my mum was one with whom he strayed."

"And how old was your mother at the time?"

"She would have been sixteen." Maggie didn't take long to consider.

"Well in that case I am sure that Charles was not your father."

"How can you be so certain?"

"Well I shall have to put this carefully, and for Heaven's sake don't let James know. It was common gossip that Charles did have affairs. But he was very careful to conduct them away from the valley. The most notable thing was that he enjoyed the company of ladies who had reached certain ages, whose husbands had become indifferent, and who were of a cushioned build. That meant I was safe on all counts." Abby could scarcely suppress a giggle; Maggie giggled too and went on.

"I would say your mother was the wrong age, she was too close to home and if your mother was built like you, then she was unsuitable to Charles also on all counts." Abby was now laughing happily.

"How do you know all this?"

"I know one or two of the ladies with whom he dallied. In fact one of them was at the Ball, not that you would think it of her now."

Abby was happy to hear this, although it didn't bring James and her closer. She would still have to await the results of the tests.

"I think that James does know his father strayed."

"Does he?" Maggie was astonished. "How does he know?"

"I am not positive, but I think Gwen knew. No, she as good as admitted it, and I would suppose she had to say something to James to back up her suspicion that I could be his sister." Maggie didn't appear surprised.

"So Gwen knew all along. I shouldn't be too surprised though, a lot of us felt that she was not exactly faithful when she was away. It must have been that kind of marriage."

"You mean a marriage of convenience?"

Maggie didn't reply for a minute as they strolled contentedly.

"Yes, I would imagine something along those lines. I suppose that a lot of couples marry for more involved reasons than simply love. Position, money, land, and to ensure that there is an heir to those lands. Having done their duty so to speak, they are free to amuse themselves discreetly. Not for me though. If Richard were to cheat on me, there would be hell to pay."

"You mean divorce?"

"If necessary. But I am sure there would be other ways to make him suffer." Maggie had a laugh in her voice.

For Abby there was no such course. "If James and I were to marry, and he cheated I would kill him."

Maggie's laugh brought her back. "Don't be so dramatic, Abby. Anyway James would never cheat on you. He has this rock-hard core of integrity and fidelity running through him. He will marry for life. You would never feel threatened with him." Their walk had taken them around the garden, most of which Abby had not really noted, so intent had she been on Maggie's revelations, and they now approached the house again.

"Time for some tea I think."

"A cup of tea would go down well." Abby agreed.

James and Richard came into the Conservatory just as Abby and Maggie entered. "Saw you coming up the garden and thought we would join you. Is there any tea going?" asked Richard.

Maggie gave a resigned shrug. "Typical man. He could have asked Josie himself, but he will leave it to me."

"Ah, but my dear. You do it so well." was Richards's rejoinder. Maggie gave him an unbelieving look and hurried off to see about the tea. Abby sat down.

"Understand you are thinking about a Farmer's Co-operative." Abby looked at James who nodded.

"Well, the farmers are. They have asked me to organise it, but I am not too sure about getting that involved."

"It's a good idea." Said Richard. "The competition from abroad is bad enough without our competing amongst ourselves. You have a good product there in the Lyney Valley. It's worth a premium from those who want the best. If the tenants cooperate, they'll all get a share of the good fortune, rather than just one or two." He said no more as Maggie re-appeared. "Mustn't talk business in front of the memsahib."

"Idiot!" Commented Maggie. "Tea's on its way," she announced gaily.

On the drive back, Abby told James that she had mentioned their possible joint parentage. He wasn't annoyed, simply saying.

"And what does she think?"

"Maggie says its rubbish." He nodded.

"That's just about what Richard said." Abby looked at him with a smile.

"So you mentioned it to him?"

"Yes. I wondered if you would say anything to Maggie, and when you disappeared down the garden with your heads close together I suspected that was the nub of your conversation." She laughed.

"Is it so easy to guess what I am thinking and talking about?" He shook his head.

"No, but I suppose I hoped you would be mentioning it to Maggie. I needed to talk to someone about this, and Richard has always been a good friend, and one who will keep a confidence. In addition he and Maggie did know my father, probably better than I, as they would have socialised from time to time. Perhaps I hoped that Richard would debunk the theory. I didn't know that father played around; but then what son would know that; Richard did know. He was very circumspect about it, but it is evident that most of his friends were well aware of father's indiscretions. He cheered me up though, when he said that the suggestion of my father being your father as well was total balderdash. It would appear that father had rather specific requirements." His demeanour was somewhat contemplative. "It is quite surreal to be talking about my father like this. I mean about his infidelity. It almost seems to me that we are talking about a distant acquaintance rather than a family member. But in many ways my father was that. Going away to boarding school when I was ten, then a brief stint at University before deciding to join the army. He died soon after that, I never really knew him." He looked at Abby. "But at least I know who my father was, even if now I find I don't like him too much." Abby realised that James was reaching out to her, and that what he had said was something that he would never discuss with anyone else. It gave her a great deal of happiness that he felt he could confide in her this way, even though the subject was painful. She reached across and laid her hand on his thigh. The contact seemed to strengthen him.

***

They drove on for another mile then he turned to her. The grin was back on his face. "If the tests prove what everyone seems to believe, I can see our dirty weekend getting closer." Abby returned the grin.

"I want luxury, James. No seedy boarding house for me. If I'm to be seduced, it has to be in the best possible comfort."

"You will have luxury. Best hotel I can find. Anyway I thought it was you who was doing the seducing?"

Abby's laughed happily. "Well we will both try, and see who

wins."

He looked at her fondly. "I suspect we will both be the winner."

CHAPTER 29

Abby did have trouble with Mary that evening, and eventually consoled her by agreeing to a bowl of soup with some bread and butter. She had enjoyed the day, not just for the visit, but because James had revealed a vulnerable side. Abby had long suspected that this was there; his behaviour when he talked about his experience in the Falklands had been a clue. Now she understood that despite an outward appearance of normality, strength and content, James' upbringing had not been ideal, and the revelations of the past few weeks about his father's weaknesses had undermined his faith in someone who hitherto he had looked up to. The comment he made about knowing who his father was yet not liking him had been painful. Abby thought about that and compared it with her experiences. She had been able to give her unknown father an exciting and honourable persona, all imagination of course, and the chances were that that image would never be shattered. In some ways therefore she was luckier than James. It made her more determined that should she and James be together, married or not, she would make sure that he was given stability and warmth, something it would appear that he had lacked when growing up. It was strange that despite all the machinations of Mary and Mavis, they had ignored one aspect of Abby's character. Her determination. An asset honed in developing her career and polished in the battlefield that was the City. She was adamant that either as a sister or a lover, she would protect and encourage James.

A little later Abby was standing chatting with Sam, when Nathaniel came into the Bar. He smiled upon seeing her, and made his way over to join them. Abby was under no illusions about what he wanted to discuss, and prepared herself for some pressure to agree to manage the co-operative. She had given this a lot of thought and intended to take up the challenge, but it would have to be on her terms. She would not reveal this decision at this moment, wanting them to cajole her a little more before agreeing. This would, she hoped then put aside any suspicion that she was trying to muscle in on them. She knew she had the agreement of

Roger, Harry and Nathaniel, but wondered about Abe Stone. She asked Nathaniel if he was likely to visit the Inn at some time so she could talk with him.

"Ah, I am sorry Miss Abby, but you will never see Abe in this place. You will have to go and see him."

"Why is that?"

"Abe is a Methodist." Sam answered. "A strict one at that. Doesn't drink, and abhors places where the sin is committed. Give him half a chance and he will preach at you from dawn to dusk."

Nathaniel agreed with Sam but was eager to soften the austere picture. "Yes Abe is a Methodist, but he's one of the kindest men you will ever meet, and he has the finest breeding stock around here. Most of my stock, and most of yours, Sam, have been bred in his herd."

"Now now, Nat, don't jump down my throat. I didn't mean anything unkind about Abe."

"So when can I meet this paragon?" Abby wanted to get back on track.

"I'll take you down tomorrow if you like," offered Sam.

Nathaniel shook his head. "Might be better if I took Miss Abby down. I've always got on better with Abe than you, Sam." He turned to Abby. "Abe's happy about the co-operative in general, but wonders where he can fit in. He has a good milk business and sells yearlings on to other farms, or at auction, rarely sells any beast to slaughter. So he feels that with the profit coming from that, he will not be in a position to benefit." Abby thought quickly.

"Surely he will. If there is a demand for more beasts, he will profit by selling more for fattening."

Sam was nodding his head sagely. "There, you see Abby; you are picking it up very quickly."

Abby viewed him wryly. "Flattering me will not make me make my mind up faster." She was smiling as she said this, and Sam knew in any case that she had made her mind up. He had been told of Abby's research, and talks with James about this, surely she would not have gone to all that trouble if she were not going to do it. Nathaniel ended the conversation as he had to leave.

"Drop by Nether Cleeve any time tomorrow, and we'll go down and chat with Abe." Abby thought quickly.

"It will be in the morning, Nathaniel."

He shrugged his shoulders. "No problem, when it suits, and Miss Abby, call me Nat please?"

She knew where Nether Cleeve Farm was, a right turn off the lane leading from the village to the station, but when she got to the turn she saw the sign which announced "Neath Cleeve Farm". Thinking that she may have been mistaken she drove on until she got to the station. There were only two of George Walker's workmen there, and neither could direct her, so she turned back towards the village and turned up the drive to Neath Cleeve Farm. No more than a rutted track, Abby drove very slowly as the drive twisted first right and then left. She was very happy to see Nathaniel waiting for her in the yard.

"I wondered where you were off to." He said by way of greeting.

"I thought I may have come to the wrong place." Abby said by apology. "I thought you said Nether Cleeve last night, and the sign at the bottom says Neath Cleeve."

Nathaniel looked a little rueful. "Ah, yes." He said guiltily." Well the place has always been called Neath Cleeve, which I don't like so I have unofficially renamed it Nether Cleeve. I am sorry Miss Abby; I should have made that clear. But you're here, and that is all that matters. Will you come in for a cup of tea or coffee, the wife's just got the kettle boiling?"

"A cup of coffee will go down very well, thanks." Nat led the way to the farmhouse, which she realised was very similar to the one at Gallow Farm. The door which was evidently not the front door opened straight into the kitchen where Nat's wife was laying out mugs on the table.

Nat introduced his wife to Abby. "Sue this is Miss Abby." Then turning to Abby said. "My wife, Susan." Abby held out her hand which Susan took after carefully wiping her hand on her apron.

"I'm pleased to meet you, Susan."

"It's nice to meet you, Miss Abby.' She paused as if unsure about what she was to say next, and then almost blurted. "We are all so pleased that you are going to marry Mr. James."

Abby was dumbstruck. "Marry?" she queried.

Susan now seemed horrified as if she had overstepped the mark. "Yes, you are to marry Mr. James aren't you?"

"Well this is the first I have heard of it."

Susan was now completely flustered, not knowing how to get out of the faux pas into which she had inadvertently blundered. "Oh dear, oh dear. I was given to understand." Abby forestalled any further explanation.

"Don't worry Susan. I have come to realise that gossip in this valley can become very fanciful, and even make truth out of fiction." Nathaniel was very red-faced, almost as much as his wife. Another occasion he thought where jumping to conclusions would mean his having to apologise. In truth he felt to blame as he had mentioned to Susan his conviction that there would be a marriage. She, in innocence, had taken this as a fact. He cleared his throat.

"I am sorry, Miss Abby. You are right though. Gossip around here can be quite imaginative. Now shall we have some coffee?" This was directed at his wife, who grateful to move the topic elsewhere asked Abby how she took her coffee.

They sat down around the table. "Everyone I meet seems to have been in this valley for years. How long have you been here Nathaniel?" Abby asked.

"Miss Abby, would you please stop calling me Nathaniel, it's Nat, God knows what my mum and dad were up to giving me that mouthful for a name, so please, just Nat if you don't mind." Abby was about to take up her old argument and stop them calling her Miss Abby, but realised that this was a battle she would never win.

"Ok, it's Nat."

He smiled. "Now let me see, I took the tenancy when the Carters retired, that would be about..." He did some mental calculations.

"Wasn't it in nineteen eighty seven?" Susan offered.

"Yes it would, no! It was eighty six. I remember now, because that was the year that Harry's wife died. Sad that."

"Was she ill?" asked Abby. Susan answered the question.

"No, Miss Abby. She was killed in the lane right outside Lydcott Farm. She was hit by a car."

"That's terrible. Poor Harry."

Nat agreed. "Yes he was in a bad way for months. The farm was going to ruin, it would have if not for Sam and Roger, and they stepped in and kept it all going until Harry got over it. Never forgot that did Harry."

"Does Harry have any children?"

"Yes he had a son, Robert. But he wasn't interested in farming. Took himself off to Bristol, I believe, working in a factory." Abby sipped her coffee.

"So how does he manage on his own?"

"Will Simmonds works for him on a casual basis." Abby remembered Will. She had met him on her first day in the valley.

"You mentioned the Carters. Would that be the same Carters as Gladys?"

"Yes that's them."

"Gladys said she was going to see them, so presumably they are still in the valley?"

"Yes. They took a little cottage when John retired. We will pass it on the way down to Abe's."

"Tell me about Abe. From what you and Sam said in the Combe Inn, he is quite a character."

"Yes he is. Best kept farm in the valley. You don't need to wear boots when you walk through his yard, it's always clean. He's a Methodist as you heard, alcohol is sinful, won't have a Television in the house. Attends the Chapel down in South Molton."

"Is he married?"

"Yes. Married a girl from the Chapel, Sheila. He has a son, called Joe or Joseph, and a daughter, Naomi. I was told that he was going to call her Mary, until Sheila pointed out the he would have sired Joseph and Mary. He decided against, thinking that it could be construed as mocking the Lord." Nat and Susan both laughed and Abby joined in.

"I understand that he doesn't get on with some of the other farmers?"

"No, that's not really true. It is possible that he can get on people's nerves as he does sometimes tend to preach at people. But someone has to say something that offends him for that to happen. You must not mind if he says he will pray for you. It is simply his way of letting you know that he respects you."

"I'll remember that."

The coffee being finished, Nat suggested to Abby that they get on down to see Abe. Susan was clearing away the mugs when she asked.

"Miss Abby, would you like to stay for a bite of lunch when you get back? Nothing fancy, but I have plenty, and you will be most welcome." Abby had to skip around this without offending them.

"May I make that another time?" she asked. "I have a constant battle with Mary, who thinks that I need feeding up. A day when I can miss lunch is a bonus for me."

Nat smiled. "I understand completely Miss Abby. Mary, I have been told believes that anyone weighing less than twelve stone is seriously undernourished. She must be despairing of you." Nat insisted that they went in his Van. "I wouldn't want you to damage that nice car over the ruts." He didn't say whether they were his ruts or Abe's.

Abe Stone's farm, Lower Valley Farm was a revelation to Abby, used as she was to the muck and general untidiness of the other farms she had seen. The yard, as Nat had promised was cleanly swept and the buildings and outhouses neatly painted. Abe himself came out to greet them, not dressed in the usual uniform of farmers of overalls and gumboots, but wearing corduroy trousers, a jacket, shirt and tie.

"Hello Abe," called Nat, "this is Miss Abby."

Abe nodded. "Good day to you Miss Abby, you are welcome. Please do come in. May we offer you some refreshment?"

"Thank you Mr. Stone, it is very good to meet you." Abe led the way into the farmhouse. He introduced his wife Sheila and invited Abby and Nat to sit down. The table gleamed with generations of polish, and sitting in the middle in pride of place sat a huge Bible. There were at least a dozen bookmarks protruding from the leaves, presumably pages that Abe would read most frequently. Sheila quickly brought tea to the table, and in addition offered Abby homemade lemonade. Abby jumped at the offer, as another tea or coffee would be too much. The Lemonade was superb, and she said as much to Sheila who accepted the praise with a small smile.

Despite his courtesy, Abe was not one to delay getting to the crux of the matter. "I have to tell you, Miss Abby that I am not altogether happy about this idea of yours for a Co-operative." Abby decided not to say anything immediately, but wanted Abe to say his piece. He was surprised that Abby did not argue straight away, so had to go on and put his case. This was in essence that fact that he had breeding stock, and rarely sent a beast to slaughter, also that if he had greater demand for yearlings, it would raise his costs, having to rent more land but that the others would not be prepared to pay any more for the stock. He would not be able to share in the increased profits that Sam, Harry and Nat would enjoy. Abby listened carefully, and when Abe seemed to have put his objections fully, tried to re-assure him.

"Mr. Stone, I thank you for being so frank with me, and if I am frank in return please do not think it discourteous." Abe waved his hands to indicate that he had no problem. "First, I must say that this was not my idea. Nat, Roger and Harry conceived the idea, and are trying to persuade me that I should manage the co-operative. I am a newcomer here, and know little about farming, but I have a background in business which they feel will be helpful to the enterprise. I haven't actually agreed as yet, because I felt it important that I listened to the views of all concerned before making that decision. And to learn more about what you do." Abe looked at Nat, who nodded his head to confirm that was the truth. Abby went on. "Your points are very important, and I am convinced that if this co-operative is to be successful, it has to be for the benefit of all," Abby emphasised the word all, "not just for some. If that were not the case I would have no part of it." Abe's countenance cleared.

"I am very pleased to hear that Miss Abby. How do you think this can be achieved?"

"Well I have to give this more consideration, as I say I am not yet completely convinced myself. But if you allow me some more time, I will try to put together a draft plan, for everyone involved to read, discuss, and if there are inequalities there, to amend. I shall depend heavily on advice, and will ask anyone who I believe can give me that advice. That will include Mr. Comberford, Sir Richard Wellings, but most importantly yourselves. Will that be in order?" Abe nodded his head. "The request I have received makes me think that there is a small, but lucrative market for the valley, and I intend to look further to find other outlets. But it has to be for the benefit of all equally. Will you give me the time to come up with a draft agreement, Mr. Stone?"

Abe's countenance had lightened as he heard Abby. "Of course I will, Miss Abby. You have put my mind at rest. I appreciate your candour, and the sentiments expressed. Thank you. And if you feel that in any way I can be of assistance, please do call upon me. I shall pray for the success of our enterprise." Abby had actually said very little, and without realising it had drawn upon all the skills she had learnt in the City negotiating her way around the office politics. It was amazing she thought, how you could say so much without substance, yet leave people believing that you had addressed their concerns. This hadn't been done cynically, as certain politicians did, but mainly to address a situation which could have damaged the idea.

With the business done, Sheila, who had remained quiet came into her own, making sure that everyone had a cup of something in front of them, and then sitting down to chat.

"Are you a churchgoer? Miss Abby."

"I am afraid not."

Sheila looked a little shocked. "If you wish to attend, we shall be very happy to take you with us to our little Church. It's very simple, but a warming place to be."

"That is very kind of you, may I give that some thought." Abe nodded in agreement with his wife, then went on to stun Abby.

"Of course. Your grandfather I am told would attend from time to time." Abby looked at him in astonishment.

"My grandfather attended?"

"Yes. We didn't know him, but we know of him from the Elders. I understand he found it very difficult to attend every week because of his duties here at the station. The congregation accepted that, as he was doing his duty, serving the community." Abby was astounded. How often did it seem that from out of nowhere, another glimpse of her grandfather came to light. No one had mentioned his religious persuasion, yet when she gave it thought, it wasn't so surprising. He was Cornish born in an area where the Wesleyan tradition was strong, and the character of the man, his sense of duty could well be another facet of his faith. She actually felt some shame, as she had none at all.

Abe would have liked to show Abby around his farm, but realised that she was hardly dressed for this and instead told her that if she was so inclined he would do that another day, when she was dressed more suitably. Abby and Nat took their leave with Sheila asking Abby to call anytime, and stay for lunch. In the car, Nat informed her that staying for lunch would inevitably involve prayers of at least five minutes duration before she could start eating. He had more to say.

"I would never believe it, but you had Abe eating out of the palm of your hand within minutes. I have never known anyone calm Abe down when he is having one of his strops. Just wait until I tell Sam and Harry. I shall have to come into the Combe tonight."

"It wasn't just blah, Nat. I meant every word I said. This thing is no good unless it is worthwhile for all of you."

Nat did agree with that. "Well that was the idea. The one thing we all need to know is how much more we can sell. If it's only an occasional carcass, then it will not make that much difference."

"I know that, that's why I have an idea, but I need to have everybody together before I talk about it."

"Miss Abby, I am convinced that whatever your idea, you will get our agreement, that is if you talk the way you did today." Nat's lugubrious face had lightened and Abby wasn't certain, but she thought she saw a little smile hovering around his mouth.

Abby had to ward off further entreaties from Susan Gaunton to stay for 'a little bite,' as she put it, and took the opportunity to call in at the station. The house echoed to the sound of hammering and an unseen voice urging another unseen voice to, 'just a little bit this way.' And, 'keep that end up.' With some trepidation she entered the house. The ground floor had been transformed. Everything had been cleared out, the furniture, the old Butler sink, the range, gone and they had started on lining the walls; clean grey sheets with a tape covering the joins. Every so often she could see wires protruding through these sheets, and on two walls pipe work as well. Heavy footsteps on the stairs heralded the entrance of George Walker.

He looked up in surprise to see Abby. "Ah, Miss Tregonney. Come to see how we are getting on?"

"Yes, Mr. Walker. I must say you seem to be getting along very quickly." He hummed as usual then said.

"It can be deceiving. It always looks at first as if the work is going quickly. Getting the dry-lining up makes it look that way, it's the details that take the time though. I'm glad you're here, I was going to call you. There are some decisions needed."

"Ok." Agreed Abby. "Tell me what you need."

"Well for a start, I have put in some wiring for the ring-main, and tails for where plugs will be, over the work surface and around the base of the walls, but if you would like anymore, perhaps you could let me know, as it is easy to do them now, better to have more than not enough, you know. And you will have to start thinking about what you are going to put there." He pointed to the space where the range had been. Abby had given this some thought, and James had managed to get her some brochures from a place in Taunton. She had seen one she liked, which looked as if it was a period piece, but was nonetheless state of the art, and would either use Gas, or Electricity, or a combination of the two. She told George about this. He hummed some more. "Yes I think I know what you mean. If you would let me have the brochure with the one you want indicated, I can get it on order. But if it's the one I think you mean it'll cost you a bit." Abby suddenly had a thought.

"Mr. Walker, I assume there is a flue there?"

"Yes of course. We would use it if you have a gas cooker fitted."

"Could you use it for a real fire?"

George looked at her. "A real fire?"

"I have suddenly had this thought. I am not a cook, so it seems a waste of time my putting this big cooker in. It would be nice if I could have a fire there instead."

George saw what she was getting at. "Tell you what. How about a wood-burning stove? I can get one which will fit in nicely, look a little bit more like the old one as well. It will have an opening front so you can enjoy real flames. Course you will have to have a separate boiler for the central heating, but those come so neat and convenient these days, you will hardly notice it." Abby thought about this and nodded.

"Yes. I like that. Would you go ahead with that?"

"No problem. But what will you cook on?"

"I'll get a microwave, and a toaster. Anything else I will go down to the Inn and Mary will feed me."

They moved around the ground floor, with Abby gesturing to where she would like electric plugs to be, George marked the positions with a soft lead pencil with which he signed a great cross and a little lightning symbol. He nodded his thanks and said.

"If you would come back next week, we can do the same with the bedroom. Does your brochure have bathroom suites in it, as I shall need to know what you want soon?"

"No it didn't. What do you suggest?"

"I have got some catalogues, shall I bring them down to the Inn? Then we can go through them."

"Yes please, that would be good, but I don't want any of these plastic things." He smiled his agreement.

"Very wise. I have got some catalogues showing cast iron, and pressed steel baths. You'll have enough room up there to put in a separate shower cabinet and a Bidet if you wish. Give it some thought and we'll discuss it when I come down with the catalogues."

As she left it suddenly occurred to Abby that she would have to start thinking about furniture. Not for the main room as her grandfather's table, dresser and chairs would go back in there, but for the backroom, and for her bedroom. Loathe as she was to get Mavis and Mary too involved, she realised that she would have to bring them in to the discussion, else they would feel slighted. She was suddenly reminded that bedroom furniture would have to include a double bed, just in case a certain gentleman would be staying. Would they get a double up those stairs? She laughed at herself. Despite what Sam and Maggie had said, and despite her own gut feelings, there was still a nagging doubt. If James turned out to be her brother, then he would certainly not be staying. Abby then cheered herself up, it was better to be prepared, you never know.

Back at the Inn, a letter awaited her. Looking at the writing she knew exactly who this was from, hurriedly she opened the envelope, not bothering with a knife to slit it. Mr. Brasher had written.

Dear Abby.

I am writing first to thank you for your hospitality, when I stayed at the Combe Inn. Your kindness made my stay a very pleasant experience.

The Joint of beef, I am pleased to say, matched the praise I had given to the delight of many members. Our Chef, a man who is only grudgingly pleased, had to admit that it was some of the finest meat he had ever had the pleasure of cooking.

The committee had a meeting from which I excluded myself on the grounds that I had a particular interest. The judgement was that the Club should take immediate steps to obtain supplies on a regular basis. Our Chef therefore will be in contact with you in the very near future, to discuss prices and quantities. I should say at this juncture, that we would like to purchase all meats and poultry as well. He will probably travel down for a day, to inspect the facilities. Please do let me know when this would be convenient.

I intend to make another visit shortly, as I would very much appreciate an opportunity to talk with Mr. Purvess, as well as seeing the friends I made when last I visited. I shall write to you soon with the dates, hoping that Mr. and Mrs. Elvesly will be able to accommodate me.

I look forward to seeing you soon, and hearing how the restoration is getting along.

Your affectionate friend,
Brasher

Abby needed to pass this good news on to Roger and Harry to start with and then to James. She immediately set off for Gallow Farm. The only one there was Mavis who could not entreat Abby to a tea or coffee, but did say that Roger was over in the fields repairing a gate, and that Sam was at Lydcott with Harry. Abby thanked Mavis and asked if she thought it would be alright to call at Lydcott.

"Bless you girl, of course. They will only be chatting if I know them. You go, they will be pleased to see you." Abby got back into her car and drove the short distance to Lydcott Farm. The drive as all these farm drives was not exactly a smooth surface, and Abby decided that if she would be doing this more frequently, perhaps she should get transport more suited to the terrain.

She drove into the yard and almost immediately Harry appeared from his shed, followed by Sam. "Miss Abby, it's so nice to see you here. Can I offer you a cuppa?"

"Harry, thank you, but I have had coffee at Nat's, and lemonade at Abe's. Any more to drink, and I will burst"

"Well come in anyway. Getting a bit chill to be standing about out here." Sam followed them in to the Kitchen. Harry looked embarrassed as the place was a bit untidy, with dirty dishes in the sink, and on the table. He quickly cleared the table, and invited Abby to sit. Abby gave him the letter from Mr. Brasher, which he read, then passed it on to Sam.

"Good news eh, Sam?" Sam had put his glasses on to read the letter, and looked up at Abby and smiled.

"Well, Abby? You will have to make your mind up quick. It looks as if we could be in business." Abby had realised that she would have to take charge now. "Yes, Sam. I would like to have a meeting with everyone involved. Obviously not at the Inn, as Abe will not set foot in the place. I need to outline a few ideas, and set about getting the co-operative up and running. Where would you suggest?" Harry and Sam exchanged glances then Harry ventured his opinion.

"I would think that Nat would let us have it at his place. What do you reckon, Sam?"

"You could be right. Abe gets on with Nat better than anyone. If he came to Gallow, Mavis and he will get into a scrap, and Susan will I am sure put on a sandwich or two for us. Yes, Nat's best."

Abby nodded. "O.K. Next thing is when. We have a day or two. I will write back to Mr. Brasher to let him know that any time will be convenient for his Chef to call, but we will need to discuss prices before-hand. I will get on the internet and find the latest prices, but we will have to take into account transport and cold storage costs as well. I will ask Nat if this is alright with him and try and have our meeting within two or three days. Is that o.k. with you?" Harry and Sam both nodded. Sam with a little inward smile. Harry, Nat and the others had imagined that getting Abby to run things would merely relieve them of the organisation and paperwork. Now he thought they were going to discover that they had let loose a Tigress. If the gossip and conjecture surrounding Abby was any-thing to go by, she had done very well in her job, and made millions for her Bank. He did not doubt that Abby was going to be just as driven with the co-operative. Although he was no longer a farmer, he would be at the meeting, if only to see the expressions on their faces when they realised what they had done.

Abby spent quite a lot of time at Lyney House, grateful for the Aga which warmed the room making the calls that would get her the details she required for the meeting. The first day she waited at the door for someone to answer her knock. There was none, nor did she see James' Land Rover about. He had said to her to come at any time, but she felt inhibited about just walking in. Eventually the importance of her work got the better of her diffidence, the door when she tried it was unlocked so she made herself at home. It was strange for her to walk into a house with no locked door, but it would appear that James had a casual approach to security. With tea freshly brewed and her papers with lists of questions requiring answers she sat down to work.

James appeared after about an hour, and did not seem perturbed that Abby was making herself at home in his breakfast room. He bent over to claim his now usual greeting. Abby needed to explain.

"There was no answer, and the door was unlocked so I just came in. I hope you don't mind?"

He shook his head totally unfazed "Not at all. I don't usually lock the door, and I did think you may be up to do some work, so I left it like that. Any tea left in that pot?" James made another pot as the tea was a little stewed. He took her mug and refilled it while he was about it.

With the cup steaming in front of her Abby wanted some advice. "Two things I want to run past you. First I want to register Combe Lyney as a brand."

He raised his eyebrows, and gave it some thought. "Now that is an excellent idea. A brand name for quality produce. Very good. Second?"

"Don't you want to discuss that?"

"Nothing to discuss." He shook his head. "It's a very good idea, I am sure the chaps will like it, and they are the ones who will have most to gain."

"Right. We have confirmation from Mr. Brasher that his Club will take meats on a regular basis. But I suspect that will not be sufficient to make that much difference. I would like to contact other Clubs, and possibly some top Hotels and see if we can get them interested. What do you think?"

James sat staring into his mug for a while before answering. "I agree that we ought to get other outlets, and yes, it has to be establishments which want the best for their clientele. I am not too sure about Hotels though. In my experience Hotels may provide you with comfortable bedrooms, but their restaurants leave a lot of room for improvement. It's all about profit margins. They tend to buy as economically as possible and sell at the highest price. I don't think they will pay a premium price for our produce." He thought for a moment. "But there are some restaurants that specialize in Traditional English Roasts. If you dined there you could have almost any meat you chose, and they usually have at least three trolleys, just for beef alone. They are very particular about quality. I think they would be a better outlet."

Abby was convinced. "Yes of course. Whenever the directors went out for lunch that was the kind of venue they chose. Well done my good ideas man. How do we get them interested though?"

James was thinking again. "I would say let the reputation speak for itself, and possibly they will come to you." He stopped waiting for Abby to comment, she didn't, so he continued. "I think the best thing is to get it all set up, and iron out the logistics. Once that is working properly, then you can have a go at other outlets, when you know what quantities are required and how the demand can be satisfied. Growing beef is done over months, Abby, not just a few weeks."

Abby was silent for a while. James was right. Her ambition was running away from her, this was going to take some time. But she couldn't resist getting back at him. "I suppose this was your Army training, you cannot advance until you have all the necessary equipment in place?"

He smiled knowingly."Yes, it was a lesson hammered into us. Or in other words, don't stick your neck out, until you know that your body can follow and you're not going to be shot at."

Abby smiled wickedly. "Speaking of bodies following." She got no further.

"Don't start on that. I will have to go and take a cold shower if you go there."

"What did you think I was going to say?"

"Something saucy I expect."

Abby was laughing. "Perhaps I was but these tests are taking far too long."

"They'll be done soon. Doctor did say about four or five weeks, and it must be almost four weeks now. I'm just as impatient."

"Where are we going for this dirty weekend then?"

"Abby! A little more decorum please."

"I have been exercising decorum for too long. I want to be very, very naughty for once in my life.

Well actually more than once, I am sure that once will not be satisfactory."

"Oh casting doubts on my ability as a lover, are we?"

"Not at all James, in fact it was more a compliment. I am certain that once tried, I shall want more."

"Oh Gawd! Definitely a cold shower beckoning. Stop this now, else I shall take you over this table now."

Abby's smile became broader if that was possible and her eyes twinkled. "Promises, promises" She laughed. "Ok, James. I shall stop teasing you."

CHAPTER 30

The letter expected was already in the post. It arrived at Lyney House two days later, the Doctor's receptionist being frugal with her employers expenses had used a second class stamp. It dropped through the door, and James collected it with his other post. Realising immediately what this was, he called Abby on her mobile straight away.

"It's here."

"What does it say?"

"I haven't opened it yet. I think as it concerns you as much as me, we should open it together."

"I'm on my way." Abby rarely drove her car quickly, but on this occasion an uncharacteristic turn of speed got Abby to Lyney House in no time at all. James had put the kettle on, using the electric kettle rather than using the Aga. They would need coffee post haste. Not bothering to knock, Abby charged straight into the Breakfast room. The letter sat in the middle of the table. James put coffee down for them both, and sat beside Abby. For a moment neither dared to pick it up and open the envelope. Eventually Abby could not wait any longer; she grabbed the letter and ripped it open, feverishly scanning the contents.

"I do not understand this." She handed the paper to James, who read it more slowly. He looked at her. His first impulse was to tease her, but better sense told him that that would not go down well. Abby was impatient.

"Well! What does it say?"

"Hang on; I am trying to make sense of it."

With little concealed anxiety, Abby waited. "Well?"

James had finished reading the report. "I don't understand why Civil Servants and Doctors cannot use simple language. There is the usual gobbledegook but it would seem there is no match at all in the DNA. We are not related!"

For a while Abby sat there taking this in. Then a serene smile came to her face, and she leaned over and kissed James in the way that she had wanted to for ages. Eventually their lips parted, only for James to bring her face to his again for another kiss.

"What are you doing this weekend coming?" James enquired of her.

"Whatever you tell me to do." Abby replied happily.

"Ok, consider yourself booked from Friday afternoon until Monday morning." Abby nodded vigorously.

"Where are we going?"

"You'll find that out when I pick you up, although as I suppose you will not want to be seen dead in my Land Rover, shall we take your car?"

"Of course, if we are going somewhere posh."

"Well it's as posh as my budget will allow. But as it's out of season most places are offering deals. I am sure that we will have the best caravan on the site." Abby looked at him suspiciously, uncertain if he was joking. James maintained his calm exterior for a while until he could sustain it no longer.

"Oh Abby! The look on your face." He blurted out with fits of laughter. She joined in, hiding the chagrin she felt at being so easily duped.

"Well Mr. Comberford. I am quite certain that that would be your usual idea of a weekend of seduction." She grabbed the front of his jacket.

"But I require a classier environment." She pulled him forwards and planted a kiss on his lips. "Anything less than classy, you won't even get so much as a kiss."

Abby and James slipped away from the Combe Inn at three fifteen that Friday. The only observer was Mary from the same vantage point that she had seen Abby and James kiss after the Ball. The significance of the suitcases was not lost on her, and within minutes she was on the telephone to Mavis. So engrossed were they in their conversation that Mavis neglected to listen out for Sam. He gathered the gist of their gossip within seconds, and exploded. Mavis had never seen him so angry in all their years together, and for the first time in her married life was very afraid of his temper. Mary on the end of the line could hear all that Sam was saying, and was at first inclined to put the phone down. She was about to do so, when Sam took the receiver from Mavis and made his displeasure very clear to Mary. Although Abby had not said anything to him, it was proof positive to him that the test had proved negative. James would not behave this way unless he was certain, not just certain of their patronage, but certain as well of his feelings towards Abby. He wished them well wherever they were heading.

The two people who were at the heart of this eruption were blissfully unaware, and were well away from the valley heading for Torquay. The hotel was very much to Abby's taste.

Abby, for the second time in recent months wondered why she could not remember the weekend in complete detail. She felt that the emotions and passions her two nights with James had stirred would have given her enough memories to write a book, yet just as she had after the Ball, only small vignettes came to her mind as she lay in bed that Sunday evening. She hadn't really known what to expect. Yes, she had encouraged James, possibly giving him the impression that she was knowledgeable in these matters, but when it came down to it, she could only let James take the lead and follow him. The overriding memory was of tenderness. James was considerate and gentle. She contemplated her wakening on Saturday. She had slept very well for the few hours that were available to her, and awoke still tingling throughout her body. She stretched like a cat even the soft cotton sheets were sensual against her skin and caused her flesh to tingle, a reminder of the excitement of last night. She was naked. Looking across the bed her gaze took in the still slumbering James, his hair tousled and with a slight growth of beard on his cheeks. During the night the bedclothes had slipped so an arm, most of his chest, and a leg were exposed. His lips fluttered gently with his breathing, and occasionally a soft snore eased gently in his sleep. He was also nude. Abby snuggled closer, and pulled the bedclothes over him to share his warmth, although her body seemed to be superheated anyway. She had never been loved so tenderly and gently before. Previous encounters had been swift with little care shown to her as if her participation was merely that of a body to be used. James had never seemed in a hurry, and explored her body with his hands, fingers and tongue, slowly, softly guiding her with love. Abby had gradually been brought to a high plateau, where her whole body seemed alive under his hands, every plane of her flesh, supersensitive to his touch. His kisses, that she enjoyed so much since the Ball were now deeper, holding more passion and far more intimate. He took control of her and carried them both to Nirvana. From her experience she thought that men just took, James had changed her view, he gave and kept on giving.

She lay awake watching him wondering where he had become such a good lover, and with whom. She hated her, whoever she was, then relented as she realised that she was enjoying the results of those lessons. James stirred. Abby moved with him, and that reminded her body of more prosaic functions, she needed the bathroom! Sitting up she looked for her robe. It was draped over a chair on the other side of the room. Her clothes lay strewn over the floor, where James had dropped them as he undressed her. The reality of the situation came to her. After the way that she and James had behaved last night, there was little point of being prudish this morning. She rose from the bed, careful not to disturb James and padded across the floor to the bathroom. She picked up her robe intending to put it on for her return, then decided that she liked being naked for James, so let it drop.

On her return she checked the kettle and switched it on, preparing the cups to make tea. Suddenly a voice came from the depths of the bed.

"Well now. There's a welcoming sight for the morning. The maid is naked. It was never like this, even in my dreams."

Abby turned completely unabashed. "Good morning Lover. I seem to have forgotten to bring my little uniform with the lace cap. I do apologise, Sir."

"Don't apologise my dear. I have absolutely no objection." He sat up. Then flinging back the sheets got off the bed, and hurried towards the bathroom.

"Oh Sir!" Abby cried, noticing his excitement "Should I make the tea or ... James grinned.

"Make the tea, and then we will explore the 'or'. I shall just be a moment." Abby was just pouring the hot water when two arms insinuated themselves around her waist and held her close.

"James!" she said rather breathlessly, "I shall spill boiling water."

"Oh! I am sorry."

"Don't be. I like you to hold me close." She turned in his embrace and lifted her face for his kiss, then another and yet another. The tea was forgotten.

Getting back to the Inn on Sunday evening was unreal for Abby. Somehow she had expected that everything would have changed, because she had changed, yet the Inn was exactly as she had left it, the first drinkers in the bar, Jack taking things easily before the rush later. Mary would be in her kitchen, although there didn't seem to be any diners wanting food. Abby was disappointed by this lack of electricity in the air, after all she had a weekend of life-changing experiences, and thought that somehow she would be sending out sparks and that someone should recognise the change in her, and want to enthuse with her. Her thoughts were contrary because actually she would not have wanted to talk about it anyway. Jack came round and carried her suitcase up stairs, but apart from asking how she was made no other comment. The knock on the door as she was unpacking came as no surprise as Mary came in. She looked at Abby with a light smile on her face.

"I won't ask questions. There is a look in your eyes that tells me that you had a good weekend."

"Is it that obvious?"

"There is a sparkle there I haven't seen before. Another woman, one who knows you will notice it, but don't worry, none of them down-stairs will see it. Will you want anything to eat?"

"Yes please, Mary. I am going to have a shower, and then I will be down. Something light please, I don't think my stomach could take anything else." Mary nodded and was going to leave, when on the spur of the moment she turned and enveloped Abby in a hug.

"I'm glad things are working out for you."

Later Abby had time to reflect, not without a little embarrass-ment, about the weekend. It was strange, as she could not recall the weekend in its entirety, but like the Ball, cameos and vignettes came to her, mainly the exciting moments. The embarrassment came as she real-ised how bold she was, walking about the room naked, showing off for James and loving his eyes on her. Then there was the language she had used, urging James on. Her cheeks burned, what must he think of her? But however ashamed she was, however much her blushes suffused her skin, she knew that should a repeat of the weekend be offered she would have no compunction about accepting.

Abby, with reluctance put her musing to one side. She had to prepare for the meeting with Roger, Harry, Nat and Abe. This should have happened last week, but there were difficulties getting all the participants together, and the Monday this week was the best time, hence the return early from Torquay. Perhaps it was chagrin that the meeting had forced this early return, or possibly the determination gained from the City, but the meeting was just as exciting as Sam had thought possible, much to his delight. Abby showed why she was successful in her job, with a firm outline of her business plan, and a forecast that acted as a splash of cold water on the assumptions of one or two. Abe was very happy with the meeting as Abby proposed a system that would allow all of them who joined the scheme to enjoy equally in the profits. This appealed to his Methodist adherence. Nat had to support Abby as he had become her champion in this matter, although he was somewhat unhappy that the extra revenue he had supposed would not be as great as his imagination had conjured. Harry and Roger were the most unhappy. It was their production that would provide the bulk of the extra business, but had assumed that they would be able to buy yearlings for fattening from Abe at similar prices as they had enjoyed in the past, ignoring his increased costs to provide them with more beasts. Abby had listened to them all and was determined to create a level playing field for all to profit.

In essence Abby was setting up a business in which they all had shares, which would buy all the production at agreed rates, for selling on. The profits would then be distributed to shareholders as dividends. It was simple, and although it would not address every individual's difficulty, it would cover most eventualities, and could expand easily if other farmers in the locality wanted to join. Sam had already heard from one who was interested.

If they came out of the meeting with somewhat shell-shocked expressions, Sam came out with a half-smile on his face. Harry had made great play of telling Abby that they wanted someone independent to run the co-operative, to avoid the arguments. Now he had got what he wished for and was bruised from the encounter. When Harry turned to Sam later and complained about Abby's direct approach, Sam had little sympathy. "Harry, you wanted Abby to run it. Well she's going to, but not as a puppet with you pulling the strings. By all accounts she made herself a lot of money in the City. Now if she can bring that sort of skill to us, and make us a lot of money, don't complain!"

Harry was still put out. "Yes and if that happens, next thing will be Mr. James putting the rents up."

Sam had thought this argument would appear sooner or later. "So? What if he does? You know damned well that the rents here are less than elsewhere. He has been subsidising us for years. Come on, Harry be fair." Harry reluctantly nodded.

He said nothing else for a few minutes, then. "You're right, Sam. I was right as well. She is the best person to run this thing. She had Abe eating out of her hand, never thought I would see that. And I like this idea of creating a brand name. We ought to get the carcasses stamped with the name." He gave that some thought. "She didn't think of that." Sam smiled ruefully. Harry was ever the same; he always had to come out on top, even if his victories were more in his own head than actual.

With things happening Abby now moved in to the old estate office. James had arranged a phone line, and Abby immediately applied for a second, to run a broadband connection for her computer. She was happy with her lap-top to begin with, but admitted to herself that she would have to get a new one for the co-operative, as she had personal stuff on the lap-top and could envisage a time when others may want to use the computer for co-operative work. James had done a good job in clearing and tidying the office, and all it needed was Abby to arrange the desk and files as she liked, then add the feminine touch. She rummaged through the kitchen and found a vase, then helped herself to the last of the roses from the garden. James found her there busy with organising all the papers she had gathered on her researches.

"Ah! The wheeler-dealer is in place."

Abby looked up. "Wheeler-dealer?" she queried.

"I have been talking to Nat and Abe this morning. Nat is astonished that you have taken the reins so soundly, and kept Harry in his place, which we all know is a difficult thing to do. Abe is totally in awe and is your confirmed supporter. He has convinced himself that you are organising this with strong Methodist principles, which means that as you have God on your side it must be good for the whole community. He also seems to believe that you will be attending Chapel with him and Sheila. Are you?"

"It wasn't part of my plans. Will he be upset if I don't go with them?"

"No. Methodists are very forgiving. They just believe that one day you will see the light and join them; all they have to do is be patient. I am going to put the kettle on, fancy a coffee?

Abby nodded enthusiastically. "Yes please."

Abby followed James into the breakfast room. The kettle was just whispering steam as it came to the boil on the Aga, and James set out the mugs, sugar and milk. Abby came close to him and waited. He turned and put his arms around her drawing her into a kiss. The steam was boiling out of the kettle when their lips grudgingly parted. Abby sat down at the table.

"Whew! They get better and better. I could get used to those."

James smiled. "I thought it was you that was doing the kissing. I was just hanging in there."

"Well you can hang in there some more."

"Now?"

"Later. I'll let you know when." Abby was pensive for a while, and James catching her mood became concerned that something was troubling her.

"What's the matter, Abby?"

"Nothing."

"Abby. You say nothing, but it means anything but. It means that there is something that you cannot talk about, or will not talk about, or don't know how to talk about. So what is it?"

Abby shook her head and suddenly blurted. "Was I over the top when we were away?"

"How do you mean, 'over the top'." Abby was quiet, not knowing quite how to say this.

"Well, did I shock you? I used some bad language, and behaved brazenly, walking around with no clothes. Did it upset you?"

James couldn't believe that Abby had asked this question. "Did it look like I was shocked? Not at all. Was I appalled by your language? Not at all. Abby, it was a tender and wonderful time. What happened there will stay with me for the rest of my life. I will never share that with anyone but you. And if you want to walk around without clothes, I have never seen a more beautiful sight. In fact the next time you feel like walking around naked, let me know, and come up here for the weekend. You will improve the look of the place no end, and give me a great deal of pleasure." Abby smiled, James' compliments were now given without that hint of flippancy that he used at first, and his emotion showed in his words.

Then her smile evolved to wicked. "James are you propositioning me?"

"Yes."

"Oh good, then I will take you up on that. One stipulation though."

"Yes, and what would that be?"

"You turn the heat up first. If I am walking around here naked, I want my nipples erect from passion, and not from the cold."

Two days later Gwen Comberford returned. The first Abby knew of it was Gwen walking into the Estate office. She didn't seem at all surprised that Abby was working there. Her information service was obviously working well. "Good morning Abby. How are you?"

"Hello Gwen, I am well. How are you? It's nice to see you back."

"No it isn't, because whilst I am here you and James cannot play House together. But don't worry, it won't be for long." Abby was flummoxed by Gwen's words, and all she could do was an embarrassed smile.

Gwen let her off the hook. "I know the results of the test, and I know that you and James could not keep your hands off each other for long, so don't be shy. It's what makes the world go around."

Abby grinned. "Well, we have acted with decorum."

"I know. Hopefully soon you will have no need to. But apart from making my son very happy, it would appear that you are making lots of changes here."

"Well James said I could use this office."

"No I don't mean this; although it was about time something was done here. I meant the scheme you are setting up for the Farmers. About time they were dragged into the twentieth century. Good for you."

"It was their idea in the first place. All I am doing is bringing some organisation to the idea." Gwen accepted Abby's explanation, although it was clear that she didn't totally believe it.

"Fancy a coffee?'

"That will go down very well. Thank you."

"Will you come into the house, or would you prefer it here?"

"I'll come in the house." Abby was sure that Gwen would not take kindly to having to bring coffee to the estate office.

They sat down at the large table as Gwen waited for the kettle to boil. Abby was apprehensive, not knowing if this was just a friendly chat, or was Gwen going to put her on the spot. Gwen, secretly was pleased as she realised Abby's fears, but with the coffee made, decided to put her mind at rest.

"Be at ease, Abby I am your friend, really. I just want to get to know you better. My son makes me out to be a dragon, well possibly with him I am, and need to be at times. You will find that in times to come you will have to put a rocket under him. He can be very forceful at times, and then he sits back and lets everything happen without lifting a finger." She took a sip of coffee. "I am so pleased that you are not my husband's daughter. There is no obstacle to you and James getting together. I think I know how you feel about James, and I am certain about his feelings for you. I shall let him know in the strongest terms that if he doesn't ask you to marry him, then I will make life so unpleasant for him that it won't be worth living."

Abby bridled. "You say that you think you know what my feelings are, and go on to tell me that James has to ask me to be his wife. I am not some baggage that has to be attended to. You fail to recognise that even if James were to ask me, irrespective of my feelings, I may not wish to marry him."

"But why?" Gwen had been certain that Abby would jump at the chance.

"I have made my own way in life, and without being boastful, I have done a good job. There are other things that I may want to do. One thing I do not wish is to become a meaningless adjunct to James. It may be that I would like our relationship to go on as it is now, so that I can pursue other interests." This shook Gwen, she had underestimated Abby and she wondered if the expression 'a meaningless adjunct' was an arrow aimed at Gwen's frivolous and irresponsible lifestyle. Abby was the one who was now secretly pleased that the firm foundations that Gwen had assumed had been shaken. The truth was that Abby would probably accept a proposal from James, but that was her decision and she wasn't going to be bullied into a marriage to please Gwen. Nor would she accept a proposal that James had been forced to make by his mother.

Gwen took some time to think, sipping at her coffee whilst trying to find a reply to Abby's forceful statement. "I am sorry, Abby. I was making assumptions. To be honest you make me feel inadequate. I have idled my life away, being as you say a meaningless adjunct to Charles and not a very good one at that so it would seem. You on the other hand have made a lot of your life and from what you say intend to do more. I can see that marriage to James, and living here would severely impair your ambitions." Gwen's apology and response hit Abby. Maybe she had gone too far.

"Gwen, I did not say that a marriage was out of the question. All I want is a bit of time to do what I think I have to. If James asks me at some time, it has to be because he wants me for his wife, and not because he has been pressured into it." There we go, thought Gwen. Nothing as simple as it being a sensible union, they wanted to be in love. What was the matter with young people these days she wondered? Wasn't friendship and common interests enough? Although this was tiresome, she had learned that Abby was not to be bullied. In fact she admired her for that. Abby was her own woman, strong and resourceful, more evidence that she was totally right for James.

She would have to be more devious though; her frontal attack had been rebuffed. "Abby, I believe I have to leave this to your best judgement. Please don't be upset if I seemed to be pushy, as you will probably realise I am not like other mothers. To tell the truth I am probably a very bad mother. But I do want the best for my son. I happen to think that you are the best for him, but if James ever gets up the gumption to ask you, it will be your decision. Now tell me about this plan of yours." Gwen knew that she would find this very boring. She had never given much consideration to the tenant farmers, their problems and struggles to make a living. That their rents allowed her to live in relative comfort was immaterial to her, and given little thought. Therefore she was hardly listening to Abby as she explained the plan.

"As I said it is not my plan, but I am getting involved if only to ensure that the organisation is correct." Abby went on to explain about the co-operative and how they could hopefully exploit a market for premium quality meat and poultry. Abby's description revealed a greater knowledge than Abby herself thought she had. Gwen gave every appearance of listening carefully. If later Abby would recall that Gwen had asked no questions she would realise that this topic had no interest for her. In fact Gwen was already thinking of another subterfuge to bring Abby's money into the family by marriage.

CHAPTER 31

Later that week Abby took a day off to drive over to Coolton Grange. She wanted to pick Richard's brains a little, and felt that time with Maggie would give her some relaxation.

Richard was a mine of information about many things, but what gave Abby great hope was his mention of refrigerated transport. The slaughter house in Paverton could do the transport, but at a huge cost as Abby would be using the lorry for a whole day with only a small load. Richard mentioned that he was using transport once a week, with a hired vehicle and an agency driver. There would be space on the lorry, for Abby to use, and it would be at proportional rates.

"The wagon is going anyway." He told her. "So what space you use will help with the hire and labour cost. Helps me, and helps you." His reaction when she told him that she applied to register Combe Lyney as a brand was very positive. "That's a damn good idea! Branding will help you establish your produce as upmarket, get you better prices."

Maggie couldn't wait to get Abby away from Richard and settle down with a drink and hear all her news. Abby immediately told her that James and she were not related.

"Oh well, we knew that anyway." Maggie sounded unsurprised. "It was confirmed when you and James went away for the weekend. James is far too honourable to do that if there was anything dodgy about it."

Abby laughed. "Well in that case there is nothing else to tell, you seem to know it all anyway." She paused for a moment. "How did you know?"

Maggie shrugged her shoulders. "I told you once before. You are of great interest to everyone around here. What you say and do is soon spread along the grapevine. But it is especially of interest when James Comberford, whose name has never been seriously linked to any girl around here, goes off with this newcomer. Eyebrows were raised, tongues wagged, and there was many an 'Ooh' and 'I see' spoken with a nod and a wink." She smiled broadly. "I won't ask if it was good, it obviously was, otherwise you wouldn't be sitting there with that beaming smile on your face."

Abby started laughing, and put her cup down in case she spilt it. "Let's just say we were very compatible, and leave it at that."

"So when's the wedding?"

"Don't you start. I have had enough of Gwen Comberford going on about that."

"I can imagine. She was on the phone to Richard, pumping him about your financial state. Richard, bless him, didn't say a thing. Be careful with Gwen, Abby, she sees you as the answer to her problems."

"You mean with James never having married."

"No. I mean that Gwen would like to spend her old age without money trouble. You, she thinks, could assist with that."

Abby was startled. "Are you sure?"

"I'm pretty sure. Richard thinks the same. Gwen has lived quite well, what with her friend in Berkshire. She had the insurance money when Charles died, but it's anybody's guess what she did with that, but I am certain that James saw none of it. I also understand that James gives her a very good allowance from his income. Richard reckons that is the reason he has never been able to improve the Estate. You know that some of the cottages need a lot of work on them. James cannot afford to do the work, so as compensation he has kept the rents low. Because the rental income is inadequate that means he can't live as he would want."

"That seems unlikely for Gwen." Abby mused. "She gives the impression of being quite organised…" She stopped as a sudden recall came to her, of Gwen wanting to employ a cook and gardener, and of James insisting that they could not afford that.

Maggie looked at her curiously. "What were you going to say?"

"I have remembered something Gwen said to James, it would appear that Gwen does not seem to have too much of a grasp of economic reality."

"You have to realise, Abby that Gwen was brought up in a society, where girls were not expected do anything except ride horses, decide on menus, look decorous and have babies, but never, ever to have any dealings with something as sordid as money. Men administering their estates, investments and property made the money, the ladies spent it. She moves in a world of good country houses, Dinners, horse racing, and limousines. She came from that world, and has never been able to leave it. She would have no more idea of budgeting than fly in the air, she was never taught how."

"That's positively Victorian. Surely those days are long gone."

Maggie had to smile. For all her success in this world, Abby was still somewhat naïve. "Oh it still exists. Times have changed but there are still families like that, and Gwen's family was one of them."

They were interrupted by Josie the help. "Lady Margaret, Sir Richard will be joining you soon. Will you want another pot of tea?"

"Good idea. Would you like another cup, Abby?" with Abby's affirmation Maggie turned to Josie.

"Yes please Josie, and if there is any of that cake left, will you bring that?" Josie nodded and left. Maggie mused somewhat.

"It must be you being here. She never calls me Lady Margaret as a rule. Makes us sound like Gwen Comberford's lot."

When Richard arrived, he had hardly sat down when Maggie announced. "Gwen Comberford is after Abby's money."

"Thought so!" He turned to Abby. "What do you think about that?"

For Abby the answer was simple. "Not a chance!"

"Good." Richard seemed pleased. Abby had been thinking about this for some time, and was quite aware that if, and at the moment it was only if, she and James got together, she would have to help him build the estate back to where it had once been. The news that James was contributing to Gwen's extravagant lifestyle was not entirely a revelation. But she would be damned if she was going to contribute as well.

"None of this comes totally as a surprise. I suspected that something was going on. Even I could work out that the rents for acreage let, should have given James a better standard of living than he has. It hasn't been spent on Lyney House, that's for certain, so unless he is an irresponsible gambler, money was going elsewhere." She paused and then said slowly. "I don't think that James is a gambler." This was said with a smile as her two companions looked ready to refute that idea. They subsided.

Richard had something to say. "Abby, from what I have learnt from talking to you, and what others have said, I am certain that you are astute. I am not going to ask questions of you, because I don't want to know, but I am sure that what capital you have is invested wisely. My advice, and I am sure you don't need it, is keep it well invested, and never let slip control of your accounts. For heaven's sake don't start subsidising Gwen, you will find that a drain that is never full. James likes you, because it is you, and for no other reason. He's too bloody upright to have any ulterior motive."

Abby smiled at them."I know." Then something that Richard had said stopped her smile. "What others."

"Pardon?"

"What others have talked about me?" She was a little angry. If others had been talking about her behind her back she was going to sort it out.

Richard relaxed. "The chap you sold your flat to, Bernard."

"Yes?"

"Well he is quite a high-flyer, and has dealings with a number of City Institutions, amongst them your ex-employer. When he mentioned that he was buying your flat the Chairman was interested and mentioned a couple of things. Bernard gathered that you were very well thought of, and sorely missed. He gave me to understand that the chap who allowed you to leave, has, as they put it, reached his ceiling." Abby's smile was involuntary, but spread slowly across her face.

"Oh good. Steve's been rumbled."

"Is that the chap who allowed you to leave?"

"He didn't have a choice. At least he thought he didn't. He dared not make waves as I let him believe that I was about to hit the Bank with the Tribunal. He would have been history after that, and he knew it, so he had little option." Maggie had listened and with women's intuition understood that Abby had left after scoring one for her side. One thing she didn't understand.

"What do they mean by reached his ceiling?"

Richard answered for Abby. "No chance of promotion, no chance of a better package, bonuses at the absolute minimum, and no point in complaining. If he doesn't like it, he can go and try elsewhere, if they will have him."

Abby nodded in agreement. "It's like a slow death in the City, where you are rated according to the last bonus you got. If your bonus doesn't increase or drops, then you are seen as un-bankable and on the way out."

Maggie shrugged her shoulders. "Sounds like boys competing to see how high they can piss up the wall if you ask me." Richard and Abby were in fits of laughter, with Abby a little shocked that Maggie would say such a thing in company.

Richard turned to Abby. "Now I have told you this, you aren't going to go back, are you?"

"It's nice to know that you are missed, but no, Richard, I am not going back. I have got my teeth into a new challenge here."

Later after Abby had left, Maggie returned to the subject of Abby's acumen. "She was good at her job, was she?"

Richard slowly nodded his head. "Yes. Bernard let on more than I mentioned to Abby. It would appear that as soon as she left her department suffered quite a reversal of fortune. The main board couldn't understand it, as this bloke Steve had always put in reports to the effect that he was responsible for the success. Consequently when bonuses were handed out he got the lion's share. As the profits tumbled they started asking questions of everyone in that department, and they realised that it had been Abby who did the business, and this man had been manipulating things to claim the glory. I imagine that Abby was aware of this, hence the outcome. I suspect she hit them for a tidy sum as well."

"She was that good then?"

"I would think she was, and even though she didn't get paid what she was due, I am sure she has got a tidy bit of capital tucked away, more than anyone would think. She's a cute girl and make no mistake."

"If James doesn't ask her to marry him then he needs his head examined."

"Ah, but will Abby say yes if he did

Maggie set her mind to this question. "I think she will, but it will be on her terms. I am glad we put her straight on Gwen though."

"Yes I am as well. Though having said that I somehow suspect that Abby would not be a fount of cash for Gwen anyway. She may help James with the estate, God knows it needs it, but as you say it will be on her terms, and I believe that it will benefit his tenants first. She said something when we were talking earlier, and she has this urge to do something to contribute to the community. This co-operative is a start. That will need some capital to get it going, and I think that Abby intends to provide it. James won't be disappointed about that, you know he always puts the tenants first."

Once Abby had got all her facts together, she wrote to Mr. Brasher informing him of the price per kilo they would ask for the supplies, and shortly after that the Club Chef, Tony Donaldson, arrived. Roger took him up to Paverton to see the Abattoir and cold storage facilities and he found nothing to fault there. He returned to the Combe Inn, and then upset Mary by wandering into her kitchen. He was forgiven only when he set to, helping Mary prepare lunch.

"I never feel comfortable out front," he explained, "here, I am in the world that I know." Mary was completely mollified when he showed her how to prepare a special Roux sauce with Herbs to go with chicken portions. The flavour was superb.

When he was introduced to Abby he took the opportunity to tackle her about the prices she was charging. They were in the Combe Inn at the time, and Abby had no wish to talk about business there, so she drove to the office at Lyney House. He followed in his own car. Abby made coffee and they sat down.

"What is the problem Mr. Donaldson?"

"It's the prices, Miss Tregonney. You're a little bit over the top on price." Abby had done her research well, and was not going to move on this at all. The price reflected the latest auction prices for the South East in general, with transport costs added, she knew that whilst a little higher than they would have paid before, it was still a fair price for what had to be described as superlative meats. She said as much. Donaldson was taken aback as Abby quoted confidently, without reference the latest prices for beef, lamb, pork and poultry.

"So you see Mr. Donaldson I cannot consider any easing of my prices, although I will track according to the market. You will have the best meats in London, in texture and taste. I am sure that would reflect very quickly on the reputation of the Club, and on your own skills as a Chef." Donaldson had to withdraw. He had already been told that by the chairman of the catering committee that the prices were acceptable, but he had hoped to impress his employers with a better deal.

The next thing he had to discuss with her was the quantities he would need on a weekly basis. Abby was taken aback by these. She had not realised that a Club could get through so much provender.

"How many covers to you serve each day?" she asked in astonishment.

"We would usually have one hundred and twenty to a hundred and fifty for Lunch, and probably about the same for Dinner. That's weekdays of course. At the weekends quite a lot less." Abby's mind worked furiously to understand this apparent anomaly. The answer when it came was simple. The Club members like the city traders were not there at the weekends.

"Would you want this amount delivered every week, or do you have storage sufficient for more than that?'

"I can at a push, store sufficient for three weeks, a little longer hanging has never harmed any meat."

Abby nodded. "So if we were to deliver roughly every ten days you would be happy with that?"

"That would be fine, unless I get an unexpected high demand. How quickly could you deliver in an emergency?"

Abby had no idea, and decided to bluff. "Within reason I would think that we could get most of your requirements within three days. But I will warn you that in that case I would probably be sending a refrigerated van half empty. An extra charge may have to be considered if it happened too frequently." He seemed unsure about that, no other suppliers had threatened an additional delivery charge for emergency supplies.

His next question was. "When can you commence deliveries?"

"I will contact you very soon about that. You are buying a Brand which can only be produced in this valley. I will not be getting carcasses from anywhere else to fill a gap. It takes months for the animals to grow, but we won't keep you waiting that long I can assure you. I would think sometime in the next four weeks should bring our initial delivery." He left with an impression of Abby as a clever business woman, a reputation which would eventually filter through to other Chefs and other Clubs. Abby felt rather pleased with herself. Having got into a new trade, she seemed to have held her own with someone who had been in it for years.

It seemed now that everyone was clamouring for her attention. George Walker caught her at the Inn. Abby knew he had phoned a couple of times, but had not found the time to get back to him as yet. "I could do with seeing you down at the house if possible. See where you will want the power points upstairs." Abby felt guilty, and shamefaced told him she would be there this afternoon if that suited him.

"That will be fine. I've got to look at another job later this morning, but I shall be there about two-thirty." Abby could not argue and agreed to meet him then. "Now I have got some catalogues here of Bathroom stuff. Would you like to look through them and let me know what you would like?" Abby flicked quickly through the first catalogue. "I'll let you know this afternoon, but from the look of it I shall be able to choose easily." That mollified George, rarely do clients make up their mind so quickly.

He then handed her a brown envelope. "We did agree stage payments, didn't we? That lists the work done so far. If you are happy with that, there is an interim invoice enclosed."

"That's fine, we did agree. I'll look through and let you have a cheque." A thought struck her. "Will there be room for all the bathroom fittings, I mean bath, Hand-basin and toilet?"

"Plenty of room. We can put you a separate shower in. Better than having one over the bath. Don't worry, there's plenty of room." Making a decision was not difficult for Abby, She had only turned four pages of the catalogue when she found exactly what she was looking for. An Edwardian style suite with a free-standing roll-top bath. The bath was cast iron, just what she wanted. She turned to the invoice. Mr. Walker had listed all the work done to date. As Abby had been down to the house so frequently, she could have written the list herself, his list coincided with her mental estimate exactly. She wrote a cheque to cover the invoice value. That was easy, the next item on her agenda was to arrange another meeting with the members of the co-operative. Armed with the knowledge of how much the Club would need, she now wanted to know if they could fulfil the demand. She would go and see Roger after settling with Mr. Walker.

George Walker was very pleased for the cheque, beaming at Abby as he said. "That's the fastest payment I have ever had. Pity there aren't more like you around."

Abby laughed. "Well I thought I would do it straight away, I know I have been difficult to contact lately. I have looked through the catalogue and decided that this suite," she pointed it out to him, "is exactly what I want." George read the specification and measurements, and looked worried.

"Just a moment Miss Tregonney." and he stalked off, taking his long tape out his pocket, humming all the while. After a few minutes he returned, and the worry was now deeply etched into his face.

"Sorry to say Miss, but as I thought, that bath won't go up the stairs."

"Oh no, are you sure?"

"Yes. I measured a couple of times just to be certain."

"Damn! I had set my heart on that as soon as I saw it."

"Well…" his voice tailed off.

Abby looked at him with a question on her face. "Did you think of something?" She asked, knowing that the answer would probably cost her a bit.

"I could do it, but the window will have to be taken out. It would go through there, no problem."

"Well that's what we'll do." George was humming again, and Abby waited for the inevitable.

"Cost a bit more. Have to be very careful taking it out, and it will all have to be set in properly after."

Abby was determined. "Do it that way, Mr. Walker." The humming didn't stop with her answer though. He walked away a couple of steps then turned back to her. Abby waited.

"About the windows." He said tentatively.

"Yes."

"If we are taking that one out, it seems silly to put the old frame back. Would you not like some new double glazed fitments? I could get some very good ones fitted. UPVC, sash windows like you have, couldn't really tell the difference, but you will never have to have them painted." Now Abby had to think. It would appear that the costs were going up all the time. She could see the benefit of having double glazed windows, and they would be sympathetic with the Victorian veranda.

"What do you think they will cost?"

Hum, hum again. "Roughly, I reckon you are looking at fifteen hundred."

"What? That's far less than I would have thought."

Mr. Walker looked a little sheepish. "I get a glazing company to do that work for me; they'll do the veranda as well. They charge me trade price, and that's what I will invoice you for."

"That's very generous of you, Mr. Walker. Why?"

"Miss Tregonney, there's a lot of work here. Keep me going for a few months, and you pay promptly. I will make a good profit out of you anyway, so no point in being greedy." What he didn't say was that he had heard the gossip around here about this lady and Mr. Comberford and thought that there was a good chance that he would get work on Lyney House at some time. Keep Miss Tregonney sweet, he thought.

Abby had no hesitation now. She smiled. "Let's do that."

***

Abby was happy as she mentally ticked off the things she had to do. She felt worthwhile again. The next most important job was to meet the co-operative. She had calculated roughly what turnover the Club could provide, and its value. It was actually worth more than she originally thought, not understanding how many meals they would serve, that surprised her. She drove up to Lyney House where she saw both Gwen's Jaguar, and James' Land-Rover. Abby was piqued, there were things that she should have noticed, but it was only now, after talking with Richard and Maggie, that the significance of the two cars became clear. James drove around in a battered old Land-Rover. Gwen enjoyed the comfort and luxury of a relatively new, top of the range Jaguar. She drove round the stable yard without announcing her presence. Her second line had been connected so she was straight onto the internet to check the latest prices.

She was working on her ideas for building the business when James put his head round the door. "Hey Miss Wheeler-Dealer, Tea and cake is on the table. Mother says to come and join us." Abby grinned. "Who made the cake?'

"Who else, but this chief cook and bottle washer that you see before you."

"I'm on my way. Before you go, James. There is something I would like to run past you." He entered the office and waited. Abby got out the list of requirements for the Club. Walking round the desk, she held her face up for a kiss. Only after that greeting would she get to the nub of her query.
"Look at this list; do you think this is possible?"

He scanned the list quickly. "Every week?"

"No, about every ten days."

"The Lamb and Pork, they could certainly do, but the beef I reckon will be at a push."

Abby then showed him the price per kilogram she had agreed.

"Good grief! That's good. A fair increase on what they get now."

"Yes, well don't forget we have to pay for transport. I have costed in the prices the abattoir quoted me, but Richard has offered me a deal sharing his transport. That will ease the burden." She put the papers back in the file, and smiled up at James. "Lead me to the tea please, James."

Gwen was as friendly as ever. "Sit down Abby, the tea's freshly made; I'll pour you a cup. James tells me you have become very busy of late, and you haven't been to see me. It won't do you know, you have to relax sometime."

"Sorry Gwen. There is a lot to do at the moment; hopefully soon I will have more time."

"How's your little house getting along?" Gwen asked sweetly, hoping that Abby would make the comparison with Lyney House. Now Abby understood Gwen's character and her devious mind, the comment did not upset her, and she determined to serve like for like.

"Oh there's such a lot of work still to be done. Every time I go down there Mr. Walker seems to coax me into spending more money. The bathroom suite I chose will not go up the stairs, so it has to go through the window, and then I end up agreeing to replace all the windows with UPVC double glazing." Gwen would have loved to ask how much money Abby was spending, but her upbringing and dignity would not allow. Instead she murmured, "I see." Abby had mentioned the money as she was aware of Gwen's pre-occupation with wealth.

"Oh well, I am sure you will be quite comfortable in your cottage, and it will have been worth it." James was aware that something was going on, but for the life of him he could not fathom what. He invited Abby to taste some his cake.

"Yes please, James." Abby was happy to move away from the sparring with Gwen. With her mouth full of cake it absolved her from making a reply to Gwen's last sally. With her mouth finally empty of the delicious cake she turned to James.

"That cake is wonderful, full marks, James. Now I have to have a meeting of the members of the co-operative. Would you have any objection if we had it in the Estate office?"

"None at all, it's your office now." Gwen wasn't too happy about this. Even though it wasn't actually in the house, it was close enough, and it rankled, having the people she thought of as inferior class in her home.

"Will there be enough room?" She queried, hoping that James would say no. James had little doubt.

"I would think so; most of them seemed to crowd in on Quarter day when father was alive."

Abby agreed. "Yes, I shall push the desk back against the wall; I think that will give us enough room for all the chairs." For Gwen the world had gone mad. They were going to be invited to sit as well. The next day she was gone again, not wishing to be there when all these farmers came to her house, and sat down!

The meeting was quite lively. Abby, with James' help had pushed the big desk against the wall, so that she would be sitting with them rather than addressing them from behind the desk. Geoff Corliss came a little early so that he could discuss with Abby how he could be part of the co-operative. He seemed pleased with her answers. With all in attendance she outlined her proposals, once more. Then asked. "You have all had time to think about it. Later you will have the chance to air any problems. In the meantime these are the requirements that the Club has." She handed round copies of the list to everyone. "And these are the prices they will pay." Again copies were handed round. Even Nat was disposed to lighten his countenance when he saw these. Abby continued.

"But you will not get those prices. The co-operative will buy from you at your normal local price per kilo deadweight."

Harry was immediately on the attack. "But that's not right!"

Abby calmed him down. "You will all trade at present prices. That means that Mr. Stone will sell yearlings as present, you Roger, Harry, Nat and Geoff, will sell to the co-op at existing rates. The co-op will sell to new customers at these higher prices. There will be a full accounting kept, and every six months, all members of the co-op; and that means all of you; will receive a dividend based on the difference, less operating expenses. The dividend will be based upon the number of your stock which is moved this way. We can use the animal's passport as a way of checking what has been sold through the co-op, and pay dividends accordingly. Mr. Stone will receive his dividend based upon the number of yearlings sold on for fattening which pass through the co-ops system. This is a Partnership, so you are still self-employed and dividends have to be declared as earnings. This system may not be perfect. It may well be that we have to fine tune it later. What we have is basically a marketing arrangement; in the future we can expand it to cover purchases of feed etc. to get better deals. If it all works well, and we get more customers it may be necessary to get our own cold-store and transport, but that is a long way in the future. Let's start small and see how it goes."

Questions then came fast and furious, and Abby was able to answer most of them to the general satisfaction. She then went on to ask her big question. "You have seen the list of requirements. Can this be done?" Abby did not get an immediate answer. Heads were put together as farmers who are notoriously secretive suddenly found that they had to reveal facts to their neighbours. Sam, who had listened and watched quietly, eventually stopped all the discussion by answering the question. "Yes, Abby it can be done. There's enough finished stock in this valley, if you include Bullocks, Beeflings and Baby Beef to see us through. It may become a problem if there are other outlets taking similar quantities, so it may be an idea if Abe gets his Bull to run with the cows a little more." Abe was quite happy and therefore laughed at Sam's suggestion. Abby had resolved all his doubts, as he would share equally with the others the profit based upon what was sold on to the co-op.

He did have one question which the others seemed to have overlooked. "Now tell me, Miss Abby. This all seems a very good thing for us, but I would imagine that it is going to need some capital to set it up. Where's that money going to come from?" There was a sudden silence. Taking profit from this new deal was good, but finding money to start the ball rolling was not anticipated.

Abby was not surprised that it would be Abe who asked this question. "Well so far it hasn't cost much at all. Mr. James will not charge the co-op for the use of this office, as he believes this venture will be good for all. The capital as such is working capital, to pay bills for slaughter, storage and transport. I don't think it right either, for you having sold to the co-op to have to wait for your money. If you will allow me, I shall cover the initial expenses myself, and recover on a six month basis over time." The silence was total. Harry and Nat were now feeling very guilty. It was they who had pressed Abby to do this, but they hadn't expected her to have to fund the thing as well.

Harry cleared his throat. "Miss Abby, I don't know what to say. This is very good of you, but I don't think it right that you should have to put money into it. Perhaps it will be best if we drop the whole idea. We managed before, and will go on managing." There was a general agreement amongst them all. This was too much to ask.

Abby held up her hands. "Harry, I appreciate your sentiment, but let me say this. Ever since I arrived here, I have been given help without stint. I am making this valley my home, but I have to do something to earn my place in your community. This is the way I can give something back to all of you, who have made me welcome here, and shown me friendship."

Abe Stone was moved by these words. "Miss Abby this is an example of the best Christian attitude." He clasped his hands together in a gesture of worship. "I shall pray to the Lord, and give thanks to Him for sending you amongst us. I will say one thing though. The Lord approves of Labour, and also approves of the Labourer being worthy of his hire. We, who will benefit from this work, should forgo part of our profit in order that you should receive your entitlement." There were nods and words of agreement from all of them. Abby kept the smile off her face with difficulty. This was something she had thought about, but had not found a way of implementing. Abe Stone had neatly resolved her problem. Before the meeting descended into too much sentimentality, Abby wanted to move on.

"I have registered a Brand for all products marketed through the co-op. It is simply Combe Lyney Produce. I shall market Combe Lyney products as a superior quality in all respects, and worthy of a premium price."

"Does this mean that we can all use the Brand for everything we sell?" This was Harry, looking for an edge again.

"No, only those products sold through the co-op can use the brand. After all the meats can be traced back through the passports and Slap marks. For our own reputation we have to be absolutely sure of the product we sell." Abby's researches were paying off now. Harry had not been too certain that Abby would know about Slap marks, the edible dye numbering applied to a carcass to identify the source. "I shall arrange for each carcass to bear the Brand name as well." Harry to do him credit smiled now. He had been trumped.

The meeting had been going on for two hours now, and so Abby asked if there was any other business. There was none. Abby did have other business though. "Before you go, I want you to read and understand this agreement." She handed everyone a copy. "This is the partnership agreement, so before you sign it, you must understand what it entails. Take it away with you and give it consideration. Any problems, phone me, any misgivings, phone me, anything you don't understand, phone me." Taking their copies they split up to go their own ways. Thanking Abby on the way out for all her hard work, and for what she was going to do for them. Abe promised to pray for her, and Nat said how right he had been to suggest she should run the enterprise.

She escaped to the house, and made herself some coffee, realising as she did so, that she ought to have offered them some refreshment.

A mental note was made to get a kettle and mugs in for the office. James' arrival was not altogether unexpected.

"I thought you would be around once the meeting was over." She welcomed him. He bent over and kissed her.

"How did it go?"

"It went well. I am surprised though that I didn't get a rougher time from them. I mean some of the conditions could have ruffled a few feathers."

"I'm not surprised at all. They are somewhat in awe of you."

"Why?"

"Well you have come here with this mysterious background. Working in the City. That means you understand business and finance. If you say this is how it should be done, they are not going to argue. They are farmers. The closest they ever get to high finance is calculating the income for the milk," He sat down with a coffee for himself. "I am glad mother has gone. Did she upset you?"

Abby shook her head. "No. I don't think she can understand why I am settling into the valley, when she can't wait to get away." Abby waited to see if that explanation would suffice. It obviously did as James then said.

"Would you like to come up for a meal on Saturday?"

"Are we talking Lunch or Dinner?"

"We are talking Dinner." He agreed.

"Is breakfast included?" Abby asked.

"What do you like for breakfast?" He answered her question.

"I accept. Do I have to dress?" Abby immediately noticed the gleam in James' eyes and waited for the glib remark.

"Now that you mention it," his voice tailed off, and a wicked smile creased his lips. Abby smiled too.

"Another cold shower?" She asked.

"In all probability, at least once a day until Saturday." The gleam was still in his eye. "Then you can be as outrageous as you wish."

"Well I hope it isn't too cold then."

Abby was going to get back to her office, and then remembered something Sam had mentioned. "James. What is a Beefling and a Baby Beef?"

"What brought that up?"

"Sam did. He was reassuring me that we could cope with the order from the Club."

"Oh I see. Well a Beefling is a young beast usually about eighteen months old. It won't have reached its full weight, but is still viable for slaughter. That's what we call them here, but it can vary around the country and other parts of the world."

"I see. And a Baby Beef?"

"That's a beast which is a bit younger. They are quite light, but as the meat is very tender, it makes up in value what it loses in weight. Why didn't you ask Sam?"

Abby looked a little sheepish. "Well I didn't want Harry to realise that I hadn't gone too deep with my research. I find him easier to handle, when he thinks I know more than I actually do."

James was grinning as she said this. "You're learning, Miss Tregonney you're learning."

Abby gave him a quick kiss as she left. "Perhaps I will learn some more this weekend?" Her eyes twinkled, and a naughty smile hovered around her lips. James for once was stuck for words.

CHAPTER 32

The Inn that evening was buzzing with all of the co-op members, except of course Abe Stone, discussing the terms of the agreement. Sam who had declared early that as he was no longer the tenant of Gallow farm, and would therefore have no interest, nonetheless found himself in the position of mediator, helping to explain clauses, and soothing tempers when arguments broke out over the meaning of the clauses. Abby watched from the bar, chatting with Mary, but keeping an ear on the conversation to see which way the wind was blowing. Harry detached from the group and approached her. Abby was expecting a complaint, and was surprised when he held out to her some rolls of cine film. "I don't know if these will be of any interest to you, Miss Abby. But they were taken in nineteen sixty four. We used to have a Fete every year, and these were taken then. To be honest I reckon they will have perished by now, and for the life of me I can't find the projector, so I've no idea if they are any good. You may be able to get one though. They are Super Eight." Sam joined them.

Abby looked closely at the rolls. "I doubt that I could get hold of a projector, that's if they still make them? But any good photographic shop will be able to transfer them onto a DVD. I'll have to go to Taunton I think though. Is there anything on them of interest to you Harry?" Harry shook his head.

"No, not to Harry." Sam remarked. "But I think there will something of interest to you, Abby." Abby looked up in surprise as Sam went on. "If my memory is correct your Mum will be in some of the shots, and even possibly your grandfather." Abby was definitely interested.

"I thought I had got rid of them years ago," said Harry apologetically, "I was turning out some cupboards yesterday and found them. Meant to give them to you this afternoon." Abby's smile was all the thanks he needed.

Harry turned the conversation then to the co-op. "Miss Abby, I feel really bad about getting you involved, especially as it is going to be you who actually funds the thing. It doesn't seem right to me."

Abby put her hand on his arm. "Harry. I meant what I said this morning. Just think of all the things you and Sam have done for me. All that work putting a fence in, and getting the Goods shed cleared out. I can't let that go by without giving something back. Sam said to me once that that is how it is here. A job needs to be done and everyone will help. Well this is a job that needs to be done, and I am determined that I will help. Anyway I will get the capital back once it is up and running, so don't give it anymore thought." She waited for argument but none came, Sam and Harry both nodding heads slowly as they thought about that.

Abby diverted away from what was obviously an embarrassing topic for Harry. "How is it going over there? Is the Agreement satisfactory? It can be modified as time goes on, if it doesn't suit the changing circumstances."

Sam answered. "I think that it's alright. The problem is that Farmers are not used to co-operating, and they are loathe to give up their independence. I have explained that they are still their own men, but the more they support the co-op, the more they will make out of it."

A little later Abby made herself scarce, as the discussion between Harry, Roger, Nat, and Geoff Corliss was obviously going on far into the night. She retired to her room and picked up one of the books she had bought; it concerned the run-down and closure of many of the branch lines.

Thomas Tregonney

The station that Thomas had joined all those years ago was now reduced to a simple, single line through the platform. The signal box had been closed last year, with Reg Purvess transferred away to another box near Exeter. The points, sidings, and signals that it had controlled had been isolated and clipped, leaving a desert of rusting rails and weed, marooning the goods shed in the process. Gone too were the steam engines, that had left a reminder of themselves every time they called at the station with a heady smell of steam, hot oil and sulphur. Now a green, two coach diesel unit growled its way up and down the line, the service calling at inconvenient times so that even the last few regular passengers had given up and got their own transport. The driver a young man; who years ago would still be cleaning Locos, not driving one; slouched casually, Cap-less in his cab, not concerned at all if the train was running empty or early or late. The guards were still Metcalfe and Bird, their job hadn't changed, but their demeanour had. They were aware, as Thomas that time was running out. The railway that they knew and took pride in was vanishing.

Thomas had officially retired in the April of this year. No replacement was appointed, so he stayed on, in the house and at the station apparently rent free, but also wage free, apart from the measly pension that his years of service had brought. It was odd though, that British Railways never followed with notice to quit the house. He presented himself just as always, Frock coat, wing collar with neatly knotted black tie, and the cap. The service was so sparse that he had plenty of time on his hands to do the jobs he would once have delegated to Porters. He weeded the flower beds, polished the windows, doors and furniture, and kept the platform edge white as always. At the back of his mind was the horrifying thought that perhaps someday someone in authority would enquire into the situation, and give him his marching orders. Until that happened Thomas would maintain the standards, even though others appeared to have little time for them.

The train approached the crossing. The gates were never closed against the railway these days, yet still the horns sounded, the two tones jarring unpleasantly on his ears as he waited to meet the service. A dirty, blue-grey miasma hovered over the coaches, vanishing as the motors were shut down to coast into the platform. Thomas stepped forward to stand where the Guards compartment should stop, but the driver overran, so he had to walk to meet Mr. Metcalf the guard. As ever their greeting was correct. "Good Morning, Mr. Metcalf."

"Good Morning, Mr. Tregonney." They stood together on the platform awaiting any sign of movement that could indicate a passenger. There was none. Thomas consulted his watch.

"You are early. I shall have to hold you for three minutes."

Metcalf shrugged his shoulders. "It's that young idiot who's driving. Had the throttle wide open all the way up from the Junction. He ignores speed limits for turn-outs and curves. Thank heaven I had something to cling onto. It's good to stand here on something that isn't rocking and rolling all over the place. It's easy for him. He just sits there and pulls the lever a bit more." There was a hint of disgust in his voice Thomas was nodding and Metcalfe carried on. "No wonder the old steam drivers thought of themselves as something special." He stopped and thought for a moment. Then looked enquiringly at Thomas "Aren't you supposed to be retired now?" In all the years he had called at Combe Lyney, he had never dared to ask a personal question of Thomas.

He was therefore surprised when Thomas answered him. "Well they wrote and told me so, but as there doesn't seem to be any intention of sending a new stationmaster I am keeping things going until someone does arrive."

Metcalf shook his head. "They don't have stationmasters now. They are called Station Managers, and there is one who is supposed to look after all the stations from Tiverton to Barnstaple. I've never seen him, so I am not surprised you haven't. Anyway the word is that they are going to close this line and the Devon and Somerset." Railwaymen were if nothing else locked in the past, and Metcalf used the name of the line from Taunton to Barnstaple as it was described when originally planned and built. Thomas didn't need to ask, as habitually he used the same description.

He looked at his watch again. "Time to be away." The guard

consulted his watch, and placed his whistle between his lips at the same time unfurling his green flag. He blew one short blast and displayed the green. The driver did nothing, just leaned out of his window and looked back.

Metcalf shrugged his shoulders. "I forgot, they don't show the flag now, I have to use the buzzer." He stepped back into his compartment, and pressed the button situated just over his door twice. The driver acknowledged the signal by repeating it. The engines surged and clouds of blue smoke hurled up from the exhausts, as the train got under way. The acrid exhaust smoke curled and billowed in its wake. It also got into Thomas's eyes and throat, and he coughed once or twice. No wonder people didn't like to travel in those things, he thought, that stuff would poison them.

As he turned away, he noticed the dishevelled figure standing by the goods shed. Thomas walked towards the end of the platform and called across to the figure. "Good morning, Woody."

Woody walked over the jungle of ballast and weeds towards the platform. "Good morning Mr. Tregonney. I trust you are well." The well modulated tones had no surprise for Thomas. Over the years the two had exchanged the time of day on many occasions, and respect had built between them. Whilst strange on the surface it sprang from the isolation that each experienced, albeit that one had chosen isolation, and the other had it imposed upon him.

"I am quite well, thank you, Woody. I am glad to see you today. Please don't take offence but I have a uniform that does not suit me. It's good quality worsted. Would you accept it?"

Woody smiled wryly. "In my position, Mr. Tregonney, taking offence is an emotion wasted. I would be grateful. As you see, my present ensemble has lost the ability to keep the chill wind at bay."

"Come down to the house, if you will. I shall fetch it for you." They made their respective journeys to the house. Thomas went immediately to the back room where the British Railways uniform hung on a hanger, it had never been worn, and although by now over twenty years old was pristine although it bore, generously, the scent of mothballs. Woody had not entered the house, so Thomas took the suit out to him. "I am sorry that it smells so much of mothballs." He apologised.

Woody demurred. "A very sensible precaution, and out in the woods there is no-one to complain, mind you, the deer and rabbits will smell me coming, at least until it has aired through. I am most exceedingly grateful, thank you." He examined the cloth. "This is a fine suit, it will last well. It looks unworn though, are you sure you can let it go?"

"It has never been worn. I have always been much happier with these." He indicated the frock coat he wore. "It reminds me of the better times, when we ran a proper railway." He paused. "I was just going to make myself a cup of tea. Would you join me?"

"I am not keeping you from your duties?"

Thomas, sadly, shook his head. "There are so few trains now that I have little to do. I am in fact officially retired, but as they haven't appointed a new stationmaster, I carry on for the while." Woody had suspected that this upright man would be retired. Thomas went to put the kettle on the hob. Whilst he waited Woody looked around. "Do you take sugar?"

"No thank you, Mr. Tregonney." Woody laughed. "Sugar is one of life's toothsome pleasures I have learned to live without." He didn't add that tea was also one of those pleasures. Thomas brought out the steaming cups.

"Perhaps you would like to sit inside?"

"It's a fine day. Having Tea is an occasion for me, it wouldn't do to take too much enjoyment all at the same time." He sipped carefully at the hot liquid. "I do miss your trains. It was delightful to see those pretty green engines and the chocolate and cream coaches passing through the valley. They somehow completed this picture of sylvan content."

Thomas had joined the Great Western Railway when he was fourteen, so his education had been limited to just reading, writing and arithmetic, at which he achieved competently. He had never heard the word sylvan before, but agreed with Woody nonetheless. "Yes. The railway never seemed out of place then. We offered services to our customers, and fitted in. It was part of the community, but never intrusive."

Woody mused. "Tell me if you know. What will happen now?"

"I have nothing official, but from what I can gather the railway will be closed down."

"That is ridiculous. Why?" Thomas shrugged his shoulders.

"I understand that they intend to close the line from Taunton to Barnstaple. That means that this line will close as well. Someone in London has decided that they aren't necessary anymore." Thomas took the empty cups and went to rinse them under the tap. He came out and closed the door. Woody folded his new suit over his arm and prepared to vanish once more into the greenwood. As he walked away he turned back for a moment.

"I notice that your coal supply is low. When will you get more?"

Thomas looked unhappily at the small stock. "I used to get supplies allowed out of the station requisition. There hasn't been any for a few months. But as officially I have quit the house, I am not surprised. I doubt that there will be any more."

"Will your stove burn wood?"

Thomas had never considered the question, and had to give it a few moments thought. "Probably. It will burn much the same way I would imagine."

"Leave it with me, Mr. Tregonney. I will find some fallen branches for you. It will keep you going for a while."

"That's very kind of you, Woody. I shall pay you of course."

"You will not! A good service," he indicated the suit. "Deserves one in return." He didn't say that money was of very little use to him.

Thomas almost smiled for a moment. "Then when you bring the wood, you will join me in another cup of tea?"

"That will be a pleasure. Good day to you, Mr. Tregonney."

***

As he walked away, making for Huish Coppice, Woody was much troubled. He wanted to tell this lonely man, who had shown him kindness, what he knew about his daughter, but he could not. Marion had made him agree to say nothing to anyone about what he had seen. A promise was a promise. He had broken a promise years ago, and as a result was spending his life as a hermit, the only way to separate himself from the shame he had brought on his family. This was not too much to endure compared with the lady to whom he had made that broken promise. She was the one who would have spent a life of total misery, probably hating him every day of her existence. Woody would not ever break a promise again, and the assurance given to Marion he would keep safe, as long as she was alive. He hoped that Marion, wherever she was, was building a good life and that she had recovered from the shame of that day.

Thomas returned to his self imposed duties. The return service from Paverton would be here soon. This perhaps would be carrying passengers, as a few would be bound for Market Day in South Molton. He busied himself running a damp cloth over the windows of the station building. He had done this only two days before, so it was hardly necessary, but he would keep busy. It surprised him that they didn't get as dirty as before. He would never think the thought that this was because the Diesel trains were cleaner than the Steam engines.

The service had come and gone, there would not be another one for three hours, so he sat at his desk and wrote up his journal. This would occupy his time well. The ornate script he had learned as a small boy took time to form. In addition he had to give thought to the instances that should rightly be put in the journal. Few would arise with just one train every two to three hours. What he did put in was the need to increase the service early morning and evening, when he was certain that passengers would present themselves. This same entry had been written on many of the pages. He had written memorandums to District Office on this subject on numerous occasions. At first they thanked him for his observations, later they just ignored him. He had the sense not to write since his official retirement. It was best if they were unaware of his continued occupation of the station and house.

His days passed slowly, there was little to do. A few days after he had seen Woody, he was pleased to see him approach coming up from the direction of the old Mill Lane. He carried a large sack slung over his shoulder. Thomas walked to meet him, as Woody made directly for the house.

"Good Morning Mr. Tregonney. I have got some firewood here for you."

"Good Morning Woody, that's extremely kind of you. You must come in and sit down for a while, that sack looks like quite a load. I'll make some tea."

"Well, I don't know if that would be appropriate, Mr. Tregonney."

"Nonsense, Man. Come in, I insist." Woody nodded his thanks, and after putting the sack down outside the door, followed Thomas indoors. He looked around strangely, almost fearfully. Thomas noted his apprehension and told him to make himself comfortable.

"I find it difficult, Mr. Tregonney; it is many years since I have been in a house. To you it is normal, but to me it is quite strange, almost discomforting." He felt the presence of Marion there. It was the way that items were placed, not regimented as a man would, but with an eye to turning everyday things into decoration as a woman would do. Thomas had never changed anything, sticking resolutely to Marion's placement, so that if she walked through the door tomorrow, she would feel at home immediately.

"I'll make the tea, and we will go and sit outside if that will make you feel more at ease."

Woody nodded. "I believe it will."

Thomas made the tea, and picked up one of the chairs. "Here, at least you can have the sit down I promised."

Woody smiled and took another chair. "This will be as comfortable as any I have used." Outside it
was cool but sunny. The coolness of the air bothered neither of them, indeed it would have to be close to freezing, before Thomas, used to standing on his platform in all weathers, would complain that it was a little chilly. Woody from years of living out in wind, rain, and even on occasion's snow, had developed an immunity to all weathers. His tattered rags in multiple layers acted as insulation, keeping him cool in summer and warm in winter. "Are you amenable to Rabbit?" Woody enquired of Thomas.

"Yes I am." Replied Thomas. "It was almost the only meat we had on the table when I grew up. So yes I am quite happy to eat rabbit. I believe the Gangers would trap them along the line, and sometimes, presumably when they had more than they needed, would leave a rabbit hanging on the porch. Marion learned to make a very tasty stew. Why do you ask?"

"I dine on rabbit frequently." Woody told him. "Like your gangers my traps are giving me more than I can use. I just wondered if you would accept one from time to time." Thomas hated accepting anything that he could class as charity, yet his pension was only a few pounds a week, and did not stretch to flesh every day. He collected his pension, travelling up the line to Paverton once a week to get to the Post office there. The Guards said little when he would climb into their compartment for the journey. He should not have taken advantage of free travel now, but why would they quibble. Their loyalty to the railway had vanished when they learned that they would be redundant within a few months anyway, so if Thomas took a free ride what did it matter? When Reg Purvess had left with the closure of the Signal box, Thomas had taken over the vegetable garden that Reg had cultivated along the line side. Reg had grown potatoes, cabbages, onions, and carrots, and kept himself, and Thomas, quite well supplied. Now Thomas used the plot to eke out his meagre pension. Grudgingly, he knew he would accept Woody's offer. But decided that he would return the favour.

"That would be most kind of you. I have been growing a few vegetables just beyond the site of the old signal box. There is a small surplus. I would be pleased in turn, if you would accept some. I don't seem to have the knack with Onions though Reg grew some beauties. Potatoes and Carrots do well, though, and Cabbage."

"Have you ever tried wild Garlic?" Asked Woody, "not as strong as the cultivated Garlic, but a very acceptable substitute for Onion."

Thomas had no idea what Garlic tasted like. His simple life style and budget had never run to what he would have described as Exotic foods. "Does it grow round here?" He asked somewhat surprised.

"Oh yes. I'll drop some by for you with the rabbit."

Thomas nodded and then a gave an almost invisible smile. "I'll put some vegetables by for you."

Woody did smile. "That is most uncommonly kind of you Mr. Tregonney."

***

Over the next few weeks Woody would drop by from time to time. Bringing wood to add to the pile, rabbits, and wild garlic. Thomas even if he didn't see Woody; and few did see Woody unless he wanted to be seen; would leave out a string bag containing a few vegetables. The truth was that his vegetable garden did not produce enough for a surplus, but Thomas could not accept gifts from Woody without returning the favour. Their relationship could not be called friendship. Thomas did not understand that concept, and Woody had for years maintained an anonymity that suited him, and prevented questions. He burned to disclose to Thomas the facts of Marion's disappearance, but had to remain silent. At the moments when he may have said something he forced himself to think of his past broken word, and that gave him the strength to keep the promise that Marion had begged of him.

It had been a habit in the past for Thomas, to walk down to the Combe Inn two or three times a week. Here he would take a simple Lunch; usually some bread and cheese; and a pint of Mild. Now his budget would not allow too many visits, but those few visits he did make were more relaxing as there were no longer any station porters to worry about. He would not accept the offer of a refill from any, knowing that he could not afford to return the courtesy, yet managed some conversation with Sam Perry and particularly Alfred Carter whose daughter had married Reg Purvess. He had always thought of Reg Purvess with respect, and was pleased to learn of him from Alfred's gossip. The times when he would see Woody, or felt he could afford a drink at the Combe became oases of small pleasure to him, interrupting as they did the idleness of his days, because the service was becoming even more sparse as the year wore on. Idleness was something that he had rarely experienced and he could not enjoy such times, feeling guilty that he was not occupied. There was a constant worry that one day someone from British Rail would arrive to demand that he quit the Station House. He didn't know what he would do then as he had absolutely nowhere to go. If he had realised that B.R. now classified Combe Lyney station as an un-staffed Halt he would have been easier in his mind. But such was the inefficient bureaucracy of the nationalised railway that no one had thought to place a sign on the station advising that detail.

It came as a terrible shock when he returned from the Combe Inn one day and found that in his absence a notice had been posted on the board at the front of the station announcing the closure of the line in that October. He had been expecting something to happen, even the most un-learned man would realise that the line could not exist with so little pat-ronage, yet he felt bitterness that they could throw away his life's work so contemptuously. Angrily he tore the poster down, scrunching it into a little ball and tossing it away. Anger was not an emotion that came to Thomas easily. Later, when he calmed down, he found the poster in the bushes where it had landed from his wild throw, and having straightened is as best he could, pinned it back up. Now his fate was decided. They would take up the rails, and level the site, including the house. Thomas was in complete despair that evening and for many days to come. He would have nowhere to live, and the pension was insufficient to rent even a simple cottage or room. The extent of his despair was demonstrat-ed by his not meeting trains as punctiliously as he once did. The Guards, Metcalfe and Bird were surprised but could not investigate, as any such enquiry would lead to the discovery of Thomas's unauthorised occupa-tion of the house.

Thus the line that had served the valley and the occupations of those who served the line gradually drew to their close.

CHAPTER 33

When Mavis and Sam came into the Combe that Saturday night, Mavis immediately looked around for Abby. She looked enquiringly at Mary, who had a very smug look. "Abby?" she asked Mary.

"Gone up to the House."

"Will she be back a bit later?"

"Don't think so," replied Mary, "had an overnight case with her."

"Oh!" In that exclamation, Mavis had invested more meaning than a sentence fifty words long could have described. Mary nodded as if she had understood every word of that sentence. Sam looked from one to the other, and that look carried a warning that neither of the women could mistake.

"That's nice." Mavis dared not say anything more

***

Abby was sitting down to a Lasagne that looked and smelt superb. She held a glass of Valpolicella and waited for James to sit down. He wiped the sweat from his brow, washed his hands and sat. He grinned at her. "This is going to be the best meal I have had in ages."

"Oh, boasting are we? Shouldn't you await my judgement before you can say that?" Abby protested.

"Doesn't matter what the food tastes like. You are sitting opposite me, and that would make any meal exquisite." Abby blushed. James did not say this with his usual flippant tone. He was quite serious, and she felt warmth spread though her body.

She lifted her glass to him. "Food and Love. What more could a girl want." She hesitated a moment. "Except possibly some Parmesan, if you have any?"

James looked over the table with horror. "I thought I put some out." He dashed off and came back with the packet. "I meant to put it into a dish. I am sorry."

"Doesn't matter, James. Everything else is right. I would hate to think that you are completely perfect. Wouldn't do at all." James had that lascivious look on his face.

"No not perfect, in fact I can be very bad at times."

"Oh good. I feel like being very bad myself tonight."

The Lasagne was very good, the wine was very good, and the company was also very good. Relaxed and with her appetite satiated, Abby sat back nursing her glass, and anticipated the rest of the evening with excitement. James suggested a tour of the house, as Abby had never before ventured further than the ground floor. They took their glasses and James picked up the bottle of wine. The staircase creaked as they went up, the wide steps allowing them to walk side by side. She toured the first floor with interest, James apologising for one or two of the rooms, which to all intents and purposes did not seem to have been used for years. At one end of the upstairs hall was another staircase, which James explained led down directly to the kitchen. Opposite another ascended towards the second floor, a steeper, less generous in width staircase. Uncarpeted their footsteps on this stair sounded loudly and hollow. The rooms up here had angled ceilings as the gables of the roof encroached on them. They were smaller and utilitarian, with just one toilet and bathroom between the four bedrooms. The servants; and these rooms had obviously been staff quarters; had been accommodated in the most utilitarian circumstances.

Her tension mounted as she realised that James was saving his bedroom until last, knowing that once they reached there, they would not be leaving until the morning. They went back down to the first floor and finally he opened the last door. She was surprised, having expected a very masculine room. Instead she walked into a well appointed room, shades of lemon and cream gave a warm and peaceful atmosphere, whilst the furniture of naturally stained Pine was a good classic but not antique style. A large two seat settee and a club chair, gave her the impression that James would spend quite a lot of time here. The double bed was Pine, with a simple slatted headboard against which the pillows rested. She stood taking this in, when James stepping up behind her wrapped his arms around her, his hands neatly cupping her breasts. Her wiggle let him know that this was encouraged, and he adroitly unbuttoned her blouse, and slid his right hand in, surprised that he was suddenly touching bare skin.

"Abby, my Darling, you seem to have forgotten something." She nodded; her eyes closed as he caressed her.

"Yes you seemed to have a problem with my bra clasp in Torquay so I thought I would save you the problem." She turned in his arms and smiled up at him. "Aren't I a thoughtful girl?"

"Totally." He murmured as his lips descended to hers.

Although Abby no longer felt that she had to keep her relationship with James a secret, she hadn't counted on her movements being discussed throughout the valley. Abby had not thought of Lizzie's contribution to the local news. Lizzie had come up to Lyney House early to feed and muck out the horses, and was surprised to see Abby's car at the front. It was covered in dew, so had not been used since the day before. At first she imagined that James and Abby were out somewhere in his Land Rover, but upon seeing that in the yard, also covered in dew, her over active imagination went into overdrive and a little smile came to her lips. Later that day the gossip was disseminated to whoever she met. Lizzie was naturally friendly, and having grown up in the valley knew everyone. Lizzie was also an incorrigible gossip so within twenty four hours the news that Abby had stayed overnight at the house had spread for miles. She enjoyed the success of passing on original news, but was dismayed that her grandmother and grandfather did not seem to be interested at all. It was almost as if they knew already, thought Lizzie despondently. There was another farm where this news was greeted with less than satisfaction. Most families being happy that James and Abby were getting together. There was no censure for the couple, it was Nature's way and they anticipating with pleasure the marriage which they felt sure would follow. The one area where the pleasure of that event was greeted with less than a smile was at Lower Valley Farm, where Abe and Sheila had worried faces. "We shall pray for the young couple," decided Abe with Sheila's agreement, "That they will see the error of their ways, and seek the Lord's blessing on their union with a marriage." His hand was laying on the large Bible, as it always did when he felt the need to invoke his Lord to strengthen his argument. He would not think any the less of Abby, nor James. His interpretation of his Methodism did not allow for pointing the finger at Sinners, as he believed that it wasn't his place to accuse nor judge. The Good Lord would do that at the day of Judgement. It gave him a jolt when Sheila suggested that this may be the Lords way of bringing the young couple together. He had to think about that. He was usually so certain in his opinions, and was used to his wife agreeing with everything he said. That she should disagree was a surprise but not upsetting. In his philosophy God had not set him as the superior in this marriage. He would not argue with her, as usual he left it to the Lord to decide.

"The Lord does move in mysterious ways. We cannot hope to fathom His reasons. We shall pray for them, and for guidance." Abe was usually long-winded in his prayers, today was going to be a bit of a marathon.

Her work on the co-op could be put on hold for a while, as she was waiting for the registration of the enterprise to come through. Abby decided to go down to her house on Monday morning to see what was happening. George Walker was there and was pleased to see her. "I was going to phone you. I have had the specification for the station from Ms. Eaton, which basically confirms what we discussed. So I want to get a crew in there soon." He handed her a letter. "That is an estimate for you. I have tried to pare it down as much as possible, but I have to stick with the specification."

Abby quickly ran her eye over the costs, and looked up saying. "Go ahead, Mr. Walker. Shall we say the same terms and stage payments?"

"Thank you, Miss Abby. It will be a first rate job I assure you. Now about the Goods Shed. I had a look at it last week, and it seems to be in sound condition. They built well in those days. So what I was thinking." He paused.

"Yes?" Abby encouraged him to say his piece.

"I can just do a tidy up job if you want. Check the roof, point and paint. Funnily enough it hasn't been listed, I can't understand why, but it hasn't."

Abby also thought that strange.. "Do you still have the photograph from Mr. Brasher?"

"No, the heritage people have it, but I can get it back. Why?"

"I wanted to check if the barge boards were carved like the station."

"I can answer that. Yes they were. If you are going to ask me to replicate those as well, it can be done but it will cost you a bit more."

"Let me know please. I will probably have it done, as it's going to be part of the atmosphere here, so it ought to be exactly as it was."

"Ok. I'll work it out as soon as possible. Then if you agree I will get my carpenter started on the whole lot. That will take him two or three months I reckon."

They turned back to the house. "I am finishing off inside. Everything will be done except the cold water tank and the bathroom. The bathroom suite will not be here for a couple of months anyway, so it seems best to do that and the cold water tank at the same time." They walked in. The change was enormous. The fitted unit with a Belfast sink gleamed. Cupboards had been built along the wall over the sink, and the walls were totally smooth, with the electric sockets flush with the surface.

"I have put in the boiler for the central heating; it's in this cupboard here." He opened one of the wall cupboards just to the left of the sink. "The balanced flue has gone through the wall and vents outside. It will not be seen when we put the veranda up. Now, have you thought about the colour you want on the walls?"

Abby blushed a little. "No I haven't given it any thought at all."

George was humming. "Well I would like to get some paint on when the plaster skim has dried completely. If I may make a suggestion?"

"Go on."

"If I get a good coat of cream on, you can over paint it easily when it suits."

"Cream?"

"Yes. It's quite traditional round here. It has a hint of Yellow in it, like Clotted Cream. With only the two small windows the lighter colour will brighten the rooms as well."

"I like that, Mr. Walker. Would you do that, please?" They continued about the house. Abby was very pleased with all the work that George had done. He did seem to be in tune with her ideas and preempted her thoughts. He did this again when they started to go up stairs.

"Miss Abby, these stairs are going to be very dark most of the time. I have put in wiring for a light, but I would like to run an idea past you, if I may."

"Go on Mr. Walker."

"As we have to remove some of the roof to get the cold water tank in, I could at the same time put a sky light in. It comes with a polished aluminium tube about two feet in diameter, so light will travel down the tube to a domed reflector, which we would put into the ceiling at the top of the stairs. Then you will only need the electric light when it's dark. They're very good and bring a lot of light in. What do you think?"

"Brilliant idea. I like it, Mr. Walker, yes please do that."

"Ok. Won't cost too much, as we have to get part of the roof off anyway, and that's already costed in."

Leaving the station site, Abby thought ruefully that people, supposedly identified as simple country folk, were anything but. George Walker seemed able to persuade her to spend more on her house every time she met him. Sam seemed to grasp her ideas for the co-op very quickly, and Harry was always on the lookout for an angle that would benefit him. James was the one who did not have an eye for a fast buck. Yet Abby admired him for his integrity, and his patriarchal concern for his tenants, which she now realised had cost him dearly. The means to help him, lay on her desk when she returned to the Estate office. A letter from Peter Adams lay on her desk. She read it carefully, making sure she understood his comments and suggestions. James' Shares would not realise a tremendous amount of Capital, but Peter had suggested a spread of investments, which would bring James a much needed boost in income. Abby went online to check the latest bid-prices. Now her City brain kicked into gear, she was sure she had heard rumours about one of the Companies. If this was so a takeover was a distinct possibility, and a better price could be had. She quickly scribbled down her thoughts to present to James, certain that he would be around soon.

Abby wandered into the house to make coffee, setting out two mugs as she did so. The complaining engine and the spitting gravel announced James' arrival. He came straight through to the kitchen, where Abby was sitting sipping the freshly made brew. He came over and bent to kiss her. It was a lingering kiss and left them both a little breathless.

"Well, hello James. Now that is how a girl likes to be greeted in the morning. The only way to improve on that is for the Kissee to be in bed with the Kisser."

"That can be arranged." James grinned.

"We shall have to talk about that, perhaps later." Abby eyed him slyly lowering her eyes. "The kettle's just boiled, if you want coffee. Then sit down there is something I want to discuss with you."

"Yes Ma'am.' He saluted theatrically, then went and made a coffee. Once he was seated, Abby pushed Peter's letter over to him. He read it twice yet still seemed unsure of the meaning. He pushed it back to her.

"I told you I know little about investments. I think I get the gist of it though, and if you recommend this guy, I shall go ahead with it."

Abby felt she ought to explain a little more. "I believe that Peter has got it about right. I do have some thoughts on that one." She pointed to the listing. "I did hear some rumours. It wasn't something that would make any difference in my job. But I believe that Company will be the object of a bid shortly, so it would be worth hanging on to those and see what transpires. Keep them until the next Tax year at least, it will reduce the Capital Gains on the sales at the least, and may net you a lot more to invest." James looked gloomy.

"I knew the Taxman would be getting a share somehow or other. I will take your advice anyway. What else."

"I like Peter's suggestions, he knows his stuff." Abby had been amused to see that Peter had proposed some of the investments that Abby had included in her Portfolio. "From what he has suggested, I would say you would be in the region of twelve thousand a year better off." James was cheered significantly.

"That's brilliant. I shall be able to start some repairs to the cottages." Abby sighed. How typical of James. Duty and obligation first, his own welfare coming second.

"Don't start spending before you get the money, although anything you do spend on repairs to the cottages, you should be able to set against income tax." James looked up in surprise.

"Can I do that?"

"I should think almost certainly."

"That's tremendous." Impulsively he got up and kissed Abby.

"What will I do without you?"

"Make certain I never go away." James made no reply, however his usual grin vanished and he looked pensive. Abby looked pensive as well. The comment had come out without thought, yet had served a purpose in a way. Letting James know that her continuing to stay in the valley depended on him. Sam would nod his head in approval, he advised her that she would have to push James. Well Abby told herself now is the time to start pushing.

James had a lot to think about. He had no doubts about his feelings for Abby, and wanted more than anything to have her as his wife. Thereby hung the problem. She had never said how she felt about him; it didn't occur to him that he had never confessed his feelings; and without some indication of her feelings he could not ask her to marry her, fearing that she would believe that her wealth was the object rather than Abby for herself, he sometimes regretted having been so open about his financial position. Yet this apart, the real truth, the actual reason he could not ask her was that he would be totally crushed if she were to reject him. Therefore he tried to maintain the status quo, keeping the relationship alive and hoping that somehow by circumstance the situation would be resolved without his having to tempt fate. Her supposed wealth; which Abby had never denied nor confirmed; was of no consequence to him. This woman had come to the valley and brought sunshine into his life. All the remaining depression from the Falklands had gone, and he knew that if she ever went away, the clouds would hang over him once more.

The object of his quandary was back in the Estate office. Abby realised that she had dropped a small bomb on James, so she left him to stew for a while. Her putting pressure on James was acceptable, pressure from anyone else was not. Would she accept him? Of that Abby had few doubts, of course she would. His company was never dull, their conversation always flitting along that middle road which could easily flip from serious to laughter. He was protective of her, but never possessive. She had proof of that at the Ball, when she danced with someone who obviously felt that dancing was merely the foreplay to some other activity. James had suddenly appeared to claim her. He had said little merely commenting that Abby had promised this dance to him. The man looked set to argue, but the look on James' face and the uniform had decided him against. There was of course their nights of love. Abby smiled secretly at the memories, and her skin heated. That was very special, and the prospect of sleeping next to James for the rest of her life was very, very appealing. She couldn't understand how this relationship had changed her. She had suddenly become an exhibitionist, and a voyeur! On Sunday morning she had sat in front of the mirror, to put some lipstick on. She was nude, and very aware of James watching her. It was thrilling! She loved showing herself off for him. In the mirror she could see him laying on the bed, he was naked too. It took a long time for that lipstick to go on. The lines of his body excited her, the taut stomach, the strong arms, but most importantly the look of desire in his eyes as he watched her. Not to mention the physical desire which was much in evidence. It was very late that Sunday before they came down to make breakfast.

Her idyll was interrupted by Sam, who poked his head round the door and asked if it was alright to come in. "Of course, Sam. You should know I am pleased to see you anytime."

"Well I didn't want to disturb you if you were busy." Abby had been smiling when he entered, and her next words gave him a clue to why.

"No not busy, Sam. Just thinking about something." The smile strengthened and she blushed. Sam chuckled.

"Well I won't ask you what you were thinking of, I can tell it was nice thoughts by your blush." Abby blushed even more.

"Sam! I wouldn't tell you anyway. You would think me terrible."

"Good weekend?" He teased her. Abby was now the colour of Beetroot.

"Stop it, Sam. Would you like a coffee? I can go and make some." Abby tried to change the subject.

"No, not for me. But thank you anyway. I just came to tell you that there is enough carcasses in the cold room for the first delivery."

"That's good. Quicker than I thought. I will ask the Club when they want to accept it and get the transport organised. Who supplied them?" Sam wasn't absolutely sure who had supplied what.

"I shall write to all of them and ask that they let me have a list. They will need to do this every time."

Sam grinned. "No need to worry. The despatch list will have all the information on it, and that will give you the originating farms. It's good job too, as otherwise all you would get is a grubby little note. Not particularly good on paperwork, farmers." Abby was relieved that it was Sam to whom she was revealing her ignorance.

"That's a relief. I still have a lot to learn, don't I, Sam?"

"You're getting it, Abby. But don't worry; just ask Mr. James or me if you are at all worried. I will say though, you have done a brilliant job so far, even Harry is amazed at how much you know. Shut him up once or twice you did. It was a pleasure to see!"

"He wasn't upset?"

"Only because he didn't think you knew. When he found out that you did know, he was stumped. Gave me a little chuckle, that's for sure." They grinned at each other, and then Sam took his leave.

"Got to meet Mr. James down at the farm, need to talk about drainage on some of the meadows."

"Ok, Sam, shall I see you tonight?"

"Yes, I shall be in about nine, we'll have a chat then. Bye."

***

The year drew to a close more quickly than any other year Abby had experienced. The last two weeks of November seemed inundated with rain; Abby had lain awake at night listening to the rain exploding in furious gusts on the window. The Lyney River became a torrent of brown swirling water, lapping up to the piers of both bridges threatening to overwhelm its banks. The threat was realised one morning when Abby intending to drive to Gallow Farm discovered the lower fields under a foot or so of water, the road on its embankment a causeway across a lake of sullen water. Looking up she saw that the hills were wearing a coverlet of snow a contrast to the dull browns of the deciduous trees and the lifeless greens of the pines. The road back to Molton was probably impassable with those steep gradients she remembered. Abby now understood what Sam had tried to tell her that the valley had moods and not all of them tranquil. Looking back at the warm spectacle of summer it was hard to envisage then the change that the winter would bring.

Work had continued at the station, but inside work only. The first delivery of meats had been made, and the second was about to leave. Feedback from the Club was extremely encouraging, and Abby turned her thoughts to where else she could place Combe Lyney produce. She was only thinking for the moment, understanding James' advice that she should get the system working, iron out the snags before taking the next step.

George Walker had redirected his workforce to the Station. There was little more that he could do at the house, until the Bathroom suite was delivered and that had been delayed until March. He wouldn't take the roof off or fit the windows until that happened, not wanting to leave the house open to the wet of the West Country winter. George believed that he would complete the station before the house. He told her why. "No Electrical or plumbing to do. Getting the old plaster off and new lime plaster on will not take too long, stripping the wood of paint and priming and re-painting is easy. The Goods shed is even easier, no plastering to do. The only hold up will be the Barge boards. So I reckon they should be finished about March time."

With little to do down at the house, and with everything organised with the Co-op, Abby could relax and turn her thoughts to Christmas. A conversation with Sam one evening changed some of her plans. She had been contemplating her gift list when he had mentioned in passing the tradition of only exchanging presents with family and no one else. He went on.

"None of us has money to throw around, so such presents we do give are always very simple and not expensive, a little bottle of perfume or aftershave is normal." He went on. "Of course on Christmas Eve we all get together for the Carol Walk."

"Carol Walk! What is that?"

"As I said it's on Christmas Eve. We start at the Combe, leaving about eight. We have lanterns and some liquid sustenance to keep out the cold, and we go round the village singing Carols. Some will come out and join us on the way, and we end by going up to Lyney House, where Mr. James will have hot Toddies and Mince Pies ready for us. It brings the whole village together."

Abby thought the idea was great. "Can I join this year."

"Of course you can Girl. You will be very welcome."

Later Abby would realise that Sam had, in a very gentle way, advised her not go overboard with presents for all and sundry. It was a sobering thought, that she could easily have embarrassed some with presents that she thought of as inexpensive, that they could not match. She was in her room at the Inn when this thought came to her.

"Oh Sam. What would I do without you." She scrapped her list, leaving just Sam, Mavis, Jack and Mary, and of course James.

***

On Christmas Eve, she came down to the bar, dressed for the cold weather. A hot, flustered but nonetheless happy Jack met her and handed her a Lantern attached to a broom handle. Mary rushed around lighting the candles in the Lanterns. All around there were people she knew, most holding Lanterns such as the one she had. For once even the weather, the farming and the bloody government were not discussed. No one appeared to be in charge until Mavis appeared. The little woman soon had everyone organised and one by one the assembly filed out into the lane. Abby was greeted immediately by Abe and Sheila, who had waited patiently outside, happy to join the Carol Walk, but not prepared to waive their condemnation of the demon drink, even for a moment. Sheila took Abby's arm. "Miss Abby, it is so good to see you on this joyous occasion, God bless you." Abe joined in the blessing with a smile, not usual for him. The throng moved off down the lane, with the strains of 'God rest ye Merry Gentlemen' at first heard quietly from the front of the file, and gathering volume as those at the back joined in.

Abby sang lustily, surprised that she could remember the words, as they patrolled the village. Her singing was frequently interrupted as greetings were exchanged with others. Nat was almost unrecognisable, his face sporting a smile which was very different to his normal mournful expression. Susan, still embarrassed by her faux pas again tried to apologise. Harry surprised her with his tuneful Bass singing voice. "You should be in the Church Choir." She told him.

He grinned. "I was when we had one, that was a few years ago though." There was no apparent programme of carols, it appeared spontaneously, when one Carol finished from somewhere in the pack another was started and the rest of the singers took up the refrain. Neither was there any one person in charge, apart from Mavis who bullied anyone she thought was not singing as lustily as possible. However the singers seemed to follow a pattern, probably brought about, thought Abby, by the years this event had taken place. The habits of yesteryear becoming tradition today. The throng grew steadily as the progress was made, until at last they climbed the lane up to Lyney House. As they gathered in the forecourt, lit by Christmas lights strung from tree to tree, and the flickering illumination of at least fifty Lanterns, the Carol 'Silent Night' was sung, with James on the doorstep adding a good baritone to the impromptu Choir. As that Carol ended Mavis led half a dozen ladies inside only to emerge within a minute, carrying trays of Mince Pies, and hot fruit punch. Abby was entranced by the whole episode, never before had she felt so involved with a community, laughing and singing and saying hello to many new friends.

Suddenly she was aware of James by her side. "Did you enjoy that?" He asked. Abby's smile was the answer.

"Absolutely magic. What happens now?"

"Many will go back to the Combe and ease their sore throats with a little drop of something."

"What will you do?" Abby asked James.

"Exactly that, are you coming?"

Abby nodded. "Let's go!"

James took her hand and led her through the bushes on a barely recognisable path to a gate that opened onto the Churchyard, following the path that wound down to the front of the church and eventually to the lane almost opposite the Combe Inn. Abby remonstrated with James. "You didn't tell me about this path, the times I have walked up that lane, when I could have taken this short-cut."

James was suitable chastised, apologising profusely. "I'm sorry. I thought you knew about it." They had made the journey fairly quickly but were not the first to arrive, already Jack and Mary were busy dispensing drinks for the thirsty throng almost overwhelmed by the demand. James took station behind the bar to help and showed himself quite proficient as a Barman.

"You could take this on as a second job." Abby remarked.

"Not likely," replied James, "too much like hard work. You know how us upper classes abhor hard work." It was quite late when James left, and Abby trudged wearily upstairs to her room.

Christmas day dawned, damp and overcast. Abby made herself a cup of tea, then returned to bed, snuggling in the warmth. If she was honest with herself, Sam's words about living in the station house and its isolation had been a wise warning. If she had been living there now, it was unlikely that she would have joined the Carol Walk last night, nor would she be contemplating with pleasure the day to come.

It had been a good day. Mary had tried to coax Abby into eating a larger breakfast giving as a reason, "Well It is Christmas Day!" Abby resisted her, pointing out that Mary would expect her to eat Lunch, of which there would be plenty. She gave Mary the choice, breakfast or lunch, she couldn't eat both. Mary retired having lost that round. The

Combe Inn opened for the Lunchtime rush, closing at two o' clock. The usual patrons with dry throats were of course in evidence, yet today their jollity was warmer compared to that of ordinary days. Abby had for a moment in an extraordinary rush, collected glasses and washed them to help Jack out, Mary being very busy in the kitchen at the time. James had arrived just before two, and helped in ushering out those who felt that today of all days they should be allowed one last drink. With shouts of 'Happy Christmas' the last and most persistent were persuaded to leave. Abby again went behind the bar and washed glasses as Jack re-stocked the shelves. James arranged two tables together in the Lounge, as Mary bustled in with tablecloth and cutlery to set up for their feast.

The Capon was indeed all that Mary had promised, and with mounds of Brussels sprouts, roast potatoes, parsnips, peas, and stuffing Abby was tempted to eat more heartily than ever before. Heartily maybe, but no match for James or Jack who attacked the meal in fine style and literally cleared their plates in quick time, and then helped themselves to more.

Around six, they drove down to Gallow Farm, where a party was just starting. Roger, Valerie their two children and Harry had arrived before them. Mavis was in her element and with Mary's help set out a table of cold meats, pork pies, salad, Christmas cake, nuts, and trifles. Abby was unable to eat anymore than a slice of cold Turkey and some Sherry Trifle, but watched in amazement as James loaded a plate and started to clear it with his usual efficiency. After the gargantuan meal he had demolished at Lunch she was amazed that he could manage yet more. The furniture had been pushed back and Sam invited Abby to dance. Her lessons with Sam and Mavis had continued, so she felt only a little consternation at dancing in front of this audience. Within a few minutes they were joined on the floor by most of the other guests. The steps of the Waltz and Quickstep were second nature to her, but the 'Hokey Cokey' gave her problems, putting the left leg in when it should have been the right leg, and turning anti clockwise, when she ought to have turned clockwise.

The party was going on long into the night, when James caught

Abby's eye, and asked if she would like to come up to the house. Her smile was all the answer he needed, and they slipped quietly away, or so they thought. An eagle eyed Mavis noted their departure and smiled.

Abby relaxed into James' arms, cocooned in the warmth of his bed. A cup of hot cocoa at the side.

"This has been the best Christmas I have ever had, and this is simply the best way to end the day." James' kiss told her he was in agreement with that.

CHAPTER 34

New Year's Eve was again very busy at the Combe Inn, and Abby once more made herself useful, collecting empties and washing them for Jack to refill. As Midnight approached she found herself unthinkingly at James' side. Jack had tuned the Radio to the BBC and as the gongs of Big Ben rang out.

He kissed her and whispered. "Happy New Year, Abby." Abby didn't realise that the cheers were more about James kissing Abby, than the New Year that dawned. With that indication of Abby's and James feelings for each other, the news was disseminated throughout the valley quite quickly. Most eagerly awaited the announcement of an engagement and when that failed to come questions were asked. Worried minds debated this with other worried minds. They could not understand the turmoil that was going on in James' mind, who had the most worried mind of all.

As before when he came back from the Falklands, James went to see Sam. Mavis had gone to Paverton, so they had the cottage to themselves. Sitting at the big table with mugs in front of them, Sam waited for James to start. After a few minutes of silence, Sam prodded James. "Was there something special you wanted to talk about?" He asked. James was still silent, so Sam had another go. "Or perhaps someone special you wanted to talk about." James nodded. But apart from that said nothing. "Would it be Abby?" Sam pushed a bit more. James nodded again. Sam took a sip from his mug. "Well it's a good conversation we are having." He paused for a moment waiting for a response. There was no response. "What about Abby?" He persevered.

At last James said something. "I don't know what to do about her."

"Ah, we have speech. But I don't understand, is she upsetting people, or poking her nose in where it isn't wanted?"

James' demeanour denied that. "No, it's nothing like that; it's about Abby and me."

Sam nodded gravely. "So, it's got to that stage has it?"

James looked up questioning the statement. "What do you mean?"

"I mean, Mr. James, that Abby is fond of you, and you are fond of Abby. That's the stage I am talking about."

"Yes Sam, but what do I do about it?" Sam laughed out loud.

"Oh, Mr. James, from the gossip I would say you are doing something about it."

James let a small grin come to his face. "No no, I am not talking about spending time together, but what do I do about keeping her here. My mother said that Abby had hinted that she had other things to do, and just the other day, Abby said something to the effect that she could move away from here."

Sam shook his head in amazement. "Mr. James. Listen to me for a moment. First of all, do you think that Abby would be spending all that money on the house and station, if she was thinking of moving on? Do you think that she would be doing all this work and putting money into the co-operative if she was thinking of moving on? And do you think she would be spending time with you, and becoming close, if she was think-ing of moving on?"

"I accept that, but I don't know where to go from here."

"I can't believe I am hearing this." Sam shook his head sorrow-fully. " Mr. James Comberford, who has run this estate for getting on fifteen years, Captain Comberford DSO. The bold and decisive officer and you don't know where you go from here. Well I will tell you what you should do. Ask Abby to marry you. Simple!" James was shocked, not so much because Sam had made that suggestion, but the tone of voice he used.

"I...I couldn't do that."

"Why? Don't you love her?" He was pleased that James did not have to think about that.

"Yes, I do."

"So why can't you ask her to marry you?"

"Because I don't know how she feels about me."

Sam with a little anger decided it was time to be blunt. "Damn you man! She sleeps with you. Do you think that Abby would do that unless she was in love with you? I certainly don't."

James went white in the face. He never thought that Sam would refer to that or even acknowledge that he knew about Abby's and his weekends. "But she's never said that she loves me."

"Have you told her that you love her?"

"Well, not sort of." Sam could not believe that James was this stupid.

"Well, not sort of." He threw James' words back at him. "I suggest that you tell her very quickly, and that you follow that up with a proposal. You say you are worried that Abby might leave. All I can say is that the way you are going on is the way to make certain that she does leave. For God's sake man! Get a grip. Talk to her, tell her how you feel."

In the face of Sam's diatribe James shook his head.. "She will probably think I am asking her because she is well off, I can't have her believe that of me."

"Abby will not believe that of you at all. I know."

"I don't understand. How do you know?"

"James, I have been here on this earth and in this valley for eighty years." Sam's voice went up an octave as he spoke. " In that time I have learned a thing or two about people. I have watched you grow up, and become the man you are today. An honest man. A man of integrity and values. You have this failing though; you don't act when sometimes you should. In the short time Abby has been here she has recognised those values in you, and understanding that, she could never believe for a moment that you would ask her to marry for any other reason than your love for her. Now go away and think about that, but don't take too long, because I want to see your wedding; and if Abby were to ask me; give her away. But I am eighty, and I don't know if I have the time left for you to dally around. So jump to it Captain Comberford!"

James left Gallow Farm having received a shock. Sam had never spoken to him in such a way before. He had gone to see Sam expecting him to understand and sympathise with the problem. Instead Sam had not sympathised, and could see no problem at all. To cap it all it appeared that Sam had lost some respect for him. Never in all these years had Sam addressed him other than as Mr. James. Now to be called just James was not; as in most cases; a sign of friendship, but more a reflection of Sam's loss of respect. It didn't matter what Sam had said, James could not believe that the solution was a simple as all that. He was certain that if he asked Abby would refuse him. There were no solid reasons for this belief, it was something that had come into his head without reason some time ago, and the passing of weeks and months had done nothing to change that idea. So entrenched was this notion that Sam's words could not convince him otherwise.

January rolled into February, cold, damp and misty. Abby felt guilty about the men who worked on the station, they had some shelter from the cold rain that fell so frequently, but with no heating, bar the small grate in the Waiting Room, the station was at best a cheerless place, how could her grandfather have put up with it? But George's workmen seemed a cheerful lot and always greeted her warmly when she went down to view the progress. Then as if by magic, at the end of February a most significant change came over the station. The new flagstones for the platform had been delivered and were down. The plastering and painting had been completed, and there in a long, plastic-wrapped package were the Barge Boards. Some of the crew had gone over to the Goods Shed and were busy stripping long-neglected paint; others were chipping out powdered mortar and re-pointing. The metamorphosis from dry chrysalis to butterfly was almost complete.

The small parcel that arrived for Abby one day was of little interest to Mary, who was surprised when Abby seemed very excited about it. The post mark was Taunton. The covering letter was from the photographic processor who explained that much of the film was beyond saving. However they had managed to rescue some thirty minutes of footage and that had been transferred to the DVD enclosed. Abby ate breakfast hurriedly, eager to get to the Estate office where she had left her lap top computer.

The first pictures were taken in a field, which Abby recognised as the one behind the Combe Inn. Tents were being erected and a small stage. Then the scene changed suddenly to one where the same field was full of people. A flickering image of a much younger Sam, Mavis and Harry were evident. Harry had a woman with him who Abby supposed was his dead wife. A tear came to her eye as it was obvious by Harry's attention that he had loved his wife with deep affection. Then there was a tall handsome man standing on the stage making a speech. He had the look of James about him. It must be Charles Comberford! She flipped back to the start of the scene and studied the people closely. Yes! There was James, a small boy. A happy smile came to her face, her James as a seven or eight year old boy…Oh, how sweet! She let the scene play on. Her finger darted quickly to the pause button frequently as faces appeared that she could identify. Then the now easily recognisable figure of her grandfather appeared in a pan shot, with a girl beside him, dressed in a pink and yellow Gingham dress. Mum! Abby tried to work it out. Her mother would have been about fourteen or fifteen at the time, but still gave the appearance of a young girl. Yet in the very short space of two years she would be giving birth to Abby. It was so hard to believe, she seemed so young and innocent. The decision to run away when she was little more than a girl was so courageous or was it a courage born of desperation? Abby let the film run a little more, studying the people, especially the young men. Did any of them take more notice of her mum than others? Was one of those boys or young men her father? There were no clues to be gained from the thirty minutes of film, as none of those young men seemed to take an interest in the young Marion. Abby was again left with no answers. She ran the film again and again, seeking some sign, a gesture from someone that would indicate a partiality. There was nothing!

Abby was no closer to the truth, yet she felt that one of those men in the film had to be her father, it stood to reason that if her mum had a teenage crush it would be with someone local, but who? She had never wondered about a father too much until she came to Combe Lyney. Getting to know more about her family did encourage speculation, but if Sam and Mavis could not tell her who her father was, how could she discover his identity from these flickering faded images? Resignedly she was now putting that question once more to the back of her mind.

Early in March the windows of the house had all been removed and a large gap had appeared in the roof. Men were pouring concrete into foundations adjacent to the front door and a huge delivery from the wholesalers was being craned off their lorry. Wrapped in protective corrugated cardboard and plastic, Abby knew that it could be nothing else but her bathroom. George Walker was there running around calling instructions, it appeared to be total chaos, but an order was found as the suite was placed gently on the ground, and other items of piping and drainage were also taken off the lorry. George noticed her, and once he was satisfied that no one was going to damage the fittings came over to see Abby. "You came at the right time, Miss Abby. We'll get the bathroom fittings in within the next three days; the bricky's will get the low walls in for the Veranda, they will be dressed rock, the same as the house, and all the windows will be in by next week."

"That's excellent, Mr. Walker. When do you think it will be habitable?"

He hummed for a moment or two. "Give me three weeks. We need to get all the plumbing connected, the gas supply tank will come tomorrow, there are lots of little things to do, and I would want to test everything before handing over. Three weeks should do it. Now I wanted to see you to ask about tiling the Bathroom. Do you want it all tiled, or just the splash areas?"

Abby was not sure. "Can I go and look; I will get a better idea there." He agreed that would be better.

George led the way in; there was a board down to cross the foundations. With all the windows out, the place felt quite cold, but Mr. Walker and his workmen seemed not to notice. Abby was encouraged to see all the electrical points fitted, and the walls painted a soft buttery cream. She had to agree that it did make the place look lighter. She inspected the bathroom with Mr. Walker and decided that two walls would be tiled, the one behind the shower cabinet, and the one where the hand basin and Bidet would go. He showed Abby some floor tiles, which looked in keeping with the style and age of the house, but were non-slip. More expense thought Abby, but agreed that it should be right from the start, rather than wishing later that it should have been done.

She left with the good news that the station would be complete, subject to final inspection by Ms. Eaton within a week. Abby had made application for grants, and had not heard anything. She felt it was time to put pressure on Ms. Eaton, so asked George if he would let her know when Ms. Eaton would be inspecting.

Abby had been in regular correspondence with Mr. Brasher, keeping him informed of the progress, and also listing questions that he alone seemed able to answer. With the news that the station building would be ready towards the end of March, he decided that he would pay another visit. Abby had not thought about a ceremonial re-opening of the station until James suggested that it would be fitting. "I think it would be right to make it a bit special. I know it will be to you, Abby, but it will be special also to the people here, especially those who remember the days when the railway operated. Perhaps I could have a word with the Reverend Hopkins, make it a sort of re-dedication ceremony. What do you think?" Abby disagreed, this was being done for her personal reasons, and her first thought was a selfish one, keeping this to herself.

"No, James. I wanted this to be private. It's my project and I am doing this for my family."

James argued. "Your grandfather ran that station to offer a service to the people of this valley. He saw it as his duty, and took pride in doing that. To me it seems fitting that the people of this valley should pay him respect in this way. You told me that he was religious, so having this blessing would be appropriate, I would have thought."

She looked at him beseechingly. "Are you really sure?"

He nodded. "Ask Sam if you are unsure. I am certain that he would think it right."

Abby did ask Sam, and he having been forewarned by James agreed. "I think it would be respectful. We let your grandfather down. I think there's a few here, not just me, who would appreciate the chance to mark the occasion properly, and in some way to say sorry for our neglect, of him, and of course your mother." Abby accepted that.

James had plans. He wanted to mark the occasion with something special for Abby's sake. As part of his plans he had enlisted the help of the Paverton Army Cadet Force, to parade with their Band. He spoke particularly to one Graham Boyce, who blew a trumpet better than any he had heard. Then he tackled Reverend Hopkins, at first the Reverend was disinclined to bless an old railway station and was persuaded to officiate upon being reminded that he had missed Combe Lyney on his circuit on many occasions, and the Diocese would not be happy about that.

Ms. Eaton came and went, approving all that had been done, yet leaving with a flea in her ear from Abby, as the Local Authority were dragging their feet over the grant. The Heritage Fund had turned them down, not surprisingly, they had more important projects to support, but locally there were grants, and Abby would not let them get away. The date was set for the third of April. Mr. Brasher had confirmed that he would be there, and Mavis had made sure that most residents of the valley would be there as well, or she would know the reason why!

Sam rarely walked the fields now. The farm had been handed over to Roger some ten years ago, and Sam had no quarrels with his methods, the management was in essence the same way that the land had been used for seventy or eighty years. Indeed he thought, if Sam's grandfather was walking with him he would not notice any great changes. However he did from time to time like to take a walk around the farm, strolling casually through Lower Penny acre; which actually was far larger than its name would suggest; the Water Meadow, Upper Penny and Lydcott Straight. He didn't know why these fields were named so; his father had used these names and probably his grandfather as well, the reasons lost in the timeless pattern of country lore. It was at the top end of Lydcott Straight that he encountered Woody; who appeared as he usually did, seemingly out of nowhere. "Good morning, Mr. Perry. It's a good day for walking the pasture."

"It is indeed, Woody. I don't often see you here though."

"I have been watching for you for some days now. May I ask first what would seem a strange question? I have seen Miss Tregonney down at the old station quite often, but I haven't seen Miss Marion. Is she not here with Miss Abby?"

"No Woody." Sam was disquieted. "I thought you knew. I am sorry to tell you, but Miss Marion is dead. She died about fifteen years ago. No one knew until Abby came here." The news affected Woody dramatically. His lifestyle of being invisible and incommunicado worked against him as well as for him. His head went down, and to Sam it appeared that he was muttering something, possibly a prayer.

"I am deeply upset to hear that."

He stopped and Sam got the feeling that he was struggling with a dilemma. Eventually he straightened and took a deep breath. "Mr. Perry, that being so I have information that rightly should be given to Miss Tregonney directly, but I must confess that I am not well enough acquainted with her to do so, nor am I equipped with sufficient courage. This information should rightly come from someone who knows her well, possibly you or perhaps Mr. James."

Sam was intrigued, what could Woody know that others in the valley could not. "Go on, Woody."

Woody hesitatingly started to tell Sam what he knew. "When Miss Marion went away, I was aware that no one knew why, even Mr. Tregonney. However I believe that I did. I had reason to believe that she could be pregnant." Sam was shocked and angry. At first he wondered if it was Woody who impregnated Marion, then cast the thought aside.

"If you knew that Woody, why the bloody hell didn't you say something. We might have had a chance of keeping her here, giving her the support she needed. Damn you Woody, Damn you!"

Woody winced, shaken by Sam's angry outburst. "I am sorry, Mr. Perry. Your condemnation of me is well deserved. I have castigated myself often enough, but I couldn't say anything. Miss Marion had made me promise that I wouldn't. I had broken one promise before with terrible consequences, I wouldn't betray another."

Sam eventually calmed down, and needed to know why Woody could have come to this conclusion. "What made you believe that?"

"I was in Higher Huish Wood one day when I heard screams. It took me some time to discover the reason. It was Miss Marion who screamed, she was dishevelled, and bleeding from a private place. I knew enough to understand that she may have been assaulted. When I looked to see if the aggressor was still around I noticed that gentleman who came to stay from time to time at Lyney House. I never knew his name, but he was hurrying away, making for Huish."

"Was he of big build with dark hair?" Woody agreed that the man was.

"I knew him, not a nice person at all. He was the son of one of Mrs. Comberford's friends." Sam told Woody. "He only came down here to escape the problems of his life. Debts I assume. I think his name was Gore, Ralph Gore. You think he raped Marion?"

"Yes, Mr. Perry. I am sure he did. Marion was very distressed and mostly unintelligible, but to me it was obvious what happened. I had some Yarrow and Comfrey at my Den and gave her some to treat herself as best she could. I offered to help her back to the station but she refused."

"And Marion made you promise not to tell anyone?"

"She did. I feel so guilty, I should never have made that promise, but Miss Marion was very insistent. Once made, I couldn't break my silence. Now that I know she is dead, I feel able to reveal what happened. I am so sorry."

"We have to tell Mr. James. He will know if Abby should be told. Let's go back to the farm, I'll telephone him."

Woody was very concerned. "No, Mr. Perry. I could not face him. Not at this moment. Please tell him yourself."

Sam understood that Woody, who had kept a low profile for all these years, had summoned just enough courage to tell him about this, but that courage was quickly failing. "Yes, Woody. I will tell him, but you must understand that he may want to speak to you."

Woody nodded unhappily. "I know, Mr. Perry, I have a debt to Miss Marion and to Miss Abby. If he has questions please tell him that if he comes to Huish, I will find him there."

***

Sam took the quick way back to Gallow Farm. He was as close to tears as he had even been in his life. If before he had felt sympathy for Marion when he first talked with Abby, his sympathy was far deeper now. She had been ignored by her father and her life ruined by a dissolute bastard. As he neared the farmhouse his sadness turned to anger. Anger at Thomas Tregonney but especially anger at Ralph Gore. He called James as soon as he got back. For once he would not tell Mavis. She would not be able to keep her mouth shut for long. Sam asked James if he could come up and see him, rather than James come down to Gallow, not wanting to take the risk that Mavis would come upon them and hear this terrible news.

"Come up, Sam." James responded happily.

"Is Abby there?" Sam asked.

"No, why do you want to speak to her as well?"

"No. It's a bit private."

"Come up now, Sam."

James was curious. His last conversation with Sam hadn't gone the way he would have wished; now he wondered if Sam was going to continue in the same way. Fifteen minutes later, Sam arrived. The speed with which he came alerted James to a possible emergency. Sam waited at the front door until James came and took him through to the Breakfast room. "Would you like some coffee, Sam?"

"Thank you Mr. James, but no. You may want something stronger though."

"Why? Sam." In a few short, terse sentences, Sam related Woody's tale. James was to say the least shocked and angry.

"The bastard!" Sam agreed with that epithet. James had more to say. "Dad always said he was trouble, but mother insisted that he should stay. I suppose because of Amelia Gore, her friend in Berkshire"

"I know Mr. Gore hasn't been here for years, but if he were to show his face… Mr. James. Accidents have been known to happen with Farm machinery."

"He will never be back, Sam. He was killed years ago." He went on. "It's a good job he is as I could not stop myself from ripping the guts out of him."

"I will not mourn him." Sam knew how James felt and agreed with him.

"I doubt that few did. He died in a car crash. He had another man's wife with him at the time, and she died as well."

Sam nodded. "It would seem that he had the same morals right to the end."

James did make coffee as this information sank in. He turned to Sam as the kettle boiled.

"Do we tell Abby?"

"I don't know, Mr. James. I suppose she has a right to know, but after finding out how her grandfather died, do you think it would be too heartbreaking for her?"

James came to a decision. "I don't think we should tell her." He decided. "She doesn't know who her father was and has accepted that she probably never will. Knowing that she was conceived in such a way and by such a man is a tragedy we can keep from her. What do you think, Sam?"

"Part of me says we shouldn't keep secrets. But then, does knowing help at all, especially under these circumstances. Woody has kept it secret all these years, perhaps it's best if goes on being secret."

James was in agreement. "Who else beside Woody knows?"

"No one."

"Good, we'll keep it to ourselves." He put a cup of coffee in front of Sam, and sat down himself.

"How much unhappiness can one family have? For all the success Abby had in the City, how do you balance that with the horrors that this valley has inflicted on her?"

Sam was pleased that Mr. James was thinking of Abby but had to point out that Abby would never know about this, and the only tragedy as far as Abby was concerned was her grandfather's death. He went on. "If you want to see Abby happy, you have it in your own hands to give her that happiness. Mr. James." James was not happy to be reminded again.

The following day, James rode up to Huish Coppice making his presence obvious. He was joined after about forty minutes by Woody. Woody gave his word once more. No one would know about the attack on Marion.

That evening James came into the Combe Inn, eagerly looking for Abby. She wasn't at the bar or in the Lounge. He asked Mary if Abby would be down that evening. She looked concerned. "No, Mr. James. I thought you would know. She paid her bill up to date, and left this afternoon. She had a suitcase with her."

CHAPTER 35

James was shocked! Abby gone? Where? Why? His first thought was that she had somehow found out what happened to her mother? The second thought dismissed that idea. He knew that Sam would not say anything, and Woody after keeping this secret for over thirty years was unlikely to break another promise after only a few hours. It could not be that. He looked around seeking Sam, if anyone knew it would be Sam. Abby would confide in him, wouldn't she? Sam was not there. He was sitting at home watching the television. Mavis couldn't understand why he was there and not at the Inn as usual. She had asked him in an oblique way and had an oblique answer, so she tackled him head on.

"Why are you here this evening? Most unusual for you."

Sam ruminated, trying to find the right words to answer her. He decided to elicit Mavis' support, but without telling her the complete truth. "Abby has gone."

"What?"

He looked at his wife, confirming the news. "Abby packed her case and left this afternoon." He stopped himself from saying that it was because of her and Mary's gossip.

"Is she coming back?" Mavis was extremely worried.

Sam shrugged his shoulders. "I don't know. I saw her leave and all she said was that she was going off. I asked her where and for how long but she didn't answer, just drove off towards Paverton. She didn't look happy."

Mavis immediately phoned Mary, who didn't know any more than Sam. "I caught sight of her putting her case in the car, and she was away before I could get out to ask what she was doing. She had left a cheque for her account on the bar for me. Paid up everything. There's some of her clothes still in the room, but in her note she said she would send for them later. Mr. James was just here, and he seemed most upset about it."

Mavis decided on some action. "Mary. I am coming up. We'll go through everything she has left to see if there is something that will tell us what she is about." Not for one moment did Mavis consider that she would be invading Abby's privacy.

Mavis rarely drove although she had a licence. This was important so she borrowed Sam's Land Rover and drove to the Inn. As she did another Land Rover passed her going in the opposite direction. She was so concerned that she didn't realise it was Mr. James, nor did he notice that it was Sam's Land Rover that was travelling towards the Inn. James had tried Abby's mobile phone five times, it rang and rang without answer, and Abby would appear to have turned the message service off. Sam sat counting the minutes. He knew that Mr. James would arrive very shortly. He got up and put the kettle on. Perhaps he would need some tea, and was quite sure that Mr. James would also.

James did arrive very shortly, just as the kettle boiled. Sam let him in, James was breathless and flustered. "You look as if you could do with a cup of tea, Mr. James."

"Abby's gone."

"Yes, I know, but would you like a cup of tea?"

"Abby's left."

"Well I want some tea anyway, so I'll pour one for you."

"Sam, this is important. Abby's gone away."

"Yes I know, Mr. James. Mavis was just on the phone to Mary, and I heard."

"You see to be remarkably calm about it."

"What's to get all hot and bothered about? If she's gone, she's gone. It's sad, but it's her decision. If she comes back, it's her decision as well. So sit down and drink the tea."

"But why?"

"Why? Because I have just made it."

"No, Sam. Why has Abby gone?"

Sam looked at James witheringly before answering him. "Mr. James. You of all people should understand why." He replied witheringly.

James was shocked into silence. Then said feebly. "But I haven't done anything, or said anything."

"Exactly, Mr. James. I told you only a few days ago, that your lack of action would send Abby away, and now it would appear that you have succeeded. Well done!"

***

James sat miserably. He didn't taste the tea, it was just warm liquid trickling over his tongue and slipping down to his stomach, where it joined the growing knot that his stomach had become. After a while he roused himself to ask Sam. "Do you know where she's gone?"

"Why would I know that? I didn't even know she had gone until a few moments ago." A little lie, but Mr. James would not know that. He went on. "I don't know if it would help but perhaps you could have a look around her office. Possibly she has left something lying around that would give some indication. If I know Abby, she will not have gone without making arrangements. See if she has left a clue."

"Yes. That's right." James clasped the straw in desperation. "She would do that. Let's go now."

"Oh no, Mr. James. I could not do that. It would be wrong for me to go looking around her personal things. But you as her landlord so to speak can. You'll have to do it yourself."

James converted himself from abject misery into the man of action. "Right. I'll go and do that now. I'll let you know if I find anything." James got up to leave.

"Aren't you going to finish your tea?" Asked Sam. James didn't hear him.

***

Sam heard the Land Rover start and the scrubbing tyres as James viciously let in the clutch. He pulled out his mobile phone and searched the memory and dialled the number.

"Hello Sam." Abby's voice held a hint of amusement.

"He's on his way to your office as we speak, Abby. Will it be easy for him to find?"

"No, Sam. He will have to search quite thoroughly. If I made it too easy, he may suspect a conspiracy."

Sam laughed. "Well it is a conspiracy, really. But you're right."

"He's called about five times, you know."

"I'm not surprised, Abby. He's frantic."

"Good." There was silence for a moment. "I am doing the right thing, aren't I, Sam."

"Yes, Abby. If you had seen him here, you would not doubt his feelings for you. The man just needs a kick to make him do something. He'll find you. I'll know when he sets off and I'll let you know."

"Thanks, Sam. How was Mavis?"

"Mavis and Mary will be ransacking your room as we speak. Now if I know those two, they will put everything away tidily, and do a lot of washing and ironing for you. Serves then right! I got so angry with the pair of them, all their manoeuvrings and plots. Now take care, Abby. I'll phone whenever I can without being overheard." Sam was well aware of the irony; it was he and Abby who were making plots at the moment.

"Ok, Sam. I owe you a drink."

At the Combe Inn, Mary and Mavis had finished their search, and found nothing to suggest why Abby had left, or where she had gone. They now sat in the lounge with their heads together, examining the likely implications raised by Abby's departure. As in all such pubs, where the same clientele would gather invariably most evenings there was an undercurrent of concern. It was not about who was there, but rather who was not. The fevered quiet conversation that Mary and Mavis were having sparked interest, and the absences were noted. So at least three new rumours for the valley were born, to be digested, rejected and resurrected over the course of the next few days.

James had started his investigation in the Estate office. At first he felt guilt for this, reasoning that this was now Abby's office and that he shouldn't be going through her papers. If he had realised that Abby had anticipated this and had not left anything too personal for him to find it would have made him feel better. James would not know this until Abby and Sam's plan had either succeeded or collapsed irretrievably. There was little pattern to his search and as a result he found nothing that evening. He retired to eat a late hasty meal before taking to his bed. It was not a comfortable night for him. The meal eaten quickly lay heavily on a stomach that was already uneasy and his mind, full of dismay and anger at the situation would not allow sleep. Even the bed reminded him of what he had had lost, as every time he turned over Abby's perfume, her invisible presence, teased his nostrils. It did have one benefit though. At some time an insidious thought crept into his head that he was the sole cause of this discomfort. He mentally kicked himself for not having the courage to declare his feelings to Abby. If he had done that Abby would either have accepted him or not. If she had rejected him he would at least know why she had gone away, misery would have been his world for a long time, but at least he would know. If she had accepted him…well happy would be the least adjective to describe his life.

The next morning he was back in the office. It was only just light when he started as he had given up on sleep around five, when the first tendrils of light were creeping through the curtains. He had decided on a more methodical approach to the task. He cleared a space on the desk, and took each file out from the cabinets one by one, replacing it when he had finished examining it. He worked the day through, pausing only to make some coffee. By seven that evening he had discovered nothing. Frustrated, angry and very hungry he returned to the house to make a sandwich. His head was aching badly, a result of too much coffee, nothing to eat, and a sleepless night. He was planning on going back to the office when his army training brought him to his senses. "Don't be a fool, man," He told himself, "take a bath, and get a good night's sleep and then start again fresh in the morning."

Sam was coming under a lot of pressure from Mavis. She felt that he didn't seem to show the same concern as others about Abby's departure. No one else would notice this, but they had lived together for over fifty years and if anyone knew Sam, it was Mavis.

"You know something, don't you?" She tackled him the next day.

"After eighty years on this Planet, yes my Love, I suppose I do know some things."

"Don't start trying anything with me, Sam Perry. I'm talking about Abby, and you know something about why she's gone."

Sam sighed heavily. "I know no more than you or Mary or even Mr. James for that matter. But if I were asked if I had thoughts on it, I would say that Abby has left because she realised that she was going nowhere with Mr. James. Now that is just a thought. I cannot say if it is right or wrong."

Mavis and Mary had come to that conclusion also. "That silly man!" Mavis was bitter. "The right woman for him, right in front of him and he couldn't see it." Mavis had tears in her eyes at that point. "Such a lovely girl, now she's gone off, all alone, just like her mother. My heart is breaking for thinking about her." She stopped to wipe her eyes. "Is there nothing we can do, Sam?"

"The only one who can do anything is Mr. James. He came down here after you had gone to the Combe. I suggested he had good look in Abby's office to see if she had left something, anything that could give him a clue to where she's gone."

"I'll go up and help him look." Mavis was determined, but Sam was equally determined.

"No you will not." He had that tone of voice that Mavis recognised as the one that she dare not ignore. "If it is as we think then it's Mr. James who has to find her, if she can be found. He has to make the running now and prove to himself and to Abby that he does care for her. The man's got to realise what he could lose."

The next morning the man in question went back to his task. Repeating his actions of the previous day. He had found nothing yesterday and similarly he discovered no clue to Abby's whereabouts this day. Frustrated and angry he returned to the house and sat morosely over a quick meal. Damn the woman! Why did she have to go away? Couldn't she see what she meant to him? Sam's words kept coming back to haunt him, that it was his own reticence in declaring his love that was the problem. The anger died and misery set in. He headed towards another sleepless night.

He returned to his task again on the third morning, casting round the office for any bit of paper he hadn't examined. The morning was spent fruitlessly searching; the methodical approach abandoned as he frantically sought for something, anything that could give him a lead. Finally he spotted a box file under the desk. He wasn't sure anymore at this point if he had gone through it or not, none the less he got it onto the desk and prepared to investigate. It was then that purely by chance he got a breakthrough. Abby had always kept a spiral bound note pad on the desk for jotting down quick notes. The top page was clean and James had ignored it, until he accidentally knocked it on the floor when he placed the box file on the desk. As it fluttered to the floor the pages opened up, and he noticed the previous pages covered with jottings. He picked it up and carefully read. Much of it was about market prices and he could recognise those as the wording was so familiar to him. There were lots of scribbling concerning the station and the house, from telephone conversations with George Walker. Then there was a telephone number with the initials B H next to the number, the area code was one he recognised as relatively local. He could spend time checking through the directory, but took the course of direct action. He picked up the phone and called it.

"Bay Hotel." James was thrown for a moment and didn't say anything; he considered putting the phone down when the voice came again.

"Bay Hotel, can I help you?"

"Eh, yes. Do you have a Miss Tregonney staying with you?"

"One moment." James waited impatiently. He heard the phone being picked up.

"Miss Tregonney is not taking calls at the moment. Is there a message?"

"No, no message. I'll call again. Thank you."

***

People say you always find things in the last place you look; the obvious reason is that you stop looking at that point. The other truism is that you overlook the obvious; James kicked himself for not looking through the notepad before. It had been there on her desk all the time! If Abby were there she would have congratulated herself. Leaving the clue in relatively plain sight, counting on James not seeing the obvious.

An instinct had told him not to leave a message, but to go and see Abby. He checked the code with the directory; it was Blue Anchor in West Somerset. From what he knew, Blue Anchor was simply a promenade with one road running back from the coast. The Bay Hotel should not be hard to find. He looked at his watch. He had time to shower, shave and dress appropriately. He left Lyney House at just after two in the afternoon; he thought he would be there by three fifteen easily.

Sam had taken to walking his pastures again, yet only those pastures that gave him a view of the road going up to Paverton. When James' Land Rover roared by leaving a cloud of blue smoke, he knew that James had found the clue. He phoned Abby. "I think he's found it, and he's on his way. Mind, Abby the way he's thrashing that motor he may not make it." He heard Abby chuckle.

"Well I am pretty sure he phoned the hotel about two hours ago. I am going out, Sam. I don't want to be here as if I was waiting for him. I'll let him cool his heels for a while."

"Good idea, Abby." They broke the connection.

***

James made good time, and found the hotel without trouble, after all the name itself gave an indication of where it could be discovered. He parked and went in. There was no one in reception so he pressed the plunger on the Brass bell. A young lady came from the rear office. "Can I help you?"

"Yes, I wonder if I could see Miss Tregonney. I believe she is staying with you." The receptionist checked the key board.

"Her key is here so I would imagine she is out at the moment. Was she expecting you?"

"No. I just hoped that I might catch her. May I wait?"

"Of course, Sir. The Lounge is just through the door there. Would you like some tea or coffee?"

"Coffee would be good, thank you."

"I'll bring it through for you." James wandered into the Lounge. He had chosen coffee as he imagined he may need the caffeine boost when he confronted Abby. Then he thought. Was it a confrontation? No it wasn't, not really. He was going to beg Abby to come back.

The preserved West Somerset Railway ran very close to the sea at Blue Anchor, and the arrival and departure of the trains was very evident to anyone in the vicinity, especially when the level crossing gates were closed to road traffic. James did not hear the arrival, nor the departure of the train from Minehead. All he was hearing was the voice in his head telling him how to manage the conversation he was about to have with Abby.

Abby had taken a quick return trip to Minehead purely to give James time to think, and as she walked back from Blue Anchor station saw James' Land Rover parked at the hotel. He was so bound up with his own thoughts that he didn't see Abby arrive. Abby was standing in the doorway when James looked up and saw her. All his planned words were forgotten.

"Abby. Thank God I found you." Abby was quite amused at this as she had intended to be found anyway. He had got up when he saw her, now she came over and took a seat near to him.

"Why? James. I wasn't lost."

He sat down again. "Eh. No of course not, but we all worried when you went off without telling anyone."

"I didn't realise that I had to tell anyone if I was going away for a few days. I did leave a note for Mary."

"Well no. But Mary, Mavis and Sam have been quite concerned."

"So! You can tell them when you get back that I am fine."

"You're not coming back then?"

"I shall be back for the blessing of the station, then......" Her voice trailed off.

"Then? He repeated.

"I have to give it some thought."

"Why? Abby. We thought you were going to settle in the station house."

"That was my intention, but I have been having second thoughts. At this moment I don't know what I will do, or where I will go. If someone made an interesting offer, that could shape my plans."

"Oh." He sounded disappointed. "You mean a Bank or something?"

"Not necessarily."

"But you could go back to London?"

"Again, not necessarily."

James seemed to grow in stature then, as he took a deep breath and summoned his courage.

"Abby, we, no I mean I, don't want you to go away. I want you with me, I need you. Damn it! Abby I love you." He slipped forward in the chair and knelt in front of her. "I want you to be my wife. Will you marry me? Please?"

Abby's heart pounded but kept her serene countenance. "Wow! That's bit sudden, James. Where did that come from?" She smiled inwardly at the contradiction of those words.

"It's my fault, Abby. I should have told you how I feel long ago. But I thought…I felt…Perhaps you would have thought…Oh Shit! I don't really know why I didn't say anything. I do love you, Abby. Please say yes. Life wouldn't mean anything if you go away." He was still on his knees. Abby made no answer.

She had thought about this on quite a few occasions, and in her mind had decided to accept. But James prevarications should not be resolved so easily. "I need to think about this, James. I am not sure if I would make a good wife to you. I can't cook, I am hopeless at housework, and I certainly would not be a meek and subservient wife."

James shook his head vehemently. "I don't need a meek and subservient wife. I need an Abby. The Abby who challenges me, make me laugh, argues with me, cuts me down to size when I get too pompous, and thrills me with her presence every day." The last sentiment thrilled Abby as well. That last phrase was the most important, if anything he had said would make her accept that was the one. But she was determined not to give in as easily as that. The receptionist came into the room at that point and noting James kneeling before Abby realised that she had interrupted something. She gave Abby a quick smile and left, closing the door behind her. James hadn't noticed. Abby gestured to him to get up.

"I will think about it, James. I will give you my answer when I return for the station blessing."

"That's a week away. Will you not come back earlier?"

"I will be back a couple of days before. I need to ask Mr. Brasher a couple of things."

***

The journey back to Combe Lyney was taken at a slower pace than the outward journey. James drove with a mixture of emotions. He felt better now he had finally told Abby of his feelings, and despondent that she had not accepted him immediately. At first there was a little anger that she hadn't accepted him, but as the miles rolled away a more temperate attitude prevailed. He couldn't really blame her, could he? He was the one who should have been brave enough to tell her how he felt. He was the one who allowed their relationship to settle into a comfortable routine. Comfortable for him, yes. He took but gave little back. Had it been comfortable for Abby? Had she thought that he was happy to have her as a Mistress, but nothing else? Shame at his perceived disrespect brought heat to his face. If she rejected him, then it was his actions that brought about that rejection.

Sam had left it until he saw James drive past Gallow farm going back to Combe Lyney. He dialled Abby's number. "Hello Sam." She picked up straight away.

"How did it go?" Sam was eager to know.

"I have never seen James so unsure of himself. Sam! He was wretched. However, he did propose."

"And?"

"I will tell him yes when I come back for the blessing of the station."

"You're making him sweat for a while then?"

"I thought it appropriate. He's got to learn that I am not a weak, simpering woman."

Sam was laughing. "I doubt that there is anyone here in Combe believes that, Abby. Remember, I saw you in action at the meeting with the co-operative."

CHAPTER 36

Abby had expected a third degree cross examination upon arrival back at the Combe Inn. But all Mary asked was. "Did you enjoy your few days away; the sea air must have been nice." Alerting Abby to the fact that James must have told at least one person where she was. In the bar that evening she saw Sam, who surreptitiously winked. Abby discreetly nodded, acknowledging his part in the conspiracy. She then gave her attention to Mr. Brasher who had arrived that day.

She and Mr. Brasher went to the station the day before the blessing. The building was pristine, looking just as it should, not new, but as an old building which had been cared for. He stood on the track bed, now devoid of weeds, with Sleepers and ballast taking their place, just looking, saying nothing, his face revealing his feelings. He nodded his head. "This Abby, is how a station should look. Great Western, through and through." They had discussed the informative signs and pictorials that would go into the station. He had obtained official and unofficial photographs and had these blown up and printed on board. From the cavernous boot of the Rolls Royce he now produced them. One of George Walker's men carried them into the station. Covered by transparent acrylic sheet they would last for years. They went round the station deciding where the hoardings should go, for each one he produced a printed explanation of what the photo showed and what work the men were doing. They too had been enlarged and sealed under an acrylic coat. George Walker came over to see what they were doing, and immediately called the man back.

"Mark these up, drill and plug. We'll get these up straight away, Miss Abby." He turned back to his workman. "Use mirror screws, and don't over tighten. If you crack the acrylic I shall have your guts for garters!" He had a smile on his face as the man hurried off. "Best to warn them of their fate before they do it wrong."

Mr. Brasher had kept the best until last. He produced the photo of Thomas Tregonney standing on his platform, which he had also had blown up. Then the chronology of Thomas's career in the service of the Great Western Railway. "In his office, I believe, Abby. Would be the best place?" Abby nodded too full of emotion for words. Each hoarding was left against the wall it would be fixed to. Mr. Walker promising that they would be affixed properly or he would know the reason why.

As Abby and Mr. Brasher left the station building he apologised that the hoardings for the goods shed were not ready. The printer, though, had promised that he would deliver within three days.

"I shall stay until then, Abby. I would like to make sure the placement is correct and to your satisfaction."

"My satisfaction?" Abby queried. "I will be happy with whatever you suggest. After all, you are the expert." Mr. Brasher acknowledged her compliment with a little smile. Abby then raised the subject of payment for all this work.

He shook his head. "Please don't mention it, Abby it was little enough, and my pleasure in contributing something to this work is more than sufficient thanks."

***

They were leaving through the wicket gate when Abby noticed the old sign, the one that she had seen broken and thrown amongst the weeds on the track. It was now whole and affixed to the diagonally slatted fence. She looked at Mr. Brasher.

"Did you organise this?"

He shook his head. "No, Abby. Nothing to do with me." Abby returned to the office building and found Mr. Walker, who was standing over his workman making sure he understood what was required of him.

"Mr. Walker. The old sign about tickets. Did you get it repaired?"'

"Yes. Miss Abby. Ms. Eaton noticed it and told me that it had to be repaired and fixed as you see it. Evidently it was shown in one of the old photographs, so she included it in her specification. I found the bits and had them welded then repainted." He looked worried. "Why? Is there a problem?"

"No problem at all. I was surprised, that's all."

***

Now that she was seeing her project coming to completion, she was grateful for James' good advice. Restoring the station was an emotional step for her, but she recognised that having a purpose for the station was just as, if not more important. Everything she had learned from Sam and particularly Mr. Brasher had indicated that this building, delightful as it was, was a tool designed to do a job. Granddad was merely the operator of the tool.

The re-dedication had been set for eleven-thirty. It was one of those spring days when the sun shone but with little warmth, the saving grace was no wind to chill. Even so it was wise to wrap up a little. Abby arrived just after James, and was astonished to see the station approach full with cars, mainly Land Rovers, the standard mode of transport in the valley. She recognised most. James' battered and scarred vehicle, Mary and Jack, Sam, of course and his family, Harry, Nat and Susan Gaunton, Abe Stone's Land Rover was easy to spot, it was the only clean one there! Then of course the elegant Rolls Royce announced the presence of Mr. Brasher. She noted a Lexus and had to wonder who owned that. James had waited for her by the wicket gate and his eyes asked for the answer to his proposal. "Later, James." She told him. She was prepared for a good turnout but when they got on the platform she was surprised at the numbers. Seeing Sir Richard and Lady Margaret, answered the question of the Lexus, then the sight of a small squad in Khaki standing on the gravel of the track bed surprised her.

She turned to James and in a voice as cool as the air asked. "What is the Army doing here?"

"Oh, I believe they are going off with the Reverend Hopkins to another function. I said it would be fine if they stopped here, swelling the numbers a bit." Abby's face told him she wasn't too sure whether to believe him of not.

James led Abby along the platform towards the newly glazed porch where the Reverend Hopkins waited, dressed in a white Surplice, bible in hand. Abby had to welcome many of the gathering, stopping and having a few words with most as they made their way. Abby was surprised when after the greetings were done, James started the proceedings.

"Sir Richard, Lady Margaret, Reverend Hopkins, Ladies and Gentlemen. No one was more surprised than I when Miss Tregonney asked to take over this station and house. To all intents and purposes the buildings were almost derelict, yet Miss Tregonney saw in them something more than a cursory examination would reveal. She saw something that no one else would ever see, no matter how hard they looked. She saw her Family." He paused to let that sink in. "That's an important concept, family. All of us here take for granted our mothers, fathers, siblings. They are there. We laugh with them, we quarrel with them, fall out with them, yet we can always return to the loving familiarity of the familial embrace, for comfort and for support. We can trace our families back through three, four or more generations, that knowledge grounds us, we know who we are." He paused again. "Miss Tregonney had none of those experiences, so this station where her grandfather worked, the house where he lived with her grandmother and where her mother grew up, assumed an importance that many of us could not understand. I think now we do understand. Re-building the past is a way of finding ourselves, and I believe that Miss Tregonney has done that. At the same time Miss Tregonney has found something else, friends as well as a family. Abby now belongs here, she is one of us." He turned to Abby. "Abby. You came here and offered friendship and courtesy to all of us and have become an essential part of this village and the valley, we want you to stay; you are part of us now, part of this little community. If you

ever go away, you will leave a vacuum here that nothing will ever fill."
He smiled, and looked at the Reverend, who cleared his throat and began
the blessing of the station.

He started by making reference to the peculiar relationship that
the clergy seemed to have with the steam railway, which bought a smile
to their faces. "Many see the Church in the same light as the steam railway. Dinosaurs that have little reference to modern life. Indeed the Great
Western Railway, known often by just its initials was humorously referred to as God's Wonderful Railway, and disparagingly as the Great
Way Round. I think that if God had indeed designed a railway, it would
have been the Great Western he used as a prototype. There was much
similarity between the Church and the railway, both gave service to a
community, the one spiritual, the other practical. We could see this station as the equivalent of the church, always open to serve those who had
need of our help and succour. From this place some would set out to pursue fame, fortune or a new life. Others left to do service for their country.
Yet the station was here to welcome them back, and many would have
seen Thomas Tregonney, sending them on their journey and facilitating
their return. In the midst of so much turmoil, Thomas Tregonney and his
station were beacons of stability, much as we hope the Church could be
seen. We will give thanks for his life, the service he gave us, and bless
this building as a symbol of all he did."

This, for most was mercifully a short service, not so for Abe
Stone who felt it was far too short, but for the others standing there was
quite sufficient. The service ended with the Lord's Prayer, and James
gestured to Abby to come inside the porch. She looked enquiringly at
him, but his smile re-assured her. On the wall between the door to the
booking office and the door to the waiting room there was a draped Union Flag.

The Reverend, Sam and others followed them in. There was insufficient room for everybody so those who could not crowd in watched
through the glazed partition. "Abby." Asked James. "It would give us a
great pleasure if you would pull away the Flag?" Abby gave him a questioning look. He nodded and gestured for her to go ahead. She did, re-

vealing a grey Slate plaque fixed to the wall. Engraved on the plaque were the words.

DEDICATED TO
THOMAS TREGONNEY
STATIONMASTER 1938 - 1966

Abby stood there silently, emotion causing a lump in her throat. Tears came to, and then overflowed her eyes. At that moment from outside they heard the drums tap, once, then twice, then three times. Graham Boyce moistened his lips, raised the Trumpet and blew, hitting perfectly, the first three notes of Aaron Copland's 'Fanfare for the Common man'; the notes hung hauntingly, bright crystals on the still clear air. Everyone turned to watch as Graham finished the first refrain, then the drum beat again and the other trumpets and bugles joined in mirroring the notes but one beat behind. James smiled to himself; the band had practiced almost without pause to get this right. He turned to Abby who was crying silently, tears cascading down her cheeks.

He took the step that brought him to her side and put his arm round her. "Are you alright, Abby"

She nodded against his chest. "Thank you, thank you so much, James. I think granddad would be proud and even have moisture in his eyes now." He gave her his handkerchief, and she dried her eyes, looking up and smiling. "Now I know why you were so insistent that we had this ceremony."

James grinned. "You had me worried when you seemed so set upon doing nothing really, and I wanted this to be a surprise."

"Well it was definitely that." They walked around, James was very interested in the large photographs, and took time to study them and read the explanations.

"It comes as a shock to realise that all this work was going into making the railway work. Most people then and now would only look at the superficial, the trains and the locomotives. Few would realise how many men were involved in getting that train with its engine to the station and from there safely to its destination. It makes you stop and think."

Abby agreed with him. "Yes. I didn't give it a thought until I started to read up on it. I only wanted to know about granddad. He was the station master, and for a while I thought that was all he was, then as I read, and talked with Mr. Brasher I realised that though isolated, he was an important part of a huge commercial enterprise." They wandered through into the office, where they were greeted with the photo of Thomas.

James grinned. "Just as I remember him. Fearsome. No one would dare lark around on his platform."

Abby was just enjoying the moment, ambling through the station and hearing his memories. She decided to put him out of his misery. "Oh, by the way James. The answers yes." she said quietly.

"Sorry, what did you say?"

"You heard. Yes, I will marry you."

James stopped and stared at her with a stupefied expression. "You mean it?"

Abby's smile widened. "You lovely, silly man, I only went away so you would come and find me, and ask that question. I had to do something knowing I loved you and wanted above everything to be your wife. Of course I mean it. James! I don't know when I fell in love with you. It may have been the Ball; it may have been when we rode together. But I do love you, and want to be married to you more than anything else. So set the date, Mr. Comberford."

"How long do you need to prepare?"

"Not long at all. I am sure that Mary and Mavis have been making plans for this from almost the first moment I stepped into the valley. But don't leave it too long, we don't want the bump showing."

"What bump?"

"The bump your baby will make, I'm pregnant!" Abby had an unsettled stomach and slight nausea for a while. Whilst not particularly indisposing, the fact that it went on for a week or two alerted her to the possibility of her condition. The Doctor had confirmed her suspicion. At first she had debated whether to tell James. Then the spectre of taking the same course as her mother filled her with despair. No, she thought, any child that she had would grow up here, knowing whence it came and where it belonged. To his credit, not for one moment did James think that he may not be the father of this child.

As the initial shock faded he found his voice. "Why didn't you tell me?"

"If I had, you would have rushed me to the altar in no time, but it would be because of the baby. I wanted you to marry me for me, just me."

"I must grab the Reverend before he goes. Arrange for the Banns to be read." Then he suddenly remembered something that Abby said.

"Did you say that you went away just so that I would come and find you and propose?"

Abby nodded with a little smile on her face. "You see, James, I will not be a meek and dutiful wife at all, I'll argue and anger you, I will also try to twist you around my little finger, but only because I love you and to get you to do the things I want."

He seemed shocked at first then grinned. The grin that had Abby go weak inside. "I told you I wanted an Abby. Any Abby within two feet of me now will do. Don't change, Abby. I need you just as you are. I'll go and speak to Reverend Hopkins."

Abby turned back to the photograph of her grandfather. What would he think she wondered? His granddaughter marrying into the Comberford family. She grinned. Definitely shocked, she thought and also of the belief that she could be getting above her station.

Sam was chatting with Mr. Brasher when he saw James hurry away. He came to find Abby. "Mr. James was in a hurry."

"He's gone to find the Reverend Hopkins."

"Is it what I suspect?"

Abby nodded smiling. "Yes to get the Banns read, Sam. I told James yes. Now I have another favour to ask of you. You have been like a father to me, ever since I came here, and not having any male relatives I need someone to give me away. Would you do me the honour of giving me away?"

Sam's face was a picture. "Abby! It will give me much pleasure to do that. Of course I will Girl." When Sam told Mavis she wanted to go and congratulate Abby immediately, but hesitated before going and came back to Sam and gave him a kiss on his cheek.

"There Sam. When I suggested all those months ago that Abby needed a dad to look after her, I knew you would do a good job. And you have." Tears came to her eyes as she continued. "And now, just as if she was our own daughter you are going to give her in marriage." She turned to go and find Abby, then turned back again. Her expression, soft before had hardened. "You know more about this than meets the eye, Sam Perry. We are going to have words soon. Depend on it." As always Mavis had to have the last word.

THE END

Author's Postscript

I hope you have enjoyed this tale. For some time I did consider a sequel. However I have rejected that idea. Abby took me five years to write when I was relatively healthy and could sit and write for eight hours or more every day. Unfortunately these days I am not able to write for more than an hour or two. Therefore a sequel would likely take me far more than the original five years.

For those readers who would like to know more I note my ideas for Abby's future.

Yes. Abby and James do marry and she gives birth to a girl. James registers the child while Abby is still in the maternity unit and calls his daughter Tregonney. His reasoning is that as Abby is now a Comberford it would be right to have a Tregonney in the valley. An unusual name for a girl but it works for me. Abby and James argue this but the deed is done. Tregonney or Comberford is immaterial, Abby is always known by everyone in the valley as Miss Abby

Abby lives in her family home for just two months, before returning to the Combe Inn from where she is married.

Gwen takes it upon herself to invite her friends from Berkshire to the wedding. She is horrified when she understands that Abby has invited all of James' tenants and rescinds her invitations to her friends as she could not ask them to sit down with the lower classes. Sometime later she buys herself a brand new Jaguar car and asks James for the money. He tells her he hasn't got that sort of money and Gwen suggests he asks Abby for the money. Abby refuses. I can imagine a rather heated row when Abby does that which ends with Gwen storming off and not being seen in the valley for quite some time. Abby does buys a good used Range Rover for James and consigns the rattletrap Land Rover to a well deserved retirement.

By a convoluted rumour ex-Sergeant 'Spade' Diggins heard that Captain Comberford was getting married and arrived in Combe Lyney with as many of the Captains' company he could find. It was therefore a surprise to James and Abby that an impromptu Guard of Honour greeted them as they left the Church. Abby spoke to Diggins, "call me Spade, Ma'am. Everybody does." She learned a lot more about James' service and why he was awarded the DSO. Spade had brought his wife, Linda who mentioned that the Bed and Breakfast business they managed was closing down. Learning that Linda had cooked and cleaned for the business a total of ten bedrooms and usually the same number of occupants Abby asked if she would like to do the same at Lyney House. Spade and Linda fitted in seamlessly. Linda was happy to cook for them and was welcomed by Mary at the Combe Inn whenever she was stretched. Spade became a very useful gardener and quickly tamed the rather overgrown garden. Seems quite appropriate, a Spade to garden! They moved in to the top floor at Lyney House.

Mr. Brasher finds a use for the station when a small preservation group are given notice to quit their site for a Supermarket development. He talks to Abby and James and they agree to have them occupy the station and track bed. The preservation group have rescued and re-built a GWR locomotive, a pannier tank. Together with their collection of goods trucks, vans, and guard vans they show the station in a very authentic guise. With eight hundred yards of track laid and the goods shed once more connected by rail, they are able to re-enact much of the shunting and movements that Thomas Tregonney would have known so intimately. School trips to the station were met by one of the members of the group (who actually was a teacher) dressed in a detailed replica of a GWR stationmaster. He would conduct the group around and explain how the station worked. The highlight for the school group was when the Pannier tank appeared, apparently from South Molton, pulling two guards vans. The children were allowed to board the vans and were treated to a short trip up and back.

Mr. Brasher was often a visitor. His affection for Abby making him the adopted Uncle that he had asked her to view him. Without realising he had found the familial affection he had missed for all his life. Abby a few years later understands when she finds herself a beneficiary in his Will.

Sam lived long enough to hear once more the rhythmic sound of steel wheels on jointed steel track, the clang as un-braked goods wagon were shunted and that never to be forgotten 'pop' followed by rush of steam as the locomotive moved the load. Yet more importantly to him, he had held Abby's daughter Tregonney in his arms when she was christened. Abby's second child, a boy is christened Samuel.

Here is a preview of another story you may also enjoy:

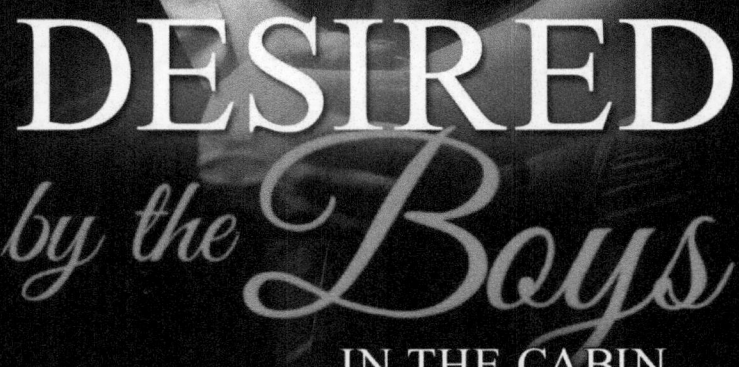

Hot Erotica
George X. Bush

DESIRED
by the _Boys_
IN THE CABIN

Mary was fed up with being left behind each month while Riley went up to the cabin with his three friends, Mark, Robert, and John, to fish, drink and just have fun. She was only 23 and she wanted some fun, too. She resented being left behind to fend for herself in this way. She poured herself another drink, her third, and flopped down onto the sofa in frustration as she sipped her drink. *I'll show him*, she thought, sipping her drink, a plan coming into her head. Quickly gulping the rest of her drink down, Mary went to her room and quickly threw a change of clothes and some toiletries into a bag, grabbing her pocketbook and keys as she locked the door behind her and got into the car. If she drove steadily, she could be there in three hours and surprise them.

Mary had to stop a couple of times on the way as she felt herself getting tired, but she finally pulled up to the cabin around four in the morning. As she let herself in, she heard the sounds of snoring coming from different areas of the cabin. She was tired and felt a bit ragged from all she had drunk during the evening, so she quietly tiptoed to the bathroom to take a shower. The water felt so good after the long drive and she stood under it enjoying the sensation.

When she got out of the shower and dried herself, she appraised what she was seeing in the mirror. Her long red hair hung down to the middle of her back. She had that pale skin with light freckles that was common to redheads. Her breasts were very full with large pale nipples on the ends. Mary cupped them in her hands, gently squeezing them as her fingers automatically sought out and found her nipples, squeezing them and pinching them, pulling on them as they screwed themselves into large hard knots. Her hands trailed down her flat stomach to where a small thatch of bright red pubic hair used to grow above her pussy. She had no hair on her pussy, having had it removed by electrolysis so that it was as smooth as a baby's. At the top of her slit, her clit hood peeked through her pussy lips and her clit, fat as a pinkie finger, stuck out from beneath its hood. Her hand trailed down and her fingers trailed up through and between her pussy lips, feeling herself and the wetness that was starting. Her legs were long and straight, as were her feet and toes. Men had always found her beautiful and at the moment she quite agreed with them.

She was still squeezing her breasts with one hand, her other still between her legs when suddenly the door opened and Robert staggered in, completely naked, his cock dangling in front of him, bigger than anything Mary had ever imagined. As he shut the door, he blinked his eyes, trying to clear the fog of alcohol and sleep so he could make sense of what he was seeing.

"Mary?" he croaked, his voice still sounding a bit drunk.

"Hi, Robert," Mary said, frozen where she stood, her hands not moving.

"What're you doin' here?" he asked, slurring his words. "And how come you're naked?"

"Uh, I thought I'd drive up and surprise Riley and I just took a shower," she replied, letting her hands fall to her sides as she stared at his cock which was beginning to grow even larger…

To purchase the book, look for **Desired by the Boys by George X. Bush**.

BBW
LOST & FOUND

THE CRUISE SERIES, BOOK 1

JESSICA JOHANNSEN

If Belinda weren't staring right at it, she never would have believed that it could be true. As Belinda peered down at the computer screen, the woman in the photo seemed to stare right back. The woman's casual grin made Belinda feel mocked; made her feel as though the woman flaunted what she possessed.

Belinda covered her mouth with both hands to contain the scream that built in her throat. The young, sexy blond was her husband's mistress; the pictures on his computer finally answered the question that she had been too afraid to ask. No, it wasn't her imagination; their marriage of fifteen years had finally passed the point of no return. She knew she had to finish getting ready for work. Sitting here at her husband's desk, wearing only a bra and skirt, she felt open, exposed, and raw.

Belinda searched the contents of her husband's hard drive, finding album after album of photos. There were hundreds of pictures of the mistress, in every state of dress and undress. Skipping back to the earliest album, she checked the upload date. Her stomach lurched when she realized that the first pictures were dated over a year ago. Almost to the day that her husband had moved out of their bedroom and taken up permanent residence in the den.

Belinda wound her long black hair up into the bun that she wore for work. She applied make-up; she puckered and blew a kiss to her reflection, a silly habit. She flinched, realizing that many of the photos her husband kept were pictures of the blond woman making just that face, the wink and kiss.

Tears threatened to fall. She closed her eyes and took a deep breath. He had already ruined their marriage; she would not let him ruin her meeting with the board.

Belinda turned her mind to work, making sure she arrived in the conference room before anyone else. She set about preparing the screen. When Mr. Whiting entered the room, she was standing at the podium, reviewing the presentation in her mind. His presence had always unnerved her; she had forgotten that he'd be there this morning until this moment. He nodded at her as he made his way to the back of the room.

"Belinda, are you ready?" he asked.

"As ready as I'll ever be," she said. She regretted how it had sounded, so unsure of herself; it wasn't fair that the blond got her husband and her self-confidence all in one fell swoop.

"You'll be great," he assured her.

Mr. Whiting always undressed her with his eyes. Today was no different; she could feel his gaze peeling away the layers of her clothes.

Tall, broad-shouldered, with blond hair and piercing blue eyes, Robert Whiting was considered quite a catch. Belinda had entertained dirty thoughts about him a time or two, turned more than once to catch a glimpse of his backside as he passed. She always shook her head and reproached herself. She was a married woman; she didn't drool over men.

Today, though… she could drool all she wanted, over anyone that caught her eye. Mr. Whiting just happened to be foremost in her mind when it came to hot, single men. Belinda ran her hands down her waist and her round hips, feeling nervous. She checked her watch. Everyone else would be arriving shortly and she couldn't help but wonder if Mr. Whiting hadn't gotten here early just to get her alone.

In her mind's eye, she imagined sauntering towards him, returning that lustful gaze. Sliding down into his lap, feeling her skirt rise on her thighs. Exposing her garters and stockings, pressing herself against what she imagined was an impressive erection. She would lick her lips as she ran her hand slowly down the front of his pants, longing to unzip them so badly and wrap her dainty fingers around his manhood.

A loud sigh escaped her lips. She flushed, embarrassed. Perspiration teased the back of her neck; her blouse was damp. This was ridiculous, but she couldn't help it. She added this moment of embarrassment to her husband's lengthy list of crimes. Cut off from sex for a year, Belinda was so needy that she was ready to risk it all to bump and grind in the boardroom. More than that, Mr. Whiting was her boss, and far too young for her. She gave herself a sharp reprimand for her unacceptable behavior, pulling herself together.

If you like this sample, look for **BBW Lost and Found-The Cruise Series, Book 1 by Jessica Johannsen**.

From the Author

If you enjoyed any of my books, then please share the love and click like on my books in Amazon.

If you write me a review and send me an email I will send you a free book, or many.
(Just know that these emails are filtered by my publisher.)

Good news is always welcome.

One Last Thing, For Kindle Readers...

When you turn the page, Kindle will give you the opportunity to rate this book and share your thoughts on Facebook and Twitter. If you enjoyed my writings, would you please take a few seconds to let your friends know about it? Because... when they enjoy they will be grateful to you and so will I.

Thank You!

Kerry James
kerry_james@awesomeauthors.org